ECORIAN
THE COMPLETE VEREDOR CHRONICLES

E J GILMOUR

HERO PAGES PUBLISHING

DEDICATED TO JED

ECORIAN
THE COMPLETE VEREDOR CHRONICLES

Ecorian: The Complete Veredor Chronicles
Copyright 2015 E J Gilmour

ISBN: 978-0-9923750-7-2

Hero Pages Publishing
www.heropagespublishing.com

www.ejgilmour.com

Cover image: © depositphotos.com/CoreyFord

MAP OF THE WESTERN LANDS

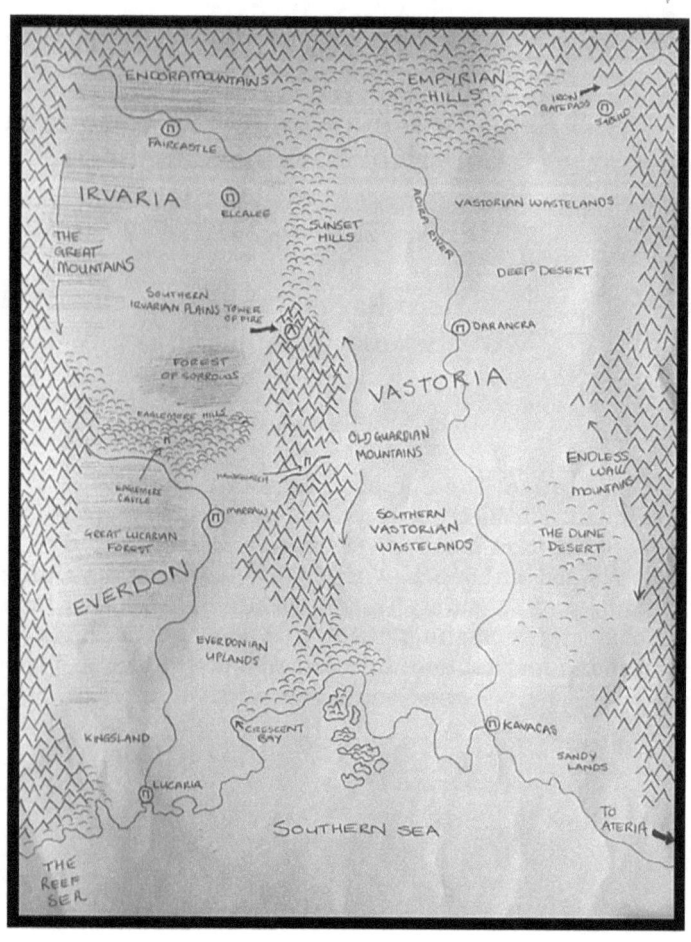

MAP OF THE EASTERN LANDS

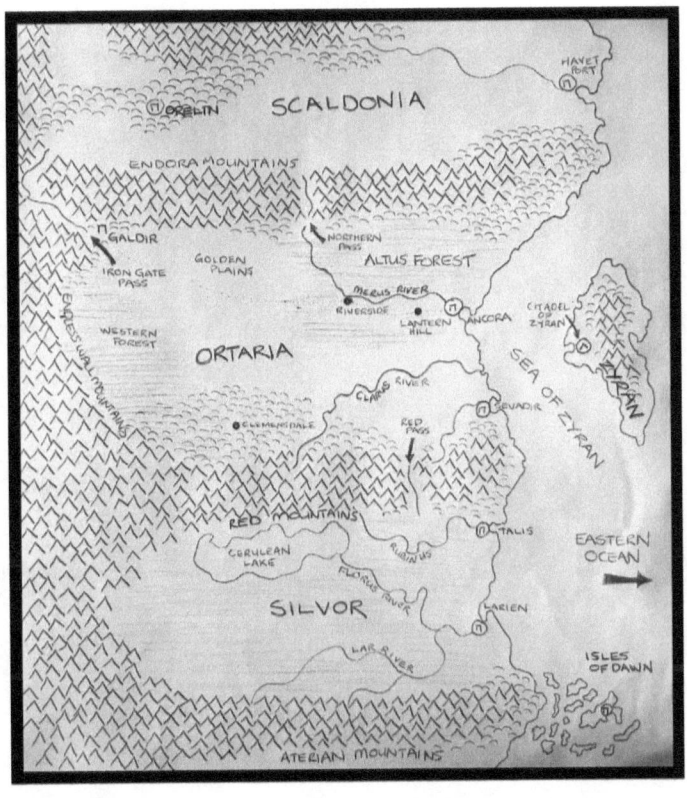

THE SWORD OF LIGHT: BOOK ONE OF THE VEREDOR CHRONICLES

CHAPTER ONE

Deep in the southern hills of the Kingdom of Ortaria, perched precariously on a mountainside, was a lonely and simply built hut. There was nothing particularly unusual about the hut, apart from its rather perilous location. A steep track led down to a little village far below, and anybody passing through the village would have thought it was a very strange place to build a home, if they noticed it at all.

A young man stood by the only window and looked out across the valley. He was tall with wavy brown hair and dark eyes. The small window presented a view of the entire village. The people of Clemensdale were scurrying about and making preparations for the approaching storm. Dark clouds were rolling across the hills to the east. Thunder rumbled from above and echoed throughout the valley. He reached out and fastened the shutters as lightning lit up the sky above.

The hut was made up of a single room with a central wooden table and two single beds against each wall. An oil lantern filled the little hut with warm light. On top of the table was a small metal box. The young man sat down and gently lifted the lid off the box. Inside was a piece of folded parchment paper. He took it out and unfolded the letter. He then began to read.

Brother Erako,

I send to you this child. His name is Eben. Lady Kaloren has requested that he be hidden from our enemies. She has assigned me the task to protect the child. I must ensure he is placed somewhere where he will not be found. She has also requested for the Ecorian Sword to remain with Eben. I know I can trust you to take care of him. It is truly important that you accept. We are living in a dangerous time. Our numbers are few in these lands. The rumours are true; the hand of evil reaches south. I will only say a few words in this letter of our troubles. We have encountered our old enemies in Ortaria. There is word they have entered Vastoria. We can only hope the Cosmic Gate holds true. We fear the time grows near. One of us will come to take Eben from you soon.

Sincerely,

Carlin.

Eben had read the letter at least a dozen times, and with each reading more questions entered his mind. The metal box had been hidden beneath Erako's bed. The contents of the letter had shocked him deeply.

For most of his life Eben had lived in the southern hills of Ortaria. He had been taught the craft of surviving in the wild rocky land by Erako, the Huntsman of Clemensdale. Erako was already an old man when Eben was entrusted to his care, and he singlehandedly raised Eben from when he was only two years old. Few memories remained of the time before his arrival, only vague recollections and faces of people who he could not clearly remember. Eben had always been told that a stranger left him and had promised to return one day to take him away, but the stranger never returned. The months turned into years without a word or message.

Over sixteen years had passed since he arrived at the small remote village. In the depths of winter a fever had overcome Erako. The old huntsman passed away peacefully in his sleep. Life in the village had not been the same since Erako's death.

Erako always said someone would eventually come to Clemensdale to explain Eben's origins, but after reading the letter he felt a deep desire to search for the answers himself. There was so much he wanted to know: who Carlin and Lady Kaloren were, and where had he come from, but mostly he hoped to find his parents.

**

After several hours the storm had passed. Questions continued to circle around in Eben's mind. He knew that he would have to leave his home and begin a dangerous journey if he was ever going to have a chance at discovering any of the answers. Clemensdale was a humble village and very far from anything evil or treacherous. The people were shy folk and went about their business without much care for the happenings of the wider world. The village was tucked away in the hills and mostly forgotten by outsiders.

Many dreadful stories had been brought to Clemensdale by peddlers, drifters, and nomads.

The Kingdom of Ortaria had once been a peaceful and beautiful land. Rumours continued to surface that something menacing was growing in the north and east of the country. The summers had grown cold and the winters long and icy. Crops had mostly failed, rivers were depleted of fish, and few animals remained in the forests. However, even with all these happenings, the village of Clemensdale continued to be largely untroubled. The farmers had little to complain about, the bakers still baked, the shepherds still tended their sheep, and the village folk were as happy as they had ever been.

Eben pondered the stories as he packed his bag. He knew the roads that led north would be dangerous. His thoughts were interrupted by a gentle tapping at the door. He opened the door and looked out to see Vera, the baker's wife, standing just outside. Vera was a very old woman with grey hair and blue eyes that were full of cheer. She looked up at him with a warm smile.

'Hello there my dear boy,' she said as she stepped inside and out of the cold.

'Vera, I wasn't expecting you.'

'I've come to bring you some bread. We baked it this morning especially for you,' she said, setting the basket down on the table. She turned to face him. 'How are you my boy? We've been worried about you living all alone up here on the hill. Is everything all right?' she asked as her eyes glanced across at his half packed bag on the floor.

'I'm fine.'

'It looks to me you are planning to go somewhere,' she said, a look of worry crossing her face.

There was a short silence as Eben thought of how best to tell Vera about his planned journey to Ancora. He knew Vera cared for him like an aunt would for a nephew, and he also knew she would probably be opposed to any suggestion of an adventure beyond the boundaries of Clemensdale.

'I am, Vera. I'm going on a journey.'

She nervously scratched her chin and shook her head. 'Eben, you should reconsider. There are many terrible things out on the roads of Ortaria. Erako would have wanted you to stay safely here in Clemensdale. You have an important place in our village. We care about you; you know we do.'

'I know, Vera, but please understand I have to go to Ancora. If my parents are out there somewhere I still may be able to find them. I know the road will be dangerous, but it's a chance I'm willing to take.'

She took his hand and warmly smiled. 'I realise what it is like to have so many questions and no answers. If you really must go then you also must stay safe. You don't know much about the outside world, none of us here in Clemensdale do. Don't trust anyone. It's not like Clemensdale out there; the people beyond the hills are only interested in what they can take from you. They say it's about take, take, take in the north. Keep your eyes wide open. Always remember your home and your people. Once you find what you seek hurry home to us. We will be waiting for you.'

'Thank you, Vera.'

**

Eben had been walking for three days. He set out from Clemensdale taking only his leather cloak, a hand axe, his hunting bow, enough food for several weeks on the road, and the Ecorian Sword that was mentioned in the letter. He had decided to take the back road from Clemensdale to the main highway.

It had rained heavily overnight and dark clouds filled the sky above the hilly terrain. Not a single bird could be heard singing that morning, and a deep gloominess had settled over the land. The road ahead looked rugged and unpleasant. He expected a long day of tough trekking along the rocky and rarely trodden way.

The back road led northeast toward the main highway, which he planned to follow all the way to the port city of Ancora. Stories of bandits and other unspeakable terrors on the northern road had convinced him the back way to the highway would be his best option. The road had already proven to be challenging; it traversed many deep valleys and unstable ridges, and often he found it difficult to know whether he was actually following the road or had strayed off onto a goat track.

The brightness of Clemensdale faded away the further he moved north. It seemed that the trees were struggling against a silent and invisible force. The leaves were withered and their branches drooped. The light of the sun struggled to make it all the way to the ground, and a murky feeling permeated the landscape. His hope pushed him to persevere, and he wasn't going to let the road or the gloominess force him to turn back. He had his sights firmly set on the great capital of Ortaria.

**

Eben's dark eyes surveyed his surroundings. He had arrived at the place where the old back road intersected the main highway that led from Ancora to the Iron Gate Pass. The landscape around was dotted with large oak trees rising up over moss covered rocky ground. Directly ahead of him were the ruins of an ancient village. Most of the stone houses were completely derelict, and all the inhabitants had long since moved on. A stream flowed through the village, pouring down out of the hill country to the south. Eben approached with caution. Erako had taught him how to pass by unnoticed. He had been educated in all that was necessary to become a huntsman; walking silently was one skill he was quite adept at.

He passed through the ruins and came to the edge of the stream where an old rock bridge spanned the fast flowing water below. For a moment he had a feeling he was being watched. Without moving his eyes darted to the left and the right.

'You there!' shouted a voice to his right. He quickly turned around as his hand went for his hunting dagger. In the centre of the ruined village was an old and very large oak tree. Hanging upside down by a rope tied around his ankles was a bedraggled young man with an unkempt red beard and long greasy dark hair. He was perhaps a year or two older than Eben. It was instantly clear his hands were tied behind his back. The rope around his ankles was attached to a chain that was wrapped around a branch high above, and his head hung about four feet from the ground. He looked at Eben with bright blue eyes and a wide smile.

Eben slowly walked toward him. 'How can I help you?'

'I think the answer to your question is obvious,' replied the young man, glancing upward toward the chain that was holding him in place. 'I've been waiting for someone like you to come by and free me.'

Eben looked up at the chain and wasn't sure if he should trust the stranger. 'I expect someone tied you up for a reason.'

'Not for a good reason,' replied the man defensively. 'I was travelling with a small group of traders. The sly backstabbing thieves robbed me and then left me here to die. Now really, why don't you just go ahead and free me? Surely that can't be too much trouble for you?'

'How can I trust you? You could be a threat to me.'

The young man released a sigh and shook his head in disbelief. 'True, I could be a threat, but when you think about it, you have a sword, an axe, and a bow, and I have nothing. By anyone's guess you are much more of a danger to me than I am to you. I won't trouble you if you just help me escape. Surely you won't leave me here to die? No one deserves to be treated in such a way. It's really quite simple; just use your axe to cut the rope, and I won't bother you ever again.'

Eben considered the situation and knew what the young man said was true; he simply couldn't leave him and walk on. He took his axe from over his shoulder and walked over to where the rope had been fixed to a lower branch.

'Hey, wait, be careful with that axe,' said the stranger, not knowing for sure what Eben was going to do. A second later Eben cut the rope just below where it was connected to the chain. The man toppled downward and was stunned for a moment. He slowly got to his feet and stumbled around as he gained his balance. Eben helped to untie his hands.

'Thanks. You have done a good deed,' he said as he brushed the dust off his dirty clothes.

'I hope so,' replied Eben as he turned to leave.

'Where are you heading?' asked the stranger as he followed.

'I thought you said you wouldn't bother me again.'

'I'm just trying to be friendly. You hill folk sure are odd. You simply don't trust anyone.'

Eben crossed the rock bridge and walked east out of the ruined village. He was hoping the stranger would take the hint and leave him alone.

'I see; you're heading for Ancora,' said the man, continuing to follow.

'Perhaps,' replied Eben, not wanting to share his plans. Eben was beginning to think he had made a mistake releasing the young man. A few moments went by in silence.

'Are you taking the highway? You won't make it. Walking the highway alone is a sure way to meet a sorry end.'

Eben stopped and looked back. 'So what would you suggest?' The stranger smiled widely.

'I would suggest not going to Ancora in the first place. Ancora is dangerous. If I were you I would return to the hills along the road you came, but if you insist on going forward to Ancora you would probably need someone to show you a different way.'

'I don't need your help if that's what you're suggesting,' said Eben, turning back around.

'But I need your help,' said the man, rushing his words and continuing to follow.

Eben looked back over his shoulder and was beginning to feel a little impatient with the stranger.

'I already helped you.'

'Yes, I agree, you did, but you must realise I'm alone with nothing to eat in a barren land. The truth is that if you leave me here I'll probably die. Yes, you freed me, but really what was the point if you were going to leave me alone with no food. If I don't starve I will be killed by bandits or something much worse,' he said, scanning Eben's face for a reaction.

Eben realised it was going to be difficult to be rid of the stranger. He remembered back to something Erako had said to him many times as a child: 'There is a purpose to everything in life. Every meeting, every action, and every outcome has a meaning. In time everything becomes clear.'

'What's your name?'

'Redding is my name, but I am known as Red.'

'I'm Eben of Clemensdale. You can come with me until we arrive somewhere safe.'

Red nodded and smiled.

**

Deep in the dark and gloomy forest, far beneath the canopy of towering oak trees, the two young men trekked slowly eastward. As they walked through the woods they were only seen by an occasional bird or squirrel, and mostly their presence went unnoticed.

Eben moved up beside Red who was crouching down and looking over a slight ridge to a shallow gully beyond. A moment earlier they had heard the sound of crunching and breaking branches ahead. It had sounded like something large was moving through the woods in their direction.

Red peered through the trees. 'It's safe,' he whispered, glancing back at Eben. Eben listened for the sound again. All was silent. 'We can continue,' whispered Red as he slowly began to get up. Eben grabbed his shoulder and dragged him back down.

Suddenly a creature came into view. It was not like any creature that Eben had seen before in all his years of hunting. It was similar to the shape of a man, but it was covered in a hide of thick dark fur. The monster snorted with each breath and walked with a menacing hunchback. Its hands were large with sharp claws, and its head was like that of a wild boar with tusks protruding from beneath a hog's snout. The monster stopped and looked about with fierce bloodshot eyes. The beast snarled and sniffed the air.

'It's a muckron,' whispered Red, his eyes wide with panic.

Eben felt a sense of disbelief, and his heart began to race. He had heard about muckrons, although he had always believed they were mythical creatures. Muckrons were frequently the adversaries of men in many old folk stories. Seeing the reality of the beast before his eyes was a shock. Eben reached for his bow and drew an arrow as quietly as he could manage. The beast leapt in their direction. The muckron was moving as fast as a hunting dog and made its way up the slope toward them.

'Run,' cried Red, leaping up and turning on his heel. Red sped off in the opposite direction. Eben focused his attention on the fast approaching monster and drew back his bowstring. He released the arrow and watched as it flew wide of its mark. The muckron howled furiously, continuing toward Eben and gaining speed. Eben quickly turned and started running, knowing he wouldn't have time to shoot again; his heart was beating like a drum. Red was almost out of sight. Eben looked back over his shoulder and saw the furious beast leap over the ridge and run after him.

He turned and drew his hunting dagger. A moment later the beast was upon him. Eben, holding his breath, stabbed forward with the dagger and felt the impact of the monster. He was knocked off his feet and crashed into the ground. The muckron was above him and had pinned him down. With both hands he reached up, grabbing beneath its foul mouth and used all his might to keep the muckron's fangs from biting into his neck. A menacing howl was followed by a dreadful hiss. Eben cried in pain, using the last of his strength to hold off the monster's yellow fangs.

Suddenly there was a heavy thud. The monster leapt back and turned around. Red stood a few feet away with a large stick. He swung the stick wildly as he stepped away, drawing the muckron's attention from Eben.

'Leave my friend alone!' shouted Red. The beast moved toward Red, howling and snorting as it prepared to pounce once again. Red, wide eyed with horror, gazed up at the monster. He swung the stick again. The muckron stamped its feet like a bull preparing to charge.

Eben struggled to his feet and stumbled across to where his backpack and sword had fallen to the ground. He grabbed the sword and drew it forth. The light of day flashed against the polished blade, and for a moment the gloom of the forest seemed to retreat. The beast turned and glared at Eben. Eben raised the sword, ready to fight, and felt courage flow through his veins. The muckron stumbled backward and was clearly bewildered. It stared at Eben in silence. The monster flung its head back and howled skyward before turning and dashing away through the woods. A moment later the beast was gone. Red sat down on a rock, catching his breath.

'Thank goodness that's over,' gasped Red, who was visibly shaking.

'You saved my life,' said Eben gratefully.

'We are even,' said Red. Eben nodded in agreement.

'We should probably move on from here just in case the muckron decides to return.'

A few minutes later they set out eastward and away from the direction the monster had fled.

CHAPTER TWO

In a grassy glade, deep in the forest, a gentle flickering light from a small campfire lit up the surrounding trees. Eben and Red had found a clearing that was well protected from the weather by a circle of shrubs and trees. It was a nice place to set up camp for the night. Red warmed his hands by the small fire.

'We are about two days walk from Ancora,' said Red as he took a stick and stoked up the fire.

'Can you tell me about Ancora?'

Red cringed at the thought. 'It's a dangerous place. A few years ago Ancora was a thriving seaport and mostly a peaceful and safe town. Slowly over the last two of three years it has changed to become a haven of thieves and cutthroats. King Ignis is mostly to blame. He doesn't care much about the people anymore. All the good men of the town were sent away three years ago to a distant fortress called Galdir in the far west of Ortaria. King Ignis told the people that the men were required to guard the Iron Gate Pass against a possible invasion. About three years ago King Ignis employed groups of vagrants and vagabonds to maintain law and order in Ancora. The problem is these new guardsmen are only interested in lining their pockets with gold and silver. The townsfolk quickly learned it wasn't safe on the streets. Everyone who had the means to leave moved to the safety of the villages around Ancora, but now the villages are very dangerous with all the groups of bandits and monsters wandering around the wilderness.'

'What about you? Are you from Ancora?'

'Me, no; I'm from Talis in the Kingdom of Silvor,' replied Red, snorting at the suggestion that he may be Ortarian. 'Don't take it the wrong way; I like Ortarian people, and I've spent a long time in your country, but at heart I'm a proud Silvorian. We're a little more relaxed than the average Ortarian and probably less money hungry.'

'I see,' said Eben. 'So what brought you to Ortaria?'

'Work and money,' replied Red, seeing the contradiction in his own words and laughing at it. 'I took a job on a trading ship out of the port of Talis about two years ago. Soon after I found the sea was not the place for me. I sailed as far south as Ateria and as far north as Scaldonia. I've probably seen a lot more of the world than the average man, but I knew when it was time to move on. I then took another job working for a small circus troupe operating around the docks of Ancora. At first I was helping mostly with setting up the stage and guarding the tent. Later I started to help out with the acts, and I learned a lot about circus performing. Unfortunately my stint in the circus didn't last all that long. About six months later a gang of local thugs burned down our circus tent in the middle of the night; that was the end of the circus.'

'So what did you do after the circus burned down?'

'I looked for a job in the town. It quickly became clear that the employment situation was constantly getting worse. Just before I had spent every last coin, I took a job working for an overland trader. I like to call him Olack the Terrible. He's a nasty individual who operates a small group of wagons. He trades with villagers all over Ortaria. Olack didn't like me from the beginning and only employed me because few people are desperate enough to work on the dangerous highways around Ortaria.'

'This Olack must be brave to take the risk?' suggested Eben.

Red laughed and shook his head. 'No, no, he doesn't do the work; he sends other people to do it and then takes the profits.'

'So how did you end up tied to that oak tree?'

'I was the leader of three wagons and eight men working for Olack. We traded our goods on a five week journey all the way out west, almost as far as the Endless Wall Mountains. We were on our way back to Ancora with the profits. The men I was leading decided to rob all the money from the expedition. They chained me to the tree when I tried to stop them. Luckily you came along. I could have died in that place. Hopefully we don't bump into Olack in Ancora. He won't be happy with me.'

'Surely you can explain what happened to Olack.'

'Olack, no, he won't understand. I was the leader, and he'll blame me for the loss. It's probably best to stay away from him and hide out in Ancora.'

'I see,' said Eben.

'What about you? Why do you want to go to Ancora?'

'I was not born in Clemensdale; I was adopted by a huntsman. I never knew my real parents. I thought the best place to look for answers about my past would be Ancora.'

'Why would a hunter adopt a child? That seems strange to me.'

'I guess that's true. It's just the way it happened. I don't really know much of the world outside the hills around Clemensdale. The village is still a safe place and is mostly unaffected by the troubles elsewhere. Although, we have suffered over the last two winters and have had some poor crops.'

'Poor crops are better than none. Most Ortarian farmers brought in next to nothing last year. I think this whole land is cursed,' said Red as his eyes drifted to look at the dark edges of the glade. 'I don't know what's happening, but it seems to be getting worse as time goes on. Once I get some money together I'm going to sail back to Silvor and leave this cursed land behind forever.'

**

Eben and Red walked east for two days. The forest eventually gave way to grass covered hills that gradually descended toward the coast. They stood on a hill about two miles from the western gate of Ancora. The entire town was set around the edge of a small bay. The sea stretched out into the distance beyond. Eben was mesmerised by the subtle light of the sun shimmering on the water.

He had never seen the sea before and he marvelled at it for some time; he felt something in his heart grow warm at the sight. High above the town several large vultures circled ominously. Smoke rose from many chimneys, clouding the sky directly above the city. Red started moving down the grassy slope that extended all the way to the main gate. The gate was arched and set in a poorly maintained grey stone wall. Eben followed after Red.

'We will have to be careful,' said Red. 'There are a lot of thugs who try to take advantage of unsuspecting folk coming to town. Keep your eyes open at all times.'

They approached the gate together and several brutish guards looked up as they walked through. For a few moments Eben thought they were going to be stopped, but they passed by the guardsmen without incident. Inside the gate a cobblestone street wound its way eastward and turned north through the town. The road led up a gradually rising slope toward a large palace which was set atop the headland at the northern edge of the bay. The Palace was a magnificent building and dominated the skyline. Three large towers rose from its highest point, and they stood like sentinels watching over the town below.

Many beggars scurried about. They were dressed in rags and the sight of such poverty shocked Eben. Further along a group of mangy dogs rummaged through the rubbish filled streets. A stench like nothing Eben had ever experienced rose from the streets and permeated the whole town. Red led the way quickly away from the gate, and apart from a few grim looks from strange men they were not bothered by anyone.

'A good friend of mine lives down by the docks. She may be able to provide us with some safe rooms for the night,' said Red. 'Do you have much money?'

'A little, how much will it cost?' asked Eben.

'Probably a few copper coins a night.'

'I have some silver coins,' said Eben.

'That's plenty.'

**

They arrived at the docks several minutes later. There were about five or six ships harboured in the bay. Many smaller boats were tied to a network of docks that were situated toward the southern side of the bay covering an area about two hundred yards in length. The docks were busy and bustling with fishmongers, sailors, and seafaring folk.

'Three years ago the harbour had a hundred anchored ships in it. Most sea merchants try to avoid Ancora these days,' said Red as they walked along the edge of the docks. Red then suddenly veered to the right and led Eben down a narrow laneway. At the far end was a small door. Above the door was an old painted sign that Eben could scarcely read. He strained his eyes and made out the words: The Sea Dragon.

'I used to drink at this place, but it closed down about a year ago. It's an old tavern that doubles as an inn,' said Red as he knocked on the door. He waited for a few moments. 'The King kept taxing places like this until they went out of business,' he added, continuing to knock loudly.

'Who's there?' asked a woman's voice from the other side.

'It's me, Red.'

There was a long pause. Red shuffled nervously.

'What do you want?' she asked warily.

'Stella, I know you probably don't want to see me, but I'm really in a bit of trouble. I need a room for a few nights. My friend can pay for both of us,' said Red, his voice becoming more urgent.

'You owe me a fortune, Red!' she shouted. 'Stay somewhere else!'

Red rubbed the back of his neck. He nervously looked at the door for a few seconds. 'Come on, Stella, just a few nights. Then I'll never bother you again.' There was only silence. He knocked again a little harder.

'Go away, Red!' she shouted.

'Oh, come on. Please, Stella, I really need your help this time. Remember the good old days when we worked in the circus together. Come on, just a night...or two. Please, Stella. You know I'll pay you everything I owe you when I can.'

There was a silence that lasted about half a minute. The door opened a few inches. Eben could see the face of an attractive young woman with dark hair cut to her shoulders, a fair complexion, and large green eyes. She stared out at the two of them unsympathetically. Her eyes narrowed as she looked Red up and down. She then gave a bemused smile.

'Red! What happened to your clothes, and why are you wearing those ridiculous rags?' she asked as she opened the door wider. Red smiled widely and stepped into the large common room of the tavern.

'Great to see you again, Stella,' he said, hugging her. She gave Eben a slightly suspicious glance as he stepped through the door. She then closed the large oak door and bolted it with a big iron latch.

'Only two nights, Red,' she said firmly.

'Sure, I get the picture. We won't bother you at all. You won't even notice us.'

'Good. You can stay in rooms four and five upstairs,' she said. 'Don't forget to make the beds when you leave and change the sheets,' she added. 'And just one last thing: you're not hiding from anyone here are you?' she asked, giving Red a doubting look.

Red took a step back. 'Hiding from someone? What? Why would I be hiding from anyone? Whatever gave you that idea?' He winked at Eben.

'If I find out you're taking advantage of my hospitality I'll throw you to the streets where you belong,' said Stella in a hardened voice.

Red laughed from his belly, 'I really would like to see you try to throw me.'

Stella turned on her heel and marched out of the common room, slamming the door as she exited. Red looked over at Eben with a wide smile.

'She's your friend?' asked Eben.

'Yeah,' answered Red. Eben realised there was some history between them and thought it best not to ask any more questions. He took his backpack up to room five, which had a small window with metal bars and a narrow bed. It was a simple but comfortable room. He set his backpack against the wall and lay down to rest.

**

Eben awoke to the smell of eggs and onions cooking. He got up, put on his clothes, and then walked down the stairwell to the common room where Red was chatting to Stella who seemed much more relaxed than she had been the night before.

'Would you like some eggs, Eben?' asked Stella as he approached the bar.

'Thanks, that sounds great,' he replied, taking a seat beside Red.

Red had some new clean clothes and had trimmed his shaggy beard into a neat style, but he had left his hair long.

'What's your plan for the day?' asked Stella, looking to Eben.

'I'm actually in Ancora to find answers about my heritage.'

'Red did say something about that,' said Stella, handing him a plate of fried eggs and onions.

The taste of eggs was delicious compared to the salted meat that he and Red had been eating for the last few days.

'Do you have any idea where you would start looking?' asked Stella.

'I am searching for a woman by the name of Lady Kaloren, I think she would probably know where I could find my parents.'

'The nobles don't tend to mix with the commoners in Ancora, especially these days,' said Stella. 'Lady Kaloren, I don't know the name, perhaps she's the wife of a knight or lord.'

'You could try the Royal Library,' suggested Red. 'They probably won't let you in, but if you pay one of the scholars they might be able to point you in the right direction.'

'I'll give it a try,' said Eben.

He looked to Stella and she smiled back at him warmly.

'So you and Red worked together in the circus?' asked Eben.

'I was an acrobat,' replied Stella. 'Unfortunately the circus burned to the ground a long time ago. I do miss those days; seeing you dressed up as a clown was always amusing,' she said to Red, a playful grin crossing her face. Red shot a nervous glance at Eben before uncomfortably looking away.

'You never said you were a clown,' said Eben, smiling at Red. Red twitched in his seat.

'I was only a clown for a little while; it was more like filling in really,' he said defensively.

'Filling in!' Stella laughed. 'Don't believe a word he says, Eben. He was employed as a clown from the very beginning.

'No! I wasn't!' he cried, blushing crimson red.

'Come on, Red. You're a wonderful clown,' she said, trying to reassure him, but still laughing.

'It's true, I was a clown,' confessed Red, glancing awkwardly up at Eben.

'You are the first clown I've ever met,' said Eben smiling.

Red nodded and his usual smile crossed his face. He was happy to hear the sound of their laughter, even though it was at his expense.
**

Dozens of vultures slowly circled high in the sky above Ancora. They peered downward through the hazy smoke cloud to the dank and filthy streets below. To the town folk their arrival was a sign of the dark times they were living in. Never before had vultures circled the skies above their town. They were a constant symbolic reminder of the ever growing oppression that filled the Kingdom of Ortaria.

Eben walked through the streets and up the main cobblestone road that led toward the palace. A deep depression and despair pervaded the entire town. Stella had given basic directions to the library and he walked along quickly, not wanting to catch the attention of any of the unsavoury looking characters he saw along the way.

The main road ascended gradually toward the palace. At the top of the rise was a large town square, and across the square were several wide stone steps that led up to a mighty arched entrance gate that was set in a gatehouse. A stone wall stood about fifteen yards high and encircled the entire palace. Ten fully armoured guards with long spears stood at the gate. It seemed like the gate was the only way in or out of the palace. He passed by unnoticed and followed the lane that edged along the outer wall on the western side of the palace.

Just down from the wall on the northwest side was a large building with a set of stone steps that led up to a solid bronze door. At first glance the library looked closed. He walked up the steps. There was a big bronze doorknocker with the face of a dragon. Eben knocked three times. There was no reply. After a minute he knocked again, but still there was no answer.

After waiting several minutes he decided to push on the door. The hinge creaked as the door slowly opened revealing a dark hall beyond. Many bookshelves had been cast down and those that were still standing were completely empty. The library had been ransacked. A dim light drifted down from several smashed windows set high in the walls. There was no one around and the abandoned library had a spooky feeling about it.

'Hello,' called Eben as he walked forward into the gloom. His voice echoed off the stone walls.

He heard someone approaching and looked to his right and saw an old man with crazy dishevelled white hair and piercing blue eyes. He was carrying a large wooden staff. The man jumped over a broken bookcase with surprising agility and started to spring forward toward Eben.

'Who said you could come in here?' he shouted as he prepared to swing his staff. 'Damn young ragamuffins coming round here looking for something to steal! Can't you see the King closed the library and burned all the books? There is no money here! I'll teach you a lesson, thief!'

'Excuse me, Sir, you're mistaken. I was looking for a librarian or scholar,' replied Eben, having to jump back to avoid being struck.

'Nonsense!' shouted the old man, swinging the staff again. Eben ducked easily out of the way and stepped backward toward the door.

'Really, I'm searching for someone who can help me find...' Eben had to dodge quickly to avoid getting hit once again. He was almost at the door.

'Please stop swinging that thing. Listen to me for a moment! I need to find someone called Lady Kaloren,' he shouted. A moment later the old man stopped and looked at him curiously.

'Lady Kaloren,' he muttered and raised his thick white eyebrows. 'Why do you want to find her?'

'I believe she may know who my parents are,' replied Eben. 'Do you know who she is?'

The old man nodded slightly and turned around; he walked back into the gloomy library. It seemed to Eben he wasn't going to answer. 'I must find her.'

'You won't find her in Ancora,' said the old man as he continued to walk away. 'Lady Kaloren is a famous Everdonian from the Western Lands beyond the Iron Gate Pass. She was a brave warrior. She fought in many wars.'

'Everdonian. What's that?'

'Everdon is a kingdom,' said the old man with a patronising tone.

'What about someone called Carlin, have you heard of him?'

The old man froze in his tracks and glanced back over his shoulder. 'What do you know about Carlin?' He turned around and started to walk back toward Eben; his piercing blue eyes staring intently.

'Nothing really; all I know is that he may be able to help me find my parents.'

'Who are your parents?' asked the old man, his curiosity increasing.

'I don't know. I'm searching for some answers; that's why I came to Ancora. You seem to know Carlin; can you tell me where I can find him?'

'I did know him once. He served King Ignis. Unfortunately Carlin died many years ago, so you can't find him,' said the old man, staring down at the ground solemnly.

'He died?' murmured Eben, feeling dismayed at the news.

'Yes, I heard, years ago, that he was killed by a monster which had been terrorising the coastal people north of Ancora. He wasn't Ortarian. He was a knight from a distant western land.'

'Why was he in Ortaria?'

'I don't know why,' said the old man, shaking his head. 'However, I do know someone who may have some answers for you. Her name is Torela; I think she knew Carlin. I vaguely remember seeing them together in the old days. She lives in a house near the north gate. I will sketch the directions for you.'

The old man took charcoal and some parchment from his pocket and quickly scribbled down directions.

'Thanks for your help,' said Eben gratefully.

'You're welcome. I should also warn you there is mandatory conscription for every Ortarian man between sixteen and forty. The King is sending all the young men out west to the Iron Gate Pass, and only those who have permission from the crown can remain in Ancora. No one really knows why he is doing it. These are perilous times we live in; you should be careful because you may be forced to join the army and find yourself on your way out to Galdir.'

'Thanks for the advice,' said Eben.

'And one last thing,' said the old man. 'I'm sorry for my haste in trying to drive you away; most of the time the only people who visit the library are thieves looking for something to steal. Once, only a few years ago, I was the Chief Royal Librarian, and this was one of the finest libraries in Veredor. Now I am homeless and living out my days frightened for my own safety.' The old librarian stared vacantly at the ransacked shelves and drew a long breath.

'I'm sorry to hear about your troubles. I hope you can rebuild the library one day,' said Eben, seeing clearly that the man was truly devastated by the way his life had turned out.

'That day won't come until King Ignis comes to his senses and ends all this insanity,' said the old man.

A moment later he shuffled about nervously, realising he was probably saying too much and that he shouldn't be talking about the King in such a way to a stranger. 'Goodbye and good luck young man,' he said as he turned away and closed the library door.

CHAPTER THREE

Eben walked toward the north gate and found his way to a long and narrow laneway that cut away to the south. There were piles of debris and waste everywhere. The laneway was especially gloomy because the buildings on either side had high walls and very little light entered from above. He weaved his way through whilst searching for the red door. At the far end he found what he was looking for. The door was set in a very grimy stone building with no windows facing the laneway.

A black cat leapt off a ledge and knocked over some empty bottles; they fell to the ground and smashed, shattering the gloomy silence. Eben was feeling edgy; the mood of the place was oppressive.

He knocked three times and waited. Nothing happened. He knocked again. A small sliding hatch opened and an angry looking eye stared out at him from the other side.

'Who are you and what do you want?' asked a deep grumbling voice of a man.

'My name is Eben, I'm looking for Torela. I was told she lives here.' There was a short silence and the man shut the hatch abruptly.

'Go away stranger!' he yelled aggressively.

Eben knocked again. 'Please, I need to talk to her. She's the only one who can help me.' A few moments silently passed. The door burst open and a hulk of a man stood pointing an oversized crossbow at him.

'Don't move!' shouted the man as he glared down at Eben. Eben took a step back and then stood completely still. The man standing in the doorway was the biggest man Eben had ever seen in his whole life. He had deep lines in his forehead, black curly hair, and arms like tree trunks. An instant later a woman with a gentle face stepped into view from around the corner of the door. Her long hair was light brown with streaks of grey, and her eyes were remarkably turquoise blue. She wore a simple long green dress and brown leather boots. It was difficult for Eben to guess her age, but he thought she was at least forty. She studied Eben for a few moments and then glanced up to the huge man.

'Torg, be still, he means us no harm.' She seemed kind and peaceful in complete contrast with the fuming giant standing by her side. 'I am Torela and this is Torg. What do you want from us?'

Eben instantly felt reassured by her. She had a sense of peace that seemed to push the gloominess away; he had a feeling she could be trusted. She also had a strange accent that he had never heard before.

'My name is Eben. I was told that you knew Carlin when he was alive. I need to ask you some questions about him if you have time?'

She stared at him and pondered what he had just said. 'Yes, I did know him. What is your association to him?'

'I came to Ancora looking for him. I went to the library. An old man there told me that he had died years ago. I hoped to find him because he may have known my parents.' She nodded slightly in response and watched him for a few moments. She appeared to be contemplating what she should do next.

'You should come in out of the cold,' said Torela, directing him inside and into a long hallway that led to the back of the house. Eben stepped in, and Torg slammed the door behind them, bolting it solidly with two large steel latches. Torela led Eben down the hallway which opened into a large room. The room was full of exotic luxurious goods: rich carpet covered the floors, the couches were draped in silk, and beautiful artworks adorned the walls. The room didn't have a single window and was lit entirely by candlelight. On the far side a staircase ascended to the second level. There was also a door to their right that led into a kitchen area.

'It's a beautiful house,' said Eben, his eyes glancing around the room.

'Thank you, Eben. Please take a seat.' Torela directed him to a comfortable cushioned chair. He sat down and she sat in the chair opposite him.

'Eben, you said that Carlin may have known your parents. What can you tell me about this?'

'I was hoping you could tell me something because I really don't know much at all,' replied Eben as he took the parchment letter from his pocket and handed it to her. She opened the letter and read it to herself. Eben saw her eyes widen as she read; she looked up at him and stared directly into his eyes for several moments. She then glanced at the sword that was latched to his belt.

'Your sword, is it the same sword mentioned in the letter?'

'Yes,' he replied.

'May I have a look?' He nodded and handed the sword to her. She unsheathed the blade. 'This sword is ancient. I never expected that I would ever come to hold the Ecorian Sword in my own hands.' She studied the blade and hilt closely for at least a minute.

'What do you know about the sword?' asked Eben, very curious to know what she was implying.

'I know it once belonged to the emperors of the Ecorian Empire.'

'But why do I have it, and why did Carlin hide me away in a remote hill village?'

'I don't know why,' replied Torela, handing the sword back to him. 'However, I know that Carlin had many secrets that he never told. He never told me about you or the sword.'

'Who exactly was Carlin?'

'He was not from Ortaria. He came from Iarthar, a land far in the west of Veredor. He was a member of an ancient order of knights, and he was a noble warrior who worked tirelessly to protect the lands from evil.' She paused for a moment and stared at Eben. 'I think you should not have come to Ancora. This city is living under a terrible curse; you are not safe here. '

'I know we are living in dark and dangerous times, but I came because I needed answers.'

'I understand your desire to find the answers you seek. I'm sure everything has a purpose, and I know that you have come at this particular time for a reason. I'm not sure what your purpose is yet.' She cast her eyes down at the sword. 'Every warrior who ever carried that sword fought for the good of all the people of Veredor.' Her voice was calm and strong. Eben could feel in his heart that she spoke the truth. He looked down at the sword.

'I want to help the people of Ortaria,' said Eben, feeling a sense of conviction rise through his body. She stared at him for a little while as if she could read his thoughts.

'Tomorrow there will be a meeting here at sunset. You may find some more answers if you come. You may also find that there are ways you can help the people of Ortaria.'

'I will come,' said Eben, eager to learn what he could do to help.

'Do you have a place to stay?'

'I'm staying with some friends at a closed down inn near the docks called The Sea Dragon.'

'Eben, you must be careful, this city has danger lurking around every corner.'

**

It was a rarity to see people out on the streets after dark in Ancora. Only vagrants, vagabonds, and other unsavoury characters would dare go out at night. There was a good reason to be cautious as many unsuspecting folk would simply disappear into the darkness never to be heard of again. Of course there was an argument to be made that the streets were actually safer at night simply because there were fewer people around. Either way the streets of Ancora were not safe at the best of times.

Early in the evening a pair of evil eyes caught sight of something peculiar. Anyone else may have thought that a young man passing by wearing a worn leather cloak was simply one of the many vagrants making a living from the misery of the townsfolk. But a glimmer of hope, like light in the darkness, lit up the murky street, and a darkened heart for a moment caught a glimpse of its own frozen state and felt powerless.

Eben walked back along the main road toward The Sea Dragon. It was getting late and he thought it best to hurry. He passed by the palace and continued to walk toward the docks. Rounding a corner he saw a hooded man mounted on a large black warhorse. The darkness and gloom seemed to accumulate around the rider. Slowing his pace, he looked up as he passed by, attempting to appear inconspicuous. The rider's dark eyes stared directly at Eben; most of his face was shrouded by the shadow of his hood. For a few moments they made eye contact. Eben felt a shiver rise up his spine. He glanced away and continued along the far side of the road and passed by without incident. He quickened his pace and looked back over his shoulder to see the rider hadn't moved.

A few minutes later Eben arrived at the inn and he knocked three times on the door. It was an icy evening and a cold gale was blowing in from the sea.

'Who's there?' asked Stella a few moments later.

'Eben,' he replied in a shivering voice.

She opened the door and smiled as she ushered him in out of the cold.

Red appeared from the bar with a smile on his face. 'We were starting to worry about you. I'm glad to see you're all right. Come over and have a warm glass of ale.' Eben followed them over to the bar and took a seat.

'Did you find any news about your parents?' asked Stella as Red poured him a mug of ale.

'No,' replied Eben. 'But I did learn a few things about my past.' Red handed him the ale. 'I found the library you told me about. It is in a state of ruin. I met an old man who was once the librarian there. He directed me on to a wise woman who lives near the north gate. She knew Carlin, the one who sent me to Clemensdale when I was very young, although she had never heard of me. She also seems to know what's going on in Ortaria. I'm going to meet her again tomorrow night.'

Stella raised her eyebrows and gave Eben a troubled look. 'You should be careful who you trust. Don't get involved in anything that's plotting against King Ignis unless you want to get yourself killed.'

'She's right,' agreed Red, nodding soberly. 'Everyone knows the reason we have these troubles is because the King doesn't care for the people anymore. Nobody likes the King; anyone and everyone who has tried to do something has been thrown in the dungeon or executed for treason.'

'Surely something needs to be done,' said Eben.

Red took another sip of his ale. 'True, something does need to be done, but it's probably best left to other people.'

**

Eben found his way back to Torela's house late the following day. The sun was setting sooner than he expected, and he was rushing because he was running late. He arrived at the laneway and quickly approached the red doorway. It was a little after sunset. A moment later the door opened.

'You're late,' grumbled Torg in his deep burly voice.

'I'm sorry,' said Eben, stepping into the hallway.

'They're all down there,' added Torg, pointing toward the room beyond the hall. Torg then closed and bolted the door.

Eben walked down the hall and came to the large furnished room. A group of about twenty people were seated in a semicircle. They were facing the far side where Torela was standing and speaking to them.

'....all of you have heard the rumours and have seen what is happening in Ancora. You know the darkness continues to grow.' She looked to Eben and directed him to a seat as she spoke. 'Each one of you is here because you are concerned. Each one of you is here because you care for the people of Ortaria and you want to see an end to all the villainy and evil.'

'How can we do anything if King Ignis won't listen to the people? Years ago he cared for us, and now he refuses to hear our cries for help,' said a man in response.

Torela nodded and paused for a moment before speaking, 'True, he doesn't listen. He refuses to give audience to anyone. He seems to have changed and hardened. He once was a much loved and honourable man. Three years ago everything changed, and for a long time there has been no explanation or reason. No one has known why, but tonight I believe you will learn the truth,' she said, and her words stunned the people. 'I want to introduce to you a young man named Cassiel. He was once a student of the magic academy on the island of Zyran. You will want to hear what he has to say.'

A tall and handsome young man stood up and walked over to stand beside Torela. He looked to be in his mid-twenties and was wearing a long brown coat. Cassiel held his chin high and his shoulders back and had a certain sense of pride about him. He had carefree dark hair, dark eyes, and a fair complexion.

'Thank you, Torela,' he said and she took a seat. He looked down at the group seated before him and cleared his throat before speaking. 'For you to understand what I have to tell you I first must inform you of a few details about myself and also about the Citadel of Zyran. Firstly about myself: I was once an apprentice at the Magic Academy of Zyran. Seven years ago I began my training; many of you know such training is rigorous and takes over a decade to complete. Honestly, I was never a talented wizard; nevertheless, I always worked hard and committed myself to the study of magic, and in my first year or two it was a pleasure to learn.'

Cassiel scanned the faces of the group and for a moment he glanced at Eben. He drew a long breath before continuing. 'And secondly, what many of you probably don't know is that beneath the Citadel of Zyran there is a dungeon where the Zyranian Order keeps only the most dangerous prisoners. The dungeon is the home of rogue sorcerers, tyrants, and other evil individuals. The prison is bound by an ancient and very mysterious enchantment which makes the stone and hewn rock impenetrable. There is no way to break in, and it's impossible to break out. The only way in and out of the dungeon is through the main prison gate and a single corridor that leads down into the dungeon. The only way to open the dungeon gate and the cell doors is by using a magical key which is held by the Gatekeeper of Zyran.'

He paused for a moment, catching his breath. The whole group were listening intently.

'The dungeon door is guarded at all times by two wizards of the academy. About three years ago I was placed on guard, which I might add is a particularly tedious job. Late that night, when I was nearing the end of my watch, I was approached by two wizards who were leading a man. The man's face was covered by a cloth sack. It's not unusual to see wizards in Zyran, especially within the grounds of the Citadel, but these two were two of the most important wizards on the island. Baltac at the time was the second in command of the Zyranian Order, and Trebax was and still is the Gatekeeper of Zyran. You also know that Baltac is now the High Commander of the Zyranian Order and the Lord of Zyran. I wondered why the prisoner's face was hidden. As they came back up from the deep I overhead Baltac say that Ortaria was defenceless now that the fool was locked away.'

There was a gasp among those seated.

'Are you saying they imprisoned King Ignis? Why would the Zyranian Order do such a thing? The Zyranian Order has stood by us for centuries.

Surely they are our allies,' said an old man near the front.

'Let me tell it plainly: I believe the Zyranians have taken an evil path and are working to sow seeds of wickedness in our lands. I also believe you are being ruled by an imposter. The real King Ignis is imprisoned in the Dungeons of Zyran.'

'We must free him!' shouted a woman who was seated next to Eben. The group started talking frantically. Eben could hear the outrage and shock in their voices. Torela stood and turned to the group.

'Please listen,' she said. The room fell silent. 'With Cassiel's help we have devised a plan to free the King. Cassiel, if you would please describe the plan.'

Cassiel nodded and waited for the room to become completely silent. 'It will not be easy. You have been called here because you are trusted, and we need some volunteers to complete this difficult task. Firstly we must sneak into the Citadel of Zyran. Secondly we must steal the key from Trebax, the Gatekeeper of Zyran; thirdly we must get to the dungeon gate without being seen, and last of all, we must free the King and safely escape the island. There is no way that any of us could take on the full force of the Zyranian Order, and the Citadel also has a dedicated group of one hundred highly skilled guardsmen. It is extremely important that we don't get seen and we complete this mission in secret. The wizards are very powerful and wouldn't hesitate to kill us if we were discovered.'

There was a silence as the group absorbed all that Cassiel had said. The silence was suddenly broken when Torg rushed down the hallway from the front of the house.

'My Lady, palace guardsmen are entering the laneway!' he cried.

Torela remained calm and closed her eyes for a few seconds. Everyone in the room looked up at her, waiting for her guidance. A few moments later her eyes opened. She looked up at Torg.

'Torg, lead the people out the back door. We have been discovered. They are coming for us,' she said. Everyone in the room stood up quickly. Torg drew his massive two handed broadsword.

Eben could feel the ground begin to shake. A groaning and screeching sound resonated down the hallway. They looked toward the entrance. An explosion blasted from the front door and shook the entire house. A wave of fire approached them at a blistering speed from the hallway, setting fire to everything in its path.

Torela lifted her hand; a ray of blue light issued forth creating a rippling energetic barrier which shielded them from the approaching fire. Eben drew his sword as Cassiel moved to stand beside Torela. The room emptied of people as Torg led the group through the kitchen and out the back door. Only Torela, Cassiel, and Eben remained in the room. The intense flames suddenly faded away. A man in a dark cape stood at the entrance to the hallway.

'Meara,' he grunted, his eyes full of hate. His lips curled down at the edges with malice. He was entirely bald which seemed to increase the look of brutality that was etched into his features. 'I thought the Irilian Order had agreed to stay out of the Eastern Lands.'

'That agreement ended when the Zyranians decided to turn against the people of Veredor,' said Torela. 'The Irilians work for the good of all people, you know that, Zarceler.' At the sound of his own name the caped man smirked and stepped forward as a group of guardsmen dashed down the hallway to stand behind him.

'Oh yes, how noble of you,' said Zarceler mockingly, with an evil grin from ear to ear. Zarceler raised his hand. There was a flash of red light. Beams of orange energy burst through the air toward Torela. Torela lifted her hands and blue light streamed forth creating a barrier that looked like a transparent shimmering wall of energy. It shielded them from the hissing fiery energy blasts. Zarceler didn't stop bombarding the shield with his sinister attacks. They hissed and smashed into the barrier.

A moment later a group of brutish guardsmen appeared in the kitchen at the back of the house.

'Cassiel, take Eben and get out of here!' cried Torela. Cassiel raised his hand and hurled several orbs of fire at the approaching soldiers in the kitchen. The blasts knocked the soldiers back, and they all tumbled away.

'We can't leave you!' shouted Cassiel.

'You must go!' she cried out, looking back over her shoulder. 'Please, Cassiel. Go!' Cassiel hesitated for a moment and then turned toward the stairs.

'Quick, up the stairs,' cried Cassiel, pushing Eben across the room toward the staircase. Eben climbed the stairs in seconds and reached the door at the top. The door opened out into a large bedroom. At the far side of the room there was a small window. Eben went to the window and started to open it. Cassiel was not far behind.

'No! Eben, climb the ladder to the roof!'

Cassiel locked the door and touched the handle. He muttered some words under his breath; an orange light streamed forth from his hand and entered the door causing it to instantly lock. In a heartbeat Eben had climbed the ladder and pushed open the trapdoor. A moment later he was on the empty rooftop. The whole house was shaking from the raging battle inside between Torela and Zarceler. Eben stood with his sword in hand as Cassiel climbed onto the roof after him.

'Eben, run and hide. I'm going back down there to help Torela.'

'I'll come too,' said Eben, not wanting to leave them to fight Zarceler and the soldiers alone.

'No!' said Cassiel firmly. 'She wanted you out...' His words were cut short.

The entire building started to groan and shake under their feet. A moment later it began to collapse around them. Cassiel managed to scurry across and grab onto the solid wall of the adjoining house, but Eben slipped backward over the edge. For a few moments he fell, completely losing control. His back struck the solid ground as a dust cloud from the collapsing building blasted out into the surrounding alleyways and lanes. He slowly got to his feet and picked up his sword. After a dazed moment he started to move down the alleyway and out of the dust. He could feel his left leg was aching and his head was throbbing from the fall. He turned and saw a great pile of rubble where Torela's house had once stood. Cassiel was nowhere in sight.

'Find them! I want them dead or alive!' cried Zarceler's furious voice in the distance.

Eben limped away as quickly as he could into the darkness and edged down through a thin gap between two buildings which opened up into a small square. He crossed the square and moved through a laneway full of waste and rotting food.

'This way!' shouted a voice from behind him. Eben looked over his shoulder and could see a group of soldiers in the distance. They hadn't noticed him yet, and he glanced around for somewhere to hide. There was a wooden crate full of waste. He jumped in, covering himself as they approached. They passed by, not noticing the crate or the young man hiding within. Lying completely still in the rot and stench he waited until all was quiet.

After a short time he lifted his head and looked over the top of the crate in the direction the guardsmen had gone. The laneway was empty. He climbed out of the crate and started searching for a side laneway to escape. He found a long and thin alley that led back in the direction of the north gate. Dragging his aching leg he quietly staggered forward. The pain was also growing in the back of his head, and blood was dripping down the back of his neck. Shouting voices echoed through the lanes and alleys behind him. He hurried along and moments later the lane opened out onto the main street that led from the north gate back toward the palace.

He crossed the road and ducked into a back street on the opposite side. He gradually stumbled his way through a network of narrow lanes and alleys until he arrived at the docks. An icy wind blew across the docks. Completely exhausted he found the door of The Sea Dragon and almost collapsed on the doorstep as he struggled to knock. A few moments passed before Stella opened the door.

'What happened to you?' asked Stella, stepping out and gently taking him by the arm.

'Really, I'm fine,' he said as he unsteadily made an attempt to step through the doorway.

A moment later Red was at the door. 'By Teodric! Eben. You smell like rotting fish,' he said, grinning.

'This isn't a time for jokes,' shouted Stella. 'He's badly hurt.'

'No really, I'm fine...' whispered Eben as he started to lose consciousness.

Stella lay him down on the floor of the common room. 'Get some clean cloth from under the bench in the kitchen! And get some water!' Red's smile disappeared instantly. He ran off quickly to the kitchen.

Eben looked up at Stella. She stared down at him; her green eyes full of concern for him.

'Eben, you will be fine. Everything is going to be...' Those were the last words he heard that night. Everything went dark.

CHAPTER FOUR

Eben awoke and looked around to find he was lying in his bed at The Sea Dragon. His head was bandaged, and he could feel his leg still hurt, but the pain had lost most of its sharpness. His body was covered in grazes and bruises, but he had been cleaned and washed. He thought back over the night before and the ill-fated meeting and wondered if any of the others had survived the raid. Everything had happened so quickly that he had no time to think. He pulled himself out of bed and slowly walked to the door, making his way down the stairs to the common room. Flickering firelight lit up the common room. Red was sitting next to the open fireplace warming his feet and hadn't heard Eben coming down the stairs.

As Eben approached Red turned and looked up. 'Eben, you're awake. I thought you were never going to get up. You've been out for two days.'

'Thanks for looking after me.'

'You should thank Stella. She's the one who cleaned you up. You must have lost a lot of blood. You have a mighty gash on the back of your head and a bruise on your leg bigger than any I've ever seen. Take a seat before you fall over again.'

Eben took the seat across from Red. He looked at the blazing fireplace and felt its calming warmth.

'Where's Stella?'

'She's gone out to visit a friend,' replied Red as he looked back over his shoulder toward the front door. 'So, what happened to you the other night? How did you end up all beaten up like that?'

'I went to the meeting I told you and Stella about. It was about the evil in Ancora...'

At that moment the front door opened and Stella stepped in carrying a leather bag. She locked the door and approached them. 'You're up,' she said, surprised. 'Are you feeling better?'

'Much better,' replied Eben. 'Thanks for taking care of me.'

'You're lucky you made it back here. If you had fallen over in the streets it would have been the end of you,' she said as she walked by them and placed the leather bag on the bar.

'At least you managed to gain us two extra nights here at The Sea Dragon,' said Red, slightly chuckling. Stella glared across at Red and then walked into the kitchen without saying another word. Red didn't seem at all troubled by her and smiled as he looked back over his shoulder toward the kitchen. Turning his head he glanced back at the fire. 'That reminds me. Remember you said you had some silver.' Eben nodded. 'We probably should give some to Stella. I think she'll let us stay a little while longer; at least until you're completely well, but we definitely have to pay her something, and you're the only one of us who has any money.'

'Sure, I will pay, but I don't want to be a burden on her. Maybe we should leave sooner rather than later.'

'Oh, don't worry,' replied Red. 'She likes having us around.' Red put his feet back up to warm them again.

'She doesn't seem to like you much.'

Red's threw his head back and laughed. 'Don't be ridiculous. Of course she likes me.'

'Are you sure?' asked Eben, not convinced.

Red didn't answer. He watched the flames of the fire for a few seconds. 'So, you were saying about your meeting,' he said, changing the topic. Eben thought he probably shouldn't ask about Red and Stella's relationship.

'Yes, the meeting was brought to an end when the house was attacked by a sorcerer.'

'A what?' cried Red, his eyes widening in shock.

'They were discussing some very serious matters and the house was attacked. I made it to the roof in an attempt to escape. I fell when the house collapsed, and that was when I was injured, but I managed to escape through the back alleys and made my way back here.'

'We did warn you. Getting involved in anything that questions the King is dangerous,' said Red, taking an unfamiliar serious tone.

'Red's right,' said Stella as she came back into the room from the kitchen. 'He may be a bad king, but King Ignis is our king...'

'He's your king, Stella. Remember I'm Silvorian,' said Red, lifting his chin proudly.

'Actually he's not a king at all. He's an imposter,' said Eben. Stella and Red froze.

'An imposter!' shouted Red, almost slipping from his chair

'That's what the meeting was called to discuss. The real King Ignis is imprisoned in a dungeon on the island of Zyran. An imposter sits on the throne of Ortaria. It's an evil plot put together by a group of Zyranian wizards,' said Eben. There was a stunned silence. Only the crackle of the fire made any sound.

'Surely this can't be true,' said Red. 'How can they be sure?' Stella looked to Red and then her eyes darted back to Eben.

'They believed it enough to put their lives at risk,' said Eben. 'And look what happened to me. I was lucky to escape. The authorities didn't want anyone to get out. They want to make sure no one knows what I just told you.'

Stella looked to be deep in thought. A moment later there was a thudding knock at the door. Stella took a quick breath and anxiously stared across at Eben.

'They don't know where you are staying do they?' asked Stella, whispering fearfully.

'I don't think so,' whispered Eben.

They stood up and walked toward the door. Again the heavy knock rang out.

'Who is it?' asked Stella.

'I'm looking for Eben. Is he staying here?' asked a man's voice from outside. Stella backed away, and she looked back at Red and Eben. Red signalled for her to reveal nothing.

'There's no one by that name here,' she answered.

There was silence for a few moments. Suddenly the locked bolt of the door started moving and opening by itself.

'Bloody magic!' gasped Red, clenching his fists. Stella stepped back behind the young men. A moment later the door opened. Cassiel stood in the doorway.

'Die Zyranian!' shouted Red, instantly leaping forward. Cassiel lifted his hand and stopped Red in his tracks; an invisible wall barred his way. Red pushed forward but couldn't move.

'Red, he's not against us,' cried Eben. Red stopped trying to press against the barrier and moved back a little. Cassiel walked into the room and gently closed the door.

'That's the kind of bravery we need,' said Cassiel with a slight smile. 'I'm sorry to surprise you like this.'

'Who is he?' asked Stella nervously, glancing across at Eben.

'This is Cassiel,' said Eben. 'He was at the meeting. He's a wizard. Cassiel, I would like you to meet my friends, Red and Stella'

Stella and Red stared at Cassiel. It was extremely rare to meet a wizard in Ortaria.

'You seem far too young to be a wizard,' said Red, still upset that he had been restrained by Cassiel's spell.

'I'm an outcast. I never finished my training,' said Cassiel, unperturbed.

'That explains it then; you're a dropout,' said Red. Stella shot Red a disapproving look.

'Yes, that's true, but under the circumstances I'm happy to be a dropout,' said Cassiel with a confident smile.

'Would you like a drink?' asked Stella politely.

'Indeed I would,' replied Cassiel as he casually took off his coat and hung it on a hook beside the door. They walked back over to the warmth of the fire.

'I was worried about you, Eben. I thought you were killed in the battle,' said Cassiel. Stella pulled up a seat for the young wizard.

'He arrived back here in a terrible state two nights ago,' said Stella as she went to grab a pitcher of ale from the bar.

'What happened to the others?' asked Eben.

'Everyone who escaped through the back door was captured by waiting guardsmen. It was a trap. Torg and the others were taken to the palace dungeons. I expect they met a terrible fate.'

'And Torela?'

'I'm not sure if she made it out or not before the building collapsed. I managed to escape along the rooftops. I returned the next day to have a look around. The city guard were still searching the area, so I had to move on. I spent yesterday and today looking for Torela to no avail.'

'How did you know where I was staying?' asked Eben.

'I had spoken about you at length with Torela earlier on the day of the meeting. She held you in high regard. She thought that you could help us in our struggle against the Zyranian Order. I think she thought you were special in some way.'

Red laughed and folded his arms across his chest as he leaned back in his chair. 'You should be careful, Eben. It looks like he wants you to join his rebel army.'

Cassiel frowned and took a sip of his ale. 'There is no army, just me,' he said coolly. 'Everyone in Ancora who wanted to help was captured two nights ago. So if something is going to be done it is up to me to do it.'

'So you're going to free King Ignis yourself?' asked Red.

Cassiel stared at Red for a long moment. He then glanced across at Stella. 'I assume you and Stella both know what's going on with King Ignis?' Red nodded curtly. 'Good. Eben trusts you. The enemy would kill you if they knew you were aware of the King's imprisonment.' Red was taken aback and scratched his chin nervously. 'You are right, Red. I do need help. I'm working on a plan to free King Ignis, and I can't do it alone. The enemy may have had an infiltrator at our meeting. They may also know some of my plan. If we're going to free King Ignis then we should do it as soon as possible.'

'We! Don't include me in your plan,' said Red sharply.

'I'll help,' said Stella.

'Stella! Don't be ridiculous. You can't get involved; it's too risky,' protested Red.

'King Ignis is my king, Red. You're Silvorian, so it doesn't matter much to you. I want Ortaria to return to how it was years ago.'

'I'm definitely in too,' said Eben.

'Good,' said Cassiel. 'I'm very grateful for any assistance.'

Red stood up and heavily sighed. 'If Stella goes I'll have to go too.' Cassiel smiled at hearing Red's words.

**

Later that evening they were sitting around a table in the kitchen. Cassiel placed a large piece of parchment on the table top. A few candles were lit and provided a soft light. It was a map of the Citadel of Zyran, which included details of the main gate, diagrams of the academy, and the location of the Dungeons of Zyran.

'The Citadel is surrounded by an outer wall and has three main gates; it is about a thousand yards in diameter. Only Zyranian Wizards and students at the academy are allowed inside, and the gates are well guarded by a fierce band of guardsmen. Outside the Citadel there is a village beside the docks; it exists mainly to serve the Citadel itself and...'

'I've been there and...,' said Red.

Cassiel stared across at him. 'Good, Red, but Stella and Eben haven't, so let me continue. The

Citadel is quite impressive and consists of over one hundred stone towers that rise high into the sky above. Many bridges make a network of pathways between the towers. In the past each wizard was given their own tower to live in; now some of the towers are used for other purposes because there are less than a hundred Zyranian wizards. Trebax, the Gatekeeper of Zyran, lives in a tower near the main front gate. He holds the key to the prison which looks like this.' He took from his pocket another small piece of paper and unfolded it, showing a picture of an octagonal crystal.

'It doesn't look like a key,' said Stella.

'It's an ancient and mysterious amulet which can be used to open any door,' said Cassiel. 'Our mission is to enter the Citadel, steal the key, free the King, and escape before anyone knows we've been there.'

'Impossible,' said Red, shaking his head. 'I don't want to dampen your enthusiasm, but even getting into the Citadel of Zyran will be a great task in itself, and trying not to be seen will probably be even harder. I've seen those towers; assuming Trebax locks his door the only way in would be through the high windows that are a hundred feet above the ground.'

'I didn't say it was going to be easy,' said Cassiel.

'I can do it,' said Stella. They were surprised by her words. 'If we can get into the Citadel then I can climb into those windows. Acrobatics, rope climbing, and trapeze were my specialties in the circus.'

'Stella, Trebax will kill you if he sees you. I don't like the sound of this plan,' said Red.

'It's risky for all of us, Red,' replied Stella.

'But we still have to get into the Citadel,' said Eben.

Red started lightly tapping on the table, and they turned and looked at him. 'When I was a sailor we delivered Silvorian wine to Zyran in big oak barrels. I know a man who may be able to smuggle us inside the Citadel. He's not the charitable type; he'll require payment.'

Cassiel took from his pocket a leather pouch and tipped the contents of gold and silver coins onto the map. A gold coin could buy a great deal in Ortaria.

'Money isn't a problem,' stated Cassiel. 'Assuming we can get into the Citadel and steal the key, we will still need a distraction to get into the dungeons. The prison is guarded by two wizards and there is only one way in and out. If there was only one wizard I could probably deal with it; two make it impossible for me. I'm simply not powerful enough to deal with two wizards at once.'

'Fireworks,' said Red with a cheeky grin.

'Fireworks!' repeated Stella, shaking her head. 'We don't want to wake the whole of Zyran.'

'Why not? I could create absolute chaos by setting off the fireworks, and everyone's focus would be on me. No one will have any idea that a prison break was happening. Maybe the guards will leave their posts long enough to investigate.'

'Hmmmm,' groaned Cassiel, not liking the idea. 'Firstly, there is no guarantee the wizards will leave their posts, and secondly, you will be completely destroyed by the Zyranians.'

'I won't!' said Red defensively. 'I can light them up and run. By the time they start looking for me I'll be long gone.'

'Do you know enough about fireworks though?' asked Cassiel hesitantly, still not convinced by the idea.

'You're talking to the unsurpassed master of fireworks himself!' said Red confidently. Both Eben and Cassiel looked to Stella for confirmation.

'Yes, it's true, Red is very experienced. In the circus he was a Fire Master and prepared a display every night,' said Stella.

'A man of many talents,' said Cassiel. Cassiel paused and reflected for a few moments on the idea. 'It's possible that fireworks could be used as a diversion within the walls which could help us escape after we free King Ignis. We should definitely bring some fireworks, yet I doubt the wizard guards will leave their posts for anything. We still have to think up a way of getting by them.'

The room fell silent. They all sat in quiet reflection, searching for a solution.

Eben broke the silence. 'I once hunted mountain deer in a special way. Mountain deer can't be shot with an ordinary arrow because they are likely to run leagues away before they collapse. I would wait for them quietly in a hidden place. When they appeared I would use a small harmless dart with a tiny amount of the common herbs Ortarian Mugwort and Valerian Root. Within seconds the dart would cause them to fall to the ground asleep. We could use this same method on the wizards.'

'Brilliant,' said Cassiel. 'This is just what we need. If you could approach the wizard guards with a long cloak and hood they would probably mistake you for a wizard, and then before they realised you weren't...they would be sound asleep.'

'But how do we escape once we free King Ignis?' asked Eben.

'That's the easy part. The supply gate near the docks is always locked except for when they're taking supplies in. If we make it that far we will have the key; we should be able to open the gate and walk straight down to the docks to our waiting boat. So that's our plan. We arrive on the island and pay your acquaintance to smuggle us into the Citadel. Stella will infiltrate Trebax's tower and steal the key. Eben will put the wizard guards to sleep, and I will then enter the prison and free King Ignis. We will then escape via the supply gate and sail back to Ortaria.'

'We have a plan at last,' said Red merrily.

'Indeed we do,' said Eben, feeling uneasy at the many difficulties such a plan may entail.

CHAPTER FIVE

They spent several days preparing for their mission. Cassiel had organised passage to Zyran aboard a small trading ship. They had gathered all the required equipment: ropes and grappling hooks for Stella, the herbs and darts for Eben, and Red had organised a supply of fireworks. They had discussed all aspects of the plan in detail, and they knew that if they could free King Ignis he would be able to rally the people and bring back all the good men who had been sent away to Galdir and the Iron Gate Pass. The liberation of Ortaria depended on their success.

Cassiel had purchased some swords for them from a local armourer. Stella now carried a short sword at her side, and Red had a broadsword. Red was in the common room practicing with his new sword. Eben, sitting by the fireplace, watched on and was surprised that Red was actually a skilled swordsman.

'When I was a sailor there was always the risk of being attacked by pirates on the high seas,' said Red as he keenly practiced his cuts and stabs against thin air.

Stella sat on a chair in the corner of the room watching Red. Cassiel had gone to gather some last minute supplies for the journey. They planned to leave the following day at sunrise.

'Are you any good with a sword?' asked Red, glancing across at Eben as he continued to practice.

'My adoptive father taught me how to use a sword when I was young, but I think I am a lot better at archery.'

A moment later the door opened and Cassiel walked into the common room. He quickly closed the door and bolted the lock. His face was flushed, and he was visibly shaking.

'What's the matter?' asked Stella, alarmed at his state.

'I saw Zarceler on my way back here. I rounded a corner and he was across the street from me. Unfortunately he recognised me and sent his guardsmen after me. I escaped through the back lanes. I managed to lose them, but only just,' he said.

'Who's Zarceler?' asked Stella.

'He is a Zyranian Enforcer. He is highly skilled in the art of battle magic. They send him to hunt the enemies of Zyran. He's not someone you want to meet in a dark alley,' answered Cassiel. Eben handed Cassiel a mug of water.

'He was the one who attacked us at the meeting,' said Eben, remembering that Torela had said his name.

'Yes, that was Zarceler,' said Cassiel, before pausing to drink from the mug. 'Torela's real name is Meara. Meara has been using the name Torela to hide herself from the Zyranians in Ancora. She's an Irilian. The Irilians are the largest order of wizards in the Far Western Lands of Veredor. Long ago the Irilians and the Zyranians went to war against each other. After many battles the Zyranians scattered and almost destroyed the Irilian Order. The Zyranian Order has patronised the Irilians ever since those days. Meara came to Ancora to contest the power of the Zyranian Order and to free the lands of the east from their evil schemes, but the Zyranians are powerful and there are many of them. Few wizards are brave enough to challenge the power of Zyran. For a long time the Zyranian Order has been the most powerful order of wizards in Veredor.'

'How many orders of wizards are there?' asked Eben curiously.

'There are four main orders and a few smaller groups of wizards here and there,' replied Cassiel. 'The Zyranians are the largest order. The Irilians live in the Far West, and they are mainly based in the land of Dravania. The Fire Order is a small and very ancient order based in the Old Guardian Mountains between Vastoria and Everdon.'

'And the fourth?' asked Red as he sheathed his sword.

'The Northern Sorcerers,' said Cassiel with a grimace. 'The Northern Sorcerers are from the Kaznor Empire in the Northern Lands of Veredor. Their magic is very different in nature to the magic of the wizards who live in the South.'

'How so?' asked Eben.

'I can't easily explain magic; it's very mysterious. The Irilians, Zyranians, and Fire Order all learn about the subtle potential hidden in their surroundings. They learn to manipulate this power. The Northern Sorcerers are different, they howl deep within; in the process they devour themselves and their bodies wither away, and they often hunger for power.'

'Which wizards are the most powerful?' asked Red.

'The Northern Sorcerers almost always defeat the wizards of the South. Usually several wizards from the South are required to overcome a single Northern Sorcerer, and on several occasions in history a Northern Sorcerer has been so powerful that the entire Zyranian Order has had to fight them. But the magic of the Northern Sorcerers is not refined. They can't do things like heal a broken arm or open a locked door. They're much more likely to blast the door open. Thankfully, they rarely come south from Kaznor and if they do they tend to come alone. Two decades ago a very powerful Northern Sorcerer came south with a small army and attacked Zyran. I was a child at the time of the invasion. It was a terrible time for the people living on the island.'

Stella stood up and walked over toward the kitchen area. 'All this talk of wizards is fascinating, but we will have to have something to eat if we're going to be at sea for a couple of days.'

**

The following morning they rose about an hour before sunrise and did a final check on their packs before leaving the inn and walking across to the docks. Anchored against a pier was a small weatherworn ship. Sailors and dockworkers were rushing about and completing the last minute preparations before setting out. Cassiel led the way along a gangplank. The old captain, standing atop a large wooden crate, was a fiery man with a bushy black beard and a heavily lined face. He was furiously shouting commands to the sailors below. They jumped and ran about, creating quite a chaotic scene.

'Come on ya naw good fish guts; work harda. We need da git moven! I aint pain ya to run a social club,' he shouted, his voice was coarse and guttural.

'Captain Orstag,' said Cassiel as he stepped up onto the deck of the ship.

'Not naw,' he blurted back, dismissively waving Cassiel away. They stood on the deck as sailors ducked and weaved about them.

'Git outda da way!' shouted Captain Orstag down at them.

'Where to?' asked Cassiel, surprised at the tone Captain Orstag was taking.

'Beelow da deck!'

They were a little taken aback by his gruffness, and it looked like Cassiel was going to say something. A moment later the fuming captain turned his back to them and began shouting at the sailors on the other side of the ship. Cassiel thought it better to hold his tongue. Red led the way down below the deck and into a dimly lit and confined area below. Barrels, wooden boxes, and many traded goods were loaded everywhere in the stuffy and exceedingly dank space. A stench of something putrid permeated the entire ship.

'What do we do now?' asked Stella.

'Wait. I assume the Captain will assign us a cabin soon,' replied Cassiel. That was the deal I made with him yesterday.' They could hear voices toward the back of the ship.

'I'll see if I can find our cabin,' said Red. He walked off toward the back and was lost from view behind large wooden crates.

Eben sat down on a barrel. 'This is cosy,' he said, trying to be positive.

Stella smiled bleakly; she looked down at the floor as two rats scurried around the edge of a crate and ran along an edge, jumping into a gap in the floorboards. Her bleak smile quickly turned to a deep frown, and she covered her mouth with her hand.

'Were there any other boats?' she asked anxiously.

'Don't worry; they won't hurt you, they're only rats,' replied Cassiel. They could hear voices merrily shouting from the back of the ship. A moment later Red appeared with a wide smile.

'Hey, come on. A friend of mine is here,' said Red cheerfully.

They followed him between the crates and made their way to the back of the ship where there was a slightly cleared area. Seated on a small wooden chair was a very overweight middle-aged man, with greasy hair, dark circles under his eyes, and a big grin on his face. He was surrounded by a group of five gangly men, all with swords at their belts. Stella cautiously glanced at Eben.

'Stella, Cassiel, Eben; I would like you to meet Falsig,' said Red, indicating toward the overweight man.

'Pleased to meet you,' said Falsig in a throaty voice, a greasy smile crossing his face.

'Years ago we worked together on a ship called the Gale Blazer,' said Red, who seemed happy to have met up with his old friend.

'Those were the days,' said Falsig, grinning across at Red.

'Remember when those crazy villagers thought we had stolen a pig. We had to swim five hundred yards out to our anchored ship!' said Red, laughing as he spoke.

'Sure do, Red. ' said Falsig, chuckling along. 'So why are you heading out to Zyran?'

'Business,' replied Cassiel coolly.

'What kind of business are you in, Cassiel?' asked Falsig, paying close attention.

'Trading rare goods,' said Cassiel quickly. 'What about you, Falsig; why are you going to Zyran?' asked Cassiel, turning the topic away from their mission.

'I work for the Zyranian Order,' said Falsig casually. 'I bring the wizards some of the finest spices and delicacies in Veredor. Whilst I'm not travelling I help govern the kitchen in the Citadel of Zyran. I also help a little to manage the Citadel's guardsmen.'

'Do you think you can get us into the Citadel?' asked Red carelessly. Cassiel's jaw dropped as Red revealed a part of their plan, and he stared harshly at Red, obviously not wanting him to say another word. Red's realised he had made a gaff and his eyes shifted from side to side.

'Why do you want to get into the Citadel?' asked Falsig inquisitively.

Red looked to Cassiel and Eben nervously, not sure what to say. Falsig could see they were uncomfortable about the subject, and he looked up to Cassiel, assuming he was the leader.

'Why don't we have a private talk a little later this evening,' suggested Falsig. Cassiel agreed.

**

The Sea of Zyran was considered by most seafaring folk to be one of the finest stretches of water in all of Veredor. It was often said that the life of a fisherman was that of a blissful dream; however, in recent times few boats journeyed between the coasts of Ortaria and Zyran. It was widely told that a foul curse blew with the wind and scourged every ship that dared to sail the stretch of sea. Many of the once numerous seafarers had sailed away in search of safer waters in the south.

After the ship had set out from Ancora they had been assigned a small cabin toward the front. The sound of the waves and the ocean seemed strangely familiar to Eben, even though he had never been on a boat before. The four of them sat on the floor of their tiny cabin.

'I shouldn't have said anything, I know,' said Red remorsefully.

'Our plan is already hanging in the balance. If we start giving everyone we meet an idea of what we're planning we are sure to be killed by the Zyranians before we even reach the front gate of the Citadel,' said Cassiel angrily.

'I won't say another word,' said Red.

'It was stupid. You may have placed us in danger and jeopardised our plan,' said Cassiel.

'Falsig was a good friend once. We should be able to trust him,' said Red, trying to reassure them, but clearly doubting his own words.

'What about the five others standing around him?' asked Cassiel sharply.

'I'm sorry. What can I do about it now? I can't take back what I've said.'

'Don't worry about it Red,' said Eben calmly. 'We'll work it out. After all they don't know anything except that we want to get inside the Citadel.'

'But that's enough to make them suspicious,' said Cassiel.

There was a tapping on the cabin door. Eben stood up and reached over to open it. Falsig stood in the doorway with a big smoking pipe in his mouth and a sly grin on his lips.

'Hello there. Thought I would come by and have a little talk. Can I come in?' he asked, stepping inside before they had answered his question.

There was scarcely enough room in the cabin to accommodate the massive man. Somehow he managed to sit cross-legged on the floor. He continued to smoke his pipe which quickly filled the room with a thick haze. Eben closed the door and resumed his place which was now beside Falsig.

'Red, you said you and your friends want to get inside the Citadel of Zyran?'

'Maybe,' said Red, not wanting to give away anything more.

'Maybe means yes with you,' said Falsig with a hoarse chuckle. 'Now let me guess. You're planning to get inside the Citadel and rob the treasury, right? It sounds like the most ridiculous thing in the world to do, and under normal conditions I'd think you wouldn't stand a chance, but I gave it some thought, and I know Red wouldn't try such a thing unless he thought the odds were good. That made me think the three of you,' he indicated to everyone except Red, 'must all be professional thieves. Am I right?'

They looked at each other, not sure what to say for a few moments.

'Perhaps we are and perhaps we're not,' said Cassiel with an expressionless face. 'What's it to you?'

'Well, well, well,' said Falsig, grinning widely. 'I've been looking for an opportunity to move out of the kitchen and into my own palace. If we can strike a deal then I think I can get you into the Citadel.'

'So you want to make some money?' asked Cassiel coolly.

'I provide the service and you pay me my money, plain and simple,' replied Falsig, his grin extending from ear to ear. Cassiel looked to be deep in thought for a few moments. He was formulating a new plan in the space of ten seconds.

'If you get us inside then we'll give you a third of everything we take,' said Cassiel with a firm tone that completely convinced Falsig. Red's mouth fell open at Cassiel's words.

'We have a deal,' agreed Falsig.

'Good, but no more than a third,' repeated Cassiel.

'I accept your offer,' said Falsig.

**

They sat in the cabin after Falsig had left. All their eyes were cast downward. They knew that Falsig was a real risk to their plan succeeding.

'He'll be furious when he discovers that we aren't thieves and there is nothing in it for him,' whispered Eben.

'He'll have to be happy with a third of nothing,' whispered Cassiel with a slightly humorous smile, which was rare for him.

'It's not honest,' whispered Stella.

'It's also not dishonest. None of us said that we were thieves; he made that assumption himself. We didn't say we were stealing anything; he assumed that too. I said that he can have a third of what we take. He will have to be happy with a third of nothing. A deal is a deal. We need a way into the Citadel of Zyran, and we can't tell anyone our plan. The truth is that if our plan succeeds Falsig will be rewarded in the end; he just might have to wait until King Ignis takes back his throne.'

'You're cunning like a Zyranian,' said Red. 'I think we should tell him what we're really up to and see if he wants to help us.'

'Firstly, I was born on the Island of Zyran; that makes me a Zyranian by birth. Naturally, I am well versed in Zyranian lore and culture. And secondly, we have to make the best of our situation and that means never letting Falsig know our real plan,' said Cassiel firmly.

Red stared at Cassiel frostily for a few moments. 'You're not the leader of our group, Cassiel.' Cassiel took a deep breath and looked away.

'We don't have a leader,' said Eben. 'We are in this together and must try to get along. We have to rely on each other to succeed. This arguing is not helping us.'

A few moments went by and no one said a word.

'Falsig won't be happy,' said Red. 'I already have enough people who want me dead. King Ignis better give him the reward after we free him.'

'Our plan is risky to say the least. I'm willing to take any opportunity that will help us succeed,' said Cassiel.

**

Eben and Red stood on the deck at the front of the ship looking out at the sea as the sunset cast flickering orange light across the gentle waves. Eben felt he had never seen such beauty as the light reflecting on the water.

Falsig appeared and walked over from the back of the ship. 'What a lovely evening,' he said, a big sly grin covering his face.

The sun was slowly sinking beneath the waves ahead. It was truly a beautiful sight. Eben felt a sense of wonder looking out over the sea at the shining light. Watching the water brought a sense of peace to his heart.

'I'm wondering, Red. What does a thief need a bag of fireworks for?' asked Falsig.

'Have you been looking in my bag?' asked Red tensely.

'Just checking on my investment,' replied Falsig, his grin instantly fading into a stony expression. 'Red, I get the feeling you're not telling me everything.'

Red looked away toward the sunset and waited for a few moments before replying. 'The full details of our plan will remain a secret, Falsig'.

Falsig roughly grabbed Red's arm. 'Listen to me. If your cheating me I'll make sure you pay,' he said fiercely.

Eben quickly turned and immediately raised himself to his full height and clenched his fists in readiness to defend his friend. Falsig sneered up at Eben. A moment later Red smiled. He was not afraid of Falsig at all.

'Relax, you'll get your reward, Falsig,' said Red as he removed his arm from Falsig's grip.

'Make sure of it,' said Falsig as he turned and walked away.

'I don't like this. I hope I haven't foiled our plan,' said Red, his eyes narrowing as he watched Falsig head toward the back of the ship.

'Maybe we should go back to our original plan of the wine barrels,' suggested Eben.

'No, it's too late. He'll probably go straight to the Zyranians if we change anything now. He can't comprehend that we would be prepared to risk our lives for anything other than treasure, and he's determined to get his share.' Red glanced back out toward the sun as it descended beneath the waves. The cool evening was growing dark.

CHAPTER SIX

It was late in the afternoon on the second day after leaving Ancora. The ship crossed a small bay and was approaching the docks. Eben looked out at the sight of the Citadel of Zyran that towered ominously above the docks. At least a hundred stone towers rose high into the sky above and a weblike network of dozens of stone bridges linked the towers together. A massive grey stone wall, at least a hundred and fifty feet high, completely surrounded the Citadel. Hundreds of ravens circled in the gloomy haze above the towers, and dark murky clouds hung low in the sky.

Cassiel, Red, and Stella stood with Eben toward the front of the deck; they stared out at the Citadel as the ship neared the docks.

'It looks intimidating,' said Stella nervously.

'The wizards of Zyran are by far the most cunning in all of Veredor. We must be careful,' said Cassiel, looking up at the Citadel uneasily.

The ship slowly approached and entered under the dark cloud which hovered not far above the tops of the towers. The gloominess was oppressive. The area of the docks was about three hundred feet down from the edge of the wall of the Citadel. A large village made up of many huts and small houses surrounded the dock area. The sailors threw ropes and tied the ship to the dock. Captain Orstag began yelling at his sailors.

Falsig approached as the ship came up beside the docks. The sailors rushed about and secured lines and placed a gangplank. Eben and the others were preparing to disembark. 'You would be wise to get a room in the inn over there,' said Falsig, pointing toward a large inn at the edge of the village. 'I'll meet you at the bar around noon tomorrow, and we'll discuss our dealings in more detail.' He shuffled down the gangplank and was followed by his five shadowy companions.

'I don't trust him,' said Stella, grimacing as she watched Falsig walk away. Eben nodded in agreement.

Cassiel walked down the plank and across the docks. Eben, Red, and Stella followed him across the way and up the slight slope toward the inn. The sign above the door read: 'The Lost Mermaid,' and had a faded picture of a sad mermaid sitting on a beach. It was a large stone building with an upper floor and a gabled roof. Cassiel pushed the door open and stepped in. Eben, Stella, and Red followed Cassiel's lead.

The common room was crowded and very warm with large open fire burning at the far end. Groups of men filled most of the tables and many others stood at the bar. A long bar stretched along the wall on the right side of the room.

Cassiel stopped and scanned the room. He then leaned toward Eben. 'Some of these people could be dangerous, so be cautious and discreet. I'm going to see if we can reserve some rooms for tonight.' He then turned and walked toward the bar. No one in the room seemed to notice the small group of newcomers.

'Let's take the table in the corner,' said Red. They walked over and sat down. 'At least this place is warm. I remember staying here once a few years ago when I was a sailor.' He looked toward the big open fire across the room; the flames were burning brightly. 'I'm going to get us some drinks.' Red jumped up out of his seat and approached the bar.

Cassiel returned at the same time as Red. 'We have rooms on the upper floor,' he said as he took the spare seat at the table. A barmaid walked over and placed the three ales down on the table in front of the three of them.

Cassiel's eyes narrowed at the sight of the three ales. He looked up at Red and raised an eyebrow. 'You don't like me much do you, Red?'

'Sorry Cassiel, you were talking with the innkeeper. I didn't know how long you would be gone,' said Red defensively. Cassiel stared at Red for a few silent seconds. He then stood up and walked over to the bar to buy himself a drink.

'Zyranians,' muttered Red when Cassiel was out of earshot.

Stella eyed Red with a harsh frown. 'Cassiel is our friend, Red. At least try to get along with him.'

Red looked down at the table and nervously scratched his forehead. 'I'll respect him when he shows me a little respect,' he muttered.

Eben was aware that tension had been growing between Cassiel and Red ever since the two of them met back in Ancora. Red was rarely serious and always tried to turn everything into a joke. Cassiel was almost always serious and stern in demeanour and rarely had time for joking around.

Cassiel returned to the table with a mug of ale. He sat down and took a sip. 'I visited this inn regularly when I was studying at the academy,' said Cassiel, glancing around the room nostalgically.

'How far did you get into your training?' asked Eben.

'Seven years,' replied Cassiel. He then took another sip of his ale. 'I was cast out of the academy.'

'Why were you cast out?' asked Stella.

'That's something I don't like to talk about; it was a rather unpleasant experience. I will say that I was glad to see the end of my time there. When an apprentice is cast out they can never return to the Citadel and they are forbidden to practice magic,' he said soberly.

Before long a barmaid appeared with steaming plates of mutton and vegetables. They hungrily devoured their meals before retiring to their beds.

**

The next day was less gloomy. Eben looked out of his window; the dark clouds had reduced above the Citadel. Sunlight was pushing its way down through small gaps in the sky. The Citadel of Zyran was a daunting sight; it dominated the skyline above the small village. Eben could see a large group of guards marching across the top of the wall in the distance.

There was a knock at his door. Cassiel stepped into Eben's room.

'Good morning, Eben. I think we should go down to the docks and buy a small boat. We're going to need one to leave after we finish our mission here.'

'How do you feel about the plan now that we are here?' asked Eben as he stood at the window and continued surveying the immense dark walls of the Citadel.

'I hope we can succeed,' replied Cassiel. 'Falsig has made our task more challenging; hopefully he won't be a problem until after King Ignis is safely away from here. Stella's task is very dangerous. I think it is doubtful that Trebax will leave the dungeon key out of sight. If he sees her he will not hesitate to kill her.'

'Maybe we should find another way,' suggested Eben, feeling concerned for Stella.

'There is no other way into the dungeon. Only the key will open the prison door and the doors to the cells within. We are the only people who know King Ignis is imprisoned in the Dungeons of Zyran. If we fail then we fail.'

Eben stood up and put on his leather cloak. Cassiel led the way down the stairs and out of the inn. They walked across to the bustling area of the docks. Sailors were offloading crates and barrels from a large ship that had only just come into port. Across the docks, on the southern side, was a smaller pier set apart from the main docks. A few smaller fishing boats were moored to the pier. Eben and Cassiel approached the smaller pier.

An old man was fixing a net at the edge of the dock. He was a bearded short man with a very big nose, weathered skin, and a dirty old sailor's hat with a big eagle's feather attached.

'Hello there,' said Cassiel as they approached.

The man glanced up at Cassiel as he continued to fix his net. 'Hello to you too.'

'Can you tell me where I could buy a boat?'

The old man stopped fixing his net and looked up. 'A boat? You don't look like a sailor or a fisherman.'

'I'm neither,' said Cassiel coolly.

'Perhaps you're wishing to sail the wild seas and see some far off lands. I've been around sea folk for a few years now, and I know a sailor when I see one. Let me give you some free advice: if you sail out to sea without experience you'll be sailing to your grave,' said the old man with a slight chuckle.

'I appreciate your interest, but if you can't assist me I will ask someone else,' said Cassiel impatiently. The old man laughed. 'What's so funny?' asked Cassiel.

'You don't remember me do you, Cassiel?'

Cassiel's eyes widened as he suddenly recognised the old man. 'Baftel!' he cried, stunned by the sudden revelation. Eben looked from Cassiel to the old fisherman. Baftel threw his net aside and stood up. 'What brings you to Zyran?'

'I was going to ask the same question of you,' said Baftel.

'What are you doing here? I heard you were banished from the Zyranian Order,' stammered Cassiel.

Baftel sighed and looked around nervously. 'Yes, I was banished from the Citadel and cast out of the Zyranian Order. The Zyranian High Council voted seven for my death and eight for my banishment.' He sadly glanced back across the docks to the walls of the Citadel of Zyran. 'I have watched as the shadows have grown in Zyran. The dark cloud constantly hovers over the island, but this morning, for the first time in years, the sun seemed to find a way through.' The old man looked to Eben for a moment. 'I believe there may be reason to hope again.'

Cassiel, still pale with shock, slowly regained his regular composure.

'I heard you betrayed the Zyranian Order and were forbidden to practice magic,' said Cassiel.

Baftel flinched at hearing Cassiel's words and then nodded his head sadly. 'Yes, I heard that was their story. The real truth was hidden beneath a shroud of lies. Now I don't suppose it matters. I can never again enter the Citadel of Zyran. I have enjoyed fixing nets and fishing for the last five years. The life of a wizard was always full of adventure, but fishing is much more fun.'

'Can you help us find a boat to sail to Ortaria?' asked Cassiel.

'As I said, sailing these seas would be dangerous for someone without any experience,' replied Baftel, shaking his head.

Cassiel looked out to sea and then back to Baftel. 'Can you take us back to Ortaria, Baftel?'

'I only have a twenty foot fishing boat. You would be better off going on one of the larger trading ships.'

'I can't wait for one of those ships. When I have to leave Zyran I will need to leave at once. I can pay you, Baftel,' said Cassiel.

Baftel's eyes narrowed. He glanced away, and a deep frown crossed his face. He picked up his net and walked down the pier a little before he answered.

'Cassiel, I know you're an outcast like me. I wonder why you would want to come back to Zyran in these dark times. There's only a coastal village here, and we both know you can't go into the Citadel. Am I correct in supposing that you are involved in something untoward?' Cassiel ignored the suggestion as Baftel threw his net into an open deck sailboat and then walked back to the two of them. 'I remember when you were at the academy. You never did like taking direction, and you always had a very strong will. I only hope whatever you have planned doesn't kill you and your friend. Your enemies may know more than you realise.'

'What do you see?' asked Cassiel nervously. He knew Baftel was renowned for his ability to see what was hidden.

'A candle left out in the rain. Sharks circling a man stranded at sea. You have brought hope into a place of shadows. You are like a man wading in the rough waves with an oil lantern in his hand,' said Baftel, seeming troubled by his own thoughts.

'Do you think my plan has been discovered?' Baftel looked to Eben for a moment and then back to Cassiel; the strain was visible on his face.

'There's a greater plan at work.'

'Can you help us? You say that I have brought hope to Zyran; would you help that hope?' Baftel drew a long breath and then whispered something they could not hear. A long silence followed before he answered.

'I will take you back to Ortaria if you succeed.'

'Thank you,' said Cassiel, bowing to the old man.

'You will have to come and tell me when I should be ready for the journey.'

'I will,' said Cassiel.

**

They walked back toward the inn and Cassiel seemed troubled by some of the things that Baftel had said.

'Who is he?' asked Eben, curious to know more.

'Baftel was once the leader of the Seers of Zyran. They were a minor fraternity within the Zyranian Order. They focused on developing an ability to see the true nature of what lies beneath the surface and what lies beyond normal perception. Five years ago Baftel was accused of using his powers to plot against the Zyranian Order. He was banished from the Citadel and cast out of the Zyranian Order. I'm concerned that he has foreseen trouble ahead for us.'

'Could we be walking into a trap?' asked Eben.

'Perhaps,' said Cassiel uneasily.

'Should we change our plan?'

'No, the longer we stay here the more at risk we are. This is our one chance,' he said as they reached the door of The Lost Mermaid.

**

At noon the four friends were seated in a small private room that was set off from the main common room. The table was large and hardly fit into the confined space. Falsig was seated across from them and was grinning slyly. They all felt uncomfortable in his presence. His pungent body odour drifted across the table.

'I assume you are ready to start the undertaking at any moment,' said Falsig. He slurped on a large mug of ale.

'That's correct,' said Cassiel with a stony expression.

'Good. Tonight there is a banquet in the hall of the Citadel and nearly all the Zyranian Order will attend. I've brought a group of servants up from the village to help with preparations and to work in the kitchen. Tonight, shortly after nightfall, I will let the servants out through the supply gate to return home to the village. Wait by the gate; I'll let you in after I let them out.'

He took another gulp of his ale and a moment later burped. Stella averted her eyes in disgust. Falsig saw her expression and smirked. 'There are a few conditions,' he continued. 'If you get caught you never knew me, and be sure I will not let you out of the gate without getting my share of the loot. If you try anything shifty I'll have you buried.'

'We will be waiting at the gate after dark,' said Cassiel.

'I'll see the four of you tonight.' Falsig skulled his remaining ale. He then stood up and nodded with approval before walking from the small room. A moment later he was gone.

'He is the foulest man I have ever met,' said Stella, grimacing at the thought of him.

'What do you think?' asked Eben, looking across to Cassiel.

'I don't trust him,' said Cassiel. 'But this is our only chance to free King Ignis. I will tell Baftel to be ready to leave tonight.'

CHAPTER SEVEN

They hid in the shadows about fifty feet from the wall and were huddled behind a group of shrubs. The supply gate was a rectangular wooden door that stood about ten feet high at the base of the wall. The gate was closed and the Citadel was completely silent. From their place behind the shrubs they had a wide view of the area. They waited and watched. Eben could sense the feeling of anticipation was growing among the small company. He looked up to the top of the wall high above and saw a brigade of guards passing by.

'I don't like this,' said Red.

'Be quiet,' whispered Stella.

The gate opened. Lantern light lit up the gateway. The group of servants who were carrying small lanterns stepped out and scurried away along the outer base of the wall in the direction of the village. Falsig stood alone in the dark entrance holding a large lantern.

'Let's go,' whispered Cassiel. They followed him quickly across to the gate.

'Come on,' whispered Falsig with urgency as they approached. He ushered them inside and locked the gate behind them. 'You're on your own now. I'll be across the way. I will wait here until you return.'

Falsig walked away leaving them in the dark just inside the gate. Eben looked up at the amazing sight above. The stone towers rose high into the dark sky. Many stone bridges crossed from tower to tower; some not far from the cobblestoned streets and others hundreds of feet above. Lanterns lit the bridges and lanes below providing a soft light that permeated the entire Citadel.

'Let's move,' whispered Cassiel. He hastily led them away from the gate. They kept to the shadows as they followed Cassiel into a small alleyway that wound back toward the main front gate. The lanes and squares were completely empty. Eben looked ahead and saw that the alley came to an end and opened into a large square. Cassiel stopped just before they reached the end of the alley. He glanced around the corner. The area beyond was dimly lit by several street lanterns, and down the way they could see the main gate. Just across the square was the base of a tower that rose high into the sky. Eben looked up and could see a bridge spanned a gap of fifty feet between the larger tower and a smaller tower further into the Citadel. The bridge was about a hundred feet above the square.

'That's the Gatekeeper's tower,' whispered Cassiel, pointing to the tower across the square. He looked at Stella. 'Are you sure you want to do this?'

'Of course,' replied Stella confidently.

'See the window above the door where the bridge meets the tower. The door will be locked and probably have a trap; you must be careful. The arched window above the door should take you into the main chamber where the key would be kept. Trebax should be at the banquet, but there is still a chance he is in there.'

Stella looked up and her green eyes flickered in the faint lantern light. She took from her bag a pair of leather gloves and a long coiled rope with a grappling hook.

'Do you want me to come with you?' asked Red nervously.

'No,' she whispered as she prepared her ropes.

'We will be waiting for you here,' whispered Cassiel.

She entered the square and edged along the near wall until she was standing directly beneath the bridge. They watched as she took the rope and started swinging it in large loops. A moment later she released the hook. The grappling hook flew upward with total accuracy and hooked onto the railing of the bridge. Stella pulled the rope tight, and a moment later she was ascending the rope with amazing skill. Within a minute she had reached the bridge. She climbed over the stone railing and hastily took from her bag a second rope and hook. She walked toward the Gatekeeper's tower and looked up at the window above.

With a small swing she sent the second rope over the ledge of the window and an instant later she was climbing. She reached the window and stood for a moment in the opening. They watched as she stepped into the tower and was gone from sight.

'She's amazing,' whispered Red, staring up in wonder.

A little time passed and she didn't reappear. Eben kept his eyes fixed on the window. Red's expression of wonder was gradually turning to one of concern. A few more moments passed and still nothing happened.

'She's probably in trouble,' whispered Red anxiously. He started to move toward the first rope.

Cassiel grabbed his arm and stopped him from leaving the dark alleyway. 'Wait,' he said firmly.

A moment later Stella leapt from the window and grasped the rope as she flew through the air and slid down to the bridge in a matter of seconds. They watched as she ran across the bridge and quickly climbed over the edge. She glided down the first rope to the square below. There was no sign of anyone chasing her. She ran over to them and was holding the crystal key.

'He was there; he saw me as I was leaving,' she said as she looked back up to the window high above. They all looked up and could see the silhouette of a robed man in the window.

'Quick, let's go,' said Cassiel.

They dashed along the alleyway in the direction they had come. They ran through the narrow laneways and squares and took many turns to the left and right. The laneways of the Citadel were like a maze. Eben had lost all sense of direction. They suddenly stopped before rounding a final corner.

'Just ahead of us is the gate to the Dungeons of Zyran. We must act quickly before Trebax raises the alarm. We have no time for any delay,' said Cassiel.

Eben took the sleeping darts from his bag. They looked around the corner toward the prison entrance. Directly ahead of them was a round cobblestoned area about forty yards in diameter.

On the far side there was a large iron door with no apparent handle.

'The wizard guards are gone,' stuttered Cassiel, his eyes scanning the area ahead. He turned to Eben with a deep frown; a moment later the blood drained from his face. 'It's a trap,' he cried.

They looked back the way they had come and saw a group of robed wizards approaching with a large number of guardsmen. Across the open area they could see other wizards were approaching from the opposite alleyway that led to the prison gate. Flames started blasting toward them. Cassiel raised his hands and created an invisible shield. The onslaught of fire smashed against the unseen barrier. There was no escape.

'Into the prison!' shouted Red, grabbing Stella's hand, he led her quickly across to the door. Eben and Cassiel followed as Stella took the key and touched it to the dungeon door. The door started to slowly open. Eben drew his sword as the Zyranian wizards rushed from the alleyways behind them. Stella and Red backed away inside the prison and were out of sight moments later. Cassiel raised both hands and sent multiple blasts of fire at the approaching wizards. The Zyranian wizards instantly retaliated. A blazing torrent of fire blasted through the air toward them. Eben and Cassiel leapt into the prison only just avoiding the onslaught. A moment later Red slammed the door as the powerful surge of fire and energy smashed against it.

They stood in the dimly lit entrance chamber. On the opposite side of the chamber was a stairwell which led down into the dungeon below. The enchanted walls glowed around them. Cassiel leaned against the door, hanging his head low. He crouched down and stared at the stone floor. 'The entire Zyranian Order will be out there waiting for us. They must have known we were going to try to steal the key and allowed us to. I think the only reason they let us take the key was because they wanted to make sure they caught all of us.'

'We're safe in here though. There's no way they can enter the dungeon,' said Red, trying to be positive about the situation.

'But how will we get out of here?' asked Eben.

'We should free King Ignis,' said Stella.

'But we won't be able to leave with him now that the Zyranians know we are here. We are completely trapped,' said Cassiel.

'We should free the King; perhaps he can help,' said Eben as he walked toward the stairwell.

Red, Stella, and Eben walked down the stairs. Cassiel followed. The stairwell led about fifty feet down through solid rock and opened into a large subterranean passageway that was about a hundred feet long with iron doors lining both sides of the way. There were at least twenty cell doors.

'We must be careful and ensure we don't free the wrong person. Who knows what's behind each door,' said Red as he led them along the passageway.

'King Ignis is in the last cell,' said Cassiel as he came into the passage from the stairwell. They walked to the door that Cassiel had indicated. Stella took the key and touched it to the door; a moment later the cell door slowly opened. They peered into the small dimly lit dungeon room; on the far side was the shape of a man curled up on the ground and clothed in rags. He lifted his head slightly and looked at them.

'Who are you?' he asked in a low and deep voice as he slowly got to his feet. The man was perhaps fifty years old with strong features. He had long brown hair that was streaked with silver, a beard that he had tied up neatly, and strong dark eyes. He looked proud and dignified, even though he was clothed in rags.

'Your Highness, we are here to rescue you,' said Stella, stepping into the cell. He walked over to them, his eyes wide with bewilderment. 'My name is Stella and these are my friends: Red, Eben, and Cassiel.'

'You are Ortarians. How did you know I was here?' asked King Ignis.

Cassiel interrupted before Stella could answer. 'Your Highness, there will be plenty of time to explain everything later. Unfortunately our attempt to rescue you was discovered by the Zyranians. The Zyranian Order is waiting for us outside the prison. We don't know how we can possibly escape.' The King nodded as he stepped out of his cell into the passageway. He looked up and down the corridor and scratched his beard as he pondered an idea.

'You have the key?' asked King Ignis.

'Yes,' replied Stella.

'In my time here I have become acquainted with the man in the cell next to mine. We have talked with each other through the walls for years, and we have become quite good friends. May I have the key so I can free him?'

Stella handed over the key. King Ignis stepped toward the door to the right of his own cell.

'No!' shouted Cassiel, leaping forward to stand in the way.

'What are you doing?' asked the King, surprised by Cassiel's move to block him.

'You can't free Azagord,' said Cassiel firmly.

'Who is Azagord?' asked Eben.

'He's a powerful and evil sorcerer,' replied Cassiel. 'He's the Northern Sorcerer who came south from Kaznor nearly twenty years ago and attacked Zyran. He's a merciless tyrant who possesses great power. Only this prison can contain him; he should never be released.'

'Cassiel, no one is beyond redemption, not even Azagord,' said King Ignis. 'Furthermore, he may be our only hope of escape.'

'I can't allow this,' said Cassiel defiantly.

'Azagord was once my personal enemy,' said King Ignis. 'I worked with the Zyranians against him and fought his army in Ortaria before he attacked Zyran. He has been imprisoned here since those days, and he is not the same man he was when he entered this place.'

'But, Your Highness...'

'Step aside,' commanded the King.

Cassiel reluctantly moved away from the door. King Ignis stepped forward and touched the key to the iron surface. The door opened and revealed a very skinny older man with thin dark hair, deep hollow cheeks, and sunken dark eyes. He was short and clothed in rags with a dishevelled beard.

'Azagord,' said King Ignis warmly.

'My King,' said Azagord in a deep foreign accent. The sorcerer stepped out of the cell and embraced his friend.

The others stepped back at the sight of him. Azagord glanced over at them with sunken eyes which were like pools of darkness. His eyes instantly fixed on Eben and the sword he was carrying. He stepped away from the King toward Eben and stared at him more intensely. Eben sensed danger as Azagord slowly approached.

'Is everything all right, Azagord?' asked King Ignis. Azagord didn't answer and kept his eyes fixed on Eben.

'It seems strange that the Sword of Light should fall into my hands after so long in exile,' answered Azagord in a rasping voice.

The King looked from Azagord to Eben. Azagord moved forward with lightning speed. Cassiel tried to step in the way, but a blast of glowing green energy sent him sliding along the floor and pinned him to the stony surface. Eben raised his sword, but before he could react the sorcerer grabbed him by the throat. He felt a shock of energy pass through his body, paralysing his arms and legs. Azagord lifted him off the ground with incredible strength.

Red tried to swing his sword at the sorcerer, but his blade struck an invisible barrier. Red then found that he was unable to move; his feet were completely frozen in place. Azagord then flicked his wrist and sent Red flying backward.

The King stepped toward Azagord. 'Azagord, stop!' he commanded. The sorcerer looked at King Ignis for a moment.

'I can't, my King. This is my duty, my reason, and my purpose. I was sent to recover the sword and to kill the one who carried it. The Master needs the Sword of Light. The Master will cast it through the Cosmic Gate,' hissed Azagord.

King Ignis placed his hand on Azagord's shoulder. 'Please, Azagord. Remember our pledge. You do not have to be a slave to the darkness. You can choose the path toward the light.'

Azagord looked over his shoulder at the King again. His body was trembling. He looked down and away from Eben and tears started to issue forth. 'I am sorry. I'm so sorry for what I am,' he said shakily. A moment later he released Eben. Azagord then fell to his knees and grasped his head in his hands, hiding his face from them.

Eben shrank back from the sorcerer and watched on as Azagord began weeping bitterly. Cassiel was also released. Stella and Red helped Eben up. Eben felt his blood returning to his limbs.

'The Zyranian Order waits outside the prison. Can you help us escape?' asked King Ignis.

Azagord glanced up at King Ignis with tortured and sorrowful eyes. 'I once fought the entire Zyranian Order and failed. I can save you, but only with my life.' The sorcerer slowly stood up and turned to look at Eben. 'I am sorry for hurting you, forgive me. I will pay my debt to you and your noble ancestors.' Azagord resolutely took the key from the hands of King Ignis and started walking toward the stairs.

They followed Azagord up the stairs and across the entrance chamber. The sorcerer touched the key to the iron door. Slowly the door opened revealing the area outside which was crowded with Zyranian wizards. The wizards watched as Azagord stepped out.

'Greetings,' said Azagord. There were several gasps and cries when they saw him.

'Azagord is free!' cried a Zyranian.

Instantly the area lit up as the wizards all raised their hands and unleashed a torrent of bright yellow energy, masses of sparks, fire, and flaming columns toward Azagord. Azagord howled and a blanket of bright green energy blasted forth, completely matching the incoming fire and creating an explosion just outside the door that shook the ground. He then raised his hands high above his head and a bright green beam of liquid light rushed up toward the clouds above. The energetic light created a twisting vortex in the sky. The Zyranians looked up at the swirling clouds. The energy whirled in a massive circular motion hundreds of feet in diameter and then suddenly started funnelling downward toward Azagord.

Azagord glanced back over his shoulder and smiled for the first time in his life. 'Run my friends!' he cried as he walked toward the Zyranians surrounded by swirls of bright green light. The battle exploded between the sorcerer and the wizards. Fire, sparks, and shockwaves of energy blasted in every direction.

Cassiel led the way out of the door and down a narrow lane that cut away from the prison. Explosions thundered and shook the ground as they ran.

'This way!' cried Cassiel. He knew the way back and they followed him. They ran quickly through the laneways and made their way toward the supply gate. Eben looked back and could see the entire Citadel was ablaze with fire and light.

He noticed silhouettes in the light coming after them.

'We are being followed,' shouted Eben as they approached the gate. Three wizards and a group of guardsmen came into view.

'Red, the fireworks!' cried Cassiel. Red took his bag of fireworks and threw it with all his might toward the approaching wizards as Cassiel sent a flame through the air that ignited the bag as it struck the ground. The fireworks started blasting in all directions and created a spectacular multi-coloured barrier of blazing light.

'Quick, to the gate!' commanded King Ignis.

They dashed down toward the gate. Falsig stood waiting for them.

'What have you done?' shouted Falsig, looking up at the fireworks exploding in the sky and the blazing fires in the distance.

'Get out of the way, Falsig!' shouted Cassiel.

'Where's my payment?' cried Falsig, his face was red like a beetroot, and his veins were clearly visible on his neck. 'We had a deal.' He drew a large dagger from his belt; the blade shone in the light of the fireworks. 'You can't leave!' he bellowed. 'I want my payment!' He stood in front of the supply gate and blocked their way. They stopped in their tracks.

'There is no gold,' said Cassiel firmly.

'The Zyranians are going to hang you up by your toes!' screamed Falsig, jumping forward and stabbing at Cassiel with his dagger. Eben reacted quickly and threw one of his sleeping darts. A moment later, to the surprise of the entire company, Falsig fell to the ground asleep.

'Well done, Eben, he needs a good nap,' said Cassiel.

Red took the gate key from Falsig's hand as he lay sleeping. A moment later he had opened the gate. They all raced outside and hurried down toward the docks. The Citadel of Zyran shook and burned behind them as they ran.

Baftel stood by his boat staring up at the Citadel; he was mesmerised by the sight. The dark clouds above were glowing from flashes of light that issued up.

'Cassiel! What's going on?' asked Baftel, not taking his eyes from the Citadel.

'Ahh, we had some help from an unexpected ally,' answered Cassiel. Baftel stared in shock as they jumped into his boat. 'We have to make haste.' Baftel nodded as he hurriedly loosened the ropes. He guided the boat away from the docks and into the night.

Before long they were out in the bay. They looked back at the Citadel as the fiery battle raged on. Suddenly there was a mighty flash of green light accompanied by a great explosion. An instant later the Citadel of Zyran became dark and silent.

'Goodbye Azagord,' said King Ignis sadly.

CHAPTER EIGHT

They had sailed west across the Sea of Zyran throughout the night. Few of them slept at all; the feeling that they were being followed kept them on edge. The morning arrived and the sun slowly rose above the horizon in the eastern sky. Baftel often looked back anxiously, but no other boats or ships could be seen. Zyran was out of sight, and the sail was fully raised; a strong wind was blowing them toward Ortaria.

'It's a good wind, and the currents favour us,' said Baftel as he took a seat at the back of the boat. 'The Zyranians may have power over fire and earth, but the weather and tides are mostly beyond them.'

Cassiel had explained to King Ignis much of what had been occurring in Ortaria since his imprisonment. King Ignis was deeply saddened by the news of how bad the situation was in his kingdom.

'Monsters roam freely in the wilderness, and the main highways around Ortaria have become mostly impassable,' said Cassiel.

'What about the port city of Sevadir; does my cousin Duke Julian still rule there?'

'Your Highness, I am sorry to say that your cousin Duke Julian died two years ago. The imposter has placed an evil ruler in his place to govern Sevadir.'

King Ignis nodded. 'It would seem our only hope is to travel to Galdir and the Iron Gate Pass where my army waits.'

'Yes, I think it would be a wise course of action,' agreed Cassiel.

'I know that the imposter was placed there by the Zyranian Order,' said King Ignis. 'I also know they will send word quickly to intercept us if we try to dock at Ancora or Sevadir. Our only choice is to dock at a smaller village or to land on a secluded beach and make our way through the wilderness. We can stock up on supplies once we find a village. It is at least a twelve day march out to the Iron Gate Pass, and the wilderness will slow us down. Perhaps we can acquire some horses.'

'You are right, Your Highness. I'm also sure our enemies will do all they can to try to stop us reaching your army,' said Cassiel.

Baftel looked up into the sky and saw a sea eagle ascending as the sun rose higher in the east. He glanced toward King Ignis anxiously. 'They will send the Zyranian Enforcers after you.'

King Ignis nodded sternly. 'Yes. I would expect them to do that; however, I believe we can avoid them,' said King Ignis confidently.

'There is something else you should be aware of,' said Baftel. 'I see a shadow like black smoke drifting across Ortaria. Something evil will stand in your way.'

'Skatheans,' said King Ignis, flinching as he said the word.

'What are Skatheans?' asked Eben.

'The Skathean Knights are an evil order from the north of Veredor,' replied King Ignis. 'They have been the bane of good folk for many ages. For a long time the Fiorian Knights matched their strength and prevented them from entering the Southern and Eastern Lands. Now there are few Fiorians remaining in Veredor, and the Skatheans have come south without hindrance.'

'I thought Fiorian Knights were a myth,' said Red.

'I believe the Fiorian Knights still exist, but their numbers have greatly diminished,' said King Ignis.

Stella interrupted the conversation and excitedly pointed out a group of five dolphins from the front of the boat. The creatures approached and swam by the small vessel. Eben looked over the edge; they were very close to the side. He reached out; gliding his hand through the water, and a dolphin came very close and was only just out of reach. Eben was sure that the beautiful creature had looked up at him for a moment before swimming onward.

'They seem to like you, Eben,' said Red.

He had never seen such beautiful creatures; they looked so graceful and gentle. Before long the dolphins were gone from sight and disappeared beneath the waves.

They continued sailing throughout the day. A brisk breeze brought them ever closer to Ortaria. Several hours passed. Red had fallen asleep and the others were also resting. Cassiel was seated at the front of the boat and was in a deep meditative trance, completely oblivious to what was happening around him. Eben reflected on the recent events as the boat became quiet. He felt that he had been caught up in a whirlwind of happenings and had barely had a chance to think about everything that had occurred since he left Clemensdale. He felt a hand on his shoulder and turned to see King Ignis was standing beside him.

'May I sit here?' asked the King, indicating to the place beside Eben. Eben nodded and the King sat down. 'It was quite a night last night. I must thank you for your bravery,' said King Ignis, lowering the volume of his voice so no one else in the boat could hear.

'You're welcome,' said Eben.

'I have wanted to talk to you about your sword; this is the first chance I have had,' he whispered.

'What do you want to know about it?'

'Where did you come across the sword?'

'It was left to me when I was a child,' said Eben, also lowering his voice.

'I see, and who bequeathed the sword to you?' asked the King.

'A man named Carlin at the request of Lady Kaloren,' replied Eben. King Ignis stared at Eben with wide eyes for a moment.

'I knew Carlin and Lady Kaloren.'

Eben felt his weariness leave him. 'Can you tell me who my parents are?'

The King raised an eyebrow and seemed puzzled by the question. 'You don't know them?'

'No, I was adopted by a hunter: Erako of Clemensdale. I have lived for most of my life in the hills in the south of Ortaria. I only recently came to Ancora.'

'A hunter...' repeated King Ignis, scratching his chin and pondering Eben's words. He stared at Eben for a few moments, and a look of surprise was clearly evident in his eyes.

'What can you tell me of Carlin and Lady Kaloren?' asked Eben.

'Carlin was a Fiorian Knight. He died twelve years ago in battle.' The King stared out to sea and was sad at recalling the memory of Carlin. Eben could see that Carlin must have been a friend to him.

'And Lady Kaloren?' asked Eben

'Lady Kaloren, she was the leader of the Fiorian Knights, the Gatekeeper of Emeril. She was the greatest and most noble warrior in all the lands of Veredor. Almost twenty years ago Ortaria and Zyran were at war with Azagord and his army from Kaznor. I requested the help of the Fiorian

Order, and they sent five Fiorian Knights. Kaloren was their leader. Carlin and the other Fiorians worked with my army and the Zyranian Order. They vanquished Azagord's army after a long and bloody war. It was Carlin who captured Azagord and imprisoned him beneath the Citadel. Kaloren at the time was pregnant, and she stayed in Ancora whilst the war was being fought in Zyran. The other Fiorians went west after the battle, but Kaloren and Carlin stayed with me in Ancora for several months. Kaloren waited on news from her husband; a great warrior who I knew as Elons. He was helping the Irilian Order in a battle against a Northern Sorcerer called Baramak in the Far Western Lands.'

King Ignis paused and looked about to make sure no one would overhear him before he continued.

'We heard news that her husband had been captured by the sorcerer Baramak who was in league with the Skatheans. Sir Dorn, an Irvarian Knight, came to tell us this terrible news, and Kaloren was deeply saddened. Not long after this time a group of Skathean assassins attacked the palace in Ancora and attempted to kill Kaloren. Carlin defeated them. We later discovered there were various Skathean plots designed to assassinate Lady Kaloren. She was forced to leave Ancora and went into hiding somewhere in Ortaria. Only Carlin knew where she was hiding. He kept it a secret because he believed the Skatheans had spies all over Ortaria. Two years later Carlin told me that she had gone west to search for her husband. I have not seen her for over eighteen years, and to be honest I do not know what became of Lady Kaloren.'

Eben took from his pocket the parchment letter and handed it to King Ignis. He opened the letter and read it to himself.

'I suspected this was so, and now I can see it is true. I think Lady Kaloren is your mother,' he said. Eben felt a rush of excitement at the news.

'My mother. Are you certain?' he asked, his heart pounding from the revelation.

'Yes, I am sure. She is a great woman, and I know she wouldn't have wanted to be separated from you. She would have left you with Carlin for your own protection. I'm certain Carlin sent you to the hunter to ensure you were safe. He did not tell me about you. It troubles me that no one ever came to take you back to your parents.'

Eben felt his elation turn to apprehension. 'Do you think she is...?' He felt distraught at the thought that something terrible had happened to his parents and couldn't finish the question.

'I don't know,' replied King Ignis as he handed the letter back to Eben.

Eben felt like a thousand thoughts of possibilities were going through his head at once. He realised that he would have to go west to find the answers.

'Your sword; it's the Ecorian Sword,' said King Ignis.

'Ecorian; what does that mean?' asked Eben.

'Your sword is one of three swords which were used to defend Veredor. In ancient times Veredor was ruled by a powerful and virtuous lineage of emperors called the Ecorians. That sword became known as the Ecorian Sword because the Ecorian

Emperor always carried it. The original name of the sword is the Sword of Light.'

Eben looked down at the sword that lay by his side in its scabbard. 'Why would my mother leave such a sword with a small child?'

'I don't know,' replied King Ignis. 'However, I do know that the Sword of Light is a powerful weapon and much more than a simple sword. It was forged out of the essence of the cosmos and has many mystical powers. Your mother wanted you to have this sword, and I know you will have to learn to use it. These are dark times, Eben. Few men stand against the darkness; a powerful evil is growing in Veredor.'

Eben felt a sudden weight of responsibility at hearing these words from the King. He thought back to his time in Clemensdale where he was safe and secure.

'Azagord said that his master wanted to cast the sword through the Cosmic Gate. What did he mean?'

King Ignis pondered the question for a few moments. 'Azagord came south to find the Sword of Light and take it back to his evil master in the north. His instructions were to recover the sword and kill the one who carried it. He believed the Zyranians had the sword. Azagord attacked Zyran because of this belief. Only now do I see that Kaloren secretly carried the Sword of Light all along.'

'What is the Cosmic Gate?' asked Eben.

'I only know of the Cosmic Gate from folk stories. I never believed that it existed until I had spoken with Azagord,' said King Ignis. 'The Cosmic Gate is a place where Veredor meets with the cosmos beyond. It is the only way to come into Veredor and the only way out of Veredor. The old stories tell that the Cosmic Gate was built by an ancient race to protect Veredor from the powers of darkness. I think Azagord's former master wanted to cast the Sword of Light out of Veredor so no one could use it against him. This news worries me deeply. If the gate has collapsed we are all at risk. The outer cosmos is said to be a realm inhabited by many creatures of darkness.'

'Did Azagord say that it had collapsed?' asked Eben.

'No, he didn't say; however, your letter from Carlin to Erako says the Fiorians were hoping for the Cosmic Gate to remain firm, and the letter was written when you were very young. This concerns me: if they were worried about it then, what now?'

'We should ask the Fiorians Knights,' suggested Eben. King Ignis cast his eyes downward.

'After Carlin died and until the time of my imprisonment I was searching for any remaining Fiorians. I never found any.'

**

They had been sailing all the first day and into the second night. The sun was high in the sky on the following day. The sight of the Ortarian coast gladdened their hearts. Eben could see high cliff faces to the north which gave way further south to a rugged coastline interspersed with small bays and inlets. A blue sky and a warm breeze welcomed them as they approached the coast.

'There's a small fishing village to the south,' said Baftel, turning the rudder and angling the boat.

Eben hadn't slept since the conversation with King Ignis. Learning that his mother was the leader of the Fiorian Knights had sent his mind into a spin. There were so many questions racing through his head. Why didn't his mother use the Sword of Light to fight the evil if it is such a powerful weapon? Why would she leave the sword with him when he was so young? Where had she gone? Why hadn't she returned? What happened to his father? What did the Fiorians know? Were there any Fiorians remaining in Veredor? He needed to know the answers.

They slowly approached a little fishing village that was set on rocky slopes around a small cove. There were various fishermen's huts and several small boats that had been pulled up onto the beach. Baftel slowly steered the boat into the small cove, and a few of the villagers stood on the beach and looked out fearfully toward them as they entered the cove.

They softly struck the sand a little back from the water's edge. Red leapt out of the boat, and waist high in the water, he started to pull the boat toward the beach. Eben jumped overboard and helped Red drag the boat to the shore.

'Ahoy!' shouted King Ignis as he stepped off the boat into his kingdom.

The others followed. A few moments later they were all on the beach just down from the village. One of the villagers approached. He was an older man with a short beard, slightly balding, and a weathered face. He seemed somewhat anxious about their arrival.

'Hello Strangers,' he said, looking at Baftel, who was the only one of their company clothed as a seafarer.

'Hello there,' said Baftel politely.

'We don't have anything for you here. It would be best for you to move on,' said the villager; his hands were trembling as he spoke.

'We don't want anything from you,' said King Ignis diplomatically.

'I assume you will you be leaving then,' said the villager.

'We were hoping to buy horses and some food for our journey.'

'We only have fish,' replied the villager grimly. 'The King has taxed all our possessions. He has left us in poverty.'

King Ignis looked concerned at hearing the news. 'We won't bother you, and we will move on in a few minutes. We would be very happy to buy some fish.'

'We can sell you some fish. I'll go back to the village and bring some back for you.' The man turned and walked back to the village and was out of sight a few moments later.

'These seaside villages were thriving a few years ago,' said King Ignis, staring up at the huts with sad eyes.

'Where will we go from here?' asked Red.

'Directly west,' said King Ignis. 'The coastal road is up on the hills just yonder. We will cross the road and travel overland through the wilderness.'

'If I come with you I will never again sail across the Sea of Zyran,' said Baftel.

'What do you mean?' questioned Cassiel, troubled by Baftel's words.

'I can also see with my magic that I will not make it to Galdir.'

'What will happen?' asked Cassiel.

'I'm not sure. I know my life will be in grave danger if I follow you, and perhaps I will die, but if I return to the sea I will live.'

'What about us. What will happen to us?' asked Red.

'I don't know,' said Baftel. 'I only see mist. Your way is hidden from my eyes. I believe a secret power is defending your company from prying eyes; the power prevents me from seeing anything about you.'

'If this is true you should return to the sea and not accompany us,' said King Ignis.

Baftel looked to the King for a moment. 'Is it better to be a dead eagle or a living toad?' he asked.

'A living toad,' answered Red, as if the answer was simple.

'But the living toad never knew what it was like to soar in the clouds,' said Baftel. He paused and his eyes drifted back to the sea. 'And eventually the toad will die as all living things do; therefore, I will come with you. If I can help you it would be better than returning to the sea. I have no skill with battle magic, yet I can see things that are hidden.' He then went back to the boat to gather his supplies and his bag.

The villager returned and handed a sack of fish to King Ignis.

'That will be a bronze piece,' said the villager. Cassiel paid him for the fish.

A few moments later Baftel came walking up from the boat. 'You can keep my boat.' The villager looked uneasy at hearing the offer. 'I won't be coming back for it.'

'We should move on,' said Cassiel, looking toward the track that led away from the village and up the slopes toward the hinterland. A few moments later they walked by the village and made their way up the hill.

**

They crossed the coastal road and entered the wilderness. King Ignis led the way. The land was hilly and wild; often they would come to small patches of forest, but mostly they were trekking through rocky treeless hills. They were all hungry and hadn't eaten a decent meal since before the rescue. It was agreed that they should find a hidden grove to set up camp. They found a small gully with a perfect clearing for camping that was hidden from view and protected from the wind. The day had started to grow cold and heavy clouds had gradually covered the sky.

Red was busy trying to get a fire started; he was clicking together flint rocks which Eben had given him from his bag.

'That's not how you do it,' said Cassiel with a slight laugh.

'I know what I'm doing,' snapped Red as he continued to strike the flint rocks.

'Let me have a try,' suggested Cassiel. He stepped over, but Red wouldn't hand him the rocks.

'Leave it to me,' said Red, raising his voice.

Cassiel pointed his hand at the fire and a magical flame shot forth instantly igniting the wood. Within a few moments the fire started blazing. Red recoiled back and stared up at Cassiel.

'Cheat,' muttered Red. He stood up, crossed his arms and turned away. Cassiel seated himself down beside the fire. Eben watched as Red walked to the edge of the gully and sat on a fallen tree trunk. The others sat around the fire and enjoyed the warmth. Eben stood up and walked over to Red.

'Is everything all right, Red?'

'Sometimes Cassiel makes me feel like a clown.' Eben sat beside Red and they both looked back toward the fire as the evening darkened. Red glanced at Eben with a smile. 'I was a clown. Now I'm in the business of rescuing kings.'

'True,' said Eben.

'You know, Eben. Some people are wizards and others are great warriors; some people are rich royals and others are respected nobles, but in the end all of that doesn't matter much.'

'What do you mean?' asked Eben.

'I mean: what good is it to have all the gold, power, and fortune if you don't have friends and people who stand by you?' Eben could see the point that Red was trying to make. 'In the end, that's all that matters in life. Remember when you freed me. I was really worried before you came walking into that abandoned village. I thought I was going to die hanging upside down from that old tree.'

'You repaid me soon after when you saved me from the muckron,' said Eben.

'I couldn't leave you there fighting that muckron alone. You saved my life and no one had ever done that before. You could have easily left me hanging there to die. The truth is that I could have been a really big problem for you; you didn't seem worried about that. You made me believe that there are good people in this world.'

They watched the fire from the edge of the clearing. King Ignis was stoking it up with a stick as Stella and Baftel prepared the fish for cooking.

**

After a meal of fish they slept by the fire and took turns keeping watch. It was a quiet night and uneventful. The following morning the company rose early and prepared for the journey further west through the wilderness. They started out, and King Ignis led the way at a marching pace. Eben could sense his impatience; the terrain was proving rough and difficult. They made slow progress westward.

'We must find some horses,' said King Ignis.

'We could go further north and stop at a village on the main highway and buy some,' suggested Cassiel.

'Our enemies will be searching the highways,' said King Ignis.

'We shouldn't go near the highway. I don't think horses will help us much,' said Red. 'I think it would be best for us to walk to Galdir. It wouldn't be wise for us to leave the wilderness.'

'I'm sure horses will help us move quickly,' said Cassiel. 'We also must buy supplies somewhere; the fish will only last a couple of days.'

'I agree with Cassiel,' said the King. 'Lantern Hill is a small town west of Ancora on the main highway and probably only a day north of where we are now. We could buy some horses and food and quickly return to the wilderness.'

'It's a bad idea,' said Red, shaking his head. 'Eben can hunt and has his bow, and we could collect mushrooms.'

'I can hunt, although it would take some time out of our day,' said Eben

'We can't afford any delay,' said Cassiel. 'The enemy will learn where we landed and will follow our tracks from the village. We can be sure they will have horses, and once they find our tracks they will catch up to us in no time.'

'Exactly,' said King Ignis. 'If we continue without stopping for horses and supplies our enemies will most likely catch us before we reach Galdir. Stopping at Lantern Hill is our best option. It may be worth the risk.'

'North it is then,' said Cassiel, happy the decision had been made

'I still don't like this idea,' said Red. 'I stopped over at Lantern Hill not so long ago. It's a dangerous town.'

'What Red says is true; it will be dangerous,' said Baftel. 'I see a menacing evil hovering over the town of Lantern Hill. We should be cautious of this idea.'

'What do you see, Baftel?' asked Cassiel.

'I can't be sure. Evil gathers further north. The highway is being watched by our enemies.'

'It is a risk we'll have to take,' said King Ignis.

CHAPTER NINE

The company journeyed north and the land flattened out as they marched toward Lantern Hill. As they progressed the trees grew more numerous and the landscape gradually turned into forest. Eben and Red had passed through the same forest weeks earlier on their way to Ancora. The forest was the magnificent Altus Forest, the largest forest in Ortaria. They found a goat track that led northward through the woods, and by the mid-afternoon the trees gave way to the muddy highway that cut directly through the forest from east to west.

'Is Lantern Hill to the east or west?' asked Cassiel as he looked from left to right.

'West,' replied Red.

'I thought east,' said King Ignis. The highway gradually curved out of sight through the forest.

'Is that horses?' questioned Stella softly.

'Quick, off the highway!' cried Baftel.

They all dashed back off the highway and made their way into the trees as the sound of galloping horses could be heard growing louder from the west. They ducked out of sight behind trees and bushes and watched as a group of at least two dozen armour clad horsemen rode by at full speed. A few moments later they were gone from sight, and the sound of the galloping faded away into the east.

When they were certain the horsemen were gone they walked back toward the highway. Baftel led the way and looked in the direction the horsemen had ridden.

'They're gone,' he said.

'We should go west,' said Red. King Ignis nodded. 'Lantern Hill is west. I travelled back and forth along this highway when I was a trader. The town is about an hour from here. We should stay off the highway for our safety.'

The group walked through the forest and kept just south of the highway to avoid the possibility of an ambush. After about half an hour the forest started to thin and gave way to a long lush field that stretched out into the distance. At the far side a line of yew trees grew along the base of a small hill that the town of Lantern Hill was built upon. They could clearly see the outline of the gabled rooftops and smoking chimneys of the stone houses and huts. They stopped short of the field and stood just within the last trees of the forest.

'How should we proceed?' asked Cassiel, looking to King Ignis.

'We can split up the tasks; that would reduce the time we spend in the town. One group can get the food, and the other group can buy the horses and the swords,' suggested King Ignis.

'There's a dark shadow covering the town. I don't think we are safe here,' said Baftel.

'What do you see,' asked King Ignis, glancing uneasily back at the wizard.

'Vultures feeding on a carcass,' said Baftel gravely.

'Keep your eyes open. If we get separated then we'll meet back here,' said King Ignis.

'I can buy the six horses we need,' said Red. 'I know a merchant in the town who sells horses and travelling goods, and we may even be able to buy some swords from him. After I buy the horses I'll lead them to the other side of the town.'

'Good,' said King Ignis. 'I'll go with Red and Baftel to buy the horses and swords. Cassiel, Eben, and Stella can gather the food supplies. We'll meet on the western side of town as quickly as we possibly can. Don't talk to anyone unless it cannot be avoided, and keep your heads down.'

Cassiel divided his gold between the two groups. They crossed the field quickly and ascended the slope of the hill up to the eastern entrance of the town. The town had no wall and was cut in two by the main road that ascended directly over the hilltop and ran straight down the opposite side. A few scruffy guardsmen near the entrance scowled as they passed by. The whole town was very dank and grimy. The streets were full of mud and rot. The people of Lantern Hill looked to be downtrodden and miserable. Eben felt dismayed by the haunted and bleak faces of the townsfolk.

Red led the King and Baftel away to the right as Cassiel, Stella, and Eben walked up the hill to the top of the town. At the top of the hill there was a large open square and in the centre was a marble statue that had been smashed and was missing its arms and head. Cassiel sighed at seeing it.

'That statue was of Teodric the Builder. He was one of the greatest kings who ever lived,' whispered Cassiel.

They walked by the broken statue and down the road leading toward the western side of the town. A little down from the top of the hill they found a merchant storehouse. Cassiel went inside to arrange the supplies whilst Stella and Eben waited at the door just outside. Eben looked over the rooftops and down across the countryside as the view from the hill was panoramic. He could see the many fields that surrounded the town. His eyes glanced up the road and his heart froze when he saw a hooded horseman passing the ruined statue and heading in their direction. The rider was dressed in black and had a deathly pale complexion. His eyes were fixed on Eben and Stella.

'Get inside,' said Eben, taking Stella by the arm; he led her into the storehouse. Cassiel was finalising his deal and had slung a large sack of food over his shoulder.

'Cassiel!' shouted Eben. Cassiel quickly turned and looked back at Eben and Stella. 'We're in trouble.'

'What is it? What did you see?' asked Cassiel.

'There's a horseman near the statue. I think he's a Skathean,' said Eben. The colour instantly drained from Cassiel's face.

'A Skathean!' he repeated as he quickly went to the window beside the door. He looked out and leapt back an instant later. The whole storehouse shuddered, and the window shattered with the sound of a mighty crash. Orange flames smashed through, knocking Cassiel to the floor, and setting fire to the far side of the storeroom.

'Zarceler! Zarceler is here, and he has Skatheans with him!' cried Cassiel. Cassiel struggled to get up off the floor; he was clearly injured from the fiery blast. The storeman ran out a side door as Eben drew his sword. Stella looked horrified and went to help Cassiel.

'Eben!' cried Stella as Eben moved toward the front door. The store around them started to burn.

'I'll protect you!' shouted Eben. He threw his bag, axe, and bow aside and looked to the Sword of Light in his hand. Courage pushed the fear from his veins. A shockwave smashed into the door, blasting it off its hinges and forcing Eben to stumble back. A moment later a fierce Skathean stepped in through the doorway. His face was deeply pale, and his piercing blue eyes revealed his murderous intention. He was clothed completely in black and wore a long dark cloak. He held a large sword in his hand, and he stared directly at Eben with malice.

Suddenly a blast of fire from the hand of Cassiel struck the Skathean, knocking the evil warrior toward the door. With great agility the Skathean recovered his balance. He leapt towards Cassiel and Stella furiously, ready to swing his blade, but Eben moved forward and stood between the Skathean and his friends. Their blades clashed with a screech of steel on steel. The Skathean fell back and stared at Eben with menacing eyes. Eben quickly advanced. He struck at the Skathean several times and forced his opponent to parry. The Skathean stepped backward and out through the doorway onto the street.

'Go out the back!' shouted Eben, glancing over his shoulder at Stella and Cassiel. Stella helped Cassiel. They went toward the back door as the fires blazed around them.

'Eben, they're Skatheans! You can't beat them!' shouted Cassiel as they exited out the back.

Feeling confident, Eben leapt out into the street after the Skathean. Instantly he was surrounded by five waiting Skatheans. Zarceler was standing across the way and grinning wickedly. Eben stood at the doorway as the storehouse burned behind him. He raised his sword and was ready for combat.

'That looks like a wonderful sword, boy!' said Zarceler with a smirk. 'You are surrounded, surrender!'

'Never!' cried Eben defiantly.

Instantly he found himself defending multiple blows from the Skatheans. He struggled to parry and counter attack as the Skatheans pushed him away from the storehouse and down the road. He kept stepping back as they advanced and strained to defend the incoming strikes, stabs, and slashes. The five of them worked together like a machine. They surrounded him and forced him further down the hill until he was eventually near the western edge of the town.

With his back against a stone wall he desperately tried to defend himself. His sword flickered in the light of day and moved so gracefully in his hand, but his faith and courage were diminishing and his weariness was growing. A moment later a flash of bright red light struck him in the chest and he dropped to the ground; the Sword of Light fell from his hand as he curled over in pain. A burning sensation of fire circulated in his abdomen. Completely breathless he curled up against the stone wall as the Skatheans pointed their swords at him and were ready to finish him off. Zarceler approached and looked down at him with a mocking smirk.

'In truth, I have never seen such a wonderful display of swordsmanship. What fool in all of history would challenge five Skatheans at once? You lasted so long. It's a pity you are not my servant. You would make a good bodyguard; unfortunately I have to kill you,' said Zarceler, grinning viciously.

'He has the Sword of Light,' hissed one of the Skatheans. Zarceler's jaw dropped, and his eyes filled with devious wonder at hearing the words.

Eben found some energy within and started to get up off the ground. He looked up at Zarceler who was grinning down at him and gloating.

'Where did you get that sword, boy?' asked Zarceler.

Eben didn't answer and stared defiantly up at the wizard.

'We will take the Sword of Light to the Master,' said Zarceler, grinning with malicious delight.

Suddenly a bright blue wave of energetic light blasted out from the stone wall behind Eben. The shockwave knocked all the Skatheans and Zarceler away from him; they tumbled to the ground. Eben grabbed his sword and regained his feet. A moment later he could see Red charging down from the top of the hill on a large horse.

'Eben!' cried Red.

Eben felt his confidence return at seeing his friend coming to his aid. He dashed away from the Skatheans and rushed back up the hill toward Red. The Skatheans were quick to regain their feet and turned to pursue him. Zarceler watched with a sneer as Eben ran. Moments later he reached

Red. Red leaned down and helped Eben up onto his horse.

'We have to get out of here! The others are already out of the town.'

'What about Stella and Cassiel?'

'They're safe with King Ignis,' said Red.

The Skatheans were almost upon them. Red turned his horse around and charged away. Zarceler snarled and was furiously enraged. Several dozen town guardsmen appeared at the top of the hill and attempted to block their escape. Red turned the horse and charged down a side lane that led out of the town.

'Kill them! Kill them all!' screamed Zarceler in the distance.

Moments later Red and Eben rode westward out of the town, leaving the Skatheans and Zarceler staring after them. They met with King Ignis and the others about three hundred yards from the eastern edge of Lantern Hill. The whole company had acquired horses and swords. Eben jumped down off Red's horse and mounted his own.

'Are you all right, Eben?' asked Stella.

'I'm fine,' said Eben.

'We have to go before they come after us,' said Red.

King Ignis turned his horse. They galloped away west toward the edge of the forest.

**

They rode west along the highway for several minutes before King Ignis led them off the road into the forest to the north. They kept moving through the woods for quite some time and eventually stopped beside a small stream.

'I can't believe you tried to fight them. They were Skatheans!' said Cassiel.

'He saved our lives,' said Stella, clearly annoyed that Cassiel was questioning Eben's choice.

'You were very brave, Eben. Thanks for saving us,' said Cassiel.

'We have to keep moving,' said King Ignis. 'They will surely follow us.'

They rode west through the forest for the remainder of the afternoon, and the day grew darker as thick clouds crossed the sky and gentle misty rain started falling. At the end of the day they set up camp beside in a wide clearing and made a small fire. They sat around the fire and tried to keep warm as the frosty evening progressed into an icy cold night.

'We have swords and horses now and enough food for the journey to Galdir,' said King Ignis. 'The Skatheans will follow our tracks through the forest, so we will have to ride constantly tomorrow to put as much distance between us and Lantern Hill.'

Baftel looked to the sky above. 'A big storm will arrive tomorrow and will slow us down.'

'We must persevere,' said King Ignis sternly.

That night few of them slept. The rain grew heavier and the horses stirred and were anxious. The morning was cold, and the rain was torrential. A little after sunrise they rode west from the clearing. By midday they arrived at a wide and slow flowing river. A thin track followed the bank.

'This is the Merus River; it flows all the way from the Endora Mountains to Ancora,' said King Ignis.

'There's a town along the river further west called Riverside. I recommend that we take my advice this time and avoid it,' said Red.

'Red is right; we must not go there,' said Baftel. 'Riverside is shrouded by a shadow that is as dark as night.'

'We will follow the river west and go around Riverside,' said King Ignis. 'I believe there may be several places where the river is shallow enough to cross. We are probably safer on the northern bank.'

They moved on and followed the river. The rain grew heavier with each passing hour. They could hear thunder booming in the east. Eben could see the dark clouds were moving in their direction. Before long the rain became torrential, and the thunder was directly above them. The track beside the river was growing muddy and difficult for the horses. They were making slow progress. They came to a shallow area of rapids; King Ignis led them across the river to the north bank. The track that followed the river on the north side was little more than a muddy goat track.

'We should find shelter from this storm,' said Red.

'No, Red, we must persist,' said King Ignis.

'This rain will wash away our tracks,' said Red. 'The Skatheans and Zarceler won't be able to follow us through this. There's no point trying to push forward.'

The thunder boomed above and flashes of lighting lit up the sky illuminating the gloom around them.

'There is an abandoned farmhouse further along the river,' said Baftel. 'It is about an hour from here.'

'Good. If it is safe we will stop there,' said King Ignis.

They continued through the heavy rain and mud. After an hour they arrived at a cleared area of forest. A farmhouse was near the riverbank. It looked to be long abandoned and mostly in disrepair. King Ignis led them over to the farmhouse and dismounted. He walked in through the front door which was hanging by one rusted hinge. Eben and the others did the same. Inside was a large living area that made up most of the lower level of the house. To the left there was an open fireplace. A few broken chairs and a half rotting table were the only other contents of the room. Cobwebs covered the interior. King Ignis cleared away the cobwebs with his sword, and Cassiel picked up the scattered chairs.

They felt relieved to be out of the rain and took off their coats and cloaks. Before long Red was busy trying to build a fire in the fireplace.

'We should stay here until the storm passes,' said King Ignis. 'Red is right, Zarceler won't ride through this wild weather. They won't be able to follow our tracks after this heavy rain.'

'We are safe here,' said Baftel. 'I can't see the Skatheans following us. There are no enemies close by.'

'Good, we must rest well whilst we can,' said King Ignis.

Red managed to get the fire started and gathered some wood from around the farmhouse. The day faded into the evening. The company huddled around the warmth of the fire. Stella and Red prepared a meal of bread and potatoes. They all ate well and felt revived after a proper meal.

It was agreed that they should take turns to keep watch through the night. Eben lay down in a corner of the room and rested. He drifted off to sleep.

CHAPTER TEN

Eben awoke to the sound of voices. He sat up and looked over to see Cassiel, Baftel, and King Ignis standing by the front door.

'Wolves,' said Baftel. 'There are packs of wolves and other forest creatures across the river.'

Eben could hear the howl of wolves in the distance. He stood up and walked over to the others.

'Is everything all right?' asked Eben.

'No, there is something else,' said Baftel. He was in a trancelike state.

'What?' asked Cassiel, staring out the doorway into the darkness.

The heavy storm had passed and the rain had mostly stopped, only a light drizzle remained.

'A wizard,' said Baftel as he stared blankly out at the darkness. King Ignis drew his sword.

'There,' said Baftel, pointing out the doorway across the river. There was a blue glow on the far bank that was gradually growing brighter. 'I can't see any ill will. The wizard may not be against us.'

Cassiel boldly stepped out of the house and walked toward the river. King Ignis, Eben, and Baftel followed him down to the bank as the blue light across the river grew even brighter. The light flew down and struck the water. The surface of the water started to freeze as the light glided across the river creating a bridge of ice. A silhouette mounted on a large horse appeared on the far bank. The rider moved out onto the ice bridge toward them.

'Look,' said King Ignis. A large wolf and a fox followed the approaching rider. They waited nervously as the wizard drew near.

'Who are you?' shouted Cassiel.

'Cassiel,' said a woman's voice.

'Meara. I can't believe you found us,' said Cassiel, his face brightening with joy.

'Meara!' said the King gladly.

'Torela,' said Eben.

'King Ignis. I am very glad to see you again,' said Meara as she arrived at the bank. The icy bridge dissolved behind her. 'I have been following you for several days.' She dismounted and stepped over to them.

'These are my friends, Kiarn and Gasta,' she said, indicating to the large wolf beside her and the smaller red fox. The mighty black wolf stared at them with fierce golden eyes, and the fox stayed some distance back.

They walked with Meara back to the farmhouse. She took a seat at the table as Kiarn the wolf sat beside the fire directly next to Red who was still sleeping. Gasta, the fox, refused to enter the house and waited outside the door.

'I bring many tidings,' said Meara as she took a seat at the table.

'Are you hungry? We have food,' said Cassiel.

'No, thank you, I'm fine. Kiarn, Gasta, and the other creatures of Altus Forest have been bringing me food.'

'What news can you tell us, Meara?' asked King Ignis.

'I will tell you what I know. I escaped my first confrontation with Zarceler in Ancora, and soon after I learned that Cassiel and Eben had left for Zyran to attempt to free you. I was very worried because I didn't expect the mission to succeed. By the time I discovered the plan it was too late for me to follow. The Zyranians would have detected my presence if I had followed you to the island. I waited in Ancora for news. Eventually the news of your escape came to me. I was astounded to hear that Azagord saved you and sacrificed his life.'

'I knew that you would not come to Ancora or Sevadir. I soon learned that the Zyranians had sent five Enforcers to find and capture all of you. I also became aware that the Zyranians have been working with the Skatheans. Soon after I discovered you had landed south of Ancora. I believe a secret power has been protecting your company. The power has prevented anyone from following you,' she said, looking to Eben for a moment. 'I met Kiarn and the wolves of Altus Forest. Kiarn showed me the plight of the forest creatures. Muckrons and other monsters have been roaming the forests and killing everything. The wolves, jackals, bears, and foxes have fought against them for two years. Only recently the wolves learned that an army of muckrons has been brought to Ortaria by the Skatheans.'

'An army of muckrons!' cried King Ignis, shocked by the revelation.

'Yes, an entire army. The forest creatures are not fond of men, yet they know that only with the help of men can they free the lands of muckrons and other monsters. Kiarn is a king among wolves. I asked for his help to find your company. The wolves helped me to follow you all the way to Lantern Hill; I almost met you there. I was in Lantern Hill when Eben fought the five Skatheans, and I helped him in the battle. You rode away without knowing of my presence. We then followed you to this farmhouse. Without the help of Kiarn and the other forest creatures I would have never found you. They had to communicate with other creatures that had seen you passing by. That is how we followed you.'

'You created the blue flash of light that saved me from the Skatheans,' said Eben. 'You saved my life.' Meara smiled warmly across at Eben.

'I'm glad that I did,' she said. 'You fought valiantly against those Skatheans'.

'Thank you,' said Eben. Meara nodded and then looked back to King Ignis.

'I told Kiarn that you, King Ignis, would help the forest creatures free the land of muckrons.'

'I will,' said King Ignis resolutely. 'Tell Kiarn that I will help.'

'You both want to free the land of this evil shadow that is destroying Ortaria. An alliance will be formed.'

King Ignis nodded and Meara looked across at Kiarn. The black wolf stared at her with his large golden eyes.

'He welcomes your offer of help,' said Meara, looking back to King Ignis.

'Good. This army of muckrons will not live long in Ortaria,' said King Ignis decisively.

'We are heading for Galdir. Once we arrive I will lead my army back to Ancora and destroy our enemies,' said King Ignis firmly.

'I have some bad news. The Imposter who sits on your throne has ordered your army to invade Scaldonia,' said Meara. The King was deeply concerned at hearing the news. 'The Imposter and the Skatheans know you are heading for Galdir and that you hope to lead your army back to Ancora. The Skatheans rule most of Scaldonia; only one resistance army remains at the town of Orelin. The Scaldonian army in Orelin is led by Duke Egil. Your army has been ordered to attack Orelin, which will destroy any remaining resistance in Scaldonia. The battle will also likely weaken the Ortarian army. Our enemies plan to destroy both the resistance in Scaldonia and to cripple the Ortarian army.'

Stella woke and walked over to join the group at the table.

'Is there time to intercept my army?' asked King Ignis, his face showing his strain and grave concern.

'If we ride quickly we may be able to catch them,' said Meara.

'Then we will have to ride like the wind to the Iron Gate Pass,' said King Ignis. He stood up and took his coat from the back of his chair. He was ready to go at once.

'It won't help,' said Baftel.

'Why?'

'Skatheans and Zyranian Enforcers are riding out to the Iron Gate Pass. They will wait there and attempt to prevent us from following the army into the pass.'

'You have shown the strength of your perception,' said Meara. She was intrigued by Baftel's skill with magic.

'There are many Skatheans, perhaps twenty, and there are five Zyranian Enforcers,' said Baftel. Meara cast her eyes downward and shook her head.

'We can't possibly defeat so many Skatheans and Zyranian Enforcers,' said Meara.

'Perhaps we can ride back to the sea and sail around the Endora Mountains. We could come to Orelin across Southern Scaldonia,' suggested Cassiel.

'No, by the time we arrived the battle would be over,' said King Ignis, shaking his head in frustration.

'Is there no other way?' asked Cassiel.

'There is one way,' said Baftel softly, as if what he was about to suggest would not be received well.

'What way?' asked King Ignis with eagerness.

'The Northern Pass,' said Baftel solemnly.

The King shook his head again and was clearly against the idea. 'No man has passed that way for hundreds of years. A powerful draug lives there.'

'The power of Eben's sword may protect us from the draug,' said Meara.

'The draug that lives in the Northern Pass is particularly formidable. I don't think the Sword of Light will help us. A draug usually won't attack directly; it will be more likely to set a trap,' said King Ignis.

'True, King Ignis is right, the draug won't attack us directly, but we have no chance against the Skatheans and Enforcers; we may have a chance at defeating a draug,' said Baftel.

'Wolf! There's a wolf!' cried Red, waking up to find the massive black wolf by his side. He bounded across the room, stumbling away from Kiarn. Kiarn leapt up and growled at him fiercely.

'Red, he's a friend!' cried Eben, but Red fumbled for his sword as Kiarn snarled. Eben crossed the room and held out his hand to Kiarn. 'Calm down, Red!'

Red stared, bewildered at the sight of Eben standing beside the wolf. He put his sword back in its scabbard and shook his head in disbelief.

'We have no choice. We will attempt the Northern Pass,' said King Ignis.

**

They left the farmhouse early the following morning and rode north away from the river. The forest slowly gave way to grassy hills. As they progressed northward the land about gradually became rockier. Kiarn and several other forest creatures followed the company, including two other wolves, Gasta the fox, and two jackals. A number of large birds also followed the company.

'How do you communicate with these animals?' asked Cassiel.

'The creatures share images with me,' replied Meara.

'What a wonderful gift you possess,' said Baftel.

'This is a secret mystery understood by all the wizards of the Irilian Order,' said Meara.

'No Zyranian can do what you do,' said Baftel.

'The Zyranian Order saw little worth in befriending the lesser creatures of Veredor. The Irilians have always included this skill as an essential part of our training, and as you can see, Zyranian, the ability has proved useful,' said Meara.

'It is very clear to me how useful such a skill is,' said Baftel. 'You should know, Irilian, that I was banished from the Zyranian Order for trying to fight against the evil that is growing in Zyran. I was once the leader of the Seers of Zyran; now I am a lone wizard and an outcast. I no longer belong to any order of wizards. You should also know the Zyranians have long known that the Irilians are stronger; however, they deny it to themselves.'

Meara looked across at Baftel. She stared at him for a few moments. Her expression softened.

'I would like to invite you to come to Dravania with me to join the Irilian Order, Baftel,' said Meara.

Baftel's jaw dropped at the suggestion, and he stared at Meara with wide eyes full of wonder. A wizard had never been known to change from one order to another in all of history.

'Are you saying that you want me to become an Irilian?' asked Baftel. 'I...I...would be honoured,' he stammered.

'It's a long journey to Dravania; I am sure the Irilian Order will welcome you,' said Meara warmly, smiling across at Baftel. Baftel was glowing with happiness.

'For a long time I have been out in the cold, banished and alone. Thank you, Meara. I accept your gracious offer.'

Meara simply nodded as they rode onward.

**

The landscape became continuously more craggy and rocky the further they journeyed north. Kiarn led the way. Gasta, the fox, often ran ahead and would frequently disappear, only to reappear soon after. In the distance Eben could see a line of tall mountains stretching across the horizon from east to west.

'The Endora Mountains,' said King Ignis. 'The Northern Pass isn't far from us. It is above the source of the Merus River. We should be there by tomorrow afternoon.'

They rode on through the rugged landscape. The day was cold, and dark clouds hung over the mountains ahead. They found that the land was gradually becoming hillier and more barren. The afternoon progressed toward the end of the day, and the company together decided to set up camp in a sheltered flat area between two small hills. Red made a campfire, and Stella gathered firewood with King Ignis and Baftel. Cassiel was talking with Meara. Eben sat by the edge of the clearing and looked down at his sword, which glinted in the soft light of the setting sun.

He pondered the grave responsibility the possession of the sword had bestowed on him. He wondered why his mother didn't use it to fight the evil in the lands. Why had she left the sword with him as an infant? Surely such a great sword would have helped her to free Eben's father from his captors. He knew he would have to travel west to search for the answers. He also knew that he would have to find a Fiorian Knight, if any remained in Veredor.

A moment later Meara approached. 'Eben, you look concerned. What is troubling you?' she asked. He looked up at her. 'King Ignis told me that you are the son of the wise and beautiful Lady Kaloren.'

'Yes, that is so,' said Eben. 'Why would she leave the Sword of Light with me if it has such great powers? Why didn't she use the sword to fight the evil in the land?'

'She wanted you to have the Sword of Light,' replied Meara. 'You must trust her. The sword has many powers; in time you will learn to understand them. The people of Veredor need you to be brave. There were three swords that once protected Veredor from the powers of darkness; you have one of those three swords. You have a duty to protect Veredor with your sword as others who carried the sword before you did.'

Eben looked down to the ground; he felt the weight of the responsibility. 'I'm a simple villager, Meara. I want to help the people of Veredor, but perhaps someone else should take the Sword of Light.'

Meara sat down beside him and stared at the campfire across the clearing. 'Eben, the power of the sword increases when you believe. The Sword of Light magnifies your skill by a measure of your belief, trust, and bravery.'

'But how can my belief change the way things are?' asked Eben. Meara continued staring across at the fire and was contemplating the question.

'What you are asking me is a deep mystery, yet I may be able to shed some light on the matter. Think of it like this: would you cross a bridge if you believed it wasn't secure?'

'Of course not,' he replied, not sure where she was leading with the question.

'Therefore what you believe changes what you would do.'

'But you said the bridge wasn't secure.'

'Only according to your belief. Because you believed the bridge wasn't secure you wouldn't cross it; therefore, you would never know what was on the far side of the river.' She paused for a moment and then glanced across at him. 'Every action, every plan, and every step in life relies on your belief. You must believe to trust, and you must trust before taking action. It is the same with your sword. If you believe you will do amazing things, yet if you do not believe the Sword of Light will diminish in power and you will never see the sword as it truly is.'

Eben glanced at her and then across to the fire. The fire was blazing and lighting up the area as the evening grew darker. His eyes followed the sparks that drifted up into the cold night air. He knew there was truth in what she was saying.

Meara gestured toward Red and Stella. Red and Stella were sitting close beside each other near the fire. 'Can you see the way they look at each other? Can you see how they are falling in love? They are shining with hope. They believe in each other, and they trust each other. They have so much hope. They will have a strong relationship. Their trust and belief will be the foundation which will allow their love to grow strong. Without trust and belief such an outcome would be impossible. Can you see they believe in each other?'

Eben looked across at his two friends. He could see Stella smiling at Red, and Red was beaming back at her. Meara was right, they were falling in love. He had been so distracted that he hadn't noticed.

'I think I'm beginning to understand,' he said, glancing back at Meara.

'You are a good young man, Eben. I will help you on your journey as much as I can. Eventually there will come a time when I can help you no longer.'

CHAPTER ELEVEN

Eben slept well that night for the first time in many nights. They left the cleared area and rode quickly toward the enormous mountains ahead. Ominous dark clouds filled the sky above, but there was no wind or rain. Kiarn and Gasta led the way through the wilderness, and the craggy slopes slowly started to become significant foothills. All the other forest creatures had left their company overnight. They turned to the west and came upon the Merus River once again. The river gushed down from the hills above. The company found an old path that followed along beside the riverbank. The path was carved from the rocks and wound a way through the hills ever upward toward the towering snow-capped mountains above.

'This path leads directly to the Northern Pass,' said King Ignis, staring sternly upward to the mountains above. 'The Northern Pass was once a well-travelled way to Scaldonia. Many knights and wizards tried to vanquish the draug; none of them ever returned. This is a cursed way.'

'Draugs often try to trap their prey. It has long been said that they flee from the goodhearted,' said Baftel. 'The draug will attack our weaknesses. They are ghostly wraiths that prey on the innocent creatures of our world. The draug of the Northern Pass is said to be very powerful, a dark shadow from the Forgotten Age.'

'Can you see the draug with your powers, Baftel?' asked Meara as they proceeded along the path.

'When I look toward the Northern Pass all I see is an image of myself staring back at me. It is like looking into a mirror. I have never seen this vision before,' replied Baftel.

They rode onwards, following the path up into the mountains. Eben stared up at the enormous icy peaks that rose high into the clouds above. The path led them along the base of a valley. At the far side of the valley they reached a wide stairway that was carved from the rock and ascended for hundreds of yards directly up the side of a great mountain. Each step was big enough for a horse to stand on, being over thirty feet wide and twenty feet in length.

'These stairs are called the Sky Steps and were built by the Ecorian Emperors in the days of old. I have always wanted to see them,' said King Ignis, looking up with wonder. 'At the top of the steps we will find the Astrum Chasm; that is where the draug is said to live.'

'Kiarn and Gasta will not go any further. They say that they will honour the forged alliance with men; however, they will not go to a place of such hopelessness,' said Meara. 'They're frightened for us. They sense evil above the Sky Steps, and they warn us not to proceed. An image of despair drifts down from the mountain.'

'We are three wizards and four warriors. If we cannot defeat this draug, no one can,' said King Ignis as he rode forward and started moving up the steps.

They followed King Ignis as he boldly ascended the Sky Steps. Eben looked back and could see the red fox and the large black wolf staring up after them. After the company had gone a short way up the fox and wolf ran off and were gone from sight. The climb was difficult for the horses, but eventually they reached the top.

Directly before them was the opening of a chasm cut between two vertical cliffs that ascended high above. The chasm was about ten feet wide at its entrance and only a pale light flowed down from above. Eben couldn't see very far into the gloom and shadows. The path led directly between the cliff faces of two adjacent mountains. A bleak feeling of dread seemed to flow out of the darkness. The horses were anxious and didn't want to continue. King Ignis jumped down from his horse and drew his sword.

'We will have to lead the horses,' he said as he took the reins and tried to pull his horse forward;

the horse wouldn't move. Cassiel tried the same; his horse also refused to go on.

'They will not enter the chasm,' said Meara.

'Then we will have to kill the draug so they will,' said King Ignis, shaking his head in frustration.

The King then turned and walked into the opening between the two cliffs, holding his sword up as he proceeded. Eben dismounted and drew his sword and followed after the King. The others weren't far behind. The way was shadowy and full of oppressive gloom. King Ignis strode forward with confidence. Red caught up to Eben and had his own sword ready. An overwhelming smell of decay permeated their surroundings.

As they advanced the distance between the cliffs widened to about forty feet. Hundreds of feet above they could see the slight gap between the two cliffs; the faintest light drifted down from above. Eben could see an object ahead on the ground. King Ignis stopped. A few moments later Eben and Red were standing by his side. The object was the skull of a horse. Various other bones were scattered about. Cassiel reached them and a moment later the others arrived.

'The draug is very close,' said Baftel, his eyes scanning the rock walls of the chasm. The group looked about and could see nothing in the gloomy shadows.

'Here, old draug,' whispered Red, attempting to lighten the mood. A nervous smile crossed his face.

'Let's keep moving,' said King Ignis. He led them forward a little further through the chasm. More and more bones were scattered across the stony ground the further they went and the smell of death grew stronger. The King stopped suddenly and seemed frozen in place.

'What is it?' whispered Eben, but King Ignis didn't answer and only stared ahead and seemed to be in a trance. Eben looked back to see that the others were all frozen and staring ahead with glazed over eyes. Only Baftel was unaffected and he quickly rushed to Eben's side.

'Eben, listen to me,' stammered Baftel urgently.

'What's going on?' asked Eben, looking towards the King who was still frozen. His eyes darted about, searching for the hidden enemy in the shadows.

'What you see you do not see; what you hear you do not...' said Baftel. He didn't finish his sentence

'Do not what?' asked Eben, looking back to Baftel. Baftel simply smiled. 'Do not what, Baftel?' repeated Eben.

Baftel pointed ahead. Eben looked further down into the chasm, and the gloom began to disappear. The area lit up with a soft warm light.

'Down there, Eben. She is waiting for you,' said Baftel calmly.

'Who?' asked Eben, feeling confused for a few moments. He looked to King Ignis, but the King was gone.

'Go and see,' said Baftel.

Eben stepped further along the way and could see someone approaching from up ahead. He stared as the person grew closer. She appeared to him, and he was taken aback by her exquisite beauty. Her long hair was blonde and like silk, her eyes like blue sapphires, and her skin was translucent. She was dressed in a fine flowing linen dress, and she smiled at him as she approached. Eben felt all his fears drift away as she grew nearer. Her exquisite beauty set his mind at ease.

'Who are you?' asked Eben softly, awestruck in her presence.

'Eben, how is it that you don't know me. I am your wife,' she said. For a moment he felt confused.

'What! My wife! Am I married?' he asked, feeling bewildered. His mind seemed to be drifting in a cloud, and he couldn't focus on anything but the woman in front of him.

'Of course,' she said as she beamed at him; her beauty was like nothing he had ever seen before. Eben looked about and saw the chasm was gone. An instant later he was standing in a field of long green grass and the sun was shining brightly. She took his arm gently.

'We must go,' she said as she tried to lead him away.

'But my friends, I can't leave them,' he said. Her smile faded from her face for a moment.

'Your friends are gone.'

'Where are they?' asked Eben, feeling the confusion was overwhelming.

'They left you, Eben. Don't you remember? They no longer have any need of you. You are a simple villager. Adventures should be left for heroes. Surely everything you want and need is here with me,' she said, smiling at him reassuringly. Again she tried to lead him away.

'They wouldn't leave me,' said Eben, resisting her. She looked back and frowned.

'They had to go. They are glad you decided to leave the important things to them. You know you could never be a hero. Eben, it is your right to be here. You deserve to be here with me after all your suffering and pain. You have had such a hard and lonely life. Look at the beauty of this place. You deserve all this.'

Eben thought of Red and Stella. He thought of Cassiel, Meara, and King Ignis. He wondered why they had left him and felt deeply disturbed. He could feel his sadness growing.

'I need to go back to them and say one last goodbye. They are my friends; I can't desert my friends. They need me,' said Eben.

'You can't go back,' said the beautiful woman, her voice becoming firm.

'Why?' asked Eben, feeling his sadness growing even stronger.

'Because your parents are waiting for us,' she said as she tried again to take him away. Eben felt a sudden sense of joy at hearing the news and the sadness melted away.

'My parents are here?' he asked as he felt his happiness growing again.

'Yes,' she said smiling. 'They want to see you so much. We must hurry before they leave,' she added.

The world around him shimmered and she faded. A flickering shadow replaced her for a moment. Eben felt like he was about to wake, but a moment later she returned.

'What was that?' he asked as he looked about the beautiful meadow.

'Nothing,' she replied and smiled appealingly. 'Absolutely nothing,' she added, trying to reassure him.

Suddenly the shimmering happened again. Her smile quickly faded into a sneer. This time the world around Eben started to collapse and dissolve like smoke being blown away by the wind. He looked about and could see the rock walls and gloom of the chasm again.

Eben could hear the gasps and moans of the others as they all woke from the illusion. He looked back and saw they were in shock. Meara sat down and King Ignis stood looking down at the ground gravely. Baftel lay beside Eben on the ground. The old wizard had aged many years and the irises of his blue eyes were almost completely white. His hair had also become as white as snow.

'Eben...' he muttered. 'Eben,' he repeated in a soft and weak voice.

'I'm here, Baftel. What happened?' He took Baftel's hand and helped him to sit up. Meara came to their side and had regained her composure.

'I vanquished the draug. It fled into the mountains and is now little more than a harmless shadow,' said Baftel with a croaky and weak voice. 'But it took much of my life essence and my eyes. I will never see again.'

'What happened?' asked Meara calmly.

'The draug set a trap for us. It tried to lead us into an illusion of what it believed was the fulfilment of our deepest desires. My ability to see beyond such lies saved me from falling into the illusion. I didn't have time to warn you properly. My will locked with the will of the draug in a fight to the death. I had to sacrifice much of my life force to defeat the monster. I had to show I was prepared to lose something of myself to save you; it was the only way I could overcome the draug.'

'Then you saved us,' said Meara. King Ignis walked over and joined them. 'Baftel destroyed the draug.'

'You did well, Baftel,' said King Ignis as he knelt beside the frail old man and tried to help him to stand up. 'Never have I seen such things as the things I have just seen.'

'What did you see?' asked Eben.

King Ignis looked at Eben with deep sadness in his eyes. 'I can't speak of what I saw,' he replied sorrowfully. 'We should move on from this cursed place.'

The company slowly recovered from the dream illusions of the draug. They collected their horses from the southern entrance to the chasm and then moved along the way heading north toward Scaldonia.

**

The chasm opened onto a stone platform that was about a hundred foot wide and long. The view of the mountains was magnificent. They could see the Kingdom of Scaldonia in the distance. A vast plain extended as far as they could see. A stairway, much like the Sky Steps they had ascended, led down the far side of the mountains. The company said very little. The trauma of being offered such temptations had shocked and tested them all.

'We will be in Scaldonia soon,' said King Ignis. 'From there we will ride quickly to intercept my army before they attack Orelin. I hope we are not too late.'

The day was slowly drifting into night. They found a place to camp in a valley between two mountains. Cassiel and Meara managed to make a fire from magic alone as there was no wood to burn in the mountains, and the night was icy cold. They sat around the warm fire in silence and rested. Baftel was now dependent on others to lead him onward.

They rested that night and very little was said. The following morning the sky was blue and there were fewer clouds. They all felt like a shadow had passed, and a renewed hope grew in their hearts. They set off and by midday the pass was leading them out of the mountains. Lush grass plains stretched out into the distant horizon. Scaldonia looked to be mostly flat with few trees.

They came out of the mountains and into the plain. King Ignis increased the pace. Baftel's frail condition kept them from galloping; at best they could move at a slow canter. The King was growing impatient.

'My army will be moving ever closer to Orelin.'

'You should ride ahead,' said Meara. 'Baftel is in no condition to move so quickly. I will stay here with him and come to meet with you at Orelin.'

'I don't want to leave you here alone on these cold plains, yet I fear that if we do not ride like the wind our mission will be in vain.'

'I will stay behind with Meara and Baftel,' said Stella.

'So will I,' said Red, obviously not wanting to go ahead without Stella.

'And you, Eben?' asked King Ignis.

'I will come with you,' said Eben.

'I'll also go with you, Your Highness,' said Cassiel. 'If we ride quickly we will reach Orelin in a matter of days.'

'Good. We will take the three fastest horses and ride as quickly as we can. If everything goes to plan we will meet with the four of you in Orelin.'

They all agreed to the plan and exchanged horses. The swiftest steeds were given to the King's company. The three of them then rode out across the flat grass plain, galloping into the northwest. For many miles they rode at a dashing pace.

'No hills, just horizon,' said Cassiel. He stared out into the distance. The flat plain stretched onwards as far as they could see with nothing but grass.

'Only Scaldonian nomads live in these cold grasslands. I admire them for making their lives out of this bleak land,' said King Ignis, his strong dark eyes scanning the distance.

They continued riding as quickly as possible.

CHAPTER TWELVE

Eben, Cassiel, and the King rode until the day was too dark to continue. They set up a basic camp. Cassiel created a small fire with his magic. The night grew cool; an icy wind constantly blew across the plain. King Ignis woke them before sunrise and was eager to continue.

'We will rest when we come to my army.'

The King led them onward. They pushed their horses to their limits, galloping as much as they would allow. Later in the day they reached the end of the plain. The land gradually grew more undulating and rocky. Small birch trees were scattered about. They crossed several crystal clear streams, and by mid-afternoon they came upon a road that led north and south.

'This is the road from the Iron Gate Pass to Orelin,' said King Ignis. The road itself looked muddy and well-trodden with fresh wagon, horse, and boot tracks. 'My army came by here not long ago. We must ride with haste!' he cried. They turned their horses and galloped northward along the winding road.

The landscape around became hillier and the trees more numerous. As the evening approached they came to a rise in the road, and when they reached the top of the ridge they could see out across a large basin dotted with stone farmhouses. In the centre of the basin was a walled town. Camped on the southern side of the town, about half a mile from the wall, was the Ortarian army. Hundreds of tents dotted the fields to the south of the town, and a multitude of banners flew above the army depicting the red flag with the golden lion of Ortaria.

Orelin was a large town; the wall that surrounded the town was almost a perfect circle. Eight towers rose from the wall, set at even intervals. At no point was the wall more than a thousand yards in diameter. A large keep was situated at the centre of Orelin, and the Scaldonian flag still flew above the town. The dark blue Scaldonian flag depicted a white eagle with outstretched wings. The road they were on led to a large gate that was securely closed. Eben could see the walls were manned with many men.

'They have not attacked the town!' shouted King Ignis happily. He charged forward. Eben and Cassiel rode after him down the slope toward the Ortarian encampment.

As they approached the camp several armoured riders broke away and rode out to meet them. They were carrying spears and were prepared to fight. They stopped about fifty feet from them.

'What is your business?' shouted one of the riders.

'Who is your commander?' asked King Ignis.

'What is your business?' repeated the same rider angrily.

'We are here to speak with your commander!' cried King Ignis. The leading rider moved his horse forward and came closer.

'I will spear you if you don't tell me your real business.'

'You would spear your own King,' responded King Ignis, staring harshly at the rider.

'What nonsense is this?' asked the rider sharply.

'Take me to your commander, now!' commanded King Ignis.

The rider stared at King Ignis for a few moments and seemed to be considering the situation. 'At very least I hear you are Ortarian by your accent. If you make any trouble for me you will pay with your life,' he said, turning his horse. 'Follow me.'

They followed the rider toward the edge of the encampment, and after the rider had spoken with several other soldiers they were asked to dismount.

'I hear that you want to see General Hugo?' asked another soldier, who was clearly of higher rank due to his impressive armour. He was an older and very skinny man with a long face and a receding chin, yet the fierce look in his eyes revealed he was a seasoned warrior.

'That's right,' replied King Ignis.

'I cannot permit you to see General Hugo unless the purpose of your visit is clearly stated,' said the soldier.

'I have a message from King Ignis,' said King Ignis.

'What message would that be?' asked the soldier.

'I will tell him myself,' said King Ignis resolutely.

'No you won't,' replied the soldier firmly, crossing his arms and standing tall.

King Ignis saw that he was clearly not going to be taken to General Hugo. He gave the situation some thought for a few moments.

'Tell him this: the shadow will never overcome the light.'

The proud soldier looked puzzled for a moment and scratched his chin. 'That is your only message?'

'Yes, that is all,' said King Ignis. 'Tell him just what I have said.'

'All right, but I will have you flogged if you are making a fool of me,' said the soldier. He then turned and walked away into the encampment.

King Ignis turned to Eben with a smile. 'I said that to Hugo just before we went into battle against Azagord's army. He never forgot those words.'

They waited for a few minutes and nothing happened. Eben could see the army was preparing for battle, swords were being sharpened, catapults were being assembled, and armour was being prepared. The whole camp was bustling.

A few minutes later they could hear some commotion. They saw a man approaching who was adorned in fine armour and wore a long red cape. He was an older man with greying hair, a noble face with large green eyes, and a big dark moustache. He moved with determination and strength, and he stood tall with pride. General Hugo looked very noble and the picture of a warrior. He was flanked by several fully armoured knights and other guardsmen. The General approached the edge of the encampment and stared at King Ignis, greatly shocked by the sight before him.

'What sorcery is this?'

'No sorcery, Hugo,' replied King Ignis.

'I see King Ignis before me. Why are you clothed like a peasant, and why are you here in Scaldonia when I received word from you in Ancora only a day ago?'

'Perhaps you are taking orders from the wrong man,' said King Ignis.

'I serve the King of Ortaria with complete loyalty; I do not question his orders,' said General Hugo.

'That was always one of your faults, Hugo,' said King Ignis, shaking his head. 'You were always a little too good at following my orders. You should remember what I said to you when I made you commander of my army.'

'If you tell me that then I will kneel before you here and now. Only King Ignis knows what he said to me that day.'

'I said there may come a day when I may order you to do something you thought was wrong and if that day should come you should question me.'

General Hugo stared in astonishment at King Ignis. He was speechless for several moments.

'My King!' he cried, and he fell upon a knee, bowing his head to the ground. All the knights and soldiers who stood around did the same. There was a sense of great shock among the men who had witnessed what had happened. Cassiel and Eben remained standing.

'What foolishness is this; why are you invading the lands of our Scaldonian friends? Why didn't you question this order?'

General Hugo looked up, confused by the question. 'I did question the order,' he said, his shock still obvious.

'Then you should know the truth. I have been imprisoned in the Dungeons of Zyran for three years. The Zyranian Order has placed an imposter on my throne. What they did not expect was that I would escape with the help of these two friends and some others,' he indicated to Cassiel and Eben. 'Now the time has come to rise up against the tyranny in our land.'

General Hugo stood up. 'There is much we need to talk about.'

**

As the day neared its end they were led through the encampment to a large command tent where a command table had been set. General Hugo sat at the table with three of his field commanders and two knights. King Ignis sat on the other side with Eben and Cassiel.

'The Imposter's commands were to invade Scaldonia and capture Orelin. He ordered me to kill Duke Egil and destroy any resistance,' said Hugo with a tone of regret. King Ignis nodded soberly at hearing the news.

'Recently I have spoken with Meara of the Irilian Order,' said King Ignis. 'She told me the enemy's plan is to have us destroy each other. Tomorrow we will make peace with Duke Egil. We will see if he needs our help. I have also heard news that an army of muckrons has landed near Ancora. We must return to Ortaria and clear the evil army from our land.'

'There are muckrons everywhere. We encountered a group of forty on the road south of here, and we saw many smaller groups near the entrance to the Iron Gate Pass. I have also heard the Scaldonians were driven south by armies of muckrons. Apparently the muckrons and Skatheans control the north of Scaldonia.'

'Perhaps we can work with Duke Egil and clear these monsters from both our kingdoms.'

'My King, it may prove difficult to convince Duke Egil that we are his allies. I sent him a message this morning; I have asked him to surrender and allow us to enter Orelin,' said General Hugo, staring down at his own hands.

King Ignis cringed at hearing the words. 'Did he send a reply?'

'Yes, he did. He said every man and woman in Orelin would fight to the end, and he also said that we are traitors.'

King Ignis stared down at the table gravely. 'This will be difficult for me to repair.'

'They blame us for much of their suffering. The Imposter closed the Iron Gate Pass and stopped all trade going north and west from Ortaria. The Scaldonians relied on our exports, and they have been impoverished by the closure of the pass. They also blame us for not assisting them when they were first invaded. An army from Kaznor attacked the north of Scaldonia several months ago, and King Vidar was taken in chains back to the Dungeons of Zarkanor. Perhaps we should not attempt to reconcile. Our army could be ready to march for Ancora tomorrow morning.'

King Ignis heavily sighed as he contemplated the situation. 'No, Hugo, I want to talk with Duke Egil. A shadow has covered both our lands. Evil is everywhere. We need our friends in these dark times. The Scaldonians are our age old allies; we must stand by them. I will talk with Duke Egil myself in the morning.'

'We will send a messenger at first light to arrange a meeting,' said General Hugo.
**

Eben was given new clothes and his own tent. He felt exhausted and realised that he hadn't slept properly for many days. He went to sleep quickly and woke to the sound of the clambering encampment. He put on his new clothing and walked outside. About ten yards away he could see Cassiel sitting by a small campfire. There were hundreds of tents surrounding them. Most of the soldiers in the encampment were busy making preparations. Cassiel was talking with two soldiers who were seated across the fire. The symbol on most of their shields and banners was a golden lion set against a dark red background. Eben walked over to Cassiel and took a seat beside him.

'These two men are called Max and Marius. They've been assigned to help us,' said Cassiel as Eben sat down. They were two young men, perhaps around the age of twenty. Both were clean shaven and dressed in chainmail armour, with shoulder plates, and swords at their sides. Eben greeted the two young soldiers.

Max looked across at Eben. 'I have been told to take you to an armourer and allow you to select some fine armour. We have also prepared breakfast for you and Cassiel.'

'The breakfast is really very good, you should try it,' said Cassiel.

'Thank you,' said Eben. Marius handed him a bowl of oats with honey.

After he had finished his oats Max led him through the camp to where a group of large wagons were situated. They approached an older man who had a thick black beard, a completely bald head, and a fierce looking face. He was busy sharpening a sword.

'Weapons Master Rufus, this is Eben, a friend of King Ignis himself. I have been instructed to bring him to you so you could provide him with some new armour.'

The weathered and rough looking man looked up at Eben and gave a curt nod. 'You're young to be a friend of the King,' said Rufus in a deep and hoarse voice. 'How old are you?'

'Eighteen,' replied Eben.

'Old enough to die in battle,' said Rufus gruffly as he looked Eben up and down and gave a tight smile. His eyes glanced at Eben's sword for a few moments. 'That sword you have is interesting. Who made it?'

'I don't know,' answered Eben.

'I haven't seen a sword like it, and I've seen thousands of swords,' said Rufus as he moved toward one of the wagons. 'So, what kind of armour do you want? If you are a swordsman you'll probably like something light that won't slow you down.'

Rufus opened the back of one of his wagons and inside were racks of swords, spears, shields, and suits of armour. He climbed up into the wagon and selected a chainmail shirt, a steel chest plate, and an open face helm.

He stepped back down with the armour. 'This is what the infantry field commanders wear,' he said, handing Eben the polished chest plate latched to a back plate. 'Here are some schybalds, you probably call them shin plates, and here are some shoulder plates, which I call pauldrons; these latch easily to the top of your back plate. You can choose between leather or metal plated vambraces to cover your forearms. This is a very light and high quality chainmail shirt; you wear it beneath your plate armour, it stops cuts and slashes. And this is an open face helm; this one is good for swordsmen because it doesn't block your view. The knights often wear them when they're using their swords. Do you need any weapons?'

'No, the armour will be enough,' said Eben.

'Good, it should be easy enough to put on yourself.'

'Thank you for your help,' said Eben.

'I'm just following orders,' said Rufus gruffly.

Eben returned to his tent and tried on the armour. It added a little weight, but he thought he would be able to move almost as well with the armour on. He noticed instantly that the soldiers greeted him with increased respect. Cassiel was still seated beside the fire outside his tent.

'Well, don't you look fine in that new armour,' said Cassiel. 'You look like a real soldier now.' Eben nodded and smiled. 'I just heard that King Ignis received word back from Duke Egil. The Duke won't come out of Orelin to meet with him. He'll only meet with him if King Ignis comes into the city. I don't think it's safe. The Scaldonians are likely to kill him once he's inside the walls. He's only permitted to take one soldier with him inside.'

'Do you think he will go?' asked Eben.

'King Ignis is keen to reforge the alliance with the Scaldonians. I think he will go, but it's not until noon tomorrow.'

'Who's going to go with him?' asked Eben.

'I don't know; probably one of his knights. We'll have to wait and see.'

**

Meara, Red, Stella, and Baftel arrived at the edge of the encampment as the sun was setting in the western sky. Eben and Cassiel greeted them and led them through the encampment toward the command tent.

Red was looking at Eben with a cheeky grin. 'When do I get my armour?'

Eben smiled across at his friend. 'I'm sure King Ignis can arrange that.'

King Ignis came out of the large tent and greeted them. 'I'm glad to see you have arrived safely.'

'We're glad to see you weren't too late,' said Meara.

'One more day and we would have been too late. My army was going to attack Orelin this morning,' said King Ignis. 'Please, come in out of the cold. We are discussing some serious matters.'

They entered the tent and took seats around the table. General Hugo, several field commanders, and two knights were also seated at the table. They greeted the newcomers warmly.

'I think this plan is simply wrong,' said Hugo.

'It is dangerous, but it's the right thing to do,' said King Ignis. 'If we don't reforge the alliance and we allow Scaldonia to fall then we can be sure Ortaria will be next. We need to work with our friends.'

'But Duke Egil's request that you enter Orelin sounds like a trap,' said Sir Victar, an older and noble knight who was seated beside General Hugo. 'He's only allowing you to take one soldier into Orelin. Duke Egil knows you will be vulnerable. Why wouldn't he let you take more guards?'

'This is about trust,' said Meara. 'Duke Egil wants to see if you trust him. Trust is shared in all friendships. He knows that if you trust him you will go. If you don't trust him he knows he cannot trust you.'

'Meara is right; this is a test of trust,' said Baftel, his voice weak and croaky. He looked very old in the dull light. 'There is one other thing that I can see within Orelin. They have one of the Fire Order with them.'

'A Fire Wizard?' asked Meara, raising her eyebrows at the revelation.

'Yes,' replied Baftel. 'He resists my seer ability. He is aware of our presence, Meara.' He paused and caught his breath. It was a struggle for Baftel to speak. 'King Ignis, if you can only take one soldier then that soldier should be Eben.' Everyone at the table looked across to Eben. 'He is the greatest warrior in the encampment.' Eben didn't know if he believed what Baftel was saying.

'This is true, Eben,' said Meara. 'I saw you fight those five Skatheans in Lantern Hill. If only one person can go you would be the best choice.'

'Five Skatheans!' gasped General Hugo.

'I didn't win,' said Eben modestly.

'But you're still alive,' said Sir Victar, amazed and awed by the revelation.

'It's true, Eben proved himself to be quite a warrior in Lantern Hill, but I can't ask you to put your life at risk,' said King Ignis.

'I will go,' said Eben.

'We may be walking into a trap.'

'We've escaped traps before.' Eben smiled. King Ignis nodded with a slight smile back at Eben.

'All right then, Eben and I will go to meet with Duke Egil tomorrow at noon.'
**

The next morning Eben awoke early. He was feeling strong after two nights of solid sleep. He put on his armour and stepped out of the tent. The sun was already fairly high in the sky; it was a couple of hours after sunrise.

Max approached. 'I was asked to let you rest.'

'Thanks.'

'I have been ordered to take you to the Horse Master to find you a warhorse,' said Max.

Eben nodded. Max led him through the large encampment to the southern side where many horses were tied to wagons and carriages. They walked over to a young man who had long hair and a very long beard.

'Horse Master Jorg, this is Eben, a friend of King Ignis. The King has requested you give him your best available warhorse.'

'Certainly,' said Jorg. The young Horse Master led them along the edge of the camp to where several horses were tied to a wagon. 'These are three of my best,' said Jorg. There were two dark brown warhorses and a grey one. They were all obviously bred for war. 'I recommend this one,' he said indicating the grey horse. 'His name is Swiftwing; he is very fast and the wisest of the three. He was given to General Hugo by a drifter who said he had ridden him all the way from the lands beyond Irvaria. The foreigner also said that Swiftwing has fought in several battles in the Western Lands.'

Eben walked up to the huge horse and touched his nose. The horse was friendly and clearly liked him.

'Good, I'll take Swiftwing,' said Eben.

'I'll saddle him up and have him taken to you. I heard you're going to go with the King into

Orelin. Swiftwing will be a good horse for your mission. He won't be frightened.'

They left Jorg and walked back toward his tent. An armoured soldier came running over to him.

'Eben, look at me,' said Red with a huge smile and a glimmer in his eyes. His new armour was shining brightly and was similar to armour Eben had been given by the Weapons Master. Red also had a new finely crafted sword latched to his side. He had his beard shaven to look neat and had tied his shaggy hair back.

'You look great,' said Eben.

'Like a knight,' cried Red heartily. 'I can't wait for Stella to see me like this,' he said as he ran off to find her.

CHAPTER THIRTEEN

The town of Orelin had served as the southern capital of Scaldonia since ancient times. It was often said that the Ecorian Emperors of old took a particular interest in the town as it was the gateway to the Scaldonian Highlands where the mysterious Scaldonian Oracle was said to live. The town's proximity to the Iron Gate Pass led to it being the central point of many battles throughout the ages. The Scaldonians who lived in the south were regarded as a rugged and battle worn people.

The day was dark and clouds rumbled with thunder in the east. King Ignis and Eben rode together toward the main gate of Orelin. King Ignis was adorned in magnificent armour with intricate designs depicting two golden lions. His long red cape was draped down over his horse.

The day was nearing noon when they reached the main gate. The wall stood about fifty feet high. Eben could see hundreds of men lining the walls.

'I am King Ignis of Ortaria! I have come to meet with Duke Egil!'

There was a silence for several moments and then the gates opened enough to let them ride through. The King led the way through the open gate. On the far side were five rugged knights on horseback waiting for them. Their armour was unpolished and dark, and their capes were dark blue. They carried shields with them that had a depiction of a white eagle with outstretched wings, and they all wore helms with visors that covered their faces. The knight in the centre looked particularly rugged and fierce. He had his visor up and stared at them with angry eyes. For a moment Eben was worried they had ridden directly into a trap.

'I am Sir Leif of Scaldonia; Gaurdian of the South; Commander of the Orelin Guard,' said the severe looking knight in a rumbling harsh voice.

'I am King Ignis of Ortaria; direct descendent of the Ecorian Arbiters and rightful ruler of Ortaria,' said King Ignis.

'Duke Egil awaits you; follow me.' Sir Leif turned his horse and led them through the dreary looking town toward the main keep. The streets were mostly empty as almost all the people were indoors. The townsfolk that they did see looked to be living in complete poverty.

The keep was surrounded by a second smaller wall about two hundred yards from the southern gate. They were taken up to the gate of the keep and entered into a large courtyard. Two lines of armoured spearmen formed an honour guard for them. Sir Leif led them up to a big arched door and then dismounted. The other knights also dismounted and King Ignis did the same. Eben followed their example.

'I will now take you to see Duke Egil,' said Sir Leif. He led them in through the door which opened into a long corridor that had no windows and was lit by burning torches at intervals along the wall. Sir Leif led the way through the corridor; the other knights followed them closely.

They reached a second door; Sir Leif pushed it open. Directly before them was a large throne room with stained glass windows and white marble floors. The hall was about a hundred feet long and had two rows of spearmen lining both the long walls. Across the marble floor was a bright silver throne. Seated upon the throne was an old man with long grey hair that fell to his shoulders, a clean shaven face, and a very fearsome look in his grey eyes. He was dressed in amour of the manner of his men, and he stared at King Ignis with a look that bordered on contempt. Beside him on the right was a knight and the left was a crazy looking man wearing a worn brown robe; his hair was frizzy and flew out in every direction. Further to the right of the Duke stood three young maidens, all wearing fine dresses, impressive jewellery, and beautiful attire. To the left of the Duke stood several men who wore no armour; they appeared to be scholars or advisors.

Eben and King Ignis followed Sir Leif across the marble floor toward the Duke.

'Duke Egil, I present to you, King Ignis of Ortaria,' said Sir Leif. He then bowed to the Duke and walked aside. The Duke clapped his hands a few times and sat back deliberately in his chair with a smug smile on his face.

'To be honest, I thought you wouldn't come,' said Duke Egil, his voice was deep and strong. 'After all that my people have suffered at your hands, I can hardly believe that you would dare to come here unprotected. Of course I will let you explain yourself, King Ignis, but only because you apparently have some courage left in your old veins. Why have you brought your army to our gates? My knights say you have over twenty thousand men. Clearly we didn't invite you. First you ask me to surrender, and now you want to make peace. It looks like a trick to me. Explain, King Ignis.'

'Duke Egil, this is no trick. I only reached my army two nights ago. I came to put an end to this madness. I never asked my army to invade Scaldonia, and I never asked for the Iron Gate Pass to be closed...'

The Duke started laughing heavily and folded his arms across his chest. 'Trying to be innocent doesn't suit you, Ignis,' he said. King Ignis frowned and his eyes narrowed. He was clearly offended by the statement.

'I have been in a dungeon for three years!' said King Ignis firmly. 'I escaped the Dungeons of Zyran only recently. I had to race north to stop my army from invading your lands. An imposter sits on my throne; he was the one who ordered this invasion. Now I have returned I plan to repair all the damage that has been done.'

The Duke stared at King Ignis with wide eyes at hearing the revelation. The throne room fell completely silent. Duke Egil looked to the man at his side in the brown robes with the crazy hair.

'Garnock, is this true?' The wizard stared intensely at King Ignis for a few moments; his eyes then darted across to Eben. He gazed at Eben with his crazy wide eyes. Eben wondered what he was thinking and felt uncomfortable.

'Yes,' replied Garnock, his extremely high tone made him sound completely insane. 'It's all true, Duke.' Garnock continued staring intently at Eben. 'You must ask the Ortarian who that is he brought with him.'

The Duke looked from the King to Eben. 'Who is your guardsman?'

'His name is Eben,' said King Ignis, surprised by the question.

'Why do you want to know about his guardsman?' asked the Duke, looking to the crazy wizard.

'He is not who we think he is,' said the wizard. 'The sea shall bend for this one.'

The Duke rolled his eyes at the cryptic reply of the wizard. 'What are you talking about? Why do you always speak in riddles?' The Duke looked from the wizard back to King Ignis. 'King Ignis, this story of your imprisonment is news to me; I knew nothing of it. We Scaldonians suspected Zyran had fallen beneath a shadow; however, we have never known for certain. You must know these are terrible times for us. Our northern city of Aldokan has fallen to the Kaznor Empire. There is an evil growing in the north, and armies of muckrons have landed on our shores. King Vidar, my brother, was captured by the enemy and taken as a prisoner to the Dungeons of Zarkanor. We have been pushed south and our people have suffered greatly. You should also know that our scouts say there is an army of muckrons camped about ten miles north of Orelin.'

'An army of muckrons!' exclaimed King Ignis, surprised that such an army was so close to Orelin. 'How many muckrons are there?'

'Thousands,' replied the Duke. 'And they have a wyvern with them.'

'A wyvern!' cried King Ignis, clearly shocked.

Eben's adoptive father Erako had told him that wyverns were very evil dragons. It was said that some wyverns flew and others crawled. Erako had also told him that real dragons were much larger than wyverns and often majestic and good creatures. Generally only the smaller wyverns were evil in nature. Eben had always thought they were just creatures in stories.

'Yes, the wyvern flies in circles above the muckron horde. It's not very big, only about five yards in length, but it is very ferocious. The beast killed two of our northern scouts and only one returned to tell the tale. It swoops down and takes them from their horses, like an eagle taking a rabbit,' said the Duke.

'An army of muckrons and a wyvern; these indeed are evil times,' said King Ignis. 'Armies of muckrons have not been seen in these lands since the Forgotten Age. I recently heard news that one such army landed on the shores of Ortaria. I plan to lead my army south to destroy the evil army that threatens my kingdom.' There were a few moments of silence as the two rulers stared at each other. 'We must rebuild our alliance of old. If we can reform our alliance we could march on this muckron army in the north, and together the Ortarians and Scaldonians could destroy all the evil that plagues our lands.'

The Duke glanced across at his knights and then uneasily looked back toward King Ignis. 'My men don't trust you or the Ortarian army beyond the gate. They told me that you would try to trick me into opening the gates of Orelin.'

'This is not a trick. You know I tell you the truth,' protested King Ignis.

'Yes, I know,' said the Duke, staring down at the white marble floor for a moment. 'But if you want the alliance restored you must prove to my men and my people that you and your army are trustworthy. If you lead your army north of Orelin and destroy the army of muckrons you will have the alliance you seek.'

King Ignis nodded and realised there was no other way. Duke Egil was resolute in what he had said.

'I see,' said King Ignis softly. 'I will consult with my commanders and inform you of our intention.'

**

They returned to the encampment and King Ignis arranged a meeting with General Hugo and the other commanders and knights. Eben, Meara, Cassiel, and Baftel sat at the command table with them.

'Garnock,' said Meara, intrigued by the revelation. 'He is a very powerful member of the Fire Order. I wonder why he is in Scaldonia, so far from the Old Guardian Mountains.'

'I don't know what he is doing here, but he was interested in Eben,' said King Ignis.

'What did he say about Eben?' asked Meara.

'He said that the sea would bend for him,' said King Ignis. Meara looked to Eben, and she pondered the saying for a moment. 'What does that mean?

'I'm not entirely sure; I think one day we will find out,' said Meara. She gave a slight smile to Eben before looking back to King Ignis.

'He will restore our alliance if we destroy the muckron army which is camped ten miles north of here,' said King Ignis.

'A muckron army!' cried General Hugo.

'Indeed, we need to assess our options. How many men do we have?'

'Almost twenty five thousand,' replied General Hugo. 'We have sixteen thousand infantry, two thousand archers, five thousand light cavalry, one thousand heavy cavalry, and fifty knights. We also have eight mobile catapults and several other siege machines, but I think we should consider turning south. If we spend our strength fighting the muckron army in Scaldonia we may risk not having the men to fight the muckron army in Ortaria. Perhaps we should forsake rebuilding the alliance. The Scaldonians only have a small army remaining here in Orelin. We would be wise to focus on the needs of Ortaria and return home.'

The King contemplated in silence what General Hugo had said. Everyone at the table was looking at him and waiting for his answer.

'No, Hugo. We must keep our honour. If we lose our honour we would forsake everything we have fought for; I will never let that happen. Ortarians don't turn away from a fight. We stand by our allies and friends. That's who we are, and we won't change now or ever. The Scaldonians have suffered, and they are our friends; we will fight for them. Anyone can be a friend in peaceful times; I have learned it is in the dark times that loyalty and honour are truly tested.'

'I will order the army to prepare,' said General Hugo.

'We will need to send scouts to assess the muckron army. There is a problem though; they have a wyvern with them.'

'A wyvern!' gasped Meara.

'Yes,' said King Ignis. 'Duke Egil said this beast has already killed some of his scouts. Send only scouts who know the danger and are prepared to take the risk.'

'It will be a challenge to find a man willing to take on this task, especially if you give him a choice,' said General Hugo.

The King thumped the table with his fist. 'Forget the scouts, if we can't beat this army of muckrons now it will eventually arrive in Ortaria and destroy us there. This battle will test our strength and bravery. Order the army to prepare; we ride north in the morning!'

**

The army started to make preparations for leaving that afternoon. Eben sat by a campfire with Cassiel.

'We are going to war in the morning,' said Cassiel. 'I have never seen a muckron. I wonder if they are as terrible as the old stories say they are?'

'I fought one once,' said Eben. Cassiel was very surprised. 'They're fast and strong.' He remembered back to the fight with the muckron in the forest. 'If I didn't have Red with me I would have been killed. He saved me.'

'Red saved you?'

Eben nodded. A moment later Red walked quickly over to where they were sitting by the campfire. His face was pale, and he was deeply frowning.

'Eben, you have to talk some sense into Stella, she's gone mad! She's preparing to fight in the battle tomorrow. You have to convince her otherwise.'

A moment later Stella came into view and marched over. Her eyes were blazing, and her face was red with anger. She was wearing a chainmail shirt, shoulder guards, shin guards, and she had two short swords latched to her belt.

'What are you talking to them about, Red?' she asked angrily.

'Stella! The danger is too great,' argued Red.

'You know I can fight, Red. So stop trying to...'

'But...but, you'll be the only woman on the battlefield.'

'Meara will be there, so I won't be the only woman,' she replied defiantly.

'That's true, Red. Meara will be there,' confirmed Cassiel.

'Shut up, Cassiel,' yelled Red.

'I've been through all this danger with you: Zyran, the wilderness, Lantern Hill, and the draug. I'm not going to stand aside now and watch from afar.'

Red didn't know what to say. Eben could see Stella was determined and would not back down.

'If we fight together and stay close we can defend each other and make sure that no one gets into trouble,' said Eben. Red reluctantly accepted the fact that Stella was going to fight.

CHAPTER FOURTEEN

The army moved out the next morning and followed the road north away from the Orelin basin. The army looked like a giant metal serpent winding its way up through the rocky hills. Thick dark clouds hung low in the sky, and the air was dense as a morning mist was rising from the ground. A little rain had fallen earlier. Eben rode with King Ignis, Red, and Stella toward the front of the troops.

'Do you feel like fighting in a battle today?' asked King Ignis, looking across at Red.

'Not really,' replied Red. The King laughed heartily.

'I'm sure you will fight well.'

'I'll do my best,' said Red.

'Not since the Forgotten Ages have armies of muckrons roamed these lands. The Prince of Shadows brought them to Veredor in those days from a dark place in the cosmos. At the end of the Forgotten Age the muckron armies were destroyed by the Astarian Fiora. The Prince of Shadows was cast into the darkness beyond the boundaries of Veredor.'

'So why have they come back now?' asked Red.

'I don't know,' said King Ignis.

'Maybe the Prince of Shadows has come back from the darkness,' suggested Red.

'I hope not. The Prince of Shadows was the most terrible adversary the people of Veredor have ever faced.'

'What's an Astarian?' asked Eben, curious to know more about the Astarian Fiora.

'The Astarians were immortals who lived in ancient times. They were a goodhearted and benevolent race.'

'Do any still live?'

'I have never heard of any who live near men. It is said the Scaldonian Oracle is an Astarian. I have also heard there is an oracle in the Far Western Lands. I don't know of any other Astarians living in Veredor other than the oracles, and many people don't believe that the oracles actually exist.'

The oracles were mystical beings that lived in the wilderness, one in Scaldonia and the other in the Far Western Lands. Eben had heard stories of heroes having to overcome many obstacles to find the oracles. It had long been said that the oracles could give insights into the deepest mysteries.

They rode on for an hour. The mist cleared. The hills came to a sudden end and a plain stretched out before them. Thick storm clouds had settled low in the sky above the plain. There was no rain at all and the air was still. From the hill they could see across a plain that extended about ten miles to another mountain range in the north. The road continued for two miles and they could see smoke rising from the encampment of the muckron army. The Ortarian Army halted. Eben could see the silhouette of the wyvern flying in circles through the smoke that hovered over the encampment of muckrons.

'How many muckrons do you think there are, Hugo?' asked King Ignis.

'Thousands, perhaps six or seven thousand,' replied General Hugo as his eyes scanned the encampment of their enemies.

The wyvern started flying toward them. Eben could see the orange and red scales of the creature as it approached. The beast had large horns, clawed feet, and batlike wings which were dark in colour. It ascended higher and within a minute was circling above the army of men and screeching in a deathly shrill tone. All the men of the army looked up in horror at the wyvern.

'I never thought I would see anything like that,' said King Ignis sternly, staring up at the evil creature high above.

Meara rode up to be beside King Ignis. 'They are said to be as intelligent as men. I believe the wyvern is spying for the enemy.'

'We must move quickly then,' said King Ignis. They moved down the slope of the hill and arrived at the plain within a few minutes. The muckron army was marshalling itself in the distance and preparing for battle.

'We will move closer until we are about five hundred yards away from them,' said General Hugo. 'Our knights and heavy cavalry will charge them. We can use the light cavalry as support. The infantry can move in as a third wave.'

'What about the archers?' asked King Ignis.

'They can support the infantry and stop the enemy flanking us.'

'Good, let's move out further across the plain and prepare our position,' said King Ignis.

Eben could hear the drums of the enemy in the distance. Deep horns were being blown, and all the muckrons howled. The sound of the beasts froze their hearts.

'Urs-shaka, Urs-shaka, Urs-shaka!' The muckrons growled as they formed several lines and started moving toward the army of men.

The Ortarian army formed several opposing lines with the heavy cavalry and the knights to the front. The light cavalry formed a line directly behind the heavy cavalry. The infantry formed about ten lines behind the last horses, and the archers stood further back. By the time the army had formed a position the muckrons were about fifteen hundred yards away and were steadily advancing across the plain.

'Are we ready, Hugo?' asked the King. General Hugo sternly nodded. King Ignis rode out in front of his army on his great white warhorse. He looked magnificent against the dark horizon and the heavy clouds. His long red cape flew in the wind, and his bright armour was shining brilliantly. He was like a light set against the gloom.

'We fight for Ortaria! Keep your honour! Be brave! Be true!' he cried. The army cheered all at once. 'We Ortarians have always fought for the good of all people! Now we are here, in a foreign land, and we are called to vanquish this evil horde of monsters from Veredor! I believe we have the courage! I believe we are brave! Fight well! Fight for your family! Fight for your people! And fight for all that is good!' he cried. The cheers of the army echoed across the field.

'Urs-shaka, Urs-shaka, Urs-shaka,' bellowed the muckron army in response. The wyvern released a bloodcurdling scream, which sent shivers through the Ortarian army.

'For Ortaria!' cried King Ignis, drawing his sword as he turned his warhorse to face the enemy.

An Ortarian trumpet sounded and rang out across the plain. The heavy cavalry started to move forward. The polished armour of the knights shimmered as the sun shone through a gap in the clouds above. A second trumpet sounded and the light cavalry followed.

Stella was riding beside Red, and Meara was a little further back with Cassiel. Baftel was standing much further back behind the lines of archers. Eben smiled across at Red. He felt his confidence growing. A feeling grew in his heart that was similar to how he had felt in Lantern Hill, a sense of courage flowed through his veins.

'Let's ride!' cried Eben, drawing the Sword of Light. The blade glimmered brightly as the light of the sun reflected on the smooth polished metal.

Swiftwing leapt forward, chasing after the cavalry. The pace was growing as their horses galloped. Stella and Red were beside Eben; Cassiel and Meara were a little further back trying to keep up. Eben stared ahead at the line of hideous muckrons. The sound of thousands of horses galloping was thunderous. The heavy cavalry were lowering their lances as the line of muckrons stood ready. The muckrons were armed with an assortment of spears, war hammers, maces, and some carried battle-axes. Some of the muckrons wore makeshift armour and others wore nothing at all. Their hideous hairy pig faces snarled and growled.

The front line of cavalry struck the line of muckrons with a mighty clash of steel. A moment later Eben was upon them. He swung his blade and watched a muckron fall. Swiftwing crashed through the enemy front line. There were howls and cries all about; the scene was wild. Eben was surrounded by monsters. He thrust his sword out again and again. His visual field was full of foul pig faces, some with tusks, and others with protruding fangs and drooling mouths. Swiftwing pushed through the field of muckrons, knocking the monsters down as he charged on.

Eben looked back and could see Stella and Red about forty feet away, side by side, fighting several muckrons together. Further away he could see waves of blue flames and swirling columns of blue fire blasting from Meara's hands. The monsters howled and ran from her. The cavalrymen were all around fiercely battling the monsters. Eben swung, stabbed, and slashed as the beasts shrieked and howled at him. The scene turned into a mad blur. The Ortarian infantry then entered the fray. The intensity of the battle increased. Eben parried and struck out again and again. His heart thumped like a drum. Swiftwing reared up on his hind legs and kicked a muckron away as Eben stabbed another.

'Eben!' cried Stella's voice from far off.

Eben turned Swiftwing about and looked to see the wyvern descending on Cassiel about a hundred feet away. The wyvern's red scales glimmered in the daylight; a menacing howl echoed out as the beast swooped downward. Cassiel held his hands up, creating a shield, but the wyvern crashed through the barrier and struck the young wizard, sending him flying through the air. The wyvern leapt after him.

Eben turned Swiftwing about and galloped across the field toward Cassiel, but Red arrived first and stood in the wyvern's path. Red swung his blade. The wyvern simply struck out, and Red's sword flew from his hand. Red stumbled back and looked up at the large fangs of the beast, his eyes full of shock. A moment later the wyvern grabbed Red around his chest and lifted him up, squeezing him tightly. Red moaned in pain as the claws buckled his armour. Stella cried out and ran to save him, but the wyvern leapt into the air and beat its wings.

A moment later Eben charged into the scene as the beast flew upward. Eben leapt from Swiftwing and grabbed onto one of the wyvern's horns. The enraged face and red eyes sneered. The beast whipped its head about, trying to shake Eben off. Eben hewed down at the creature's arm which was holding Red; the severed arm fell away, and Red landed in the mud below. The wyvern gave a bloodcurdling scream and crashed into the field. Eben rolled away from the fierce beast and quickly got to his feet, holding up the Sword of Light.

The wyvern moaned in pain and roared in defiance. Eben dashed forward as the wyvern leapt at him. He brought his blade down and cut through its scales; a moment later the beast dropped, writhed on the ground, and then fell still.

The muckrons backed away as Eben lifted his sword high above his head, the daylight seemed to collect around the blade. The muckrons stumbled back further and moaned in fear. The soldiers and cavalrymen cheered for Eben. The remaining muckrons started to run, and several riders chased them down. Further out there were some small skirmishes, but the area directly around them was clearing of muckrons as the monsters were running for their lives.

Stella went quickly to Red's side. He was dazed and disoriented. Cassiel limped over a few moments later; the left side of Cassiel's face was covered in blood from a gash above his eyebrow.

'Red, are you all right?' asked Stella. 'Please, Red, say something!'

'Stella...I think I have some broken ribs,' muttered Red as he opened his eyes. Stella held him close and was thankful he was speaking.

Moments later Meara walked over. 'The muckron army is retreating,' she said as she looked out across the plain.

Eben sheathed his sword and helped Stella to sit Red up. Meara walked over and put her hand on Red's shoulder. A gentle blue light emanated from her hands, and Red suddenly looked brighter and happier.

'You have three broken ribs,' said Meara. 'This spell will reduce the pain and help to heal you more quickly, but just because the pain is mostly gone doesn't mean you are free from an injury. You should take care.'

'Red, I thought I was finished. You saved me from the wyvern.' said Cassiel.

'Anytime,' said Red as he stood up.
**

Eben sat in the command tent. Red, Stella, Baftel, King Ignis, and General Hugo were seated around the table. Meara and Cassiel walked in to join them, followed by two knights.

'Sadly we lost two thousand men, and about a thousand are severely injured,' said General Hugo. 'Our riders say about a thousand muckrons escaped north and are continuing to move away from us. Several smaller groups of the monsters have been hunted down by our cavalry.'

King Ignis nodded. 'We will give all our fallen the full burial rights and honours that they deserve. They showed courage and gave the ultimate sacrifice. We shall always remember the victory we had here over the muckron horde. We will never forget those who fell in the battle.'

'The heavy cavalry did the most damage to the muckrons...and Eben.' said General Hugo.

'The men are calling you the Dragon Slayer,' said King Ignis, looking to Eben with a proud smile. 'I watched you riding through the lines of muckrons. You were alone and ahead of everyone else. They scattered at your feet. I have not seen anything like that in all the battles I have fought.'

'Such things haven't been seen since the Forgotten Age,' said Meara.

Eben looked down at the Sword of Light at his side. He knew that much of his ability came from the sword he carried.

'We will have to turn south soon,' said General Hugo. 'The Imposter in Ancora ordered us to invade Scaldonia with only enough food and supplies for three weeks from Galdir. We should make haste to return to Galdir.'

'Galdir? No, the Zyranians will expect us to come back that way,' said King Ignis. 'We will ride through the Northern Pass and make directly for Ancora.'

'The draug is gone, but it would prove very difficult to take wagons and catapults up the Sky Steps,' said Meara.

'Yes, what you say is true,' agreed King Ignis. 'Baftel, can you see where the muckron army is in Ortaria?' asked the King, looking across at the frail wizard.

'There is a dark shadow near Ancora, perhaps the muckron army is there. It is difficult for me to know for sure. I have been looking south, and I can see the Skatheans are planning something. They have moved from the Iron Gate Pass and away from Galdir. They are heading eastward back toward Ancora.'

The King scratched his beard; for a few moments he was deep in thought. 'It would take us about eight days to ride back to Ancora if we took the Northern Pass. If we went through the Iron Gate Pass it would take us an extra week.'

'By now the Imposter and the Zyranians would be aware that you have taken control of the army,' said General Hugo. 'He would be preparing for you to come south; that's probably why the Skatheans have gone east. They may also know that you killed the draug, so he may expect us to come back through the Northern Pass. If we go through the Iron Gate Pass, we can restock at Galdir, and clear the villages and towns along the highway of all the tyrants and bandits who rule them. We can sweep across Ortaria and return victoriously to Ancora knowing that our enemies have all been destroyed.'

'It's a good plan,' agreed King Ignis. 'We shall vanquish the evil in Ortaria from west to east. We will head for Galdir.'

**

By the evening the army had started to prepare to move south. Meara and Cassiel were working with the injured, healing as many as they could with their skills. Eben, Red, and Stella worked with them assisting with bandaging. By nightfall Meara was exhausted. They sat around a small campfire discussing the journey south.

'If the muckrons are as they were here then we should do fine in Ortaria,' said Red.

'There were only seven thousand here,' said Meara. 'We greatly outnumbered them. I believe they were here waiting to attack the Ortarians after they had fought with the Scaldonians. They were waiting for the Ortarians and Scaldonians to destroy each other; their task was to finish off whoever was left. They never expected the Ortarians to help the Scaldonians. If we were to fight a larger muckron army I believe we would then learn what they are truly capable of.'

'We will likely get the opportunity soon,' said Cassiel. Meara nodded.

All of a sudden a small blackbird flew down and landed on Meara's shoulder. It sang a short sweet song and then leapt away. The bird was gone from sight a few moments later. Meara looked into the flames of the fire and for some time didn't say a word.

'That small bird was a messenger from the Irilian Order,' she said. 'I have been called to an urgent meeting in Dravania.' They fell silent and stared at her. 'I must go to the Iril Fortress in Dravania.'

Eben felt his heart sink at hearing these words. Meara was a great support to their group.

'Must you go, Meara?' asked Red.

'Yes,' she replied regretfully. 'Please excuse me; I will talk with King Ignis.' She stood up and walked away from the campfire in the direction of the command tent. Cassiel followed after her.

**

Later in the evening Eben was talking with Max, Marius, and some other soldiers. Word had spread about Eben's bravery and skill in the battle.

'Eben, can we talk?' asked Cassiel as he approached.

'Of course,' replied Eben. They walked back toward the campfire.

'I have some good news; Meara has accepted me as her apprentice. I will finish my training and eventually become an Irilian,' said Cassiel gladly.

'I'm happy to hear it,' said Eben.

'Baftel will be going west with Meara.' There was a short silence. 'Meara must go to Dravania; she has no choice in the matter. A great war is raging in the kingdoms of Iarthar and Dravania. The Irilians face a large threat, and Meara is one of the strongest Irilians. The Irilian Order needs her now.'

'So what are you going to do, Cassiel?'

'I have decided to stay with you, Red, and Stella. I want to stay here and finish what we started. Meara said that she will take me to the Iril Fortress in Dravania and begin my training after the war.'

'I'm glad you're going to stay,' said Eben, feeling relieved.

CHAPTER FIFTEEN

The army set off early the following day. By midmorning they had reached the basin of Orelin. The company of friends rode at the front of the troops with King Ignis. They watched as Duke Egil rode out from the gates of Orelin on a mighty black warhorse; he was followed closely by ten of his knights. Their dark blue capes flew in the wind as they galloped across the field toward the Ortarian army.

'I salute you, King Ignis,' said Duke Egil as he drew near.

'And I you, Duke Egil,' said King Ignis.

'My scouts have told me that you destroyed the army of muckrons and the wyvern. Consider our alliance reformed,' said the Duke happily.

'I am glad to hear it. We are now heading for the Iron Gate Pass to liberate Ortaria,' said King Ignis.

'I have eight thousand fighting men in Orelin,' said Duke Egil. 'Now we will ride north and attempt to clear our northern lands of the enemy.'

'I wish you all the best,' said King Ignis. 'When I complete my campaign in Ortaria I will send reinforcements to you. We must also consider that the Zyranian Order is working against us. There may come a time when I ask for your help.'

'And I will send you men if I can. I should also tell you that Garnock has sent word to the Fire Order to tell them the Zyranians have turned to evil ways. You should also form an alliance with Silvor, Ateria, and the Isles of Dawn. Perhaps they can help us deal with Zyran.'

'Once I reclaim Ancora I will send word to the kings in the south, yet I fear that Zyran will already be influencing them.'

'Perhaps the Irvarians in the west can help us,' suggested Duke Egil.

Meara rode up to bring her horse beside King Ignis. 'I am going to Irvaria. I will take word to King Edric of Irvaria and inform him of your troubles. I am the Irilian Meara. You should know the Irilians are also your allies.'

'I'm happy to hear that,' said Duke Egil. 'The forces in Veredor are gathering their strength, and hopefully we are not too late. A great darkness is coming to our lands. We must be ready.'

'It seems to me that the darkness has already arrived,' said King Ignis, raising an eyebrow.

'Garnock said what we have seen is only the beginning. He was sent by the Fire Order to watch the north. The Kaznor Empire has a new emperor; they simply call him "Master" and he is known by no other name. All the Skatheans and muckrons are loyal to him. I believe he is the force behind the evil we face, including what is happening in Zyran.'

'I have heard of him,' said King Ignis. 'Azagord told me about him when I was imprisoned in Zyran. He is mysterious and powerful. Azagord told me that he is a powerful sorcerer, greater than the Northern Sorcerers. Azagord was forced to submit to his will. He had to fight for his mind against the forces of darkness; thankfully in the end Azagord redeemed himself.'

'I think this person we speak of is actually an Astarian,' said Duke Egil.

'Perhaps he is the Prince of Shadows,' suggested Red, recalling the earlier mention of the evil adversary from the Forgotten Age.

'I hope not,' said King Ignis nervously. 'I always thought those old stories were just legends and myths. Until recently I thought the same about wyverns. We are going to see many dark times ahead if the Prince of Shadows has returned to Veredor.'

'We will fight these enemies together, whoever they are,' said Duke Egil.

King Ignis was happy at hearing his confidence. 'Indeed, we will not allow the forces of darkness to take hold.'

**

They left the Orelin basin and journeyed south along the road toward the Iron Gate Pass for the rest of the afternoon. It was a fine day, and the clouds had mostly dispersed allowing the warmth of the sun to shine down. The soldiers were glad to be heading home. There was a growing sense of hope that they would soon see their families again and see an end to the evil reign in their homeland. All the men felt encouraged by their victory against the muckron horde.

That evening they made a camp beside a small river. Eben, Red, and Stella were sitting around a campfire. Max had joined them and was playing a wooden flute. The sound of the music was soothing to their tired minds.

'That tune was lovely. You play so well,' said Stella.

'I bring my flute everywhere with me. My father gave it to me before he died. I grew up in Ancora near the western gate. I haven't heard from my mother and sisters for nearly two years. I often wonder how they are.'

'You will see them again soon,' said Red as he took the wooden spoon from the pot and tasted the stew he had been preparing. He then brought out some wooden bowls from his leather bag. Eben had no idea where he had found his cooking equipment. He served the four of them some of his delicious mushroom stew.

'Very nice, Red,' said Eben.

'I was a cook for a little while when I was still living in Silvor,' said Red.

'You've done just about everything,' said Stella.

Red nodded and a big smile crossed his face. 'Twenty years old and seen it all,' he said proudly.

'Probably you should think about settling down,' suggested Eben.

'That's the plan,' said Red, his smile becoming even wider as he glanced across at Stella. Stella shyly looked away.

'What about you, Eben. After the war, what will you do?' asked Red.

'All I really want to do is find my parents.'

'Where will you go?' asked Stella.

'I plan to travel to the lands beyond the Endless Wall Mountains. I hope to find the remaining Fiorian Knights. King Ignis told me that my mother was once the leader of the Fiorian

Order. They may be able to tell me what happened to my mother and father.'

'Your mother was a Fiorian; that's amazing,' said Stella, her eyes widening at the revelation.

'I hope she's still out there somewhere,' said Eben.

'If she is I'm sure you will find her,' said Red confidently.

'I have heard the Western Lands are beautiful. Especially Irvaria and Everdon,' said Stella. 'I hope you find your parents.'

'I will search until I do,' said Eben, feeling he would not rest until he knew what happened to his mother and father.

**

The following morning the army moved further south. The towering Endora Mountains covered the entire southern skyline. The landscape gradually flattened out and looked much like the plains they had ridden across when they had first come out of the Northern Pass. The army was marching quite quickly, mostly due to the enthusiasm of the men. The road curved gradually toward the southwest as they progressed. The Iron Gate Pass was set at the collision point of the Endora Mountains and the Endless Wall Mountains. The pass had always been the only road to Vastoria from Ortaria and Scaldonia; this fact had caused it to be the focal point of numerous wars throughout the ages.

Eben had heard that the land of Vastoria beyond the pass was a harsh and inhospitable desert. The Vastorians were mostly a tribal and nomadic people. They lived in the wastelands and made a living from the unforgiving environment.

This gave Vastorians a reputation as a rough and ruthless people. Further west, beyond the borders of Vastoria, was the famed Kingdom of Irvaria. Irvaria was said to be a land of grand castles, lush rolling hills, beautiful lakes, enchanting forests, and noble people. Eben wondered how far he would have to go to find the answers he sought.

'Eben, if I was to ever get married would you be my best man?' asked Red.

Eben looked over to Red who was riding beside him. He then looked back over his shoulder and saw that Stella was riding quite a long way back with Meara and Baftel.

'Of course,' he replied.

'Good. Great,' said Red, nodding and smiling. Red slowed his horse and waited for Stella to catch up. Eben continued to ride at the front of the army with King Ignis.

'He's an interesting young man, that Red,' said King Ignis. 'He never takes anything seriously, yet he is always there when you need his help; such a strange combination.'

'He's my best friend,' said Eben as he looked over his shoulder at Red and Stella riding further back.

'I'll have to make him into a knight for his service to Ortaria, even though he was born in Silvor,' said King Ignis. 'Keep this a secret; I'll make it a surprise for him on our return to Ancora.'

'I won't say a word.' Eben felt happy about what King Ignis had said. He knew Red would be overjoyed at being offered a knighthood.

**

Late in the morning on the following day the Ortarian army was approaching the meeting place of the two mountain ranges in the southwest corner of Scaldonia. The land grew hilly the further they proceeded south. Ahead of them were two great mountains and a deep valley. They moved along the well maintained road that cut into the hillsides and led up through the great valley between the two snow-capped mountains. After midday King Ignis halted the army on a hilltop, and from their position they had a wide view of the mountains.

'The Iron Gate Pass,' said King Ignis. 'In two days we will be in Galdir.'

The King led the way along the road as it curved up through the mountains. The road led them through deep valleys and was often carved into mountainsides. Often there were sheer cliffs that descended into deep and craggy valleys below. There was always enough room for at least two wagons side by side.

When evening arrived they set up camp at the base of a valley high in the mountains. The army had prepared for the cold by bringing firewood from the wooded lands below, and before long hundreds of fires lit up the valley in the early evening. Meara, Red, Stella, Baftel, and Cassiel were sitting with Eben around a blazing campfire.

'Tomorrow we will part ways,' said Meara. 'Before long I will return to Ortaria. There will be a great need for the Irilians in these lands. I hope to bring many wizards to assist the people of the Eastern Lands.'

'Do you think the Zyranians can be stopped?' asked Red.

'Yes, I do. I also believe there are still some good Zyranians; however, the High Commander and the Gatekeeper have certainly turned to evil ways. I am convinced they are in the service of the evil Master in the north. I hope to bring about a revolution within the Zyranian Order. Magic was always intended to be used for good. In ancient times men had no magic. The Astarian Lumen instructed men in the ways of Astarian magic to help men defend Veredor. Those first few wizards formed the Fire Order. They built the Tower of Fire in the Old Guardian Mountains; the Fire Order has lived there ever since. From the Fire Order came the Irilians and the Zyranians. The primary intention always remained the same: to use magic for the good of all and to protect Veredor from evil. Therefore I believe the way to overcome the Zyranian Order is to call on the good Zyranians who still hold to the true ways of old.'

'When Baltac became the High Commander all those who were good were pushed down or out of the Zyranian Order.' said Baftel. 'The good wizards who remained have been given the lowliest positions in the order, and there are several others like myself, outcasts.'

'Soon we will gather the outcasts and help them to retake control of Zyran,' said Meara.
      **

The next morning the army moved onward through the Iron Gate Pass. The road continued to take them higher into the icy mountains. By early afternoon the way opened out onto a wide flat area situated between three enormous snow covered peaks. They had come to the crossroads of the pass. Three roads led away from the area. Each way had ancient stone gateways set into towering walls, but the old gates were long since gone. The flattened area between the gates was about the size of a large farmer's field, about four hundred yards across. Each gateway opened the way to the three respective countries. West led to Vastoria, north to Scaldonia, and east to Ortaria.

'This place is called the Edius Plateau,' said King Ignis as his eyes scanned the empty area. 'Many wars have been fought between these three gates.'

The army stopped on the plateau as it was the place where Meara and Baftel would be leaving them. The two wizards rode to the front of the lines of soldiers.

'King Ignis, I will return as quickly as possible,' said Meara. 'I wish you the best for the trials that are ahead of you.'

'I look forward to your return to Ancora,' said King Ignis warmly. Meara then turned to Eben.

'Eben, remember what I told you about crossing the bridge. I'm sure you will do amazing things. We will meet again soon. Be brave and strong.'

'I will,' said Eben.

She then looked to Cassiel. 'You are now my apprentice and a wizard of the Irilian Order. Represent us with honour in Ortaria. I will send word to you, and we will meet again soon. Serve King Ignis loyally.'

'I will be true to the Irilian Order and serve King Ignis,' said Cassiel, bowing to Meara.

'Goodbye my friends,' she said, turning her horse toward the gate that led to Vastoria.

Baftel raised his hand and waved to the company as they departed. 'I will see you all again,' said the old wizard. Meara was leading Baftel's horse behind her own horse. They rode away slowly, and before long they were out of sight.

'Let's continue,' said King Ignis. The army moved away from the Edius Plateau and through the eastern gateway toward Ortaria. As the evening arrived the army came to a wide valley with a waterfall which fell down from the heights above to a fast flowing stream that rushed through the base of the valley. They set up camp again beside the waterfall.

Later in the evening Eben sat by the stream with Red and Stella.

'It's going to be different with Meara and Baftel gone,' said Stella, a hint of sadness in her voice.

'We will be fine,' said Red. 'Meara said she'll return to Ortaria as soon as possible, and she'll bring with her more wizards to teach those Zyranians a thing or two.'

'You're right, Red. She won't be gone for long.'

CHAPTER SIXTEEN

The following day they came out of the mountains and into the foothills on the Ortarian side of the range. The air was clear, and the sun was shining brightly down on them. From a high hill Eben could see the Kingdom of Ortaria stretching out into the distance. He could see the hills below and emerald green plains that faded into the distant horizon. His eyes were drawn to a hill about three miles away. A mighty fortress was set at the height of the hill. A small town covered the steep hillsides surrounding the tower.

'Galdir!' cried King Ignis excitedly.

The general mood in the army was hopeful; Eben could feel the excitement in the air. They continued to move forward toward the fortress, and within two hours they were rounding the last hill.

A group of riders rode out from the fortress to meet them; their leader was wearing bright armour in the manner of a knight, but without a helm. A large moustache dominated his face, and he was mostly bald with hair growing out only above his ears. The other riders were Ortarian cavalrymen.

'Hail! General Hugo!' shouted the leading rider. 'I expect to hear good news. Has Orelin fallen?'

'Baron Doriak, there is much we must discuss,' replied General Hugo. Baron Doriak's posture stiffened; he took a quick breath as he stared in shock at King Ignis. A few moments passed in complete silence.

'I don't see how this can be,' said the Baron, visibly shaking. 'I received word from King Ignis in Ancora only yesterday, and yet, here I see that King Ignis rides with the army. Surely there is something wrong.'

'I am King Ignis. The message you received was from an imposter,' said the King firmly.

'I don't know if this can possibly be true,' said Baron Doriak, his eyes narrowing.

'It is true,' said General Hugo. 'We have been the victims of grave treachery. King Ignis has been imprisoned in the Dungeons of Zyran for three years. An imposter has been ruling our lands. Now that King Ignis has returned we will make all things right in Ortaria.'

'I trust you, General Hugo; however, this news is difficult for me to understand. I must say that I am shocked. Let me lead you to the fortress. We will discuss this matter further in private. Follow me, Your Highness,' said Baron Doriak as he turned his horse.

The army marched onward toward the fortress. The towering fortress was a thin structure made of dark bluestone and looked to be as old as the mountains themselves. The tower was about fifty yards across at the base and about a hundred and fifty yards in height. The fortress only had narrow vertical windows set high above the ground. On top of the fortress three flags of Ortaria blew gently in the wind; the flags depicted the golden lion of Ortaria set against a red background. A defensive wall, standing about forty feet in height, encircled the town at the base of the hill. Several small towers were set at intervals along the wall. The army marched up to the main gate.

King Ignis turned to General Hugo. 'Hugo, tell the men to set up camp here. Allow them to enter the town if they wish, but tell them to be respectful toward the townsfolk. Have your commanders organise supplies for the journey to Ancora. I want to leave at first light.'

'It will be done,' said General Hugo with a curt nod.

The King then turned to Eben. 'Eben, come with me up to the fortress. I'm not yet sure this place is completely safe, so keep your eyes open.' A few moments later General Hugo returned.

Baron Doriak led King Ignis and Eben up toward the fortress. General Hugo, Cassiel, Red, and Stella followed after them. The town was depressed and desolate; however, it was in a far better state than Ancora or Lantern Hill. The people stared as they rode by. Eben could hear the surprised shouts as the people of the town saw King Ignis riding with the Baron.

They arrived at the top of the hill. At the base of the fortress was a great iron door set above several stone steps. There were many depictions carved into the surface of the great door. Two guardsmen stood on each side of the entrance. They all dismounted and tied up their horses. A few moments later they walked through the doorway into a hall. Mighty pillars lined the walls, rising about eighty feet to the ceiling above, and the floor was covered with grey slate. On the far side of the hall was an empty bronze throne. To their left and right stone stairways led up to the higher level. Several doorways led off from the main hall on both sides.

'The Hall of Galdir, it has been too many years since I was last here,' said King Ignis as he walked toward the bronze throne.

'I would not sit there if I was you,' said Baron Doriak as the iron door slammed shut. The doors lining the walls burst open, and groups of armed Ortarian guardsmen charged into the hall. About forty guardsmen surrounded the group as Baron Doriak walked toward the throne and sat down, relaxing back with a smug grin on his face.

'What is the meaning of this?' shouted King Ignis, his hand going to the hilt of his sword.

'The real King Ignis has instructed me, by royal decree, to capture the pretender and to remove General Hugo's rank. I will take control of the army.'

'This is madness!' cried General Hugo. 'The army will never allow it!'

'Yes they will. Because I am the highest ranked man in Galdir, now that you, Hugo, have had your rank and nobility taken from you. This pretender will be put in chains and taken back to Ancora. You will be punished for trying to masquerade as the King of Ortaria.' King Ignis looked across at Eben who was standing at his side.

Cassiel began to lift his hands; Baron Doriak's snorted and then glared at him. 'Ah, yes, the young Zyranian. My reports say you are an impatient fool and that your skills are feeble at best. Do you think using your magic now will save you or your friends?' Several of the guardsmen pointed their spears at Cassiel. Cassiel lowered his hands and looked across at King Ignis for direction. The King turned to Eben.

'Eben,' whispered King Ignis. 'These guardsmen are Ortarians; they don't deserve to die for following the orders of this mad fool. I saw you slay a hundred muckrons and a wyvern.'

'What are you plotting?' shouted the Baron, clenching his fists.

Eben glanced around at the guardsmen and drew his sword. He nodded back to King Ignis confidently. A moment later Eben stepped forward toward Baron Doriak.

'You cannot take the King,' said Eben boldly.

'Do you want to die, boy? Your group is outnumbered at least five to one!' shouted Baron

Doriak, his lips curling in anger. Eben continued walking toward Baron Doriak. 'Kill him!' cried the Baron.

The guardsmen charged at Eben. Eben easily parried several attacks and sliced a spear in two as he kicked a guardsman back. He parried and threw another to the ground as he continued walking toward Baron Doriak. More guardsmen charged at him and again he parried and threw a man down as he tripped another up and knocked the man's sword away. A moment later he held his sword inches from the Baron's chest. Baron Doriak stared up at Eben in shock.

'Tell them to drop their weapons!' said Eben in a low voice.

The Baron shrunk back in fear. He looked to the guardsmen who had been knocked to the ground and the others who were stumbling away; none of them were seriously hurt, but they had all been completely outmatched.

'Drop your weapons,' he muttered, trembling in fear as he stared up at Eben. 'Who are you?'

'He's a loyal Ortarian,' said King Ignis, stepping forward to stand beside Eben. 'Now get off my throne, Doriak! You will never sit in my place again!' Doriak stood up and cautiously stepped away from the throne. 'Hugo, have the town secured. I want to make sure there are no other traps or traitors. Also have the entire fortress searched.'

'Yes, Sire,' said General Hugo as he went to the iron door and pushed it open. He took from his belt a horn and blew it three times.

King Ignis then walked over toward the group of guardsmen. 'You men are Ortarians. You have seen the evil growing in our lands. Your families have faced hardships. I am King Ignis, rightful ruler of Ortaria. I am a true descendent of the Ecorian Arbiters of the Ecorian Empire. I have been imprisoned for three years by people who plan to make you into slaves. Now I have returned, and I intend to free our lands of evil and bring back freedom and happiness to Ortaria. If you serve the Kingdom of Ortaria you should take up your weapons and fight for what is good and true. I give you this opportunity, an amnesty; pick up your swords and pledge your allegiance to Ortaria.'

They looked bewildered and some of them hung their heads in shame. One of the guardsmen stepped forward.

'We serve you, Your Highness. Baron Doriak told us you were a pretender. We see now that you are the real King of Ortaria.' He then fell on one knee and pledged his allegiance, and the others followed his example.

General Hugo walked over from the iron doors. 'The army is coming up the hill through the town.'

'Good,' said King Ignis, turning back to look at Baron Doriak.

'Doriak, I have always trusted you; now I see my mistake.'

The Baron looked up at King Ignis with a smug grin. 'King Ignis, you have no idea what you are facing. You think that you can retake Ortaria. Only days ago there were dozens of Skatheans here; they knew you were coming, and they have prepared for you. Soon Ortaria will be a land of muckrons.'

The King stared at Baron Doriak. A few moments of harsh silence passed.

'Put him in the dungeon,' commanded King Ignis. 'I remove your rank and nobility, Doriak. You shall answer for your crimes, your dishonour, and your treason.'

'When the army of muckrons arrives here they will free me, and you will learn the hard truth, King Ignis. I look forward to seeing what they do to you when you are captured. The days of the Ecorian Arbiters are at an end. The Master in the north will utterly destroy you and the fools who choose to stand by your side.'

'Take him away!' commanded King Ignis.

Several of the guardsmen took Doriak by his arms and led him away through one of the side doors. Moments later about twenty soldiers from the army burst in through the iron doors, all of them ready for a fight, having just run up the hill at Hugo's call. King Ignis walked over and sat down on the bronze throne.

'We must prepare.'

**

In the upper level of the fortress was a large chamber with a long oak table and a great fireplace. A fire burned brightly and kept the entire room warm. King Ignis sat at the table looking through piles of parchment that had been sent between the Imposter and Baron Doriak. Eben sat across the table whilst Stella and Red sat by the fireplace. General Hugo stood near the King.

'Doriak was working with the Imposter for years,' said King Ignis. 'He knew I was imprisoned in Zyran. They were initially planning to use the army to invade Vastoria; they then planned to march across into Irvaria. After I was freed they made a desperate move as they knew the army would be a threat to them if I could regain control. It seems that several nobles have been in on the Zyranian plan. Earl Zalmar and Baron Ardok were working with Baron Doriak. This explains a lot; Baron Ardok had a meeting with me the afternoon I was taken away to the Dungeons of Zyran. I'm sure he infused my wine with a potion that put me to sleep. He must have been working with the Zyranians all along.'

'I'm surprised that Earl Zalmar is a turncoat. I always thought he was a good man,' said General Hugo.

'We will question him on our return to Ancora,' said King Ignis. 'This last note sent to Doriak worries me the most. He was told to attempt to capture us and take control of the army. The note then goes on to say that they are making preparations in the east. They say they will come west and crush the Ortarian army if he fails to take control of it. This would refer to the muckron army Doriak was talking about. Perhaps they plan to meet us on the road.'

'We should send scouts across the plains in the morning,' said Hugo.

'Yes, we should. The fact they think they can match us is what concerns me the most. They're aware of our numbers, and they're confident enough to come west to meet us.'

'Perhaps we should remain in Galdir and wait for them,' suggested Hugo. 'We have walls and the fortress here.'

The King gave it some thought before answering. 'No, Hugo, I want to go east and recapture Ancora as soon as possible. They could starve us out by laying siege to Galdir, and our cavalry would give us no advantage here. We know the cavalry helped us a lot on the battlefield in Scaldonia. It's an advantage I don't want to give up.'

'So we will ride out in the morning as planned?' asked General Hugo.

'Yes, we must. I also want you to choose a loyal knight from the army. I will place him in charge of Galdir.'

'I believe Sir Victar would be the best knight to govern Galdir,' replied General Hugo. It was agreed that Sir Victar would be given control of the fortress.

**

Eben slept that night in one of the upper chambers of the fortress. He woke as the sun rose in the east and cast long beams of light through his chamber window. The town below was already bustling as the army was preparing to march onward. He drew the sword and looked at the light reflecting off the blade. The steel seemed to collect the light. The Sword of Light didn't glow, but it was as if the light of the sun curved toward the blade making it seem slightly brighter than it should be. The Ecorian Sword, an ancient and powerful weapon used to protect Veredor from the powers of darkness. The thought that his mother had left the sword with him still caused many questions to flow through his mind. He knew that only the Fiorians would have the answers he sought.

He walked out of his room and down a stone stairwell to the command chamber. King Ignis was talking with some of his knights and General Hugo.

'We sent eight scouts east at first light. They will check the highway and report back. The army will be ready to move within an hour,' said Sir Rocco, a burly and dark haired knight.

'Well done, Sir Rocco. We will head for Riverside.'

A guardsman came walking into the chamber carrying a small piece of paper. 'This arrived by carrier pigeon several minutes ago.' General Hugo took the note and handed it to King Ignis. He unfolded the note and read it to himself.

'A message from our enemy,' said King Ignis with a disdainful grimace. 'The Imposter has asked us to surrender. He says there is no need for a war and that we should know our place as slaves to the Lord of Veredor.'

King Ignis cast the note in the fire. He then turned to face the company of knights. 'We are men of honour and freed from bondage because of our service to the truth. Chains, prisons, and even death; all these things cannot possibly enslave those who have freedom in their hearts. We will fight these enslavers, and they will see freedom by our example.'

**

The army marched away from Galdir as the sun rose higher in the eastern sky. Eben rode with the King and Cassiel at the front of the army. Red and Stella were riding further back among the troops. They slowly came out of the foothills and into a land of lush green plains. There were very few trees, but occasionally a huge tree would rise up from the flat land.

'These are the Golden Plains,' said King Ignis. 'These plains are home to several nomadic clans. I expect we will see some shepherds before we cross the plain and reach the western edge of Altus Forest; although with all the Skatheans and bandits around they will have probably moved far away from the main highway.'

They rode on throughout the day. Clouds were rolling across the sky from the east; by the late afternoon a light rain was falling. As the evening arrived they set up camp beside the highway. Red was trying to get a fire started with some wood he had gathered along the roadside.

'Do you need some help with that?' asked Cassiel.

Red looked up and nodded. 'Sure, if you could use your magic it might help.' Cassiel pointed his hand at the wood and a flame shot forth. The fire instantly started blazing.

'You'll have to teach me that trick one day,' said Red with his usual cheeky grin. Cassiel smiled and nodded as he sat down beside Red.

'It would take about five years to teach you. It's not just about making a flame appear; it's about understanding the nature of things around you and learning to bring about a change in that nature. You would have to learn to focus like a wizard.'

'Five years! Ha, I think I'll keep using my flint rocks,' said Red, warming his hands by the fire. 'I know a few simple coin and card tricks; that's as far as I want to take it. After the war is over I want to focus on my swordsmanship.'

'You're already a great swordsman,' said Stella.

Red shook his head at Stella's comment. 'You saw that wyvern knock the sword out of my hand so easily. I don't want that to happen again. I want to learn to fight like you, Eben.'

Eben knew it was the Sword of Light and not so much his skill that was making him a good swordsman. 'This sword gives me a great advantage.'

'No, it's more than the sword; you're brave. I couldn't believe what I was seeing when I saw you jump from your horse and grab the wyvern by the horns; that was truly amazing. Then I saw you fight those guardsmen in Galdir. What you have is a lot more than an old sword.'

Eben nodded and wasn't sure if he agreed. Erako had taught him to use a sword, and he knew he was a proficient swordsman, but his skills with the Sword of Light were far beyond any skill level he had previously possessed.

**

The next day was spent marching eastward. The open grass plains appeared to go on endlessly. There were no other travellers on the highway. Occasionally they caught sight of a stranded cow or goat. That night they set up camp again and slept well.

The following day the army set out early. By the midmorning Eben could see a horseman in the distance galloping along the road in their direction. As the rider came closer it was clear he was injured and struggling to stay on his horse. He was one of the scouts they had sent out on the first day. Several of the front riders rode out to meet him and helped him down from his horse.

King Ignis dismounted and walked over to meet the scout as two soldiers helped him to stand. Eben, General Hugo, and Cassiel walked with the King.

'Sire... I bring... bad news,' he said in a stammering voice.

'What news?' asked King Ignis.

'We rode out across the Golden Plains... to the edge of Altus Forest. There is an army of muckrons waiting for us camped just outside the forest... I was the only one to escape. We were firstly set upon by a group of Skatheans, but their warhorses couldn't keep pace with our scouting horses... Then the enemy wizards rained fire down on us from above... Four of my companions were killed. The four of us who survived the attack rode on as quickly as our horses would gallop. That's when we were set upon by three wyverns... Only I escaped. My injuries aren't bad; I think I can still fight.'

'Three wyverns,' repeated King Ignis gravely, nervously scratching his beard.

'Yes, Sire.'

'And how many muckrons did you see?'

'Many more than we fought in Scaldonia. It's difficult to say how many; I think about twenty thousand.' King Ignis looked disturbed at hearing the number.

'You have done well and shown much courage. I will reward you when we return to Ancora for your bravery. What is your name?'

'Tullis,' answered the scout.

'Well done, Tullis,' said King Ignis. He then turned to Eben and Hugo.

'Three wyverns, Skatheans, and Zyranians; we are in for a fight this time.'

'We are still two days march to the forest's edge,' said General Hugo.

'You killed a wyvern, Eben; how about three?'

'I can try.'

CHAPTER SEVENTEEN

'Three wyverns!' exclaimed Red, shaking his head in disbelief.

'That's what the scout said,' said Eben.

'You're going to have quite a task,' said Red, laughing nervously. They were sitting around the fire with Cassiel and Stella in the early evening.

'I'll do my best,' said Eben.

'I think King Ignis is very troubled by this news,' said Cassiel. 'We beat the small army of muckrons in Scaldonia without too much trouble. This one is much larger, and they have Skatheans and the Zyranian Enforcers with them.'

'Most of the men are very confident. They think we will win and return home soon,' said Stella.

'They are fighting for their homeland, so they will fight bravely,' said Cassiel.

They slept in their tents and woke early. The feeling of anticipation was growing among the troops. Rumours about the enemy army were circulating throughout the camp; however, the men kept up their confidence as they knew they were fighting for their families and homeland and that there was simply no option to fail.

The army set out about an hour after sunrise and moved quickly. The men seemed restless to get to the battle; they all knew it was the last task before a triumphant return home to Ancora. Eben rode in full armour at the front of the army with King Ignis. He felt ready for battle. He could feel his fingers tingling from the anticipation.

'It's going to be quite a fight, Eben. They have assembled an army of Skatheans, wyverns, and wizards. We only have soldiers, archers, and cavalry' said King Ignis.

'We will fight bravely. The men are ready,' said Eben.

They continued marching across the plain. By mid-afternoon they could see a distant line of trees of the Altus Forest. Smoke rose in a thick column forming a dark cloud directly ahead. As they marched closer they could see the smoke was rising from an area between two small hills.

'We are not far from them now,' said King Ignis.

Another hour passed as they marched onward. They could see the encampment of the enemy in the distance just outside the forest at the beginning of the plain. General Hugo rode up beside King Ignis and Eben.

'We will use our cavalry again,' said King Ignis as his eyes scanned the distance.

Eben could see the muckron army was marshalling itself into long lines parallel to the forest. It was instantly clear that the enemy army was massive.

'How many muckrons are there, Hugo?' asked the King.

'Twenty thousand at least,' said General Hugo stoically. They could see the dark shapes of three wyverns rising up from the ground into the sky above the muckron horde; two of them were red and one was green. Their scales glimmered in the sunlight.

'What do you think, Hugo?'

'We face a difficult fight,' said General Hugo. The King turned to Eben. 'And you, Eben?'

'We can either fight or retreat, but if we retreat we'll have to fight them again at Galdir anyway.'

'You're right, Eben. We must fight them either way. Hugo, assemble the cavalry. Tell the men to be ready'

General Hugo rode off and began shouting commands to the army. The army began to move into an attack formation. The cavalry moved to the front with the heavy cavalry making up the first line with five lines of light cavalry behind. The infantry formed about ten lines behind the cavalry, and the archers stood not far behind the infantry.

Red and Stella rode up toward Eben. Stella had acquired a knight's shield, which was flat on the top edge and curved downward to a point at the bottom edge. The shield was dark red with a golden lion painted across it. She also carried a new sword at her side instead of the two short swords she had carried into the previous battle. Eben noticed that she had a rope coiled with a grappling hook. Red wore shining new armour and an open-faced helm.

'What's the rope and grappling hook for?' asked Eben.

'For catching wyverns and pulling them out of the sky,' replied Stella with a confident smile.

'Stay near me. This is going to be much bigger than the last battle,' said Eben.

'We won't let you get away from us,' said Stella.

They looked toward the enemy lines and could see two riders crossing the field, one of them carrying a blue banner.

'It's the banner of terms. They want to negotiate,' said General Hugo.

'Eben, follow me. Let's ride to meet them,' said King Ignis. The King rode out across the field. Eben turned Swiftwing about and charged after the King. A minute later they were nearing the two riders. One was a Skathean, revealed by his deathly pale skin and cold piercing eyes. He carried a long sword and no other weapon, and he wore the dark attire and a black cloak. The other rider was also wearing a long dark cloak. As the King and Eben approached they both recognised the familiar face of Falsig.

King Ignis halted about thirty feet from the two enemy riders, and Eben came up to be beside him. Sweat was dripping from Falsig's swollen and ugly face. His eyes were red and bloodshot.

'What terms do you bring?' asked King Ignis firmly.

'We ask you to surrender!' answered the Skathean, his voice cold and harsh. 'If you surrender you will be disarmed and allowed to return to your homes after taking an oath of allegiance to the Lord of Veredor.'

'We will never surrender. Your evil army will die today unless you leave our lands and return to where you came from! We will never serve your master,' shouted King Ignis, his voice deep and strong.

The Skathean slowly moved his horse forward. 'Is this the son of Elons? Did you know your father, boy?' asked the Skathean with a sly grin. Eben felt his heart drop and was astonished that this Skathean knew his father's name. He was speechless. The Skathean looked back to the King. 'His father couldn't save himself. Do you think the son of Elons will save you, King Ignis?'

'What do you know of my father?' asked Eben. The Skathean simply grinned evilly and said nothing.

'Even if we die today we will die with our honour,' said King Ignis firmly.

The Skathean scoffed and sneered. 'Honour! Your honour is nothing but a lie; it is your greatest mistake,' said the Skathean, sneering at King Ignis with contempt. 'You hope to hide yourself from the real truth: there is always a price on a man's honour. And freedom, we Skatheans are free from the burden of your foolish morality. We possess real freedom.'

King Ignis held his head high and stared directly into the eyes of the Skathean. 'You are completely enslaved by your evil desire; freedom has no place in you.' The King's voice was clear and strong. 'Today you will see our honour in all its glory, and you will see that these good Ortarian men are prepared to sacrifice themselves for the good of all people. What I speak of is real freedom. Freedom is the choice not to be ruled by fear, pain, and desire. Such freedom has no place in you, Skathean. Today you will see real courage, and you will realise that you are mistaken. You have taken the dark path because you believe you will gain something for yourself, but nothing is ever truly gained that isn't given.'

The Skathean backed away and stared at King Ignis in silence. He then looked from the King to Eben.

'I look forward to taking possession of the Sword of Light.' He sneered contemptuously and then turned his horse back toward the enemy lines. Falsig waited a moment before turning his horse and following after the Skathean. King Ignis and Eben then rode back to the waiting company.

**

King Ignis and General Hugo were riding at the front of the army. The lines had slowly advanced to be within a thousand yards of the enemy ranks. Eben rode with Red, Cassiel, and Stella. They looked across the plain toward their enemies. The army of muckrons was waiting in the flat area between the two small hills. Smoke rose above the monstrous army, creating a thick dark cloud that hovered low. The three wyverns circled in the smoky sky as the sound of deep booming drums echoed across the plain.

'They are using the hills and forest as a natural shield to stop our cavalry flanking them,' said General Hugo.

'We will ride directly at them and smash through their front lines like we did in Scaldonia,' said King Ignis. 'Eben, I've told my knights to challenge the Skatheans. I'm hoping that you, Red, Stella, and Cassiel can focus your strength on the wyverns.'

'We will,' said Red proudly. King Ignis nodded and then turned to General Hugo.

'Hugo, tell the archers to position themselves on the two hills and to shoot at the muckrons below. Tell them to hold those hills.'

King Ignis then looked back at his army. The army was eager to make a move. Hugo rode through the ranks of the men and shouted orders. The King rode over to be beside Eben.

'This will be a mighty battle. If we are overwhelmed I will blow a horn four times to tell the army to retreat.'

General Hugo returned from giving the orders a moment later. 'We are ready to advance,' he said. King Ignis rode in front of his army.

'Today we are called to rise up and fight for our freedom!' he cried. 'We will show our enemies that this is our land! Ortaria is our country! We will live free from oppression, now and always! Let courage and bravery be your weapon! Be strong! Be true! Fight for your family! Fight for all that is good!' A loud cheer rose from the lines of troops.

The men were ready to advance. King Ignis turned to face the enemy. He drew his sword and pointed the blade at the muckron horde. A moment later the first line of heavy cavalry started moving forward.

Swiftwing leapt after them and the pace rapidly increased. Red, Stella, and Cassiel followed closely behind. The light cavalry followed further back. King Ignis rode ahead with the knights toward the left of the advance. Eben stared ahead at the front line of muckrons. They had crossed five hundred yards. The smoke cloud above them was darkening. Several moments later the cloud above began to swirl.

'For Ortaria!' cried King Ignis. The knights brought their horses to a gallop.

The swirling dark cloud began to glow red. Eben could see wizards standing on both the small hills with their hands held high above their heads. The sound of a mighty boom echoed across the plain; a moment later fire began raining down on them from above.

Massive flaming blasts exploded around them. Cavalrymen were being thrown from their horses as the rapid charge continued. Eben felt the heat of an explosion beside him; Swiftwing leapt over burning ground and charged onward through the heat and smoke. Eben drew his sword. The muckron lines were fast approaching. The knights and heavy cavalry crashed through the front lines, and a moment later Eben was among them. He hewed down a muckron as he rode forward into the enemy ranks. Red and Stella were beside him, both of them swinging their swords wildly. Cassiel was throwing bright flames to the left and right as he rode a little back from them. Eben continuously cut and stabbed in all directions. The muckrons scattered before him. Swiftwing pushed forward through the throng of monsters.

Twenty feet away a wyvern swooped down and dragged a knight from his horse, casting him to the ground. Eben turned Swiftwing and saw Red struggling with a muckron and Stella backing away as two muckrons attacked her. He charged forward and cut down one of the muckrons that was attacking Stella. Meanwhile Red cut down the muckron he was fighting.

'We have to kill that wyvern!' shouted Eben above the calamity of the battle. Cassiel rode over. His hands were glowing brightly.

'You lead the way!' shouted Red.

'Follow me!' cried Eben.

Swiftwing dashed forward through the battlefield toward the red wyvern. The four of them smashed their way through the horde of hideous pig headed muckrons. Directly ahead the wyvern was causing havoc among the Ortarian cavalry. The beast was leaping from rider to rider, ripping them from their horses. Eben charged onward. The wyvern turned itself around and howled. It then jumped at him ferociously. Eben stabbed out with the Sword of Light, but the wyvern parried the blade with the edge of its scaled arm. The beast then pounced forward and knocked Swiftwing over. Eben fell to the ground and rolled away. Stella swung her rope, and the grappling hook caught on the wyvern's horns. The creature howled ferociously and whipped its head, dragging Stella off her horse. She leapt through the air and flipped backwards in a feat of acrobatic mastery. Eben had lost sight of Swiftwing in the heat of the battle.

Eben, now on foot, ran at the fierce beast. He propelled himself at the howling wyvern, stabbing out with the Sword of Light. A flash of red light struck him in the same moment, sending him tumbling back. He fell in the grass and for a moment felt breathless. Zarceler appeared and was standing near the wyvern with two Skatheans beside him. His hands were surrounded by a bright red glow.

Eben quickly regained his feet. An instant later one of the Skatheans charged. He parried the incoming strikes and counterattacked with several cuts and stabs, but the Skathean blocked his counterattacks. The other Skathean came into view.

'Hand over the Sword of Light!' hissed the Skathean, leaping at Eben. Eben deflected the first cut and the second. He then struck back, knocking the Skathean off balance.

He felt the claw of the wyvern grab him around the chest from behind. The beast lifted him off his feet and squeezed him tightly as it beat its wings and flew skyward. Eben turned himself in the wyvern's grip and drove his blade deep into the beast's scaly neck. The wyvern shrieked in pain and released him. The ground approached rapidly, and a moment later Eben slammed into the field, dropping his sword. The dragon simultaneously plummeted into the ground and heaved around for a moment before it lay lifeless. Eben, in a daze, struggled to get up and looked around for his sword. It had fallen a little way off and he scrambled across the field toward his weapon.

The shadow of a Skathean moved between Eben and the Sword of Light. Eben stopped in his tracks. The Skathean grinned as he approached Eben. Stella quietly picked up the Sword of Light from the ground behind the Skathean. The dark knight, catching sight of her, turned and sneered, and an instant later he charged at Stella. Stella struck out with the Sword of Light. The Skathean parried and counterattacked, but Stella was quick to defend and deflected the stab. Again the

Skathean struck out, and again she parried. She thrust the Skathean's sword to the ground as she kicked out, knocking him off his feet. The Skathean rolled backward and lay stunned on the muddy ground.

In that moment a great horn sounded, ringing out across the battlefield. It blew again and again, and then a fourth time. Eben looked back and could see the Ortarian army was retreating and being forced back by the horde of monsters. Clearly the army of men were being completely overwhelmed. The Skathean regained his feet as Stella handed the Sword of Light back to Eben. A moment later Red came into view. The muckrons were crowding the battlefield around them.

'The army is leaving!' shouted Red.

The Skathean laughed evilly as he stood up. 'Your army is finished!' he said in a heckling voice. 'Ortaria is ours!'

Eben looked about and could only see muckrons and Skatheans; the main Ortarian lines had fallen back about fifty yards and were being pursued by thousands of muckrons. Stella and Red looked at Eben, worry etched into their faces. They were trapped with enemies all around. Eben could see the situation was becoming hopeless as packs of muckrons approached from all sides.

A moment later a great howl echoed out across the battlefield and every eye turned to see its origin. A massive black wolf stood on top of the hill to the north.

'Kiarn!' shouted Eben, feeling his heart leap in his chest.

They all watched as hundreds of wolves, bears, jackals, and other creatures emerged from the edge of the forest, flanking the muckron army. The wild animals charged into the monstrous horde. The Skathean's face became deathly pale as he stared at the army of forest creatures tearing into the muckron ranks. The evil knight dashed away at great speed toward the rear of the battlefield and was gone from sight moments later.

The horn sounded again, ringing out just once, which was the call to attack. The Ortarians cried out as they pressed forward against the lines of muckrons.

Cassiel rode over a moment later. 'The creatures of Altus; they've come to save us!' he shouted as he looked across the battlefield in wonder.

'Let's help them!' cried Eben, rushing forward with his friends following closely.

The muckrons howled in horror, and in a short time the tide of the battle had turned. The muckron army was being pushed toward the southern side of the battlefield. The wolves and bears attacked them with savage ferocity, and the Ortarians grew in confidence at seeing the monsters in retreat and knowing they had such powerful allies fighting with them.

Eben fought his way through the horde. He looked ahead and could see a giant bear pick up a muckron and cast it at another pig headed monster. Packs of wolves were circling the muckrons and forcing them to back away toward the southern side of the battlefield. To his right Stella and Red were pursuing a small group of muckrons that were trying to escape to the south of the battlefield.

Eben caught sight of Zarceler. The evil wizard was blasting the wild animals and Ortarian soldiers with his magic. Eben rushed toward Zarceler.

'Have you come for more pain?' screamed Zarceler, lifting his glowing hands. A bright beam of red light shot across the distance at Eben. Eben held his sword up. The energetic blast of light was deflected and struck the ground. Zarceler sneered and again raised his hands and flames burst forth through the air. Again Eben used the Sword of Light to shield himself from the fire. Eben advanced as Zarceler turned and started to run. Moments later Eben was at his heels. Zarceler fell to the ground and looked up at Eben with terror in his eyes. Eben raised his sword and was ready to strike.

Zarceler cowered on the ground, covering his face with his hands. 'No! Don't!' he cried, begging for his life.

Eben delayed for a moment. 'You deserve to die!'

Cassiel appeared beside Eben a moment later. They looked down at Zarceler. 'Let me live. I can change,' begged Zarceler. 'I was following orders. I'm not evil. It's the Master, not me...'

Cassiel considered the situation for a moment. 'We can tie his hands behind his back; his magic would be much reduced,' said Cassiel. 'We could take him as a prisoner back to Ancora.'

'Stand up!' said Eben firmly, pointing his sword at Zarceler. The wizard stood up.

'Hands behind your back!' ordered Cassiel. Zarceler complied. Cassiel went to tie his hands.

Suddenly Zarceler turned and grabbed Cassiel. He held a small knife up against Cassiel's throat.

'Drop your sword or Cassiel dies!' hissed Zarceler.

Cassiel stood completely still. He looked across at Eben and shook his head. Eben stared into Zarceler's mad eyes and could see he would surely kill Cassiel.

'Drop it!' screamed Zarceler wrathfully.

Eben reluctantly dropped his sword. Zarceler grinned as he looked down at the sword on the ground.

'Now step back!' cried Zarceler. Eben took several steps back from the wizard. Zarceler threw Cassiel aside and then picked up the sword. 'Now the Sword of Light is mine!' he said, cruel glee filling his eyes.

A great cluster of Ortarian troops were nearing them as the muckrons were in full retreat and were rushing up and over the slopes of the southern hill. Zarceler laughed like a madman and waved his hand; a shockwave of glowing red energy struck Eben. Eben felt the heavy impact as he flew back several feet and crashed into the ground. He was dazed and shaken and looked up at Zarceler. The wizard slowly walked toward him and was grinning evilly. He cast another red burst of painful energy at Eben. Eben felt his body cramp and shake. He could hardly take a breath. Cassiel began to get up. Zarceler knocked him back down again with a spell and smirked.

'I knew it would come to this. Now you will both die for causing this foolish revolt,' said Zarceler. He lifted his hands once again.

Eben caught the rapid movement of something dark out of the corner of his eye. A moment later Kiarn leapt from left field. The dark shape of the wolf throttled the wizard. The Sword of Light fell from the Zarceler's hand as he cried out in horror. In an instant Kiarn's mighty jaws ended the life of the evil wizard. Zarceler's body lay still and lifeless. Kiarn's golden eyes glanced across at Eben for a moment. An instant later the wolf ran off after the retreating muckron army.

Eben pulled himself up off the ground. His body was aching all over. He walked over to Cassiel and helped him to stand up. He then picked up the Sword of Light, and together they looked southward at the fleeing muckrons.

'It is done,' said Cassiel.

Red and Stella walked over and were completely exhausted. The four friends hugged and embraced.

**

The army set up camp beside the forest. Eben sat in a command tent with King Ignis, Red, Stella, Cassiel, several knights, and field commanders. King Ignis had his face bandaged. He looked very weary.

'I am sad to say that we lost many good men. Brave General Hugo also died in the battle,' said King Ignis. Eben felt the sadness in the room at the news of the death of General Hugo 'We have completely destroyed the muckron army. The archers on the southern hill stopped most of them from escaping; only a few muckrons breached their lines. Two of the wyverns escaped, and another was found dead on the battlefield. We have also captured several Zyranians. General

Hugo and all the men who died here today will be remembered forever. We will ride to Ancora and free our people from tyranny. Today we have brought light back to Ortaria. We will take that light to every corner of our land.'

They heard the strength in his voice. There was a sense of hope growing in their hearts.

CHAPTER EIGHTEEN

They rode eastward over the days that followed and arrived at the gates of Ancora. The day was bright and sunny and spring flowers covered the fields surrounding the city. The city gates were open and King Ignis led the army through the western gate. Word had already reached Ancora of the victory in the west over the muckrons, Skatheans, and Zyranians.

The Imposter had fled Ancora before the arrival of the army. The story of the King's imprisonment in the Dungeons of Zyran was known by all, and the people were overjoyed at the homecoming of their true king. The people shouted and cheered as King Ignis led the army through the town toward the palace. A great crowd had gathered in the large town square outside the palace; celebrations and cries of joy could be heard in all directions. The shroud of gloom had completely left the city and a sense of joy permeated Ancora.

Eben rode Swiftwing along beside King Ignis. Red, Stella, and Cassiel followed closely behind. The King led them through the crowd to the steps of his palace. A group of Ortarian guardsmen were waiting at the palace gate. They had been sent ahead to secure the city. King Ignis dismounted as the crowds continued cheering. He walked up the steps and turned to face the crowds of people and his army. The multitude became silent and looked to the King.

'Today we have brought justice and peace back to Ancora. No longer will you live under an evil shadow. Today every Ortarian is free. We will remember every man who died fighting for our freedom. We will remember every sacrifice that was given. They fought for the good of all Ortarians and all people everywhere. Together we will rebuild Ortaria. Today peace has returned to our land!'

With this the people cheered. King Ignis bowed to his people before turning and walking through his palace gate. Eben, Red, Stella, and Cassiel followed the King into the palace.

**

'Sir Redding,' said Red, a wide smile crossing his face. 'Can you believe it?'

Eben was happy for his friend. They were sitting in a beautiful chamber in the palace with large arched windows, marble floors, and a great oak table. The large chamber was adorned with all manner of royal luxury. There were paintings on the walls, crystal chandeliers, and marble pillars that rose up to a white ceiling above. The room was the royal guest chamber.

'And you, Eben; Champion of Ortaria,' said Red. Eben nodded and smiled across at Red. King Ignis had declared that Eben was the Champion of Ortaria. King Ignis had also declared that he would grant Eben any wish, if it was in his power to grant. Eben had told him that he only really wanted to go west to find his parents, and the King had said he would do whatever he could to help Eben complete his quest.

Red looked across at Stella with a smile. 'I like the sound of Lady Stella.' Stella smiled happily. 'We have something to announce,' added Red cheerfully. Eben could easily guess what it was. 'We're going be be married.'

**

Two weeks later Eben stood beside Red in the great hall of the royal palace of Ancora. Red shuffled nervously. He was clothed in fine linen and had his hair combed back and his beard had been neatly styled. An Ortarian guard of honour created two lines, and a crowd of notable citizens of Ancora had gathered for the wedding. King Ignis sat on his golden throne and watched the proceedings. Cassiel, Max, and some of the other soldiers who they had come to know stood a little way away. Eben could also see the old librarian in the audience. He had a great big smile on his face.

Trumpets sounded and a moment later Stella entered the great hall through the massive entrance doorway. Sweet music filled the great hall. She walked toward them across the marble floor in a long flowing white dress. She looked ever so beautiful, and everyone in the hall stared at her, amazed by her loveliness.

'She's so incredible,' whispered Red in awe of his bride. She was being followed by two bridesmaids; both had been performers in the circus. She slowly approached Red, looking into his eyes with immense happiness.

King Ignis stood up and stepped down toward them. He took from a small table two candles and handed one to Red and the other to Stella. It was the custom of marriage in Veredor that two candles should be lit from a single flame and that both the bride and groom would then declare their love and commitment to each other in their own words, both swearing an oath to always be true.

A candle stood on a stand and burned brightly. Stella took her candle and lit it from the larger candle, and Red followed her example, and they stood together holding their candles. It was also the custom in Veredor that the man should declare his love first. Red looked to Stella with great love and tenderness.

'Stella, from this day onward I will be your husband. I promise to always be true to you, and I will always love you. I will always stand by your side, defend your honour, and protect you. You are and will forever be my one true love.'

Stella smiled at Red lovingly. 'Red, my love; I will be your wife. I will love you truly and forever. I will honour you and be true to you always. I will hold you in my heart and together we shall build our life together.'

They embraced and kissed and then turned to the people who all applauded and cheered. King Ignis then walked over and stood beside them. 'I present to you, Sir Redding and Lady Stella, husband and wife,' he announced. The people clapped and cheered again. Red and Stella kissed again and held each other close in a joyful embrace.

**

For two weeks the four friends had been staying in the palace. Eben was sitting in the royal guest chamber reading a book about the history of Ortaria and the other Eastern Lands of Veredor. Cassiel entered the room and was holding a letter in his hand. He handed the letter to Eben.

'This message came from Meara this morning.'

Dear Cassiel and Eben,

I write to you from Dravania. I have attended a meeting with the Irilian High Council and told them of the troubles in Ortaria. I hope this message reaches you in time. I write to inform you that a council will be held in the Irvarian city of Faircastle on the first day of summer. This council is being arranged by King Edric of Irvaria at the request of the last remaining Fiorian Knights. They have requested representatives from all of the magic orders, the major orders of knights, and the southern monarchs of Veredor.

I will be travelling to Irvaria to be the Irilian representative. I hope to meet you there.

Your friend,

Meara of the Irilian Order.

'We must go,' said Eben, feeling excited that the Fiorians would be at the council.

'We will go together,' said Cassiel. 'We should leave soon because summer is not far off.'

'We can head for the Iron Gate Pass and cross into Vastoria,' suggested Eben.

'I will start to prepare for the journey today,' said Cassiel. Eben could feel they were on the verge of a new adventure.

**

Later in the day Eben was packing his backpack and making preparations to leave Ancora. Red and Stella entered his chamber without knocking.

'There is no way you and Cassiel are going to Irvaria without us,' declared Red.

'Wouldn't you rather stay in Ancora?'

'No way,' said Stella firmly. 'We're going west with you.'

Eben felt happy that his friends were so keen to join him on the journey west. 'It will be a long and dangerous adventure.'

Red and Stella both smiled.

THE JOURNEY WEST: BOOK TWO OF THE VEREDOR CHRONICLES

CHAPTER ONE

The sound of galloping hooves echoed in the night. A flash of white light hastened through the dark woods. Eben could not see clearly because of the murkiness of his surroundings. A light in the distance caught his attention. He watched as a glowing unicorn approached through the gloomy forest. The beast was surrounded by shining light that lit up the tangled trees at the edge of the clearing.

Eben awoke and abruptly sat up. He felt so wide awake that it could have been the middle of the day. The vivid dream remained clearly imprinted in his mind. He leaned over and lit the oil lantern beside his bed. His chamber was situated on an upper level of the palace and was adorned with all manner of royal luxury. King Ignis had been generous in rewarding him and his friends for all they had done for the Kingdom of Ortaria. He put on clothes and then went to the window and looked down to the palace courtyard far below. Across the far side of the courtyard was a large gatehouse. Several guardsmen stood just within the walls and kept a watch on the night.

A moment later Eben caught sight of movement at the top of the wall. A cloaked figure emerged from the far side. The shadowy man quietly lowered himself down a rope to the courtyard below and then edged along, keeping to the shadows, until he arrived at the palace wall. Eben kept his eyes fixed on the dark figure who had carefully avoided being seen by the palace guard. The cloaked man quickly climbed up the palace outer wall. A few moments later he slid through a lower level window and was gone from sight.

Eben drew a deep breath and picked up his sword. He dashed out of his chamber into a long lantern lit corridor. Moments later he was descending a stone stairwell that led down to the great hall on the first floor. The hall was only dimly lit by a single oil lantern that was set beside the main entrance door. His eyes scanned the area; there was no one in sight. Across the hall he could see the open window. Eben slowly walked out across the marble floor into the centre of the hall. Suddenly the dark figure came into sight from behind one of the large stone pillars that lined the outer walls.

'Who are you?'

The hooded man walked forward and did not respond. Eben drew his sword. The man stopped about twenty feet from Eben and stood still for a few moments; his face was shrouded by the shadow of his hood. His hand went to his side, and he drew a sword.

'Getting by the guards was too easy. I see you have saved me the bother of finding you,' hissed the man frostily.

'What do you want?' asked Eben firmly.

'The Sword of Light; you will give it to me or you will die.'

Eben shook his head at the man's words. He knew that one man was no match for him whilst he carried the Sword of Light. 'I don't think you know who you are dealing with.'

'Yes I do,' hissed the cloaked man. 'You are the one they call the Champion of Ortaria. You are nothing without the Sword of Light.'

'I'm not going to give my sword to you,' said Eben, turning the blade to point it at the cloaked man. 'If you want the Sword of Light you're going to have to take it from me.'

'With pleasure,' said the cloaked man, suddenly launching himself at Eben.

Eben quickly parried and stepped back as his opponent swiftly advanced. The clash of blades rang out, shattering the eerie silence of the hall. Eben was forced back toward the stairwell and had to focus to hold off the attack. For a moment Eben felt that he was being overwhelmed. He struck back again and again, and with great effort he pushed the cloaked man back across the hall. Eben pressed forward with all his skill and experience until his opponent was forced into the far corner. With a quick circular motion his enemy's sword was sent bouncing across the marble floor.

The man, now unhooded, stared at Eben with piercing dark eyes. His skin was deathly pale, and a sneer was etched deeply into his features. Eben knew in that moment he was dealing with a powerful Skathean. He held his sword at the Skathean's neck, ready to finish him. The doors of the hall burst open and a large group of palace guardsmen rushed toward them.

'What's happening here?' cried a guardsman.

'An infiltrator!' replied Eben as the palace guardsmen approached.

'It's Eben the Champion,' shouted one of the guardsmen.

'This man is a Skathean. Bind him and then take him to the dungeon. We must inform King Ignis. I am sure the King will want to question you.'

The Skathean scoffed and laughed evilly. 'You will find that I give you no answer but this: the Lord of Veredor wants your sword. He will soon come south to take the Sword of Light from you. You are a fool if you think you're safe in Ancora; there is no place in Veredor where you can hide. Every servant of the Master is hunting you. You may escape the servants, but you will never escape the Master. Your meagre hands will tremble in his presence and in that moment all your hope will fade. You will soon see what real power is.' His voice hissed, and his evil eyes were fixed on Eben.

'The shadow will never overcome the light,' replied Eben firmly. The Skathean's cold eyes stared at Eben as the Ortarian guardsmen placed him in manacles. Eben watched as the guardsmen dragged him away across the cold marble floor. He then returned to his chamber and pondered what he had heard from the Skathean.

**

Eben sat with King Ignis, Cassiel, Red, and Stella around the table in the royal guest chamber.

'It would be best for you to make a move soon,' said King Ignis. 'It's not safe for you here if Skatheans can so easily sneak by my palace guard. I will have to double the guard as we simply can't accept an intrusion like this. You should know that I had the Skathean questioned. He refuses to speak.'

'He said enough last night,' said Eben. 'You're right; we should leave for Faircastle soon.'

'The council will be held on the first day of summer,' said Cassiel. 'We must make a move if we hope to arrive on time.'

'This council is of great importance to us,' said King Ignis. 'King Edric of Irvaria sent a messenger pigeon and requested a representative from Ortaria be present. Sir Red has graciously agreed to be our representative.'

'It is an honour and a privilege,' said Red.

'Most importantly we need you to ask the Irvarians for help. This is a desperate time. We are in great need of assistance. I received word from Duke Egil yesterday. He marched his army north to liberate the far northern Scaldonian town of Aldokan. He found the way blocked by large armies of muckrons. He also said there are other unknown evil creatures lurking in the north. He has returned to the relative safety of Orelin and has asked for our assistance to liberate Scaldonia. I plan to send him several thousand men, but we still must also deal with the Zyranian Order.'

'You should wait for Meara to return with the Irilians and then set sail for Zyran,' said Cassiel 'I believe breaching the walls of the Citadel would prove impossible without the help of wizards. Even if you had one hundred thousand men you could not capture the Citadel of Zyran.'

'You must speak with Meara about this. Tell her that I hope to cross the Sea of Zyran soon.' King Ignis looked sadly around the table at the four of them. 'I will miss the four of you. You have become very important to me. I feel that you are like my own children.'

'We will return as soon as we can,' said Stella, smiling kindly at the King.

'I look forward to the day,' he said, his sadness melting away. 'You must be careful. We have taken back Ortaria, yet there is still much evil in the land. The Vastorian Wastelands are particularly dangerous; you must always travel cautiously. The Vastorians are a fierce people; you should be cautious about giving your trust to them. If there are Skatheans in Ortaria there will surely be some in Vastoria.'

**

The following morning they galloped away leaving the walls of Ancora behind. Eben rode Swiftwing and led the way along the highway as they entered Altus Forest. The day was bright, and the sky was perfectly blue with not a single cloud in sight. The birds of the forest were singing, and a feeling of joy permeated their surroundings.

As the evening approached they arrived at the small town of Lantern Hill. They stopped their horses at the edge of the forest and looked at the town ahead. Lantern Hill was set on the hill at the far side of a large field. The sunset sent long golden streaks of light through the smoke that drifted upward from the many chimneys. Eben remembered back to when they were last in Lantern Hill and the experience of fighting the group of Skatheans. He replayed the events in his mind; the memories made him slightly lightheaded.

'Do you think we should stay in Lantern Hill?' asked Eben.

'King Ignis said the town is safe. There is a small brigade of Ortarian infantrymen based here. I think we should be fine,' said Cassiel.

'I agree,' said Red. 'Once we leave Ortaria we'll have to do a lot of camping, especially when we pass through the deserts of Vastoria.'

They rode across the field and two guardsmen greeted them as they approached the base of the hill.

'I'm Sir Red, and this here is Eben, Champion of Ortaria, Lady Stella, and Lord Cassiel.' The two guardsmen bowed and saluted them.

'We were informed that you were coming. We will tell Baron Sabin of your arrival,' said one of the guardsmen. He then turned and ran up through the town toward the manor house which was set at the pinnacle of the hill. Eben dismounted Swiftwing and led his horse up the main cobblestone street. The people stared as they passed by. Red was outfitted in the elaborate armour of a knight and looked the most dazzling of their group. Most of the villagers watched Red, and he enjoyed the attention. Eben preferred less armour and wore only a light chainmail shirt, a leather overcoat, and gloves. He found it was much easier to fight with less weight.

A short man approached them and was followed by about a dozen Ortarian guardsmen. He was a thickset man with dusty brown hair and bushy eyebrows. A big welcoming smile crossed his face as he reached them.

'Welcome my friends. Champion Eben, Sir Red, Lady Stella, and Lord Cassiel, I am overjoyed you have come to Lantern Hill. You probably don't remember me; I fought with you in the Battle of Scaldonia and the Battle of Ortaria.'

Eben thought he recognised Baron Sabin's face from the many faces of the knights who had travelled with them from Scaldonia to Ortaria.

'We are just passing through on our way west to Galdir,' said Cassiel. 'We will stay in the town inn if you have no other lodgings for us.'

'The town inn...no, you can't stay there,' exclaimed Baron Sabin, horrified at the suggestion. 'I have guest rooms in the manor house. Please follow me and be my guests.'

They followed Baron Sabin up the hill and arrived outside the rather large house. The manor house didn't have any battlements and was simply the largest house in Lantern Hill. Two guardsmen in full Ortarian armour stood by the front door and saluted them as they approached.

'I will have the stableboy take care of your horses,' said the Baron. 'Please, come in and meet my wife and family.'

**

Baron Sabin had his chef prepare a banquet to honour their arrival. The Baron proved to be a gracious host and made sure they were completely comfortable. Stella and Red had wanted to explore the town, but Baron Sabin had planned the entire evening. He insisted that they attend his banquet; he had entertainers and musicians perform for them, and he introduced them to a host of noble families who lived in and around Lantern Hill. By the time they retired to bed they were all very tired but also in good spirits.

The following morning they set out early and rode west along the highway, heading in the direction of Riverside.

CHAPTER TWO

The town of Riverside was set on the banks of the Merus River at a place where the river widened and slowed significantly to form what looked like a lake. The river was about five hundred yards across at its widest point. The surface of the water was completely still and reflected the trees on the far bank with almost perfect accuracy. The town was much larger than Lantern Hill with hundreds of houses lining the waterside south of the river. They sat on their horses and stared down from the top of the hill above the town. Twilight was fast approaching; the sun had already set in the western sky leaving a faint blue glow above the horizon. The evening was growing cool and dark.

'Wouldn't you prefer staying in an inn?' asked Red. 'It sure is nice staying in a palace or manor house and being treated like royalty, but I'm starting to miss the cheerfulness of a bar and the smell of ale.'

'You will never make a good noble if that's how you feel,' said Cassiel.

'I think the novelty of nobility is wearing off. I like the idea of being a noble much more than the reality.'

'I once stayed in a nice inn down by the river,' said Cassiel. 'I'm sure the Lord of Riverside will invite us to stay if he knows we are here. I agree with you, Red; I think I would prefer to stay at an inn as well. We simply won't announce our arrival. The Lord of Riverside won't even know we are here.'

They entered the town through the eastern gate and followed the lantern lit cobblestoned streets down to the river where many large and illustrious stone houses lined the waterfront. The cobblestones were paved all the way down to the water's edge. There were various small piers and hundreds of boats and barges anchored beside them. The sound of lively music could be heard from the numerous small inns which were set along the riverbank.

Cassiel led the way toward a fine looking inn that was right at the water's edge. It looked very welcoming and was a two levelled wooden building with a high gabled roof. The inn was painted completely white with ivy climbing up the walls on every side. Sweet music could be heard from the common room. Cassiel led them up to the door where they handed their horses to a waiting stableboy. Eben looked up and saw the sign above the door: Welcome to the House of Einin.

The common room was warm and almost completely full. Two men were playing flutes in the corner as a crowd of men and women laughed and conversed loudly and cheerfully.

'Perfect,' said Red happily. His eyes sparkled as he looked at the crowds of merry people.

'I'll see if I can get us some rooms,' said Cassiel. He approached the bar as the others found a table beside a window. They could see the lake through the window; the moon was rising up over the line of trees on the far side. The moonlight shimmered on the still water.

'This is a beautiful town,' said Stella. Red put his arm around his wife and held her close.

'We should move here one day and settle down,' said Red. 'You could move here too, Eben. We could all live here happily beside the lake.'

'That sounds lovely,' said Stella.

Cassiel walked over from the bar. 'We have rooms. I especially chose rooms with a view to the lake.'

'We should have a good meal tonight because there are no towns from here all the way to Galdir,' said Red.

The evening was pleasant and merry. They enjoyed roast chicken and a few too many mugs of ale. They were welcomed like they were old friends. The locals were a happy group of people and were still celebrating the liberation of Ortaria. They heard stories that Riverside had seen some terribly evil times until the arrival of the Ortarian army only three weeks earlier. The Skatheans were all gone, and the town was in the process of cleaning up and returning to the joyful peace of former days.

Eben retired to his room late in the evening and felt happy and full of cheer. His room was small but very pleasant. It was situated on the lower level. The lake lapped at a rock wall only several feet from his window. He placed his sword beside his bed and sat down on a cushioned chair by the window to watch the moonlight shimmer on the lake.

Something caught his eye outside the window. There were large ripples crossing the surface of the water. He leaned toward the window and peered outside. Whatever was causing the ripples was moving closer. He strained his eyes to see if there was a boat, but it was too dark. A few moments later the ripples abated, and the lake became still once again. He thought nothing more of it. After a few minutes he stepped back across to his bed and pulled back the covers. His eye caught the movement of a dark shadow passing by his window. A feeling of apprehension was growing in his chest.

Suddenly the glass shattered; the frame of the window gave way as a dark shape smashed inward. The face of a furious wyvern snarled as it crashed forward toward Eben. The beast wasn't like the wyverns he had seen on the battlefield; its head was much larger, and its scales were a glimmering dark blue. The wyvern howled and whipped its head from left to right, tearing a huge hole in the side of the inn and ripping the entire outer wall away. Eben grabbed the Sword of Light and drew the blade. The beast pounced forward as he cut downward, but the wingless wyvern raised an edged arm and deflected the blade. Eben stumbled and fell back away from the fierce beast.

The wyvern's huge fangs snapped forward. Eben desperately scurried back out of the way. He dashed out of the bedroom. The wyvern roared and smashed a way through the wall into the hallway. It chased him down the corridor toward the common room, tearing the inn apart as it pursued him. The common room was mostly empty; the few remaining patrons stared in horror as Eben burst into the room with a howling wyvern at his heels.

Eben turned to face the beast and lifted his sword. The wyvern pounced as he quickly stepped back and cut out, missing the beast's neck by only inches. The snarling beast recoiled and started to circle him menacingly. It smashed and knocked over chairs and tables. The few remaining terrified patrons rushed out the front door. Eben could feel his strength growing. He stared into the wyvern's fierce red eyes.

Suddenly Stella and Red dashed into the room from the hallway. The monstrous beast turned to face them, howling madly. They both drew their swords. Red, without considering the situation, jumped at the creature, cutting down with all his might. The wyvern raised its clawed arm and parried the strike. It then whipped its long tail. Stella quickly ducked, but the scaly tail struck Red and knocked him across the room, sending him crashing into the far wall. Meanwhile Eben charged at the beast and stabbed forward. The sword pierced through the thick blue scales; the wyvern howled in pain. Eben pushed the sword deeper and the wyvern struck out with the back of its massive clawed hand and knocked Eben across the room. Eben stumbled and for a few moments felt dizzy from the impact.

Cassiel then stepped into the room from the hallway. His jaw dropped as he looked at the beast. He raised his right hand and a bright orange beam of flame rushed through the air and blasted into the wyvern's face.

'It's a lindworm!' cried Cassiel.

The beast writhed about the room and shook the sparks away from its eyes. It then violently crashed through the front wall to the cobblestoned street beyond. Several town guardsmen had gathered outside, having heard the commotion. They looked up at the creature in terror and backed away.

Eben gathered himself and shook off the daze. He charged outside after the lindworm. The beast turned to face him and lifted its head high, attempting to intimidate him with its size. It then howled loud enough to wake the entire town. More guardsmen rushed down toward the scene of the battle, and they stared in shock as Eben stepped forward defiantly.

'I am Eben, Champion of Ortaria. You will never take the Sword of Light from me!'

The beast shrieked and pounced, snapping out with its massive fangs. Eben jumped aside, dodging the ferocious bite, and in a single motion brought his blade down at the lindworm's scaly neck. The beast fell to the ground and screamed in pain. Without delay Eben hewed down again; a moment later the hideous lindworm fell still and lifeless.

Red and Stella walked over from the ruined inn and were followed closely by Cassiel.

'How many is that now?' asked Red, a bewildered smile crossing his face.

Eben looked across to his friends. 'Three,' he replied. 'But I think they're getting larger.'

'No, this wyvern was of the lindworm variety,' said Cassiel as he stared down at the dead beast. 'Lindworms do not have wings, but they are larger and stronger than their flying cousins.'

A group of a dozen Riverside guardsmen approached. 'Who are you?' asked their leader, who was a tall and skinny man with a thin gaunt face.

'I'm Sir Red, and this is my wife Lady Stella. That's Eben, Champion of Ortaria. Over there is Cassiel, the wizard.'

The guardsmen stared in awe from Eben to the dead lindworm. They stared at the lifeless beast in a stunned silence. Eben glanced back at the half demolished inn. The whole front wall had been knocked down, and the common room was completely ruined from the battle.

'Maybe we won't settle down here after all,' said Red.

**

They sat beside a large brightly burning open fire with Earl Carlo of Riverside. They had been invited up to the palace after the battle. The Earl was a large man with a gentle demeanour and long dark hair. He was clothed in fine linen and was softly spoken.

'I had no idea that you were in Riverside. If I had known I would have invited you to stay with me.'

'We didn't want to bother you,' said Red politely.

'It would have been an honour to have you as my guests,' said Earl Carlo. 'Stories of the four of you are being told everywhere. Your deeds are known by all, and I see from viewing the dead wyvern that everything they say is true.' Eben nodded. 'I'm sorry we couldn't provide you with more protection. The wyvern entered the town from the lake; it was simply impossible for the town guards to know the creature was coming.'

'We dealt with the situation anyway,' said Red.

'Yes, you did well,' said the Earl. 'The people of Riverside have risen from their beds to have a look at the dead wyvern. No one really believed in such creatures until recently; now their existence is beyond doubt.'

**

They stayed that night in Earl Carlo's palace. The next morning they rode west from Riverside along the highway through the Altus Forest. The day was warm and the sky blue. A soft breeze blew from the south. They rode briskly and around midday they stopped by a small crystal clear stream that ran through a glade beside the highway. Red prepared some buttered bread for lunch. They sat in the grass beside the stream and rested for a while.

'How did the lindworm find us?' asked Stella.

'I don't know,' replied Cassiel. 'However, I think it clearly came for Eben's sword.'

'The Skathean in Ancora said every servant of his master would be hunting me.'

'Perhaps we are not being careful enough travelling so openly through Ortaria,' said Cassiel, his eyes uneasily scanning the edge of the forest.

'I agree, we should try to be more cautious,' said Eben. 'Azagord said the master in the north wants to throw the Sword of Light through the Cosmic Gate. I think he doesn't want anyone using the sword against him; that's also what King Ignis believes. The Sword of Light has been used to fight evil for thousands of years.'

'The sword must be able to stop him,' suggested Red. 'Why else would he want to take the sword from you?'

'I'm sure most of our questions will be answered when we arrive at the council in Faircastle,' said Cassiel.

**

After a short time they remounted their horses and left the glade. They rode west for the remainder of the day. As the evening approached the company found a clearing off the highway and out of sight. Red made a small campfire and placed a pot full of vegetables over the flames. The evening was cool and still. The moon rose over a line of trees, lighting up their surroundings.

Eben looked across the fire and saw that Red was staring intensely at the full moon. 'What's troubling you, Red?'

'The full moon always brings back memories of my childhood when I lived in Talis.'

'What memories?' asked Stella.

'Some sad memories; the night my parents died was a full moon night.'

'You never told me what happened to your parents, Red,' said Stella gently. Red looked into the flames of the fire and for a moment fell into a thoughtful trance.

'The memories are difficult to talk about,' he said, pausing for a few moments. 'At the time I was fourteen. I spent most of my days working with my father. He was a candle maker and had a small workshop in the backstreets of Talis. We lived behind the workshop in a small one bedroom cottage. I was out late with some friends one night and returned home to find my parents were gone. Everything was taken from our house, and the workshop had been ransacked. I didn't know where they had gone or what had happened. I asked everyone in the neighbourhood; no one knew what had happened to them. I searched every corner of Talis and asked everyone if they had seen my parents. My father never owned his workshop, and he had large debts to various bankers in the town. The bankers sold the workshop and our cottage. I was left to fend for myself on the streets of Talis. I worked hard to support myself and lived on the streets for years. I spent all my spare time searching for my parents. I never found them. It took me years to accept the possibility that they were probably murdered.'

'I'm sorry to hear this,' said Cassiel. 'Those years must have been very difficult for you.'

Red nodded and glanced up at the moon. 'Every time I see the full moon I think of them. I miss them so much. I think they are still with me in a sense, looking after me and keeping watch over me.'

Eben felt sad for Red. He understood what it was like to not know what happened to your parents. Hearing about Red's past made him feel an even stronger kinship with his friend.

'Hey look, dinner is ready,' said Red as he leaned over and pulled the pot off the flames. He took four bowls from his bag and served them boiled vegetables.

**

They moved quickly the following day and came to the edge of Altus Forest. They stopped their horses at the site of the Battle of Ortaria where they had fought weeks earlier. Few signs of the battle remained. After a short stopover they followed the highway out across the Golden Plains.

The highway was mostly empty apart from occasional peddlers or trading caravans. The blue skies were passing away. The weather was becoming cool again as grey clouds rolled in from the north. As night fell they set up camp by the side of the road. They sat around the campfire and kept warm as the night grew dark.

'I'm looking forward to seeing Vastoria and Irvaria,' said Red. 'I've heard many stories about the Western Lands. Irvaria is said to be the most beautiful kingdom in all Veredor.'

'I've also heard Irvaria is beautiful,' said Cassiel. 'They say Faircastle was built by the first Ecorian, Jeriel the Just; it was the seat of the Ecorian Emperor and the capital of the old Empire. Faircastle is said to be a glorious city. Faircastle was known as the Star of the Ecorian Empire.'

'What ever happened to the Ecorian Empire?' asked Stella.

'The Ecorian Empire was ruled by a line of powerful and noble men who were direct descendants of Jeriel the Just. Jeriel's only son, Aldis Ecorian, married a mermaid and from that time the emperors became known as the Ecorians. The Ecorians were not quite men and not quite mer; they belonged to both races. There were never any other unions between men and mer in all of the history of Veredor. The mer by nature could only have two children, a son and a daughter, and the Ecorians inherited only half this trait, being only able to have one child, either a son or a daughter. The last Ecorian died without an heir, and the Ecorian Arbiters, the men who governed the provinces of the empire, argued over who should succeed the Ecorians. Eventually they decided to form independent kingdoms. Ortaria, Silvor, Scaldonia, Irvaria, Everdon, Vastoria, Ateria, and the lands of the Far West became independent kingdoms. King Ignis is a direct descendent of the Ortarian Magistrate of the Ecorian Empire. The Ecorian Arbiters have since been regarded as the highest degree of nobility in Veredor.'

'I would like to know more about the history of Veredor,' said Stella.

'There is a lot to learn. So much has occurred across the ages. There is a great library in Faircastle. Hopefully we will be able to read some of the old books when we arrive.'

They sat around the fire and rested. The night grew cold, but the fire burned brightly and kept them warm.

**

The days that followed were much the same. The Golden Plains were mostly empty. The weather had taken a turn for the worse, and they often found themselves riding through heavy rain. Around midday on the third day they could see Galdir set on the hill in the distance. Misty clouds hung low above the fortress, and the tops of the mountains beyond Galdir were hidden from view.

'This is our last stop in Ortaria,' said Cassiel.

'The Vastorian Wastelands await us,' said Red, his eyes studying the towering mountains ahead. Red had been looking forward to the adventure beyond the mountains. They were excited about the prospect of seeing Vastoria and Irvaria.

'The wastes are very dangerous. Meara told me they are mostly ruled by warlords and tribal leaders,' said Cassiel. 'We will cross them as quickly as we can. I expect it to be a two week journey from Galdir to Faircastle. We will probably have to stop at the city of Sabulo just beyond the Iron Gate Pass. We will need to find a guide to take us across the desert. Once we cross the wasteland we will make for the Adira River. From there we can take a barge up the river all the way to Faircastle.'

They rode onward toward the gate of Galdir. The large reinforced ironclad gates opened as they approached. Two Ortarian guardsmen stood on each side of the great archway and allowed them to pass. They rode up through the town to the top of the hill where the dark stone fortress towered high above the town. The townsfolk appeared much happier since they had been liberated from the rule of Baron Doriak. Several guardsmen walked down the fortress steps to greet them.

'I salute you, Champion Eben, Sir Red, Lady Stella, and Lord Cassiel. We were not expecting you so soon,' said their leader, who was a very short man with a completely bald head. A dozen or so guardsmen stood behind him. 'I have sent someone to fetch Sir Victar.'

Moments later the great iron doors opened. Sir Victar stepped out and stood at the top of the steps. He was a tall and gaunt looking man with high cheekbones and bright blue eyes. His dark hair was oiled back, and he wore the same armour as the guardsmen of the town. He was around forty years old and looked very lordly, but at the same time very exhausted.

'The Dragon Slayer himself,' said Sir Victar, walking down the steps toward them.

'Greetings, Sir Victar,' said Eben. 'We are passing through on our way to Irvaria. We are hoping to only stay one night at Galdir.'

'King Ignis sent word that you were on your way. You're most welcome to stay in the fortress. Please come in. I'll have a banquet prepared in your honour,' said Sir Victar. They followed him through the iron doors into the magnificent hall of Galdir.

'Did you see any muckrons on the highway?' he asked as he led them up the stairs to the upper hall where an open fireplace was burning brightly.

'No, we rode across Ortaria and didn't see one, but we did get attacked by a lindworm in Riverside,' said Cassiel as they all took seats around the long oak table.

'A lindworm!' exclaimed Sir Victar.

'It was really nasty, but it didn't last long against Eben,' said Red. Sir Victar looked to Eben and nodded respectfully.

'We haven't seen any wyvern around Galdir; however, there are still many stray muckrons in the wilderness. I only have a garrison of eighty men here at Galdir, and they are all that is protecting the whole west of Ortaria from the borders of Altus to the Endless Wall Mountains. I've sent word to King Ignis for more men; I don't know if he can spare any at this time.'

'The King has sent brigades to all the small villages and settlements around Ortaria,' said Cassiel. 'He's also sending men to Scaldonia through the Northern Pass. I'm sure when he can spare more men he will send them.'

'I hope that day is not far off. I worry because we are exposed to a raid from Vastoria with such a little force based here in Galdir.'

'Why would the Vastorians attack?' asked Cassiel, surprised at the suggestion.

'I am mostly worried about bands of raiders and renegade warlords. The Vastorian Wastelands are a complete mess. The warlords are tearing each other apart, and there's a threat that it could spill across the mountains. There is also word that the Skatheans control the south of Vastoria. They have also been pressing into the northern wastelands. It wouldn't take much for the Skatheans to gather an army and cross the Iron Gate Pass. Then they could enter the Golden Plains and even reach as far as Riverside. There have also been reports of muckrons and other monsters beyond the pass. Most troubling is the word from Scaldonia. Duke Egil faces monsters that don't even have names.'

'That sounds grim,' said Red.

'It's very grim,' said Sir Victar sternly. 'Galdir is a great fortress; we can stand against a large army, but eighty men...it's such a small number.'

They could clearly see that Sir Victar was deeply strained; the dark circles under his eyes showed his exhaustion. They knew there was little they could do to help his situation.

'We are travelling to Irvaria and will cross the Vastorian Wastelands. Can you share any knowledge regarding the road ahead of us?' asked Cassiel.

'The road forward will be treacherous,' said Sir Victar in a low and uneasy voice. 'If you weren't experienced warriors I would suggest not going west at all. Beyond the Iron Gate Pass you will find the city of Sabulo, a pit of despair. The city is ruled by a tyrant warlord. I believe he is in league with the Skatheans. You would do well avoiding the town altogether; however, Sabulo is perhaps the best place to find a guide to take you onward through the wasteland.' Sir Victar paused and looked toward the large arched windows before continuing.

'There is no road west through the desert. You will surely need a guide to take you across the dry lands. The main risk is accidently stumbling on unfriendly tribes or being ambushed by bandits. You could angle to the north and follow the path through the Empyrian Hills; the tribal people of the Empyrian Hills are noble, but they're also very unpredictable. You will need to pack your horses well and carry enough water for many days. The land is completely barren. There are wells in the desert, but the wells are hidden and well-guarded by the local tribes and clans. You are welcome to take whatever you need from the fortress stores.'

'Thank you, we appreciate your help,' said Eben. 'We will stock up before we leave in the morning.'

They rested beside the fire in the upper hall of the fortress. Sir Victar provided them with a sumptuous banquet. The night was quiet and uneventful, and the following morning they rose early. Cassiel had already prepared the horses and gathered supplies. The cloud cover of the previous day had mostly passed.

They rode out of Galdir along the winding road that led up through the mountains into the Iron Gate Pass.

CHAPTER THREE

They had passed by the Edius Plateau and hadn't seen another person since they entered the Iron Gate Pass. They set up their small tents about half a day's ride west of the plateau in a small dale that was out of sight of the mountain path. A veil of fog had descended and hid the craggy mountainside from view. An icy wind blew down from the snow-capped peaks. They wrapped their cloaks closely and sat by the campfire as an icy night approached.

'We should come out of the pass tomorrow morning,' said Cassiel.

'If we don't die from this cold first,' said Red, intensely shivering. 'I don't think I've ever been this cold in my entire life.'

Cassiel pointed his hand at the fire; the flames instantly doubled in size, warming the entire area.

'Nice trick,' said Red gladly. They huddled closer to the fire.

Stella brought the horses into the circle of warmth, and Cassiel used his magic so that the fire burned brightly all night, keeping the icy cold away from the campsite. The sunrise promised a warmer day; the clouds had cleared away revealing a bright and clear sky. They packed up the camp and set off early. The mountain path gradually descended; before long they had entered the foothills on the far side.

They stood on a high ridge with a view to the dry and arid plain beyond the mountains. Beyond a group of foothills a dry and dusty plain extended out into the hazy distance. They couldn't see a single tree in Vastoria; only dry shrubs and prickly weeds grew beyond the Endless Wall Mountains. The land looked rugged and bleak. To the north the Endora Mountain range stretched away westward like giant fangs rising from the plain.

'Vastoria looks like it's the opposite of Ortaria,' said Red.

'So harsh,' added Stella.

'Only tribal nomads survive in the dry deserts,' said Cassiel.

Eben could see the road led out of the Iron Gate Pass and cut toward the south across the parched plain. Further south there was a wide and lone hill that looked to have a town built on it.

'I think that's Sabulo over there,' he said, pointing toward the southwest.

The others looked and could see the outline of the town in the distance.

'Sir Victar told us to stay away from Sabulo,' said Stella.

'True, he did, but we must find a guide to take us across the wasteland. As far as I know there is no other town around here,' said Cassiel, his eyes searching the plain. 'We'll have to keep our wits about us. If the lord of the town has dealings with the Skatheans then it will be dangerous for us.'

'Maybe we should just try to cross the wastes without a guide,' suggested Red.

Cassiel pondered the idea for a few moments. 'If any of us had ever crossed the wasteland I would probably think we could. The real issue is the possibility of crossing tribal boundaries by accident. The Vastorians are very territorial. Only an experienced guide can make sure we don't become the victims of an accidental trespass.'

'Sir Victar mentioned the Empyrian Hills,' said Eben. 'Perhaps we should follow the Endora Mountains and cross the Empyrian Hills.'

'The tribes of the Empyrian Hills are supposedly good and noble,' said Cassiel. 'They are closely related to the Irvarians. It would probably be safer for us to go that way. However, I read about the Empyrian Hills before we left Ancora, and I learned it would take us twice the time to cross the Empyrian Hills as it would to cross the wastelands. They are said to be riddled with hundreds of gorges formed by streams that flow down from the Endora Mountains. We probably wouldn't make it to Faircastle on time for the council if we went that way.'

'Sabulo it is,' declared Red.

'It seems like the most reasonable choice,' said Cassiel.

**

They followed the road that led southwest and passed through the craggy foothills as they descended toward the plain. Within an hour they had reached the beginnings of the plain. Sabulo was built on a lone hill that jutted out about two miles from the last of the foothills of the Endless Wall Mountains. The hill had steep slopes leading up each side and was completely flat on top, being about five hundred yards from end to end. An old wall made of a yellow ochre coloured stone completely surrounded the town and mostly appeared to be in a state of ruin. They approached the hole in the wall that was the town's northern gate. The gatehouse and the towers had completely crumbled into ruins, and there were no guards. Groups of grubby looking vagrants, vagabonds, and beggars culminated around the entrance.

They rode up toward the gate. As they approached three rough looking men stood up and walked over to meet them.

'If ya need anyfing in Sabulo we can get it for ya,' said their leader in a deep burly voice. He was a massive man with a big moustache and long straw like hair. His two companions stood a little back from him, one had a severely hunched back and the other was a young man with a snarl etched into his face. They all had curved Vastorian swords slung over their shoulders.

'We are looking for a guide to take us across the wasteland to the Adira River,' said Cassiel.

'Wez can organise that for ya,' said the huge man. 'Iz can take ya to a place where da guides drink. For a silver piece dat is.'

'That seems a little costly for such a little service,' said Cassiel.

'You sayen I arnt deserve me pay,' said the Vastorian, his nostrils instantly flared and his lips curled downward. 'You tink you, an outsida, can come ear and make demands on me, a worken man,' he added as he angrily stepped toward Cassiel.

Red looked across at Cassiel and shook his head. 'Let me handle this,' said Red firmly. 'I'll give a bronze and that's it, you got it, otherwise get out of the way!' The man frowned up at Red and then sneered as his hand went to the axe that was hanging on his belt. Red's hand went to his sword hilt. The man took a few steps back. They both severely eyed each other for a few moments.

'All right, we'll make it a bronze,' said the Vastorian, finally backing down.

'Berp, take em to da Old Guard Station Tavern.' The young man with the snarl stepped forward. Red flicked a bronze coin to the huge Vastorian.

'Follow me,' said Berp. He led them through the gate.

'I learned how to deal with people like that when I was living on the streets; some people don't respond to reason and only speak the language of toughness,' said Red, glancing back at the Vastorian as they rode onwards.

The street was covered in waste, and the buildings looked derelict. Almost every window had been smashed and boarded up. Every second house was either a pile of ruins or a makeshift structure. The people living in the city were all covered in filth; everyone looked frightened and deeply troubled. A putrid smell permeated the whole town and was like nothing that Eben had ever inhaled in his life...simply terrible.

'We won't stay long,' said Cassiel as they followed Berp along the main road.

After about a hundred yards Berp turned and led them down a side lane toward the west side of the town.

'We almost dare; just a bit fuver,' said Berp. About a minute later he stopped and pointed down a long and dark alleyway.

'Down dare,' he grunted before walking away.

'I don't like the look of this,' said Stella, her eyes narrowing as she stared down the foul and grimy alleyway. She shook her head uneasily.

'I can't see a tavern,' said Cassiel.

'Follow me,' said Red as he turned his horse and led them forward.

Rats scurried away as they proceeded. About a hundred feet ahead the alleyway came to a sudden end and a second lane bent away to the right.

'They rode onward and then suddenly came up against an abrupt dead end. There was nothing but a grimy brick wall in front of them.

'I think we were fooled,' said Cassiel.

Suddenly a multitude of masked men, all in black attire, appeared from over the edge of the rooftops. Others rushed out from a door behind them and blocked their exit. Most of them had crossbows, others had spears and swords. Eben drew his sword and Cassiel raised his hands, ready to use his magic.

'You would be fools to resist,' said a masked man who walked across the rooftop to stand on top of the grimy brick wall.

'What do you want?' asked Cassiel, looking up at the man in black. There were at least thirty masked men surrounding them.

'I want you to drop your weapons and get off your horses,' replied the man in black.

'We won't be doing that,' said Red, turning his horse around and staring fiercely up at the leader of the bandits. There was a deathly silence for a few moments. Eben's eyes scanned the bandits; he counted at least ten crossbows pointed at them. He wondered if he could possibly take on so many at once.

'Red!' exclaimed the man on the wall, breaking the silence. 'Is that you?'

'Who wants to know?' asked Red.

The man quickly pulled off his mask and revealed his face. He was a handsome young man with dark mischievous eyes, an olive complexion, and curly brown hair.

'Quade,' said Red with a surprised laugh.

'I never thought I'd see you again, Red,' said Quade with a smile from ear to ear. He slid down off the wall to the alleyway below and sheathed his sword.

'Another friend, Red?' asked Cassiel suspiciously. Red glanced at Cassiel, understanding that he was referring to the experience with Falsig. He gave a wary smile and then looked back to Quade.

'Do you treat everyone who comes to Sabulo like this?' asked Red.

'No, we're actually not what we look like; we are the remaining members of the Baker's Guild. There's a bounty out on your head big enough to make everyone want to capture you...even bakers. We were not going to harm you; we just wanted the bounty. Everyone in Vastoria is searching for the four of you. We were told that you had come down from the Iron Gate Pass and were heading this way, so we set a trap for you.'

'What now?' asked Red, looking up at the other bakers on the rooftops.

'You and your friends aren't safe here in Sabulo. You have to get off the streets. Follow me. I'll take you somewhere secure.' Quade then looked to one of the crossbowmen. 'Tell Big Bill it was a false alarm.'

The bandit nodded and was about to leave, but another masked bandit grabbed his arm, stopping him in his tracks. 'I don't think you can make that decision, Quade,' he said viciously.

Quade looked across at the masked man defiantly. 'I command these men, Raulok, not you. Red is like a brother to me; I can't hand him over to Big Bill.'

'We don't want to give up the reward, and we don't care about your friendship. The Skatheans are saying the bounty is one hundred gold pieces. You can be sure I will take them to Big Bill if you won't.'

Eben could sense the situation was about to explode. Quade looked up at the bandits on both rooftops and then back to those in the alleyway.

'Are you going to take orders from this little upstart or me?' asked Quade angrily.

'I think you'll find when gold is on the table loyalty is cast into the furnace,' said Raulok. 'You haven't been in the Baker's Guild long enough to learn what we are truly like.' He then looked up at the bandits on the rooftops above. 'I promise to divide the gold evenly among you. That's three gold each!'

'He's lying, and he can't even bake! Don't listen to a word he's saying!' cried Quade.

'Capture them!' commanded Raulok. A moment passed. The bakers didn't move. 'Do it!' repeated Raulok fiercely.

Several of the bakers threw nets from the rooftop. Cassiel raised his hand. The nets stopped in mid-air and flew back at the men who had thrown them. Raulok was speechless for a few moments as he watched the men on the rooftops become entangled in their own nets.

'Get them!' cried Raulok furiously. The bandits in the alleyway rushed forward.

Cassiel sent a magic shockwave through the air at the approaching bandits. They all tumbled back. Simultaneously he protected them from many crossbow bolts with an invisible shield.

'Let's get out of here!' cried Red, turning his horse and drawing his sword.

Swiftwing spun around and leapt forward. One of the fallen men jumped to his feet and thrust his spear at Swiftwing. Eben deflected the attack and kicked the bandit down as he rode by. Stella and Cassiel were right beside him. A moment later they galloped out of the alleyway. Red heaved Quade up onto the back of his horse and charged away from the bandits. The ragtag group of baker bandits chased after them.

'Get the horses! Catch them!' cried Raulok madly, watching as they sped away.

They raced down the main street and turned toward the northern gate. Within seconds they were out of the town and descending the slope toward the plain. They arrived on the dusty plain and stopped to look back at Sabulo.

'Quade, can you take us across the wasteland?' asked Red.

'Looks like I don't have a choice,' said Quade, looking back at Sabulo, his face pale with shock at having his men turn on him.

'We found our guide,' said Red with a smile. A moment later a large group of riders stormed out of Sabulo.

'Those bandits are coming after us!' said Cassiel, turning his horse toward the desert.

'Ride,' cried Eben. They galloped westward and charged out across the dusty plain.

CHAPTER FOUR

The bandit's mangy horses couldn't keep pace with their warhorses. Before long they were far out on the flat desert plain and out of sight of the pursuers. The dry environment was already taking its toll on them. The horses were starting to tire and an unrelenting dry wind blew from the south. The plain was becoming sandier the further they went. Swarms of flies were constantly circling them and irritating the horses.

'I can't believe they turned on me,' said Quade despondently, his dull eyes staring down at the ground.

'Wouldn't you expect bandits to do that?' asked Stella. Quade glanced glumly in Stella's direction and didn't reply.

'Are we heading in the right direction?' asked Red as he waved the sand flies away from his eyes.

Quade looked about for a few moments. 'Soon we'll have to turn south. If we continue west for too much longer we'll ride into the tribal regions.'

'We only have enough water for a few days. I think the horses are going to struggle in these conditions,' said Eben.

'There's a desert well one day from here,' said Quade. 'It's guarded by the Eastern Well Keeper. He'll want to be paid. The Skatheans may expect us to go in the direction of the well because they'll soon learn that you were in Sabulo looking for a guide.'

'Are there any other ways?' asked Cassiel.

'Not unless you want to brave the tribal regions west of here. We can either go through the Deep Desert or north to the Empyrian Hills. The people of the Empyrian Hills are very territorial, especially with all the troubles lately. The Deep Desert is dangerous, but probably the best way forward. We could follow the northern edge of the Deep Desert tomorrow. Once we arrive at the well we will be able to restock our water skins and the horses can drink. '

'The Deep Desert it is,' said Cassiel.

They rode onward across the plain and turned south later in the afternoon. Before sunset the plain came to an end. Further south they could see large sand dunes rising above the desert.

'Welcome to the Deep Desert. We can pitch our camp here and wait until the morning before we move onward,' said Quade.

They set up camp and rested as the sun descended behind the large dunes. The heat of the day gave way to a cool night. Quade sat on the sandy ground and counted the coins in his leather pouch.

'Five silver pieces. I'm almost broke. This is all I have left in the world. Red, please explain why I had to give up everything to save your skin?'

'We could have handled the bakers without your help, so don't blame me that your guild turned on you,' said Red defensively.

'I know; I shouldn't have been there with those bakers. The plan was to capture and take you to the Skatheans. None of them can really fight, and they're typically not violent people. They didn't really want to hurt you. They're just fools looking to get rich quickly,' said Quade as he stared eastward across the plain. He then glanced back at Red. 'Why are we going west? We are a long way from Silvor.'

'We're going to Irvaria to attend an important council,' said Cassiel.

'What council do you mean?'

'A council to do something about the Skatheans and muckrons in our lands,' said Red.

'Why do you care, Red?' asked Quade, surprised that Red was involved in anything so important.

'I'm a knight; it's my duty to care,' said Red with a glimmer of pride in his eyes.

'A what?' exclaimed Quade, his jaw dropping at Red's words.

'A knight,' repeated Red with a smile.

Quade's shook his head in disbelief. 'I never thought I'd see the day. I can't believe it! Whatever happened to your idea of going back to Silvor and living the easy life?'

'It's a long story, Quade. Last time I saw you I was just about to join the circus in Ancora. That's where I met Stella. After the circus burned down I started working for an overland trader and travelled around Ortaria. Soon after I met Eben and Cassiel, and a little later we became friends with King Ignis of Ortaria. Life has been an adventure since then, and I'm married too,' said Red, taking Stella's hand affectionately.

'What! Married! I can't believe it!' shouted Quade, shaking his head and laughing.

'It's true. I've become a little respectable,' said Red.

'A little?' questioned Quade, rolling his eyes.

'Yeah, just a bit,' replied Red.

'Amazing! I remember the streetwise kid living rough in Talis, and here you are...a knight, married, and a friend of a king.'

'It's been an adventure,' said Red. 'What about you, Quade? What are you doing in Vastoria?'

'Ah, yes, that's a story. I went west from Ancora after we arrived there. I planned to keep going all the way to Iarthar and the Far Western Lands. I ran out of money in Sabulo and had to work as a peddler. I learned to navigate the wastelands and deserts between the Adira River and Sabulo. The way across the desert gradually became more and more dangerous. In the end I had to look for something else to do. I started working as a bodyguard which didn't last long. I got desperate in the end and I found myself working as a baker. I worked my way up through the ranks of the Baker's Guild. The old guilds of Sabulo have lost their power in recent years, that's why they were going after the bounty on the four of you.'

The evening went on with more stories and conversations. Eben enjoyed Quade's company; he was a friendly drifter. They rested well that night. Eben awoke early the next morning and watched the sun rising over the dunes.

**

They followed the northern edge of the Deep Desert. By midday they were exhausted. The horses were struggling and dehydrated.

'I can't stand this place,' said Red. 'What happened to this land to make it this way?' he asked, not expecting to be answered.

'They say the Prince of Shadows cursed Vastoria,' said Cassiel. 'These were once beautiful lands in the Forgotten Age. They belonged to the Astarian Fiora. The Prince of Shadows came and burned down the forests and killed everything that lived here. It is also said that he destroyed Vastoria because he was jealous of Fiora. The wind blew away all the soil and only the sand and clay remained. This land was called Fairaria in those days.'

'The quicker we cross the better,' said Red, irritated by the swarm of sand flies buzzing around his head.

'You should try living here for a few years; you'd have nothing to complain about then,' said Quade with a laugh.

'No thanks.'

They rode on for the remainder of the day. As the evening approached they came to a place where there was a deep gorge and a dry river bed.

'This is the desert well I was telling you about,' said Quade.

Down in the deep of the gorge there were actually small trees growing. It was an oasis in the desert. Quade led them down the slope and along the dry riverbed where they were protected from the wind. Further ahead they could see a small grouping of mud huts.

'Let me do the talking,' said Quade. He walked ahead of them toward the huts.

'We've come to buy water!' he shouted. A few moments later two men appeared. They were wearing long overcoats and black turbans. Only their eyes could be seen as their faces were covered by cloth.

'We don't sell to anyone,' replied the Well Keeper.

'Why not?' asked Quade, surprised by the answer.

'Orders from the Skatheans, no one buys water or they will kill us.'

'Since when?'

'For the last month. The Skatheans are trying to stop anyone crossing the Deep Desert.'

'How do you survive then? Don't you trade water for food?' asked Quade.

'We do, but the Skatheans say no,' said the Well Keeper.

'You shouldn't listen to the Skatheans. The time of the Skatheans is coming to an end in these lands,' said Cassiel as he rode up beside Quade.

'Their time is not at an end yet,' said the Well Keeper. 'The Skatheans rule the Vastorian Wastelands, and until they don't we will listen to them.'

'We have a problem then,' said Quade sternly. 'Because we can't go on without water, and we certainly can't turn back to Sabulo.'

'It's not our problem,' said the Well Keeper gruffly.

From behind the huts another man walked over. He was clothed in the same manner of the two others, but he had a curved Vastorian sword at his belt and a small circular bronze badge affixed to his chest. His face was covered by a black metal mask.

'Is there a problem?' he asked in a deep and strong voice.

'They won't leave without water,' said the Well Keeper.

The man with the sword stepped forward fearlessly. 'We have nothing for you. Move along.'

'You're a Desert Knight?' asked Quade coolly.

'Yes,' replied the man.

'I didn't realise the Desert Knight's took orders from Skatheans,' said Quade, taking a tone that mocked the Desert Knight.

'We don't,' said the Desert Knight firmly.

'The Well Keeper says he won't sell us water because of the Skatheans. You're serving the Skatheans by telling us to move on without letting us take any water.' There were a few moments of uncomfortable silence.

'Who do you serve?' asked the Desert Knight.

'I serve no one,' replied Quade.

'Everybody serves somebody; you're a fool if you haven't learned that yet,' stated the Desert Knight sharply.

'We serve the King of Ortaria. We are on our way to Faircastle,' said Cassiel.

'You mean you're going to the council?' asked the Desert Knight.

'You know of the council?' asked Cassiel, surprised.

'Indeed, we have sent our own envoy to attend.'

'This is Sir Red of Ortaria; he is the Ortarian envoy. We need water to continue our journey. If the Desert Knights have sent a representative you must realise that we are on an important mission.'

The Desert Knight looked at Red for a few moments and then back to Cassiel. It was impossible to know what he was thinking because of his mask.

'If the Ortarian Knight asks for water he can take it,' he said firmly

'I ask for it,' said Red instantly.

The Desert Knight turned to the Well Keeper. 'Let them have water. The Desert Knights are bound by an oath to give assistance to the Ortarian, Scaldonian, and Irvarian Knights. It is our tradition. I therefore will not stand in your way, Sir Red.'

'Thank you,' said Red.

They were then led beyond the huts to a place where there was a small pond. The horses were allowed to drink. They refilled their water skins and then rested by the water. After several minutes the Desert Knight walked over to them.

'You must be the one who they call Eben?' he asked.

'Yes, I am Eben.'

'Word came to Vastoria that a hero by the name of Eben has appeared in Ortaria. I have heard you helped the Ortarians win a battle in Scaldonia. They say your skills with the sword are unmatched and muckrons scatter before you.'

'I do my best,' said Eben modestly.

'I am a swordsman and a master of Grecob's Method. I am wondering who you studied with and which method you use?'

'A hunter taught me how to use the sword.'

'He must have been a master,' suggested the Desert Knight.

'He was a good swordsman, but I knew him as more of a huntsman. I don't follow any particular method.'

'Interesting, then you must be a natural.'

'I suppose,' said Eben. He didn't want to mention the Sword of Light to the Desert Knight.

'My name is Arthur. I am pleased to have met you.' Eben stood up and politely shook Arthur's hand. 'I am sure we will meet again,' he said. He then nodded and walked away.

The night grew cool and dark. They camped beside the pond with the permission of the Well Keeper. The gorge kept the wind away and there were few sand flies. The following morning they set out early. They felt refreshed and rode quickly westward. They entered the plains of the Deep Desert which were completely flat and extended as far as the eye could see. The ground gradually became hard clay. Not even weeds grew, and the entire plain was completely devoid of any life.

'Many people meet their end out here. If you try to cross without enough water this place consumes you,' said Quade, his dark eyes scanning the horizon.

'Are we likely to meet anyone?' asked Cassiel.

'Sometimes I see people out here, and other times I've crossed and haven't seen a soul, but I doubt we will see anyone since the Skatheans have closed the wells. This place can send you a little crazy; it's something to do with being alone with so much space. The main problem out here is running into groups of Blue Caps.'

'Blue Caps, out here?' asked Cassiel, concerned at the revelation.

'What are Blue Caps?' asked Stella.

'They're nasty little men who bore deep into the desert. If you stray too close to a colony they come out in groups of hundreds and swarm you. They then take you away and keep you as a prisoner deep beneath the desert'

'What do they look like?' asked Stella nervously, her eyes searching their direct surroundings.

'They look like miniature men. They are not taller than the height of your knee, and they are incredibly ugly. We should be fine with the horses. If you're ever out here without a horse it would be difficult to outrun them. You'd probably end up as a Blue Cap breakfast.'

They rode on throughout the day and saw no other men and no signs of any Blue Caps. The hazy horizon extended out before them as far as they could see. As night fell they set up camp. Cassiel used his magic to make a fire. At first light the following morning they set out again. The day was a little warmer and the wind had subsided. They struggled onward, and by late in the afternoon they had come to a place where the clay surface gave way to white salt lakes that extended as far as the eye could see. Not a drop of water remained in the lakes.

'The Adira River is across these dry salt lakes. If we move quickly we should arrive at the western side of the Deep Desert tomorrow. The river is not far,' said Quade.

'The sooner the better,' said Red, clearly flustered.

'Look,' said Stella, pointing westward toward the horizon.

In the distance they could see horsemen galloping toward them. The sun was low in the sky, and the riders shimmered on the desert horizon.

'Are they Skatheans?' asked Red.

'It's hard to tell,' said Quade. 'There are three of them.'

'I think we can handle three Skatheans,' said Red confidently.

'Maybe,' said Cassiel anxiously.

Eben stared as the riders slowly approached across the plain. When they came into view it was clear they were not Skatheans, but they were dressed in the same manner as Arthur with their faces covered by dark metal masks. They wore the small round bronze badges over their chests which revealed they were Desert Knights.

'They're Desert Knights. Be careful; not all Desert Knights can be trusted,' said Quade.

'What do you think they want?' asked Cassiel.

'I'm sure we are about to find out,' replied Quade.

They waited in silence as the three riders approached. The Desert Knights halted their horses about twenty yards away.

'We greet you, Ortarians,' said the leader. 'I am Dillon of the Desert Knights. We have come to warn you. Word came to us from our kinsman, Arthur. He said that you are being pursued by a large group of Skatheans. The Skatheans arrived at the Eastern Well shortly after you were there.'

'How many Skatheans?' asked Quade.

'At least twenty,' replied Dillon.

'Twenty,' repeated Cassiel, shaking his head in shock.

'Yes, they are not far from you now. We have come to offer you safe passage through the tribal regions to the north. From there you can come to the Adira River further away from Darancra. The Skatheans won't be able to follow you. If you continue west from here you will find the Skatheans rule the southern reaches of the Adira River and you will meet your doom.'

'Why do you want to help us?' asked Cassiel coolly. Dillon didn't answer straight away. He looked to his two companions, and they whispered among themselves.

'We do not want to help you,' he answered flatly. 'Arthur, our kinsman, has requested this. We would have avoided contact with you if not for his request as we have little care for you or your business. Now that we have met we are bound by oath to help the Ortarian Knight who rides with you.'

Eben looked to Cassiel. 'Should we accept?' he asked in a whisper.

'It seems that Arthur is on our side even if these Desert Knights are not,' replied Cassiel, also whispering. 'If what they are saying is true we would be fools to go west from here. The tribal regions are probably our best option. I think we should go with them.' Eben nodded and gave it a little thought. The last thing he wanted to do was to walk into a trap set by Skatheans. Knowing that they were being followed so closely was cause for great concern.

'We accept your offer of help,' said Eben.

'Follow us,' said Dillon as he turned his horse around and galloped north.

CHAPTER FIVE

They rode north quickly and came to the edge of the plains of salt. As the day progressed they entered an arid land where only small brambles grew from the dry sandy soil. The landscape became ever so slightly undulating. The harsh wind of the salt plain had been left behind.

'At least something grows here,' said Red, looking sullenly down at a prickly bush.

The Desert Knights led them onward and continued northward without delay. Eventually, as the day was drawing to an end, they came upon a shallow gorge, and the knights led them down and along the base. The temperature had dropped significantly, and they could feel moisture in the air. They followed the dry base of the gorge westward. After a few minutes they came upon a small settlement of mud huts. The Desert Knights halted their horses and indicated for the others to remain in place. Dillon dismounted and walked toward the mud huts. Several rugged tribesmen approached him from the settlement.

'We request sanctuary for the night,' said Dillon.

'And you will have it,' said an older tribesman. The tribesman had a long dark beard and a deeply weathered face. A few quiet words were exchanged between Dillon and the tribesmen who nodded several times and then indicated for them to pass.

Dillon led them beyond the huts as the gorge curved around toward the north. The area widened significantly as they rounded a final corner. Before them was a shallow lake surrounded by hundreds of mud huts. Across the lake was the entrance to a large dark cave. A trickle of water slowly poured down from the cave into the crystal clear lake below.

'This is the home of the Jeanians. They're a large Vastorian tribe. They have no allegiance to the Skatheans,' said Dillon. 'We will be safe here until the morning. Tomorrow we will ride northwest toward the Adira River. The river is about a day and a half away from here.'

Dillon led them over to the side of the lake. The locals kept their distance and refused to speak within earshot of them. Eben felt that if the Desert Knights had not been with them that the Jeanians would not have welcomed the company. They set up camp beside the still lake.

'They are very aloof,' said Stella.

'They don't trust outsiders,' said Dillon, glancing from Stella back toward the grouping of huts where a small gathering of Jeanians kept a watch on them from a distance. 'That's why they have survived here for so long. In the old days they were the largest tribe in Vastoria, and they subjugated the lands to the west of the Adira River and most of the Deep Desert. In recent times they keep to this hidden gorge and several other concealed springs throughout the desert.'

Dillon looked back to Stella and then across to Eben. His dark metal mask made it impossible to see his expression

'They say the Jeanians were here when the Ecorian Emperors ruled Veredor. They follow the old ways of that ancient empire. They will serve no one but the Ecorians. For a long time they waited for the return of the Ecorian Empire. Of course the Ecorians are no more. The Jeanians have a legend that says the Ecorian Emperor once lived in the cave across the lake for a year. They say that the water came up from the deep to greet him. Supposedly the Ecorian could mysteriously draw the water from the deep and create springs in the desert. This is the last large lake; there were once many throughout the Vastorian deserts. The cave across the water is revered by these people.'

'I had no idea there was this much water this far out in the wasteland,' said Quade.

'They guard this place with their lives, and they only allow Desert Knights to stay here. No other outsiders are ever allowed to pass through this place. They would kill you if we weren't here accompanying you.'

They looked across the lake at the trickle of water that splashed down from the cave creating ripples in the clear shallow water.

**

The sound of a commotion woke Eben from a deep sleep. He quickly sat up and could see their camp was surrounded by a multitude of Jeanian tribesmen. The sun was just beginning to rise. At first Eben thought they were in danger, but then he could see that the Jeanians were actually gazing out across the small lake with wonder in their eyes. A raging torrent of water was rushing from the cave. The lake below was rapidly deepening, and a stream was starting to flow through the gorge. The group stood and watched with the Jeanians as the flow of water grew.

'This is a sign!' cried an old Jeanian tribesman. 'We have waited for sixteen hundred years. Our time has come again! The Ecorian Empire will return! The water flows like the days of old!'

More Jeanians gathered as the lake filled, and they cried with joy. They all believed it to have great significance.

As the Jeanians celebrated a lone hawk descended from the skies above. Dillon raised his hand. The hawk landed on his wrist. He took a small piece of paper from its claws. Moments later Dillon released the hawk. The bird of prey quickly ascended back toward the sky.

'We must make a move. The Skatheans have gathered a small army of mercenaries in Darancra and are following the Adira River northward. They hope to intercept you before you cross the river. The twenty Skatheans are at our heels; they are camped just south of this hidden gorge. They are using their vultures to keep track of us. We must leave this place and make for the river. Arthur has organised a single boat for you to cross at the Mooring of Gastrell where a brigade of my kinsmen await us. Once you reach the far side of the river you will be much safer.' Dillon paused and stared at them for a few moments. 'I wonder what is so important that the Skatheans require an army to intercept you?'

'Our business will remain a secret, Sir Dillon,' said Cassiel. 'You should know that you do well protecting us from the Skatheans.' Dillon nodded and accepted the fact that they were not going to reveal anything.

'Gather your horses. We must leave immediately.'

**

Without delay the company rode away westward from the gorge. Dillon galloped out ahead with his two companions and kept a blistering pace. All the horses apart from Swiftwing strained to keep up. After riding for at least half a day Dillon halted his horse and stared back across the desert. Eben did the same. They could see on the horizon the dark shapes of riders pursuing them.

'Skatheans! They intend to catch us before we reach the river. We must ride like the wind!'

They rode on as quickly as their horses would take them. Eben looked back over his shoulder and could see the Skatheans were gaining on them. After another hour the landscape gradually changed. The soil was becoming darker; bushes and shrubs were dotted all about.

'Can you see the rise ahead? Beyond that ridge we will come to the Adira River and the Mooring of Gastrell.' In the distance there was a slight rise and a line of small trees.

'Look!' cried Red, pointing toward the southwest. A great cloud of dust was rising from beyond the ridge.

'It's the Skathean army!' shouted Dillon. 'We must hurry!'

They pressed ahead as fast as their horses could manage. Before long they arrived at the rise, and the exhausted horses rushed up the slope to the top of the ridge. From the height of the ridge they could see the mighty Adira River. A gradual slope led downward about four hundred yards to the riverbank. The river was wide, at least five hundred yards across, and flowed slowly to the south. Shrubs and trees lined the banks, and a dusty road led along the side of the river. They could see the stone landing which served as a small place for passing boats and barges to dock. Directly beside the landing a large group of fifty Desert Knights were mounted on their horses and waiting.

Toward the south, perhaps only a mile away, an army of horsemen were charging toward the Mooring of Gastrell. A group of Skatheans were leading the mercenary army from the front.

'We have no time!' cried Dillon. 'Follow me!'

They followed Dillon and the two other Desert Knights as they charged down the slope. Within a minute they were nearing the landing. It was instantly apparent that there was only one small wooden canoe. The group of Desert Knights directed them out onto the landing.

'You will have to leave your horses. On the far side of the river you will be safe for a time. The Skatheans will have to ride a long way south to find a boat or barge to follow you across. Follow the river north as quickly as possible. The further north you go the safer you will be,' said Dillon.

The sound of the approaching army was growing. Eben dismounted Swiftwing and quickly gathered his backpack and sword. He felt sad at having to leave Swiftwing behind. He had come to appreciate his great warhorse.

'Make haste!' cried Dillon.

Stella and Red were already in the small canoe and Cassiel was stepping in. The top edge of the canoe was nearing the surface of the water; it was obviously not built to carry any more than one or two passengers. Eben was next to step in. The water almost came over the edge, leaving only an inch or two.

Quade stood on the landing and looked down at them. He realised the boat couldn't possibly carry another. 'Goodbye my friends,' he said, warmly smiling down at them.

'Come on, Quade, there's enough room,' said Red, dismayed and not wanting to leave his friend behind.

'No, there's not,' said Dillon firmly. 'The boat cannot take another. You must go now! The Skatheans are almost upon us!'

'We can't leave you,' insisted Red.

'Don't worry about me. I have survived worse than this, and besides, this was always your quest. I was just tagging along for a while. Vastoria is my home now, and I mean to defend it,' said Quade as he turned back toward the horses. 'I hope you don't mind if I borrow Swiftwing. Of course I'll return him if we ever meet again.'

Quade mounted Swiftwing and drew his curved Vastorian sword. Simultaneously the fifty Desert Knights turned their horses to face the approaching army of Skatheans and mercenaries. The army was charging toward the landing with a terrible roar. The thunderous sound of a thousand galloping horses echoed between the two opposing ridges and grew louder with each passing moment.

'Go!' cried Dillon. 'We have risked much to see you safely through the desert. You must go now!'

Cassiel and Eben took oars and started to row the canoe out across the water. They watched as the fifty Desert Knights formed a line to face the approaching army. Suddenly the Desert Knights charged forward at the army. Within seconds they smashed into the leading ranks of the Skatheans and mercenaries. The battle raged. It was difficult to make out exactly what was happening amid the calamity. Eben and Cassiel continued to row the small vessel across the river as they watched the battle intently. The Desert Knights were fighting valiantly, but the task at hand was simply too great. They were being crushed and overwhelmed.

'Look,' cried Stella as about a dozen remaining Desert Knights broke away from the battle and rode up the slope to the top of the ridge. 'Quade is with them!'

The Skatheans and mercenaries were in close pursuit and within seconds the Desert Knights and Quade galloped over the ridge and were beyond sight. All fell silent on the shoreline in the wake of the battle. Several Skatheans approached the edge of the water and stared out at them. Eben and Cassiel continued to row, and they stared back at the Skatheans in the eerie silence.

CHAPTER SIX

The Adira River had always been a source of life to those who lived in the deserts of Vastoria. The river flowed out of the lush land of Irvaria to the northwest and was sacred to the people of the desert. The vast majority of the population of Vastoria lived on the banks of the river, and the surrounding areas provided fertile soils for farming and grazing of cattle. The river dwellers considered themselves to be true Vastorians, an ancient people with a distinct culture.

Eben stepped onto the western bank of the river and the others followed.

'I hope Quade got away safely,' said Red, staring back across the wide river.

'I'm sure he'll be fine. Swiftwing is amazing; he can outrun any Skathean horse,' said Eben.

'I hope so,' said Red.

'We should move on,' said Cassiel. 'We still have an hour or two before sunset.'

They followed the course of a dusty and well-trodden road that led beside the river. As dusk approached they moved away from the shore and set up camp a few hundred yards in the hinterland. Red built a small fire and prepared a meal.

'We could have met an ill fate without the help of the Desert Knights. We were very fortunate to gain their assistance,' said Cassiel. 'The Skatheans seem desperate to stop you taking the Sword of Light to Faircastle.'

'Thank goodness we're beyond their reach now?' said Red assuredly.

'I don't think we are safe yet,' said Cassiel, shaking his head. 'They may be able to cross the river somewhere. Dillon said the further we go north the safer we will be. The Skatheans will not dare to follow us further once we cross the border of Irvaria.'

'How much further is the border?' asked Eben.

'A few days if we move quickly,' replied Cassiel.

'Then we should move as quickly as we can. I'm tired of this game of cat and mouse,' said Red. 'We always seem to be running away from something. I look forward to the day they are running from us.'

'As long as we don't meet too many of them at once I believe we will have the upper hand,' said Eben confidently.

'You are probably right,' said Cassiel. 'But the Skatheans know what we are capable of. Surely they will only attack us if they believe they can overwhelm us. We should remain cautious.'

That evening they took turns keeping watch.

**

The following day they moved quickly north along the river road, and as noon approached they came upon a small river settlement. A group of ten mud huts surrounded a stone landing where two small barges were moored. As they approached several villagers quickly gathered staffs and spears and stood ready to defend their settlement.

'We mean you no harm. We're just passing through,' said Cassiel calmly.

'Find another way around our village,' said a young Vastorian man. 'Everyone who comes out of the south is evil these days. We doubt you are any different.'

'We are not a threat to you,' stated Cassiel.

'We don't care what you are,' said the young villager with a sneer.

Eben caught sight of a large group of barges drifting down the wide river. More barges followed and within a minute there were dozens. The villagers turned around and watched the river as the barges came closer and floated by.

'It's an army from Irvaria,' said Cassiel gladly. 'Look, they are flying the banner of their kingdom. They must be going south to challenge the Skatheans.'

Eben could see the red flags flying high with a depiction of a white dragon. The barges were full of armoured soldiers.

'That should keep the Skatheans from bothering us,' said Red happily.

'I dare say you may be right,' said Cassiel.

Before long the barges had all passed out of sight. The villagers turned back to face them.

'If you're against the Skatheans you're on our side,' said the young man. 'The river settlements from here to Irvaria have opposed the Skatheans since they arrived in Vastoria.'

'The Skatheans are our enemies too,' said Red. 'We fought them in Ortaria.'

'We have tried to stop them from taking control of our settlements for months. They hope to turn us into their slaves by dividing our people. They didn't expect our bonds to go so deep. We won't turn against our brothers for silver or gold. These have been troubling times for us. Now the Irvarians are coming we have reason to hope. Can you stay and help us fight the Skatheans?'

'I'm sorry,' replied Eben. 'We are urgently on our way to Faircastle and can't afford any delay.'

The young man nodded. 'You should know that something evil lurks in the wilderness to the north of here. It's not safe for men to be out in the night. Several caravans have completely disappeared on the river road between here and Irvaria. Men are telling stories of a shadow that walks in the darkness.'

'What kind of shadow?' asked Red in a low voice.

'We don't know. About two weeks ago a group of our tribesmen were camped half a day north of here. Their camp was attacked by something they couldn't see because it kept to the shadows. Several men were dragged into the night and were never seen again. The survivors said they felt unusually cold the night when they were attacked.'

'We will be careful,' said Eben.

**

They walked quickly for the remainder of the day and passed by two more river settlements before dusk. Once again they set up camp in the hinterland and found a cleared grove surrounded with trees and out of sight of the road. Red and Stella collected firewood while Cassiel and Eben set up the camp.

'What's your opinion of the warning we received?' asked Eben.

'It's probably nothing to worry about,' answered Cassiel. 'The people are strained from fighting the Skatheans. It could be the Skatheans trying to create a state of fear among the village folk. I'm hoping we don't have to fight another draug. I think we should keep a vigilant watch tonight.'

'Do you think we could beat a draug,' asked Eben.

'I think I understand the method a draug uses to attack. They tempt their victims with their deepest desires. The answer is simple; whatever they offer you, understand it's a lie, and then simply reject it,' said Cassiel assuredly.

'Easier said than done,' said Red as he returned to the camp with Stella. 'None of us beat the draug, and we knew the things we were tempted with were not real. If Baftel hadn't been there we probably would have been victims.'

Cassiel nodded. 'You are right, Red; although once you touch the fire you're unlikely to touch it again. We all saw what the draug could do. I think we would do better if we ever face such a challenge again.'

'Perhaps,' said Stella. 'But let's hope that we never have to.'

**

Eben awoke as Cassiel shook his shoulder. 'Eben, wake up,' he whispered uneasily.

'What's happening?' whispered Eben, sitting up quickly. He could see in the firelight that Cassiel was intensely staring out toward the edge of the clearing.

'There's something out there,' whispered Cassiel, continuing to watch with wide eyes.

'What did you see?' asked Eben, looking in the direction Cassiel was staring.

'I didn't see anything; I felt it, an evil intention. A terrible feeling in my heart.'

Eben quickly shook Red and Stella and they both sat up.

'What's wrong?' asked Stella.

'Cassiel thinks there's something out there,' whispered Eben.

'I knew we should have insisted on staying in one of those villagers by the river,' said Red as he drew his sword and stood up.

'Quiet,' whispered Cassiel. 'Listen, can you hear that?'

'No, I don't hear anything,' whispered Red.

A cold breeze blew across the clearing. The flames of the campfire reduced until only the hot coals remained. Only a little red light from the coals lit their faces, and the edge of the clearing had fallen into complete darkness.

'Reveal yourself,' said Cassiel, lifting his hand. For a moment nothing happened. There was complete silence. A blast of icy wind struck them. The light of the coals dimmed until almost no light remained. Cassiel fell to his knees and hunched over, groaning in pain. He struggled in an attempt to get up. Immediately he fell back down and lay still on the ground. Eben and Stella quickly went to his side as Red stood with his sword in hand.

Eben could see the colour was draining from Cassiel's face. He seemed to be struggling within himself. The cold wind continued to blow.

'Cassiel, what is it?' asked Stella, trying to help him to sit up.

Cassiel held his chest with his right hand and was in a state of shock. His face was pale.

'All I see is darkness,' replied Cassiel as he stared up at Eben. A shroud of darkness cast itself over his eyes, and the blood drained from his face. His eyes stared up absently as he lay still and unresponsive. Eben stood up and drew his sword. He knew whatever it was beyond the clearing would have to be destroyed, but he had no light beyond the faint glow of the coals. Suddenly Cassiel stirred. For a moment a glimmer of hope entered the young wizard's eyes.

He strained to half sit up and raised his hand. 'All that is true in life give us hope with your light,' he whispered. An instant later his hand started to glow with bright white light. A bright light that looked like a small star, far brighter than any lantern, ascended upward above the height of the trees and lit the entire clearing. The bright white light shone out through the surrounding trees.

Red suddenly dashed across the clearing with a shout resembling a battle cry. Stella drew her sword and followed after Red.

'Go, Eben, they'll need your help,' said Cassiel faintly.

Eben nodded and quickly jumped up and ran after Red and Stella. He followed their silhouettes through the trees. Red was already beyond the clearing. A moment later Red cried out fiercely, and a second later a cry of pain followed. Eben arrived at the scene. He saw Red had fallen to the ground. An instant later Eben caught sight of the creature. It looked like a living shadow in the shape of a man. The light seemed not to be able to reach it. All they could see were its two red glowing eyes floating in the darkness. The shadow glided over the ground like a ghost and moved with great speed and agility.

Stella leapt at the spectre and thrust her sword forward. The shadow leapt away.

'Don't let it touch you,' cried Red.

The shadow dodged another of Stella's attempts to cut it down and then reached out toward her with an obscure hand which extended well beyond the normal reach of a man. She managed to duck just in time and stepped back. Meanwhile Eben stepped forward to join the fight. The shadow halted and stared at him. The air was icy.

'What are you?' asked Eben, staring into the swirling darkness before him.

The shadowy creature gave a terrifying shriek and then retreated back into the woods to be further away from the light. Eben pursued it, and Stella followed. The creature was moving swiftly. Eben was struggling to keep up. He chased it down into another clearing which was far from the light of the bright star. The shadow stopped in the centre of the clearing and turned to face him.

'There will be no light,' it hissed in an icy and hollow voice that sent shivers through Eben's body.

Eben held up his sword and pointed the blade at the shadow. 'This is the Sword of Light,' he cried. 'We will show you light, and you will no longer hide in the shadows.'

The shadow shrieked and leapt at Eben. Eben stepped back several times as he dodged the shadowy arms as they violently reached for him. He then cut forward with perfect precision. The shadow hissed and screeched as the blade sliced through its body. The creature shuddered and writhed about. Eben watched as it evaporated before his eyes. The ghostly foe gave one final howl and then was gone.

Stella arrived a moment later. 'What happened?' she asked, looking about for the shadowy enemy. Red arrived a few seconds later.

'I put an end to it,' said Eben.

'Good,' said Red, clutching his aching arm.

'Are you okay?' asked Eben.

'It feels like a burn from ice. My arm feels a bit numb, but I think I'm all right,' replied Red, shaking his arm so that the blood could flow back into the limb.

They returned to the camp. Cassiel was sitting by the fire waiting for them. The bright star was gone, and the flames of the fire had rekindled. Cassiel was wrapped in a blanket and was recovering from his ordeal.

'Did you catch the creature?' he asked as they approached.

'Eben slew it,' said Stella.

'It was a shadow in the shape of a man,' said Red.

'This creature was something different, a monster I am not familiar with,' said Cassiel. 'It matched my power and then attempted to shroud my heart in a frozen darkness. I felt the cold night descending as I fell into an unsettling dream. I reached toward the only light I could see. At first the light was far away from me, a faint glimmer in the distance. Then the light came closer. All I could hear was the sound of sweet voices singing around me. I felt at peace. The bright light grew larger, and the icy shroud of darkness was lifted.'

'That's when you made the star appear,' said Red.

'I'm not sure where the star came from. It was certainly not created by any magic skill that I have. Perhaps the voices I heard came to our aid.'

'I don't know how we would have fought the creature without the light,' said Eben. Cassiel nodded in agreement.

As the night progressed they built up the fire until it was burning brightly and lighting up the entire clearing. They took turns to keep a vigilant watch until dawn.

CHAPTER SEVEN

The following day the four friends continued their journey. They were determined to reach the border of Irvaria as quickly as possible. They passed many small river settlements. The further they went north the more welcoming the people became. As dusk approached the river turned toward the west. In the distance they could see a line of small hills

'The Sunset Hills,' said Cassiel. 'Irvaria is beyond those hills.'

They marched onward with renewed energy and had almost reached the Sunset Hills as the night fell. They set up camp beside the river and rested well that night. Knowing that Irvaria was so close gave them a feeling of confidence.

After sunrise they made a move and within an hour came upon the hills. The Adira River wound its way through a shallow gorge. The river road was hewn into the hillsides and followed the path of the river. Almost instantly the land about became green and fertile. The grass was lush, and majestic golden elm trees filled the groves and hillsides.

After about half an hour of walking the company rounded a bend in the road. A hundred yards ahead the way widened significantly. They could see a stone watchtower built on the hillside adjacent to the river. Down from the watchtower was a stone landing where several boats were moored. The river road passed between the tower and the landing. The watchtower stood about seventy yards tall; at its height flew the red flag of Irvaria depicting the white dragon. Dozens of fully armoured Irvarian soldiers were gathered down by the river.

'This is one of the watchtowers of the Sunset Hills. There are many of them scattered along the border,' said Cassiel. They walked ahead toward the tower. The group of soldiers noticed them approaching and walked up from the riverbank.

'What is your business in the Kingdom of Irvaria?' asked the leader, a lean and tall man with a noble face and short auburn hair.

'I am Sir Red of Ortaria,' said Red proudly. 'We are on a mission to Faircastle to appear at the council by invitation of King Edric of Irvaria. This is my wife, Lady Stella, and my two friends, Eben and Cassiel.'

The soldiers murmured between themselves for a few moments. The captain stared up at them and seemed very surprised.

'We did not expect anyone to come this way. Vastoria is said to be impassable. They said you would likely go by sea to Everdon and come to Irvaria from the south. I'm surprised you managed to cross Vastoria.'

'I'm surprised too,' said Red with a smile. The captain nodded and smiled back at Red.

'My name is Commander Jon. These are the men of the Brigade of the Sunset Hills. I will give you horses and have an escort take you as far as Stonehaven. There you will be safe and can rest for the night. From Stonehaven you can take the road that follows the river to Faircastle.'

'Thank you for your assistance,' said Red.

'It's an honour to help you, Sir Red,' said Commander Jon.

Commander Jon led them to the watchtower. They were given Irvarian tea and biscuits as the four horses were being saddled and prepared for them. They sat around a small wooden table situated in the lower level of the watchtower.

'Did you encounter the Skatheans in Vastoria?' asked Commander Jon.

'Many of them,' replied Cassiel. 'The Desert Knights told us that the Skatheans rule Darancra and the south of Vastoria. They are preventing anyone from crossing the Deep Desert.'

'Yes, we have heard they control Darancra. Fortunately their days are at an end. Only recently an army left to liberate Darancra from their evil rule. The Skatheans arrived in Vastoria three years ago in the port city of Kavacas. They have since progressively moved north. It is interesting to me that the Desert Knights told you this. Did they assist you?'

'Yes, they sacrificed a lot to help us cross the desert,' said Eben.

'This news is surprising. We have not been sure about the allegiances of the Desert Knights. They have sent an envoy to the council, yet we have long thought they may have been working with the Skatheans.'

'No, you can be sure they are not in league with the Skatheans,' said Cassiel. 'Only days ago there was a battle at the Mooring of Gastrell. The Desert Knights fought bravely against the Skatheans. Many of them were killed that day.'

A moment later there was a knock at the door and a young soldier entered the small room. He was perhaps eighteen years old with curly brown hair and a determined look in his eyes.

'The horses are ready, Commander,' he declared.

'Good, well done. Sir Red, this is Charles. He and two others will lead you to Stonehaven. You should arrive there before nightfall. I wish you all the best for your remaining journey.'

'Thank you for your hospitality,' said Red, bowing to Commander Jon.

Commander Jon nodded and smiled warmly. He followed them out to their horses. The four horses were majestic creatures. Eben could see that Irvarian horses were indeed a noble breed, each of them in some way was similar to Swiftwing in stature; although Swiftwing was clearly a prince among horses. They mounted their horses and galloped away from the watchtower heading steadily westward.

**

The land about grew ever more beautiful the further they progressed. The treed hillsides and lush valleys were a picture of splendour. Small crystal clear streams poured down from the hills above and flowed into the Adira River. The river followed a wide gorge that wound its way through the Sunset Hills.

'I never expected Irvaria to be so beautiful,' said Red, his eyes surveying the magnificent landscape.

'This is why the Ecorian Emperors of old chose Irvaria as their home,' said Charles, a glimmer of pride in his eyes.

As the day unfolded they came to the far side of the hills and descended toward the lowlands which were also incredibly beautiful. The road passed through long meadows full of colourful spring flowers. Later in the day the road led them back to the Adira River.

'Soon we shall arrive at Stonehaven,' said Charles.

They continued along the river road for another hour. In the distance they could see a solitary hill to the south of the river. They entered a shallow dale surrounded by vineyards. The road led them around the base of the hill. As they rounded the western side they could see a very large and old stone house; it looked to be almost a part of the hillside. The grey stone walls were covered in moss and ivy and a gabled roof rose high above the many arched windows. A short wall surrounded the house, and an open gate led them into a stunningly beautiful rose garden within the wall.

An old man stepped down from the threshold. He wore a red woollen overcoat, and his long grey beard descended all the way down to his belly. His aged face showed a certain degree of gentleness. He walked toward them slowly and warmly smiled as he approached.

'My name is Sir Norman of the Sunset Hills. I am the Guardian of Stonehaven.'

'I introduce to you Sir Red of Ortaria, Lady Stella his wife, and his two servants. They are guests of King Edric and on a journey to Faircastle for the council,' said Charles. Eben and Cassiel smiled across at each other at the mention of being Red's servants.

'You are most welcome here at Stonehaven,' said Sir Norman. 'Please, come down from your horses. I will have the house cook prepare a feast to honour your arrival.'

'I must say what a beautiful garden you have,' said Stella as she dismounted.

'Thank you, Lady Stella. For centuries these gardens have been kept mostly the same as they are now. Stonehaven is the furthest westerly abode of the Irvarian Royal Family; a stopover for royalty that take the journey into the Eastern Lands. It is rare that we have any of the royal family staying with us these days; however, we must always keep the gardens and house ready. Mostly we serve as a guesthouse for noble travellers and knights passing this way along the river road.'

'Are there any soldiers stationed here?' asked Red as they tied the horses to a water trough.

'Only the house guard. We have six guardsmen who protect us. Of course they rarely see any action. The Brigades of the Sunset Hills keep anything wicked from crossing into Irvaria. Please, come inside. I will show you the house.'

Sir Norman led them through the front door. They were immediately amazed by the lavish surroundings. The wooden floors were polished to shine, the whitewashed stone walls were adorned with magnificent paintings, and wonderful crystal chandeliers hung from the high ceilings above. A long hallway led them down to a large open room with a sitting area beside a burning open fireplace. On either side of the fireplace were two large bookcases that stood wide and tall, reaching up toward the ceiling above. Thousands of leather bound books adorned the shelves. Cassiel gazed on the books with wonder.

'You are welcome to read any book you desire,' said Sir Norman, having spotted Cassiel's interest.

'This is only a small part of the royal collection. It is rather unfortunate that they are rarely read. Occasionally I read a little, but mostly they are left as they are, apart from the regular dusting they receive.'

'Thank you,' said Cassiel as he walked over and browsed the shelves.

'Please, Sir Red, consider Stonehaven as you would your own home. I will have your rooms prepared and inform the house staff of your arrival. I expect that you will be leaving in the morning for Faircastle. The journey is a three day ride, or five days on a barge, but I dare say that you should ride because the first day of summer is only five days from now, and I'm sure you would prefer to be early for the council.'

'Of course,' said Red. 'Thank you for your kind hospitality.'

'It's a pleasure,' said Sir Norman warmly. 'I must say you are the first Ortarian Knight I have ever met. I'm very glad to have you as my guests.'

With this Sir Norman left the room. They sat down on the large comfortable chairs.

'I think I like the Sunset Hills,' said Red, smiling at Stella. 'Perhaps it would be a good place to raise our children.'

'We'll see Red,' answered Stella, smiling back at her husband.

'Look at this,' interrupted Cassiel as he took an old leather bound book from the bookcase. 'Rare Creatures of the Forgotten Age – by Baron Monte of the Endora Mountains.' Cassiel gently opened the old book and stared down at the pages with a glow of excitement in his eyes. He turned the pages lightly and then suddenly gasped.

'Here it is! Ghouls! Creatures of darkness brought to Veredor by the Prince of Shadows in the Forgotten Age. Ghouls are servants of the Prince of Shadows. They are related to draugs and are said to have a similar origin. They were brought through the Cosmic Gate in small numbers. Ghouls were used as the personal guardians of the Prince of Shadows. They can pass directly through solid objects, move with great speed through the night, and they retreat underground during the day. All the ghouls were slain by the Astarian Fiora in the Battle of Shidon. No sightings of them were ever documented after the end of the Forgotten Age.'

'No sightings. That means we are the first to see one in ages,' said Red.

'It would seem so,' said Cassiel. 'This is clear evidence that the Prince of Shadows has returned and the Cosmic Gate has been reopened. If ghouls are his personal guardians then the one we fought must have been sent by him.'

'So the evil Master is the Prince of Shadows as we suspected,' said Eben grimly.

'It makes perfect sense. He must have planned to establish himself in the north where the Skatheans and Northern Sorcerers are based.'

Cassiel went back to the bookcase and took another large leather bound book. '- The Account of the Forgotten Age - By Holmia the Mystic.' He opened the book and flipped through a few pages. 'Recognise this,' he said as he turned the book toward them.' A clear illustration of the Sword of Light was sketched on the page.

Cassiel read from the book. 'The Sword of Light, one of the three swords of the Astarian people. The Sword of Light belonged to the Astarian Fiora. The Sword of Light was used to protect Veredor in the first wars of the Forgotten Age. The Sword of Light was later wielded by the Astarian Fiora against the Prince of Shadows in the Battle of Shidon. Fiora vanquished the Prince of Shadows and cast the evil Astarian into the darkness beyond Veredor. Fiora sealed the Cosmic Gate against his return. The Sword of Light is the only weapon powerful enough to match the power of the Sword of Darkness. The Sword of Light stands as a sign of hope for the people of Veredor.'

'Is there a Sword of Darkness too?' asked Red.

'Of course there's a Sword of Darkness, and there is also a third Astarian sword called the Sword of Midlight. Can you see why this is significant? The Prince of Shadows wants to take the Sword of Light from Eben because the sword was used against him successfully in the Forgotten Age. He wants to remove the one weapon that can stop him. That's why Azagord said he wanted to cast the sword through the Cosmic Gate, because if he can remove the Sword of Light from Veredor there would be no weapon powerful enough to be used against him.'

They looked across at Eben. Eben felt his heart thumping in his chest. The idea that he held the only weapon that could stop the Prince of Shadows conquering Veredor was overwhelming. A silence fell upon the company for a few moments.

'Don't worry, Eben. Whatever happens you can be sure we will stand by your side,' said Stella kindly.

Suddenly Sir Norman entered the room. 'I have informed the cook to prepare a roast dinner, and my butler has informed the house staff to prepare your rooms. For the next hour I suggest you enjoy the books and the gardens around Stonehaven. I will send someone to find you when dinner is served.'

'Thank you. You have made us feel very welcome,' said Red.

'It is an honour.' With this Sir Norman left the room. They turned to face Eben again.

'Of course we will stand by you no matter what happens,' repeated Stella. 'We're all in this together until the end.'

Red and Cassiel both nodded. Eben felt his confidence return at knowing his loyal friends genuinely cared about him. He knew they would be there by his side no matter how events eventually turned out.

**

Sir Norman served up a mighty feast in the grand dining room of Stonehaven as he had promised. Roast chicken, potatoes, pumpkin, peas, gravy, and the finest red wine Eben had ever tasted.

'This is an excellent wine,' said Cassiel.

Sir Norman smiled and a glimmer of pride could be seen in his eyes. 'Stonehaven's wine is famous throughout Veredor. We have even sent barrels as far as Scaldonia. Irvarians have always loved wine; winemaking is a highly regarded craft in our country, we take it very seriously.'

They continued with the meal and the house staff continued to bring dish after dish and finished with a lavish date pudding covered in fresh cream and strawberries. They stared wide eyed with delight.

'You will find the road to Faircastle is safe and very pleasant. It will take you through the lowlands and several forests. The road will then return to follow the Adira River before you arrive at Faircastle.'

'Is Faircastle as magnificent as they say?' asked Cassiel.

'Indeed it is. The castle is said to be the most marvellous in Veredor. I'm sure when you come to see it you will agree. Faircastle was built by Jerial the Just and the Ecorian Emperors who followed him. Now Faircastle is the home of King Edric, who of course is a direct descendent of the Irvarian Ecorian Arbiter.'

'We look forward to meeting your king,' said Eben.

'I am sure you will be impressed by him,' said Sir Norman. 'King Edric is dearly loved by his people.'

After dinner they were shown to their charming rooms on the upper floor. They rested and slept peacefully under the roof of Stonehaven.

CHAPTER EIGHT

The following morning they gathered in the front garden of Stonehaven. The house servants had prepared their horses and brought them to the front gate.

'It has been a most pleasant stay,' said Red, bowing to Sir Norman.

'Please come again if you pass this way on your journey home. You, Lady Stella, and your friends are always welcome to lodge at Stonehaven.'

'It's been an honour; thanks again,' said Red, climbing up on his horse. They all mounted their horses and prepared to leave. Sir Norman waved them goodbye as they rode through the front gate and turned their horses westward. The day was bright and a gentle breeze blew from the east. They rode quickly away from Stonehaven.

For several hours the company kept a swift pace. The land about was simply splendid, a picture of enchanting beauty. Spring flowers filled meadows of lush green grass and colourful butterflies could be seen flying all about. Occasionally the road would take them through golden elm forests, but always within a few minutes the forests would clear and they would once again come upon beautiful meadows in full bloom.

'Irvaria is even more beautiful than the stories make it out to be,' said Eben.

'Superb,' said Cassiel.

As the afternoon advanced they entered a forest and left the grasslands behind. The forest was also beautiful and mostly populated with majestic elm trees. Gentle sunlight filtered down from the canopy above. The road was well maintained and small arched bridges crossed many crystal clear streams throughout the forest. As night approached they stopped in a forest glade beside the road and set up camp.

'I don't think I'll ever want to leave this kingdom,' said Red as he gathered some wood at the edge of the glade.

'I feel the same. There is a sense of peace and joy throughout this land,' said Cassiel.

The four of them sat around the campfire and enjoyed the peaceful evening.

**

The next day they rode out and came back upon the river. Within an hour of setting out they found themselves approaching a small settlement. The village was mostly made up of humble stone houses and a few larger farmhouses dotted the fields between the river and the forest. A large wooden sign read: Welcome to Easthome.

'Look at that; they actually have a sign welcoming people to their village,' said Red, smiling as they passed by.

As they rode through the village the village folk walked up from the riverbank to greet them. The atmosphere was very welcoming and the locals invited them to stop for tea.

'We appreciate your invitation, but unfortunately we cannot stop. We are urgently on our way to Faircastle,' said Cassiel.

The villagers followed them all the way to the edge of the village and waved them farewell and continued to watch until they were out of sight.

'The people in Irvaria are so friendly,' said Stella.

'It makes me realise how suspicious everyone is in Ortaria and Silvor,' said Red. 'No one at home would ever invite a stranger in for tea and biscuits.'

'They would in Clemensdale where I come from,' said Eben, remembering the kind-hearted people of his home village. For a moment he felt a pang of nostalgia. At heart he knew he was a simple villager. No one in Clemensdale cared much for what happened beyond the valley. They were simple folk with happy lives. He missed his home and looked forward to the day that he could return.

**

For two days they rode onward. The river road took them northwest and they passed through many beautiful villages along the way. Most of the villages were similar to Easthome.

On the morning of the fourth day from Stonehaven they came out of the forest into cleared farmland. As they progressed the land became exceptionally beautiful and undulating. The road followed the river as it wound its way through various valleys and shallow gorges. Often they would pass lovely farmhouses, and regularly they saw shepherds with flocks of sheep on the slopes of surrounding hills. The further they went the more frequently they saw barges, boats, and smaller canoes on the river.

In the mid-afternoon the road turned away from the river and led them up along a lengthy final ridge. The far side of the ridge descended downward to an emerald green plain below. From the height of the ridge they could see far into the distance.

They caught sight of a majestic and magnificent castle about seven miles away across the plain. The castle was built on a solitary hill with incredibly high walls. Twelve soaring towers rose at intervals along the outer wall. Irvarian flags flew at the height of each tower. In the centre of the city stood an enormous palace, rising high above the level of the outer wall, with its own seven towers ascending a great distance into the sky above. The Adira River curved around the base of the city on the northern side. They could see many villages and towns outside the walls. It was difficult to make out the details from the ridge, but they were all sure the castle was far greater than any they had seen before.

'There it is, Faircastle! The pride of the Aecorisians,' said Cassiel, wonder lighting up his face.

'Is it really so big, or are my eyes playing tricks on me?' asked Red.

'Faircastle is simply amazing,' answered Cassiel. 'The outer walls are at least two hundred yards in height. The Palace is a city in itself. At the pinnacle of the palace is the Ecorian Hall. Within the hall is the Sapphire Throne of the Ecorian Emperor, a throne made completely of blue sapphires, a treasure beyond all treasures. Faircastle is the heart of Veredor.'

There was a long silence as they stared into the distance.

'Let's go closer,' said Eben. He started moving his horse quickly down the slope. The others followed him, and before long they were galloping across the plain with their eyes fixed on the high walls of Faircastle. After little more than half an hour they were approaching the towering outer wall. They turned toward the southern side where they could see a great gate. Villages were dotted all about on the plain surrounding the enormous castle. They rode on toward the great arched gateway. Seven armoured guards with long spears stood on either side of the gate.

As they approached they slowed their horses to a trot. Ahead of them stood a figure in a long green robe waiting just outside the gate.

'Meara,' cried Cassiel with delight, being the first to recognise her.

'Welcome to Faircastle,' said Meara as they rode closer. 'I am so happy that you arrived safely. Baftel told me you were drawing near, and I thought I would come to greet you at the gate. We heard news from the border when you entered Irvaria.' They all embraced her happily. 'I was very worried when I learned that you had decided to cross the deserts. I knew you weren't aware the Skatheans had moved north through Vastoria. I feared that you would be walking into a trap. Thankfully you have arrived safely and just in time for the council.'

'We have had quite an adventure,' said Cassiel.

'I think you will find the adventure is just beginning. ' said Meara. 'Please, follow me. I will take you to the palace where all the guests of the council are staying. We have much to discuss.'

They dismounted and led their horses through the great arched gateway. The main street led in a straight line up a gradual rise to the majestic palace at the top of the hill. They were amazed by the beauty of the city. They passed hundreds of splendid houses as they ascended the gentle rise. Street lanterns and flower beds lined the way, and all the people of Faircastle seemed joyful. The Irvarians obviously took great pride in making things look beautiful.

In wonder and silence they ascended the gentle hill and arrived at a large and almost perfectly flat square at the top. There were many people in the square; groups of men and women were talking, and various street performers played pleasant music. Eben couldn't help but feel happy. The palace towered into the sky above. An enormous golden arched door stood at the entrance; thousands of carvings were etched into its surface.

'The Ecorian Gate,' said Cassiel. 'The engravings tell the story of the rise of the Ecorian Empire. We are blessed to have this opportunity to see it.'

They led their horses across the square to the gate. Three guardsmen in shining armour stood on either side of the arched entrance. The gate started to open and the guardsmen moved aside. The guardsmen at the gate took their horses. They then stepped forward into the palace.

Directly before them was a magnificent hall lined with white marble pillars that rose up at least eighty yards to the ceiling above. The polished marble tiles of the floor were a mixture of blue and white. At the far side stood a large obelisk that was painted purple with a depiction of a white unicorn. Three well-dressed men approached from the far side of the hall, each with a sword at his side. One was much older with greying hair and a friendly open face. The two younger men followed closely behind.

'Greetings, Sir Red, Lady Stella, Eben, and Cassiel. My name is Earl Evander; these young men are my sons: Gelson and Tom. We have been sent to welcome you to Faircastle and make sure you are comfortable and aware of the proceedings of the council. My sons will show you to the guest chambers on the upper levels. If you require anything you can ask any of the palace staff to bring a message to me and I will see to it. The council will commence at noon the day after tomorrow. We are very glad you arrived safely.'

Gelson and Tom looked like identical twins. They were both conventionally handsome with light blond hair and bright blue eyes.

'We are pleased to meet you, Earl Evander,' said Red. 'It has been a long journey across Vastoria. Thank you for your welcome. Will we meet King Edric soon?'

'Yes, you will. At the moment King Edric is very busy preparing for the council; this is the reason why he has sent me to greet you. You are the last of the envoys to arrive. Thus far we have received envoys from Dravania, Iarthar, the Tabarian Knights, Everdon, the Desert Knights, Ateria, The Isles of Dawn, Scaldonia, the Takalian Knights, the Fire Order, the Fiorian Knights, and of course Meara, Arlen, and Baftel from the Irilian Order. Unfortunately we heard word that the Silvorian envoy's ship was destroyed by the Skatheans in the Southern Sea.'

Red looked horrified at hearing that his own countrymen had been killed by the enemy.

'Please, follow my sons to your chambers,' said Earl Evander. The Earl then bowed and walked away leaving his two sons to show them to their rooms.

The young men led them across to the far side of the hall. They entered an adjacent corridor that took them into a large room with a perfectly square wooden door.

'The top levels of the palace are so high that the wise men of our city had to devise a way for us to reach the upper levels without having to climb thousands of steps,' said Gelson as he opened the large door. Before them were two seats suspended in mid-air by ropes that were tied to a chain above. On their right was a large lever beside a bell which was hanging from an oversized hook. Eben stepped into the room and looked up to see a long shaft that ascended directly upward for hundreds of feet.

'Please, Eben, take a seat,' said Tom. Eben sat in one of the seats and Cassiel sat in the one beside him. 'This will take you directly to the Ecorian Hall.'

'How does it work?' asked Cassiel, amazed by the ingenuity.

'I am really not sure,' answered Gelson, shaking his head slightly. 'I think it's something to do with springs and tension. Whatever you do don't let go. When you reach the top and are safely off simply ring the bell and pull the lever to send the seats back down.'

Gelson proceeded to ring the bell loudly, and for about five seconds nothing happened. Then suddenly there was a heave and a moment later they were both ascending quickly. After about a minute they arrived at the top of the shaft; a stone landing allowed them to disembark.

'These Irvarians are amazing folk,' said Cassiel, a look of wonder in his eyes. 'I always thought the Zyranians were the craftiest people in Veredor. I'm starting to have doubts.'

They disembarked and rang the bell. Cassiel pulled the lever and the chairs quickly descended. They then opened the door before them. They were amazed by the sight. The upper hall was not as large as the lower entrance hall but instantly struck them with its outstanding beauty. The pillars were pure white marble with intricate carvings and rose up to the ceiling above which was painted blue like the sky. The floor was covered with large marble tiles that formed the picture of a white unicorn in flight. Great stained glass windows lined either side of the wall; each window showed scenes of the ancient history of Veredor. By far the most astonishing sight before their eyes was the large Sapphire Throne of the Ecorian Empire. The throne was made entirely of swirling crystal blue sapphire. It seemed to glow; the light from the windows above reflected in a manner that made the sapphire glisten. Standing on either side of the throne were five fully armoured guardsmen.

'Magnificent,' whispered Cassiel in awe. 'The throne has remained empty for many ages.' He walked forward toward the throne and Eben followed.

'Why doesn't King Edric take it as his own throne? asked Eben.

'He wouldn't dare. When the Ecorian Arbiters divided the Ecorian Empire they agreed that no man would ever sit on the Sapphire Throne. Such an action would cause a war. It would mean a king was declaring himself to be the new emperor and greater than all the other kings in Veredor. Only an Ecorian can sit on the throne.'

Eben followed Cassiel across the marble floor. As they approached two of the guardsmen stepped forward to block their way.

'No closer!' commanded a guardsman firmly. They stopped in their tracks.

'We were just looking and would not dare...,' said Cassiel.

'Look, but come no closer. Our duty is to protect the Sapphire Throne. By order of King Edric no man can come within twenty feet.'

They stared for a while at the throne and then suddenly heard footsteps coming up behind them.

'Are you looking for somewhere to sit?' asked Meara, smiling at Eben. She then turned and looked across at Cassiel.

'The throne is even more magnificent than in my dreams,' said Cassiel. Meara nodded in agreement and glanced around the hall.

'The Ecorians were exceptional people. They united the people of Veredor in a way that no one has ever repeated.'

Moments later Gelson and Red walked over from the shaft and not long after Tom followed.

'Let us take you to your chambers,' said Gelson. 'All the guests of the council are staying on the level below. Please follow us.'

Gelson and Tom led them back across the hall and down a stairwell that led them to a wide corridor on the level below the Ecorian Hall. Beautiful paintings, sculptures, and freshly cut flowers were placed all along the way. They followed the corridor for about fifty yards and then took a turn to the right, descending a short stairwell that opened up into another corridor. On the right side of the corridor were several short arched windows and a view outward across the city below; a door led out to the stone balcony. Along the left wall were two doors.

'These are your chambers. The first rooms are for you, Sir Red and Lady Stella,' said Gelson.

'Lord Eben, the second door leads to your rooms. Your chambers, Lord Cassiel, are on the far side of the palace where the Irilians are residing. Each room has a bell beside the door. If you ring the bell the palace staff will come to your assistance. You can ask the palace staff to find us if you require anything that they cannot provide. Everything you require will be provided. The council will be held at noon the day after tomorrow in the Ecorian Hall. We hope you enjoy your time here in the palace.' Gelson and Tom bowed before leaving.

'You will find the chambers are comfortable indeed,' said Meara. 'You should all get some rest. Tonight we will have dinner together with Baftel in my chambers. The palace staff can take you to my chambers at sunset. We have a lot to talk about.'

With this Meara turned and left with Cassiel. Eben entered his lavish and luxurious chamber. He came firstly into a large carpeted sitting room with cushioned chairs and couches, beautiful paintings on the walls, a desk by a window, and a round wooden table with four chairs. An archway led him into a second room where he found a large bed that took up almost the entire room. A doorway led out to a small stone balcony. He stepped out onto the balcony and looked down at the city below and out at the picturesque land; it was a beautiful sight to behold. He smiled.

CHAPTER NINE

Eben rested for an hour and felt he could finally relax. As the day neared its end he changed out of his worn dirty clothes. He chose a loose fitting white shirt and dark trousers. The house staff also brought him new leather boots of the highest quality. He attached his sword to his belt and looked in the mirror. He was feeling completely refreshed.

When the day was nearing its end he rang the bell at the door. Within a minute a very short and a man with curly red hair and bright blue eyes arrived at his door.

'How can I help you, Sir?' he asked, a large and friendly smile crossing his face.

'I wish to be taken to the Irilian Meara's chambers.'

'Certainly, Sir,' replied the man.

Eben followed the man as he made his way down the corridor and up the stone steps. He then opened another door which revealed a thin corridor that cut through the centre of the palace and was lit only by lantern light.

'This is the short cut, Sir. Otherwise you have to follow the outer corridors.'

Eben followed him along the long corridor. They arrived at the opposite door within two minutes. The man opened the door and turned left. On their right side were arched windows, which revealed a wide view from the far side of the palace. They continued a little way and then followed a flight of steps downward. The steps curved toward the left. There were three doors spaced about thirty feet apart.

'The second door is the one you seek, Sir.'

'Thank you,' said Eben appreciatively.

'Most welcome, Sir,' said the man as he turned to leave.

Eben approached Meara's door and knocked three times. Moments later the door opened, and Red looked out at him.

'Eben, you must see the sunset,' he said excitedly. Eben followed Red into Meara's rooms and could instantly see the blazing red sun shining through the large west facing windows. Everyone in the room watched in silence for several minutes as the sun set over the horizon, leaving a subtle blue twilight sky.

'Even the sun shines more beautifully in Irvaria,' said Meara, after the sun had fallen below the horizon. Eben looked around the room and saw Baftel sitting at the table with a man he didn't recognise.

'This is the Irilian Arlen,' said Meara, indicating toward the man. Arlen was an old man with high cheekbones and an overly big nose. His hair was very long and silvery grey, and he also had a long silver beard. His dark eyes had a look of deep attentiveness. 'Arlen, this is Eben, Champion of Ortaria.'

'I am most pleased to meet you. I have heard much about you,' said Arlen as he stood up to shake Eben's hand.

'I'm pleased to meet you too,' said Eben.

'It is good to hear your voice again, Eben,' said Baftel with a smile.

'I'm glad to see you again, Baftel,' Eben walked over and hugged his old friend.

'Please take a seat, Eben,' said Meara as she took a bottle of wine from a shelf beside the table. 'This is one of the finest wines in Irvaria, grown in the Springs of Adira in the foothills of the Great Mountains. She poured them each a glass. 'I can't express how happy I am to have you arrive unharmed. I have been deeply concerned for your safety.'

'We almost didn't make it. We have passed through many trials on our way here from Ancora,' said Cassiel.

'Yes, the road you chose was dangerous, but perhaps it may have been just as dangerous to come by sea. I can only hope the council yields the benefits that we hope it will. There is much history between the kingdoms and orders that are attending.'

'Have you heard anything we should know?' asked Cassiel.

'There are some things I would like to inform you about. The council was called by King Edric at the request of the Fiorian Acartor. Acartor has been staying in Faircastle since he escaped the Dungeons of Zarkanor in Kaznor where the evil Master had imprisoned him for many years. You should also know that the situation in many kingdoms has become desperate. The Kingdoms of Coran and the Kingdom of Glenia in the Far West have fallen into enemy hands. Iarthar and Dravania are still holding their borders, but the Far Western Lands are overrun with muckrons. Word also came several days ago that Orelin is under siege, and an army of muckrons have occupied the Iron Gate Pass. King Ignis has sent an army to Galdir to protect Ortaria from invasion; it is not known how many enemies he is facing. Acartor has personally met the one who is known as the Master, and he knows much about the plans of our enemy. He has not revealed much yet; however, I expect he will reveal everything he knows at the council.'

'Do you think this evil Master is the Prince of Shadows? We have come to believe he most likely is,' said Cassiel.

'I do not know. I believe the Fiorian Acartor will reveal his true nature.'

'Can the Irvarians send an army to help King Ignis?' asked Red.

'I can assure you the Tabarian Knights and monarchs in the Far West will also be requesting reinforcements from Irvaria and Everdon,' said Meara gravely. 'I doubt that any can be sent. We have become aware of two hundred enemy ships sailing around the Cape of Ateria. They are carrying a large army of muckrons, at least forty thousand, with one purpose and one purpose only: to invade Everdon and Irvaria. Baftel has seen the fleet with his powers. King Edric is also aware of this impending threat. It is unlikely that King Edric will send troops to a foreign land if he faces such a threat at home.'

'This is very disturbing news,' said Cassiel.

'There is always hope,' replied Meara with a confident smile.

'We believe the Master in the north has made a fundamental mistake. He has sent the greater part of his army to attack Irvaria for one reason. I believe that reason is to capture the Sword of Light.' The entire company turned to look at Eben.

'Perhaps he will not attack if the sword is not in Irvaria,' suggested Eben.

'It is unlikely that our enemy knows the Sword of Light is in Irvaria. The sword does not reveal itself to anyone, and no seer can unveil its location. The most crucial information we have gained is that the Master is coming south with the fleet. We may have a chance to defeat him once and for all.' Meara stared directly at Eben. 'Someone will have to face this evil Master eventually, and you, Eben, are the greatest swordsman I have ever seen. I believe this task may be your destiny.'

Eben nodded and considered the situation. He remembered back to when he was fighting the lindworm in Riverside and all the other battles. Perhaps Meara was right. Perhaps it was his destiny.

'No one outside this room knows that you carry the Sword of Light,' said Meara as she looked around the table at the whole company. 'We should not tell anyone at the council that Eben possesses the sword until such a time is required. We still don't know what we will learn from the other envoys. Keep the Sword of Light with you at all times. There are many people here who would risk much to have such a weapon.'

**

Eben returned to his rooms and tried to sleep. He felt restless and couldn't stop thinking of the endless possibilities. He finally fell asleep late in the night and slept until late the following morning when he heard someone knocking loudly on his door. He stumbled out of bed and quickly clothed himself. Again someone knocked heavily. He went to the door and unlatched the lock. Stella and Red stood outside and stepped in.

'It's nearly noon, Eben. Don't you want to explore Faircastle?' asked Red as he walked over to the windows to take in the view. 'We had breakfast already. The palace chef is a true master. You can order anything you feel like,' said Red, turning back to look at Eben with a happy smile.

'Perhaps you can order some fried eggs and toasted bread,' said Stella as she took a seat at the table.

'No, I'm not really hungry,' said Eben as he poured himself a cup of water.

'We've decided to stay here in Faircastle after the war,' said Red. Eben smiled, knowing that Red had said the same about so many places before. 'Irvaria is perfect. The land is beautiful and the people are the most noble and decent we have ever met.' Eben could see Red and Stella were in perfect agreement.

'I can understand why you would want to live here; there's no other place like Irvaria. Let's hope that we win the war. If the evil Master is coming with forty thousand muckrons I think we are going to have a fight on our hands.'

'I'm sure we can win. We won in Scaldonia and Ortaria. We know how to fight muckrons, and we can repeat what we've done before,' said Red decisively.

'I hope you're right,' said Eben.

For the remainder of the day they explored the palace and the city within the wall. Faircastle was a maze of lovely streets and laneways. Each turn presented a pleasant picture. The greatest care had been taken by the townsfolk to keep their city clean and presentable. Probably the most striking feature of the city was the pursuit of architectural excellence. In the evening they returned to the palace. They met with Cassiel and sat in his chambers and watched the sunset.

'Tomorrow will be an important day for us,' said Cassiel.

'I only hope that we can convince the Irvarians to send an army to help King Ignis,' said Stella.

'I'm sure they will seek to do what is best for everyone,' said Cassiel. 'These Irvarians are a proud and brave people. They have a natural sense of honour. I believe they will send help to King Ignis if they are able to.'

'And we will finally meet the Fiorian Knights,' said Eben gladly.

'Many of our questions will be answered tomorrow. Let's hope the answers we receive bring us hope,' said Cassiel.

**

Eben woke early in the morning of the following day. He prepared himself for the council. After breakfast he went to the window and drew the Sword of Light from its scabbard. The morning light reflected off the blade.

'Today we'll see where the journey is going to take us,' he said to himself.

He sat on a cushioned chair and placed the sword on his lap. For a long time he stared out the window into the distance. Many thoughts and questions passed through his mind. He knew his time was coming. If anyone had any knowledge of what happened to his mother and father they would surely be at the council. He thought that if his mother was the leader of the Fiorians they would surely know what happened to her. A feeling of anticipation swirled in his chest.

After some time the silence was broken by a sharp knock at the door. He sheathed his sword and walked to the door, unlatching the lock. The door opened and Cassiel walked into his room.

'It is almost time. How do you feel?' he asked, clapping Eben firmly on the shoulder as he walked by.

'I feel fine.'

'I will be seated with the Irilians on the far side of the table from you. King Edric has arranged all the people from the west to sit on the western side of the table and those from the east on the eastern side. Because I am now an Irilian apprentice I have been placed to sit with the Irilian Order. You will be seated with Red and Stella near the Scaldonians and Dawnians.' Cassiel sat down at the table and took and apple from the fruit bowl.

'I have a feeling we are about to see into the unknown,' said Eben.

'I don't doubt it,' said Cassiel. 'Remember what Stella said: we're all in this together. We have travelled a long road. We shall stand by each other until the end.'

CHAPTER TEN

Red, Stella, and Eben entered the Ecorian hall. A large round and polished wooden table had been placed in the centre of the hall. Dozens of beautifully carved wooden chairs surrounded the table, and all but one chair was empty. Seated at the head of the table was an older man with striking features. He had high cheek bones, dark eyes, auburn coloured hair, and a neatly trimmed beard. He was the only person in the hall; all the guards were gone. He stood up as they entered.

'I told you we shouldn't be early,' whispered Stella, realising they were the first to arrive.

'Welcome to the Hall of the Ecorians,' said the old man in a deep and noble voice. 'I am King Edric of Irvaria.'

Eben and Stella followed Red across the marble floor toward the table.

'It is an honour to meet you, King Edric,' said Red, bowing politely. 'I am Sir Redding of Ortaria, this is my wife, Lady Stella, and this is Eben, the Champion of Ortaria.'

'I am pleased to have you as guests in my kingdom,' said King Edric. 'Please take your seats and make yourself comfortable.' King Edric indicated towards the chairs to his left. Red led them over and they sat down.

'I trust your stay thus far has been to your liking,' said King Edric as he sat back down.

'Yes, Your Majesty. We have been amazed by the beauty of your kingdom,' answered Red. 'We were even talking about the possibility of settling in Irvaria after the war.'

King Edric smiled and nodded. 'I'm sure we can accommodate such a possibility.'

'Thank you,' said Red.

Suddenly a pair of men entered the hall. Eben watched as they approached. They were both rugged looking men and dressed in dark armour with broadswords fastened to their sides. They both had long dark hair and deeply weathered faces. Both of them carried themselves confidently.

'Welcome to the Hall of the Ecorians,' repeated King Edric. 'I am King Edric of Irvaria.'

'I am Sir Tierran and this is Sir Cian. We are Tabarian Knights.' The two knights bowed low, and King Edric directed them to their seats. As he did so another group of envoys entered from the back of the hall and the process repeated itself until all but two of the chairs were taken, which were on the left and right side of King Edric.

Finally a young woman followed by an older woman entered the hall. They proceeded to take the last two seats beside King Edric. Eben, along with several others sitting at the table, was instantly transfixed by the beauty of the younger woman. She was surely the most beautiful woman in Veredor. Her radiant eyes were the colour of the sea, and her face was the image of perfection. Her long golden brown hair could only be compared with the finest silk. She held herself gracefully. Eben couldn't take his eyes off her. She glanced across at him and gave the slightest smile. Eben's trancelike stare was suddenly interrupted by King Edric.

'I must express my gratitude that you have all journeyed so far to be at this council. I know you have faced many dangers to be here. I thank you for risking your lives so we can work together against our common enemy. Firstly, let me introduce to you my wife, Queen Sera, and my daughter and heir, Princess Apherah. We welcome you to Faircastle and trust your stay here has been pleasant. Secondly, as your host, I will introduce everyone present.'

Queen Sera was an old and dignified woman who had maintained much of the beauty of her youth. She had slightly greying dark hair and deep green eyes. Princess Apherah glanced at Eben again, and he looked away, not wanting to seem rude.

'This council was called at the request of the Fiorian Acartor.'

On the far side of the table a man clothed in a long brown cloak stood up. His hair was sandy blond, and his eyes were bright blue; he looked to be about forty years old and was clean shaven. Eben found it very difficult to read his expression. It was almost like a shroud was covering his eyes or that he had learned to protect himself from other people reading his expressions. He stood up and looked down at them.

'I am the Fiorian Acartor. I am pleased to introduce the leader of the Fiorian Order, the Fiorian Chiara, Gatekeeper of Emeril.' The woman beside Acartor stood up and bowed. She appeared slightly older than Acartor. Her hair was bright red, the colour of fire, and her eyes were emerald green. She had a sense of gentle wisdom about her. Eben at once felt he could trust her simply by looking at her. 'I would also like to introduce to you Sir Ronan.' Sir Ronan was a short man with a bald head, big nose, and a jolly look. He didn't look like a knight at all.

'Thank you for the introductions, Sir Acartor,' said King Edric. 'I will now continue to introduce everyone. To my right are seated the Irilians Meara, Arlen, Baftel, and Cassiel. Beside them are Sir Tieran and Sir Cian of the Tabarian Knights. Further along are Prince Fergal of Dravania and Duke Curran of Iarthar.' Prince Fergal was a stocky redheaded man with fair skin and a stern look in his eyes. Duke Curran was a handsome man with dark hair and a sallow complexion. Eben caught him glancing at Princess Apherah. It was clear that the Duke was also awestruck by her beauty.

'I introduce you to Sir Artur of the Takalian Knights.' Sir Artur was a young man and appeared to be very calm and composed. His hair was dark and his skin pale. 'Beside Sir Artur is seated Mostyn of the Fire Order.' Mostyn was a short man with knotted dark hair to his shoulders and a deep look of concentration in his dark and sunken eyes. His beard was shaggy and tangled. He was wearing a dusty brown leather cloak and looked like a homeless vagrant.

'Beside Mostyn are seated Sir Acel and Sir Leron of the Desert Knights.' They both had their faces covered by black metal masks and were clothed in the manner of the Desert Knights. 'To the right of Sir Leron are seated Eben, Champion of Ortaria, Sir Red, and Lady Stella of Ortaria. Beside Lady Stella is King Lenard of Everdon.' King Lenard was a thin and tall man with dark hair and a sickly complexion. He was young, perhaps only in his mid-twenties, and he was adorned in some of the finest silk clothing Eben had ever seen, but he was certainly not a good looking man by anyone's summation. He had an awkward expression fixed constantly to his face, as if he was in a constant state of discomfort.

'Beside King Lenard is seated Prince Armida of Ateria.' Prince Armida was a sharp looking man with curly black hair. The Prince was considering each person as King Edric introduced the council. 'Beside Prince Armida of Ateria are seated Duke

Ettore and Duchess Cornelia of the Isles of Dawn.'
Both the Duke and Duchess were very old; they
looked to be scholars rather than warriors. 'And
finally, beside Queen Sera is seated Sir Aksel of
Scaldonia.' Sir Aksel was a man of great stature
and had strong features, a weathered face, and
long blond hair. He was wearing the dark rough
armour of the Scaldonian Knights.

'You are all aware of the evil that is growing in
Veredor, and many of you have already expressed
to me the dire circumstances that you face in
your homelands,' said King Edric. 'I believe if we
work together, like in the ancient days of the
Ecorian Empire, we could match anything that
could come against us. Now I will ask Sir Acartor
to inform you of what he knows about our
enemy.'

King Edric sat down. They turned to look at
the Fiorian Acartor. Acartor stood up and looked
around at all those seated for several moments.

'My story begins twenty eight years ago. At
that time the Fiorian Order became aware of the
presence of two powerful Northern Sorcerers who
had risen from obscurity to rule the Kaznor
Empire in the north. You are all aware of these
two sorcerers; the kinsmen, Baramak and
Azagord. They were sorcerers of a level of power
previously unknown in Veredor. In two years they
subdued the Kaznor Empire and divided it
between themselves. Azagord ruled the capital
Zarkanor and the lands surrounding the Golden
Sea, and Baramak ruled the Magor Forest and the
lands in the west of Kaznor. For a single year they
reigned and were completely unmatched. Not a
Skathean and certainly no other Northern

Sorcerer had the power to challenge them. They ruled Kaznor as unchallenged tyrants. There was little that the Fiorians could do; the Kaznor Empire was beyond the reach of our order.'

'A year later something changed. At the time we thought a third Northern Sorcerer had risen to challenge the power of Azagord and Baramak. Little was known about this new individual. The only news we heard was that he called himself the Master. Within a year he had taken control of all of Kaznor. This Master was different to other sorcerers; he didn't only defeat his enemies, he subdued and subjugated them. Azagord and Baramak became his servants, and before long he united all the Northern Sorcerers for the first time in history. Within that same year he had also taken control of the entire Skathean Order.'

'At the time a decision was made by the Fiorians to leave Kaznor alone. Perhaps this was the greatest mistake the Fiorians have ever made. As time progressed news was reaching us that this new Master was training armies of Skatheans. Twenty one years ago we finally decided to act. We sent thirty of our greatest knights into Kaznor to investigate and deal with the Master once and for all. Unfortunately we didn't know who we were dealing with. Our brigade of knights attacked the Fortress of Zarkanor. They walked into a trap. Hundreds of Skatheans surrounded them. The Master sat back on the Throne of Zarkanor and watched as our knights were slaughtered. Only two escaped to tell us what had occurred. We still knew nothing about the true nature of the Master.'

'Six months later our home in the Great Mountains, the Tower of Emeril, was attacked by an army of Skatheans. Kaloren, our former Gatekeeper, managed to overcome the attack. The remnants of the Skathean army fled back to Kaznor. Many of our remaining knights were slain in the assault, and the Fiorian Order was reduced to less than forty knights. Shortly after the assault on Emeril the Sorcerers Baramak and Azagord sailed south with their armies. It didn't take us long to discover that their task was to capture the Sword of Light for the Master.'

'What most people didn't know was that the Fiorian Order actually possessed the Sword of Light.' There was a gasp among the council. Acartor paused for a few moments. 'Kaloren, Gatekeeper of Emeril, and our leader, was the bearer of the Sword of Light.'

'Why wasn't the Sword of Light used against Azagord and Baramak?' asked Sir Aksel of Scaldonia.

'I can assure you that the Sword of Light did play a part in our victory against the evil sorcerer Azagord. You all know that Azagord was imprisoned in the Dungeons of Zyran, and until recently he remained so. Baramak, on the other hand, remains a threat even to this day. After Azagord had been imprisoned an urgent task came to our attention. One of our important allies was captured by Baramak and the Skatheans. They imprisoned our ally in the Dungeons of Zarkanor.'

'Who was this ally?' asked Prince Fergal of Dravania.

'Some of you know him. He was the hero known as Elons,' replied Acartor.

'Yes, I know of him. He was a great warrior in the battles we fought against Baramak,' said Prince Fergal.

'Indeed he was. Kaloren devised a plan to free Elons from the Dungeons of Zarkanor. The Sword of Midlight had always belonged to Elons, and after his capture the sword was returned to Kaloren. Kaloren formed a small group of our best knights. With the Sword of Midlight she infiltrated Kaznor and attacked the Fortress of Zarkanor. No one ever returned from the mission to tell us anything. We assumed she had failed and that the Sword of Midlight had fallen into the hands of the Master.'

Acartor paused for a few moments as the council took in what he had already told them.

'Time wore on with no news, and for almost a decade we knew nothing of what the Master was planning. We were completely blind to everything north of the Endora Mountains. The Master sent no one south again, and the Skatheans retreated back into the Northern Lands. For a time we thought that the Master had mellowed and grown tired of war, but we were tragically wrong.'

'During this time he was preparing to conquer Veredor. Because we knew nothing of his larger schemes we devised a plan to attempt to recapture the Sword of Midlight. Ten years ago I led the assault on Zarkanor, and at first I thought we would be victorious. I entered the fortress with four other Fiorians fighting by my side. The battle was fierce. We fought all the way to the Throne of Zarkanor. We found the Master waiting for us.'

'We had no idea who we were dealing with. It is still difficult for me to talk about what we encountered on that dreadful night. We were utterly defeated. The Master held the Sword of Darkness and took pleasure in seeing us desperately fail in our attempts to match him. He only let me live for one purpose: to extract the secrets of the Fiorian Order from me. I was imprisoned in the Dungeons of Zarkanor and tortured relentlessly. Thankfully my training held true; I gave him nothing. Often he would question me in person, and I listened to him carefully, deciphering his true nature. In those years I learned his true nature. He is the Astarian known as the Prince of Shadows. He has returned from the darkness to claim Veredor as his own. We are gathered here today to devise a plan to stop him.'

A deathly silence fell over the council; no one said a word. Finally King Edric broke the silence. 'You said the Fiorian Knights possess the Sword of Light. Surely it can be used against the Prince of Shadows. It was used to defeat him in the Forgotten Age by the Astarian Fiora; perhaps the sword can be used again.'

Acartor nodded soberly. 'Yes, the Sword of Light is a powerful weapon, but it has been lost since our leader Kaloren was lost. We know she didn't take the Sword of Light with her when she attacked Zarkanor; however, we have no knowledge of what became of the Sword of Light. We believe that Carlin, one of our knights, knew where the Sword of Light was hidden. Unfortunately Carlin died years ago. The Sword of Light remains lost.'

'Then surely we must find it,' said Sir Cian of the Tabarian Knights.

'Yes, I'm sure finding the Sword of Light will be one of the tasks we set at this council,' said Acartor. 'But, to my surprise, I learned one other important piece of knowledge when I was imprisoned in the Dungeons of Zarkanor. The Prince of Shadows is not afraid of the Sword of Light, otherwise he would have continued to come south looking for it over the last two decades. No, the Sword of Light doesn't concern him as much as we had thought.'

'But you said he sent Azagord and Baramak south to capture the Sword of Light,' said Prince Armida.

'That was what we thought at the time. The truth was more complex. The Prince of Shadows is not afraid of the Sword of Light itself; he is afraid of the one man who could wield it against him.'

'Who is that man?' asked King Edric.

'That man was the hero Elons. The Prince of Shadows sent Azagord and Baramak south to capture the sword, but the greater part of their task was to capture or kill Elons.'

'Why was Elons so important to the Prince of Shadows?' asked Meara. She glanced at Eben for a moment, knowing full well they were discussing his father. Acartor looked across at Chiara; he then retook his seat. Chiara stood up.

She looked around at the group and took a deep breath. 'What I am about to tell you may shock some of you deeply. All of you have a good knowledge of history, and therefore you all know of the Ecorian Emperors. After the fall of the

Ecorian Empire it was widely thought that Aluin Ecorian, the last Ecorian Emperor, died without an heir and that the line of Ecorians had ended. This was not true. Aluin Ecorian married and had a son in secret. His full reason for doing this was never explained.'

'The Fiorian Order became aware that the Ecorian line still existed about fifty years after the death of Aluin Ecorian. The Ecorian Arbiters had formed their kingdoms thinking the Ecorian line had ended; no one knew the Ecorians still lived in Veredor. For thousands of years the Fiorian Gatekeepers have alone kept a watch over the Ecorians. They have played a secret part in much of our history. Until recently we thought Elons was the last of that line. After Elons was captured by the Prince of Shadows we assumed the Ecorians were lost forever. We now believe we were wrong.'

Eben felt deeply shocked; his heart beat so heavily he thought it would stop. He looked across at Meara who was staring directly at him; she was also wide eyed and profoundly surprised. Eben turned to face Red, and Red looked at him with an expression of awe.

'The Ecorians live!' cried King Edric.

'One Ecorian lives,' announced Chiara.

Acartor stood up to continue speaking with Chiara. 'There is more that you must know. Before I escaped the Dungeons of Zarkanor I was questioned and tortured about the possibility of one last Ecorian. Three years ago the Prince of Shadows captured the Scaldonian Oracle. He discovered from the Scaldonian Oracle that Elons had a son who had been hidden. The Ecorians are not men, and they are not mer. They are a people unto themselves, a race beyond men and mer, with the gifts and blessings of both races. That is why the Prince of Shadows is afraid of them, and that's why he has renewed his attack on our kingdoms. He is afraid of the last Ecorian. He is coming south with an army of forty thousand muckrons. He desires to find and kill the Ecorian before the Ecorian can be prepared to fight him.'

'Then surely we must find this last Ecorian before our enemy does,' declared King Edric resolutely.

Meara was staring directly at Eben. Eben knew he had to say something. Meara smiled and nodded, understanding what he was thinking.

'Perhaps he has already found you,' said Meara softly. The group fell completely silent; they all looked across at her. She looked back at Eben. 'Eben, are you the last Ecorian?' she asked gently. All the eyes quickly shifted across to Eben. Eben slowly stood up. He took the Sword of Light from his belt and placed it on the table so everyone could see.

'This is the Sword of Light. My mother is the Fiorian Kaloren, and my father is Elons, the Ecorian. I am the last Ecorian,' he said, surprised by his own confidence

A stunned silence pervaded the group. They stared in awe at Eben. The silence lasted a full minute and would have lasted much longer if Red hadn't spoken.

'Let me understand this,' said Red. 'Are you saying my best friend isn't really a man?'

'Apparently not,' replied Eben.

'You are of men and mer, completely a man and completely mer,' said Meara.

For a few moments no one spoke a word. The emotional tension in the air was palpable.

'Lady Chiara, you said that the Ecorians deliberately gave up their position as emperors,' said King Lenard of Everdon in a scathing voice. 'If they willingly gave up the Ecorian Empire they can't expect to come back now and rebuild it. I will never bow to any man, and I will oppose any attempt to reform the Ecorian Empire.'

There were some grumbling murmurs from across the table. Sir Tierran of the Tabarian Knights stood up. The rugged warrior fiercely stared at King Lenard.

'The Tabarian Knights are allies of the Ecorians from ancient times. We are sworn to protect the Ecorians,' he said firmly. 'If Eben Ecorian requires our assistance to retake the Sapphire Throne we will give it!'

King Lenard leapt up. 'You speak of war!' he shouted angrily.

'If the Emperor wishes!' bellowed Sir Tierran in response.

'There is no Emperor! I will not bow to this boy!' shouted King Lenard with a sneer.

'I agree with King Lenard,' said Prince Armida of Ateria. 'If it is true the Ecorians willingly stepped down then Eben Ecorian can't expect to return now after thousands of years.'

'I disagree,' shouted Prince Fergal of Dravania. 'The ancient charter of the Ecorian Arbiters states that should Aluin Ecorian prove to have an heir we would all work together to reinstate the Ecorian Empire. If Eben Ecorian wishes to take the Sapphire Throne it is our duty to help him to do so.'

The hall erupted in heated argument. Eben sat down and tried to ignore the fury he had unleashed simply by being who he was. His mind was swirling with all he had learned. The arguing continued until King Edric cried out.

'Please, be silent, all of you! Sit down and be silent!' he commanded. 'Let me ask Eben Ecorian what he intends to do.' Their eyes returned to Eben. He glanced around at their tense faces.

'I only intend to help save Veredor from the Prince of Shadows,' said Eben.

'What about the Sapphire Throne? Do you intend to make a claim to power?' asked Prince Armida.

'I don't want power. I only want peace and justice,' replied Eben. 'I will have nothing to do with anything that causes division among men.' His answer reduced the tension in the room considerably.

'Thank you, Eben,' said Meara. 'You can now see that you have nothing to fear. Eben has not come to conquer you; he has come to help save you from being conquered.'

King Lenard huffed and turned away. Chiara stood up and looked at Eben. 'You are much like your father; I should have realised you were the son of Elons when you were introduced. It is a blessing that you are here. We believe the Prince of Shadows intends to land his army on the shores of Everdon within weeks. He is coming south to find you before we do. His impatience has proved to be his weakness. If we unite we can destroy the army of muckrons and defeat the Prince of Shadows once and for all.'

'How do you know the Prince of Shadows is actually coming himself?' asked Sir Artur of the Takalian Knights.

'Both Mostyn and Baftel are seers. Baftel first saw that a great fleet is sailing from Kaznor to Everdon, and Mostyn has seen that an Astarian sails with the fleet,' replied Chiara.

'It is true what Mostyn has seen,' said Acartor. 'Before I escaped Zarkanor, the Prince of Shadows came to me and told me that he planned to go south to find and kill the last Ecorian. He never expected me to escape and carry this information ahead of him. The Prince of Shadows is overconfident. He doesn't consider anyone but the Ecorian to be a threat. He looks at us as we would look at vermin, something he must exterminate, but not a real threat to his survival. The Ecorian, on the other hand, frightens him. He believes the Ecorian has the power to defeat him. I believe if Eben has this power we should assist him to complete this task. When the Prince of Shadows falls his evil empire will also fall, and our lands will be free from oppression. When he is gone his army will collapse on itself. His armies of muckrons, wyverns, and Skatheans will surely fight each other without a powerful leader controlling them.'

Eben glanced toward Princess Apherah and found she was looking at him. She smiled warmly. Her exquisite beauty distracted him and interrupted the torrent of thoughts swirling in his head.

'For several weeks I have been gathering an army in the south of Irvaria,' said King Edric. 'I have twenty thousand men ready to march now; another ten thousand will be ready in a few days. King Lenard has twenty thousand in Everdon. We will have at least fifty thousand men against the forty thousand muckrons of the Prince of Shadows. I also have an army of four thousand men near Darancra that I sent to deal with the Skatheans in Vastoria. They will join us if they complete their task in time. If we strike the Prince of Shadows decisively we may end all our troubles. We can lead Eben Ecorian directly to the Prince of Shadows and give him the opportunity to finish him once and for all.'

It was agreed by all the envoys of the council that this plan was the best way forward.

'Let us now end this council and prepare for the battle ahead. Much has been revealed. I believe we have a lot to think about,' said King Edric.

CHAPTER ELEVEN

Eben returned to his chambers directly after the council. Red and Stella joined him. They sat around the table. Eben's mind raced as he digested the massive amount of information he had been given at the council. The revelations had deeply rattled and overwhelmed him.

The door opened and Meara entered and was followed closely by Cassiel. She walked over to the table and looked directly at Eben. 'This indeed is an unexpected turn of events,' she said. Eben glanced up at her; his eyes were deeply strained.

'What shall I do, Meara?' he asked. She pondered the question in silence.

'You are the Ecorian. I should be asking you what I should do.'

Eben glanced away and stared out the window. He felt a deep sense of responsibility weighing on his shoulders. 'I don't know if I can be the Ecorian.'

'You're wrong about that, Eben. You have already done amazing things. You helped to free King Ignis from the Dungeons of Zyran; you led the battle against the muckron horde in Scaldonia, and without you Ortaria would never have been liberated. You are the Ecorian, the only descendent of the Ecorian Emperors; this is your birth right. Acartor believes you are the only one who the Prince of Shadows is afraid of. Without you Veredor will become a world of monsters. You must believe in yourself. You must take up this mantle and walk this path that has been handed to you; because if you do not every person living in Veredor will either become a slave or die. Your friends and the people of Veredor need you. You must find the courage and be who you truly are.'

Eben felt his heart lift at hearing Meara speak these words. He looked up at Meara with renewed confidence. 'I will fight for you. I will fight for Baftel, Red, Stella, and Cassiel. I will fight for all the people of Veredor.'

Meara smiled warmly. 'There is hope in your heart; may it never fade.'

**

Eben awoke early the following morning. His head was still spinning. He sat up in his bed and looked out the window as the sun rose and sent beams of golden light across the morning sky. He put on clothes and picked up the Sword of Light, attaching the scabbard to his belt. Eben gently unlocked his door and stepped out. He walked quietly down the corridor, not wanting to wake anyone else so early in the morning.

Before long he found a spiral stairwell that led downward to the levels below. He took the stairs and continued for almost ten minutes until he reached the ground floor and entered the lower hall. Several palace guardsmen were on duty, but few of them took much notice of him as he crossed the marble floor toward the gate. He felt he needed some time to think about everything that had been revealed at the council. The thought that his parents had been captured by the Prince of Shadows was foremost in his mind, and the revelation that he was also not just a man, but rather a combination of two races.

The palace gate was guarded by several armoured guards in red capes. They looked at him as he passed by.

'Are you off for an early walk through the town?' asked a tall and gaunt looking guardsman with a large red moustache.

'Yes, I shouldn't be too long,' replied Eben. 'I just wanted to get some fresh air.'

'Leave your name here with us if you don't mind.'

'Eben is my name.'

The guard stared at him and his jaw dropped. 'There is a rumour going around that the Ecorian Emperor has returned; they say his name is

Eben.' Eben looked away nervously. 'Are you Eben Ecorian?'

'I must be on my way,' said Eben.

'It is you,' said the guardsman. Eben stood there and felt stunned for a moment.

'Yes, my name is Eben Ecorian.'

'Sire, Bradley is my name. If you would shake my hand I would be honoured.' Bradley reached out, and Eben, of course, shook his hand.

'I am pleased to meet you, Bradley,' said Eben politely. 'If you would excuse me I will be on my way.'

'Yes, Sire,' said Bradley.

Eben turned and followed the main street down toward the gate. Many people were going about their early morning tasks throughout the town. He walked almost all the way to the southern gate. A large tavern caught his eye. A sign out the front read: The Drifters Rest, serving a hearty breakfast for the working man. Eben pushed through the door and entered the common room, which was clean and well-kept. Standing behind the bar was a thickset barkeeper with greying hair and a weathered face.

Eben approached the bar. 'I'll have a mug of your strongest ale.'

The barkeeper grinned, thinking Eben was surely joking. 'Ale, at this hour; the sun has hardly risen yet.'

Eben looked at the barkeeper and nodded. 'If you don't mind I'll have ale all the same.'

'If you must,' said the barkeeper as he turned back to one of the large barrels that lined the back wall. 'You shouldn't drink your life away. A young man like you has the world at your feet.

Anything is possible. In my trade I have seen too many people give their life to the bottle.'

Eben nodded again as the barkeeper turned back and handed him the mug of ale. 'Thanks for the advice,' he said as he took a big gulp of the bitter Irvarian brew.

'Where are you from, young man? Your accent is strange.'

'I'm Ortarian,' replied Eben, as he reached for some coins to pay the barkeeper.

'I have only met a handful of Ortarians in the twenty years I've been keeping this bar. The drink is on the house.'

'Thanks,' said Eben, returning the coins to his pocket.

'So what brings you to Faircastle?'

Eben was about to answer, but before he could say a word an old man entered the common room and took the barkeeper's attention. He approached the bar with a spring in his step that revealed his excitement. He was short in stature and had long grey hair.

'Wendell! You will never guess what news I heard this morning,' said the old man.

'Good news I hope,' replied the barkeeper with a smile.

'My news is always better than good!' said the old man with a grin from ear to ear.

'All right, Tim, let's hear it.'

'The word on the street is that the Ecorian Emperor has returned.'

'Rubbish!' replied Wendell, chuckling and shaking his head. Eben took another sip of his ale.

'No, it's not rubbish. I went up to ask my contacts in the palace. They say it is as true as the sky is blue.'

'An Ecorian here in Faircastle; I would have to see him to believe it.'

'Well, you just may see,' said old Tim excitedly.

'What do you think of that, Ortarian?' asked Wendell, turning to Eben.

'I don't know,' replied Eben hesitantly. 'Maybe he is not really like an Ecorian. Perhaps he is just like everyone else.'

'Don't speak such words,' said old Tim, shaking his head at Eben and waving dismissively. 'Ecorians are majestic, noble, and pure of heart. Every Ecorian in history was a hero. If an Ecorian truly has returned then our people have been blessed.'

Suddenly there was a commotion in the street outside. Eben and old Tim went to the window and looked out. The large shutters had been pulled back to let the morning sun in. Wendell joined them by the window a moment later. A fine carriage, drawn by two mighty white horses, was swiftly moving down the main street toward the main southern gate. Two knights, in full shining armour and long red capes, rode out before the carriage, and two riders followed a little way back. The carriage itself was a work of art, almost completely made of silver with a cabin and small windows.

'It is the carriage of Princess Apherah,' said Wendell. Eben felt his heart jump at the mention of her name.

'Her beauty is unmatched in all the realms of Veredor,' said old Tim proudly.

'Agreed,' said Wendell with a sharp nod.

They watched as the carriage drew near. First the leading riders passed. They appeared flustered and were clearly rushing. Eben looked to see if Princess Apherah was visible through the carriage windows.

'I wonder what the hurry is?' asked old Tim.

'Look, there she is,' gasped Wendell.

Eben could see Princess Apherah seated in the carriage. Again he was awestruck by her beauty. He stared as she passed by. Her eyes drifted to their side of the road, and at the very last moment she caught sight of Eben watching her from the common room window. Her eyes widened with surprise. A moment later the carriage stopped.

'What's this?' asked Wendell. 'Why is the carriage stopping?'

'No idea,' replied old Tim as he watched on intently.

The knights dismounted as Princess Apherah stepped out of the carriage. The people in the street knelt down on one knee and bowed their heads to the ground. The Princess was wearing a long flowing blue dress and was a picture of grace, elegance, and beauty. A few words passed between her and one of her knights. The four knights then led her back toward the inn.

'She looks like she is coming in here,' cried old Tim, almost choking on his words.

One of her knights entered the common room first. Wendell nodded to the knight. 'Good morning, Sir,' he said as the knight took a position by the front door. A few moments later

Princess Apherah entered. Her ocean blue eyes stared directly at Eben as she stepped through the door. Wendell and Tim both instantly knelt down on a knee and bowed their heads low. Eben remained standing.

'It is truly an honour, Your Highness,' stammered Wendell. 'I don't know what to say. How can I be of service?'

Princess Apherah looked down at Wendell for a moment. 'Please stand. I have only come here to talk with your honoured guest.' She looked back to Eben. 'What are you doing here, Eben Ecorian?'

Eben felt lost for words. He looked to Wendell who stared up, the blood draining from the barkeeper's face. 'I...I was just having a drink with my two new friends.'

Apherah laughed and raised an eyebrow. 'At this hour! Surely it is much too early for ale.'

'That's what I told the Ecorian, Your Highness,' said Wendell.

'Yesterday's revelations were a big shock. I just felt like going for a walk. Before long I found myself here,' said Eben.

'Your arrival surprised us all,' said Apherah, eyeing Eben curiously.

A knight entered from the street and whispered to the knight who was waiting at the door. The knight then approached Princess Apherah. He was an older man with heavily wrinkled skin, a noble face, and greying hair.

'Your father is sending Royal Guard to retrieve you, Your Majesty. They will be here any minute. The King has also sealed the southern gate. It is now impossible for us to escape.' Princess Apherah's eyes narrowed.

'Your Majesty, you should return to the palace,' said the knight.

Apherah shook her head defiantly. 'I'm certainly not going back.'

'Are you running away?' asked Eben.

Apherah looked to Eben for a moment before returning her eyes to the old knight. 'Sir Giles. Will you lead me on to the west gate?'

Sir Giles wiped his sweaty forehead and shook his head. 'I was happy to help you leave the palace and take you south to Elcalee. You know I am bound to follow your command. However, Your Majesty, you must understand that I cannot defy your father. He is my king, and I am sworn to follow his command above all others. Now that he has sent the Royal Guards after you it would be treason for me to assist you to escape Faircastle. I am sorry, Your Majesty; I simply cannot help you.'

The Princess looked away from Sir Giles; her eyes found Eben. 'Ecorian, would you like to come with me to Elcalee.'

Eben stared into her eyes and felt stunned by the question. He didn't want to say no, yet he also didn't see how he could simply leave Faircastle with her and run away. 'I....' he began, but before he could finish she had grabbed hold of his hand and was leading him toward the back of the inn.

'Is there a way out through the back?' she asked Wendell.

'Indeed, Your Highness,' answered Wendell, pointing to a hallway that led away from the common room.

Sir Giles stepped forward. 'Your Majesty, I must object to this course of action.'

'Oh, Sir Giles, please, just this once,' said Apherah, her sweet smile charming the old knight.

'I am also charged with your protection,' argued Sir Giles in a gentle voice.

'I am sure the Ecorian can protect me.' She then led Eben down the hallway and out the back door, leaving Sir Giles standing in the common room with Wendell and Tim. They found themselves in a back alley.

'We must hurry. My father has sent his best men to bring me back to the palace.'

Apherah led the way into a network of back alleys that took them away from the main street.

'Why are we running? What's this all about?'

Apherah looked up at Eben; she was about to answer, but in that moment three fully armoured guardsmen in long red capes appeared at the far side of the laneway. Eben grabbed her hand and led her through a narrow gap between two buildings. The Royal Guards hurried after them. 'Stop! Princess! By order of the King!'

Eben and Apherah entered a wider alley. Barrels were piled high on one side of the way. Eben pushed over the barrels as they ran by. He looked back and could see the guardsmen struggling after them. Eben led her down another thin alleyway and out into a side street. The townsfolk looked at them. They then ran across the street and dashed between two houses and crossed a small square. Eben saw a tavern with an open door. He led the Princess into a small and smoky common room. The greasy haired barkeeper, who was smoking a large pipe, looked up and gave a wide smile.

Eben looked out the window and saw the Royal Guards pass the tavern. 'We should wait in here for a minute,' he said, looking back to Apherah. She smiled excitedly.

'Can I pour you two a drink?' asked the barkeeper.

'Certainly,' replied Eben. 'Make it two ales.'

'I only drink wine,' said Apherah.

'Actually, one wine and one ale,' corrected Eben.

The barkeeper shook his head. 'We only serve Irvarian ale.'

'Ale will be fine,' said Apherah as she took a seat at a small wooden table in the corner of the room.

Eben sat down across from her. Apherah smiled widely as she looked at him. 'That was fun.'

'What is this all about?' asked Eben as the barkeeper placed two mugs of ale down on the table. Eben handed him some coins.

'I simply must escape Faircastle before my father forces me to marry King Lenard of Everdon.'

'Why would he do that?' asked Eben, feeling his heart drop in his chest at the idea of her marrying such an unpleasant man. He remembered King Lenard was the most unfriendly of all the dignitaries at the council.

Her concerned eyes drifted toward the small window. 'For centuries the Everdonians have been our allies. King Lenard has been on the Everdonian throne for three years. He has thus far proven very difficult for my father to work with. Unfortunately he has placed conditions on our continued alliance. Chief among those conditions is my hand in marriage. My father has promised King Lenard that he alone will be given permission to court me. I am expected to marry him.'

'But surely who you marry is your decision,' said Eben, feeling horrified that she didn't have a say in the matter.

'Exactly!' cried Apherah in agreement. 'That's what I have been saying for months, yet my father said I should meet King Lenard before I make any judgements on the matter. King Lenard arrived three days ago, and I was taken to meet him in the royal guest chambers. We talked for about a minute, and as we conversed I started to feel very unwell. I almost fainted for the first time in my life. I tried to see the best in him, yet there was nothing, not one good quality. King Lenard is quite possibly the most horrid man in Veredor.' She cast her eyes sadly down at the mug of ale. 'And I am betrothed to him.'

Eben laughed, seeing the stupidity in the situation.

Apherah looked up and frowned. 'What are you laughing at?'

'Surely all you have to do is say no. Really, this is not so complicated.'

'You speak like a commoner, Eben Ecorian,' she said, shaking her head. 'Surely you know that royal marriage is more complicated than simply choosing to marry whoever I like. I cannot simply meet someone in the street and marry them. There is so much to consider: alliances, tradition, and the fact that they must also belong to an Ecorian Arbiter bloodline.'

'That sounds very unromantic. No wonder you want to run away.'

Apherah stared at Eben for a long moment. Eben could feel she was contemplating something. 'Are you going to help me escape?'

'Of course,' said Eben, sipping at his ale.

Suddenly several Royal Guards appeared outside the tavern. 'They can't possibly have gone that way!' shouted a guardsman. 'They must have gone inside one of these buildings. Eben jumped up at hearing their words.

'Time to go,' he said, taking her hand and leading her out a side door.

They ran from the tavern without being seen. Eben turned down an alleyway that led toward the west gate. They rushed along and entered a square surrounded by high buildings.

'Do you know where you are going?' asked Apherah, looking at Eben with a doubtful expression.

'Not exactly,' replied Eben. 'Didn't you say the west gate would be still open?'

'It may be open, yet my father will probably have people watching all the gates by now.'

'Do you have any other ideas?' asked Eben.

Suddenly they could see the red capes of the Royal Guards charging down an alley that led to the square. Eben took Apherah's hand and they dashed toward the opposing alleyway, but more guardsmen approached, blocking their escape. Apherah fearfully clung to Eben's arm.

Eben backed away and looked for an exit as the two groups of guardsmen approached. A few moments later more than a dozen guardsmen entered the square. They drew their swords and cut off the exits.

'Release the Princess!' ordered the lead guardsman.

Eben scanned their faces as several more guardsmen arrived in the square. 'No,' said Eben firmly. 'I certainly will not.'

'We don't want to have to hurt you,' said the lead guardsman, stepping forward with his large broadsword pointed directly at Eben.

Eben drew the Sword of Light. Instantly Apherah stepped forward. She looked back at Eben and winked. 'Royal Guards, I know my father has ordered you to return me to the palace, but let it be known that one with more authority than my father stands before you. My father's claim to the throne is based on the fact that he is a direct descendent of the Ecorian Arbiters, yet here, before you stands the Ecorian himself.'

The guardsmen stared at Eben. A few moments later they lowered their swords.

'We have heard the rumour that the Ecorian has returned to Faircastle. Are you saying this man is the Ecorian?' asked the lead guardsman.

'Yes, I tell you the truth; this is Eben Ecorian.' The Royal Guards stared at Eben in awe. They also looked conflicted, not knowing what to say or do. Eben put away the Sword of Light as Apherah took his hand. 'Now, you will let us pass.' The guardsmen bowed their heads and they stood aside to let them pass. Once they were out of sight they started to run again. They rushed through the city backstreets and lanes toward the western gate. After a few minutes they came to the gate and found it was still open.

'Perfect,' said Eben as he led her through the gate and out of the city. Instantly they came upon a group of fifty Irvarian mounted guards. King Edric, in full shining armour, sat high on a warhorse and looked down at them sternly. They had run directly into his trap.

'I knew if I left one gate open you would eventually come through it,' said King Edric. 'I did not expect to see you, Eben, helping my daughter escape her duty.'

'Eben has nothing to do with this,' said Apherah defiantly.

King Edric stared down at his daughter. 'Dearest Apherah, I do not know what you hoped to achieve by running. You know your duty.' A moment later Apherah's carriage came through the gate and stopped beside her.

'She should be able to marry whoever she wants!' said Eben firmly.

King Edric stared harshly down at Eben. 'And who would you suggest?' asked the King angrily. Eben had no answer for the King. He looked across at Apherah. She stared deeply into his eyes; she then reached up gently and touched his face.

'Thank you, Eben Ecorian,' she said. A moment later she stepped up into the carriage. Instantly the carriage was led away.

King Edric looked down at Eben. 'I'm sorry that my daughter drew you into this.' With these words the King turned his horse and rode back into the city.

**

Later that same day Eben sat with Cassiel and Red in his chambers as the sun was setting, casting long beams of light through the misty sky surrounding the palace.

'I must say that I'm proud to be a friend of an Ecorian Emperor,' said Cassiel. Eben looked at Cassiel and wondered if this new revelation would change their friendship.

'I'm not an emperor, Cassiel. I just happen to belong to a certain family.'

'The Ecorians are more than a family. They're a race in their own right,' said Cassiel assuredly.

'But I feel and look just like everyone else,' said Eben.

'I have read that the Ecorians have exceptional and extraordinary abilities,' said Cassiel.

'If I have any powers I haven't discovered them yet. As far as I know I'm just like everyone else,' replied Eben.

There was a gentle tapping at the door. Red crossed the floor quickly and opened the door. A beautiful dark haired maiden was standing in the corridor. She was wearing a long flowing red cotton dress.

'Greetings, Eben Ecorian,' she said to Red, nodding her head as a sign of respect.

'Ahh, I'm not the Ecorian,' stated Red, indicating back over his shoulder toward Eben.

A moment later Eben was at the door and standing beside Red. She looked up and her bright eyes glanced across to Eben. 'Greetings, Eben Ecorian. My name is Lila. I am a personal attendant of Princess Apherah. Princess Apherah sent me to personally hand you this letter.'

Eben stared down at the letter which had a red wax seal in the shape of an intricately designed A. 'Thank you,' he replied.

Lila nodded once again handed him the letter. She then stood there and seemed to be waiting for something. Red glanced across at Eben, not knowing what to do, and then took from his pocket a few coins. He went to hand them to Lila as gratuity, but her dark eyes looked away and revealed her embarrassment. Red quickly returned the coins to his pocket, blushing from his mistake.

'Do you have a message for Princess Apherah?' asked Lila, a look of excitement was in the young maiden's eyes.

'Yes. Tell her that I was pleased to meet her today, and I hope we can meet again. Tell her not to make any decisions she does not want to make.'

'I will take your message to her,' she said, smiling as she turned to leave. Red closed the door and looked across at Eben.

'You met the Princess today?' he asked with a laugh.

'Yes, when I went for a walk I met her in the town.'

'What is she like?' asked Cassiel.

Eben thought about how best to answer the question. He opened the letter as he spoke. 'She is actually a lot of fun and very nice.'

He began to read: Dear Eben Ecorian, I must thank you for assisting me today. You are truly a gracious and noble man. It was a pleasure to spend some time with you. My father has asked me to apologise to you and to explain that it is my duty as the Princess of Irvaria to marry King Lenard of Everdon. Regrettably I must accept this duty. Thank you for understanding me. I hope one day we will meet again. Sincerely, Princess Apherah of Irvaria.

Eben felt his heart thump in his chest and a lump in his throat. He couldn't stand the idea of her marrying King Lenard against her will.

'What does it say?' asked Red.

'I think she is going to marry King Lenard,' said Eben as he read the letter again.

'What a pity; he's a horrid man,' said Red.

**

It was early in the morning on the following day and a crisp chill had fallen over all the land. Many fireplaces throughout the palace were burning brightly, which was a very rare event in summer. Eben stepped into the Ecorian Hall from the stairwell and saw that at least twenty guardsmen stood around the Sapphire Throne. They stood to attention as they became aware of him. Eben looked across the marble floor at the throne; an air of anticipation pervaded the hall.

Eben moved on and continued to follow the stairwell up to the royal quarters which were on the level above the Ecorian Hall. He arrived at the top of the stairwell. A large ironclad door and four palace guardsmen stood in his way. One of the guardsmen, a stout and sturdy man with black hair, stepped forward.

'How can we help you, Ecorian?' he asked in a respectful but somewhat firm tone.

'I wish to see Princess Apherah if she is able to see me,' said Eben.

They whispered among themselves for a few moments and then one of the guardsmen entered the ironclad door.

'We will see if she is available.'

Eben waited in silence. After about two minutes the door opened, and the guardsman returned.

'She is not available to see you, Ecorian. The King himself will have a word with you. Follow me.'

Two of the guardsmen led Eben through the door and down a long corridor with doors lining the walls. They arrived at the far side and the guardsman knocked on a solid wooden door. The door opened into a large chamber with a massive polished desk, bookcases lining the walls, and a small fireplace burning in the corner. King Edric was seated at the desk and sternly looked up at Eben as he entered.

'Guardsmen, please leave us,' said the King, the guards bowed low before leaving and closed the door.

'I must say your arrival has caused quite a stir among my guests,' said King Edric. 'Please, take a seat. We need to have a discussion about a few important issues.'

'I do not wish to cause you any trouble,' said Eben calmly.

'I am glad to hear you say that. I want you to know that I am very happy the Ecorian line has not been extinguished. Unfortunately it has proved to be a diplomatic nightmare assuring some of the envoys that you are not a threat to them, and this is not my only problem at the moment. A rumour of your existence is circulating throughout the city. The Irvarian people want to know the truth. A crowd is waiting outside the palace as we speak. My people are seeking answers.'

'Why not tell them the truth?' suggested Eben steadily.

'Of course I will have to tell my people everything; however, my main focus at the moment is maintaining our alliances. Much hangs in the balance as we speak. You must understand that if we do not unite we will be conquered by the Prince of Shadows. This brings me to a new problem; one that may prove a decisive blow to our survival. This problem has much to do with you.'

'What problem?' asked Eben.

'Can I have your word that you will be discreet about what I tell you?' asked King Edric.

'Of course,' replied Eben.

The King nodded with relief. 'You know, as it was evident at the council, that King Lenard of Everdon is not happy about your sudden emergence. He is concerned that you plan to take the Sapphire Throne; no amount of reassurance can calm him. I must say he is not the easiest man to deal with. His parents were both noble people, and my hope is that their young son will someday come to be like his late father. Alas, this is what I must deal with if we are to have an alliance with Everdon. We need this alliance to stand against the muckron invasion. If we do not work together we will fall. Thankfully, as it stands, we do have an agreement to work together.'

King Edric picked up a glass and took a sip of water. He eyed Eben for a few moments before continuing. 'To form the alliance with Everdon I have promised my daughter's hand in marriage to King Lenard. She is the only heir I have. I believe a marriage between the Crowns of Irvaria and Everdon at this time would forge the alliance we need and ensure our survival.'

Eben felt a lump gathering in his throat. 'As I said to you yesterday: surely she can choose who she wants to marry,' he said, trying to keep a polite tone but failing.

'Yes, it is the eternal law; she can marry whoever she wishes, yet my daughter knows her duty, and she will do what is right to save her people,' replied King Edric. 'My agreement with King Lenard is bound by honour. King Lenard knows she does not wish to be courted by him, but he believes strongly that with time she will agree to marry him. You requested to see her. I do not doubt from her behaviour yesterday that she would also like to see you again. I can only assume that your intentions are to begin a courtship. Regrettably, I cannot give my permission; I am sorry, but I must forbid you to see or court my daughter.'

Eben fell silent. He knew he could not accept the King's mandate, and he was aware that the King knew his thoughts.

'Can you assure me you will not attempt to see her again?' asked King Edric tensely.

Eben remained silent. 'I cannot make this promise,' he said firmly.

'You leave me no choice, Eben Ecorian. I have given my word to King Lenard. I must keep my word. If you attempt to see my daughter I will send you from Faircastle and forbid you to return. As long as you stay away from her you will remain as free as you are now. I realise you are a man of honour; I know you will follow your heart, but I am also a man of honour, and I must keep my word to King Lenard. I am glad to have you as a guest in my palace. I wish to honour you as the Ecorian should be honoured; however, you must accept that this is my home. These are my rules, and you must obey them.'

**

'Forbidden! But why?' asked Red, shocked at hearing of the King's mandate.

'I gave my word I wouldn't tell the reason, but I cannot accept this.'

'But how will you see her?' asked Stella.

'You could climb the outer wall,' suggested Red.

'Don't make such a suggestion,' said Stella crossly. 'Eben would surely die if he fell.'

'True, climbing the wall would be very dangerous,' said Cassiel. 'But I just can't think of any other way to enter the royal chambers.'

'If the outer wall is the only option I will have to take it. At least I won't have to worry about any guards out there.'

'How will you know which is her window?' asked Cassiel.

'I will have to hope for the best,' said Eben with a smile as he stepped out onto the balcony and looked up toward the levels above. The outer stone wall was vertical; small gaps between the stones where the only place for him to take a grip. The others followed him out onto the balcony. They looked up.

'Eben, it looks very dangerous,' said Stella.

'Stella is right; this is too risky,' said Red, shaking his head. 'Actually, I think it's probably impossible. You should reconsider and wait to see her another time.'

Eben stood on the railing. He found a place to grip and edged upward, ascending the sheer wall gradually. He climbed slowly, taking as much care as possible.

'Be careful, Eben,' called Stella softly. He glanced down and was surprised how far he had already ascended. The solid ground was at least two hundred and fifty yards below. He felt slightly dizzy as he realised how high up he actually was. His fingers ached as he continued to climb. His friends watched on anxiously. Eventually, after several minutes, he found he was near the upper windows.

He finally reached a window. Climbing onto the ledge below, he glanced inside. There was an empty sitting room, with a small desk, several wooden cabinets, a table with three bottles of wine, and a bowl of fruit.

The window was not locked and Eben found it easily opened. He slid through into the sitting room. He crossed the room to the door and gently turned the handle, opening the door just enough to see outside. An empty hallway was revealed. He stepped out and tread lightly, listening for any voices as he went. Suddenly a door opened; two men stepped out of a room ahead. He quickly opened a door and dashed into a small room. The two men passed by outside, not aware of him at all.

'What are you doing here, Eben Ecorian?' asked a woman's voice. He turned to see Lila sitting at a desk, staring up at him in shock. He was in a small bedchamber with a desk, some shelves, and a single window.

'I'm looking for Princess Apherah.' Lila smiled at hearing his words.

'You won't find her here. This level is the royal staff quarters. Princess Apherah lives on the uppermost floor.'

'Can you take me to her?'

'If I was caught I would be punished for helping you. King Edric has banished me to my quarters for a week for delivering your message to Princess Apherah yesterday. If I took you to the Princess he would probably have me thrown into the dungeons.'

'Can you tell me where to go?'

'Of course,' she said, taking a piece of paper from her desk. With some charcoal she sketched some directions. He took the paper and smiled at her.

'Thank you, Lila.'

'The map will lead you to the stairs used by the royal staff. They will take you directly to the main royal living quarters,' she said. 'Take this key; it opens the door at the top of the stairs. I hope you find her.'

'I'll do my best,' said Eben, stepping into the corridor.

He edged forward along the corridor in the direction of the stairs. After a few minutes the map led him to a small ascending stairwell. He could hear voices in the distance growing louder. He quickly climbed the stairs; after about twenty feet the stairs turned back on themselves sharply. At the top of the stairwell he came to a small landing and a solid ironclad door. A brass bell was hanging on a hook beside the door. He could hear heated voices inside.

'I simply cannot marry the Everdonian. He is completely mad! I will never agree!'

'Listen clearly,' said another woman's voice firmly. 'King Lenard is our ally, and he belongs to a good family. We simply cannot afford to go back on our promise. You are not yet twenty years old. You do not know what is best for you.'

'Mother, I know well enough that marrying him is not good for me.'

'This is not about you, Apherah. This is about the kingdom you will one day rule. We are facing an enemy we have never faced before; our days may be at an end. Our alliance with Everdon hangs in the balance. Your marriage to King Lenard will ensure our two kingdoms are united against the Prince of Shadows. This marriage is not about what you want. You must put aside your own wishes for the good of Irvaria. This is the way a good ruler should act.'

The Princess was silenced by these words. Eben wondered what he should do. He simply couldn't enter the room with Queen Sera present, and he didn't want to go back down the stairs because of the risk of being seen.

'But it doesn't matter if we have an alliance or not. Without Eben Ecorian we don't stand a chance against the Prince of Shadows. We should be trying to build an alliance with him.'

Again there was a long silence before Queen Sera spoke. 'Eben Ecorian is young; I hope that he is not as foolish as you. Be sure that we do have an alliance with him through our friendship with Ortaria. Your father knows we cannot overcome the invading army unless we have an alliance with King Lenard. Even with Eben Ecorian on our side we will not win without Everdon.' There was a short pause. 'Apherah, you will forget about the Ecorian when you begin to place your people above yourself. I know you met with him when you tried to escape to Elcalee. The Ecorian is handsome but so is King Lenard in his own way.'

'Eben Ecorian understands me. He was prepared to fight the Royal Guards to protect me. He cares about me,' she said softly.

'Don't be foolish, Apherah. Such thoughts are not for someone of your level of responsibility,' said the Queen. 'I am sure you will make the right decision. We will conduct your wedding with King Lenard before the army marches south. The alliance between Irvaria and Everdon must continue. I will leave you to reflect on this conversation.'

A few moments later Eben heard the creaking sound of a door opening and then the thump of it closing. He waited for at least thirty seconds and then placed the key in the door. He opened the lock and gently pushed the door. A large sitting room was revealed. He looked around and couldn't see anyone. The room was indeed luxurious, with fine silk pillowed chairs, fine couches, and wooden tea tables. Royal red curtains fell beside the windows, and crystal chandeliers hung from the ceilings above. The wide windows revealed a magnificent view over the city. Eben glanced around and Princess Apherah was nowhere in sight. He stepped into the room and quietly crossed the floor.

There was movement from out of the corner of his eye. He saw a blade fast approaching. In an instant he drew his sword and deflected the incoming blade. Princess Apherah dropped the short sword and stared at him in a state of shock.

'I'm sorry, Eben. I thought you were an assassin. Why didn't you ring the bell?' Her eyes were wide with surprise. 'How did you get by the guards without being seen?' she asked as the initial shock melted away.

'That was the easy part.' he replied, placing the Sword of Light back in its scabbard. Eben looked at her and was again struck by her immense beauty.

'You really shouldn't be here, Eben. My father will banish you from Faircastle if he catches us together.'

'I don't mind if he does,' he replied, feeling untroubled by the consequences. 'I came because I wanted to see you again.'

She stared at him for a moment, expecting him to say something more. 'Is that all?' she asked, raising an eyebrow.

'I have to say I was disappointed to read that you are actually considering the possibility of marrying King Lenard.'

'It is not an easy decision,' said Apherah, frowning and looking away. 'I am only considering the marriage because my people are threatened. We need the Everdonians.' She looked sadly toward the window. 'I have little choice, Eben. My father is insisting that I go through with the marriage. My attempt to escape Faircastle was a desperate move to avoid the inevitable.'

'There must be another way,' said Eben.

'Why do you care so much, Eben?' she asked, staring at him with sad eyes.

'Because I want to protect you, and I...'

Footsteps could be heard coming from behind a door. Apherah grabbed him by the hand. They dashed behind the red curtains just as a door opened and someone entered the room. She looked up at him with a sweet nervous smile as they stood completely still.

'Apherah!' called King Edric's voice. They both held their breath and listened as the footsteps crossed the room and then faded away.

'It's my father,' she whispered. 'Let's go.'

Apherah led him across the room and to a stairwell that ascended sharply. In seconds they had climbed the steps to an upper doorway. She pushed open the door at the top and the rooftop of the palace was revealed. A completely flat stone surface was surrounded by a waist high wall that followed the outer edge. Seven towers rose high into the sky above. Eben looked at Apherah as he watched her silky hair blow in the wind. She looked at him and smiled sweetly. A moment later she glanced up at the flags flying high above.

'The White Unicorn once flew where the White Dragon now flies. I wonder if it will fly again?' she asked, looking back to him. Eben glanced up at the red flags. For a few moments he thought about what she had said. He then looked back to her, her ocean coloured eyes were fixed on him, and her beauty was overwhelming.

'The White Unicorn will only fly here again if you are the one to raise the flag.'

'Only an Ecorian has the right to raise the flag of the Ecorian Empire,' she said, staring at him inquisitively.

Eben nodded and smiled. She beamed at him when she realised what he really meant. They moved closer, and he took her hands. He looked into her eyes and knew in that moment she understood. Apherah smiled radiantly as all her sadness drifted away and was replaced with hope and joy.

'Apherah, would you consider...'

The door from the stairwell burst open. King Edric stepped onto the rooftop followed by a dozen guardsmen. He marched toward them with hard and angry eyes. They turned to face her furious father.

'You have both disobeyed my orders. Eben Ecorian, I don't know how you got into the royal chambers unseen; I can assure you that it won't happen again. Apherah, you will stay in your chambers until the Ecorian is safely away from our city.'

'Father please don't!' pleaded Apherah.

'Take Princess Apherah to her chambers and place a guard at her door. She must not be allowed out until the Ecorian is gone. Eben Ecorian, you should know I am a man of honour. I will not go against my word. I regret to say that you are banished from Faircastle. Guards, lead Eben Ecorian to his chambers. You have an hour to leave Faircastle.'

'I think you're making a grave mistake, Your Majesty,' said Eben.

'I will be the judge of that,' said King Edric. He then turned and stormed away. Eben watched as

Princess Apherah was led from him. She looked back over her shoulder, smiled sadly, and then was gone.

CHAPTER TWELVE

'I can't believe we have been banished from Faircastle,' said Red, shaking his head as he stepped into Eben's chamber with Stella. 'I was really starting to enjoy living here.'

'You don't have to come with me, Red. King Edric said that only I am banished,' replied Eben.

'You're not leaving without us, Eben,' said Stella.

Meara and Cassiel suddenly appeared in the doorway. 'What's the meaning of this? Why are you leaving?' asked Meara, shocked at seeing them packing their bags.

'Eben went to see Princess Apherah when he had been forbidden from seeing her by the King,' said Stella.

'I see. I have heard that she has been promised to King Lenard. I can see why King Edric would be concerned. King Lenard is a quick tempered man. He is also an important ally in our struggle. We cannot afford to lose the Everdonians. I think you should respect the King's wishes and stay away from her.'

'Apherah does not want to marry King Lenard,' said Eben resolutely.

The room fell silent. Meara shut the door, leaving the palace guardsmen outside. She directed them to sit at the table.

'This situation is more dangerous than you think. Let us assume that you can overcome all the possible obstacles and are able to start a courtship with Princess Apherah. The end result would mean that the Ecorian would rule Faircastle and the Sapphire Throne. I doubt the Ecorian Arbiters would accept this. I believe you would gain Dravania and Iarthar as allies, and probably King Ignis, but Everdon, Ateria, Silvor, and the Isles of Dawn would probably oppose you. This is a division we can't accept at this time.'

'I don't want to cause any divisions,' said Eben.

There was a knock at the door. Red sprang to his feet and opened the door. The Fiorians Chiara and Acartor stood outside.

'Please, come in and join us,' said Red, indicating for them to enter.

Chiara looked at Eben with a furrowed brow as she entered the room. 'Eben Ecorian. We heard that you are being banished from Faircastle for attempting to begin a courtship with Princess Apherah. Is this true?'

'Yes,' replied Eben.

'Surely you must know that Irvaria and Everdon have only a tentative alliance at best. Unfortunately King Lenard has been promised Princess Apherah's hand in marriage. It is important for the united armies of Everdon and Irvaria to face the Prince of Shadows together. If you attempt to prevent this marriage the Everdonians may fight alone and refuse Irvarian help. The Prince of Shadows will crush the Everdonians and then march to the gates of Faircastle and destroy us. We need an alliance between Irvaria and Everdon. You must respect

King Lenard and not stand between him and Princess Apherah.'

Eben felt a rising anger at the unfair demands being made on him. 'Should I really show respect to King Lenard? He has little regard for me. I know Apherah does not want to marry the Everdonian. I simply can't agree to this.'

'I understand the Ecorian's point of view,' said Acartor. 'We need the Ecorian as much as we need the Everdonians.'

'What you say is true, Acartor, yet it is important for Eben to understands what is at risk,' said Chiara.

'I will fight for the people of Veredor regardless of what happens with Princess Apherah. But you also must know that Princess Apherah can marry whoever she wants; King Edric also knows this. She will never marry King Lenard. In four days King Edric will march south, and King Lenard will march with him even if he hasn't yet married Princess Apherah. The union between Irvaria and Everdon will not be important after the Prince of Shadows has been destroyed'

A loud knock made them turn. Again Red opened the door. More guardsmen had gathered outside to escort Eben out of the castle; they were growing impatient.

'By order of the King we must go now,' said the palace guardsman. Eben, Red, Stella, and Cassiel stood up and were ready to leave.

'If you ride south to Elcalee I will come with Baftel and Arlen the day after you arrive,' said Meara.

'I will go south with you, Ecorian,' said Acartor. 'There is much the Fiorians should share with you, and perhaps I can personally share some things that may help you in the battle against the Prince of Shadows.'

'No, Acartor, it is best that you stay here with King Edric and come south later,' said Chiara. 'You know most of the envoys well. You can do a lot to help foster the alliances. I will go with Eben and his friends to Elcalee.'

'As you wish, Gatekeeper,' said Acartor.

**

The palace guardsman led them to their horses; the four horses were prepared and waiting for them outside the palace. Chiara had agreed to meet them at the southern gate of the city. They mounted their horses and looked up at the majestic palace one last time.

'I hope we will have an opportunity to come back here one day,' said Red sombrely.

They turned their horses and rode slowly toward the southern gate of the city. The townsfolk took little notice of them. Even though the news had spread through the city that the Ecorian had returned they had no way of knowing that Eben was the Ecorian. They arrived at the southern gate and waited for Chiara about fifty yards outside the towering city walls.

Eben looked out across the land beyond the city. It was a cool and misty afternoon, unusually cold for summer in Irvaria, but the land of Irvaria held to its natural beauty in any weather. The small villages surrounding Faircastle were splendid. Emerald green meadows stretched far and wide. Blooming colourful flowers could be seen in all directions.

From the gate a hooded person approached in a long brown cloak. The person was carrying a parcel wrapped in brown leather tied together with twine. She pulled back her hood; Lila's face was revealed.

'Lady Lila, I thought you were confined to your chambers,' said Eben, surprised to see her.

She smiled and nodded. 'Some matters are worth being thrown into the dungeons for.' She handed Eben the leather bound parcel. 'This is a gift from Princess Apherah. She asked that you open it when you are alone.'

'Thank you, Lila. Please tell Apherah I will return as soon as I can.' He could feel the contents of the parcel were soft.

'I will, Eben Ecorian. I must hurry back. I wish you the best for your journey,' she said, smiling brightly. She then turned and walked quickly away toward the gate.

**

The road south from Faircastle to Elcalee led them through some of the most beautiful countryside they had ever seen. Hillsides of alders and groves full of silver birches frequented the roadside. Often they passed elaborate farmhouses and small picturesque villages where friendly village folk would always welcome them and ask them to stop for tea. Eben rode toward the back of the group with Chiara. Chiara's fiery red hair was unusually bright, and her eyes were emerald green, and had a distinct gemstone quality.

'I first entered the Fiorian Order twenty one years ago. Your mother was my teacher in those early days; I knew her well. I was fortunate that she personally instructed me for my first year,' said Chiara.

'Can you tell me about her?' asked Eben.

'She was exceptionally graceful and a brave warrior, unsurpassed in the history of the Fiorian Order. She was a kind woman and wise beyond her years. Your father was also a courageous and honourable man. He was a pilgrim who walked the lands of Veredor. He stood against evil wherever it appeared. He carried the Sword of Midlight in those days. I remember when Kaloren and Elons first met in the halls of Emeril. He was visiting Emeril, the home of the Fiorian Knights, and had come to request assistance in the battle against the Northern Sorcerer Baramak in the Far Western Lands. He fell in love with your mother and followed her to Ancora. It's exceptionally rare for a Fiorian to marry. We have to receive permission from the Gatekeeper of Emeril; such permission is rarely granted. I heard your parents married in the gardens of Stonehaven.'

'Stonehaven!' exclaimed Eben.

'Yes, they stopped there on their journey to Ortaria. They were going east to battle Azagord and his army.'

'Do you think my parents could still be alive?'

Chiara stared ahead and pondered the question. 'Eben, I doubt they are living in Veredor. I'm truly sorry to tell you this. We tried to find your parents and discover what had happened. All our efforts failed. I believe the Prince of Shadows is the only one who can answer your question.'

'I will ask him,' said Eben resolutely, feeling anger and determination rise through his body.

'I believe you will have the chance to,' said Chiara.

**

The company stopped at a small village called Far Field. The inn was situated at the southern edge of the village. Later in the evening Eben sat in his small room and opened the leather wrapping of Apherah's gift. Instantly he could see carefully folded purple material. He gently unfolded the material. The Ecorian white unicorn was revealed; he realised that he was holding the Ecorian flag. His heart skipped a beat when he fully unfolded the flag. He found a sealed letter and a rectangular glass case holding two wedding candles. The white wax seal showed the emblem of the Irvarian white dragon. He broke the seal and opened the letter.

Dearest Eben,

I will wait until you return with these candles to Faircastle. We will raise this flag together.

With love,

Princess Apherah of Irvaria

Eben felt his heart fill with joy. A renewed sense of energy and hope filled his body. In that moment he wanted to ride back to Faircastle to see her again, but with a little consideration he decided things were as they were meant to be. He would first fight the Prince of Shadows and then return triumphantly to Faircastle and marry Princess Apherah.

He lay on his bed and stared at the ceiling with a smile. He couldn't sleep; happy thoughts swirled in his head.

**

The following morning they set out early and made for Elcalee. Eben rode quietly at the rear of the group, watching the countryside pass by as they made their way south through Irvaria. Red slowed his horse to ride beside Eben.

'You seem quiet today,' said Red.

'I'm just thinking about the future.' Eben knew Red could read him well. He glanced across at his best friend.

'You mean that you're thinking about Princess Apherah?' Eben looked ahead and didn't answer. They rode on for a little while longer 'It's clear you have fallen for her. You're glowing with happiness.'

Eben looked across at Red and nodded. 'Yes, Red, I only hope this campaign in the south doesn't last too long. I want to ride back to Faircastle now.'

'A few more weeks and we will be on our way back.'

Eben laughed. 'I can hardly imagine this feeling being stronger.'

'It will grow stronger and more real, I guarantee it,' said Red, looking forward at Stella who was riding thirty yards ahead with Chiara. 'And the gift she sent. What was that about?'

'Just a flag,' replied Eben, not wanting to reveal anything about the candles and the letter.

'What kind of flag?' asked Red curiously.

'The flag of the Ecorian Empire,' said Eben.

Red was stunned by this admission. 'She wants you to be the Ecorian Emperor. Perhaps King Edric won't have much of a say after all. If you marry Apherah then you will eventually rule Irvaria and the Sapphire Throne. From such a position it would be easy for you to become the new Ecorian Emperor.'

'You know me well, Red; I'm a hunter, a villager, and these days I'm an adventurer, but I'm not a ruler. It would cause a lot of tension and perhaps even a war if I made a claim to the Sapphire Throne. You saw the hostility when my existence was revealed. I couldn't be responsible for causing a war.'

'If you were Emperor I could be one of your knights.'

'Thanks, Red, but I don't think it will ever happen. It's not something I want. My hopes are similar to yours. I just want a simple and quiet life. I want to find a peaceful place somewhere and settle down and live happily.'

'We will just have to wait and see what the future holds,' said Red.

They rode on throughout the day. The light of day started to fade. In the distance they could see three towers rising from a grey stone fortress which was shaped like a giant square block. As the road took them over a hill they could clearly see the town and fortress of Elcalee ahead. The fortress rose about a hundred yards in height above the surrounding town. Three towers ascended about another forty yards further from the top of the main structure. To Eben Elcalee looked more like a massive watchtower than a fortress.

The town below the fortress was surrounded by a short wall, only about five meters in height, and a twenty foot moat followed the base of the wall. A drawbridge extended across the moat. There were also several villages outside the town wall, and farmhouses were dotted about the countryside. To the south was a massive encampment where the Irvarian army had gathered. Thousands of men were making preparations for the march south. Eben watched as hundreds of Irvarian banners gently blew in the breeze.

'Welcome to Elcalee,' said Chiara, surveying the land ahead. 'As you can see this fortress is not nearly as impressive as Faircastle, yet Elcalee has earned a place in legend and has seen many battles.'

Chiara led them down through the countryside and villages. Within half an hour they had arrived at the gate of Elcalee.

'Duke Emont is expecting us. We will be his guests. King Edric told me he would send word ahead of us to make sure our stay in Elcalee is comfortable.'

They entered into the town and were led by a guardsman up to the fortress, which was situated at the top of the hill. Eben could see that much care had been taken by the townsfolk to make sure their town was beautiful, from small rose gardens lining the streets to elegantly made street lanterns. Even the wooden front doors of all the houses and terraces were adorned with beautiful carvings and intricate cast-iron doorknockers.

Waiting at the gate of the fortress was a tall and gaunt man who was wearing shining armour that looked too heavy for him. He was an old man with long dark hair and brown eyes. He stared at them with his chin held high and proud. Three knights stood on his left and three on his right. One bore the banner of Irvaria with the white dragon on the red background, the other flag was obviously the standard of Duke Emont's family, which depicted a shield with a white dragon on one side and a lion on the other. Above the shield was an eagle with outstretched wings and a red and white striped background.

Trumpets blared out from the towers above, and Duke Emont stepped forward and bowed low.

'I welcome you, Eben Ecorian, and your fine company to Elcalee. What an exceptional honour it is to have the Ecorian and the Gatekeeper of Emeril as my guests.'

People from the town started to gather around the company and looked up at Eben with awe in their eyes. He felt overwhelmed and self-conscious as more people surrounded the company.

'Thank you for your welcome, Duke Emont,' said Eben. He dismounted and walked over to the Duke and shook his hand. Chiara and Cassiel followed closely.

'I have a banquet prepared in the main dining chambers,' said Duke Emont.

The stable master took their horses. They then followed Duke Emont into the fortress and entered a large and sparse entrance chamber. Two flights of stone stairs ascended on the left and right. The stairs circled upward to join at a landing on the level above. Across the entrance chamber, directly in front of them, was a large iron door. Duke Emont led them up the right hand stairs, and the upper door opened as they approached. Two guardsmen stood within and bowed respectfully.

'I am very glad to have you as my guest, Eben Ecorian,' said Duke Emont as he led them through the door and into a long corridor. 'When news that an Ecorian had returned there were celebrations in the streets of Elcalee. I ordered the celebrations myself. I support your return, and I believe you should retake the Sapphire Throne. The throne is your birthright.'

'Duke Emont, not everyone shares your opinion,' said Chiara. 'Even your cousin, King Edric, opposes such a course of action.'

'Of course he does. He must be seen to be diplomatic, especially with all the envoys from other realms staying in Faircastle. I can assure you, Lady Chiara, that my cousin has been amazed by the return of the Ecorian. Time will tell his true position on the matter. Hopefully after the war we will have the coronation of the Ecorian Emperor and a new age of peace and happiness will arrive in Veredor.'

'Duke Emont, I thank you for your support, but please understand that I do not know how to rule,' said Eben. 'I do not want to cause any divisions. All I wish to do is help fight the Prince of Shadows. Perhaps the Ecorians won't return in the way you are hoping.'

Duke Emont smiled and nodded. 'Spoken like a true leader. I expected a certain level of humility from the Ecorian. As for ruling, there are many people who can help you do that. No king rules without advisors and magistrates, I don't expect it would be any different for an emperor. All you must know is that you have many supporters and many hope for the Sapphire Throne to be occupied as it was in the days of old.'

Eben cast his eyes downward, not knowing what to say. The Duke turned to the right and opened two large double doors. Before them was a large candlelit dining chamber with a long table and windows overlooking the town below. A banquet fit for an emperor was set out on the table with roast lamb, gravy, potatoes, baked pumpkins, broccoli, nuts, bowls of sweets, apple sauce, and several bottles of fine Irvarian wine.

Red put his hand on Eben's shoulder and smiled across at his friend. 'There are some benefits to being an emperor.'

Duke Emont then showed them to their seats. 'I know you have journeyed far today, and you must be tired. If there is anything you need please do not hesitate to ask. I have planned a meeting tomorrow at noon. There are several things we must discuss. Please rest now and enjoy the hospitality of Elcalee.'

CHAPTER THIRTEEN

The next day Eben and Chiara met in a small upper hall of the fortress. Chiara had insisted on complete privacy, and Duke Emont assured her that no one would disturb them. The hall was about thirty yards long with a very high arched ceiling and thin stained glass windows. The floor was made of grey stone, and the walls were completely sparse with no paintings or wall hangings of any kind. Chiara stood across from Eben. She was dressed in simple brown canvas clothing. She wore no armour and had bare feet. She drew her sword, which was a magnificent blade, finely built, and rather ancient in appearance.

'This is my sword; the Star of Emeril, an ancient blade that has been handed down through the Fiorian Order. The Star of Emeril was made by an exceptional Fiorian swordsmith nearly a thousand years ago.' The sword had a silver hilt and a woven pattern across the handle. 'I brought you here to teach you what I can. The Fiorians have many secret fighting techniques. Some of these methods may help you overcome the Prince of Shadows. I would like to test your skills to know your capabilities.' She lifted her sword slightly.

Eben drew the Sword of Light and held up the blade.

'I have heard your skills are amazing,' said Chiara with a smile. 'I am sure both of us are skilled enough to ensure the other doesn't get hurt.' She lifted her blade, pointing it directly at Eben and stared at him with intense focus. 'Begin.'

Eben moved to the left and began to circle Chiara. She turned on her heel to keep facing him directly. A hint of a smile passed her lips. In an instant she leapt forward. Eben skipped back as a torrent of precise and powerful strikes and slashes raced toward him. In moments he found he was almost against the wall. He had never encountered such skill and knew he would have to lift or be beaten. He leapt back, stepping up and using the wall to project himself away from Chiara. He flew through the air and rolled upon landing, quickly regaining his feet and stance. He swung his blade back at Chiara. Chiara spun around to face him and easily deflected his strike.

'Not bad,' said Chiara. Eben focused and leapt forward, unleashing a surge of attacks. Chiara held her ground and calmly deflected all his attacks. She halted his advance and pushed him back with a burst of strikes. Eben nearly fell and stumbled back as he regained his balance.

She pounced forward and her blade cut toward him. Eben deflected and again she launched herself at him. Their blades flashed like lightning; Eben tried to hold his ground but found he was being pushed back across the hall. He strained to defend himself. He was losing control and focus. Salty sweat was dripping into his eyes. A moment later he felt his sword leave his hand and heard it bounce along the cold stone floor. Chiara held her sword only inches from his neck.

'You win,' he muttered, amazed by her great skill.

Chiara placed her sword back its scabbard. 'You are exceptional, Eben. You are far better than any warrior I have ever encountered; however, I doubt you will overcome the Prince of Shadows with the skills you have.'

'How can I do better?' asked Eben, picking up his sword from the floor.

'Your technique is good; the main problem is that you reveal your intention to your opponent. You have to learn to calm your mind and not show what you are going to do. This is how I beat you; I was aware of what you intended to do. I could predict the outcome. This gave you the impression that I was faster than you. The reality was that you were much faster than me.'

'How can I change?'

'You need to relax your mind and not focus on the outcome. Focus on what you are doing in the moment and try not to overcompensate. Simplicity is often far better than complexity. You have successfully fought muckrons, Skatheans, and wyverns. The Prince of Shadows is in a different league. You must have a clear focus if you are going to stand a chance against him.'

'Perhaps I should give the Sword of Light to you; even without it you easily beat me.'

'Not easily. If you had not revealed your intention I would have lost. As for the Sword of Light, I believe the Prince of Shadows is afraid of you for reasons other than your ability to fight. The Ecorians were gifted with the ability to unite and inspire the people of Veredor. He may be more afraid of your ability to lead an army against him. There may be one other reason why he fears you, but it is a deep secret. I don't know much of it.'

'What secret?'

'It is said in our ancient records that the Astarian Fiora did not overcome the Prince of Shadows with the Sword of Light alone. The records refer to something that the Knights of Shidon knew little about, a mystical power of some kind. I know nothing of the power other than the fact that it existed.'

'Can I learn this secret magic?'

Chiara looked up toward the windows and pondered the question. 'This power may be what the Prince of Shadows is afraid of. Fiora left Veredor after she used this mystical power against the Prince of Shadows. Her fate has forever been shrouded in mystery. Somehow she closed the Cosmic Gate and sealed the Prince of Shadows out of Veredor. In theory this should have been impossible. All the Astarians can freely pass through the Cosmic Gate, but the gate was sealed against the Prince of Shadows.'

'How then did he return to Veredor?'

'I think it is important for you to understand why Fiora and the Prince of Shadows fought in the first place. The Astarians were the original people of our world. They were a majestic and beautiful people who possessed great knowledge and wisdom. They planted the trees and brought the lesser creatures to Veredor in ancient times. Fiora was one of their three leaders, graceful beyond measure, and a magnificent warrior.'

'In the beginning there was a war; the Astarians fought against an army of evil creatures from the darkness beyond. These enemies invaded Veredor to take it for themselves. The Astarians fought until few of their race remained. In the final days of that ancient war they built the Cosmic Gate to protect Veredor from the creatures of darkness. The Cosmic Gate ended the first war of the Forgotten Age and protected Veredor from further invasion. Few Astarians lived on in Veredor after the war. It was decided by a council of remaining Astarians that they should welcome others to Veredor to tend to the lands and bring joy back to their much loved world. That was when they welcomed men and mer to Veredor.'

'The Prince of Shadows is an Astarian. Why did he fight Fiora?'

'The Prince of Shadows was one of the three leaders of the Astarian people. His original name was lost in antiquity. The Prince of Shadows voted against welcoming men and mer to Veredor, yet the majority of remaining Astarians wanted to welcome men and mer to populate their lonely lands. Men and mer, who closely resembled the Astarians physically, were welcomed to Veredor in the Forgotten Age. They came and settled the lands and built towns and cities. Men especially flourished. The mer retreated to the oceans and diminished beneath the waves.'

'Why then did the Prince of Shadows turn against us?'

'At first he accepted our arrival and allowed us to prosper. Soon after this time he left Veredor and wandered through other worlds and dark places far from Veredor. When he returned he had changed. He called a council of Astarians and demanded that he be made the Lord of Veredor. He wanted the remaining Astarians, men, and mer to submit to his rule. The Astarians refused his request. Without warning he opened the Cosmic Gate and brought forth an army of muckrons, wyverns, draugs, and other creatures of darkness to destroy anyone who opposed his plan to rule Veredor.'

'The remaining Astarians rose up against him and his evil army. Most of the Astarians were slain. Fiora escaped and went to men and mer seeking their help. She formed the Knights of

Shidon, who later became the Fiorian Knights, and built a fortress called Shidon in the icy lands far in the north of Veredor. A mighty battle was fought in the land of Alber. Fiora wielded the Sword of Light, and the Prince of Shadows, leading his evil army, carried the Sword of Darkness. The Knights of Shidon were victorious over the army of monsters, and Fiora defeated the Prince of Shadows. With the secret power she sealed the Cosmic Gate against his return. From that day she was never again seen in Veredor. Her final act was to hand over the Sword of Light to the remaining Knights of Shidon.'

'So now the Cosmic Gate has been reopened,' said Eben. 'The Prince of Shadows has once again brought an evil army. Only now there are no Astarians to prevent him becoming the Lord of Veredor.'

'At the beginning of the First Age there were several Astarians who lived secretly in the wilderness of Veredor. If any remain today they are choosing to remain silent. Only the Voran Oracle lives in the Far West; our attempts to find her have failed. Thus far the Prince of Shadows has subdued all who have stood in his way. I fear that muckrons, wyverns, and draugs are only some of the evil creatures he has serving him. His impatience may be our only chance at overcoming him. If Acartor is right we may be able to defeat him, but you must prepare yourself. Acartor believes you are the only one who can do this. If you fail Veredor will become a world of darkness.'

Chiara drew her sword again. 'This time try to stay calm. Simplicity is the key.'
**

They went from training in the upper hall to the meeting with Duke Emont in a small command room on the uppermost floor of the fortress. Covering almost the entire surface of the table was a large map depicting the surrounding lands. Eben was seated at the head of the rectangular table with Red, Stella, Cassiel, and Chiara. Meara entered the room followed by Baftel and Arlen. Eben stood up to greet them.

'I trust your journey here was without incident,' said Meara as she took a seat at the table.

'A leisurely ride through the countryside,' answered Red, smiling broadly.

'We have much to talk about. Duke Emont is coming with Sir Walter, Commander of the Irvarian army. They should be here any minute.'

A moment later the door opened and Duke Emont entered the command room from the opposite side of the room. He was followed by a large burly middle aged man with a long black beard and strong dark eyes.

'Greetings,' said Duke Emont, bowing toward Eben. 'Eben Ecorian, I would like you to meet Sir Walter of the Great Mountains, Knight of Irvaria and Commander of the Irvarian Army.'

Eben quickly stood up and walked over to shake the Commander's hand before he could bow.

'I am very pleased to meet you, Sir Walter,' said Eben politely.

'And I you, Ecorian,' replied Sir Walter in a deep and strong voice.

'Now, let us begin our meeting,' said Duke Emont as he took the seat at the opposite head of the table. Sir Walter sat down beside Cassiel. 'As you all know the main force of the Irvarian army is preparing to set out to join with the Everdonian army north of the port city of Lucaria. The Prince of Shadows plans to land his fleet somewhere on the coast of Everdon. We doubt he will attempt to attack Lucaria from the sea because of the city's strong battlements. Any invasion from the sea would most likely be repelled. We believe he will want to establish a base away from Lucaria in order to prepare his army for a full scale land invasion of Everdon.'

'The Prince of Shadows has power far beyond any seer. He has shrouded many of his plans in darkness,' said Baftel. 'Yet the Prince of Shadows cannot protect the intentions of those who captain his ships. I have seen the intentions of the fleet. They do not intend to directly attack Lucaria.'

'Good, it is as we expect,' said Duke Emont. 'Our main concern is the ship of Zyranian wizards sailing with the enemy fleet.'

'At least fifty Zyranians have set sail to help the enemy invade Everdon,' said Meara. 'King Ignis now has spies in Zyran. He sent news of this Zyranian ship to Faircastle, which arrived just before we left for Elcalee. It is cause for concern; fifty Zyranians could alter the outcome of any battle fought in Everdon. I have made a request for the Irilians to send a brigade of wizards. They can only spare five at this time. War rages in Iarthar and our wizards are scattered across many lands. These five Irilians are crossing the Great Mountains as we speak and should enter Irvaria in the coming days. We are still vastly outnumbered by Zyranians. The only wizards we have to help us are those at this table and the five Irilians who will join us on the road south.'

'What about the Fire Order?' asked Red. He pointed to the map and the Old Guardian Mountains which were not far from Elcalee.

'That is precisely what this meeting is about,' said Duke Emont.

'Surely they will help,' said Cassiel. 'They had a representative at the council.'

'Yes, the wizard Mostyn was at the council,' said Meara. 'He left soon after the council concluded and returned to the Tower of Fire in the Old Guardian Mountains. He didn't commit anything to help our cause. When we asked for his help he wouldn't answer us.'

'Why wouldn't they want to help?' asked Eben.

'The Fire Order is a meditative and reclusive order of wizards,' said Meara. 'They have had little to do with the happenings of men over the last two thousand years. They keep to themselves and rarely mingle with others. It was a great feat that they even sent an envoy to the council. They live out solitary lives in their ancient tower hidden high in the Old Guardian Mountains.'

'Surely they must see the danger we face,' said Stella. 'The Prince of Shadows will also destroy them if they don't help us.'

'They do see this possibility. Unfortunately they have few loyalties to anyone outside their own order. They simply don't trust anyone but their own people,' said Arlen.

'How many of them are there?' asked Red.

'At least forty,' replied Duke Emont. 'There may be more. The reality is that the Fire Order will only help us if an ancient oath is called upon.'

'What oath?' asked Eben.

'The Fire Order is a sworn ally of the Ecorians; this oath is actually written into their rule. If you request their assistance they must help you.'

'Then I will have to go to the Tower of Fire to ask for their help,' said Eben.

'Precisely,' said Duke Emont. 'They simply can't refuse to help you if you make the request. Although there is one possible problem; to enter the Tower of Fire you must pass through the Gate of Fire. Only a wizard can repel the flames of the Gate of Fire, anyone else would be completely consumed.'

'I will go with you, Eben,' said Cassiel instantly.

'That is brave of you to offer,' said Duke Emont. 'I dare say that an Irilian would not be welcomed by the Fire Order. The Gate of Fire is only one of the ways the Fire Order protect their home. The road to the Tower of Fire may prove dangerous.'

'How is it possible for Eben to pass through the gate if a wizard can't go with him?' asked Red, scratching his chin.

'There is a way,' said Meara in a low and sombre voice. 'Before you arrive at the Gate of Fire you will find a cave which leads to an ancient place called the Chamber of Ash. In the chamber there is said to be a pool of water that glows as if it was infused with sunlight. If you drink the glowing water of the Pool of Radiance the flames of the Gate of Fire will not harm you.'

'What does the water do?' asked Eben.

'It will cause you great pain,' said Arlen sternly. 'An unnatural pain will come over you of a kind unknown to men or mer. For a time you will be completely crippled and blind. Eventually the pain will pass and when it does you will be immune to fire brought about by magic. All the wizards of the Fire Order drink from the Pool of Radiance; therefore they can pass through fire unharmed.'

'How long will the pain last?' asked Eben, looking to Meara for an answer. He felt a little anxious about the idea of being blind and crippled.

'I don't know for sure, an entire day I would guess,' said Meara. 'You don't have to accept this mission.'

Eben thought about the implications. He could see that it was necessary to gain the support of the Fire Order in the coming battle. He also thought that being immune to fire caused by magic would be of great benefit. He remembered back to when Zarceler had used fire spells against him and how the Zyranian wizards had rained fire down on them on the battlefield in Ortaria.

'I will drink from the pool,' said Eben resolutely.

'The journey to the Tower of Fire will take several days. I believe I am the only one here who knows the way,' said Chiara. 'I will lead you there.'

**

The following morning Eben, Red, Stella, and Chiara set out for the Old Guardian Mountains. Cassiel had been instructed by Meara to remain behind as she felt that it would be unwise for him to go anywhere near the Tower of Fire. She also wanted to continue his training as an Irilian and prepare him for the coming battle.

The weather had taken a turn for the worse. A solid wind was blowing from the south. The further they journeyed away from Elcalee the less they encountered settlements. The beauty of Irvaria seemed to fade away. The land mostly flattened out into large grass plains with occasional thin clusters of trees.

As they rode on Eben became aware of the Old Guardian Mountains in the distance. The mountain range rose up like craggy dark fangs into the sky above. They were approaching the northern edge of the range where the Old Guardian Mountains intersected the Sunset Hills. The main highway was curving westward. Chiara led them off the road and into the grasslands. By the time the day came to an end the mountains were only a few hours ride away.

The Old Guardian Mountains and the Sunset Hills had long been a natural shield that protected the lands of Everdon and Irvaria from the desolate curse of Vastoria. The only way across the mountains was by way of the ancient Grey Pass, a dangerous road which passed through deep valleys and traversed high ledges. The lone fortress of Hawkwatch stood at the height of the Grey Pass. The fortress stood like a lone sentry high in the mountains and had guarded the people of Everdon for centuries. It had long been considered an honour among young Everdonian soldiers to serve in the garrison of Hawkwatch.

The only other inhabitants of the Old Guardian Mountains were the Fire Order, but the Tower of Fire was situated in such a remote location that few ever gave much thought to its presence. The Fire Order lived out their lives far from the affairs of the wider world.

The company set up camp under a group of trees and lit a small campfire. Chiara meditated for some time outside the camp and watched the sunset over the hills. After the sun had fully retreated behind the hills she returned to sit by the fire with the others. Red was cooking up a mushroom stew, and a sweet aroma filled the campsite.

'Dinner should be ready in a few minutes,' he said cheerfully.

'It smells nice,' said Stella.

'I managed to take a few ingredients from the kitchen pantries in Elcalee,' said Red, lifting the wooden spoon to his lips to taste his success. 'Even better than it smells.'

Red prepared a bowl for each of them. They sat around the fire enjoying his wonderful stew as the night grew dark.

'Tomorrow morning we will come upon the northern edge of the Old Guardian Mountains,' said Chiara. 'The path to the Tower of Fire will be difficult and very steep. We should reach the Fire Steps by midday. From then onwards you will go alone, Eben. Just beyond the cave you will see a long natural rock bridge that crosses a deep chasm. The bridge will lead you to the Gate of Fire. We will wait at the base of the Fire Steps for you to return. You must be careful; the Fire Order is known for their ability to defend the Tower of Fire.'

**

Eben woke to the rumbling sound of thunder. Dark storm clouds were crossing the mountains and heading west toward their camp. They set out early and before long they were pushing forward through heavy wind and rain. Chiara led the way onward. Eben pulled his leather cloak tightly around himself in an attempt to keep the weather out. They rode on with determination. Around midday they entered hilly moorlands that led upward toward the craggy peaks. They followed a goat track through a valley and up a steep hill. The summer rain continued to shower down from the dark swirling clouds above.

Gradually the way became rockier and difficult. The horses were struggling with the terrain. Eventually they decided to continue on foot and left their horses in a grassy dale. They pushed onward up a steep hillside. At the height of the hill they could see an outstanding view of the snow-capped mountains ahead. The Old Guardian Mountains rose like contorted spikes toward the sky.

Chiara stopped and gazed out on the mountains. In silence they stood and stared ahead. 'We are not far from the stairs,' she said.

Chiara led them onward. They traversed a ridge that led to a gradual descent and came to a place between two steep mountainsides. A crystal clear stream flowed through the base of a mighty chasm. An ancient walkway had been hewn from the rock and followed the course of the rushing water. For several minutes they moved upward through the chasm. As they rounded a final corner Eben's eyes caught sight of a long flight of steps that ascended directly up the side of an enormous mountain. The steps went on for hundreds of yards and rose in a straight line.

'The Fire Steps,' said Chiara. 'From here you must go on alone. At the height of the stairs you will find the cave which leads to the Chamber of Ash and the Pool of Radiance.'

An icy wind blew toward them. Eben stared up at the mountain peak above. He couldn't see any tower, only the thick dark clouds. He slung his backpack and sword over his shoulder.

'I will return as quickly as I can,' said Eben, walking forward toward the base of the steps.

'Be careful,' shouted Stella as he bounded up the first few steps.

The Fire Steps were made of slippery grey stones slabs that ascended on an almost vertical angle. A practical man would have thought that they were built by a fool, but the wise knew that the Fire Order had deliberately made the way to the Tower of Fire challenging.

Eben began his ascent and found he could use his hands for extra support. The wind blasted across the side of the mountain; he often had to hold on tight to stop himself from being blown away. After several minutes of climbing he looked down and could see his friends far below. A slight sense of dizziness came over him as he realised how far he had already come. He climbed onwards and focused forward and upward. After a difficult climb he arrived at the top of the steps.

A stone path led across the top of the mountain. He walked forward and followed the path; the way curved through jagged outcroppings of rock. As he crossed to the far side of the mountain he could see a large stone bridge that spanned hundreds of feet across a deep valley to the adjacent peak. Atop the opposite mountain was a daunting fortress which was carved into the pinnacle. The fortress soared high toward the clouds above. Dark smoke rose from the tallest tower.

Eben followed the way forward. Just before he came to the rock bridge he caught sight of the dark entrance to the cave. It looked very murky and uninviting, but he knew he would have to continue. He lit his small lantern and walked into the darkness. The tunnel descended deep into the mountainside. He followed the way downward for several minutes. The cave widened, and he caught sight of a faint glow ahead. As he proceeded the light grew brighter and the tunnel opened into a large cavern. Directly before him was a small stone landing, and beyond the landing was a shallow pool of shimmering water that lit up the cavern. The water itself seemed to be infused with bright light; it appeared as if the sun was shining from beneath the pool itself.

Eben stepped toward the edge of the pool and knelt down. He reached out and scooped up a small amount of water. The water was glowing and shimmering in his hands. Without delay he lifted his cupped hands to his lips and drank the glowing water. At first he felt nothing. A few moments passed without any change. He wondered if anything would happen.

Suddenly he felt a burning sensation deep within which was followed by a twisting pain in his stomach. The pain began like a swirling sword and gradually spread outwards to his hands and feet. He focused, resisting the sensation, thinking that it was only a matter of controlling his attention and not focusing on the pain, but the pain grew the more he tried not to focus on it.

He sat beside the Pool of Radiance and stared down at the glimmering water. He attempted to distract himself. The pain was steadily worsening; he realised, in that moment, that the pain was going far beyond what he had prepared for. He found himself in excruciating agony. He held his head in his hands as he felt every part of his body burn as if struck with blades of fire. His breathing quickened and he let out a groan, hoping it would pass, but the pain didn't pass. He lay down on his side and held his knees to his chest. He cried deep in his soul and begged for someone, something, anything to liberate him from the agony but nothing came. Wave after wave blasted his flesh. He felt his vision fade and his body weaken. All went dark.

CHAPTER FOURTEEN

Eben awoke and the pain had passed. He felt light headed and sat up and looked at the shimmering pool for a moment. A shiver went up his spine. Nothing could have prepared him for the intensity of the experience. He felt that he had pushed through a barrier in his mind, and he knew many things would be different in the future.

He found his way out of the cave and stood for a moment in the faint light of the morning as soft rain fell from above. He looked up at the sky in silence and felt a sense of peace in his heart. He turned toward the stone bridge and slowly walked toward the Tower of Fire. Ahead of him, standing in the middle of the stone bridge, was a ten foot tall bronze statue of a man with the head of a fearsome eagle. The statue held a massive battle axe in its right hand. The bronze gargoyle stared at him, frozen in place, as the light rain fell. He continued to cross.

Suddenly the bronze statue took a step toward him. The metal screeched as it took another step. 'Go No Further!' bellowed the gargoyle. The inhuman voice boomed across expanse between them and echoed back off the mountainsides.

Eben stopped in his tracks and stared at the massive statue. 'I am Eben Ecorian. I have come seeking the help of the Fire Order!' he cried out in return.

The gargoyle stood completely still and gave no reply. Eben waited and nothing happened. The only sound was the passing of the mountain winds. He waited for a minute and then decided to move forward again. Suddenly the massive bronze eagle head lifted and the bronze statue took two steps toward him.

'Go no further!' repeated the gargoyle in exactly the same tone.

Eben knew that he would have to pass this guardian if he was to ever meet with the Fire Order. He continued to walk forward. 'I mean you no harm. I have only come seeking help.'

Suddenly the gargoyle's eyes started to glow brightly, and the bronze of its body became hot; the rain steamed and hissed as it fell on the metal. The gargoyle lifted its axe and with heavy grinding steps started moving toward Eben. Eben drew the Sword of Light and waited on the bridge.

'You must let me pass,' he cried as the massive metal gargoyle approached. The gargoyle lifted its huge battle axe. Eben knew in that moment he would have to fight. He focused his mind and held the Sword of Light between himself and the approaching metal creature. The massive axe came swinging with tremendous power and might. Eben was quick to react. He dashed out of the way and quickly struck back. The gargoyle deflected his blade with ease.

Again the axe hurtled down with a great amount of power. Eben dodged the blow, and the axe caused sparks to blast up from the rocky surface of the bridge. He rushed behind the gargoyle and brought his sword down with all his might as the gargoyle turned to face him. The sword cut through the statue's metal shoulder, slicing through the solid bronze. The gargoyle was untroubled by the damage and struck Eben with its free hand. Eben tumbled back away from the living statue and staggered along the bridge.

The crippled gargoyle closely trailed him. He found his balance just in time to dodge another blow from the huge axe. He quickly stepped back and held up his sword. The eagle headed statue again cut down at him. Eben waited until the last possible moment and then dashed aside and simultaneously cut off one of the statue's metal legs. The gargoyle instantly collapsed and floundered on the ground. Moments later it attempted to rise up but lost balance and toppled over the edge of the bridge. Eben watched as the emotionless bronze statue fell silently away into the misty chasm below.

He waited a moment to catch his breath before turning to continue across the bridge. At the far side a large stone archway led into a tunnel that was at least fifty yards long and cut directly into the mountainside. Above the archway were carved words in an unknown ancient script. Eben knew in his heart that this was the Gate of Fire. He stepped forward and held his sword ready. The tunnel walls around him started to glow red. He continued as the glow became bright. Suddenly the flames blasted out from the wall and completely swamped him. He felt no heat at all and knew the experience of the Pool of Radiance had protected him. After a few moments the flames retreated. Not even his clothes were affected by the flames.

He arrived at the far side of the tunnel where a large ironclad door stood in his way. The door had no lock. He pushed through and found a dark stairwell that ascended upward for hundreds of yards. In the distance he could see a faint light. He quickly ascended the stairs and came to a large, dimly lit, and long chamber. Faint light drifted down from several small portholes cut high into the ceiling above. The chamber was completely sparse. Directly ahead of him, opposite the stairwell, was another large ironclad door. He walked across the chamber and pushed open the door.

Just ahead was a short corridor that led to a door made of solid bronze. A moment later he pushed the second door open and instantly he found himself stepping into a great amphitheatre. The massive area was circular with walls ascending to an open ceiling high above. Stone seats lined the rising edges. The wizards were seated and facing the centre of the amphitheatre where a single stone block stood with a bright flame burning intensely atop it. The wizards turned to face him as he entered. They appeared to be a bedraggled bunch of misfits; they were mostly bearded and wearing rags. The wizards silently stared at him as he walked toward the flaming stone in the centre of the amphitheatre.

'What is the meaning of this? How did you pass the Gate of Fire and the guardian?' cried out one of the company.

'My name is Eben Ecorian. I am the last of the Ecorians. I have come here to request your assistance in the battle against the Prince of Shadows who has returned to Veredor to destroy men and mer.'

The room became deathly silent and the wizards stared down at Eben. Almost a minute of silence followed as Eben waited for their response.

'The Ecorians are extinct,' cried a wizard. 'You cannot be an Ecorian.'

Eben turned around and stared up at the wizards as he walked around the flaming stone.

'I tell you the truth. I am the Ecorian, a descendent of both men and mer. I know that you have taken an oath to help me if I should request your help. I have come here to make such a request. The Prince of Shadows will soon land his army of muckrons on the shores of Everdon. The Zyranians are working with him. Without the Fire Order we may not win the battle.' Again the room fell silent.

'We are not convinced,' said an extremely ragged and old wizard who was seated at the back of the amphitheatre.

Eben caught sight of Mostyn, the wizard who had been at the council in Faircastle. 'Mostyn, you were at the council. You know what I say is true.'

'Yes, he tells the truth. He is the only remaining descendent of the Ecorians, but he is not an Ecorian Emperor. We are required in our rule to help the Ecorian Emperor, not an Ecorian descendent.'

'Surely you must see the danger we face and the evil forces that will enslave us all. You must help us in our struggle against the Prince of Shadows.'

The wizards murmured among themselves and after some time discussing the matter Mostyn spoke. 'We will only follow the Ecorian Emperor. I was at the council. I saw you refuse your birthright. The Sapphire Throne was built by the Astarians as a gift to Jeriel the Just and his descendants. It was your right to take your throne. You refused; therefore we believe you are not the Ecorian Emperor. You conceded to the wishes of the Ecorian Arbiters.'

'I only want to help save our world from evil. I cannot force you to assist me, but you should know this: if you do not the Prince of Shadows will be the next person to enter this place. I am sure you will regret your refusal in that moment. You are the Fire Order; your power was granted to you by the Astarian Lumen with the hope that you could help save Veredor from evil. Now you have arrived at a crucial moment in the history of your order, the moment where you are called to follow your original mandate. If you refuse to help me then I say your days are numbered, and the memory of the Fire Order will fade from Veredor forever. These are the words of the Ecorian; you know they are true.' The wizards were stunned to silence by his words.

'We will not help,' said Mostyn.

'So be it; may the light of the Fire Order fade from Veredor.'

With Eben's words a strong wind blew through the amphitheatre and circled around the wizards and then blasted around Eben. The flame that burned on the stone suddenly blew out. The wizards cried in horror.

'For thousands of years the Pure Flame has burned here in this place. You, Ecorian, have caused it to go out?' cried Mostyn.

'Only an Astarian can do what he just did,' cried a wizard with tangled red hair who was seated beside Mostyn. The amphitheatre fell eerily silent.

'I am an Ecorian, not an Astarian,' replied Eben.

'This indeed is something we did not expect,' murmured Mostyn. His dark sunken eyes stared at Eben for a long moment. 'He has taken our flame from us, and in doing so he has revealed a deep secret. Fiora's Bridge may yet be crossed. I believe we should follow him to Everdon.' The wizards whispered among themselves.

'I don't understand. What do you mean? What is Fiora's Bridge?' asked Eben, looking up at the many wizards. They had their eyes fixed on him.

'It would not be wise for me to tell you what I may or may not know about such things,' said Mostyn. 'In time you will find the truth for yourself, and hopefully the truth will save us all. It is agreed among us; we will follow you to Everdon and help you fight the Prince of Shadows. Tomorrow we will come down from the Tower of Fire and march toward Everdon. Know this Ecorian: we will not belong to any army or work under any leader.'

Eben was amazed by what he had witnessed. Shortly after this he departed and made his way back down the Fire Steps.

**

The sun was shining once again and the storm clouds had passed into the west, leaving a bright blue sky above. Eben could see the small camp set at the base of the Fire Steps. He slowly navigated his way down toward his friends.

'Will the Fire Order join us?' asked Red as Eben arrived at the base of the steps.

'Yes, they will come down tomorrow and follow us to Everdon.'

Chiara walked over and nodded. 'This is a blessing. I feared they would reject your request. Only once in all of history has the Fire Order come down from the Tower of Fire and that was to help one of your ancestors.'

'They almost refused. There are things they know that I do not understand? They speak of something called Fiora's Bridge. Do you know what Fiora's Bridge is?'

'I do know a little about Fiora's Bridge. When men and mer first came to Veredor the Astarian Fiora wanted our races to become a part of the fabric of this world as the Astarians were. She could not complete her plan because Veredor rejected us. We could not form a relationship with Veredor. The Astarians thought the reason for this was a fault in our nature. The quest to find an answer became known as Fiora's Bridge. Fiora's Bridge was never crossed. Men and mer have always remained guests in Veredor.'

'What does this have to do with me?'

'Fiora's Bridge is important to the story of men and mer in Veredor.' She paused for a moment and stared into Eben's eyes. She often seemed to know much more than she would say. 'Two and a half thousand years have passed since the Forgotten Age and much knowledge has been lost. Why Veredor rejected us remains a mystery. I do not know what would have happened if our race had crossed Fiora's Bridge. This is all I can tell you.'

**

They collected their horses and camped for a night in the moorlands. Chiara led them away from the Old Guardian Mountains toward the southwest.

'We will make for the Forest of Sorrows. There we will come again to the highway. The highway will take us through the forest to the town of Marraw in Everdon,' said Chiara. 'The Irvarian army have already left Elcalee and will be taking the main road south. Meara and the other Irilians will have already made their way south ahead of us. They will be waiting for us to join them somewhere near Marraw.'

They came out of the moorlands and into lush grasslands that seemed to grow greener and brighter the further they travelled south. They moved quickly throughout the day. As the night approached they could see the northern border of the Forest of Sorrows. Chiara led them up to the edge of the forest, and they followed the line of trees westward. The forest was predominantly made up of tall alder trees which grew closely together. Toward the end of the day they set up camp just beyond the edge of the forest.

Eben and Stella gathered some wood for the fire as Red was busy preparing a meal. Chiara sat away from the campsite meditating as she usually did around sunset.

'Today is the seventh day of summer,' said Eben with a smile.

'Is it significant for some reason?' asked Stella, glancing in his direction as she picked up some dry sticks and branches.

'It's my nineteenth birthday,' said Eben, having just realised.

'Happy birthday!' said Stella happily.

'Did I hear it's your birthday?' called out Red from the campsite.

'Nineteen today,' repeated Stella.

'We should celebrate,' said Red. He fumbled about in his backpack and drew out a small metal flask. 'This is a bottle of rare Silvorian rum that I was given by the palace staff in Faircastle. I was keeping it for after our victory, but since it's your birthday I think we should have a drink now.' Red poured four cups as Chiara returned to the camp.

'No rum for me, Red,' said Chiara as she glanced at the edge of the Forest of Sorrows. 'Tonight should be calm indeed.'

Red proceeded to kindle the fire. They sat around the campfire as Red started cooking another mushroom stew. The night grew dark and Eben sipped at his rum and looked into the flames dancing over the coals. The soft sound of singing filled his ears.

Eben stood up and looked toward the forest. A voice was softly singing in the distance. Stella and Red got to their feet and also looked toward the forest edge.

'Can you hear that?' asked Eben, peering toward the edge of the forest. The woman's voice was gentle and soft.

'What's she singing about?' asked Red.

'I can't make out the words,' answered Stella. They listened for a few moments longer.

'She sings from her heart,' said Chiara, who hadn't stood up. She remained seated calmly by the campfire. They looked down at her and waited for an explanation. She glanced up at them for a moment as the singing continued. Her eyes then looked back toward the flames. Eben turned and looked back to the forest. The beautiful voice was fading into the distance and finally disappeared.

'She is called the Maiden of Sorrows,' said Chiara, not lifting her eyes from the fire.

'Who is she?' asked Eben, sitting down again by the fire.

'No one has ever seen her. Those who try to follow the voice never find her. The story of her origins has been told for many generations.'

'Can you tell us the story, Chiara?' asked Eben.

Chiara's eyes watched the flickering flames. 'Many centuries ago she was once the daughter of a farmer who lived in the grasslands to the north of the forest. Her beauty was said to be so great that many men from distant lands came to court her. Their hopes were all in vain because she dearly loved another. She had given her heart to a shepherd's son from these northern grasslands. Her father agreed to the marriage and organised a wedding. Before the wedding had occurred a baron from the south came to visit the fair maiden; he had heard the legend of her enchanting beauty. Upon seeing her he instantly wanted to take her as his wife. He asked the farmer to abandon the wedding and allow him to marry her.'

'The farmer refused because he knew his daughter's love for the shepherd's son was true. The Baron was angered by the farmer's decision but appeared to accept his will. His only request was that he could attend the wedding, and the farmer could not refuse a nobleman such a request. And so the wedding proceeded in a glade deep in the forest.'

Chiara paused for a few moments and stared up at the bright stars above. 'Out of envy and desire the Baron had secretly plotted to take over the wedding. He brought with him a troop of guardsmen and had the shepherd's son dragged away. He attempted to marry the farmer's daughter there and then. She would not light wedding candles with him. When he threatened to kill the shepherd's son, her true love, she agreed to marry the Baron, but only on any other day apart from the day she intended to marry her true love. The Baron agreed, and she was taken in a carriage away through the forest.'

'On the way south she learned they intended to kill her true love. She leapt from the carriage and escaped into the woods. She was pursued by the soldiers of the Baron. She made her way back through the forest to the glade. When she arrived her heart broke. Her true love lay murdered in the grass. She wept tears of such sorrow that have rarely been seen in Veredor. From that day on she was never seen again. Her voice is sometimes heard singing at night deep in the forest as we heard tonight. That is why the forest is called the Forest of Sorrows.'

'Why then is the song so beautiful?' asked Red.

Chiara glanced up from the fire. 'Because her sorrow was turned into joy,' she answered.

'But how?' asked Red.

Chiara looked across at Red for a moment in silence. She seemed to be pondering the best way to answer his question. 'This is a deep mystery, Red. Even the wisest in Veredor do not know how to answer your question.'

The peaceful night went on. They sat around the fire and rested. Eben listened until late, but the voice of the maiden did not return. The following morning they were greeted with a clear blue sky and a warm summer sun. They packed up their camp quickly and continued following the northern edge of the Forest of Sorrows.

CHAPTER FIFTEEN

The Forest of Sorrows was enchantingly beautiful and full of life. To a traveller it seemed more like a garden than a natural forest. It rose like a lone sanctuary from the wide grasslands that covered the south of Irvaria. The forest was made up of a diverse selection of trees: alders and silver birches in the north, and further south the clusters of alders gave way to beautiful old beeches. Toward the southern border pockets of oaks towered high above all the other trees, and groups of linden trees filled splendid groves. The woodsmen of the forest were a solitary folk and kept to themselves in the deep glades and small valleys, preferring the peaceful solitude of the deep forest.

**

By noon they came upon the main highway. Chiara looked down at the road for a little while before they proceeded south into the forest.

'The Irilians have already passed this way. The Fiorian Acartor is with them.'

'You can see that from these tracks?' asked Red, staring down at the faint tracks.

'Yes, Fiorians are trained to remember the unique tracks of horses and men,' she said. 'We should come to the other side of the forest by nightfall. There we can stay in a small village in the hills on the southern side.'

They turned south and rode onward into the woods. The forest was full of life. Birds could be heard singing in all directions. They rode for several hours, and around the middle of the afternoon the company came to a place where the forest fell eerily silent. Chiara stopped her horse and stared ahead. Her bright blue eyes were scanning the canopy.

'What's wrong?' asked Eben softly, halting his horse beside her. He looked ahead to see what she was looking at. She watched in silence for a few moments.

'Skathean Vultures,' she murmured. 'They're spying on us.' Eben strained his eyes; he couldn't see anything at first. He looked from tree to tree. Suddenly two large black vultures revealed themselves as they leapt into the air from the canopy. They ascended quickly. 'We can be sure the enemy knows our movements now.'

'Do you think the Skatheans have entered Everdon?' asked Eben, his eyes watched the vultures fly away and out of sight.

'No, I doubt it. The Brigades of the Sunset Hills keep any enemies from crossing in the north, and the Grey Pass is well guarded by an Everdonian fortress. Everdon is not yet afflicted by the Skatheans, but they can still use their spies.'

They rode on and as the day was nearing its end they came to the southern border of the forest. The trees gave way to grasslands that stretched out toward a line of short hills several miles to the south.

'The village of Dunefort is not far from here,' said Chiara. 'We can stay in the village inn for the night.'

They rode onward and followed the road across the grasslands. Thousands of flowers grew on the sides of the road. Eben caught sight of several brightly coloured butterflies hovering above the meadows. After a few minutes they came to a crossroads. The road that led east and west appeared more of a dirt track than a well-travelled road. A single old willow tree rose up beside the crossroads, and a crystal clear stream flowed by. Chiara stopped her horse and examined the ground for tracks.

'The Irilians have taken the road west from here and are being led by Acartor. There are also others travelling with them. They met here at these crossroads. Acartor has left an indicator for us to follow.'

Red's eyes searched the ground for the indicator that Acartor had left.

'See those stones just off the road. They have been placed there deliberately to tell me that our friends have gone to Eaglemere. Sir Evander of Eaglemere has always been a friend to the Fiorian Order. He is a strong and noble knight, one of the few remaining honourable nobles living in Everdon.'

Red stared down at the stones; his eyes revealed his confusion, and he shook his head in disbelief. The stones did not seem significant; they certainly didn't look like they had been placed there deliberately. Chiara turned her horse toward the east and the others followed as she galloped away.

   **

As the sun was setting the road turned sharply to the south and they found themselves riding through the hills in the soft golden light of the early evening. Chiara galloped ahead as she wanted to arrive at Eaglemere before nightfall. The way led them through several rocky valleys and followed the base of a large treeless hill. They passed a final corner; a long lake was revealed. The lake was about two hundred yards wide and at least a thousand yards in length. It filled the entire base of the shallow valley and was fed by a small waterfall on the far side. The road followed the northern shore and led to a small stone castle which was built on a craggy outcrop beside the lake. The castle had only a single watchtower and was encircled by a short outer wall.

As they approached two large reinforced wooden gates opened. They followed Chiara into a small lantern lit courtyard. Meara stood across the far side of the courtyard with Arlen, Baftel, Cassiel, and an old man with long white hair and white eyebrows who Eben rightly assumed was Sir Evander. Acartor was also with them, and beside him stood the two rugged Tabarian knights: Sir Tierran and Sir Cian, who were at the council in Faircastle. Eben remembered that they had defended him against King Lenard and had said they would assist him to claim the Sapphire Throne if he wished to. Both the Tabarian Knights bowed to Eben as he rode into the courtyard; Eben nodded and acknowledged the Tabarians. There were also several Everdonian guardsmen who stood guard at the edges of the courtyard.

'Welcome, my dear leader and friends,' said Acartor warmly. 'Was your mission to the Tower of Fire a success?'

'We have good news,' said Chiara as she dismounted. 'The Fire Order will come south to help us in Everdon.'

'This is welcome news. Your mission was successful indeed,' said Acartor.

'Eben Ecorian is to thank for this,' said Chiara.

'He truly is the Ecorian Emperor,' said Sir Tierran, his voice deep and rough. 'This is to be expected. The Ecorians have always commanded such respect.'

'The presence of the Fire Order will remove any advantage the Zyranians could have given the Prince of Shadows,' said the Irilian Arlen.

'But the real problem is not the Zyranians,' said Acartor. 'We must develop a clear plan to defeat the Prince of Shadows himself. No amount of wizards will help us if we fail to deal with him. Astarians are indeed powerful, and the Prince of Shadows is the strongest of all the Astarians. Not only is he a great warrior, he also has powers far beyond even the greatest wizard. We must plan to fight our way through the enemy army and deliver Eben directly to the Prince of Shadows. Then the Ecorian can finish this war once and for all.'

'Sir Evander, I would like to introduce you to Eben Ecorian, Sir Red of Ortaria, and Lady Stella his wife,' said Chiara.

Sir Evander bowed slightly and smiled. Eben realised how exceptionally old he actually was. His face was extremely wrinkled and his hair as white as snow. Sir Evander stood tall and proud and hadn't lost any of his knightly nobility with the progression of age.

'You are all welcome here at Eaglemere,' said Sir Evander.

'Thank you for your hospitality,' said Red. Sir Evander nodded and then glanced across to Eben.

'I knew your father, Eben Ecorian. Elons was a brave and noble man. He visited Eaglemere once when he was travelling through Everdon. You look a lot like your father. I heard the sad news that he was lost to the enemy. I am sorry for your loss.'

'Thank you, Sir Evander. My hope is to honour his memory.'

**

Eaglemere was an austere castle. Sir Evander led them all up into a large chamber in the upper level. The room was empty apart from a long wooden command table. The floor was covered in slate tiles and there were no windows at all. Several lanterns and candles lit the room. Acartor and Sir Evander took seats and indicated for the entire company to sit down.

'I should inform everyone why we must have this meeting at Eaglemere and not at Marraw,' said Acartor, glancing across at Eben for a moment. 'After you left Faircastle King Lenard threatened to end all alliances with Irvaria because Princess Apherah abruptly swore an oath to never marry him in front of the envoys. King Lenard became furious and blamed you, Eben Ecorian, for his misfortunes. Apherah apparently made no secret of her affection for you when she confronted King Lenard with her poorly timed declaration. King Edric almost had King Lenard banished from Faircastle because of his furious response. Regrettably Princess Apherah is not as discreet as she is beautiful.'

'Fortunately I managed to calm King Lenard's anger,' continued Acartor. 'He has agreed to wait until after the war to deal with his courtship problems. Unfortunately Princess Apherah rejection of him has made him even more interested in winning her hand in marriage. Thankfully everything is again proceeding as we planned; although I believe Eben should avoid King Lenard until the tensions have diminished. King Edric and the Irvarian army are marching south. They are camped north of the Forest of Sorrows as we speak. When they pass the crossroads tomorrow we will meet with the army. The main Everdonian army waits to the north of Lucaria. Within a week the two armies will merge into one and prepare for war.'

'Well done, Acartor,' said Chiara. 'I'm sure you helped to avert a disaster. We are gathered here to discuss how we will defeat the Prince of Shadows. I believe he will not fight at the front of his army. We will have to battle our way to him. We cannot allow him a chance to escape. This may be our only opportunity to stop him.'

'This is why we have come with you,' said Sir Cian resolutely. Sir Cian was stockier and older than Sir Tierran, and his dark eyes revealed a certain fierceness that was rare among men. His hair was long and dark, and his face was very weathered and a deep and long scar marked his left cheek, adding to his severe appearance. To Eben he looked like the complete picture of a battle-hardened warrior. 'We will be the spearhead of the attack and carve a way through the muckron ranks. We will lead Emperor Eben directly to the enemy.' He bowed his head to Eben.

'This is very brave of you and Sir Tierran,' said Chiara appreciatively. 'I'm sure we will face many formidable adversaries. You must be aware that the Prince of Shadows will have more than muckrons protecting him. We are likely to face wizards, wyverns, and other monsters, some that may not have names.'

'We are ready for anything,' said Sir Tierran with conviction. Sir Tierran looked like a younger version of Sir Cian; he was clean shaven with long tangled hair. The fierce look in his eye was much the same as his fellow Tabarian.

'I'm sure you are,' agreed Acartor. 'Baftel has seen the enemy fleet is planning to land to the east of Lucaria, yet the full details of the enemy's strategy remain hidden.'

'The Astarian is using powerful magic to prevent me or any other seer seeing his plans,' said Baftel. 'I am not sure what he is preparing; however, I know he is hiding his plans from us. There is a shroud over much of Veredor, like a dark blanket of smoke covering the land. I cannot see north beyond the Endora Mountains, and the entire fleet of muckrons has been completely hidden this last week. Only occasionally, at the height of my strength, I can see where the fleet is in the Southern Sea, and only once I gained a glimpse of their plan to land east of Lucaria at Crescent Bay.'

'Crescent Bay,' repeated Chiara.

'Yes, from there I don't know what they plan to do,' said Baftel.

'King Lenard has fortified Lucaria with a garrison of five thousand men,' said Acartor. 'I doubt even forty thousand muckrons could breach the towering walls of that city. The muckrons would have to dig in for a long siege. I believe the Prince of Shadows may be planning to march north to cut the supply route to Lucaria and to invade northern Everdon. In any case we will fight his army somewhere. Because Baftel has seen his plan we may be able to hold the enemy at Crescent Bay.'

'Surely the Prince of Shadows will know we are preparing for him,' said Meara.

'Yes, he would know our strength and our numbers,' replied Acartor, pondering Meara's words for a moment. 'You must understand that he does not consider the armies of men a threat to his overall plan. He is only afraid of Eben Ecorian and the Sword of Light. This is why our plan to lead Eben to him is so important. The Prince of Shadows is so confident in his own strength that he expects us to flee like a group of cockroaches would run from us. He would never expect us to bring his one fear directly to him. This will work to our advantage.'

'Who will lead the charge?' asked Chiara.

'I believe we should keep the number to around six or seven, any more than this and we are bound to be scattered on the battlefield,' said Acartor. 'Eben Ecorian, Gatekeeper Chiara, Sir Cian, Sir Tierran, and Meara should be in the attacking group.'

'What about me and Stella,' said Red suddenly. 'We want to be there too. We have fought in many battles with Eben. It's always good to have friends by your side in such situations. I don't plan to leave Eben to fight the Prince of Shadows alone.'

Acartor's eyes narrowed. He looked at Red for a few moments before answering. 'Sir Red, you must understand this group will attempt to break through their last line of defence. We will require help reaching that point, and I'm sure that you, Stella, Cassiel, Arlen, and many others will be in the thick of the action right up until this time and perhaps even until the end. Our objective is not just to fight his army; our real objective is to provide an opportunity for the Ecorian to challenge the Prince of Shadows. If we can do this we may be able to save our world, if not, we will see an evil shadow pour out over all the lands and men and mer will be completely subjugated.'

**

That night the company rested in the castle. They were given simple chambers and were happy to be sleeping under a roof. The following morning Eben woke early and decided to walk down to the lake. The day was overcast, and a gentle cool breeze blew from the east. A rocky track led down from the castle gate to the water's edge. The surface of the lake was very still. A group of swallows flew in circles over the clear water. Eben was surprised when he caught sight of Acartor sitting on the rocky shore a little further along. Acartor was staring at him and seemed to be pondering something deeply. Eben walked over to the Fiorian.

'Good morning, Acartor.'

'Yes it is,' replied Acartor as he stood up. 'I see you also had the good idea of a morning walk. Eaglemere Lake is very beautiful.' Eben turned and looked out at the lake. They both stood there for several moments in the peaceful silence. 'Chiara told me that she beat you when you were training in Elcalee.' Eben glanced at Acartor and nodded, not knowing what to say. 'She still has faith in your ability. She said you are the greatest warrior she has ever faced.'

'Chiara's skills are far superior,' said Eben. Acartor frowned and lowered his eyes.

'Eben, you are the only one who can challenge the Prince of Shadows. If you fail, we will all die.' Acartor paused for a moment; his eyes glanced at the Sword of Light. 'It has long been said that the Prince of Shadows feared the Knights of Shidon. The Astarian Fiora tutored the Knights of Shidon so they could fight the Prince of Shadows and his servants. The Fiorians are the descendants of the Knights of Shidon, and Chiara is the greatest knight in our order. If you can match her I believe you can also match the Prince of Shadows. Our success depends on our mission to lead you to him. You have the Sword of Light; I think you can do this.'

Eben looked back out toward the lake again. For a few moments neither of them said anything.

'When I was in the Dungeons of Zarkanor I learned about the deep agony of loneliness and despair. I learned what it feels like to lose hope. I was imprisoned in a dark place, Eben; a terrible place for any man. In the end I found a way out of my torment. Sometimes men must make difficult decisions.'

'What decision are you talking about?' asked Eben, sensing a certain degree of anxiety in Acartor's words. The Fiorian's cast his blue eyes downward and revealed some of his despair for a moment; it was rare for Acartor to show any expression at all. He took a deep breath before answering.

'This is difficult for me to talk about now. A time will come when I will reveal to you what I had to face in the Dungeons of Zarkanor,' replied Acartor, his voice almost a whisper. He then glanced away from Eben and lifted his eyes to look up at the castle. 'We will set out at noon to meet with the Irvarian army,' he said, his tone of voice lifting. 'There is one last thing I should say,

Ecorian. A time will come when you will face two possible ways forward. I believe you will make the right decision.' Acartor then turned to leave. Eben's eyes followed the Fiorian as he walked away.
**

For about an hour Eben sat by the lake and rested. He reflected on all that had happened since they left Ortaria. So much had happened and at such a quick pace that he had scarce enough time to reflect. He thought about the reality of having to fight the Prince of Shadows in the looming battle.

Cassiel came into view and walked down the track from the castle. He was wearing new clothing and a new brown cloak.

'Acartor told me you were down here,' he said, taking a seat on the rocks beside Eben.

'This lake has such a peace about it. See the swallows flying just above the surface?' said Eben.

'These lands are beautiful,' said Cassiel, his eyes scanning the lake.

Eben glanced across at Cassiel and wondered what advice his good friend could offer. He knew that Cassiel had always been steadfast and coolheaded in the face of danger.

'What do you think of the plan to fight the Prince of Shadows?'

'The Fiorians seem to think the plan is the only way.'

'But what do you think, Cassiel?'

Cassiel looked from Eben toward the lake and pondered the question deeply before answering.

'We have fought many evil creatures together since we met in Ancora. I think to overcome the

Prince of Shadows we will need more than the ability to fight. In the Forgotten Age the Astarian Fiora could not slay the Prince of Shadows; she had to banish him to the darkness beyond the Cosmic Gate. The Fiorians believe that the Sword of Light in your hands can end this war, but I do not know if fighting him is the entire answer. Whatever happens we are all in this together.'

'Friends until the end,' said Eben. Cassiel nodded and smiled.

They sat by the lake for a little while and enjoyed the scenery in silence.

'Red and Stella are taking new armour from the Eaglemere armoury,' said Cassiel 'Sir Evander has told us we can take whatever we want, and he gave me these new clothes. There is a lot of good armour if you want to replace anything.'

**

Eben arrived at the entrance to the armoury and saw Red and Stella were busy trying on their new armour. Red had replaced his rusting and dented Ortarian armour with polished new plate armour. He looked like a new knight. Eben stepped into the room.

'Eben, have a look at all this armour. Sir Evander said we can take anything we want,' said Red.

The room was small and completely crammed full of all manner of weapons and armour. There were racks of swords, axes, bows, crossbows, and wooden barrels full of arrows.

Eben didn't so much like wearing heavy armour. He preferred to feel free and mobile on the battlefield and felt wearing heavy plate armour would slow him down too much and reduce his ability to use his sword. Red, on the other hand, felt that heavier armour provided him with more protection and made him feel safer whilst charging into enemy ranks. Eben selected a leather shirt with a triple layer around his torso, metal elbow guards, knee guards, leather boots that reached almost to his knees, new leather gloves, and wrist guards.

'Maybe I should take one of these,' said Red, picking up a large crossbow.

'Don't bother,' said Stella, shaking her head. 'They take too long to reload.'

Stella picked up a new shield. The shield was round with the heraldic yellow hawk of Everdon painted across it. She also took a middle length arming sword and attached a second shorter sword to her belt; giving her the ability to release the shield and fight with two swords as she had done on the battlefield in Scaldonia.

'We are ready for battle once again,' said Eben.
**

Sir Evander had organised new warhorses for the company. Eben was given a large brown warhorse named Arrow. He thanked Sir Evander for providing them with the armour and horses.

The company rode away from Eaglemere and headed back toward the main highway. Sir Cian and Sir Tierran led the group. They both rode massive black warhorses, and they seemed to be ever on guard. Eben rode at the back of the group with Meara and Baftel. After an hour they arrived at the crossroads. The Irvarian army was nowhere in sight.

Acartor rode out into the middle of the crossroads and looked down. 'The army must be on their way,' he said.

'They are not far away,' said Baftel. 'They are passing through the Forest of Sorrows as we speak.'

The company rested and waited for the Irvarians. After about an hour they could hear the sound of hundreds of soldiers singing from the direction of the forest. A few minutes later the first troops came into view across the plain and were followed by thousands more. King Edric was leading his army, riding a great black warhorse; his red cape flew in the wind. He was adorned in shining armour and his helm was crowned in gold. They watched as he led the line of troops toward the crossroads.

'We expected we would be meeting you in Marraw,' said King Edric as he approached. He was followed by six of his fully armoured and mounted knights.

'We have been guests at Eaglemere,' replied Acartor.

'Eaglemere! How is Sir Evander these days?' asked King Edric, his eyes revealing his happiness at the memory of his old friend.

'As knightly as he ever was,' replied Chiara.

'He must be getting on in years. I will pay him a visit after the war.' He looked from them to Eben, and his expression became stony. 'I see you found each other,' he said gruffly. 'Is the Fire Order coming down from the mountains?'

'They will come,' replied Eben.

'Good, everything is proceeding as we planned,' said King Edric gladly. 'King Lenard has ridden ahead and will meet us north of Lucaria where the Everdonian army awaits. We will wait for the enemy to land and then we will bring the battle directly to him.'

'We have learned the Prince of Shadows plans to land his fleet at Crescent Bay,' said Acartor.

King Edric nodded sternly. 'Crescent Bay is well protected. He will be able to safely harbour his ships there and prepare for an invasion of Everdon.'

'He won't expect us to hedge him in between the land and sea,' said Acartor. 'We could prevent him from advancing into Everdon and destroy his chance of escaping by sea. He doesn't know that we are aware of his plan to land at Crescent Bay. We could surprise him and catch him off guard.'

King Edric nodded in agreement. 'The Prince of Shadows will see the terrible mistake he has made coming south to our lands.'

**

The army of thirty thousand men moved south for the remainder of the day and passed by three small Everdonian villages in the hills. The villagers watched in amazement as the army passed by. The hills they were marching through were lovely with rounded grassy hilltops and gullies full of alder, linden, and oak trees. Occasionally they would see shepherds tending to their flocks of sheep on the hills. Eben spent most of the time riding beside Red, Stella, and Cassiel near the front of the army.

King Edric had remained gruff with Eben all afternoon. He was still bothered by situation with Princess Apherah. Eben felt that it was best to steer clear of the King and stayed a little back from the very front of the army. Often he could hear the troops talking about him, but more often than not they were pointing at Red. They thought that Red was the Ecorian because of his shining new armour. Red held his chin high and enjoyed the attention.

'Even with all that new armour you don't look like an emperor. I'm surprised they think you are,' said Stella.

'What! Why not?' asked Red defensively. 'I could have easily been a king if I was born into a royal family. In a certain sense I am a king: nobody ever tells me what to do, and for years I have been completely free to go wherever I choose.'

'I was just thinking that you lack a certain regal quality. Maybe you worked as a clown for too long,' teased Stella with a slight chuckle. Red shook his head and grinned, knowing Stella was playing games with him.

'What about you, Stella. You practically lived in the circus,' said Red, raising an eyebrow. Stella smiled self-assuredly.

'Yes, I did, Red, but remember that I was always walking the tightropes and swinging on the trapeze high above.' She winked at Red with a victorious beam. Red shook his head; he knew Stella was much better at this game.

They rode onward for the remainder of the day and the army camped at the southern side of the hills where the road entered into gentle and somewhat beautiful land. The hilly landscape was partially treed with silver birches.

CHAPTER SIXTEEN

For three days the Irvarian army marched south toward the port city of Lucaria. The further they moved south the more beautiful the land became. Everdon was a kingdom of rolling hills, lush green forests, and wide flowering meadows. On the second day they passed by the town of Marraw. Marraw was set on the banks of the Everdon River.

The Everdon River flowed down from the Great Mountains to the west and carved a winding way through the kingdom all the way to the port city of Lucaria where it flowed into the Southern Sea. The town of Marraw was surrounded by a tall grey stone wall which was lined with fifteen watchtowers. A large keep rose up about eighty yards above the town. Atop the keep flew the flag of Everdon; a blue banner depicting a yellow hawk with outstretched wings.

The Irvarian army continued to march without stopping. King Edric was determined to move as quickly south as possible now they knew where the Prince of Shadows planned to land his fleet. The King seemed almost impatient to see an end to the war.

There was a feeling of concern among the troops. The Irvarians were a proud people and for the most part they held brave faces, but Eben could sense the discomfort they felt about marching away from their homeland to fight in a foreign land against a monstrous and mostly unknown enemy.

On the night of the third day of marching the army stopped beside the Everdon River in a place of wide flowering meadows. Meara had their tents set up beside the river. As the evening approached they rested by a large fire beside the slow flowing water. Meara, Arlen, Baftel, Eben, Cassiel, Sir Tierran, Sir Cian, Red, and Stella all sat around the fire. To everyone's surprise Sir Cian played a wooden flute for them.

'Two more days and we will meet with our Everdonian friends,' said Sir Tierran gruffly. 'Then we are off to meet our enemy the following day. We should make light work of forty thousand muckrons.'

Meara shook her head slightly. 'We must not underestimate our enemy,' she said, glancing across at Sir Tierran sternly. 'The Prince of Shadows is bringing more than half of the Zyranian Order, and we don't know what other evil creatures serve in this army. At very least there will be wyverns, Skatheans, and Northern Sorcerers.'

'Bring it on,' said Sir Tierran brashly. 'I've fought Skatheans and Northern Sorcerers in Dravania, Iarthar, and Coran; they're no match for the Tabarian Knights. We will take the Ecorian Emperor directly to the Prince of Shadows; the war will be over in a matter of days.'

Sir Cian stopped playing his flute for a few moments and gave a curt nod to agree with the bold statements of his fellow knight.

Eben still felt uncomfortable about being referred to as Emperor by the Tabarians. Sir Cian and Sir Tierran would have it no other way; they considered the Ecorians royal by birth. Sir Cian had told Eben that all the Tabarian Knights took three oaths when initiated into the Tabarian

Order: to serve the Ecorian family, to defend the people of Veredor against evil, and to protect and shelter widows and orphans. Therefore the two knights were bound by oaths to serve Eben, whether he liked it or not.

'I hope you are right, Sir Tierran,' said Meara calmly. 'You know as well as I do that your sword cannot parry the magic of an enemy wizard. The agility you depend on may fail you if you find you are facing so many wizards at once. Imagine the damage that fifty Zyranians could do.'

Sir Tierran harshly looked down toward the blazing fire and pondered Meara's words for a few moments.

'The Fire Order should handle those turncoat Zyranians,' said Sir Tierran.

'The Fire Order are camped a league or two north of us,' said Baftel. 'They seem to not want to come close to the main Irvarian army.'

'At least we know they're coming,' said Sir Tierran, taking from his bag an oversized pipe and a pouch of tobacco.

'They said they would come. They do tend to keep their word,' said Meara.

'And what about the five other Irilians who are supposed to be coming from Iarthar?' asked Sir Tierran.

'They are coming as quickly as they can to meet us,' replied Arlen. 'The Irilians are currently passing through the Forest of Sorrows. They have been moving day and night to arrive on time.'

'Then we will meet up together before the battle,' said Sir Tierran as he lit his pipe.

The night progressed with a lot of conversation about the approaching battle. The

Tabarian Knights were completely confident in their own ability to complete the task. Eben felt somewhat happy at hearing their confidence, regardless of the fact that they were probably underestimating the opposition. Meara and most of the others retired early to their tents. By the end of the evening Eben found he was sitting only with Red, Stella, and Cassiel.

'How do you feel about the coming battle,' asked Cassiel.

'Fine,' answered Red. 'The Tabarians are very certain of victory.'

'I doubt that the Prince of Shadows would be landing in Everdon without a plan of his own,' said Cassiel. He glanced across a Red through the flames of the fire. 'I think Meara is right; we shouldn't underestimate our enemy.'

'What if I can't match him?' asked Eben. They stared at Eben and fell silent for a few moments.

'The Fiorian Acartor believes you can,' said Stella. 'We believe in your ability, and we have seen what you are capable of in the last few months. If you can't defeat him, no one can. You have to be confident, Eben. Don't let fear get the better of you.'

'Stella is right,' agreed Cassiel. 'The Fiorians would not have formulated this plan if they didn't believe we could succeed.'

'You're right, Cassiel,' said Eben. 'I just feel something is missing. I can't understand what it is.'

'It's natural to feel a little nervous before a battle,' said Cassiel. 'Especially when so much hope is placed in your ability to succeed. Don't worry about anything. Just be yourself. I'm sure everything will be fine.'

**

For two more days the army marched south through the enchanting countryside of Everdon. They passed through many beautiful villages and small towns. Around noon on the second day they marched over a ridge and before them, about a mile ahead, was a large field with thousands of pitched tents and hundreds of blue Everdonian banners.

'It's the Everdonian army!' said Red, his eyes scanning the field.

A great horn sounded and blew five times from the encampment. Within a minute a group of twenty riders rode out to meet the approaching Irvarian army.

King Lenard led the group and was adorned in golden armour with intricate carvings. His long blue cape blew in the wind as he galloped towards them. His helm had two large golden wings proceeding from both sides. Eben thought he looked a little ridiculous. King Edric moved his horse forward to meet with the approaching riders.

'King Edric. I welcome you and your army to my kingdom,' said King Lenard.

'Thank you for the welcome,' answered King Edric.

'My army will be ready to march when we learn where the enemy has landed his fleet,' said King Lenard, his eyes glanced across at Eben, and he smirked. 'I see the Ecorian descendent rides at the front with your knights. I think you give him too much honour.'

King Edric looked back at Eben. His eyes slowly returned to King Lenard. 'The Ecorian is our honoured ally; if he wants to ride by my side I will allow him to.'

'You should be careful where you choose to place your allegiance, King Edric. You may find this Ecorian wants to take your throne. He has tried to lead your daughter astray; he may try to do the same to you.'

'That's enough!' shouted Red, riding forward boldly. King Lenard's lip curled as he looked viciously at Red.

'Sir Red of Ortaria. Let me remind you that you are a long way from home. You should be aware I will not take kindly to any...'

'I won't have you insult my friend, apologise!' demanded Red.

King Lenard sneered and lifted his chin. His face became crimson red, and his hand went to his sword hilt. Red followed in kind, ready to draw his own sword to take up the challenge. Eben rode up beside Red. In an instant Stella and Cassiel were also beside them. Both Sir Cian and Sir Tierran were also moving forward.

'We don't have time for this!' shouted King Edric.

'That man...that thing...is trying to steal Princess Apherah from me!' cried King Lenard.

'Princess Apherah has not yet decided to marry you, King Lenard!' bellowed King Edric. King Lenard shot a menacing glance at King Edric. The Irvarian king held his head high and gave a commanding stare that silenced the younger king. A stony silence followed before King Lenard spoke.

'I will concede this time for the sake of our common interests. After the war I will not be so kind and patient,' said King Lenard as he looked away bitterly. 'Unfortunately I need you as much as you need me.'

'This matter is settled for now,' said King Edric. 'King Lenard, you will be glad to know the Irilians have learned the Prince of Shadows plans to land his army at Crescent Bay.'

'I will command my army to be ready to advance south tomorrow morning,' said King Lenard. 'Crescent Bay is only a day or two from here.'

**

Eben sat alone in the early evening by a small campfire a little away from the main Irvarian encampment. The Everdon River flowed peacefully by. He was thinking about Princess Apherah and looking forward to the battle being over so he could return to Faircastle. He watched as sparks floated upward into the twilight air above and smiled to himself. Hope filled his heart and soul when he thought of the possibility of a life with Princess Apherah. His thoughts then drifted; he knew he had to discover what happened to his mother and father. He also knew the Prince of Shadows would know the answers. Eben planned to ask him directly before he completed his task.

Suddenly Eben felt a hand on his shoulder and looked up. He was surprised to see Baftel's blind eyes looking down at him.

'Eben, I have been looking for you and had to use my magic to find you,' said Baftel, a slight tremor was revealed in his aged voice.

'Baftel, please take a seat and enjoy the warmth of the fire.'

'Eben, we must talk. There is something disturbing I must tell you.'

Eben helped the aged wizard sit down and then sat by his side.

'What's wrong, Baftel?' asked Eben, wondering what could be bothering the old wizard so much.

'I had a vision today, clear and strong; a terrifying vision of a giant spider ready to pounce. I then saw the Ecorian flag covered in blood. Last of all I saw an image of you falling into a deep abyss.'

The feeling of hope diminished in Eben's heart at hearing Baftel's words. 'What does it mean, Baftel?'

'This is a dark vision. I do not know what it means. You must be careful, Eben.'

Suddenly Acartor and Chiara walked over from the encampment. 'Ecorian, we have been looking for you,' said Acartor. 'We just heard news that the Prince of Shadows has landed his fleet at Crescent Bay as you predicted he would, Baftel.' Baftel nodded at hearing the news.

'We will likely attack the enemy army tomorrow,' said Chiara. 'King Lenard is insisting that we attack as soon as we arrive. We intend to keep the element of surprise as much as we possibly can. Tomorrow we will set our attack plan in motion and strike the muckron army with all our strength.'

'I'm ready for the fight,' said Eben, feeling he had much to fight for: his father, mother, Princess Apherah, his friends, and all the people of Veredor.

'I'm happy to see you're feeling more assured of yourself,' said Acartor. 'I believe you can do this, Eben. You were born to.'

**

An hour before dawn the army started to prepare to march. During the night the company of five Irilians from Iarthar and Dravania had joined their group. They were three men and two women. The Irilians names were: Senan, a very tall and lanky man with a long brown beard; Aengus, a young and handsome man who was clean shaven with short dark hair; Elan, an older woman with long auburn hair; Cathal, a very short and stout man with a gigantic nose and a concentrated look etched onto his face; and Nuala, a young beautiful woman with golden hair and deep green eyes.

Eben stood near the front of the army with the Irilians, Tabarians, and his three best friends.

'So this is the day,' said Red, looking up to the clouded sky above.

'The day of reckoning,' said Cassiel coolly.

A great horn sounded once and resonated across the field. The lines of troops and cavalry started to move forward. Eben rode with Red, Stella, and Cassiel near the front of the Irvarian army. He felt a sense of anticipation growing in his heart.

**

As the day progressed the weather worsened and the overcast sky grew darker and more ominous.

'There is evil magic at work in the sky,' said Meara, lifting her eyes toward the southern sky where the darkness intensified.

They could see the shadowy clouds gathering in the south; it looked like a veil was covering the land. The army marched onward, and a feeling of anxiety was growing among the men.

'The enemy knows we are coming,' said Baftel. 'He is trying to threaten us with this sky.'

'The man who makes threats is always a coward,' said Chiara.

They rode on throughout the day, and the sky darkened until the entire land about was shrouded in a gloomy shadow. By mid-afternoon the road led them toward the coast, and from the uplands Eben could see the Southern Sea in the distance. The road then led toward the coast and wound through valleys and over treeless hilltops.

In the late afternoon the army came to the height of a ridge with a clear view over the coast. Before them was a large bay in the shape of a crescent with a rising headland on the western side. The headland towered above the bay with a flattened top and vertical cliffs descending toward crashing waves below. Hundreds of ships were anchored in the bay. Smoke rose from a multitude of fires in the muckron encampment on the foreshore. A group of half a dozen wyverns circled in the black swirling clouds above.

The two kings looked out at the scene of the monstrous army before them. The muckrons had already formed ranks and were prepared for their arrival. Half the enemy army had formed about twenty lines protecting the shoreline of the bay and the anchored ships. The other twenty thousand muckrons were situated around and on the slopes leading to the headland; they were guarding all the approaches from the land.

'The Prince of Shadows has taken a position at the height of the headland,' said Chiara. 'It will be an uphill battle to reach him.'

'The Zyranians are with the army protecting the bay,' said Baftel.

'The answer is simple,' said King Lenard. 'We will strike the headland with all our might.'

'No, such a move would allow the muckrons guarding the shoreline to flank us. We shouldn't allow them to cut off our possibility of retreat,' said King Edric.

'Retreat! If we don't have victory today we are unlikely to have victory ever again,' said King Lenard sharply. 'The enemy only has about twenty thousand muckrons protecting him on the headland. We have fifty thousand men.'

'King Lenard is right,' said Acartor. 'We should focus our attack on the headland.' King Edric nodded, conceding the fact that King Lenard's plan was probably the best way to attack.

A great horn sounded and the allied army of Irvaria and Everdon started to march toward Crescent Bay. Red, Stella, and Cassiel rode with Eben at the front of the army.

'I know the plan is for you to push forward toward the Prince of Shadows with Meara, the Fiorians, and the Tabarians,' said Red. 'Stella and I plan to be there with you until the end.'

'Thanks, Red,' said Eben, happy that Red and Stella were always such good friends to him.

'I will also follow if I can,' said Cassiel.

CHAPTER SEVENTEEN

The army of men moved down the gradual slope. As the land flattened out they formed ranks with the Everdonian army on the eastern side and the Irvarians on the west. The dark clouds in the sky were swirling above, and the smell of smoke drifted up from the pits of fire that were burning among the muckron ranks. Six wyverns circled in the sky. They were swooping down and screeching to intimidate the army of men. Eben sat on his warhorse and watched as the formation developed.

'The Fire Order has arrived,' said Meara, looking back toward the top of the rise. Eben looked and saw the fifty wizards of the Fire Order standing behind the ranks of the army.

Acartor and Chiara approached on their horses. They were followed by Sir Cian and Sir Tierran.

'This is it,' said Acartor.

'We will ride with the first cavalry advance. The cavalry will charge the muckron lines at the base of the hill and push toward the headland,' said Chiara. 'From there we will climb the rise and hopefully breach the enemy's defences. The Prince of Shadows will be commanding his army from the height of the headland. He is sure to be well protected by more than muckrons, so be prepared for anything. The key is to keep moving to prevent the enemy focusing his strength on us. We mustn't slow, and we certainly shouldn't turn back. The survival of men and mer in Veredor depends on our success.'

Eben took the glass case with the two candles from his backpack and placed it beneath his leather armour. He then tied his backpack to his saddle. King Edric and King Lenard were out in front of the army with their knights. They were discussing the best way to attack.

King Edric rode over. 'Are you ready?' he asked Chiara.

'We are,' she replied.

'And you, Eben Ecorian, are you ready?

'I am.'

'Good. We will send a first wave of three thousand heavy cavalry and a hundred knights. They will be followed directly by our main cavalry force. Finally we will send the infantry. Be ready to ride; the charge is about to start.'

A few minutes passed and the feeling of anticipation was growing. King Edric rode forward and lifted his sword. For several moments the King stared out at the enemy ranks. He then turned his mighty warhorse to face his army.

'For Veredor and freedom!' he cried as he pointed his sword at the headland. A great horn resounded out across the ranks of men. All at once the heavy cavalry advanced at the pace of a gradual trot. Two hundred Irvarian and Everdonian knights rode out and formed a line at the front.

'It is time,' said Chiara as she drew her sword.

Chiara rode forward. Sir Cian and Sir Tierran were quick to follow. Eben moved his horse to a trot. Red was right by his side. Stella, Cassiel, Meara, and Arlen were further back.

'Here we go again,' said Red, drawing his sword.

Eben eyes were focused at the enemy front line which was about five hundred yards ahead. The muckrons were forming positions around the base of the rise in order to protect the approaches to the height of the headland. Suddenly the dark clouds above started to glow red.

'Not fire from the sky again,' said Red, looking up as they advanced.

Suddenly a flaming beam of bright radiating energy flew over their heads and exploded in the muckron ranks. Dozens of muckrons were sent flying in all directions.

'That one was from the Fire Order! Watch out! The Zyranians are going to rain fire down on us!' cried Meara.

A blast of fire shot from the sky and several riders ahead of them fell from their horses. In response a second flaming beam of energy blasted into the muckron ranks and caused an even bigger explosion. A moment later the sky above started to rain fire down on the charging cavalry.

'Charge!' cried a knight at the front as he brought his horse to a gallop. The first line of knights all lowered their lances and charged after the leading knight. Eben drew his sword. Fireballs exploded all around, and smoke rose from the burning field. Bright beams of fire continued to smash into the muckron ranks. Meara raised her hand and shielded those around her from the raining fire with a blue shimmering layer of light.

Chiara looked across at Eben and nodded. The howls of the muckron horde filled their ears. A moment later they crashed into the enemy front line. Eben hewed down at a howling muckron as his warhorse knocked over another. The monstrous pig faced monsters surrounded them.

The battle raged ahead as the knights pressed forward toward the rise.

Chiara and Acartor were cutting down muckron after muckron. Eben stabbed out as he charged after them with Red, Stella, and Meara by his side. Cassiel had fallen back with Arlen. To the right Sir Cian and Sir Tierran were cutting their way through groups of shrieking muckrons.

'Follow me!' cried Chiara, breaking away from the cavalry. She rode onward and carved a path forward. Acartor was battling numerous foes not far behind. Eben brought his horse up beside Chiara and cut down at the muckrons again and again; muckron after muckron fell under his sword. The smell of smoke, the howls of muckrons, and the cries of men filled the air.

Meara raised her hands, and a great blast of fizzing blue fire shot forth, tearing a path through the muckron horde. Sir Cian and Sir Tierran were in the thick of the battle, whilst Stella and Red were a little further back. Eben couldn't see Cassiel or Arlen anywhere.

'Keep moving!' cried Acartor from a little further ahead as he moved up the beginning of the rise.

Eben's heart was thumping heavily. He moved his horse up the slope. A moment later a wyvern with bright green scales swooped down, aiming itself directly for Eben. Eben turned his warhorse and held his sword ready, but before the beast reached him Sir Cian leapt from his horse at the wyvern. The Tabarian sliced one of the wyvern's wings off. The beast screeched and crashed to the ground, smashing through a group of muckrons. Sir Cian instantly leapt after the fallen wyvern.

He rammed his sword into the beast's head, and a moment later the wyvern fell lifeless to the ground. Meanwhile another muckron slew Sir Cian's horse. Eben cut down the same muckron an instant later. He turned back to Sir Cian who had engaged a group of the pig headed monsters on the opposite side.

Meanwhile Chiara and Acartor, a little further up the hill, were cutting out a path through the hideous monsters. Eben charged forward and suddenly a green blast of energetic light struck his warhorse, sending him tumbling to the ground. He quickly regained his feet, but, Arrow, his warhorse, lay dead on the battlefield. An instant later Sir Cian was by his side.

'Watch out! There's a Northern Sorcerer!' cried Sir Cian as he fought his way forward with Eben toward Acartor and Meara. Eben looked ahead and could see a man in a black cloak with sunken eyes and greasy hair. The Northern Sorcerer raised his hand, and a green streak of light powered toward Chiara. Meara created a blue energy shield and stopped the attack; a mighty boom echoed out across the battlefield. Meara retaliated with three spirals of blue hissing energy that struck the Northern Sorcerer down.

'Where is Sir Tierran?' asked Eben.

'He's dead,' said Sir Cian stoically.

Eben felt deeply shocked, but he had no time to reflect on what he had just been told. He looked back down the slope to see Red and Stella struggling against a large group of muckrons about fifty yards away. They had both fallen from their horses and had been unable to keep up with the advance toward the top of the headland. They were clearly being overwhelmed. A muckron was smashing Stella's shield with a massive battle axe as Red was wrestling with another hideous monster. Eben was about to turn back to help them, but Acartor grabbed his arm.

'No, Eben. We must move onward!'

'I can't leave my friends to die,' cried Eben.

'You have to!' shouted Acartor desperately.

'Eben, I will protect them,' said Meara, realising Eben's predicament. 'I'll see you when this is all over.'

Eben nodded. Meara then dashed down the slope toward Stella and Red. Acartor and Eben turned and charged up the hill with Sir Cian and Chiara just behind. The throng of muckrons scattered before them, their snouts howling and hissing as the Fiorians forced a way forward. Both Acartor and Chiara were amazing. Their skill and agility was second to none. They cut down the enemies to the left and right, creating a path through the hideous monsters.

'We're almost there,' cried Acartor.

For a moment Eben caught a glimpse of the battlefield below; the whole field was completely alight. Thousands of men and muckrons were fighting to the death. Flames shot across the field from the multitude of wizards involved in the battle. Eben could see the second army of muckrons, which had been protecting the shoreline, were circling around behind the army of men.

As he was distracted a huge muckron struck him on the back with a war hammer. Eben stumbled and lifted his sword to parry a second incoming strike. His ribs ached from the impact.

The drooling yellow tusked monster struck out again. Eben ducked aside, simultaneously swinging his sword down; the muckron fell at his feet. He dashed forward to join Chiara and Acartor, but Sir Cian was nowhere to be seen.

Eben quickly scanned the battlefield. He caught sight of Sir Cian's lifeless body a little way back, a muckron spear protruding from his side. There was no time to stop as three muckrons assailed him an instant later. He cut them down as he dashed to the top of the headland where Chiara and Acartor were fighting through the last lines of monsters. A moment later they forced their way through and dashed forward.

Eben looked ahead. About forty yards across a flat rock surface was a man who was sitting on a chair made of twisted metal. He was middle aged with greying hair and deep blue eyes. He wore fine black clothing. His human face carried an expression of indifference. Placed across his knees was a sword that appeared to be a perfect replica of the Sword of Light.

To his left stood a man in a long black cloak who looked like a Northern Sorcerer. His eyes were deeply sunken and his thin hair was dry and grey. To the man's right stood a huge muckron who was holding a massive bronze mace. The beastly muckron was wearing intricately designed golden armour. Ten Skatheans stood behind them, and two large black lindworms waited, completely still, on a rock outcrop behind the Skatheans. Directly behind the lindworms was a sheer cliff that descended hundreds of feet to the crashing waves below.

'Well done,' said the man in black, clapping as they approached. 'I must compliment you on your achievement. Honestly, I didn't expect you to make it this far. I have to admit that you are truly remarkable warriors.'

Chiara and Acartor walked ahead of Eben.

'Your evil reign is at an end,' said Chiara boldly.

The Astarian looked at Chiara and shook his head and slyly grinned. 'Is this the Gatekeeper of Emeril herself?' asked the Astarian. 'I expected you to have better manners.' He paused and then looked to Acartor. 'Acartor; I must say you have done splendidly. You have achieved what few of us thought you ever could. Now, if you could please finish your task.'

Acartor suddenly turned and stabbed Chiara through the chest, his blade penetrated out through her back. Eben's heart nearly stopped. Chiara's stared at the traitor, her eyes filled with shock and grief. She dropped her sword and fell to her knees as Acartor withdrew his sword and stepped away from her.

'No!' cried Eben, leaping forward to intervene. Acartor turned his bloody sword and pointed the blade at Eben. Eben stabbed out at the traitor, but Acartor was quick to deflect and counterattacked with a torrent of blows. Eben focused and turned each strike away, but found he was being pushed back across the rocky ground. He felt his body straining as he only just managed to parry each incoming attack.

Eben felt grief and anger surging through his body. He struck back with an array of furious cuts and stabs. Using all his skill he managed to push

Acartor back. Acartor struggled to defend himself. Eben forced him into the centre of the headland. He swung and stabbed again and again. Acartor lost his footing and fell. Eben went to strike, but an instant later he was knocked off his feet by a blast of green energetic light.

'Well done, Baramak,' said the Astarian. Acartor grabbed his sword and leapt up, ready to finish Eben off. 'No, Acartor. Step back! I want to have a word with the Ecorian.' Acartor bowed and moved away from Eben to stand with the Skatheans.

Eben looked across at Chiara. She lay beside him on the rocky ground in a pool of blood.

'Eben,' she whispered, her voice weak and near death. 'I'm so sorry. I should have known; please forgive me.'

'Chiara, I'm going to get you out of here,' said Eben, feeling raw emotion flow through his veins. He slowly got up off the ground and moved closer to Chiara.

'Eben, it's too late for me...Fiora's Bridge, it is...it...' with this Chiara's spirit left. She lay still and lifeless.

Eben's eyes filled with tears as he turned to face his enemy. He lifted the Sword of Light.

'This could not be helped,' said the Astarian. 'The leader of the Fiorians had to die. You, Ecorian, will be offered something greater than this unfortunate fate.'

'I want nothing you can offer me, Prince of Shadows.'

The Astarian clapped gleefully, delighted with Eben's words. 'Ecorian, do you really think the Lord of Veredor would come here with only forty thousand muckrons and a few dozen wyverns? I am sorry to disappoint you; I am not the Prince of Shadows who you refer to, yet I am an Astarian, my name is Callidus. I serve the Lord of Veredor, and I have been instructed by him to offer you a great place in this world if you bow down and accept the rule of your rightful master.'

'I want nothing he can give,' said Eben angrily.

'Well, obviously the alternative is certain death. Of course men never stood a chance. If you look down at the battlefield below you will see this pathetic army of men is already preparing to retreat. What they don't realise is that they will have no home to return to. A hundred thousand muckrons entered Vastoria yesterday from the Iron Gate Pass. They are marching toward Faircastle as we speak, and they will burn the city to the ground. The Sapphire Throne will be ground into dust.'

Eben felt his fear growing. He thought about Princess Apherah unprotected in Faircastle.

'I see; there is someone who you care for in Faircastle,' said Callidus with a sly grin.

'He hopes to marry Princess Apherah,' said Acartor coldly.

Callidus nodded and grinned again at hearing this news. 'How sweet young love is. Perhaps you can save her by swearing allegiance to the Lord of Veredor. We could use you to end this ridiculous war. Men and mer would follow you. You could teach them to bow down before the Lord of Veredor.'

'Princess Apherah will not be a slave and neither will I,' cried Eben. 'I challenge you,

Astarian, to a duel to the death!' Callidus shook his head contemptuously.

'Foolish indeed, I expected more from you, Ecorian. Unfortunately I have promised Tuskhead the pleasure of killing you if you refused to serve the Lord of Veredor.'

Callidus looked up at the massive muckron standing by his side. Tuskhead was a huge muckron, being at least eight feet tall.

'Tuskhead is one of the five kings of the muckron race,' said Callidus. 'He carries the Muckmace, a weapon akin to the Astarian swords. If you want to duel me you will have to duel him first; nevertheless, I doubt your ability to survive after witnessing your pitiful attempt to overcome Acartor. You really are such a disappointment, Ecorian. Tuskhead, kill him.'

Tuskhead stepped forward and snorted loudly as drool flowed from his gaping mouth. He raised the massive mace, which was surrounded by an orange glow. The monster's red bloodshot eyes glared directly at Eben. Tuskhead then threw his head back and let out a horrific howl. Eben raised the Sword of Light and focused his full attention on his opponent. The beast then approached, swinging the Muckmace in a circular fashion.

Tuskhead then suddenly bounded forward; the Muckmace descended from above. Eben leapt aside as the mace smashed into the ground, causing the rocky surface to quake and orange sparks to fly in all directions. Eben retaliated quickly and stabbed out, but Tuskhead just as quickly raised the Muckmace to deflect the stab. Again Tuskhead swung his great weapon; Eben attempted to parry, but the sheer size of the

Muckmace crashed through his defence. He felt the heavy impact thump into his shoulder. Eben fell and almost lost his grip on his sword. Tuskhead stood above him, gloating with a throaty laugh.

'Superbly executed, Tuskhead,' said Callidus gleefully. The Astarian clapped loudly and was enjoying the show.

Eben struggled to his feet. He remembered back to Chiara telling him not to reveal his intention. He lifted the Sword of Light and pointed the blade directly at the monster.

'Come on,' cried Eben as he wiped the sweat from his forehead.

Tuskhead snorted through his hairy snout and raised the Muckmace again. The foul monster charged forward. Eben waited, completely still until the last possible moment and then sidestepped whilst simultaneously cutting out. He felt the blade connect with the flesh of the muckron. Tuskhead roared in pain and stumbled backward, his shoulder bleeding from a large wound.

Eben felt his confidence increasing. He dashed after Tuskhead and unleashed a burst of stabs and slashes. Tuskhead parried as he was forced back toward where Callidus was seated. Eben then faked a move to the left, forcing his much larger opponent to adjust to face him; he then went to the right and stabbed out, pressing the blade into the hideous monster. Tuskhead wailed and dropped the Muckmace. Eben withdrew the Sword of Light as Tuskhead fell to the ground at his feet.

Callidus looked down at the dead muckron, puzzled by what he had witnessed. The Astarian shook his head in disbelief. Eben then turned to face his remaining enemies.

'Now, Callidus, I will deal with you,' he said firmly.

Callidus stood up and drew his sword. 'This is the Sword of Midlight. I believe this sword was once carried by both your father and mother.' A confident grin crossed the Astarian's face. 'Of course this sword truly belongs to the Astarians, as does the Sword of Light. I intend to take the Sword of Light from you as I took the Sword of Midlight from your mother's hands.' The Astarian stepped forward and lifted his blade.

Eben charged at the Astarian and thrust the Sword of Light forward. Callidus easily deflected the attack and dashed to the side with incredible speed. He then struck back, forcing Eben to stumble. Almost instantly a flurry of attacks followed. Eben found himself retreating and simply not being able to find an opportunity to counterattack. He desperately tried to parry each blow and was straining to his limits. Callidus then cut a deliberate shallow blow across Eben's upper chest and stepped back.

Eben felt exhausted. He could feel blood streaming out of the gash across his chest. He raised his eyes to Callidus and lifted his sword, but Callidus stepped back away from him.

'Do you see now, Ecorian? You have completely failed. Or do you still refuse to acknowledge the truth?' Callidus shook his head scornfully. 'Fiora's plans failed long ago. Most of the Astarians were too unwise to see the truth. The old plan was foolish from the beginning. Men are much too fickle. Betrayal is the way of men.'

'I won't betray anyone,' said Eben, his voice low and hoarse.

'You're a man; betrayal is simply in your nature,' said Callidus contemptuously, turning away in disgust. 'Look how little it took for us to convince Acartor to betray his friends, his people, and his entire race. He so easily chose his own life over the thousands who have died here today. He brought you and all those men on the battlefield here because we asked him to. He brought you all to your deaths. This is the way of men: you deliberately cut each other down only to gain a pittance for yourself. How can your race survive with such weakness? Men are so insecure, so fearful, and so reckless. Often betrayal is the only way they can feel they have any power at all. Men have stained the purity of Veredor long enough. We are doing a good service eradicating your race from our world.'

Eben looked across at Acartor. The traitor stepped back and looked away shamefully.

'Some of us stand by our friends,' said Eben.

'You are no different from your father and mother. They both said almost exactly those words. They paid the price for their foolishness.'

'What happened to my parents?' asked Eben shakily.

'I will tell you when you give me the Sword of Light,' said Callidus with a snickering laugh.

Eben, seizing the moment, launched himself at the Astarian and stabbed out with all his remaining focus and energy. Callidus raised the Sword of Midlight, easily deflecting the incoming attack. The Astarian then turned his sword and thrust the blade through Eben's chest. Eben felt the pain and shock as he realised the sword had completely passed through his chest and out his back. In that moment he knew he had lost. Callidus sneered and grabbed Eben by the throat with his free hand, squeezing tightly. Eben couldn't breathe.

'This is not your world!' cried Callidus. He then withdrew his sword and pushed Eben to the ground. Eben felt his blood leaking from his body. He grasped the Sword of Light with his weakening hands. He tried to speak but found he lacked the energy to muster any words.

'Now, as your last living act, give me the Sword of Light. The sword belongs to the Astarian race. I will use the Sword of Light when I lead the attack on Faircastle.'

Eben looked down at the sword he was still clutching. He knew in his heart he could never allow Callidus to take it. He summoned his last remaining strength and cast the sword over the cliff. He then lay down on the cold stone surface and was ready to die.

'No!' cried Callidus, dashing to the edge of the cliff. Callidus watched the Sword of Light disappear beneath the waves far below. He shook his head in disbelief. 'You stupid fool!'

Eben felt the light fading from his eyes as he watched Callidus stride over and grab him by the scruff of his neck. The Astarian lifted him up off the ground. 'Die, Ecorian!' cried Callidus as he cast Eben from the cliff top.

Eben saw the water quickly approaching and the giant waves smashing into the cliff face below. A moment later he crashed into the turbulent sea and gently drifted beneath the waves. All went dark.

CHAPTER EIGHTEEN

Red parried an incoming spear and cut down the muckron who had charged him.

'Red, we have to get out of here!' cried Stella. He looked back over his shoulder to where Stella and Meara were battling a group of muckrons about ten feet away. The three of them had been forced back from the slope and pushed toward the shore of the bay. The main army of men was retreating further away from them as they fell back toward the hinterland.

'We have to help Eben and the others!' shouted Red, trying to fight his way back toward the headland.

'Red, we can't help them. The army is retreating!' cried Meara as she blasted a group of muckrons with a shockwave of raw blue energy.

'I'm not leaving without Eben!' cried Red as he cut down another muckron.

A moment later Stella was by his side; together they fought toward the slope that led up to the headland. They battled their way forward, following the edge of the cliff, with Meara not far behind. A swarm of at least a dozen muckrons charged down the hill toward them.

'Meara!' cried Stella, knowing they couldn't fight so many at once.

Meara raised her hands and shot dozens of glowing blue darts at the monsters; the muckrons all fell. Meara's turquoise blue eyes looked back to the battlefield; she knew if they continued to fight they would be cut off from any possible retreat. The Irvarians and Everdonians were fleeing the battlefield. They had been completely overwhelmed.

'Look!' cried Stella, pointing ahead beyond the multitude of muckrons to the top of the headland.

At the height of the cliff, about a hundred yards away, they could see a man clothed in black who was holding Eben's limp body above his head.

'No!' cried Red hysterically. Meara watched in horror as the Astarian cast Eben from the cliff top. The three of them stood and watched as Eben's body fell into the raging waves below.

'No!' screamed Red, dashing toward the edge of the cliff.

Meara rushed to Red's side and grabbed his arm; thinking if she hadn't Red would have jumped off the cliff after Eben.

'Red, it's too late. He's gone!' she shouted.

'No!' cried Red, tears streaming down his face.

'We have to go!'

'Maybe he's alive! I have to try to save him!' cried Red. Meara shook her head, knowing Eben would have surely died from the fall if he wasn't already dead. Stella stared down at the raging water. Her face was pale from shock.

'Red, Eben is dead,' said Meara, the words burning her heart. 'If we don't leave now we will die here!' Red looked across to Stella. Blood was dripping down his wife's face from a cut across her forehead. 'Listen to me, Red. We have done all we can. We must go!' Red nodded sadly.

Meara led the way back down toward the shoreline and cleared a path through the muckrons that stood in their way. The vast majority of monsters were either chasing the retreating army of men toward the north or guarding the approaches to the headland. This gave the three of them a clear path to escape along the coast. Within minutes they had escaped the battlefield. Meara led them for about ten minutes through the hinterland until they came to a forested area where they could hide and rest.

A dark twilight fell across the land. They sat down in a hidden forest glade and wept for their lost friends.

**

'The shroud has now been lifted and all our fears have been realised,' said Baftel.

Baftel had used his powers to lead Cassiel, Arlen, and a group of five stranded Irvarian soldiers away from the battlefield and through the wilderness. They had found a small abandoned farmhouse in the hinterland to the north of Crescent Bay.

'What about the others, Baftel? Can you see Eben, Stella, and Red? What about Meara and the Fiorians?' asked Cassiel.

'I cannot see Eben at all. I know that Red, Stella, and Meara live. They are somewhere in the wilderness to the south of us. As for the Fiorians, Tabarians, and the five other Irilians; I fear they may have been slain in the battle because they have fallen from my vision. King Edric managed to escape with what is left of his army; they are retreating north along the highway. As for King Lenard, he was killed in the battle. The Fire Order was scattered after the battle. More than half of the Fire Order was killed.'

'How did this happen?' asked Cassiel, still in shock and aching from the battle.

'The knights and men simply couldn't match the wyverns,' said Baftel. 'The enemy's lindworms caused havoc on the battlefield. The muckrons also overwhelmed our attack on the headland because they controlled the higher ground. The plan to attack the headland was foolish. The battle was completely lost when we were flanked by the second muckron army. Many men fell trying to fight their way uphill. Those that fell back were slain by the muckron army behind us.'

'What now. Is this the end?' asked Cassiel, wondering if there was any hope left.

'We must move north quickly; we won't be safe here for long, yet I fear the north will not be safe either,' said Baftel. 'An enormous muckron army has entered Vastoria from the Iron Gate Pass. The muckron horde will soon invade Irvaria.'

Cassiel stared at the table and shook his head in disbelief. He couldn't see a way they could possibly go on.

**

THE GATE AND BEYOND: BOOK THREE OF THE VEREDOR CHRONICLES

CHAPTER ONE

The Southern Sea had long been considered the most treacherous of all the seas in Veredor. Many believed that the seas of the south were even more dangerous than the icy waters to the north of Scaldonia. Reefs were scattered throughout the sea and monsters of the deep thrived in the warm waters. Storms and hurricanes were common in the summer months, and countless ships had been lost beneath the waves or wrecked on the rocky coastlines of Everdon, Vastoria, and Ateria. It was agreed by most seafaring folk that the greatest caution should be taken when venturing out after the first day of summer, and only the brave would dare sail far from shore at such a time of year.

On such a summer day a group of rare creatures came across a peculiar sight beneath the waves. In the tranquillity of the deep something was drifting; not one of their kind, but a strange creature that they had never seen before.

The ocean sprites darted through the water toward the creature and circled around it several times before deciding to venture closer. The sprites looked a lot like miniature men, and they were no taller than a foot in height. Their eyes were exceptionally large and glimmered like jewels, and they wore long pointy hats made of ocean silk which were at least as long as they were tall. They formed a circle around the peculiar creature and realised that he resembled a mer, yet he also had the appearance of a man. This confused the ocean sprites, as no such creature existed in the extensive records of their people.

They looked at one another and wondered what they should do. It was clear to them that this strange creature was injured and very close to death. They hummed a sweet song which echoed throughout the deep. The blood of the creature was leaking into the water, and they knew if they didn't do something soon he would surely die.

In a moment they decided where they would take him. They gathered around and wrapped him in a silky material, and they covered his wound to stop the bleeding. Together they then drew him far away beneath the surface of the sea.

**

Eben Awoke. The sound of water droplets echoed in the distance. He opened his eyes and could see a suspended layer of water floating about ten feet above. The upside down layer of water was acting as a ceiling. A school of fish slowly drifted by just above the surface. He turned his head and looked around. He was lying on the sandy floor of the ocean in a chamber with suspended walls of rippling water. The Sword of Light and the small glass case with the two candles had been placed beside him. He was clothed in a strange silky green material.

'Welcome,' said a soft voice.

He looked back. A man with an aged face, a thick grey beard, and big emerald green eyes was seated on the ground a little way back from him. The man was clothed in the same green material.

His bright eyes glimmered in the soft light of the ocean floor.

'Who are you? ' asked Eben as he sat up. His hand went to where the wound should have been on his chest, but he found his injuries had been completely healed.

'You were brought to us by a group of ocean sprites. They found you drifting beneath the waves. You were very close to death. You have been with us for seven days,' said the old man. 'My name is Casimir. I'm a friend of the mer. This place is the southern home of the merfolk.'

'You are an Astarian,' said Eben, sensing that Casimir was not a man.

'Yes,' said Casimir softly. 'I am one of the three remaining Astarians in Veredor. Once my people were numerous, yet now my race is close to extinction. Veredor, our cherished home, shall pass on to others. We will be forgotten like a dream.'

Eben stared at him for some time before speaking again. 'My name is Eben.'

'And you are the Ecorian,' said Casimir, smiling warmly. 'I know who you are. I have been watching you from afar. I first became aware of you when you were in Zyran; I protected you and your friends from the ghoul in Vastoria, I watched when you arrived at Faircastle, I saw you drink from the Pool of Radiance, I saw you duel with Callidus and I saw you fall beneath the waves. Of course you cannot possibly drown; this event simply woke up the mer which was dormant deep within you.'

Eben stared at the aged Astarian, his eyes wide with wonder.

'If you are an Astarian why didn't you help me? Surely you could have helped us fight Callidus. Many good people died in the battle at Crescent Bay.' A deep feeling of grief rose in his chest. 'Why didn't you help us, Casimir?' Eben thought of Chiara at the moment she was murdered and the fallen Tabarian Knights who had been so loyal to him.

Casimir looked down at the sandy ground. Eben could clearly see the burden of grief the Astarian was carrying. 'If I had intervened I would not have been able to help you now. There was more at risk than you know. I am the last living Astarian who opposes the Prince of Shadows. I resist his desire to completely control the Cosmic Gate. If I die the Prince of Shadows could instantly expel all men and mer into the deserts beyond Veredor. He would then rule Veredor completely unopposed, and he would entirely control the Cosmic Gate. Veredor would then fall beneath a veil of eternal darkness. Since you were in Zyran I have been protecting you from the eyes of the Prince of Shadows and his seers. When you arrived here I used most of my remaining strength to heal you; now I am greatly weakened. Saving you from death was the best way I could help you and our world.'

'Thank you for saving me,' said Eben. 'But how can we defeat the Prince of Shadows. Is there any hope left?'

'The battle is not over. The Prince of Shadows does not yet fully control the Cosmic Gate. There is still time to defeat him.'

'But how? The Irvarians and Evedonians were completely overwhelmed by his army. Callidus said there is another army of one hundred thousand muckrons marching on Faircastle. Who can possibly stand in their way?'

'There are other men who will rise up to fight the invasion. You are the Ecorian; you must find a way to save our world. The Prince of Shadows is preparing for his final victory. He believes the battle is all but over. There is still a chance to save us all.'

'But how can I? I was completely outmatched by Callidus.'

Casimir stared at Eben for a long moment. He pondered Eben's question. 'War is not the ultimate answer to this quest. If you are going to overcome the Prince of Shadows you must take control of the Cosmic Gate. It is the only way that you can expel him from Veredor.'

'How can I take control of the Cosmic Gate?'

The Astarians eyes drifted to look at the rippling wall of water. A small shark swam by just beyond. A few moments passed in silence. 'When we first welcomed men and mer to Veredor we expected they would be able to cross the Cosmic Gate as freely as the Astarians. We were perplexed when they could not. We were surprised in those days when men began to build walls and fences to keep each other out. Men revere power. They seek power all their lives. The Cosmic Gate was built from the essence of Veredor, and Astarians are a part of that essence; this is how we are able to open the Cosmic Gate. My race formed a relationship with Veredor when we first arrived. Our connection has endured for many ages. If you are to defeat the Prince of Shadows you must find a way to establish what was never established. Fiora's Bridge must be crossed.'

'Fiora's Bridge, what is it?'

'Fiora's Bridge is a way that few men ever choose to travel but when they do anything is possible.'

'How can I cross Fiora's Bridge?' asked Eben, hoping Casimir could give him a direct answer.

'I know there is a way. I also know you must find the way. The way to cross Fiora's Bridge is shrouded in mystery. I cannot tell you how because I do not know, yet the secret is closer than you think.'

'What about the mer people? Can they help men defeat the Prince of Shadows?'

'There are few mer remaining in Veredor. Their race has diminished gradually since the end of the Forgotten Age. They cannot help you complete your task. You are the representative of the mer and you are also a man. If you succeed Veredor will continue to be a world of men and the mer will remain deep in the oceans. If you fail Veredor will fall under an everlasting shadow.'

Eben looked down at the sandy surface of the ocean floor. His mind raced. The mystery of the Cosmic Gate was beyond him. His thoughts then returned to his friends. He wondered if Red, Stella, Cassiel, and Meara had survived the battle.

'Casimir, you say that you can see things that are far away. Can you see if my friends survived the battle at Crescent Bay?'

Casimir nodded. 'Yes, your friends are alive, but they will face many trials on the road ahead. Soon you must go; your friends and the people of Veredor will need your help.

CHAPTER TWO

'They're coming over the hill!' cried Cassiel.

A large pack of muckrons were rushing over a ridge about a hundred yards behind them. Just ahead of him Arlen was leading Baftel slowly through the forest. The old frail wizard was struggling onward. The five Irvarian soldiers had remained with them since they had escaped the battlefield at Crescent Bay. The soldiers were helping Arlen to lead Baftel onward.

'Uhka Sharh!!!' howled a muckron.

'Hurry!' cried Alren as they entered a small grove which was mostly cleared of trees. Cassiel focused his mind and lifted his glowing hands as the muckrons charged through the trees at a blistering speed. Lightning shot forward from Cassiel's hands, cutting down a wailing muckron and another just behind it. Another muckron cast a spear, narrowly missing Cassiel's head. Cassiel blasted the muckron with intense flames. The monster recoiled back and screeched in pain.

Arlen left Baftel sitting by a tree trunk and dashed back to help Cassiel. The wizard's long grey hair blew back in the wind as his dark eyes looked ahead at the approaching muckrons. Instantly the whole grove lit up as whirls of swirling blue power rushed forward from Arlen's hands. A large muckron with a boar's head and massive tusks was sent flying back by the impact. Arlen focused his power. Intense blue flames knocked down two more monsters. Meanwhile Cassiel sent dozens of glowing blue darts at a group of muckrons who were trying to move around behind them.

'We are outnumbered,' cried Arlen. Cassiel felt his power was depleting as more muckrons appeared on every side.

Suddenly the muckrons turned and retreated back through the woods. Cassiel looked over at Arlen and smiled, feeling relieved that the monsters had given up. Arlen's eyes narrowed as he looked back through the woods in the direction the muckrons had fled.

'What do you see?' asked Cassiel.

'There is something coming,' said Arlen in a low voice.

Cassiel's eyes scanned the woods; he caught sight of three dark figures approaching.

'Northern Sorcerers,' whispered Arlen, wiping the sweat from his brow. 'They sent the muckrons first to weaken us.' Arlen looked across to Cassiel. 'Prepare yourself, Cassiel. This will indeed test our strength.'

The leader was a tall man in a long black cloak. His short grey hair was oiled back, and he had a deathly pale face. His eyes revealed his confidence; a sly smirk crossed his thin lips. On his right was a short man with long black hair and a very thin face. On his left was an overweight man with a bald head and a nasty snarl etched into his features.

'Irilians,' said the leader in a mocking tone. 'Did you really think you could escape our grip?'

Arlen stared directly into the eyes of the leader. 'We are not afraid of you.'

'Of course you would like me to think that,' said the leader. 'The time of the Irilians has come to an end. The kingdoms of the Ecorian Arbiters have all but fallen under the hand of the Lord of

Veredor. Soon Faircastle will be destroyed, and the remnants of the Irilian Order will be crushed. You are weak, Irilian. Your power is no match for the power that grows in the north.'

'We will fight until the end,' said Arlen firmly.

The leader shook his head and smirked. 'My name is Kazmok. Remember my name when you pass out of this world.'

The Northern Sorcerer raised his hands. A beam of green energy blasted forward at Arlen. Arlen formed a shield of shimmering blue light, and the beam struck the shield like thunder. Arlen strained to hold off the attack as Cassiel prepared a counterattack. Cassiel raised his hands and sent dozens of glowing blue darts at the three sorcerers. Instantly a green rippling shield of energy appeared. The darts were easily deflected by Kazmok's shield.

Kazmok laughed. 'Is that all you have, Irilian.' A swirl of green energy blasted forward at Cassiel. Cassiel formed a shield, but his shield was instantly fractured from the enormous power of the attack. Cassiel tumbled back and hit the ground heavily. Meanwhile Arlen sent several bolts of lightning at the Northern Sorcerers. The evil sorcerers combined their strength to hold off Arlen's power.

'You are strong for an Irilian,' said Kazmok. 'But you are not strong enough.' The three sorcerers lifted their hands together; a massive surge of raw power shot through the air at Arlen. Arlen again formed a shimmering shield of blue light. His shield was no match for the surge of raw power, and he was knocked to the ground. Cassiel quickly got to his feet and went to Arlen's side. The old wizard looked exhausted. His strained eyes glanced up at Cassiel.

'We cannot win,' admitted Arlen as the Northern Sorcerers approached.

The five Irvarian soldiers stepped forward to protect Arlen and Cassiel. The Northern Sorcerers laughed and froze them in place with an enchantment. The soldiers were horrified at not being able to move at all.

'Now you see the truth,' said Kazmok, laughing down at them.

Instantly a shockwave of blue light knocked the three Northern Sorcerers off their feet. The sorcerers struggled to get up and stumbled back as another shockwave powered into them. A moment later Meara appeared from the woods with Red and Stella by her side. She held in her hand a brightly glowing gemstone. Kazmok unleashed a torrent of power at Meara, but Meara deflected the attack and struck back with a massive lightning bolt that lit up the entire forest. Kazmok's face twisted in horror.

'How are you so powerful?' he cried in disbelief.

'You should not underestimate the Irilian Order,' said Meara.

The Northern Sorcerers backed away to the edge of the grove. They raised their hands together; a wave of bright green power surged toward Meara. Meara formed a shield, and their attack fizzled away into nothing. She countered with thousands of bright blue darts. The Northern Sorcerers attempted to shield themselves, but several of the glowing darts penetrated their shield. Kazmok was the first to flee. He turned and ran away through the woods and was followed closely by his two cohorts. A few moments later they were gone from sight.

'Should we go after them?' asked Cassiel.

'No, let them go,' replied Meara. 'We must leave before they send an army of muckrons against us.'

'I am glad you found us,' said Arlen. 'I thought we were finished.'

'We have been following your tracks for several days,' said Stella.

'We are heading for Faircastle,' said Arlen. 'Everdon has fallen to the enemy. We plan to follow the path that leads along the edge of the Old Guardian Mountains.'

'The main highways through Everdon are overrun with monsters,' said Baftel. 'Only the lesser known paths provide a way out.'

'Can you see King Edric with your power, Baftel?' asked Meara.

Baftel looked up toward Meara and nodded. 'Yes, he has escaped the enemy and is now in the Southern Irvaria Plains with several thousand Irvarian soldiers. He is on his way to Faircastle.'

'We must hurry to join him there,' said Meara, her turquoise blue eyes revealing her deep concern.

**

Meara looked out at the gloomy road ahead. The way that followed the edge of the Old Guardian Mountains toward Irvaria was little more than a goat track. They had continued north after the battle with the Northern Sorcerers and progressed as far as they could manage through the wild country in the east of Everdon. The day was darkening. Thick clouds hovered low in the sky. The company set up camp in a shallow gully in the foothills of the mountains. Red and Stella sat together at the edge of the camp where a small stream flowed quickly by.

Red had hardly spoken since witnessing Eben's death. He felt a deep sense of responsibility about not being able to save Eben. Stella had attempted to console him, but he still felt there must have been something he could have done. Baftel, Arlen, Meara, and Cassiel were discussing the battle of Crescent Bay and the impending invasion of Irvaria.

'Even the walls of Faircastle will not stand long against such a powerful army of muckrons.' said Arlen. 'The defeat at Crescent Bay has left Irvaria defenceless. King Edric simply does not have enough men to contest such an invasion.'

'What about the Empyrians and Vastorians?' asked Cassiel. 'Surely they will see the threat that such an army poses to us all.'

'The Vastorian tribes are not united,' said Baftel. 'Even if they were united we still would not have enough soldiers to stop the muckron army.'

'The only choice we have is to hold back the enemy as long as we possibly can,' said Meara.

'I have searched the lands for a light. I fear all hope has been lost,' said Baftel. 'A shadow is shrouding Veredor. With each day the darkness grows stronger. I fear that the battle at Crescent Bay was our last hope. I cannot see a way onward.'

'We must not lose hope,' said Meara, her voice remaining strong. 'The Prince of Shadows conquered all the lands of Veredor at the end of the Forgotten Age. Only a single fortress stood in his way. Fiora and the Knights of Shidon overwhelmed his army and the Prince of Shadows was banished beyond the boundaries of Veredor. The Astarian Fiora never lost hope; we must follow her example.'

They slept very little that night. The following morning the company continued north as quickly as they could toward Irvaria. The road onward wound its way through the rocky foothills of the Old Guardian Mountains.

**

Eben walked with Casimir through a tunnel of suspended water along the floor of the ocean. He could see up through the sea to the surface hundreds of feet above. Schools of fish were frequently passing above and often he would see other creatures of the deep: stingrays, sharks, and glowing jelly fish.

'How is it that the water stays in place and does not fall in on us? Is this because of your magic?'

The Astarian smiled and laughed a little. 'No, it is a gift of the mer. Mer can manipulate water. They can also breathe underwater, yet the ability to breathe underwater is secondary to their ability to create these underwater chambers. It is a magic that is instilled in them by nature.'

'You said that the sea awakened the mer in me. Can I also manipulate water?' asked Eben.

'Of course you can. I'm sure you can do everything the mer can do,' said Casimir.

'Will I meet the mer?'

'Indeed you will, but you must understand the mer are very shy. When you arrived here they did not know what to think about you. Men are as mysterious to the mer as mer are to men. You must be gentle with them. After all, they are your people as much as men are.'

Casimir led Eben through a long tunnel for quite some time. Eventually the tunnel opened into a large chamber with high walls of suspended water that arched upward. Four stone pillars stood about twenty feet in height and were positioned in the corners of the chamber. At the top of each pillar was a large crystal ball, and each crystal emanated a soft white light that lit the entire area.

Casimir smiled and looked around. 'They are still very nervous of you.'

In the distance Eben could see people in a chamber that was cut off from where he was standing with Casimir. They were about fifty meters away through the sea. Suddenly the water between the two chambers started to form a corridor. In the space of twenty seconds the tunnel through the water had fully formed. Five people approached from the far chamber. They looked like men, and yet there was something different about them. They were all exceptionally beautiful, and their skin was soft and fair. Their hair fell long and was like silk, and their eyes were like gemstones and glittered in the subtle light of the ocean floor. Two of them were mermen and three were mermaids. They slowly approached and stood still just outside the main chamber.

'Eben, these are your people. This is Algorus, King of the Southern Sea.'

One of the mer stepped forward and bowed low. He was proud and tall. His hair was long and dark and his complexion was very fair. His large blue eyes were remarkable; they glowed with a gentle light.

'It is also a pleasure to meet you,' said Eben, aware that he had heard their voices in his mind welcoming him to their home. 'You do not speak as men do?'

'No, they can, but they mostly choose not to,' said Casimir. 'Often the mer spend long periods of time in the water. The mer have always had the ability to speak to each other without words.'

One of the beautiful mermaids stepped forward and handed Eben a small crystal ball. The crystal ball had a shimmering glow at its centre.

'This is the greatest treasure of the mer,' said Casimir. 'It is the Sun Stone of the Astarians; one of the most treasured relics brought by the Astarians when my race first arrived in Veredor. The Sun Stone was given to the mer by the Astarian Fiora shortly after they arrived in Veredor. They have treasured it ever since.'

'Why are they giving the Sun Stone to me?'

'You must take the Sun Stone with you when you return to the world above. It is a great sacrifice for them to hand it to you, yet they know this is the only way they can help you defeat the Prince of Shadows. There will come a time when you will need the Sun Stone to move onward in your quest. One day you will meet someone who has only one hand; you must give the Sun Stone to such a person, and you must not show the Sun Stone to anyone else until that day.'

'Who is this person you speak of?'

'You will know when the time is right. A dark shadow is passing over the world above. Soon the shadow will cross the ocean and enter the deep. There is much evil afoot. I must warn you; the Prince of Shadows has brought a creature to Veredor that is evil beyond measure, a beast that rose out of a dark pit at the edge of the cosmos. He is planning his final victory, and you must go soon if you are to stand against him.'

CHAPTER THREE

Algorus walked with Eben through a tunnel of suspended water. They were descending ever downward into the depths of the ocean. The rocky ground formed a gradual slope that seemed to have no end. Eben could see a dim glow ahead in the darkness of the deep. Very little sunlight managed to push through to such depths.

'Where are you taking me, Algorus?'

Algorus looked across at Eben and smiled before speaking. 'For thousands of years the mer have maintained crystal gardens in the depths of the oceans. We call them the Gardens of Light. The great power of the Sun Stone has allowed us to do this. Sadly the light we treasure will fade away when you take the Sun Stone to the world above.'

They continued and the dim light ahead gradually grew brighter and shimmered through the water. The darkness faded away and the suspended tunnel opened into a great domed area which was several hundred yards in diameter. The water was magically being held back hundreds of feet above the ocean floor.

Eben stood still and stared out at the sight with wonder in his eyes. Many towers of shimmering crystal rose up toward the ceiling of water. Hundreds of glowing crystal balls stood at the height of tall columns and many statues of mer people, carved from pure crystal, stood throughout the Garden of Light and reflected the sparkling white light in all directions.

Algorus turned to Eben and smiled again. 'This place is called Eryna's Garden. Princess Eryna of the mer built this Garden of Light after returning to the sea. She was your ancestor, and this is why I wanted to take you here. She built this garden to honour her husband who had died in the world above. She would have wanted you to see the beauty of her creation.' Algorus stared out at the garden for some time with bright and joyful eyes. He then turned back to Eben. 'For many centuries Eryna's descendants have remained a mystery to us. We never knew if one of our people still lived in the world above. You were lost to us, and now that you have returned we see this as a great sign.'

Eben's eyes scanned his surroundings. He was transfixed by the beauty of Eryna's Garden. They continued onward along a walkway, which was made entirely of crystal. The way took them directly through the Garden of Light.

'Is there no other way to light this place after the Sun Stone is taken away?' asked Eben.

'Sadly, there is no way. The Gardens of Light will be lost to us.'

'Perhaps I will return the Sun Stone after I complete my journey.'

Algorus shook his head and his eyes became sorrowful as he looked out on the garden. 'Casimir has told us that the Sun Stone will never return. The Gardens of Light will only exist in our memories. We have accepted this, for it is the only way we can help you save our world.'

**

Meara and Arlen led the way forward through the rocky and undulating landscape of Southern Irvaria. They had travelled away from the Old Guardian Mountains and were making for the main road to the west of Elcalee. Red looked up and saw swirling dark clouds had filled the sky above.

Baftel pointed ahead. 'King Edric and his men are camped just beyond that rise.'

They walked on and ascended the gradual slope and came to the top. Two guardsmen, in full Irvarian armour, stood at the height of the hill and were clearly keeping watch. One of the guardsmen stepped forward.

'Welcome Irilians,' he said as they approached.

'You must take us to meet with King Edric,' said Meara.

The company followed the two guardsmen down to a shallow grove where the remaining Irvarian army was camped. They could see the soldiers all looked weary and many carried injuries from the battle at Crescent Bay. They were led through the encampment as the sun was setting. Red caught sight of King Edric sitting beside a campfire. The King was staring into the flames and his stern expression revealed his deep concern. He looked up as they approached and a glimmer of hope entered his distressed eyes.

'Meara, Arlen, Baftel,' he said as he stood up. 'I thought you had died in the battle. I am so happy to see you survived.' They approached and the King walked over to meet them.

'We are glad that we found you. We have been trekking through the wilderness for days,' said Meara.

'Is the Ecorian with you? Have you seen or heard from Chiara?' asked King Edric.

They fell silent at hearing the question.

'I believe all those who attempted to attack the Prince of Shadows on the headland were slain,' said Meara.

'So it is true: the last Ecorian is dead,' said King Edric, shaking his head in disbelief. 'We were wholly beaten at Crescent Bay, but there is still hope. The muckron army is conquering Everdon as we speak. I will be able to gather several thousand men when I return to Faircastle. Perhaps we will have enough soldiers to halt their advance northward into Irvaria.'

Meara cast her eyes downward as she realised he was not aware of the muckron army crossing Vastoria.

'Regrettably, the muckron army in Everdon is only one of our concerns,' said Baftel in a low and concerned voice. 'An army of one hundred thousand muckrons has entered Vastoria from the Iron Gate Pass. They are marching directly to Faircastle. We will need more than several thousand men if we are to stop them.'

King Edric's face grew pale and he nearly lost his balance at hearing the news. He stared down at the ground in silence for several long moments.

'Is there a way, Baftel?'

'I am sorry, King Edric. I cannot see a way.'

'I never thought I would see such dark times,' said King Edric. 'When I was young we fought Skathean armies in Vastoria. That war was difficult for my people. We faced many hardships, but we were victorious after a long and difficult struggle, and there was always hope that victory would one day come. I fear the enemy we face now is beyond us, and I cannot see a way through the darkness.'

'We must persevere,' said Meara in a firm voice. 'We must fight on until the end.'

'My heart is weary, Meara. I fear I may not be able to protect my people from the Prince of Shadows.' They could see King Edric was carrying a heavy burden of guilt.

'You have done everything you can,' said Meara firmly. 'You have always been a good king, and your people have confidence in you.'

'We may be able to hold them at the walls of Faircastle for a while,' said King Edric. His concerned eyes scanned the army encampment. 'But I simply don't have enough soldiers to stop so many muckrons.'

**

The following day the Irvarian army marched further north. Throughout the day several wizards of the Fire Order joined their ranks. More than half the wizards of the Fire Order had been slain at Crescent Bay and the remaining wizards had been scattered.

Toward the end of the day a single rider entered the encampment. King Edric was sitting with Meara, Arlen, and Baftel at the centre of the camp. The King looked up and smiled as he saw a man approaching. Meara turned around and looked to see who it was.

'Acartor,' said King Edric as he stood up.

'King Edric. I was lucky enough to find a stranded horse in the wilderness after the battle.'

'I thought you had died with the others when you attacked the headland,' said Meara.

'Yes, Meara, unfortunately I never made it to the headland. I was overwhelmed as I attempted to follow Eben and Chiara. From a distance I saw Chiara die, and then I saw Eben being overpowered when he challenged the Prince of Shadows. I tried to fight my way to them; I did all that I could, but in the end there was nothing I could do.' Acartor looked away and hid his eyes from them.

'We saw the Prince of Shadows throw Eben from the cliff top,' said Meara sadly.

'It is difficult for me to speak about this,' said Acartor, shaking his head and looking away again. 'I placed much of my hope in the Ecorian, and now that hope has been lost.'

'We all placed our hope in Eben,' said Meara.

Acartor stared at Meara for several moments. He then looked back to the King. 'We must find a way to stop the muckron army. They are burning every town and village in Everdon. Many of the people of Everdon have escaped into the forest and the wild regions, but it will not be long before they are rounded up by the muckrons.'

'The muckron army in Everdon is not our only concern,' said Baftel. 'There is a much larger army advancing across Vastoria and they will soon cross the Sunset Hills.'

'How many?' asked Acartor sternly.

'One hundred thousand,' replied Baftel.

Acartor shook his head and took a deep breath. 'This is terrible news. Clearly you must understand there is no way we can stop them.'

'I understand,' said King Edric sternly. 'I plan to hold them back for as long as possible. The walls of Faircastle should shield us for quite some time. Acartor, you are the only Fiorian among us; can you give us any hope?'

Acartor shook his head. 'You will need to give me time to consider the situation. I believe we have few options remaining.'

**

The towering walls of Faircastle stood as the last hope for mankind. The Irvarian folk from the surrounding countryside had retreated behind the ancient walls. The people of Irvaria could hardly believe that so few of their fighting men had returned from Everdon. A deep grief permeated the city. Only four thousand of the thirty thousand who left for Everdon had returned. Another four thousand had returned after defeating the Skatheans in Vastoria, and the city guardsmen of Faircastle numbered two thousand. All together only ten thousand men and twenty wizards of the Fire Order protected the city walls. Everyone in Faircastle knew that the shadow of night was advancing across their beloved land.

Red stood at the height of the outer wall near the main front gate. He watched as a massive swarm of muckrons crossed the plain before Faircastle. All the small villages surrounding the city were set alight as the monstrous army marched onward. Thick plumes of dark smoke rose above the plain. Stella reached out and took Red's hand. Drums heavily beat, and the howls of monsters echoed out across the distance. Dozens of wyverns circled above the muckron horde, and many more lindworms marched with the evil army.

'We have to prepare,' said Cassiel. 'Baftel believes the wyverns are going to attack from the air.'

The wyverns circled the city at blistering speed. Their bloodcurdling screams resonated throughout the town below. Dark clouds gathered in the skies above. A shadow was cast over the city and the surrounding lands.

Suddenly the wyverns descended from above. Red and Stella drew their swords. Cassiel looked up in horror as twenty wyverns hurtled toward the city.

'They are going to attack the town,' cried Cassiel as he dashed down a long flight of stone steps toward the streets below. Red and Stella followed after him.

Most of the army were manning the main front gate and the high walls surrounding the city. They hadn't expected the wyverns to attack the townsfolk in their homes. Hundreds of Irvarian soldiers were descending from the height of the great wall to protect the people. Red watched as a bright green wyvern crashed into the tiled roof of a nearby house and tore its way inside.

They dashed up the street toward the terrace house which was being torn apart by the wyvern. An old woman ran out of the front door as the house shook behind her. Her face was stricken, and she screamed for help as she stumbled across the street.

The Wyvern smashed its way through the door. Stella leapt forward and cut out at the snarling beast. The wyvern recoiled; its nostrils flared. The old woman ran away screaming. Dozens of glowing blue darts blasted out from Cassiel's hands and pounded into the wyvern's scaly body. The wyvern howled in pain and jumped at Stella, clawing forward at her. Stella skipped back and swung her sword at the beast's claw.

Meanwhile Red leapt forward and cut down with all his might. His sword sliced into the wyvern's back. Crimson red blood spattered out from the wound. The wyvern howled and then whirled about. The beast snapped at Red; its large fangs coming within inches of his head. Red jumped back and held his sword up in defence. A second wave of blue glowing darts blasted out from Cassiel's hands. The wyvern moaned and leapt into the air to escape. Stella cut out one last time before the creature flew skyward and was out of reach.

A moment later a loud boom echoed out across the city. The ground shook, and the great city gate shuddered. Red, Cassiel, and Stella looked back toward the ancient gateway. Again a second blast struck the gate.

They looked skyward and could see the wyverns were retreating back over the walls. Red led Stella and Cassiel up the stairs to the top of the wall. They surveyed a sea of hideous pig headed muckrons. The muckron army were massing just outside of arrow shot. Suddenly a bright green light lit up the enemy front line. Red saw that a group of about a dozen sorcerers were standing at the front of the multitude of monsters. They lifted their glowing hands. Each sorcerer sent a ray of green energetic light into a central glowing orb of raw power. The orb grew brighter and brighter. Suddenly the orb fractured, and a thick beam of light blasted across the field and smashed into the city gate. Again the boom echoed out.

'Northern Sorcerers,' said Cassiel in a low voice.

A moment later Meara approached with Arlen. They were followed by several wizards of the Fire Order. 'We must respond,' she said firmly.

Cassiel nodded resolutely. Meara walked to the edge of the wall and raised her hands. A blue misty light surrounded her arms. Arlen and Cassiel stood on each side of her. Arlen raised his glowing hands. Cassiel did the same.

'Focus together,' said Meara.

Suddenly a bright beam of fizzing light rushed forth from Meara's hands and shot toward where the Northern Sorcerers were standing on the field below. A second ray of light shot forth from Arlen's hands and the light beams united. Cassiel did the same. The blue energy beam blasted forward. The Northern Sorcerers responded quickly and created a rippling wall of glowing green energy. The blue beam of light smashed into the shimmering green energy shield. The sound of the impact was like thunder.

'Focus!' cried Meara as the blue light blasted into the shield of the Northern Sorcerers. 'We're almost there...'

Suddenly the blue beam of light dissipated. Meara watched in horror as blades of green energy swirled up from the field below and hurtled toward them.

'It's Baramak!' cried Meara.

The wizards of the Fire Order stepped forward and raised their hands. A bright hot layer of plasma formed a shield to protect Meara, Arlen, and Cassiel. Baramak's green blades of energy smashed into the wall of plasma; the sound was deafening. Baramak didn't stop. He pounded the shield with his powerful attacks. The three wizards strained to hold off the vast power of the evil sorcerer. Red and Stella watched on in horror.

After several minutes Baramak ended his bombardment, and the Fire Wizards lowered their hands. The plasma shield instantly dissipated. The six wizards on the wall stared down at Baramak who was looking up at them with a vicious grin. He knew they were no match for him.

'You don't stand a chance! Surrender or die!' His voice was sharp and crude with a thick northern accent. He then lifted his hand and a blast of green energy shot across the field and struck the main gate. There was an explosion at the gate; the ancient gate shook and wavered.

'We must use our remaining strength to fortify the gate,' said Meara wearily.

Meara led the way down a flight of stone steps. A group of soldiers were jamming large logs at angles between the gate and the street. They looked exhausted and dismayed. Every time Baramak unleashed his power the gate would violently shudder and the logs would dislodge. The soldiers would again have to heave them into position.

Arlen and Meara raised their hands and blue misty light issued forth and surrounded the gate. Slowly the gate absorbed the glowing energy. Again Baramak's attack struck the outside of the gate, but this time the gate stood firm.

'That will hold him off for a while,' said Arlen. He wiped his brow with a handkerchief.

'We must inform King Edric that Baramak is outside the city walls,' said Meara as she turned and walked toward the palace.

They followed Meara up the street. Most of the people of the town were hiding inside their houses. The attack of the wyverns had completely emptied the streets and lanes. A dark gloomy feeling of impending doom permeated the once hopeful and happy town.

**

'We cannot possibly hold the gate for more than two days,' said Meara. 'Baramak is simply too powerful.'

They were seated in the Ecorian Hall at the same round table that had been used for the council weeks earlier. The company in the hall included: King Edric, Queen Sera, Princess Apherah, Baftel, Mostyn, Red, Cassiel, Stella, and several other high ranking commanders of the city guard.

'Baramak is not our greatest problem,' said Mostyn. Mostyn brushed his tangled black hair off his face and then looked across at Baftel. 'There are fifty thousand muckrons surrounding Faircastle as we speak. Another fifty thousand are marching across Irvaria and will be here in two days. This second wave is being led by an Astarian. When he arrives we will have to deal with magic far superior to that of Baramak.'

'The Prince of Shadows,' said Meara.

'No, we don't think he is the Prince of Shadows; however, he was the same Astarian who was present at Crescent Bay.'

'Where is the Prince of Shadows? Have we been deceived? If it was not the Prince of Shadows at Crescent Bay who was it?' asked Meara, looking across to Mostyn.

'I believe we walked into a trap in Everdon. I don't know how we were led astray, but I do know that the Prince of Shadows is coming south. I can see that he rides high on the winds of Veredor. He has left the Fortress of Zarkanor; he is flying here by means we don't understand.'

'Flying?' questioned Meara, raising an eyebrow.

'Indeed,' said Mostyn. 'Possibly he has a steed carrying him; we don't know for sure.'

'One hundred thousand muckrons, an Astarian, Northern Sorcerers, and now the Prince of Shadows; how can we possibly save Faircastle?' asked King Edric, his eyes conveyed his deep concern. 'Is there a way?'

Acartor walked into the Ecorian Hall. The company looked at him as he approached.

'Acartor, can you give us any assistance or guidance? Can the Fiorians help us in our darkest hour?' asked King Edric, a level of desperation evident in his voice.

'Our world is falling into darkness. The sun is setting on the days of men,' said Acartor as he took a seat at the table. 'Few of my order remain. If only I could have been there to save Chiara and Eben Ecorian.' Acartor looked away for a moment and shook his head grimly. 'I think we should consider surrendering the city.' His words darkened their hearts.

'And give Irvaria to the Prince of Shadows. I can never agree to this. Surely there must be another way,' said King Edric.

'If there is another way I cannot see it. I think the choice is simple. We are facing a threat that is far beyond our ability. We should consider our capacity to save the lives of the people of Irvaria and not let them be slaughtered.'

'Are you suggesting that we become slaves to the Prince of Shadows?' asked Meara.

'There are possibly other options,' said Acartor, staring at Meara without emotion.

Meara's eyes narrowed for a moment. 'Acartor, who do you serve: the people of our world or the Prince of Shadows?'

'How dare you make such an inference? I have sacrificed so much for the survival of men. I am simply suggesting a possibility. You know as well as I do, Meara, that we can't overcome the muckron army outside the city gates. You also know the kingdoms in the west have all but fallen, and in the east King Ignis is hedged in with enemies all around. It is only a matter of time before Silvor and Ateria are forced to submit. We cannot stand much longer against the Prince of

Shadows. He is simply too powerful. We can allow him to destroy us, or we can search for another possibility.'

'It would be better for us to die free,' said Meara. 'I will never take the lower road.'

Acartor shook his head. His face was unresponsive 'I believe you are clinging to a faint hope that we can somehow still win. If you continue in such foolishness you will surely be killed. I witnessed the faith you had in the young Ecorian. We learned our hope was misplaced. Eben failed us completely; surely you can see that now. Let us not let false hope fail us again. We must be practical. We must see the situation as it is. We can save the lives of the Irvarian people, or we can let them die, but I will not be involved in such futile plans again.'

'It was your plan to lead Eben to Everdon,' said Red angrily. 'The Fiorians caused Eben's death, not Meara. You first suggested the idea. If there is anyone to blame it is surely you!' Red's voice was fiery and strong.

Acartor looked across at Red. His cold emotionless face said nothing of what he was thinking. 'I was a fool to have had faith in the Ecorian. However, what you say is true; I did have hope that Eben could overcome the Prince of Shadows, but surely now you can see the truth. The Ecorian is dead. Our shared expectation killed thousands of men and gave Everdon to the enemy. We must learn from our mistakes and be practical.'

The company fell silent for a few moments.

'This is a difficult decision,' said King Edric grimly. 'Perhaps you are right, Acartor. Perhaps there is a way I can save my people.'

'I'm happy to hear that you are seeing reason,' said Acartor.

'No, Father, we must not surrender,' said Princess Apherah.

'Acartor speaks the truth,' said King Edric. 'The Prince of Shadows will kill us all if we don't surrender.'

'Father, we are not slaves,' argued Princess Apherah. 'You always told me that integrity and honour is what makes us who we are. If we surrender who would we be? You are a noble king, not a slave. Irvaria is a kingdom of free people. We should fight for our freedom until the end. We should never give up hope. Eben Ecorian died fighting. Eben died free and kept his honour until the end.'

King Edric looked across at his daughter. His anxious face softened at hearing her words. 'You are right, Apherah. We will stand against the Prince of Shadows until the end.'

Acartor's emotionless eyes remained fixed on Princess Apherah.

CHAPTER FOUR

Red stood with Stella and Cassiel near the front gate. Baramak and the other Northern Sorcerers had bombarded the gate constantly throughout the day and night. The Irvarians were preparing for the gate to collapse and had set up a makeshift wall of wooden spikes just within the city wall. The sun was rising slowly in the eastern sky. A dark ominous cloud hovered low over the city. The wyverns had not attacked the town again, but they would often fly over to intimidate the townsfolk and were always just outside of the range of the archers.

King Edric had commanded the entire population of Faircastle to retreat into the palace. Many of the women of the city had donned armour and taken up weapons to fight with the men against the invaders.

'How long do you think we have before the gate gives way?' asked Red, looking across at Cassiel.

'Let's hope it holds for the rest of the day. The enemy is going to try to capture the palace,' said Cassiel. 'They will want to destroy the Sapphire Throne. Once they break down the gate we should hold them as long as we can before falling back to the palace. King Edric has ordered the army to hold the main street and attempt to force the enemy into a bottleneck to reduce the advantage of their greater numbers. They have been building barricades in the side streets and lanes to prevent the enemy dispersing through the city.'

'Do you think the barricades will hold?' asked Red, shaking his head.

'They might hold them off for a while,' said Cassiel. 'Red, it's only a matter of time. We are just going to show them what we are made of before we die.'

Red nodded soberly.

**

Quade rode Swiftwing up a sandy slope. Three Desert Knights rode ahead of him. A few moments later they arrived at the height of the huge sand dune. The view from the top gave them a wide vista of the plains to the west.

'There,' said Arthur, pointing into the distance. Quade strained his eyes. Far in the west across the plain he could see a dark area. It was difficult to make out because of the haze rising from the surface of the desert. 'That is the camp of the Aterian army the nomads spoke of.'

'Aterians, do you think they are going to Irvaria to help King Edric?' asked Dillon.

'I think they may be doing just that. We will ride back to the Jeanians and tell them to prepare for war. If we could unite the Jeanians and the Aterians our army would be formidable indeed.'

'Even with the Aterians and the Jeanians we still wouldn't be able to match the muckron army that crossed into Irvaria. They say there were muckrons as far as the eye could see,' said Dillon. 'There is also the fact the Jeanians will not move unless the Ecorian calls for them.'

'The rumours of the return of the Ecorian Emperor are just rumours,' said Arthur. 'We will try to convince them to march west. If we allow the muckrons to destroy Faircastle it will not be long before all of Vastoria is under their control. Uniting the Aterians and the Jeanians may be our only hope.'

'What about the tribes of the Empyrian Hills?' asked Quade.

'We have sent envoys north to request their assistance. I hope we are not too late.'

**

The army of Aterians were preparing to march north. Hundreds of orange banners depicting the white bear of Ateria flew above the long lines of troops. Prince Armida rode on his great warhorse at the front of his army with his leading knights and commanders beside him.

'Your Highness, there are three riders approaching from the east,' said one of the knights. The Prince looked out across the desert and saw the three silhouettes of the riders in the hazy distance. Prince Armida halted the march and waited for the riders to arrive. He could see that two of them were Desert Knights by their appearance. Several of his knights rode out to meet the approaching riders and then escorted them back to Prince Armida.

As they approached the lead knight announced them. 'Your Highness, I present to you Sir Arthur and Sir Dillon of the Desert Knights.'

'Why have you come here?' asked Prince Armida in a gruff voice, which showed he had little respect for Desert Knights.

'We heard news that an Aterian army was marching north toward Irvaria,' said Arthur. 'We wanted to ask you what your intentions are.'

'Our intentions are clear,' said Prince Armida. 'A powerful muckron army is marching on Faircastle as we speak. We are going there to fight them.'

'But have you heard the rumours about the size of the muckron army?' asked Dillon.

'We know what we face,' replied the Prince. 'Zyranian outcasts march with my army. Their seers say there are more than one hundred thousand.'

'Then surely you would know you don't have enough men to challenge such a large force,' said Dillon.

Prince Armida's eyes narrowed as he stared sternly at Dillon. 'Are you suggesting we turn around and march back to Ateria?'

'The only chance you have is if you unite with the tribes of Vastoria,' said Arthur.

The Prince shook his head deridingly and laughed at the suggestion. 'The tribes of Vastoria are not united. I believe this conversation is leading nowhere.'

'You have not considered the Jeanians. The Jeanians are powerful; if we could convince them to come out of the desert you would have twice as many soldiers fighting with you,' said Arthur.

'Have you come here to ask if I would be interested in such an allegiance?'

'Yes,' replied Arthur.

Prince Armida didn't answer straight away. He gave the idea some thought. He knew of the Jeanians and had heard of how reclusive they were. He also didn't trust Desert Knights; he could never trust a man who refused to show his face, but he knew there was truth in much of what the Desert Knights were saying.

'This is a difficult time,' said the Prince. 'We have never faced such an army, and I would be a fool to refuse the help of anyone. In a time like this those who are not our enemies are our friends. If you can convince the Jeanians to come out of the desert we would be interested in an allegiance, but I know the Jeanians are said to be the allies of no one, so I doubt you will achieve this task.'

Arthur nodded. 'We will do what we can and report back to you.'

**

Quade charged across the desert plain after Dillon and Arthur. Their galloping horses left a cloud of dust in their wake. The warhorses of the Desert Knights were hardened from a difficult life in the arid lands; they were a unique breed, smaller and much less majestic than Swiftwing; however, they were as tough and resilient as the surrounding deserts.

They came to a place where a shallow canyon crossed their path. The sun was setting and sending long red beams of light across the dry desert landscape. Dillon led the way down a steep path that took them to the base of the canyon.

They could see fire light flickering about a hundred yards away across the dry canyon floor.

'Nomads,' said Arthur. 'Let's hear what news they can share.'

Dillon and Arthur rode slowly up to the camp where several leather tents surrounded a small central fire. A group of men were sitting around the fire and they stood up when they saw they had company.

'Desert Knights, what tidings do you bring?' asked the leader, who was an old man with leathery skin, deep blue eyes, and a tangled grey beard. His four companions were much younger men, and Quade could see they were probably his sons, or at least close relatives.

'We were going to ask you the same question,' said Dillon as he dismounted. 'Do you mind if we join you?'

'Desert Knights are always welcome to share our fire,' said the old man. 'My name is Tomas; we are nomads from the northern regions of the Deep Desert.'

'You have come a long way south,' said Arthur.

'We are fleeing the muckrons,' said Tomas. 'Many nomads of the Deep Desert have been escaping into the southern regions. We saw the muckrons flow across the desert like rivers of death. Their numbers are endless; our only choice was to flee. I fear for those who have been left behind.'

'Endless?' questioned Arthur gravely.

'Indeed.'

'Have you spoken with the Jeanians?' asked Dillon.

'No, but we know they have brought their army south. They are waiting about half a day from here at the southern side of the Deep Desert. We have heard they are expecting the return of their emperor.'

'The Ecorian,' muttered Dillon as he shook his head. 'So they allowed the muckron army to cross their tribal lands and chose not to fight?'

'They did,' answered Tomas. 'They lack the numbers to challenge such a huge army. They would have been completely vanquished if they had chosen to fight. They chose to retreat south and wait for their liberator. They will not fight without the Ecorian.'

'The Ecorian will not come,' said Dillon as he shook his head again and kicked the sand. 'It is well known that the Ecorian line died out long ago. Such rumours arise from the desperation of the people.'

'In the morning we will ride north to the Jeanian encampment,' said Arthur.

'They may not listen. Jeanians take council from no one, not even the Desert Knights,' said Tomas.

'These are desperate times we live in,' said Arthur. 'If we do not unite now then the Kingdom of Vastoria will cease to exist.'

**

Dillon and Arthur rode ahead through the desert. The landscape around was becoming more undulating. They rode into an area of sand dunes. They galloped up a steep rise and when they reached the top Quade could see out into the distance. The great sand dunes extended toward the horizon.

'Look over there,' said Dillon, pointing toward the northwest. They could see there was a plume of smoke rising into the hazy blue sky about a mile away.

'Could it be muckrons?' asked Quade.

'We will see,' said Dillon harshly. They rode out across the sandy landscape and followed the base of a valley between two huge sand dunes. They could see a burnt out trader's wagon which was still smoking. There were also several leather tents which were scorched and had been torn down. There were no people in sight.

Arthur rode around the smoking wagon and examined the ground for tracks. 'There were muckrons here not long ago; at least twenty in the raiding party. It looks like the nomads knew they were coming. They escaped on foot toward the south and the muckrons didn't follow them.'

'They are heading north,' said Dillon as he started to follow the muckron tracks that led away from the burnt out camp. 'We should be able to intercept them.'

'But there are more than twenty,' said Quade, feeling a little disconcerted.

Dillon laughed. 'Don't worry, Quade. There will be enough for you too.'

'But I'm not much of a fighter,' said Quade, feeling a lump gather in his throat.

'There's no better time to learn,' said Arthur as he led the way out of the camp.

Quade rode after the two Desert Knights as they crossed the sandy undulating landscape. They traversed several large sand dunes and followed the muckrons tracks along the base of a valley. Quade could feel his heart beginning to thump in his chest.

They came to the top of a large sandy hill and from the height they had a good view of a plain below that extended for several miles into the distance. Dillon and Arthur halted their horses. They could see a group of more than twenty muckrons crossing the flat desert plain. Dillon drew his sword and looked across at his companions.

'For the people of Vastoria!' he shouted at the top of his lungs. Arthur then drew his curved sword and cried out as they galloped down the sandy slope. The two desert knights charged onward. Quade drew his sword and hesitated for a moment, shaking his head.

'Looks like this is it,' he whispered to himself.

He then charged forward. Swiftwing easily kept pace with the horses of the Desert Knights. The muckron raiding party turned around as they approached. Their pig heads howled and moaned as they shook their spears and war hammers in defiance.

Dillon rode out in front and lifted his sword. He smashed into their ranks and rammed his sword into a muckron as his horse galloped over another. Arthur followed and cut down another monster as he charged by the left side of the raiding party. Swiftwing leapt directly into the muckron group. Quade stabbed out, but a muckron deflected his strike as another monster hacked out at Quade with a small axe. Quade leaned back, only just avoiding the strike as Swiftwing reared up and kicked out.

For a moment Quade lost his balance and he felt himself falling. His face struck the sand and he rolled away as a spear pelted into the ground beside him. A muckron then leapt on top of him; its hideous face was inches from his own. Quade struck forward with his elbow, bashing the monster on the snout as he crawled back along the sandy ground.

He caught sight of Arthur fighting several muckrons and Dillon was in the midst of the monsters. Quade leapt up as a muckron with a pinkish head and a huge pig's snout swung its war hammer at him. He stumbled back and lifted his sword between himself and the monster. The muckron hissed.

'Ursh-shaka!'

Quade cried out as he ran at the beast. He thrust forward with all his might. The muckron deflected the attack and whirled about as it swung the war hammer again. Quade deflected the blow, but he lost his footing and fell face first into the sand, losing his grip on his sword. The muckron stood above him and snorted as it lifted its weapon. Quade pushed himself back along the sandy ground as he gazed up in horror at the ugly monster. He reached out, but his sword had fallen too far away.

The muckron howled and Quade closed his eyes, knowing death would soon follow. The sound of steel on steel rang out.

'No you don't,' said Dillon's harsh voice.

Quade opened one eye and looked up. Dillon had deflected the strike and was holding off the muckron's war hammer only inches from his head. The pink headed muckron hissed and screamed, its bloodshot eyes sneering at Dillon as drool spattered out from its gaping mouth. The monster drew back its hammer and lifted it again, but Dillon was much too quick for the beast. He instantly rammed his Vastorian blade through the muckron's hairy chest. The foul monster moaned and then fell to the ground.

Quade lifted himself up and observed the scene. All the muckrons were dead.

Arthur walked over. 'Now that wasn't too hard was it?' he asked.

Quade shook his head. 'I wasn't much help. I couldn't even slay one.'

'You were a good distraction,' said Dillon, laughing.

'Maybe that's all I'll ever be,' said Quade, shaking his head. 'I've never been that good at fighting.'

'You could always arm yourself with a crossbow,' said Arthur. 'Some distance between you and the enemy may help next time.'

'I'll keep it in mind,' said Quade as he brushed the sand off his clothes.

Shortly after the battle they gathered the horses and prepared to set out to meet with the Jeanians.

**

Eben stood on a long sandy beach with Casimir. They were completely alone. A gentle breeze blew over the sea from the south. Deep and dark clouds hovered low in the sky.

'Time is running out. Your people need you. The hand of evil has reached out, and the shadow grows darker with each day, yet a glimmer of hope remains, like a single candle in a darkening world. You are brave, Eben. I believe the walls that bind you will fall when the time is right. Fiora's Bridge can be crossed.'

'Thank you for saving me, Casimir. I will do all I can to save our world.'

Casimir nodded, and his eyes drifted toward the headland. 'It is a sign!' he cried, pointing toward the headland. Eben turned to see atop the rocky headland stood a shining white unicorn. 'Go Ecorian! Go before he leaves! The eternal light has sent you a steed to take you through the darkening night! Go Ecorian!'

Eben sprinted along the beach toward the headland and climbed the rocky rise as quickly as he could. Within minutes he had reached the height of the headland. The white unicorn stared at him as he arrived. The majestic creature glowed against the shadowy background of thick dark clouds. Eben slowly approached and the unicorn gently bowed its head.

'I am Eben Ecorian,' he said softly.

**

King Edric watched the city below from one of the great arched windows of the Ecorian Hall. A feeling of impending doom filled his heart and mind. He knew it was only a matter of time, and he felt a deep sense of failure that he couldn't protect his people from the enemy army beyond the gate.

Acartor approached and stood beside him and looked outward over the city. 'The second muckron army has arrived. The Astarian from Crescent Bay is with them. The gate will fall. They will be upon us soon.'

King Edric's eyes drifted to the area beyond the wall where the muckron horde was camped. 'I know it is over, Acartor. All we can do is fight until the end.'

Acartor stood in silence for a minute with the king. 'The decision to fight is foolish and reckless. If you would allow me to negotiate I believe I could salvage something from this hopeless situation. At least then some men would remain living. We must think logically. Survival should be our priority.'

'There are some things that an honourable man cannot accept,' said King Edric firmly.

'But everyone will die,' muttered Acartor.

'Everyone dies eventually. It is not about when you die; it is about how you live. We will die as we have lived, with our honour,' said King Edric firmly.

The doors of the Ecorian Hall opened and Princess Apherah quickly crossed the marble floor toward them. She was carrying a small piece of parchment in her hand.

'Father, a messenger falcon just arrived from King Ignis of Ortaria. He has crossed into Vastoria with his army and is nearing the Sunset Hills. The tribes of the Empyrian Hills and the Scaldonians are with him. They are coming to save us.'

King Edric's eyes opened wide. He took the message from Apherah's hands.

'He is coming with an army of nearly fifty thousand soldiers,' said King Edric, his voice growing hopeful.

Acartor took a step back at hearing his words. 'This army is not enough to match the army of the Prince of Shadows. They will be utterly crushed.'

Princess Apherah looked at Acartor with surprise. 'But there may be a chance.'

'What chance?' growled Acartor. 'This is foolish. Our only chance was when we fought the enemy at Crescent Bay. We were completely overwhelmed. King Ignis is a fool for leading his army to their end. This is a barbaric move that will have a brutal outcome. This will not help us come to a resolution.'

'I don't see it that way, Acartor,' said King Edric. 'There is still some hope. We will hold out for as long as we can. Perhaps King Ignis will arrive before we are destroyed.'

Acartor shook his head. 'It is your decision, King Edric, but I think you should not hope where there is no hope.' Acartor turned and walked across the hall toward the stairwell that led down to the lower levels.

'Father, the Ortarians are strong and noble. If we can just hold off the enemy for a few more days they may be able to save us.'

King Edric smiled at his daughter. 'I am very proud of you, Apherah. You are brave and strong, and you never give up hope. I'm sorry for standing between you and the Ecorian. I should have never stepped in the way of your chance to find love.'

Apherah's sad eyes glanced away. 'I know you wanted what was best for our people. Eben Ecorian was a noble warrior. He gave his life to defend our kingdom. I will always hold the memory of him in my heart.'

King Edric smiled and hugged his daughter. 'We will honour the Ecorian by fighting as he fought. We will give our lives as he did.'

CHAPTER FIVE

An army of fifteen thousand Jeanian tribal warriors filled a wide valley between two large sandy hills deep in the desert of Vastoria. Their banners depicted the white Ecorian unicorn on a purple background and hundreds flew high above their encampment.

Quade stood with Arthur and Dillon outside the tent of the High Chief of the Jeanians. 'Do they always make you wait so long?' he asked Dillon.

Dillon's masked face looked across at him. 'Yes, they believe we gave up the noble ways of the Ecorian Empire. Making us wait is one of their ways of showing their disapproval that we no longer follow the old Ecorian ways. They only regard the Desert Knights as friends because we have fought to protect the Jeanians in the past.'

After nearly an hour of waiting they were finally called into the tent by the tribesmen. The leather tent was large and several oil lanterns burned and provided a soft light. Three old Jeanian tribesmen sat cross-legged on the ground. They all had thick beards and deeply weathered faces. A haze filled the tent from the large wooden pipes the chiefs were smoking. They turned their attention to Quade and the two Desert Knights.

'Welcome, Sir Arthur,' said the oldest of the three tribesmen.

'Greetings, Chief Parco,' said Arthur.

'Why have you come to our camp?' asked one of the other tribesmen.

'We have come to ask for your help,' said Arthur. 'We have arrived at a very perilous time for the people of Vastoria. The Desert Knights believe it is time for all Vastorians to work together. We spoke with Prince Armida of Ateria. He has brought an army of fifteen thousand men from Ateria. They are in league with the outcasts of the Zyranian Order and are marching north to battle the muckron horde which has invaded Irvaria. The Desert Knights will ride with the Aterians. We have come to ask you to join us.'

Chief Parco looked up at Arthur and shook his head. 'I'm sorry to disappoint you, Sir Arthur, but we will only follow the command of the Ecorian.'

'The return of the Ecorian is nothing more than a rumour,' stated Dillon, annoyed by the response. 'The rumour is a result of the people hoping for a liberator in such a time of darkness.

The hour of need is now. We can't wait for an extinct line of emperors to return to save us.'

'We realise the danger,' said Chief Parco in a low voice. 'Nevertheless, we are not interested in fighting in any war without the Ecorian. The Jeanians have waited for many ages for the return of our emperor. We have seen the signs, and we are prepared to wait.'

'But for how long?' asked Dillon impatiently.

'For however long it takes,' replied Chief Parco as he puffed on his pipe. Suddenly a deep horn sounded in the distance and was instantly followed by several others. 'It seems you are not the only visitors we will have today.'

Chief Parco stood up and walked out of the tent with the other two tribesmen. Quade, Arthur, and Dillon followed. The Jeanians were gathering and many had drawn their curved Vastorian swords in readiness to fight.

'That horn is a warning,' said Dillon. 'Something is coming.'

They watched the top of the hills in the distance and waited.

'Look,' said Arthur, pointing to the height of the dune to the south.

A single rider on a great white horse was traversing a high ridge parallel to the camp. He turned his horse and descended the sandy slope.

'I don't believe it,' said Dillon, shaking his head in shock.

'Don't believe what?' asked Quade as he stared at the approaching rider.

'That's not a horse he's riding; it's a unicorn.'

They watched as the rider entered the valley and neared the camp. He was not wearing any armour and only had a single sword at his belt.

'It's him!' cried Chief Parco in joy. 'It truly is him! The Emperor has returned!' The army of Jeanian tribesmen watched on in astonishment as the rider entered their camp. The unicorn glowed brightly. They could hardly believe their eyes. A complete silence fell over the entire multitude of tribesmen.

'It's Eben,' said Quade, shaking his head and smiling.

Eben rode toward them slowly as all the Jeanians watched on in awe. He halted his unicorn about twenty feet from where Quade was standing with the Desert Knights and the chiefs.

'We have waited so long for your return,' said Chief Parco. 'Are you the Ecorian?'

'My name is Eben Ecorian,' said Eben as he dismounted. 'I have come to ask for the help of the Jeanians. The Irvarians need your help. Will you help me save them?'

Chief Parco bowed down. 'We will prepare at once.'

**

King Edric had called a council in the Ecorian Hall. Already most of the seats of the table were taken by the commanders and knights of the city guard. Red, Cassiel, and Stella entered the hall. Baftel, Mostyn, Meara, Arlen, Princess Apherah, and Acartor were also seated at the table.

'The muckron army is leaving,' said King Edric. 'King Ignis has moved his army across the Sunset Hills and has entered the east of Irvaria. Clearly the Astarian does not want to wait for

King Ignis and his army to arrive at Faircastle. He is moving his army to intercept the Ortarians. I want to lead what remains of my army into the battle. My commanders have assessed our resources. We have two thousand cavalry and ten thousand soldiers. We also have another ten thousand men who are willing to fight.'

'You mean the elderly men of the city?' asked Acartor, shaking his head at the idea.

'Yes, many of the older men of our city are willing to take up arms, and many brave women have already been assisting in the defence of Faircastle. They will also march with us.'

'With such an army we will be completely destroyed,' said Acartor. 'We must face the reality that defeat is imminent.'

King Edric stared sternly at Acartor for a few seconds and then looked around at the others seated at the table.

'I believe this course of action is our best and only chance. King Ignis will not be able to overcome the enemy army alone, but with our help we may stand a chance.'

'What chance!' scoffed Acartor. 'There simply is no chance. Even with King Ignis and his army there is still no hope. The muckrons, Skatheans, and wyverns will completely destroy us.'

'I'm ready to die fighting,' said Red with deep conviction. 'Eben died fighting for freedom. We will fight as Eben fought.'

'Do you think you are being brave, Sir Red?' asked Acartor. 'We will be fools if we take this path. Men can survive and continue to live in Veredor, but if we choose to fight we will surely die. We should negotiate with the Prince of Shadows.'

The mention of the Prince of Shadows silenced the company. King Edric stared across at Acartor for some time before speaking. 'Acartor, I have already made the decision to march. We will fight with all our remaining courage. I sent a messenger falcon to King Ignis and received one back just before I called this council. He is waiting with his army at Jeriel's Field. If we march on the north bank of the Adira River we will avoid the muckron army. We can then cross the river at the Morris Bridge. Jeriel's Field is only a three day march. We must move quickly to outpace the enemy army. This will be our last stand.'

**

King Ignis, Duke Egil, and Sir Victar were standing at the height of a ridge at the edge of the Sunset Hills and looking westward into the Kingdom of Irvaria. The muckron horde was out of sight, but the enemy army had left a trail of destruction. Irvaria had been burned and deserted. The golden forests were gone and only smoking stumps and blackened trees with a skeletal appearance. The ground was covered in ash and the forest creatures, burned or slaughtered, scattered the landscape.

'This is what they will do to Ortaria and all of Veredor if we don't stop them,' said the King.

'Muckrons have no respect for life,' said Duke Egil, shaking his head as he looked out at the forsaken landscape. 'They kill for pleasure and enjoy watching the forests burn. They did the same to our lands in Northern Scaldonia. They are creatures of darkness and they have no place in Veredor. If we do not stop them they will destroy our world and Veredor will become a lifeless desert.'

'Do you think we can stop them?' asked Sir Victar.

'We have a large army; fifty thousand, and King Edric has a small army with him at Faircastle; but even with so many soldiers we are still greatly outnumbered,' said King Ignis. The King scanned the distance and then looked back to Duke Egil. 'I have always believed that courage and bravery will win out in the end. All my men are ready to give everything to win.'

'We will all sacrifice our lives to save our world if we have to,' said Duke Egil.

**

Eben looked across the table at Prince Armida of Ateria. The Aterian Prince had not moved his eyes from Eben since he had entered the command tent of the Aterian army. Chief Parco, Quade, Arthur, Dillon, and several other commanders and chiefs of the Jeanians and Aterians were seated at the table. Three wizards entered the tent and bowed to Prince Armida and then to Eben. They were clothed in long dark cloaks. The leader was an old man with greying hair, bushy eyebrows, and a large moustache.

'My name is Aperio. I am an outcast of Zyran and a former wizard of the Seers of Zyran. I am honoured to meet you, Eben Ecorian.' He bowed to Eben. 'These are my companions: the Zyranians Cardo and Tuor. They are also outcasts of Zyran.' Cardo was a stocky and short man with blond hair and dark eyes. Tuor was much the opposite; he was very tall and lanky with a sallow complexion and a youthful face; although his age was given away by the strands of grey in his hair.

Eben stood up and stepped toward the Zyranians and shook their hands. 'It is also an honour to meet you.'

They all took seats at the table. Prince Armida waited until everyone was ready before he started the council. 'Tomorrow we will march further north; we will follow the Adira River into Irvaria. We are aware that King Ignis of Ortaria is leading a combined army of Ortarians and Scaldonians across the Sunset Hills. We also believe he has the support of the Empyrians. His army numbers about fifty thousand men. He plans to attack the muckron army which is currently laying siege to Faircastle.'

'We must march to meet with King Ignis. With our armies combined we will crush the muckron horde,' said Chief Parco.

'No, such a plan would lead to our defeat,' replied Prince Armida bluntly. 'The walls of Faircastle have thus far repelled the enemy army. We believe it will not be long before the city falls.'

'Why wouldn't we want to join with the Ortarian army?' asked Eben.

'Because by the time we arrive at Faircastle the Prince of Shadows will hold the city. Once they win the city it will be impossible for us to win it back,' said Prince Armida.

'What other options do we have?' asked Chief Parco, his brow deeply furrowed. Prince Armida glanced across at Aperio and indicated for him to speak. The wizard looked at Eben.

'We have been using magic to hide our army from the eyes of the Prince of Shadows and his sorcerers. The enemy is not aware of the presence of the Aterian army in Vastoria. Furthermore, the Prince of Shadows is so confident that he no longer hides his plans from us. He believes his ultimate victory is near. He considers King Ignis to be the only thorn in his side. He will want to destroy the Ortarians as quickly as possible. Therefore, our plan is to allow King Ignis to draw the muckron horde away from Faircastle. When the stage has been set we will reveal ourselves.'

'Do you think we can defeat the Prince of Shadows?' asked Dillon.

The company fell silent. Prince Armida sternly looked to Eben. 'Perhaps we should ask the Ecorian.' They all turned to look at Eben.

Eben pondered the question. He glanced down at the Sword of Light that was at his side. 'The Prince of Shadows will wish that he never returned to Veredor,' he said with conviction.

CHAPTER SIX

The gate of Faircastle creaked as it opened. It was clearly evident that the hinges were buckled and twisted. The gate had little strength remaining. The Irvarian army had gathered along the main road that led between the gate and the palace. A sea of red Irvarian flags flew in the brisk breeze of the morning. Several long beams of sunlight shone over the city and lifted the hearts of the gathering soldiers. King Edric rode out through the gate, and Princess Apherah, wearing shining silver armour, rode her magnificent white warhorse after her father. The long lines of Irvarian troops began to march out of the city.

The horde of muckrons had completely departed the area, but their presence had left the fields and villages surrounding Faircastle in a state of complete ruin. Not one building remained standing outside the city walls; each and every structure had been burned to the ground, and all the old stone buildings had been destroyed by the invaders. Every tree had suffered a similar fate. Only smouldering stumps and blackened muddy fields remained.

King Edric surveyed the area and shook his head in anger. He turned his dark warhorse and led the army out along the river road with a look of determination in his eyes. Red, Cassiel, Stella, Meara, and Baftel rode just back from the front of the army.

'All of Veredor will look like this if the Prince of Shadows is victorious,' said Meara, her sad eyes scanning their surroundings.

'Not if we have anything to do with it,' said Red. Meara smiled at Red's brash confidence.

'We will do all we can,' said Meara.

'King Ignis may just have something up his sleeve,' said Red. 'I know King Ignis, and I'm sure he will have a plan that will get us out of trouble.'

'Let's hope so.'

The army rode on eastward for several miles and crossed a large stone bridge to the north side of the river. For the rest of the day they followed the river road. The forest north of the river had been left untouched and hadn't suffered the fiery fate of the forests on the southern bank. The beauty of Irvaria gave them hope and rekindled a feeling of courage among the Irvarian soldiers. Late in the afternoon they passed through a forest of golden elms and set up camp in a meadow on the east side of the woods and near to the river.

Red and Stella sat by the river and watched the gentle flow of the water pass by. Cassiel was sitting on a rock a little further down the bank and was watching the southern side of the wide river with intent eyes. A feeling of anger swelled in Red's heart. Memories of seeing Eben being cast from the cliff top were always at the forefront of his mind. He felt stricken that he couldn't be there to save his friend. Red had never had a friend like Eben before, and he knew that he would never again meet anyone like Eben.

'I'm going to avenge Eben,' he said to Stella. 'When the battle starts I'm going to fight my way directly to the Prince of Shadows. Just before I finish him I'll tell him I'm avenging the death of Eben Ecorian.'

'I miss Eben too,' said Stella sadly.

'I should have been there on the cliffs to help him.'

'Red, you did all you could do. We tried to keep up with Eben and the others. There were just too many muckrons. If Meara hadn't come to save us we too would have been killed on the battlefield.'

Red looked away and nodded reluctantly. He still felt there must have been something he could have done to save his friend.

Cassiel stood up and walked over to them. 'There are muckron scouts on the far bank,' he said as he pointed out across the river.

Red and Stella quickly turned and looked out at the far bank. About a hundred and fifty yards away across the water stood four hairy pig headed muckrons. Red drew his sword, but it was more of a symbolic gesture as the muckrons were no danger to them. For a few moments the muckrons watched them; they then turned and ran into the hinterland.

'Foul creatures,' said Red disdainfully.

**

The Irvarian army set out before dawn and kept a solid pace throughout the day. King Edric was keen to arrive at the Morris Bridge as quickly as possible. He didn't want to allow the enemy army to cut off the road to Jeriel's Field. Red, Meara, and Stella rode near to the front of the column of troops. Acartor, Mostyn, Princess Apherah, and King Edric rode at the very front of the army.

'There are three riders approaching,' said King Edric, pointing toward the hilly country to the north.

The riders galloped across the meadows toward the Irvarian army. Red instantly recognised the lead rider as Sir Ronan, the Fiorian who had been introduced with Chiara and Acartor at the council in Faircastle. He was followed by two other riders.

'Welcome, Sir Ronan,' said King Edric, a sense of gladness in his voice.

'We are happy to have found you,' said Sir Ronan. 'I would like to introduce you to the Fiorian Clare and the Fiorian Winfred. Clare was a young woman, perhaps in her early twenties. Her beauty was enchanting; she had long dark hair and large grey eyes. Winfred was a stern looking man with a shaggy red beard and bright red hair.

'What news do you bring of the Far Western Lands?' asked Acartor.

Sir Ronan shook his head sorrowfully. 'Little remains in the west. We have been consistently outmatched by the muckron armies. Several weeks ago our forts in Iarthar were overrun. We retreated into Dravania, but the muckrons were relentless in their pursuit. We then joined with the main Dravanian army and hoped to push back the muckron advance. Ten days ago we challenged the enemy force in the south of Dravania. We were massively outnumbered and were forced to retreat to the Iril Fortress. The three of us then left to seek your assistance. We didn't expect to find you facing such a powerful enemy army so close to Faircastle.'

'The end is near,' said Acartor flatly. 'The Prince of Shadows has sent one hundred thousand muckrons to finish us.'

'Then you will not be able to send reinforcements to the Iril Fortress.'

'Regrettably we have no soldiers to spare,' said King Edric. 'However, if we win we will send help, and the battle is only days away.'

'We cannot win. All hope has already been lost,' muttered Acartor.

Sir Ronan stared harshly at Acartor for several moments. 'Such words are not keeping with a knight of the Fiorian Order.'

'My words are nothing but the truth, Ronan. It seems that I am the only man who is being practical. You know as well as I do that death will be the only outcome if we choose to fight the Prince of Shadows. There is still a chance to negotiate. We can end all this destruction.'

'Acartor, surely you know there can be no negotiation with such an enemy,' said Ronan.

'The Prince of Shadows would make us less than slaves and take our humanity from us. It is better to live free and die free; you should know that, Acartor.'

'Ordinarily I would agree with you, Ronan,' replied Acartor coolly. 'Yet such a choice will extinguish the race of men. Will you stand by, Ronan, and watch as our race is completely destroyed? We can make the right choice and end this war, or we can follow a foolish path into oblivion.'

Sir Ronan pondered Acartor's words for a moment before speaking. 'Men are only men if they are free. The spirit rises only in the light of truth. We are free, and because we are free we can freely choose to be true. The Prince of Shadows would enslave our minds if we took the path that you suggest. Why do you seek to influence us to choose a path into darkness? You belong to the Fiorian Knights; you should know better.' For several moments the two Fiorians stared at each other harshly. 'You also know our race lives elsewhere in the cosmos. We came to Veredor as invited guests in the Forgotten Age. The world of men still abides far across the cosmos. Men will live on regardless of the outcome of this battle. You know these secrets, Acartor. Why do you make such suggestions?'

Acartor sneered at Ronan as he turned his horse. He rode away toward the back of the army without saying another word.

'I apologize for my kinsman's words,' said Ronan, a look of worry etched into his face. 'It seems that he has not coped well with his Fiorian responsibilities. I will speak to him privately later.'

King Edric's eyes followed Acartor as he rode away.

'Will you ride with us to meet with our allies at Jeriel's Field?' asked Apherah.

'Certainly,' replied Ronan. 'We would be honoured to fight by your side.'

**

The army continued for the remainder of the day. As the evening approached they arrived at the Morris Bridge. The bluestone bridge spanned the river at a point where the banks came within a hundred yards of each other. The bridge was wide enough for a wagon to pass and formed a gradual arch across the water. The clear water of the Adira River rushed by. Across the river were wide meadows with patchy groups of elm trees dotted about the landscape.

'We will set up camp on the southern side of the river,' said King Edric. 'Tomorrow we will march to Jeriel's Field. King Ignis and his army will be waiting for us.'

The army slowly crossed the bridge and began pitching tents and building campfires in one of the meadows about five hundred yards east of the bridge. Red and Stella pitched their tent and built a small campfire. As twilight descended they walked down to the riverside and watched the water flow by.

'I am looking forward to seeing King Ignis again,' said Stella. 'He is like the father I never had.'

'It will be difficult to tell him about Eben's death,' said Red.

'We will tell him that Eben died a hero and fought to the very end. In the coming days we may face the very same fate.'

Red nodded as his eyes watched the fast flowing water. The image of Eben descending into the crashing waves again flashed through his mind. He knew his opportunity to avenge Eben was near.

Suddenly his eyes caught sight of a dark shape in the water further upstream. The body of a man was being washed downstream. Within seconds the current of the river brought the man near to where Red and Stella were sitting. Instantly they could see he was still alive and bleeding from a wound to his chest.

'Look, it is Ronan,' cried Red.

Red immediately leapt into the river. The swift current pulled Red downstream as he swam furiously to reach Ronan. Within a few moments he grabbed a hold of the Fiorian. With all his might he dragged him to the shore. Stella reached down and helped Red pull Ronan onto the riverbank. The Fiorian's complexion was deathly pale, and his wound was deep. His head fell back. Stella pressed some cloth over the wound and supported his head.

'Sir Red...you have to...save King Edric...' stammered Ronan in a weak voice that was little more than a whisper. 'Acartor...he is a traitor...he's a Skathean...the Morris Bridge...go, Sir Red.'

'A Skathean!' repeated Stella in shock.

'It is... too late...the wound is to my heart...you... must go...now...save the King!'

Ronan closed his eyes and could not say another word. Red stood up and drew his sword.

'Go, Red! I will stay with Ronan!' Stella grabbed his hand. 'Be careful, Red.'

Red kissed Stella and then ran upstream toward the Morris Bridge. His heart thumped in his chest. He sprinted along the bank with all the energy he could muster. The bridge wasn't far, perhaps several hundred yards away.

Ahead he could see two figures on the bridge in the darkening twilight. The image grew clearer as he approached. King Edric was on his knees, battered and wounded, and above him stood Acartor who was holding his sword up and ready to strike. Red stepped onto the bridge and with his sword ready. Acartor turned to face him, a sly grin crossing his face.

'Sir Red, what a pleasant surprise. You are just in time to witness the execution of an Irvarian king. Are you so intent on interrupting such an important occasion?'

'It was you!' cried Red. A few moments passed, and the blood drained from Red's face. 'You led Eben into a trap! You killed my friend.'

Acartor laughed with contempt. 'Don't be so sentimental. Eben Ecorian was a fool and deserved to die. Yes, I gave him the opportunity to end this war in the only way that it could be ended. He caused his own death when he refused to serve the Prince of Shadows. Veredor belongs to the Lord of Veredor. Eben made the wrong decision and died for his foolishness.'

Red cried out and charged at the Skathean. He swung his blade with all his might, but Acartor dodged the attack with ease and slashed Red across the chest, penetrating his armour and leaving a long shallow gash. Red stumbled back as Acartor smirked and stepped after him.

'You disgust me, Sir Red. You are nothing more than a fool with some powerful friends. Killing you will be a pleasure,' hissed Acartor with a sly grin.

Red cried out in fury and again charged forward, but Acartor dashed aside and tripped him over. As Red fell Acartor thumped him in the back of the head with the hilt of his sword. Red's sword fell from his hand. He lay in a heavy daze on the cold stony surface of the bridge. The world was spinning around him. He couldn't clearly see Acartor or where his sword had fallen.

King Edric started to get up. Acartor turned and pointed his sword at the monarch. 'Patience, Your Highness, I will attend to you shortly. Just give me a moment to finish this reckless fool.'

'Enough!' cried Meara's voice. Red looked to see Meara had stepped onto the bridge. Her hands were glowing with blue light, and her bright turquoise coloured eyes stared defiantly at Acartor. The Skathean glared back at Meara; the sly gloating expression left his face and was replaced by a cold scowl. 'I see you have betrayed the Fiorian Order and joined the Skatheans. Prepare yourself, Acartor; your consequences have arrived.'

Acartor laughed. 'You are no match for me, Irilian.'

'We will see!' said Meara coolly.

A moment later a hundred glowing blue darts raced through the air. The entire bridge lit up with shimmering blue light. Acartor leapt back and used his sword to deflect the darts as he simultaneously dodged others with an awesome display of agility. Several of the darts struck him, but he seemed uninjured. Meanwhile Red got to his feet and helped King Edric away from the confrontation. Acartor then advanced with great speed. Meara lifted her hands and forks of lightning blasted toward the Skathean. Acartor howled and a black smoke gathered around him and protected him from the lightning. Meara lowered her hands and stared at him.

'What have you become, Acartor? Have you given over everything to the enemy?'

'I was instructed in the ways of power by the Lord of Veredor. He has given me power beyond anything you can imagine. My power has grown beyond all that men can hope for.' He slowly approached her.

'The shadow you have allowed into your heart has taken all your power from you, Acartor. You have allowed yourself to become a slave. You must turn away from the darkness.'

Acartor laughed and mocked Meara. 'Is this your way of pleading for your life? Do you really hope to save me? Foolish, Meara, very foolish. Know this: I chose to walk into the night. I knew exactly what I was choosing. I am not afraid of the darkness because I am the most dangerous being living in the darkness. I conspired to destroy the last hope of men. I led the Ecorian into a trap and watched him die.' A shady grin crossed Acartor's lips. 'Now, Meara, I will give you a glimpse of the shadow living within me. In a few moments you will wish you were never born.' He continued to approach her.

Meara shook her head regrettably. She reached into her cloak and drew forth a bright glowing crystal. The sight of the crystal stopped Acartor in his tracks. He stood and stared at Meara with wide eyes for a moment. 'The Irilian Star, surely you are not the leader of the Irilians!'

'Yes, I am. From antiquity the Irilians have prepared the Irilian Star to shine as a light against the darkness. The vision and hope of the Irilian Order stands with me. Your heart lies beneath a veil of shadows. You cannot hide in the shadows forever, Acartor. '

The bridge started to shake and beams of light rushed up from the cold stones. The dark smoke surrounding Acartor instantly dissipated. Meara raised her hand and a bright blue shockwave blasted forth. Acartor lifted his sword to parry, but the shockwave knocked him over and sent him tumbling backward. He staggered to his feet and stumbled back along the bridge with his sword still in hand. Fear was clearly evident in his eyes as he wiped the sweat from his brow.

'You may have won today, but we both know this army of men will never defeat the Prince of Shadows! We will meet again, Meara; then I will repay you for what you have done here tonight.' He leapt from the bridge into the fast flowing water below and drifted away into the night. Meara watched the water for a few moments and then returned to King Edric and Red.

**

Later in the evening King Edric was seated in the command tent with Red, Stella, Baftel, Meara, Cassiel, Arlen, Mostyn, the Fiorians Clare and Winfred, and several other wizards of the Fire

Order. Princess Apherah sat at King Edric's side. They had been informed that the Fiorian Ronan had died from his wounds.

King Edric had recovered from the ordeal on the bridge. He was battered and bruised, yet he had not been seriously injured by Acartor. The revelation they had been betrayed had hurt him deeply. A strong anger had taken hold of the King. Red could sense that beneath the anger was a overwhelming feeling of guilt for allowing himself to be misled.

'I have failed my people. From the beginning Acartor has been working against us. I trusted him blindly. He has been serving the Prince of Shadows ever since he first came to Faircastle. He requested that I call a council of all the southern monarchs in order to set a trap. He was never a prisoner in the Dungeons of Zarkanor; he was a co-conspirator and a servant of the enemy. Crescent Bay was a ploy to divert our forces away from Irvaria. His plan was to draw out the Ecorian and to leave our lands defenceless. We have been completely betrayed.'

'None of us knew Acartor was a traitor,' said Baftel. 'His treachery was even hidden from me and I am a seer.'

'It is likely that Acartor was trained in such treachery by the Prince of Shadows,' said Meara.

'Yes. What Meara says is true,' said the Fiorian Clare. 'Acartor, in turning to the shadow, has joined the Skathean Order, but his powers are beyond that of a normal Skathean. He has been trained by the Prince of Shadows. He was one of the most powerful Fiorians. Now that he has fallen he will be one of the most powerful

Skatheans. Deception, lies, deceit; this he has learned from the enemy. It is not surprising that he deceived us all.'

King Edric nodded, but Clare's words did little to reduce his feeling of responsibility. He looked to Red. 'Sir Red, without you I would be dead. Your bravery saved my life.'

'I did what I could, but I was no match for the traitor. Without Meara we would both be dead.'

King Edric looked to Meara. 'What Sir Red says is true, without you, Meara, we would have both been victims of the traitor. I will send several brigades to capture him in the morning. He will pay dearly for his treachery.'

'Acartor would kill anyone you sent after him,' said Meara. 'I doubt any of your men could come close to matching his skills. By now he would be far beyond our reach.'

'Meara is right,' said Baftel. 'Acartor fled quickly into the south. He is making his way to join the enemy army.'

'Then he will take our plans back to the Prince of Shadows,' said King Edric.

'I can assure you the enemy already knows our plan,' said Mostyn. 'Astarians can see things that are far away as if they were near. Whatever Acartor tells him will not alter the outcome of the battle. The Prince of Shadows already knows we are marching to join with the Ortarians. He knows we plan to make a final stand. Even with all this knowledge he doesn't doubt his ability to destroy us.'

'Tomorrow we will join with our allies at Jeriel's Field,' said King Edric. 'Together we will show the Prince of Shadows that we are not afraid.'

**

Red rode with Stella toward the front of the long line of troops. Thick rolling clouds covered the entire sky and a deep gloominess had settled over all the land. King Edric insisted that they keep a great pace. The deepening gloom was taking its toll on the morale of the army. Red could feel a certain sense of hopelessness had been growing throughout the day. They knew they were marching to face an enemy army that was far beyond their capability. As the day progressed a song broke out among the ranks. It wasn't clear who wrote the words, but before long the entire army was singing the song and it brought hope back to all the soldiers.

Even as the night falls, the Irvarians people will stand tall. Even if the sunlight fades, Irvarians will always be brave. Forever let it be known, that we stood tall to protect our home. And even in the darkest night, in our hearts we hold the light.

Late in the afternoon the Irvarian army crossed over a ridge. The Ortarian army came into sight. Jeriel's Field was a wide meadow, about four hundred yards across, that covered an area at the base of a shallow valley. Only a few old elm trees grew in the valley, and a crystal clear stream wound its way toward the north in the direction of the Adira River. Gradual slopes rose toward two opposing ridges at either sides of the meadow. The Ortarians, Scaldonians, and Empyrian armies had gathered on the eastern rise above the field and had already formed ranks. A sea of red Ortarian flags blew in the gentle breeze. A strong feeling of hope grew among the Irvarian troops at the sight of their allies.

'Sir Red, Lady Stella, ride with us,' said King Edric.

King Edric rode out ahead of the army with Princess Apherah. Red and Stella rode after them. They were followed by Mostyn, Meara, Cassiel, and the Fiorian Winfred. King Ignis, in full shining plate armour, rode out across the meadow on a mighty white warhorse. His armour shone against the background of red Ortarian flags. He was followed by Duke Egil of Scaldonia, a group of commanders, and several other warriors who were dressed in the manner of Vastorian tribesmen. As the two groups approached each other King Ignis recognised Red and Stella and smiled gladly. He then looked to King Edric and saluted his fellow king.

'King Edric, I cannot express enough how happy we are that you are joining us in such a dark hour. We face a powerful enemy. My scouts have reported they are almost upon us.'

'I am honoured you have come here to help liberate us. What are your feelings, King Ignis; can we defeat the enemy?'

King Ignis sternly looked toward the western ridge. 'It is doubtful. My scouts have reported a great multitude: muckrons, wyverns, and dark shadows that appear in the shape of men. They also have many Skatheans and Northern Sorcerers. We our greatly outnumbered, but my men are ready to fight until the end. The muckron horde is less than an hour from here.'

'We are the last hope of mankind in Veredor,' said the Fiorian Winfred. 'Only the Iril Fortress remains in the Far Western Lands. We are all that stands in the way of the Prince of Shadows completing his conquest of Veredor.'

'Then we will show him how brave men can be,' said King Ignis boldly. 'Many have already died fighting. Word reached me in Ancora that Eben was the last Ecorian. I can't express how much this surprised me. I accepted the news joyfully. Then word reached me that he had died fighting our enemies in Everdon. I still feel the grief deep in my heart at losing Eben. Upon hearing about Eben's death I decided to cross into Vastoria and follow the muckron army toward Irvaria. I believe we must be prepared to sacrifice ourselves to save our world as Eben did. We will show the Prince of Shadows the meaning of bravery.'

CHAPTER SEVEN

Red, Stella, Cassiel, and Meara had joined the Ortarian army and stood beside King Ignis. The Irvarian army had moved up beside the Ortarians and Empyrians. The entire force had formed ranks facing the opposing western ridge. Several thousand Ortarian heavy cavalry had moved to the front. King Ignis had positioned the archers to the rear. The infantry made up the majority of the army and formed ranks just behind the cavalry and knights.

'I am very glad we are all together again,' said King Ignis, looking kindly toward Red, Stella, and Cassiel. 'I will fight for Eben. I believe the Prince of Shadows will want to be here today to witness his victory over men. There may still be hope. The muckrons and monsters serve the Prince of Shadows and will scatter if he falls. If we could focus all our remaining strength on him we may still be able to win today.'

'He will be well protected,' said Meara.

'I'm sure we can fight our way through anything,' said Red.

'Slaying the Prince of Shadows may be our only hope,' said King Ignis.

Suddenly a hideous moan echoed out across the valley. A lindworm dashed over the opposing ridge and stopped halfway down the rise. Its green scales glimmered in the faint sunlight.

'Urs-shaka, Urs-shaka, Urs-shaka!' cried the muckron horde in the distance.

'They are coming,' said King Ignis.

All the men watched as the enemy army appeared at the top of the opposing ridge. The muckron horde poured across the rise and formed ranks. Thick lines of muckrons flowed like rivers of monsters. Before long it was clear that the monstrous horde was far larger than the army of men waiting at the eastern side of Jeriel's Field. Dozens of wyverns flew in circles above them, and clusters of lindworms were gathering at the front of the enemy lines. A feeling of impending doom struck the army of men.

Red scanned the army of monsters. He was looking for the Prince of Shadows, but he saw no sign of the evil leader among the muckron horde.

A shadow fell over the battlefield as the clouds above darkened. The gloom shrouded the entire army of men. Red could see fear growing in the eyes of the soldiers who surrounded him. The sun faded as more dark clouds rolled over the sky. Hope faded with the coming of the shadow.

'This is the evil of the Prince of Shadows,' said Baftel. 'He is destroying the light of our world. He is near, but he remains hidden from my vision.'

Red, Stella, Arlen, and Meara kept searching the enemy ranks, all of them hoping to locate the Prince of Shadows.

'What exactly do you see, Baftel?' asked Meara.

'I see a shadow gathering that is darker than the darkest night. It moves through the clouds above. He is watching us.'

They looked up at the swirling clouds as the light continued to fade. King Edric rode over from the front of the Irvarian army. He met with King Ignis at the front of the Ortarian army. A few moments later Duke Egil rode over and joined them. Red and Stella watched as the two kings and Duke Egil decided on a plan of attack with their commanders. King Ignis turned his white warhorse and looked sternly toward his army. King Edric was at his side, and the two kings drew their swords.

'For truth and light!' cried King Ignis. The kings then turned their horses to face the army of monsters. King Ignis pointed his sword at the enemy army. His warhorse leapt forward. The cavalry and knights charged after him. The horns of the Ortarian army sounded across the field.

Red turned to Stella. 'Stay with me, Stella.'

'Forever,' said Stella, a single tear rolling down her face. They gripped hands for a moment and then rode forward together. Cassiel was riding close beside them. Meara and Arlen were also nearby. The Ortarian cavalry advanced quickly across the field, and the howling monsters waited for them at the base of the opposing rise. Red drew his sword.

A moment later the knights and cavalry crashed into the front line of lindworms. The howls of the lindworms were hideous; knights were thrown from their horses, men cried in pain, and many horses were crushed into the ground. The second wave of cavalry struck an instant later. Red caught sight of a lance piecing a lindworm's neck. The beast howled in pain and fell to the ground. The pig headed muckrons then entered the fray. Almost instantly Red and Stella were among the enemy lines. Red swung his sword and a muckron fell under his blade.

Stella cut down a muckron. Her horse whirled around as a wave of muckrons charged toward her. Red rode forward, cutting down several muckrons as he moved his warhorse toward Stella. He didn't want them to be separated on the battlefield. There were monsters everywhere. Stella stabbed out again and again as another crowd of muckrons charged at them.

Meanwhile Red kicked out at a muckron, knocking the monster down as he thrust his sword out at another beast. A smaller muckron leapt at him from behind and bit into his horse's side, its flaring snout was hideous to behold. Red rammed his sword into the monster.

He turned to see Stella stab her sword at a lindworm. The beast raised its claw in defence and then struck back. Stella was knocked from her horse and fell into the grass below. Red jumped down to help his wife and found the lindworm was instantly upon them. He stabbed forward, but the scaly beast was too quick. It dodged, snapping back with its huge fangs.

A blue beam of light struck the lindworm before the bite could be finished. Cassiel raised his hands and dozens of glowing blue darts blasted into the scaly beast. The lindworm struggled for a moment under the attack and writhed around in pain. Red then leapt forward and hewed down with all his might, his blade cutting deep into the lindworm's neck. The beast fell and lay dead on the ground.

'Watch out!' cried Stella.

A group of muckrons were advancing directly at Red. A moment later Cassiel was at his side.

'Watch this,' said Cassiel as he lifted his glowing hands. Forked lightning blasted from his palms, and the monsters were stopped in their tracks and scattered. Stella gathered herself and joined them as another wave of muckrons approached. The flow of muckrons from the western rise was relentless. The cavalry advance had been halted. The Ortarian infantry then smashed into the enemy lines, and the enthusiasm of the men pressed the monsters back across the field. Red cut out again and again, but he found for every monster he defeated another two appeared.

'Red! The King! He needs us!' cried Stella, pointing through the throng of monsters.

Red turned to see that King Ignis was being pulled down from his warhorse by a group of muckrons. He grabbed Cassiel by the shoulder and the three of them dashed across the battlefield. They furiously fought their way forward. King Ignis wasn't going to give in easily. He swung his sword wildly and held the monsters at bay. Red and Stella were the first to reach him. Red stabbed out and a muckron fell as Stella cut down two. King Ignis turned to face them and smiled.

'Always there when I need you,' he said with a relieved laugh. His shining armour was battered, but the look of determination in the King's eyes was intense.

Together they pushed into the muckron ranks. Wyverns swooped through the air above, blasts of green lightning lit up the battlefield, and riders were being torn from their horses. The howls of the muckrons never ceased.

King Ignis led the way, but as they progressed across the field they found the lines of muckrons were increasingly difficult to hold back. Red looked ahead through the fray and saw the muckrons were allowing something to pass through their ranks. They all witnessed the sight of a ghoul walking across the field toward them. Intense darkness surrounded the spectre like swirling smoke. Its red glowing eyes were staring directly at King Ignis.

'What is that?' asked the King, his eyes wide with shock.

Cassiel lifted his hand and a bright blue beam of light shot across at the creature of darkness. The ghoul recoiled and then grew larger. An instant later it bounded toward them. Red dashed forward, cutting down with all his might, but his blade struck the ground. Instantly he felt himself being lifted up by the icy hands of the evil being. Red could feel the cold grip was burning his skin like fire.

'I take your light from you,' hissed the ghoul.

'Never!' cried Red as he reached out and grabbed the ghoul's shadowy neck.

Instantly a powerful beam of bright white light struck the ghoul. Red fell to the ground and away. Stella took his arm and pulled him back. Arlen stepped forward and stood before the ghoul. He lifted his hands and a light shone forth that was as bright as the sun. The shadow recoiled, and the muckrons surrounding them fled in fear. Arlen reached out to grab the ghoul with his glowing hands. The spectre fell back and cowered on the ground.

'You can no longer hide from the light,' shouted Arlen. 'The shadows gradually dissipated, and the ghoul curled up. The ghoul's faint red eyes stared up at Arlen in terror.

'It is too late,' hissed the ghoul in a thin and trembling voice. 'He is coming now. There is nothing you can do.'

A powerful howl blasted down from the clouds above and resonated across the battlefield. Every creature looked up to see the origin of the mighty roar. Red lifted his eyes to see the dark shape of a massive dragon swooping down toward the battlefield. Its dark scales shone like polished metal, and its huge batlike wings cast a shadow over the land below. From head to tail the beast was at least a hundred yards in length. The dragon's entire back was covered with sharp horns that rose like large spears. Its head was the size of a wagon, and hundreds of giant fangs protruded like blades from its gaping mouth. The fierce face of the beast drove fear into the hearts of all below.

Atop the dragon was a rider who was adorned in dark armour. Several horns rose from his helm and a menacing metal visor covered his face. He sat just behind the dragon's head, and he stared down at the battlefield below. In his hand he carried the Sword of Darkness, and a misty shadow swirled around him.

'The Prince of Shadows,' gasped Stella.

The dragon swooped over the battlefield and moments later smashed into the army of men. Men and horses scattered before the beast. Red, Stella, Cassiel, and King Ignis watched on as the men backed away; their courage fading at the sight of such an enormous and powerful creature. Scorching flames blasted from the dragon's mouth and incinerated several lines of soldiers. Hundreds of soldiers fled from the flames. Many horses threw their riders and galloped from the battlefield.

The Prince of Shadows halted his mighty beast. The entire battlefield fell eerily silent as all eyes looked up at the great enemy. A heckling laughed rang out across the field. The Prince of Shadows then lifted the Sword of Darkness above his head.

'Kneel!' he howled, his deep voice resonating over Jeriel's Field. The command was followed by deathly silence. For almost a minute not a single soldier or monster moved. All the men and muckrons stared up at the Prince of Shadows in terror.

A single rider then left the ranks of men and rode out across the field. Her armour was shining in the faint light of the shadowy day. Her large white warhorse held its ground before the face of the hideous dragon. Princess Apherah lifted her sword defiantly and looked up at the Prince of Shadows. 'We choose freedom!' she cried.

For a few moments the Prince of Shadows stared down at her in silence before answering. 'There will be no freedom in Veredor!' His voice reverberated across Jeriel's Field. Suddenly the dragon leapt forward. Apherah turned her warhorse and galloped across the battlefield as flames burst forth from the dragon's mouth after her. A group of brave men charged forward and were met by intense flame; they were all incinerated. The Ortarian archers started to shoot at the dragon, but their arrows bounced off the thick dark scales of the beast.

'Come on!' shouted King Ignis as he ran forward toward the dragon.

The battle erupted once again. The muckrons were given confidence by the arrival of their leader. Red and Stella ran after King Ignis. Cassiel fell behind and started to battle the muckron horde alongside a group of Irvarian soldiers.

Red focused his full attention ahead at the massive beast as he charged toward it. He lifted his sword as a group of muckrons crossed their path. The grass around them was burning brightly. The heat was becoming unbearable, and the smoky haze made it difficult to see.

Red hewed down a muckron and cleared the path to the dragon. Stella was by his side, but King Ignis had fallen back. Dozens of muckrons surrounded them. Suddenly a rider came into view and charged through the smoke and flames. Red looked up and saw King Edric holding a lance and galloping toward the dragon.

The dragon whirled around to face the King. Its massive horned tail smashed into King Edric's horse. The King fell and crashed heavily to the ground. His warhorse lay lifeless. King Edric's leg had snapped and blood flowed from a wound in his chest. The Prince of Shadows directed his dragon forward. Red and Stella dashed across the battlefield. Together they stood in the dragon's path and held up their swords. The Prince of Shadows stared down at them.

'Kneel before me!'

'Never!' cried Red as he lifted his sword and pointed the blade at the Astarian.

The Prince of Shadows halted his dragon for a moment and stared down at Red and Stella. Thousands of muckrons gathered behind the dragon. The courage of the army of men was lost save for a few brave soldiers.

'At last, Veredor is mine!' cried the Prince of Shadows, and his words shook the ground.

The shadow deepened, and all the men trembled in fear as nearly all the light of the day faded away. Red felt the hope in his heart begin to fade. He looked to Stella and saw tears welling up in her eyes. He knew in that moment the end had arrived. He cast his eyes downward and waited for death.

Suddenly a trumpet blew out from the top of the eastern ridge. Red lifted his eyes. Hundreds of purple flags depicting the white unicorn rose above the rise. A rider, adorned in shining armour, appeared on a great white unicorn. A mystic light shone over the battlefield. The Prince of Shadows roared in defiance. The trumpets of the Aterian army blew out again as a great army of men crossed the ridge and came into view. The horns of the Jeanian tribesmen followed.

'Ecorian!' roared the Prince of Shadows. The hideous dragon howled.

'Eben!' cried Red, hardly believing his eyes. 'He's alive!'

Eben drew the Sword of Light as the Aterian and Jeanian armies charged forward. The dragon leapt into the air and flew upward as the muckrons charged to meet the advancing Aterians and Jeanians. The Ortarians, Empyrians, Scaldonians, and Irvarians felt a renewed courage and once again advanced. The mighty dragon circled above Jeriel's Field.

The speed of the unicorn was incredible. Eben smashed through the enemy lines. The monsters fled and scattered before him as he cut down any lindworm or muckron that stood in his path. The Jeanians and Aterians charged into the muckrons and followed after Eben.

He looked up and watched the dragon circling above. The Prince of Shadow's eyes were fixed on Eben and the unicorn. The massive beast suddenly plunged and howled as it descended. A shockwave of bright light rose up from the field and the unicorn leapt as no other creature could. Eben swung his sword and cut through the dragon's dark scales. The evil beast howled in pain and landed on the ground as Eben passed by. The unicorn quickly circled around. Eben faced the Prince of Shadows. The dragon was injured, but the cut had only increased the beast's fury.

Meanwhile the Aterians and Jeanians were pushing the muckron horde back. The tide of the battle had turned and the muckrons were retreating toward the western ridge. Quade, riding his mighty warhorse, Swiftwing, led the charge toward the western ridge.

The Prince of Shadows stared at Eben without saying a word. He turned to see his army retreating. Only a few muckrons fought on.

'You are beaten, Astarian! Your army has been destroyed. Now I will finish you and your dragon,' shouted Eben as he moved forward cautiously.

The Prince of Shadows laughed. 'Ecorian, you have defied me for the last time. Soon you will see my victory is inevitable. I will break down any wall you build to stop me!'

Suddenly the dragon leapt skyward. The terrible creature ascended and menacingly circled the battlefield several times. Its hideous howls were deafening. The beast then swooped and in a moment snatched Princess Apherah from her horse. She struggled hopelessly in the dragon's grip as the mighty creature ascended toward the dark clouds above.

'No!' cried Eben, but there was nothing he could do. The dragon disappeared behind the dark veil of clouds and Princess Apherah was gone.

CHAPTER EIGHT

Eben came to the side of King Edric. The Irvarian King was lying on the battlefield. Red and Stella were already at his side. Cassiel, Meara, Baftel, and Arlen were standing nearby with a large group of Irvarian soldiers. The King looked up at Eben and smiled. He was struggling to keep his eyes open; his complexion had become deathly pale, and he was clearly very close to death.

'You...live, Eben Ecorian,' he said in a weak voice. 'He took her...he took Apherah...'

'I promise you, my King, that I will find her and bring her safely home.'

King Edric reached up with his last remaining strength and grabbed Eben's shoulder. 'I am sorry, Eben...You are the Ecorian...the rightful emperor...you have my blessing...save my daughter...you have my blessing...Eben...save her...'

'I promise I will save her,' said Eben. With these words King Edric closed his eyes and his spirit passed away. Eben then covered the King's face with a veil. He stood up and looked to his friends. 'King Edric has died for his people. Let us forever honour him. We will return his body to Faircastle. Then we will deal with our enemy once and for all.'

**

In the days that followed the army of men marched back to Faircastle. The feeling of grief at the loss of King Edric went alongside the feeling of hope that had returned after the victory.

The gate of Faircastle opened as the allied army approached the city. Eben rode the unicorn at the front of the procession with Red, Stella, King Ignis, Prince Armida, and Cassiel riding beside him. News of King Edric's death had already reached the city. The people of Irvaria lined the streets to welcome back the body of their slain king. The Irvarians wept for their king, but there was also a sense of elation at the victory they had over their enemies and the return of the Ecorian.

A carriage covered with an Irvarian flag led the way through the city up toward the Ecorian Gate. The golden arched gate stood open and Queen Sera, dressed in black, waited to receive King Edric's body. Tears flowed down her face as the carriage drew near. The Queen stepped toward the carriage and reached out to touch the hand of her dead husband. She bowed her head in sorrow. For several minutes the multitude and the army watched on in complete silence. Queen Sera then raised her eyes and looked to Eben.

'I welcome you home, Eben Ecorian.'

Eben dismounted and knelt down on one knee before Queen Sera. 'I am your humble servant. Your wish is my command.'

Queen Sera stepped toward Eben and stared down at him. The people of the city and the army watched on intently. The Queen's eyes were full of sorrow and pride. She placed her hand on Eben's shoulder.

'You are the Ecorian Emperor, Eben; however, if you would grant me a wish it would be that you rescue my daughter and bring her safely home to Faircastle.'

Eben looked up into the eyes of the Queen. 'I swear to you that I will not rest until Princess Apherah is returned safely to Faircastle.'

**

Eben, Red, Stella and Cassiel were seated around a table which was situated in one of the upper guest chambers of the palace. The chamber had large windows that overlooked the north side of the city. Eben stared out the window toward the northern horizon. He knew that Apherah had been taken far away into the north and his mind couldn't rest.

Red looked across at Eben and smiled widely. 'I'm still amazed that you are alive,' he said. 'We saw you die when you were thrown from the cliff top at Crescent Bay. What happened to you? How did you survive?'

'I was rescued by the ocean sprites after I fell into the water. They took me far beneath the sea to the mer city of South Deep. I was healed and then returned to the world above.'

'Well, you made it just in time,' said Red cheerfully. 'I thought the Prince of Shadows had won the battle. I was just about to give up and then I saw you riding over the hill.' Red chuckled and shook his head with a wide smile. 'You made quite an entry. Your arrival shocked the socks off the Prince of Shadows.'

'Unfortunately he escaped,' said Cassiel. 'But it is clear he is afraid of you, Eben. It seems that the tide of the war is turning. The Prince of Shadows expected to win at Jeriel's Field. This defeat will have significantly damaged his plans. He may have lost his advantage.'

'But he captured Princess Apherah. He may attempt to use her as a hostage against me,' added Eben grimly.

'Don't worry, Eben. We will find a way to rescue her,' said Stella.

'That's right,' said Red with a confident nod. 'Remember we are in the business of rescuing royalty from difficult situations. If anyone is going to stage a rescue we are probably the most qualified. We managed to free King Ignis from the Dungeons of Zyran. Rescuing Princess Apherah shouldn't be too difficult, especially for us.'

Eben smiled at Red's brash confidence. 'Tomorrow there will be a council to discuss the way forward. Rescuing Princess Apherah will be my first priority. Then we will have to deal with the Prince of Shadows and his armies. I think there will be a lot of fighting ahead of us.'

'I'm ready for anything,' said Red.

**

Eben sat at the round table in the Ecorian Hall. Seated at the table were the leaders of the tribes and nations that made up the last army of men. They included: Prince Armida of Ateria, Chief Parco of the Jeanians, Chief Soral of the Empyrians, Duke Egil of Scaldonia, Garnock of the Fire Order, King Ignis, Meara, Baftel, Red, Stella, Cassiel, Arlen, Mostyn, Aperio of the Zyranian Outcasts, and the Fiorians Winfred and Clare.

'We are gathered today to discuss how we will defeat the Prince of Shadows,' said Eben. 'You all know that the muckron army at Jeriel's Field was only one of the enemy's armies. In Dravania a great army of muckrons is laying siege to the Iril

Fortress. There is also a smaller army of muckrons in northern Scaldonia. Baftel, please share what you have witnessed with your power.'

Baftel nodded toward Eben before speaking. 'The enemy is deliberately allowing me to see what we face. The Prince of Shadows has returned north to Zarkanor with his dragon. He has imprisoned Princess Apherah in one of the towers of Zarkanor. She is being guarded by the dragon. Zarkanor is surrounded by an army far greater than the one we fought at Jeriel's Field. Hundreds of thousands of muckrons guard the ancient fortress, and each day the Prince of Shadows brings more muckrons and wyverns through the Cosmic Gate. He is filling our world with monsters. His evil hissing voice moans across the subtle world. He has threatened to execute Princess Apherah if we don't come north to fight him'

'But with such a large army protecting him how could we ever successfully attack Zarkanor?' asked King Ignis.

'The Prince of Shadows knows we can't defeat him. He hopes for us to make this desperate move in order to crush us,' said Mostyn. 'His army grows with each passing day. The longer we wait the more difficult the task will become.'

'We must devise a plan,' said Eben.

'Invading Kaznor would be very difficult,' said King Ignis. 'We would need hundreds of ships to sail around the Icy Cape. There is no other way to Kaznor. There are few ships remaining in Ortaria; perhaps we could ask the Silvorians for assistance.'

'The Zyranians control most of Silvor,' said Prince Armida. 'The Aterian navy has been battered by the Zyranians for months. We only have about a dozen warships left,' said Prince Armida.

'We could build ships in Ancora,' said King Ignis.

'It would take much too long,' said Prince Armida. 'How much time do we have?'

'Not long, perhaps several weeks,' said Mostyn sternly.

'We should consider other options,' said Meara. 'There may be alternative ways we can defeat our enemies. The Prince of Shadows controls the Cosmic Gate. That is how he is bringing the monsters to Veredor. If we could somehow take control of the Cosmic Gate we could stop him bringing more monsters from the outer darkness.'

'What is the Cosmic Gate?' asked Chief Parco, looking to Meara for an explanation.

'The Cosmic Gate is a mystical barrier which was built by the Astarians to protect Veredor in the wars of the Forgotten Age. It has protected Veredor for many ages,' said Meara. 'The Cosmic Gate is said to be made from the essence of Veredor. The Astarian Fiora sealed the Cosmic Gate against the Prince of Shadows at the end of the Forgotten Age. The gate has kept him out of Veredor for thousands of years.'

'How can we take control of the Cosmic Gate?' asked King Ignis.

'I don't know,' replied Meara. 'Yet the Astarians once believed there was a way.'

The company fell silent, and for several moments no one said a word.

Eben broke the silence. 'When I fell into the sea I was taken by the ocean sprites to the southern home of the mer,' he revealed. 'Living with the mer is an Astarian named Casimir. He is one of the last three remaining Astarians in Veredor. He told me that it is possible for men to take control of the Cosmic Gate. Only those who belong to Veredor can control the Cosmic Gate; that is why the Astarians can control it. When men first came to Veredor we were not received by Veredor as the Astarians had hoped we would be. There is something in the nature of men that prevented us from crossing this barrier. The quest to overcome the problem was called Fiora's Bridge because the Astarian Fiora held to the hope that men would one day be welcomed by Veredor. That day has not yet come. For us to control the Cosmic Gate we must find a way to forge the relationship with Veredor that was never forged.'

'Did Casimir tell you how to forge such a relationship?' asked Meara.

Eben shook his head. 'He didn't say. He only said that we revere power and seek it all of our lives.'

'Wait a minute,' interrupted Duke Egil, shaking his head. 'If we came to Veredor in the Forgotten Age then where did we come from?'

'Men come from a world far across the cosmos,' said Meara. 'The Astarians, who were the first people of Veredor, welcomed us toward the end of the Forgotten Age. The Prince of Shadows hopes to annihilate us and replace us with creatures that will be his slaves.' Duke Egil shook his head in disbelief. The company were looking to Eben for an answer.

'I do not know how to take control of the Cosmic Gate, but I know that I'm going to save Princess Apherah. I plan to leave soon with whoever is brave enough to go with me.'

'I doubt you would make it to the Fortress of Zarkanor even with your mighty unicorn and the Sword of Light,' said Baftel. 'The walls of Zarkanor are surrounded by hundreds of thousands of muckrons, hundreds of wyverns, and a multitude of lindworms. There are also many Northern Sorcerers and Skatheans among the enemy army. The dragon is waiting for you in the tower where the Princess is imprisoned. The Prince of Shadows is using Princess Apherah as bait. He knows you care deeply for her, and he wants you to try to rescue her. It would be impossible to attack the fortress alone.'

'Baftel is right,' said Meara. 'You cannot attack the fortress directly without an army, and we cannot possibly bring an army to Kaznor without ships.'

'What about sneaking into the fortress,' suggested Red.

'Much too risky,' replied Baftel, shaking his head.

'There is one person who could help you sneak into the fortress,' said Garnock of the Fire Order. They looked to Garnock. 'High in the Great Mountains there is a secluded cave. In the cave lives a mysterious individual. His name is the Star King. He is a relic from the Forgotten Age. It has long been said that he can open gateways to any place in Veredor. With his help you may be able to open a gateway directly into Zarkanor. You could secretly enter Zarkanor without the Prince of Shadows knowing.'

'The Star King is an evil monster and cannot be trusted,' stated Mostyn firmly.

'True, the Star King is not known for his hospitality or generosity' said Garnock. 'But desperate times require desperate measures. You know the place that I speak of, Mostyn; it is a dangerous place to visit, but even so, the Star King has the skill you require to enter Zarkanor and save your princess.'

'What if he tries to kill us when we request his help?' asked Meara sternly.

'He may just do that,' said Mostyn. 'That's another reason this is not a good idea. The Star King is not a man, neither is he an Astarian. He is of some other race not related to anything else in Veredor. He has been a menace to men throughout the ages; a one handed creature in the shape of a man, but he is nothing like a man in his heart or mind. I do not think he will help us. He hates all creatures that live in Veredor.'

Eben stared at Mostyn for a moment. 'You said he only has one hand?'

'Yes. There is an old song which tells that the Star King stole the Chalai from the Oran Oracle. The Oran Oracle set a trap for him and cut off his hand.'

'Do you know the words of the song?' asked Eben.

Mostyn nodded and began to recite.

In the west far from home, high he walked through ice and snow. The Star King searched for a way, across valley deep through night and day. In a place where few have stood, he reached for life as he thought he could, but fall he did into the night, without the hand he sacrificed. For the oracle knew of all his plans, and traded the Chalai for his right hand. For his home he sought above the winds, far away from anything.

Eben nodded and pondered the words of the old song. He knew that the Star King was the one who Casimir had referred to as "the person with one hand."

'We must seek out the Star King. If he could open a gateway into Zarkanor we could rescue Princess Apherah and face the Prince of Shadows without having to fight his army. I believe I can defeat the Prince of Shadows. I also believe the Star King will help us.'

Mostyn shook his head. 'You cannot be so sure, Ecorian. Many people have been victims of the Star King throughout the ages. He is unpredictable and very powerful.'

'Mostyn, you must trust me. I know this is the way onward.'

'I believe Eben is right,' said Baftel. 'The path to the Star King may yield fruit, but know this, Eben: those who choose to follow you on this path may never return. The journey will be very dangerous. I see a glimmer of hope, like a faint star in a world of darkness. You must also be aware: do not underestimate the power of the dragon that serves the Prince of Shadows. It is a beast of utter darkness. This dragon possesses power far beyond any other creature in Veredor. From a forgotten pit at the edge of the cosmos it came, risen from the darkness, a beast evil beyond measure. It was for this reason the unicorn was sent to Veredor, to contest the evil shadow of the dragon.'

'You know I will go with you, Eben,' said Red. Eben smiled across at Red. He knew well that his best friend's sense of loyalty and courage was unending.

'And I shall go with you too,' said Stella.

'I'll be glad to have you both with me. You were there in the beginning; I'm sure you will be there in the end.'

'Eben, you must assemble a company,' said Meara. 'I would also like to go with you, but I believe you should carefully choose your companions. The fate of mankind may depend on your success.'

'Surely I will go,' said King Ignis.

'And I would like to go,' said Cassiel.

CHAPTER NINE

Meara stood with Arlen on a high balcony which overlooked the city. Arlen's eyes scanned the town below. A sense of hope had returned to Faircastle. The people believed there was a chance they could succeed in the struggle against the Prince of Shadows. All the people had placed their hope in the Ecorian.

'The news from the Far Western Lands is not good,' said Arlen. 'The Muckrons have conquered Dravania City and only the Iril Fortress is holding. The Tabarians have brought their army back into the northern wilderness of Dravania, but the Irilians are cut off. Many wizards of our order have died fighting, and few of our most powerful wizards remain in the Iril Fortress. I believe I can help the Tabarians break the siege of the Iril Fortress and save our home from destruction.'

Meara looked across at Arlen and could see the deep concern in his eyes. 'Are you asking for my permission to go to Dravania?'

'The Fiorians are going to cross the Great Mountains through the ancient pass. They have invited me to join them on the journey. I may be able to help prevent our home being completely destroyed, but I will only return to Dravania with your permission.'

Meara looked out across the city and gave the request some thought. She knew Arlen was one of the most powerful Irilians. 'Eben will choose a small company to go with him on his quest to Zarkanor. It is probably best that only one wizard of the Irilian Order join him on this mission, and I believe that I should represent us.'

'Then you will allow me to return to the Iril Fortress?'

'Yes, Arlen; you will be needed there.'

A few moments of silence passed. Arlen looked across at Meara with concerned eyes. 'Meara, do you think the Star King will listen to Eben?' he asked in a low voice.

'I do not know, Arlen. The Star King is obsessed with a deep desire to return to his home world, yet he does have the skill we need to infiltrate Zarkanor. It has long been said that he does not care about the people of Veredor. I hope we are not being foolish, but I know we have very few choices; there still may be a chance.' Meara looked to the west as the last beams of light crossed the dark blue sky. The sun fell below the horizon and darkness descended on the land.

**

Eben, in consultation with the council, assembled a brave group to accompany him on the mission to seek out the Star King, rescue Princess Apherah, infiltrate the Fortress of Zarkanor, and face the Prince of Shadows. Those chosen for the mission were: King Ignis, Meara, Red, Stella, Cassiel, Mostyn, the Desert Knights Arthur and Dillon, Duke Egil, and Quade. It was agreed that Prince Armida would stay behind and take control of the united army of men. Baftel declared that he was too old and frail to make the journey into the Great Mountains. It was decided that Mostyn would go in Baftel's place and act as the guide and seer of the company as he also knew the way to the secluded cave.

Eben sat in the royal guest chamber that was situated just below the Ecorian Hall. The chambers were beautifully adorned with woven carpets, enchanting paintings, and crystal chandeliers hanging from the ceiling. Red and Stella were sitting at a small oak table, and Red had poured cups of ale for the three of them. Eben stood at the window and looked toward the north. The setting sun was casting long red beams across the sky through slight gaps in the clouds. His mind was concerned only for Apherah.

'Come and have a mug of ale, Eben,' said Red. 'It may be your last one for a long time'

Eben glanced back at Red. He knew that he could not enjoy such things as ale whilst Apherah was imprisoned in Zarkanor. Meara entered the room before he could refuse the ale.

'We have prepared supplies and horses for the journey, and we are ready to leave in the morning.' Meara took a seat at the table. She looked to Eben. 'The people of the city have been asking why you are refusing to take the Sapphire Throne. They want to know why you have not raised the Ecorian flag above Faircastle. The Ecorian flag is flying all over the city, yet it does not fly over the palace.'

'It is right that the Irvarian flag remains above the palace.'

'The nations and tribes of men have united under your leadership, Eben. It is also right that you raise the Ecorian flag.'

Eben looked out the window as the last rays of sun shone over the land. 'Only Princess Apherah can raise the Ecorian flag above Faircastle. I will not take the Sapphire Throne until that day.' He looked back to Meara. 'You know I am not a ruler, Meara. At heart I am a villager; all I want is a simple life. I would be happy to return to Clemensdale when this is over and live in the hut I grew up in.'

'It is right that power is given to those who do not desire power,' said Meara. Before Eben could speak there was a knock at the door and Cassiel entered the chamber.

'Acartor has been captured. The Brigades of the Sunset Hills have brought him here in chains.'

'We should question the traitor,' said Meara. Eben nodded.

**

The lower hall of the palace was lit by soft lantern light. Eben stood waiting with Meara, King Ignis, Red, Stella, Cassiel, Baftel, Duke Egil, Prince Armida, and several dozen Irvarian guardsmen. The Ecorian Gate opened and two soldiers led Acartor across the blue and white marble floor. Acartor was covered in mud, appeared battered and shaggy, and his hair was a mess. His hands were shackled behind his back, and he stared down at the ground as they led him toward Eben.

'This is all wrong!' hissed Acartor as he scanned the faces before him and stared intently at Eben. 'Ecorian...so it is true what they say. You live!' Acartor's eyes shot from side to side, and he strained against his bonds.

The soldier to the right was a tall and fully armoured Irvarian cavalryman. His hair was bright red, and his face was as rough as jagged rock. The soldier bowed to Eben.

'Sire, my name is Aron of the Sunset Hills. We captured this traitor as he was trying to cross into Vastoria. We were going to execute him for his crimes against Irvaria, but we thought it would be better to take him to Faircastle to be judged by you.'

'You don't know what you are doing. The Prince of Shadows promised me...' howled Acartor as he madly threw his head back.

'Promised you what?' asked Meara.

Acartor looked at Meara and scowled. 'The Prince of Shadows showed me a vision of all the power I would possess. He promised that I would rule over all men. He promised that I would govern the kingdoms of Veredor. He promised me power over all.'

'At what price?' asked Meara sternly.

Acartor looked away and waited several moments before answering. 'That I kneel down before him,' he moaned, a guttural sound exiting his mouth.

'And you made yourself into his slave?' asked Meara firmly.

Acartor howled and fell to his knees. 'What good is my answer, Meara! You know what I have done. I have spilled innocent blood, I have betrayed the trust of many, and I tried to lead our race into slavery. What was my reward? Power...no, he lied to me, Meara. It was all a lie! After the battle at Crescent Bay I was sent by the Astarian Callidus to convince the Irvarians to surrender and become slaves of the Prince of Shadows. I failed. When I returned Callidus made me give an account of what I had achieved. He was sorely disappointed in me. He handed me over to the Skatheans and muckrons. He had me brutally tortured. Callidus laughed as he watched me be tormented. My wages were nothing: an illusion, torture, pain, and death! Arhhhhh! I know you are going to kill me, Ecorian. You saw me murder Chiara. You were there and witnessed what I did. I know what I deserve!'

Meara looked to Eben. Acartor hit his head on the floor like a madman. He howled deeply and frothed at the mouth. Eben drew the Sword of Light and walked forward. He felt anger well up within. So many deaths had been caused by the deeds of the traitor. Acartor howled deeply, knowing his fate; he writhed on the floor and wept bitterly. Eben stood over him and looked down at the condemned man. Acartor's bloodshot eyes looked up and were full of anxiety, horror, and desperation.

Eben saw, in that moment, the deep loneliness and desolation that Acartor was living in and the prison and the bonds that the traitor had taken on. He looked down and saw nothing but a wretched slave. Everyone watched on intently as Eben reached down and grabbed Acartor by his shirt and lifted him to his feet.

'There is one last choice you can make, Acartor,' whispered Eben into the traitor's ear.

Acartor stared at Eben with wide eyes and in shock. 'You know I deserve to die, Ecorian,' whispered Acartor desperately. He looked away as he was not able to look into Eben's eyes.

'You gave yourself as a slave to the Prince of Shadows,' whispered Eben. 'And here you come as a slave before us. You made a terrible choice. Would you free yourself from slavery if you had one last choice?'

'But why would you offer me that?'

'I know you are a murderer and traitor, Acartor. The consequences of your actions can never be undone, yet there is something the Prince of Shadows cannot conquer in men. You can still choose to shake off the shackles he has enslaved you with.'

Acartor bowed his head and cried bitterly. 'Don't give me that choice, Eben. A shadow abides in my heart that I cannot live without. If I take such a path I will surely die.'

'Then you will die free and not as a slave to the darkness.'

Acartor stared at the ground for several moments. He then raised his sunken eyes. A single tear rolled down his cheek. Eben then stepped away.

'Remove his shackles,' commanded Eben.

'What are you doing, Eben?' asked Meara, alarmed at the command. Everyone in the room looked on in disbelief.

'Trust me, Meara. This is the only way.'

The guardsman at first hesitated, but he then reluctantly released Acartor's shackles. The traitor stood up and looked at his freed wrists. He then fell to his knees again and clutched his head in his hands. The company watched as a dark shadow rose out of the back of Acartor's neck. The shadow drifted up into the air and in a few moments dissipated.

'Was that a ghoul?' asked Red, staring wide eyed into the air above.

'No, it was a shadow that belonged to Acartor,' replied Eben.

Acartor looked up sadly. 'I am sorry for the terrible things I have done.' Suddenly he clutched his chest, and his face showed his deep agony. 'Oh. I am so sorry,' he groaned as he lay back. His life was draining from his body. His skin withered and grew deathly pale.

Meara went to his side. 'Acartor, what's happening to you?' There was no reply. Acartor's body fell still and lifeless within moments.

'This was a curse of the Prince of Shadows,' said Baftel. 'He poisoned Acartor's heart to stop him from ever turning away from the darkness.'

Eben stared down at the dead man. The company looked down at the body of Acartor, and they all were astonished at what they had seen.

**

The following morning the company gathered in the lower hall of the palace in readiness to begin the journey. The warriors of the company were wearing the finest armour and carrying the best weapons available. Red wore a combination of plate armour and chainmail, whilst Stella wore a chainmail shirt and plates on her forearms and knees. Red had kept the sword he had been given at Eaglemere as it had served him well, but Stella had replaced her sword and taken a new shield. Eben was surprised that she had found a shield with the Ecorian unicorn painted across it. Eben had also taken some fine new armour. He wore a light chainmail shirt, a silver plate that covered his chest with a carved unicorn, leather gauntlets, and metal plates that protected his shins.

Duke Egil was wearing full Scaldonian armour which was rough and battle worn. He carried a mighty broadsword at his side. Quade was wearing new Irvarian armour and had a curved Vastorian sword. He also had a crossbow latched to his back. The Desert Knights Dillon and Arthur were clothed in the same dark attire of their order. King Ignis was outfitted in finely crafted Ortarian armour. He had a sword slung over his shoulder and a short sword and dagger at his belt. Mostyn wore his usual old brown cloak that looked like it had never been washed, and Meara was wearing a light blue dress and a new leather overcoat. Cassiel looked the same as always and was wearing his dark brown coat and chose not to wear any armour.

Their horses were waiting outside the hall. The unicorn shone brightly among the horses. Queen Sera, Prince Armida, and a multitude of other commanders, lords, and knights watched on as they walked out of the Ecorian Gate. Eben walked over to the unicorn and leapt up onto its back. The others mounted their horses.

'The hopes of us all go with you,' said Queen Sera.

'We will not fail you, my Queen,' said Eben. He nodded to Queen Sera and then turned the mighty unicorn around and led the company through the city. The people of Faircastle had come out of their houses and looked up with wonder at Eben riding the unicorn down the main street. The Ecorian flag was being waved alongside the Irvarian flag throughout the city. The people cheered joyously as the company passed by, and a feeling of excitement permeated the air.

Before long the company exited the front gate and turned to the west. Eben led the company with Mostyn and Red by his side. They maintained a quick pace for several hours and passed the area of land that had been destroyed by the muckrons. They entered into the beautiful back country of Irvaria where the sound of birds singing rang out over lush green hills. Toward midday they stopped at a small stream surrounded by old yew trees. They sat beside the clear flowing water and rested.

'I have used my power to hide us from the eyes of the Prince of Shadows,' said Mostyn. 'However,

I could not hide the fact that we left Faircastle as a company of eleven.'

'It doesn't matter that he knows,' said Meara. 'There is no way that he could know our plan to seek the help of the Star King.'

'That is true, but he knows we are up to something,' said Duke Egil. 'He may have the Skatheans send vultures to spy on us. They used vultures against us in Scaldonia to keep track of our movements.'

'They won't last long against me,' said Quade as he tapped his crossbow.

'I don't doubt it,' said Mostyn.

'We will be in the Great Mountains in a matter of days,' said Meara. 'I do not think the Skathean vultures would brave contesting the eagles of the Great Mountains. Even if the Prince of Shadows learns we are going west he would assume we were going to Emeril or to help the Irilians in Dravania.'

'The Prince of Shadows may not even know of the Star King,' said Mostyn. 'I am aware of many old stories and some of the legends from the Forgotten Age. The only reference to the Star King in the Forgotten Age is that he helped the Astarian Fiora escape into the north when the Prince of Shadows was pursuing her. The other stories about the Star King cover the period of two thousand years since, and for the most part they are not pleasant stories.'

'Two thousand years!' exclaimed Red. 'The Star King is old.'

'Many of the ancient races have exceedingly long lives. The Chalai he stole from the Oran Oracle also stopped him from aging,' said Mostyn.

'However, the Star King was never concerned with immortality. He was searching for a way to return to his home far across the cosmos. That is precisely why he is useful to us. He alone discovered how to open gateways to any place in Veredor.'

For the remainder of the day they travelled west across the pristine Irvarian countryside. As they progressed the road took them through old forests, across rolling green hills, and through abandoned villages. All the village folk had retreated to Faircastle at the news of the coming of the enemy army, and they had not yet returned to their homes. Occasionally the company would come across a lone shepherd who had refused to leave his sheep, but otherwise they were alone on the road.

That evening they built a fire beside a crystal clear stream. The company sat around the fire and the aroma of Mostyn's pipe filled the air.

'Ah, tobacco from Iarthar; nothing quite like it in all of Veredor,' said Mostyn as he scratched his black shaggy beard.

Red was busy cooking them a delicious smelling stew over the fire.

'Tomorrow we will enter the western forests of Irvaria,' said Meara. 'I expect the journey to the Great Mountains to take another two days. I hope you remember the way to the Star King's cave.'

'Indeed I do,' said Mostyn. 'The Fire Order has long kept a watch on the Star King. He was once our enemy in an age long gone. Long ago the Star King built a castle high in the Great Mountains. At the time he hoped to construct a machine to help him travel across the stars, and because the sprites are a crafty race he employed them to complete the task. Later, when it became apparent that they could not achieve his request, he grew angry and went to war with the mountain sprites. The Star King destroyed many of the remote mountain sprite sanctuaries.'

'Yes, I know the story,' said Meara. 'The mountain sprites suffered many losses in the war.'

'If it wasn't for the Fire Order there would be no mountain sprites left. We saw what the Star King was doing, and we set out to stop him. Since those days the mountain sprites have been our friends; although they typically avoid the world of men. In recent times their numbers have greatly diminished. There are none remaining in the Old Guardian Mountains, and few sprites remain in the Great Mountains.'

They slept well beside the stream and the soft sound of flowing water soothed their minds. A little after sunrise the company set out again and made a blistering pace into the west. By midmorning they had entered the western forests. The tall trees of the forest provided a thick canopy that kept much of the light from the forest floor. All about them were moss covered stones and ferns. Toward the end of the day Meara took them from the main road along a track the wound on through the forest.

As the sun set they made a camp on top of a grassy hill where few trees grew. The base of the hill was surrounded by forest. Red and Stella set about building a small campfire and the company rested again after a hard day of riding. Later in the evening Eben lay back on the grass and looked up at the stars high above. His thoughts had been focused on Apherah since the company left Faircastle.

'I sense the presence of something dangerous,' said Mostyn, breaking the calm silence of the later evening. Eben instantly sat up.

'What is it?' Eben looked to the edges of the campsite.

Meara stood up and looked to the east. 'Yes, I feel it,' she said. 'Quick, prepare yourselves.'

Mostyn closed his eyes and concentrated. 'If I had the skills of Baftel I would be able to clearly see.' Eben mounted the unicorn.

'Horses,' said Quade. 'Can you hear them galloping in the distance?'

'Yes,' said King Ignis as he drew his sword. Duke Egil also drew his broadsword, and the Desert Knights stood up.

'They are not horses,' said Mostyn.

As he spoke they could see dark shapes and flickering flames approaching through the trees below the hill and lighting up the forest with a red and orange glow. Quade loaded his crossbow as Red and Stella drew their swords.

'Stone Horsemen!' cried Mostyn.

Then they were in sight. Six mighty horses, which appeared to be made completely of a dark stone, appeared at the base of the hill. Atop each horse rode a stone rider. They carried mighty flaming battle axes that lit up the surrounding forest. Flames burst from the eyes of the riders. A howling moan bellowed up the hillside as the Stone Horsemen charged at the company. The riders lifted their flaming axes. Quade fired his crossbow as Meara and Cassiel stepped forward.

'Be gone!' cried Meara as she raised her hands. Swirling columns of blue flame burst through the night at the fast approaching riders. Five of the Stone Horsemen managed to dodge the flames, but one fell; the stone horse and rider instantly disintegrated into ashes and sparks.

Eben charged forward at the five remaining Stone Horsemen. He drew the Sword of Light and in moments was among them. He cut out at one of the riders. The stone rider exploded into ash and fire. Eben then turned on another. Orange flames burst from the mouth of the stone horse, but the unicorn's speed was unmatched. The mighty steed avoided the flames and brought Eben up beside another rider. Again he hewed down. The horseman raised its battle axe and parried. Sparks blasted out from the clash of steel. The stone rider then struck back. Eben whirled around, deflected the incoming axe, and thrust the Sword of Light forward. Instantly the rider burst into flames and ash; the stone horse and rider disintegrated. The three remaining Stone Horsemen then entered the campsite.

Fire blasted from the snarling mouths of the horses. Stella raised her shield and was knocked over by a heavy impact. Meanwhile King Ignis charged directly forward and boldly swung his sword up at a Stone Horseman. The rider exploded, and the King was thrown back several yards by the shockwave of fire and sparks. The two remaining Stone Horsemen then turned and charged from the campsite. Eben gave chase through the woods.

The pace was incredible. The trees flickered by as a trail of sparks was left by the stone horses.

The horsemen split apart and turned in different directions. The unicorn chased after one, lighting up the forest with pure white light. The stone rider howled in fear, the sound was more like the roar of a bear than any sound a man could make. Eben hewed down and the stone creature disintegrated into ash, flame, and a trail of sparks. He then halted the unicorn and looked through the darkened woods for the other Stone Horseman, but the rider was gone from sight.

The whole company was still on guard and watching for the remaining Stone Horseman to return, but the evil creature had fled in fear of Eben and the unicorn.

'I destroyed one of them, but the other escaped,' said Eben as he returned to the camp.

'The Prince of Shadows sent these Stone Horsemen,' said Mostyn. 'I think he has underestimated us.'

'I doubt it. He knows our capabilities,' said Meara sternly. 'It is more likely that this was a warning. He wants us to know that we are not beyond his reach. Most of all he wants us to be afraid.'

'We are not afraid of his monsters,' said King Ignis.

'Stone Horsemen served the Prince of Shadows in the Forgotten Age,' said Mostyn. 'They have not been seen in Veredor for thousands of years.'

'Muckrons, draugs, wyverns, and Stone Horsemen; none of them scare me,' said Duke Egil. 'We have proven we can defeat all of these creatures of darkness, but the dragon that guards the tower where Princess Apherah is being held. I don't know how we will match such a creature.'

'Yes, the dragon may prove to be our greatest challenge,' said Meara soberly. 'Perhaps the dragon is even more powerful than the Prince of Shadows himself. Dragons are very rare; they are creatures that have endured in the cosmos since the dawn of time. Most of them are good natured, but the one that serves the Prince of Shadows is a beast with power far beyond any other creature in Veredor. It has a heart darker than the darkest night. We must destroy it.'

CHAPTER TEN

The Great Mountains were known to be the most imposing mountain range in all the lands of Veredor. They had always been a natural barrier that made the passage to the Far Western Lands incredibly difficult. Crossing the Great Mountains was considered by all to be a perilous and terrifying proposition. Many people had perished attempting to traverse the icy peaks, and it had long been said the mountains were the home of numerous rare creatures and strange monsters that had been mostly forgotten through the passage of time.

As the sun rose the company rode on through the forest. The land about became progressively hillier. They rode on and kept a great pace, and gradually the forest began to thin. They could see the mountains in the west. The Great Mountains were the tallest range that Eben had ever seen. Their snow-capped jagged peaks rose high into the clouds above.

'The Great Mountains; they are home to many dangerous and mysterious creatures,' said Meara, her bright eyes staring with wonder at the mountains above.

Mostyn led them onward through the last part of the forest. They then entered the rocky foothills of the Great Mountains. Before long the track completely disappeared; although Mostyn seemed to know where he was going. They came upon what looked to be an old worn track that wound its way onward across the rocky hills toward the towering mountains.

'Yes, here it is: the Path of Saidrin,' said Mostyn. He raised his eyes and looked at the mountains above. 'Many brave people have died trying to take this way across the mountains. In winter it is impassable; even in summer the way is treacherous. Few who attempt this pass ever make it across the mountains. Luckily we are not trying to cross the mountains. Our path will lead us south on a lesser known mountain track that crosses the Path of Saidrin. The way we will take has no name as it is only known to the mountain sprites, the Fire Order, and the Star King. The path will lead us onward to the cave.'

They persevered, but the going was slow as the path took them ever upward, traversing high ridges and deep valleys. Often they found themselves walking close to the edge of cliffs that descended into deep and dark valleys below. The warhorses, trained to endure hardship, managed the path without complaint. The unicorn had no trouble at all with the difficult terrain. Before long the old path had taken them high into the mountains. An icy breeze blew down from the snow-capped peaks above. Eben led the way onward, with Mostyn and Red following close behind.

'This wind is piercing,' said Red as he drew his cloak tightly around himself.

'Ah, yes, the Great Mountains are the tallest and the coldest mountain range in all of Veredor. Their peaks are covered in ice even at the height of summer,' said Mostyn.

'Surely it can't get much colder than this?' asked Red, shaking his head in protest.

'We still have a long way to go, and the wind will become much colder,' said Mostyn flatly.

Suddenly they rounded a corner. Before them the track came to the edge of a cliff and only a small portion of an old stone bridge remained. Beyond them was a deep crevasse that descended a thousand yards into a craggy valley below. It was clearly evident that a bridge had once joined the opposing ridge which was about fifty yards across.

Mostyn rode forward to the edge and stared out across the deep chasm. His concerned eyes looked back at the company. 'This indeed is very unfortunate.'

'Is there another way around?' asked King Ignis.

'No,' replied Mostyn. 'We would have to scale the ridges and cliff faces if we took any other way.'

'There must be another way,' said Meara. Mostyn shook his head.

'Can you make a bridge with your magic?' asked Mostyn, looking to Meara.

Meara stared across the crevasse. 'No, it is too far and beyond my ability.'

'Perhaps we should return to Faircastle,' said Mostyn.

'We cannot return. We must find the Star King,' said Eben.

'I am afraid there is no way onward, Ecorian,' said Mostyn.

Stella rode forward with a coiled rope and grappling hook in her hand. 'There is a way. We will have to leave the horses behind.'

'But can you secure the hook from such a distance?' asked Dillon.

'I can try,' said Stella. 'If we use two ropes we can make a basic rope bridge; one rope to walk on and another to hold. I can do it, but it would be far easier if there was someone on the other side.'

The unicorn suddenly burst forward. Eben held on as his steed launched itself across the wide chasm. For several moments the unicorn glided through the air and then landed with ease on the opposing ridge. Eben stared back at the company who were standing fifty yards back across the crevasse.

'Eben, I'm going to throw you the first rope!'

Eben leapt down from the unicorn and walked to the edge of the cliff. 'When you are ready!' he shouted.

Stella swung the coiled rope in large circles and then sent it flying across the chasm with perfect precision. Eben caught the rope and drew it back to secure it around a jagged rock. Meanwhile Stella prepared her second rope. She cast the second rope across the deep abyss. Eben repeated the process and within minutes they had secured both ropes tightly about five feet apart.

The company unpacked their supplies from the horses and secured their packs to their backs. Stella was the first to attempt the rope bridge. She edged out with ease and within a minute she had crossed and stood with Eben on the far side. Red followed closely behind and the others started to edge out on the rope. Within a few minutes Red, King Ignis, Meara, Cassiel and Mostyn had crossed. Dillon, Arthur, Quade, and Duke Egil were still out on the rope. A scream howled out across the sky; the entire company looked up. Three dark shapes descended from the clouds above. Eben drew the Sword of Light.

'Wyverns!' cried Meara.

Quade edged as quickly as possible along the rope, and the others still out on the bridge realised how vulnerable they were to an attack. The wyverns descended at a frightening pace toward the rope bridge. Meara stepped forward and raised her glowing hands. Swirls of bright light blasted toward the three monsters. A wing of one of the wyverns was torn from its body; it spiralled out of control and smashed into the mountainside.

Molten plasma shot out from Mostyn's hands and incinerated the wings of the second wyvern, sending it howling into the chasm below. The third wyvern nosedived and in moments whipped its tail and cut through both ropes. Quade leapt for the edge and managed to grab a hold of the cliff, but Arthur, Dillon, and the Duke Egil fell, all of them clutching to the severed rope. They swung down in an arch and crashed heavily into the mountainside. Dillon lost his grip and fell away from the cliff face. The remaining wyvern instantly swooped after him.

Eben watched, completely powerless, as Dillon descended quickly into the valley below. The red scales of the wyvern glimmered in the daylight as it dived after the Desert Knight. Dillon drew his curved Vastorian sword as he fell. In moments the beast was upon him. It snapped out with its large fangs and bit into Dillon's chest. Dillon, with the last of his strength, swung his blade and cut through the wyvern's right wing. Bright red blood sprayed from the wound. A moment later the wyvern spiralled out of control as it descended rapidly into the deep. Dillon and the wyvern crashed heavily into the rocky valley below.

'Quick, pull the rope!' cried Stella. The entire company heaved the rope and dragged both Arthur and Duke Egil to the top. Both of them were bruised and battered from the impact with the cliff face.

Arthur stood up and went to the edge. He looked into the deep. 'Dillon is gone,' he said in a low voice.

The company went to join Arthur at the edge. They felt the shock at losing one of their own so suddenly. 'He was brave until the end as a true Desert Knight should be.'

The company watched on in silence. Arthur then removed his mask and revealed his face for the first time. He was an older man with strong dark eyes and black hair. His complexion was weathered and like leather, and he had a short dark beard.

The company watched on in silence for some time and paid their respects to their fallen companion.

**

The path took them continuously upward into the Great Mountains. Without horses the going was much slower. The company had remained mostly silent since Dillon's death. Arthur had not said a word. There was a feeling that the Prince of Shadows was one step ahead of them and that he may already know their plan.

'The Prince of Shadows sent the three wyverns to follow us and watch us from afar,' said Mostyn. 'They took advantage of us at our most vulnerable moment.'

'Do you think there are others?' asked Eben, looking to the sky.

'No, but the enemy has many monsters in his service. We must be vigilant. Soon we will take the path to the Star King. In two days we will arrive at his cave, and then we will see if our efforts have been worthwhile.'

That evening they huddled on a high ledge of a mighty mountain. Nothing grew so high in the mountains. Mostyn created a fire with his magic that kept the entire campsite warm. Eben sat beside the fire with Red and Stella. Mostyn smoked his pipe; he was sitting on a rocky outcrop and looking out across the vista of majestic mountains.

'We have come a long way from Ancora,' said King Ignis as he warmed his hands by the fire.

'It won't be long before we are back there and celebrating our victory,' said Red confidently.

'I hope you are right, Red,' replied the King. 'I miss my home and my people.'

'We must succeed,' said Duke Egil. 'There is simply no other way. The fate of mankind relies on us defeating the Prince of Shadows once and for all.' Duke Egil looked across the fire at Eben. 'We saw you challenge the Prince of Shadows at Jeriel's Field. He was afraid of you and the unicorn. He must know that you can defeat him. If the Star King can deliver us to him we can put an end to all this.'

Eben nodded and looked into the flickering flames of the fire. He remembered back to his childhood when he would explore the forests surrounding Clemensdale. He remembered Erako and the humble kind-hearted folk of his village. The world was so much smaller in those days. He lifted his eyes and looked to the glimmering stars in the night sky and wondered how much larger the cosmos was than he knew. He then thought of Apherah and hoped she could also see the stars.

'There is also the other Astarian. He carries the Sword of Midlight. We must not underestimate his power,' said Meara.

'Callidus,' said Eben. 'He is a slave of the Prince of Shadows. I fought him on the headland at Crescent Bay.'

'And you were beaten by Callidus?' asked Arthur.

'Yes,' answered Eben solemnly; the images of the battle at Crescent Bay flashed through his mind, and the pain of seeing Chiara murdered surged in his heart. 'I was overwhelmed by his skill and power.'

'Can you defeat the Prince of Shadows when we assail Zarkanor?' asked Duke Egil, his voice never lost its rough edge.

Eben glanced across at Red, Stella, and Cassiel. He then looked back to Arthur and Duke Egil. 'I am fighting for something the Prince of Shadows does not understand, something that does not exist in his heart. This time I will not fail.'

'You believe?' asked Meara. Eben nodded across the flames at Meara.

'If you don't cross the bridge then you never know what is on the other side,' he said, repeating the words that Meara had said to him long ago.

**

The fire burned brightly through the entire night. Shortly after sunrise they set out and trekked further into the mountains. Mostyn led them onward as the track grew progressively more perilous. By midmorning the path led them through a crevice and up a rocky slope to an icy ridge. At the height of the ridge they came upon a second track that led away toward the south along a thin ledge. The track was barely visible to the eye, and the company would have missed it entirely if Mostyn wasn't there to point it out.

'This is the path to the cave,' said Mostyn as he turned toward the south.

Eben followed after Mostyn on foot. The unicorn led the way onward, and the company walked in single file as Mostyn guided them ever upward. The track took them south along a thin ledge and then over a jagged mountain top. They then continued on through snow and ice. The cold was biting, but no one complained. Dillon's death had brought a sense of stoicism to the group.

They all knew they had been chosen and that their task was immensely important for the survival of men.

They persevered deeper into the icy mountains. The cold wind blew down on them from the peaks above. Eben drew his leather cloak tightly around himself. He looked back and saw Red's eyebrows were covered in frost and his red beard had grown icicles. The company trudged onward, and it was clear that they were all struggling with the exception of the unicorn. The mountain track was often covered entirely in ice. After several hours of continuing upward they came upon a chasm; the path led onward through the base of the icy chasm. Great frozen chunks of ice had fallen from the mountainsides above and blocked the way onward.

Mostyn raised his hands and columns of flame shot out. The ice steamed and hissed as it melted away. Several minutes later the path was cleared. Without a word Mostyn led them onward. As the day progressed the wind picked up and blew heavily across the mountain path. Snow blasted into their faces and the cold was bordering on unbearable. Mostyn looked back at the company; his dark tangled hair was covered in snow.

'We will not survive long in this!' he cried above the howling wind. 'There is a cave just up ahead where we can shelter until this blizzard has passed.'

Mostyn led them on a little further and they entered the cave that was about twenty feet deep with a wide entrance. It provided enough protection from the wind and snow. Mostyn instantly made a fire and shielded the entrance with an invisible barrier that kept the cold out. Within a few minutes the fire had warmed up the entire cave.

'We must wait for the snowstorm to pass,' said Meara. The company removed their ice covered cloaks and laid them against the wall of the cave. They then huddled close to the fire.

'I have never felt so cold,' said Cassiel as he held his pale hands near the fire.

'Tomorrow we will arrive at the Star King's cave,' said Mostyn. 'We are about two hours from the entrance. He is not known for his hospitality, but we can hope for a warm welcome.'

The blizzard continued for the entire day and into the night. Mostyn's magical barrier and fire kept the cold at bay. The company slept that night in the warmth of the cave. By morning the icy weather had passed. As the sun rose across the mountains Eben stepped out of the cave. He looked out at the majestic vista of towering snow covered mountains that surrounded the thin ledge. Many questions flowed through his mind; chief among his question was how he could cross Fiora's Bridge. What was the secret? A few moments later Red walked over and stood beside him.

'Quite a view,' said Red as he stared out at the beams of light reflecting off the mountainsides.

'Beautiful,' said Eben. 'I hope the day will never come when men have to leave Veredor behind.' Eben lifted his eyes and looked to the cloudy sky above.

'That day will never come,' said Red confidently.

'You are always optimistic, Red.' Eben had realised that much of Red's character had been formed by the hardships he had faced early in life. 'The snow falls from the clouds onto the mountains. It then melts and flows into the rivers. Eventually the water reaches the sea. All life depends on the flow of the water and that flow starts up here in the mountains. Everything in Veredor is connected, but for some reason men were not accepted by Veredor. Understanding this riddle is the key to us defeating the Prince of Shadows.'

'I have no idea,' said Red, shaking his head.

A moment later Cassiel came and stood with them on the ledge. 'Have you ever seen such enormous mountains in all your life?' he asked as he stared out with wonder in his dark eyes. 'We must be close to the height of the range. It's like standing on the roof of Veredor.'

'It's cold up on the roof,' said Red.

'Enjoy the cold while it lasts. Soon we may be facing the heat of dragon fire,' said Cassiel.

A few moments later the rest of the company exited the cave. They were ready to move on. Mostyn led the way. They followed as the track continued along the ridge and then drove deeper into the mountains. The wind had ceased, and the bitter cold of the previous day had passed. The company made good progress throughout the morning. The mountain path led them around several massive peaks and then followed a high ridge covered with ice. The ridge led them to the side of the largest mountain they had seen since entering the Great Mountains.

'This is it!' exclaimed Mostyn.

They continued onward, and the trail led them around the side of the mountain. They came upon a large opening in the side of the mountain. Several mountain eagles circled high in the sky above the entrance. Mostyn led them up to the opening. It was about twenty feet wide and thirty feet high and looked to Eben like a natural cave.

'No wizard of the Fire Order has ever entered this cave before,' said Mostyn as he took from his pack a small oil lantern and proceeded to light it with a magic spark that danced on the tip of his finger. 'We must be cautious. The Star King may not welcome our arrival.'

King Ignis, Duke Egil, and Red also lit their lanterns. It was then agreed that Eben should lead the way forward. Eben mounted the unicorn and rode slowly into the dark cave. The shimmering glow of the unicorn gave off a subtle white light that illuminated the way. The company followed closely after Eben. The cave took them deep into the mountainside. Eben rode forward and the way gradually descended. For at least ten minutes they continued. The cave was becoming damp, and Eben could taste moisture in the air.

The way opened into a great underground cavern. The company stared out at a large lake that was directly in front of them. The ceiling of the cavern was made up entirely of glimmering crystals and reached hundreds of yards above the still surface of the lake. They stood at the edge of the water. It became instantly apparent that there was no way onward. The lake was about three hundred yards across, but they couldn't clearly make out the opposing bank due to the lack of light.

Meara raised her hands; a bright white light ascended and lit the entire cavern. The crystal ceiling shimmered magnificently as the light reflected back. Eben looked out across the water and saw there was no bank on the other side, nothing but a cavern wall. His eyes scanned the edges of the lake, but there was no way onward.

'Is this it? Is this the home of the Star King?' asked Meara, looking to Mostyn.

'No,' said Mostyn. 'He has built this lake to protect himself from the Fire Order. I can sense there is a way forward; however, the cave onward is completely submerged beneath the lake.'

'Is it possible to swim?' asked King Ignis.

'No, it's impossible. No one could swim so far.'

'What about your magic?' asked Duke Egil, looking to Mostyn.

'I am of the Fire Order, not water,' said Mostyn, shaking his head.

'What about your magic, Meara?' asked King Ignis.

'I can freeze water to create bridges of ice, and I can move water, but I cannot move an entire lake.'

'Then we cannot proceed. Maybe we can wait here for the Star King to come out,' said Duke Egil gruffly.

Eben leapt down from the unicorn and went to the edge of the water. He closed his eyes and reached down to touch the surface. He felt the icy water and several gentle ripples crossed the lake. He focused his mind, and a moment later the water started to part. The company watched in amazement as the water retreated and a tunnel formed.

'Eben, you're a wizard!' said Red. Eben didn't answer. He focused his mind and the tunnel extended forward across the bottom of the lake and into the submerged cave on the opposite side.

'He is of the mer,' said Meara. 'So it is true. The mer can manipulate water.'

Eben stood up and looked back at the company. 'We should move quickly. I'm not sure how long I can hold back the lake.'

Without delay the company entered the tunnel through the water. They moved quickly forward and were amazed by the suspension of the water around them. They crossed the bottom of the lake and entered the cave opposite. The cave descended for a little time and then took a turn to the right and ascended and widened gradually before ascending for some time. Directly ahead they could see a dim light. The cave led them into a small cavern.

CHAPTER ELEVEN

On the far side of the cavern was a giant man seated on a huge stone throne that was hewn out of the mountain itself. The man, if he could be called a man, was dressed in furs and was at least ten feet in height. His long grey beard descended to his knees and his white eyebrows were thicker than any Eben had ever seen. His large grey eyes stared at them as they entered the cavern. He examined the company with an expression that was similar to a child examining ants in a garden. When the unicorn entered the chamber his eyes shifted and revealed a flicker of interest, but his curiosity quickly faded away.

The company stared at the Star King for several moments before Eben stepped forward. 'My name is Eben Ecorian. I greet you with respect, Star King. I have come to seek your help. The Prince of Shadows has returned to Veredor. He has brought armies of monsters. Our race is threatened as are all who are good in Veredor.'

The Star King stared at Eben from behind his bushy eyebrows and remained silent. An entire minute passed and nothing was said.

'Will you hear our request?' asked Eben, thinking the ancient one wouldn't answer at all.

The Star King shook his head and looked down. In a deep grumbling voice he answered. 'What is it to me if men are destroyed? Men have only given me trouble since I arrived in Veredor thousands of years ago.'

'Don't you want men to survive? Do you want the good of our world to be destroyed?'

The Star King laughed. 'Ecorian, have you not seen the evil that men do? I would question your assumption that men are good. Men seek power, men build walls and barriers, men exploit the vulnerable, and men feed off the innocent creatures of Veredor. No, Ecorian, my opinion of men is that they are not good.'

Eben was shocked by the Star King's answer, but he quickly gathered himself and thought of a reply. 'But men can be good. Men can choose to do what is right.'

'That may be so, yet mostly they choose not to. There was a time when the Astarians hoped that men would make such choices, yet they did not then and they will not now.'

'You refer to Fiora's Bridge?'

The Star King laughed again. 'You know of what I speak, Ecorian. Yes, I refer to Fiora's Bridge. It was not crossed, and as far as I can see it cannot be crossed, at least not by any man from Veredor.'

'Why not?' asked Eben, hoping the Star King could shed some light on the matter.

'Because the Cosmic Gate is built from the essence of Veredor. For thousands of years I have also tried to pass through the Cosmic Gate, but I, like you, am not of Veredor. To control the Cosmic Gate you must be in relationship with this world because the Cosmic Gate is fused to the essence of Veredor. To be in a true relationship with anything requires something that men, by their nature, cannot give.'

'What must we give?'

'Such things are obvious to the innocent and hidden from the powerful,' grumbled the ancient one. He then slowly stood up and took his wooden staff that had been perched beside his throne. Eben could then see he only had one hand. The Star King then slowly walked toward the company. 'What a powerful group of men you have gathered together, Ecorian. I am sure they make you feel safe. Do you think they are powerful enough to challenge the Prince of Shadows? Do you think they can protect you from such deadly enemies?'

'We are powerful enough,' said Duke Egil boldly.

The imposing giant stared down at Duke Egil and laughed again. 'Perhaps you are; nevertheless, I am sure the Prince of Shadows will test your strength, and you may find you have less power than you think.'

The Star King then stepped toward Eben. He slowly moved his staff forward and gently tapped it on Eben's plate armour. 'Tell me, Ecorian. Is the purpose of this fine armour to keep your enemies out or to keep you in?'

'Of course my armour protects me from my enemies,' replied Eben, feeling the question must be a riddle.

'Do you wear your armour when you are at home with your friends and safe behind the walls of Faircastle?'

'No,' replied Eben, wondering what the Star King could mean.

'Why not? Why not wear armour to protect yourself from your friends? Do you trust your friends enough not to wear your armour around them?' asked the ancient one as if his question was quite valid.

'That makes no sense; why would I wear armour to protect myself from my friends?'

'I see,' said the Star King as he looked away. 'Walls, barriers, weapons, armour; it's all the same.' The Star King then walked back to his stone throne and sat down. 'I cannot help you, Ecorian. The time of men in Veredor has finished. It would be best for you and your brave companions to leave and return to your homes. Celebrate and enjoy your final days before the Prince of Shadows destroys your race.'

'There must be a way!' said Eben, a tone of desperation in his voice. 'Fiora's Bridge must be crossed. Surely there must be a way.'

The Star King looked up for a moment and pondered Eben's words. 'A way has already been found but not by a man from Veredor.

'Then why must Fiora's Bridge be crossed again?'

'Each man must walk the path. Each man must climb the mountain. If you want to stay in Veredor you must do what was never done.'

'But I don't understand how to do that!' said Eben.

'Then you simply cannot defeat the Prince of Shadows,' said the Star King impatiently. 'Now you must leave my home before I become angry. My patience has been tested long enough. You should be aware that I do not appreciate visitors.'

Mostyn stepped forward. 'We came here to ask of you a favour. Could you open a gateway for us into Zarkanor?'

The Star King groaned deeply. His large grey eyes widened and revealed his anger. 'A wizard of the Fire Order comes here to ask for my help. How times have changed! I have already helped you by not killing you for trespassing. If not for the Ecorian I would have already crushed your bones to dust. As a gift I will allow you to leave peacefully. Do not ask me for anything or I will make you wish you never entered this place.'

Mostyn was silenced and stepped back to join the company. For a few moments nothing was said.

'Perhaps there is something we can give you in exchange,' said Eben.

The Star King laughed deeply for quite some time. 'There is nothing I want from men. There is nothing men can give me, not even you, Ecorian.'

Eben reached into his armour and drew forth the Sun Stone that had been given to him by the mer. He held up the glowing crystal so all the company could see it.

'See this stone I hold. It is the Sun Stone of the Astarians. Would you open a gateway for us if I was to give this to you?'

The ancient one stood up and stared wide-eyed with wonder at the crystal. 'You would willingly trade the Sun Stone for this simple task?'

'If you would open a gateway for us to Zarkanor,' replied Eben.

'For ages I have dreamt of the Sun Stone. Long has it been far from my grasp in the depths of the ocean. Indeed, for this I will open a gateway into the Fortress of Zarkanor. Yes, for this I would give anything.'

**

The Star King came down from his throne. 'Follow me. I will take you to the Chamber of Gates. From there I will open a gateway to Zarkanor.' The giant walked to the right side of the chamber and touched the wall of rock with his wooden staff. Instantly the rocks parted. They groaned and cracked as they formed an entrance into a secret tunnel that led away from the main chamber. The Star King looked back at the company.

'I have never taken anyone through to the Chamber of Gates. Now that I have the Sun Stone I doubt I will come this way ever again. Follow me.' The Star King's entire demeanour had changed; his eyes were glowing, and he walked forward with a sense of vigour and purpose. Eben was first to follow, and Meara came quickly to his side.

'You never told me that you possessed the Sun Stone,' she said as they followed the Star King down the long tunnel.

'Casimir told me not to mention it to anyone. He told me to give it to a person who I would meet with only one hand.'

'Then Casimir knew we would seek out the Star King,' said Meara. 'He must have also known we would attempt to infiltrate Zarkanor. Let us hope the Prince of Shadows does not see what Casimir can see, for he also has the Astarian ability to see what is hidden.' Meara's eyes looked to the Star King who was leading them onward. 'The Sun Stone is a powerful relic of the Astarian people. With the Sun Stone he will be able to pass through the Cosmic Gate and find his way back to his home across the cosmos.'

They came to the far side of the tunnel which opened into a chamber with a perfectly domed ceiling. The shining floor of the chamber was made entirely of smooth crystal. The chamber was about forty yards in diameter, and the ceiling was about as high as the room was wide. A gentle light drifted up from the crystal floor and lit up their surroundings. The company entered the chamber.

The Star King walked into the centre. 'Zarkanor is a mighty fortress. Nothing, not even Faircastle, compares to it,' said the ancient one. 'I come from a world of builders and was brought to Veredor by the Prince of Shadows thousands of years ago. Over the course of a hundred years I built Zarkanor as a home for the Prince of

Shadows. However, I was betrayed; when I had finished my task he refused to send me back to my world. I grew angry and attempted to force him to keep his side of our arrangement. Unfortunately, I was no match for the Prince of Shadows. He cast me out of Zarkanor. I was left for dead in the wilderness of Veredor where I wandered for many years. I then agreed to help the Astarian Fiora in her ongoing battle with the Prince of Shadows. I built the Fortress of Shidon in the north so she could contest the Prince of Shadows, but I did this only out of a desire for revenge.'

The Star King looked to the ceiling and raised his wooden staff. A blast of bright white lightning shot up from his staff and struck the top of the dome. It swirled for a moment and then disappeared.

'The Prince of Shadows is entirely evil and desires nothing but power. If you do not stop him he will destroy Veredor.' Again he lifted his staff and a second blast of lightning shot up and struck the height of the dome. 'Zarkanor consists of three mighty outer towers, each a fortress in their own right. At the centre of the three towers is a central fourth tower, the mightiest fortress in all of Veredor. Your enemy will be waiting for you there. I will open a gateway into the lower levels of the northeast tower. From there you should be able to find your way onward. The gateway will remain open for an hour; only you can re-enter the gate, it will be invisible to all others. If you enter the gate from the other side it will take you back to the hills to the east of Faircastle.'

Again he lifted his staff and a mighty blast of lightning shot out. This time the raw white lightning didn't dissipate. The pure lightning circled the dome ceiling at a blistering pace. The Star King held his staff up and the swirls of lightning gradually descended from the ceiling and back into the staff. He then vertically cut the air with his staff. A few moments later he reached forward and pulled apart the space in front of him like he was pulling back a curtain. He created an opening in thin air that led into darkness.

'Are you ready, Ecorian?' he asked as he looked back at the company.

'Yes,' replied Eben.

'All your companions must go first. After you hand me the Sun Stone you can also go.'

The company walked forward and one by one they stepped through the gate into the darkness beyond. Last of all Eben was left with the unicorn. He then handed the Sun Stone to the Star King. The ancient one smiled as he lifted the glowing crystal in his hand, and his large happy eyes examined it closely.

'Thank you, Ecorian. For a long time I have waited for this moment. I shall now return home to my people.' The Star King then looked down at Eben. 'I hope you understand the way to overcome the Prince of Shadows. Remember what I said about walls, barriers, armour, and weapons. Perhaps you will see the way across Fiora's Bridge.'

Eben reached up and shook the hand of the ancient one. He then stepped toward the gateway with the unicorn at his side. 'I hope you journey home brings you happiness.' The Star King smiled one last time. With these words Eben and the unicorn stepped through the gateway.

Instantly they arrived in a dank and gloomy basement. A foul stench of rot permeated the room. The company were standing around and waiting to make a move. The room was small and looked to be an abandoned cellar. The only contents were many smashed bottles of wine. The stone walls were covered in thick mould and several rats huddled in the corner, frightened of the newcomers. A single tunnel led up and out of the cellar.

CHAPTER TWELVE

Mostyn concentrated and closed his eyes. For several minutes he focused his magic as they waited in the gloomy stench of the abandoned cellar.

'I see the Princess is being held in a cage in the main hall of the south-western tower. The dragon lies curled up on the floor beside her. We will have to fight the dragon to save her. We must also attempt to reach her without being seen. If we are discovered we will be inundated and overwhelmed quickly by muckrons.'

'Can we cross from this tower to the other without being seen?' asked Meara.

'I doubt it. The distance between the towers is about two hundred yards and completely in the open. I am sure there will be watchers and guards outside. There is another way; a tunnel joins this tower to the south-western tower, but I think it is guarded by something.'

'What something?' asked Red.

'I do not know exactly,' replied Mostyn. 'It is not clear to me. A monster of some kind; my vision shows me nothing about its nature.'

'If you believe the tunnel is safer then we should probably go that way,' said Meara.

'Either way we can't stay here in this dark hole. We should make a move,' said Duke Egil.

'It may be wise to fight one thing rather than risk fighting hundreds of wyverns and thousands of muckrons,' said Mostyn.

'I agree,' said Eben, not comfortable with the possibility of battling so many foes at once. 'The tunnel is probably the best option. Can you lead us onward?'

'Of course,' said the wizard. 'We must be ready for battle at any moment.'

Mostyn led the way out of the cellar. The tunnel was just large enough for the unicorn to pass through. At the far side they came to an old rotten door. The wizard opened it, just a little, to peek out. He watched for a few moments before turning back to the company.

They walked out into a long corridor that was almost as dark and dank as the cellar they had come from. 'Follow me,' whispered Mostyn. He led them on, and they walked down the shadowy corridor for about fifty feet. They then came to a tunnel that bore away to the left. The tunnel, hewn out of the stone, was about fifteen feet in height and about twenty feet wide. 'This is it.' Mostyn led them onward. After about thirty feet they came to a large iron door.

'This door has been enchanted with a powerful spell,' said Meara. 'I may be able to lift the enchantment long enough to allow us to enter the tunnel.' She reached out and placed the palm of her hand against the surface of the metal. A gentle blue light issued forth. 'The spell was cast by an Astarian. I can break it, but it will take some time. Cassiel, I will need your help.' Cassiel stepped forward and reached out, placing both his hands against the door. 'Do you feel it?'

'Yes. It's very heavy,' replied Cassiel as he closed his eyes and concentrated.

'Together we can do this.'

Instantly Cassiel's hands began to glow. For several minutes the company waited as Meara and Cassiel worked on the enchantment. Gradually the door started to slightly glow. Suddenly the light faded away. Meara then looked back at the company.

'It is done,' she said as she reached for the handle. 'But the enchantment will return in several seconds. We must not delay.' The door opened inwardly and the large hinges creaked; clearly the door had not been opened for a long time. The tunnel beyond was completely shrouded in darkness. Mostyn stepped forward and raised his hands. Several lights, like fireflies, shot forward along the length of the tunnel and lit the way onward. They could see the tunnel was very long, about two hundred yards, and at the far side there was a door, which was an exact copy as the one they had just opened.

'Be on guard,' said Mostyn as he walked forward.

Mostyn led them onwards with Quade by his side. Quade held his crossbow ready to fire at anything that moved. As they approached the midway point it became apparent the left side of the floor was flooded with a dark slimy liquid that gave off a rancid smell. They kept to the right as they passed by the sludge.

'Disgusting,' said Arthur, grimacing from the smell. They continued to the end of the corridor and arrived at the second iron door. Meara reached out and touched the metal surface.

'This one is also enchanted,' she said, looking to Cassiel for help.

'Look,' said Stella, pointing back to the sludge. The dark liquid was moving toward them across the floor.

'What in Veredor is that?' asked King Ignis.

Mostyn stared at the dark sludge; the sight of it seemed to press heavily on the wizard's heart. 'This is not a tunnel; it is a prison.'

'Cassiel, quick, help me with the door!' said Meara. Cassiel reached out, and they both started to work on breaking the enchantment.

Eben watched the pool of sludge as it slid along the floor toward them. Suddenly it stopped moving, about thirty feet from them. They watched as the sludge gathered together and began to grow and develop into a humanoid shape.

'Enough of this waiting!' cried Duke Egil. He drew his broadsword and dashed forward.

'Wait!' cried Mostyn.

'Egil!' cried King Ignis, but Duke Egil continued toward the monster.

He swung his blade, and his large sword passed directly through the dark liquid sludge without having any effect. The Duke grunted and again stabbed out. His blade pressed into the chest of the sludge creature. The monster lifted its hand with lightning speed and grabbed Duke Egil's wrist. The Duke tried to pull away but found he couldn't move. The monster then reached up and took the Duke by the throat with its other hand. Duke Egil groaned deeply, his eyes widened with shock.

Mostyn raised his hands and a bright beam of fire flew out and struck the monster; it recoiled and released its grip. Duke Egil fell heavily to the ground, and his body instantly crumbled into dust. They looked on with shock at seeing their friend disintegrate.

'No!' cried King Ignis. Eben and King Ignis dashed forward, but Mostyn grabbed their arms and ushered them back.

'Step back! Only magic can be used against this foe.'

The sludge creature, in the shape of a man, then stepped toward them, dragging its muddy inhuman feet along the tunnel floor. Again Mostyn raised his hands. Large swirls of fire blasted out and struck the foul creature, but the flames only slowed the monster a little. Quade fired his crossbow, but the bolt did nothing at all.

'Meara!' cried Mostyn.

'Almost!' said Meara, strain evident in her voice.

Eben leapt up onto the unicorn's back and drew the Sword of Light. Mostyn looked to Eben and shook his head. 'No, Ecorian. Leave this one for me.' Mostyn again raised his hands and an intense flaming barrier formed between the company and the monster. The creature of darkness approached the barrier and reached out. Mostyn concentrated as the monster pushed against his flaming shield. Beads of sweat rolled down the wizards face; he was straining to his limit.

'Lower the barrier. Let me destroy it!' shouted Eben.

'No!' replied the wizard. 'There is a reason the Prince of Shadows imprisoned this monster down here. Not even he could control or destroy it. Go whilst you still can. I will hold the monster back as long as possible. If I lower the shield we will all be killed.'

'We won't leave you here,' said Red.

'Then you will die here with me!' shouted Mostyn. The creature of darkness was pressing through the flaming shield.

Cassiel then opened the door. Meara turned and rushed back to help Mostyn. She lifted her glowing hands. 'We have to go now. The door will not remain open for long.'

'Go Meara! Save yourselves!' shouted Mostyn, fiercely concentrating on holding up his barrier of flame.

'Quick! The door is closing!' cried Cassiel.

'Mostyn!' cried Meara.

'Go!' groaned the wizard. 'You must go.'

'We won't forget you, Mostyn,' said Meara. She turned and grabbed Red's arm and dragged him back toward the door. 'Eben!'

Quade, Cassiel, Stella, King Ignis, and Arthur had already gone through the door. Meara and Red passed through a second later. Eben waited a moment, still not wanting to leave Mostyn alone to fight the monster.

Mostyn's strained eyes looked up. 'Eben, save the Princess, you must, please...go!'

Eben then reluctantly turned the unicorn and rode out of the tunnel as the iron door closed behind him.

**

The company stood in the darkness just beyond the enchanted iron door. Eben stared back in silence. The entire company felt the shock of losing Mostyn and Duke Egil.

'We are all prepared to sacrifice ourselves for this mission to succeed,' said Meara.

'We must continue onwards,' said King Ignis. 'Princess Apherah is being held in this tower.'

Meara led the company onward. The tunnel gradually ascended. They arrived at a place where two large tunnels led away to the left and the right. Meara led them to the left. The way ascended; several smaller passageways veered away. There were no monsters around and the tower was completely quiet.

Before long they arrived at a large group of steps that led up to two arched cast iron doors.

'This is it,' said Meara. 'These doors lead to the where the dragon is holding Princess Apherah.'

Eben concentrated on the doors. 'Is everyone ready?' he asked.

Meara nodded and looked back at the others for confirmation. 'We are ready.'

Eben then rode on with the Sword of Light. The others followed him as the unicorn leapt up the flight of steps. He reached a landing where the two large metal doors stood. The unicorn reared up and kicked out, bashing the doors open. Meara, Red, Stella, and King Ignis were at his side. Quade, Arthur, and Cassiel were further back.

Before them was a large hall which was about a one hundred and fifty yards in length and eighty yards in width. Towering stone pillars lined the edges and rose up to the ceiling about eighty yards above the dark stone floor. Directly ahead the dragon was curled up like a giant snake. Its fierce red eyes instantly opened as Eben rode into the hall. The beast leapt up and uncoiled the length of its enormous body. The dragon's massive batlike wings stretched out.

Eben looked across the hall and could see Apherah. She was dressed in a long flowing white gown and was being held in a cage made completely of crystal glass. She looked to Eben.

Eben didn't delay his attack. He galloped forward. The beast lunged at him. The unicorn leapt to the side in a display of awesome agility. Eben swung his blade at the shining scales of the mighty beast. Dragon blood poured out from the wound as a deafening howl issued forth. The unicorn backed away, and Eben turned to see the dragon desperately whirling around to face him.

The dragon snarled furiously, bearing its huge fangs. Intense flames burst out of its gaping mouth. The unicorn dashed aside, only just dodging the torrent of fire. Again the unicorn brought Eben into striking range. Eben struck again, cutting through the dragon's scales. The furious beast whipped around and reached out with its claw. Eben thrust his blade forward.

Suddenly Eben felt a massive impact. The beast's barbed tail struck the unicorn from the side. Eben tumbled heavily to the ground, and his head struck the solid floor. The Sword of Light flew from his hand and slid away across the cold stone ground. Eben, with blurred vision, saw the unicorn struggling to get back up. The dragon took advantage; its huge jaws wrapped around the body of the unicorn and ripped the majestic steed up from the ground. The unicorn thrashed for a moment in the fearsome jaws of the beast. Eben watched hopelessly as his unicorn was cast aside and fell to the ground lifeless. The dragon then turned on Eben. He desperately crawled away as the huge dragon pounced.

A blue blanket of flaming light struck the terrible beast at the last possible moment. An instant later Red grabbed Eben's arm and dragged him back as Meara stepped forward. She lifted a brightly glowing crystal, the Irilian Star, and swirls of lightning whirled around her. Meanwhile King Ignis picked up the Sword of Light from the floor and dashed forward to help Meara.

Meara lifted her hands; the entire hall lit up. Blue light rose from the stone floor, and a shockwave of energy struck the dragon, pushing it back toward the far side of the hall. The dragon howled in defiance. Flames burst toward Meara. Meara shielded herself and again sent another shockwave of energy at the beast. This time the dragon smashed through the spell and bounded forward.

Meara cracked the Irilian Star on the stone floor, which caused an explosion of raw power. The bright blue light was almost blinding. The dragon tumbled back and crashed heavily into the far wall. An entire pillar collapsed from the impact, and a gaping hole appeared in the opposite wall. For several moments no one could see the dragon at all as blue light swelled around the beast.

As the light faded the wounded dragon reappeared, howling furiously. Meara looked up in horror as the massive beast leapt at her. In an instant the dragon snatched her up in its claws. King Ignis charged forward with the Sword of Light and drove the blade into the dragon's side. The dragon cast Meara away; she flew through the air and crashed heavily into the wall, falling to the ground unconscious. The beast, growling horrifically, then turned to face the King. King Ignis heaved the Sword of Light out of the dragon. The dragon struck him with the back of its claw, sending him tumbling back. He staggered to his feet and stumbled away.

Meanwhile Quade fired his crossbow as Arthur, Cassiel, and Stella charged forward. The dragon turned about and unleashed intense flames. Stella ducked behind her shield as Arthur dodged the flames and leapt through the air at the dragon. He thrust his curved Vastorian blade out with perfect precision and pierced the dragon's left eye. The beast screeched in pain and whipped its tail at Arthur. The Desert Knight, displaying awesome agility, ducked away as Stella and Cassiel dashed forward. Cassiel lifted his hands and several bolts of lightning shot out and hit the beast.

Stella then stabbed at the dragon's neck, her sword only just piercing the thick scales. She quickly ducked back, avoiding the dragon's barbed tail as it raced by. Meanwhile Cassiel sent a lightning bolt into the dragon's face. The beast covered its remaining eye. Arthur, seeing an opportunity, dashed in once again. He leapt forward and thrust his blade at the dragon's massive body. His sword cut through the scales and bright red dragon blood sprayed from the wound. The dragon howled and snapped its huge jaws at the Desert Knight as he tried to retreat. Arthur narrowly avoided the jaws, but a moment later the dragon unleashed a surge of fire. The Desert Knight fell to the ground, completely incinerated by the flames.

'No!' cried Quade.

Eben stood up and tried to shake off his daze. 'We have to do something!'

King Ignis was standing on the far side of the hall. Stella and Cassiel were backing away toward where Red, Eben, and Quade were standing. King Ignis looked to Eben. The King was still holding the Sword of Light and preparing to attack the dragon again. Eben watched as King Ignis rushed in at the beast. The dragon whirled around to face him. Simultaneously Red, Eben, and Quade dashed forward.

The dragon swung its tail at the three of them. Red was knocked back and stumbled away. Quade again fired his crossbow, but the crossbow bolt simply bounced off the thick scales. He then cried out and threw the entire crossbow at the dragon as he drew his curved Vastorian sword.

Meanwhile, Eben, without a weapon, charged at the dragon. The dragon unleashed intense flames in his path. Eben ran directly into the flames; the fire circled around him. He was completely unharmed by the flames because of the power given to him by drinking from the Pool of Radiance. Eben leapt through the flames and grabbed hold of the horns directly behind the dragon's head. The beast tried to shake him off.

Meanwhile King Ignis lunged forward and stabbed out. The dragon recoiled quickly and struck back at the King, sending him flying across the hall. King Ignis landed heavily on his back, still clutching the Sword of Light. The dragon then thrashed its head about, trying to shake Eben off. Eben held on with all his strength.

'The sword!' cried Eben.

King Ignis threw the Sword of Light. Eben reached out and grabbed his sword from the air. He lifted the sword and with all his might plunged the blade into the back of the dragon's neck, driving it up to the hilt. The dragon wailed; flames and sparks burst up from where the Sword of Light had pierced its thick scales. Eben tried to withdraw his sword, but the dragon thrashed its head wildly, causing him to fall. Eben stumbled away from the massive beast.

The dragon's remaining eye fiercely ogled Eben. A moment later its neck exploded; flames and liquid fire surged out from the wound. The Sword of Light, broken in two pieces, fell away. The dragon then collapsed and lay lifeless on the cold stone floor.

CHAPTER THIRTEEN

The company rushed to help Meara; she was still unconscious on the floor. King Ignis limped toward them as Eben dashed for the glass cage that was holding Apherah. Apherah came to the edge of the glass as Eben pulled back the latch and unlocked the glass door. They embraced and held each other.

'Eben!' she cried, tears of relief rolling down her face.

'Apherah.' For a few moments they held each other in a close embrace. 'We have to go before the Prince of Shadows comes after us.'

Eben, holding Apherah's hand, ran back to the others. Red and Quade had already lifted Meara from the ground.

'She is still alive, but we can't wake her up,' said Red. Meara's eyes were closed, and her face was very pale.

'We have to get back to the Star King's gate,' said Cassiel. 'It won't stay open much longer.'

'What gate are you talking about?' asked an icy voice from across the hall. The company turned to see a dark figure approaching the lifeless body of the dragon. Eben instantly recognised Callidus. He was clothed in the same manner as he had been on the headland of Crescent Bay, simple black clothing and no armour. The Sword of Midlight was at his side. Callidus reached down and picked up the hilt of the Sword of Light.

'What a shame. You destroyed the Sword of Light and our dragon.' He examined the hilt and then threw it aside.

'What do you want, Callidus?' asked Eben.

Callidus smirked and stepped toward them. 'We want to rule Veredor and to fully control the Cosmic Gate. If it wasn't for you getting in the way we would have accomplished these tasks long ago.'

'The Prince of Shadows will never rule Veredor,' said Eben boldly.

'Are you so sure, Ecorian?' asked Callidus, shaking his head. 'How do you mean to stop him? You have no weapon, your army is insignificant, and most of your friends are dead. Soon this will all be over.' Eben watched as the Astarian walked closer. 'I could kill you now, Ecorian, yet that would be much too easy. I have thought of a more unpleasant fate. Beyond Veredor there is a place of utter darkness. For thousands of years the Lord of Veredor drifted through the deserts of the outer darkness. Now I will give your friends the punishment that Fiora gave to my master.'

Callidus reached up and pulled apart the air before him like he was drawing back a curtain. A dark rift appeared and its edges glowed with a bright white light. They all stared into the dark gateway.

'I reveal to you the Cosmic Gate. Unfortunately we do not fully control it. Casimir still works against us. It will not be long before he pays the price for his foolish resistance. Once we kill Casimir we will fully control the Cosmic Gate. Then we will be able to instantly banish all men and mer from Veredor. Such power is not yet in my hands; however, forcing you through this gateway will not be difficult.'

Callidus lifted his hands. A moment later Eben felt a heavy pressure pushing him toward the gate. Apherah fell forward. Eben reached out and grabbed her hand. The entire company was being pushed toward the gate by an invisible force. Eben struggled to resist the pressure, but it was impossible to fight the Astarian's spell. Callidus stood back, his arms crossed, and laughed. He mocked them as they desperately struggled against his magic. Stella attempted to use one of her ropes and a grappling hook, but the pressure was too intense; she couldn't swing the rope. Eben held Apherah's hand with all his strength as they slid along the floor toward the dark gateway.

Suddenly a blue rippling barrier appeared between them and the Cosmic Gate. Eben and Apherah struck the barrier first. The shimmering transparent shield held them from being pushed any further. A moment later Red, Stella, Quade, King Ignis, and Meara reached the glowing barrier. Cassiel's hands were shining brightly as he slid through the barrier he had created. The young wizard was being drawn uncontrollably toward the darkness.

'Cassiel!' cried Eben, powerless to help his friend.

'I can't shield against myself! Go! Save yourselves!' cried Cassiel as he was pulled into the dark gateway.

'Cassiel!'

Cassiel, straining with his last strength, pushed the barrier of blue light across the floor of the hall, moving them all back toward the iron doors at the far side. In moments the company was beyond the iron doors. Eben watched the gateway for Cassiel, but he was gone from sight. Callidus then closed the Cosmic Gate, sealing Cassiel in the dark world beyond. His furious eyes looked at Eben and the others. A moment later Cassiel's shield began to fade away.

'I will not be defied!' howled Callidus, drawing the Sword of Midlight. They were all completely shocked at losing Cassiel so suddenly. Eben felt a sense of horror flowing through his veins.

'We must go before this shield is completely gone,' said King Ignis.

Red and Quade carried Meara as they ran down the steps. Stella led the way, her sword in hand. They rushed from the hall and through several dark and dank corridors. Stella kicked open a door. They followed her outside into the twilight. Only a little light of day remained.

Eben looked up and could see a dark fortress that towered high into the sky. Zarkanor was built from dark stone. At its highest point, about four hundred yards above the ground, six twisted metal horns rose as a symbol of horror. The three smaller towers, which were also incredibly large, stood like giant fangs surrounding the main fortress. A tall and dark wall joined the three towers and created a barrier around the central fortress. Not a single tree, not even a blade of grass, grew within the grounds of Zarkanor. A gloomy gate stood open at the base of the main fortress.

They could hear the snorts and growls of muckrons in the distance, but the way across the gravel to the northwest tower was completely free, and there were no monsters in sight. Stella continued to lead the way onward and back to the gateway that would lead them home to Faircastle. Eben and Apherah ran together. King Ignis struggled with his injured leg. Red and Quade carried Meara.

Eben looked again at the dark gate of the fortress as they passed by. Something in his heart stirred. He knew that this was his last chance to face the Prince of Shadows. A sorrowful cry, deep within, beckoned him toward the shadowy gate.

'Stella, wait,' said Eben. Stella stopped and looked back. 'I have to face the Prince of Shadows. If I return now to Faircastle I will never have this chance again.'

King Ignis shook his head. 'Don't be ridiculous, Eben. The Sword of Light has been destroyed. There is no way you can protect yourself against him.'

'Eben, we have to get out of here,' said Red hastily, not wanting to delay their escape.

'Red. I know this is my one and only chance to stop him.'

'But how? We could not even stop Callidus,' said Stella. 'Eben, we have to get back to the safety of Faircastle.'

'Eben, please, I do not want to lose you again,' said Princess Apherah.

Eben looked to Apherah. Her eyes pleaded for him not to leave.

'Apherah, I have to go. I have to try to save our world.' Eben lifted her hand and gently kissed it. He then turned away toward the dark gate.

'Then we are going with you,' said Red, turning to follow after Eben.

Eben stopped in his tracks and looked back at Red 'I must go alone.'

'Why?'

'Red, please trust me. If I go alone there may be a chance.'

'Eben, take this,' said Quade. Quade handed Eben his Vastorian sword. Eben nodded to Quade and the others before turning toward the central fortress.

He walked across the gravel and came to the dark gate. A gloomy shadow shrouded the entire entrance. He stepped forward, and his eyes found it difficult to adjust to the intense darkness. There was no one around. The murky gloominess of the place pressed down upon his spirit and sickened his heart. He walked through the gatehouse and came to a large entrance chamber. Four Skatheans stood guard at a large iron door on the opposite side. Their eyes were fixed on him the moment he appeared.

'My name is Eben Ecorian. I request an audience with the Prince of Shadows,' he announced firmly.

The Skatheans stepped forward and drew their swords. The palest and most deathly Skathean approached him. His blue piercing eyes examined Eben for several moments.

'The Lord of Veredor has been expecting you, Ecorian,' hissed his stony voice; a deathly grin appeared on his thin lips. Eben was shocked by the revelation. How could the Prince of Shadows know he was coming? Was he walking into a trap? 'Follow me.'

Eben expected them to take the sword that Quade had given him, but the Skathean turned and walked toward the large iron door without another word. One of the other Skatheans opened the door and revealed an entrance hall that was lined with dark pillars. The floor was covered in black marble. Small lanterns lit the way, but the light did little to push back the oppressive gloom.

The Skathean led Eben down the hall to a second door which was made of bronze and depicted carvings of horrific creatures: dragons, wyverns, ghouls, muckrons, serpents, and other evil creatures that Eben had never seen. The Skathean turned and looked back at Eben.

'Beyond this door you will enter the Hall of Zarkanor. At the far side you will see the throne. There you will find the Lord of Veredor. From here you must go alone.'

The Skathean opened the bronze door. The hall beyond was far larger than any hall Eben had ever seen. He stepped forward and looked up at the towering ceiling hundreds of yards above. Mighty black pillars rose along the edge, and high above, large portholes revealed the darkening sky beyond. Black polished marble covered the entire floor of the hall. The hall was over a hundred and fifty yards in length. At the far side a group of wide steps led up to a stone platform. In the centre of the platform was a throne of twisted metal. The metal turned in on itself and rose up to form six large metal horns above. Sitting on the throne was the Prince of Shadows, adorned in his full dark armour, with his face covered by a visor.

Baramak stood directly beside the Prince of Shadows. At first Eben didn't notice, but he suddenly became aware that ghouls were standing at intervals around the walls. There were at least forty of the living shadows. Their red glowing eyes watched Eben as he entered.

Eben walked across the black marble toward the steps that led up to the throne. He knew that without the Sword of Light he was no match for the Prince of Shadows. He remembered the words of the Star King. He remembered what Casimir had said in the depths of the ocean. All the lessons he had learned on his journey whirled around in his mind. Walls, barriers, weapons, and power. Men desire power; they seek it all their lives. Walls, barriers, armour, weapons...power. His mind raced. The riddle pulsed through his being. What kept men from forming a relationship with Veredor? Why couldn't men control the Cosmic Gate? Walls, barriers, armour, weapons...power.

Eben reached up and unlatched his armour at his shoulder. He removed his chest plate as he continued to walk across the floor. He then removed his gauntlets and chainmail and dropped them as he continued. The Prince of Shadows stood up as he approached. Eben looked at Quade's curved Vastorian sword.

'Power,' whispered Eben as he drew the sword and examined the finely crafted blade. He then raised his eyes to the Prince of Shadows. The Prince of Shadows, fully armoured, stepped forward to the edge of the stone platform and stared down at Eben. Eben cast the sword aside and it slid away across the marble floor. He then walked forward to meet his enemy.

The Prince of Shadows clapped several times. 'This I did not foresee,' he said, his hissing voice was difficult for Eben to bear. 'Finally you see that surrender is the only way.'

Eben walked up to the edge of the platform and stared up at the Prince of Shadows, who was only several feet away. He focused his full attention on the dark metal visor that covered his enemy's face.

'I have not come here to surrender,' said Eben boldly.

The Prince of Shadows stared at him for a moment. He then leapt down from the platform, landing directly in front of Eben. Eben held his head high and stared directly into the Astarian's face.

'If you have not come to surrender then what have you come for...death?' Suddenly the Prince of Shadows struck him with the back of his armour clad hand. The impact was heavy, and Eben was knocked to the ground and dazed for a moment. Eben took a deep breath and shook off the pain. He gathered himself and slowly stood back up. Again he looked defiantly at the Prince of Shadows.

'What happened to my parents? What did you do to them?'

The Prince of Shadows stared at Eben and pondered the question before answering. 'Your father was captured by Baramak and Callidus. He was brought here in chains. I kept him in the dungeons. When it became apparent the Fiorians wanted to rescue him I had him executed for resisting my right to rule Veredor. I could not allow an Ecorian the chance to be free. He was a threat to me.'

Eben looked down and felt his heart fall in his chest. A deep grief took hold of him. For several moments he couldn't speak. 'And my mother?' asked Eben, almost whispering.

'Your mother infiltrated Zarkanor to rescue your father. She arrived not long after I had the Ecorian executed. Kaloren presented a problem for me. She was an impressive warrior and carried the Sword of Midlight. I was forced to lie to her; I told her your father still lived. I promised her that

I would reunite her with your father, who she loved, if she gave me the Sword of Midlight. She agreed to exchange the Sword of Midlight for your father. When I had taken the Sword of Midlight from her I had her executed for challenging my right to rule Veredor. She tried to resist, but without the Sword of Midlight she stood no chance.'

Eben fell to his knees; his hands covered his face. His heart burned inside his chest. He dropped his head and bent forward. The pain in his heart was unbearable. The Prince of Shadows stared coldly down at him.

'Such is the fate of all who choose to resist me. You, Ecorian, do not have to choose such a path. Return to Faircastle and convince men to fall down upon their knees and worship me. If you do this I will allow you to live. Serve me and you shall be revered by men, mer, and muckrons. You will have power over all.'

Eben didn't raise his head. He remained on his knees and stared down at the cold marble floor. His heart was in so much pain that he could barely move. The hope he had carried for so long was ripped away. Slowly he lifted his head and looked up at the Prince of Shadows, the murderer of his parents. The Prince of Shadows then removed his helm, revealing his deathly pale face. His eyes were sunken and devoid of any light, and his mouth turned sharply down at the edges. His head was completely bald, and an expression of bitterness was etched into his features.

'Before I killed the Gerish Oracle she told me an Ecorian would kill my dragon. Until that moment I thought the Ecorians were extinct. This is how I came to know of your existence. I allowed you to kill my dragon because I knew it was your destiny. I then sent Callidus to banish your friends into the outer darkness. I could not allow them to get in the way of my great plan. Unfortunately Callidus failed; most of your friends have escaped my grip, but this does not concern me because you are here as I planned you to be. Your destiny has brought you to me.'

'You do not know my fate,' said Eben defiantly.

'Yes, Ecorian, I do. I have foreseen all this. I knew this day would come.' The Prince of Shadows clapped his hands and laughed gleefully. 'Yes, I also saw that you would one day kneel before me as you do now.'

Eben lifted himself up and stood, not wanting to give the Prince of Shadows a moment more pleasure.

'I will never kneel before you. I will never serve you! You have nothing. Your power will only bring you loneliness. Your strength is an illusion. Nothing you have is eternal. Everything you possess is worthless. The truth has no place in you.'

The Prince of Shadows sneered at Eben. He then reached up and grabbed Eben by the throat and squeezed tightly. Eben couldn't breathe. The pain was excruciating.

'This doesn't feel like an illusion,' he roared as he slammed Eben heavily into the ground. Eben almost lost consciousness and lay on the ground in a heavy daze. A moment later he felt a heavy boot crunch into the side of his face. Eben could feel blood dribbling down the side of his head. The dark figure stood above him, gloating with a grin from ear to ear.

'Ecorian, you have nothing to protect you. You are completely alone. You have no armour, no weapons, and no walls to hide behind. I have taken your power from you. Look on me now; you will see my power is complete. You, Ecorian, are the one who has nothing!'

Eben opened his mouth and tried to speak, but little more than a faint mutter came out. '...Such is...'

'Speak up, boy, or do you also lack the power to speak?

Eben, heavily stunned, lifted his eyes and looked up to a porthole situated high in the wall above. Two bright stars drew his attention. They shone intensely in the darkness. For some time he watched the stars shimmering in the distance. A glimmer of hope returned to his heart. He turned his head and stared at the cold black marble for a moment. 'Veredor,' he whispered, ever so quietly. 'Let there be no more barriers between us. Please, in this moment receive us.' For a few seconds there was nothing but silence.

'If you will not serve me you will die!' said the Prince of Shadows as he drew the Sword of Darkness.

Eben, with his last remaining strength, pulled himself up off the floor. He struggled to stand and looked directly into the eyes of his enemy. The Prince of Shadows held the Sword of Darkness, ready to strike.

Eben took several breaths before speaking. 'Prince of Shadows, you are not welcome in

Veredor. I banish you and all those who serve you into the darkness beyond!'

The Prince of Shadows threw his head back and laughed deeply. 'I would expect such words to come from a fool such as you.'

A moment later the ground started to tremble. The Prince of Shadows frantically looked around. 'What have you done!' he cried, his eyes widening as he realised what had just occurred.

'Fiora's Bridge has been crossed!' whispered Eben.

Suddenly a great rift appeared at the centre of the hall as the Cosmic Gate opened. Bright white light lined the edge of the gateway and lit up the darkness. Eben looked back as the Cosmic Gate formed a large opening into the darkness beyond Veredor. A howling wind blew through the hall. First the ghouls were sucked into the rift. Baramak grabbed hold of the throne, but his fingers could not hold on, and he tumbled across the floor. The Northern Sorcerer screamed hysterically, and a moment later he was drawn into the darkness. The Prince of Shadows resisted with all his power and struggled against the force that was dragging him across the marble floor.

'This is my world! Veredor is mine!' he moaned, his rasping voice full of terror.

'Whilst men and mer live in Veredor you shall never return.'

The Prince of Shadows, losing control, staggered back toward the gateway. He stared at Eben, howled deeply, and then was gone.

CHAPTER FOURTEEN

Stella was the first to step through the gateway from the dark basement. Instantly she found herself in a quiet grove full of tall golden elm trees. A little light of day remained. The gateway was formed into a gnarly rock wall. Red and Quade, carrying Meara, who was still unconscious, instantly appeared. A moment later King Ignis and Princess Apherah stepped through.

Red and Quade lay Meara down on the soft grass. 'What do you think Eben was planning?' asked Quade.

'I don't know, but if he's not here in a few minutes I'm going back for him,' said Red.

'I'll go with you,' said Stella.

'No, it's much too dangerous. Zarkanor will be crawling with muckrons by now. Both of you should stay. Too many of us have already been killed,' said King Ignis soberly. 'We must trust that Eben knows what he is doing. He said he had to go alone. I do not understand what Eben is planning, but I trust his judgement.'

Meara suddenly stirred and opened her turquoise blue eyes. She sat up and scanned the company and her surroundings.

'Where are Eben and Cassiel?' she asked in a broken and weak voice.

'I am sorry, Meara. Cassiel is gone,' said King Ignis. 'He sacrificed himself to save us from Callidus. The Astarian opened the Cosmic Gate and attempted to force us out of Veredor with his magic. Cassiel saved us, but he fell through the Cosmic Gate into the outer darkness.' Meara closed her eyes, her pale face revealed her pain at the loss of her friend and apprentice.

'And Eben?' she asked.

'He went on alone to fight the Prince of Shadows,' said King Ignis.

'Alone?' asked Meara, shocked by the revelation.

'Yes, we were prepared to go with him. He insisted that he go on without us,' said Quade. 'At first he was going to go without a weapon. I had to give him my sword.'

'What about the Sword of Light?' asked Meara, her eyes narrowing.

'The Sword of Light was destroyed when Eben killed the dragon,' said King Ignis.

Meara's shock was clearly evident. She looked toward the gateway. 'Then perhaps he has learned a way to cross Fiora's Bridge, because without the Sword of Light he cannot defeat the Prince of Shadows.'

'I still think we should return to Zarkanor to help him,' said Red.

'Red, you have done everything you can to stand by your friend. He has chosen to go on alone. It is a bridge only he can cross,' said Meara.

Suddenly the shimmering gateway fizzled and began to close. Within seconds there was only the rock wall.

**

Eben stood in the silence of the Hall of Zarkanor. He was completely alone. The shadow had lifted, and the gloom had all been sucked away. He looked up to the ceiling high above and saw through the portholes that the stars were shining brightly in the night sky. He scanned the surroundings; not a single monster remained. He walked over and picked up Quade's sword.

He could feel the Cosmic Gate surrounding him. It was like he had suddenly become aware of something that had always been just out of sight. The Cosmic Gate was everywhere; it was all around. It permeated the entire world. The Cosmic Gate was Veredor, and to control the Cosmic Gate and cross Fiora's Bridge meant one would have to be of Veredor. Eben knew that no matter how far he travelled through the cosmos he could always return to his home. The Cosmic Gate would always open for him.

A thought of Cassiel being forced out through the Cosmic Gate entered his mind. He had to try to save his friend. Lifting his hands he cried out. Suddenly a bright shimmering light appeared directly in front of him. In moments the light formed a gateway into the darkness. Eben stepped forward and instantly found himself in a barren and rocky desert. A subtle orange light lit his surroundings. All about him there were red rocky hills and sandy barren valleys. Nothing grew in the desolate wasteland he had entered. There was no sun; only a dark orange sky above which gave off a little light. As far as Eben could see there was no one around. His eyes searched the rocky hills, but he couldn't see a single soul.

'Cassiel!' he cried, his voice echoing off the hillsides.

There was no reply, only complete silence. Eben looked back at the Cosmic Gate shimmering in the air. He wondered where he was and what had become of Cassiel.

'Cassiel!' he cried out, again there was no reply.

Eben walked ahead into the desert and came to the side of a large rocky hill. He made his way up the slope, hoping to get a better view from the top. Several minutes later he arrived at the summit. The desert stretched on endlessly into the distance. In every direction there was nothing but sandy valleys and red hills.

Suddenly a cry echoed out across the plain. Eben looked up and saw the dark shape of a giant bird of prey circling high above. The bird was many times larger than a man. It descended quickly and landed on the rocks about fifty feet from Eben. Its bright yellow eyes had a glow about them and they were staring directly at him. Eben could see it was a giant falcon as he had often seen falcons in the hills around Clemensdale.

'What do you want?' asked Eben, his hand going to the hilt of Quade's sword.

'How peculiar,' said the giant falcon in a smooth and powerful voice. 'You speak an Astarian tongue, yet you are not an Astarian.'

'I am a man,' said Eben firmly.

'Then you are very far from your home,' said the giant falcon. 'I have not seen a man in these parts for nearly two thousand years. What brings you so far out into such a lost and desolate place?'

'I am looking for a friend. I believe he is somewhere out here in this desert,' replied Eben, wondering if the strange creature could assist him to find Cassiel. 'Do you know your way around?'

The creature turned its head and looked out toward the hills and into the distance.

'Yes, I have searched the Desert of Eternal Loneliness for many years seeking after what was lost. The desert extends further than you can imagine; just about as far as people can possibly be away from each other without ceasing to exist.'

Eben felt his heart drop at hearing the creature's words. 'If the desert is so large then how can I possibly find my friend?'

The creature stared into Eben's eyes for a few moments before answering. 'Do not fear, man. I am sure your friend is fine.'

'How do you know?'

'Trust, yes, trust is the key; the Ecorian should already know that.'

'You know my name! How do you know my name?'

The creature squawked and turned away, realising that it had revealed something it did not intend to. 'Your name...yes, I know such things. It is my business to know such things.'

'If you know my name then what else do you know?'

'All manner of things,' said the giant falcon.

'Then you know of my friend and where I can find him?' asked Eben, stepping forward eagerly.

The creature paused and eyed Eben for a few moments. 'I know you will not find him, even if you searched for a thousand years.'

'Why?'

'Because his path has already led him far away from here. There are others who need him just as there are people on Veredor who need you.'

'Will I ever see Cassiel again?'

'Of course you will. When the time comes Cassiel will be led home. He is your true friend, and what is true is eternal. Such truth binds the cosmos together. Truth is the foundation of all things. The truth cannot become untruth, nor can untruth become the truth. Therefore, the truth is always the truth. Furthermore, what is true can never be taken from you. Often those who we think have been taken from us have actually been with us all along; they shine like stars down upon us in our darkest moments; they bring us hope when hope is lost. You see, Eben, not even death can stand in the way of the truth.'

Eben stared at the giant falcon, intrigued by his words. He wondered who this creature really was and why they had met on this rocky hill in such a desolate place.

'Who are you?' asked Eben in a low and steady voice.

'My name is Pilgrim,' said the falcon softly.

'Where are you from?'

Pilgrim looked deeply into Eben's eyes and considered the question for a few moments before answering. 'I serve the truth that exists beyond the furthest gate and above the highest height. There is a place where fields of flowers grow, above the still lakes, and deep in the Timeless Mountains. That is my home. It is the dwelling place of the Eternal One.'

'The Eternal One? Who is the Eternal One?' asked Eben, wondering who Pilgrim could possibly mean.

'One day we shall meet again when you are old and many years have passed. On that day I will take you there, and you shall meet the one who I speak of.' Pilgrim's eyes scanned the distant ridges and mountains for several moments. He then looked back to Eben. 'I believe all I need to say has been said. I will be on my way now. There are many things I must attend to. It has been a pleasure talking with you, Eben Ecorian. May the sun guide your path, and may the wind always be at your back. Goodbye my friend.'

'But wait, there are other things I must know,' said Eben.

Pilgrim looked back. 'Trust, Eben; everything will be revealed in time.'

With these final words Pilgrim leapt into the air and quickly ascended. Eben watched after him as he disappeared into the horizon.

**

Queen Sera had called a council in the Ecorian Hall. Red sat with Stella by his side at the great round table. King Ignis, Baftel, Prince Armida, Princess Apherah, the Zyranian Outcast Aperio, Garnock, Chief Parco, Quade, and Meara were also seated around the table.

Meara stood up and looked around at the company. 'Veredor has been freed of the Prince of Shadows. Fiora's Bridge has been crossed. All the servants of the Prince of Shadows have been expelled from our world. Baftel has seen all of this.'

'It is true. It also appears that nearly all the Skatheans and Northern Sorcerers have been expelled, and most of the Zyranian Order,' said Baftel. 'Our world has been liberated from the powers of darkness.'

'What about Eben?' asked Red.

Baftel stared down at the table. 'Shortly after the liberation I lost sight of him. I believe he deliberately left Veredor and entered the darkness beyond.'

'Why would he do that?' asked Quade, shaking his head in disbelief.

'Cassiel,' gasped Stella. 'He's gone to save Cassiel. Why else would he go beyond the Cosmic Gate?'

'You are right,' said Meara. 'We all know that Eben would walk into the abyss to save his friends.'

'But that's where he sent the Prince of Shadows and all his servants. Will he be safe out there?' asked Red, his eyes revealing his concern.

'I do not know,' replied Baftel. 'Little is known of the darkness beyond Veredor. The old accounts tell that it is a desolate place.'

Suddenly a line of white light appeared in mid-air across the hall. The company at the round table all turned to see a gateway open into darkness. Shimmering white light surrounded the gateway. A moment later Eben stepped through. He was covered in red dust and looked to be bruised and battered. Apherah cried out in happiness and ran to him. They embraced in front of the Sapphire Throne. The others approached, and Eben, still holding Apherah close, looked across to his friends.

'You saved us from the Prince of Shadows,' said Queen Sera

Eben nodded and smiled. 'Our enemies have been cast into the Desert of Eternal Loneliness where they belong. As long as men and mer remain in Veredor the Prince of Shadows cannot return.'

Slowly the Cosmic Gate closed and shrank away before completely disappearing.

'Did you find Cassiel?' asked Meara, anxious to hear news.

Eben cast his eyes downward and shook his head. 'I went to the deserts beyond the Cosmic Gate to search for him. I was told by a strange being that Cassiel is still alive, but his path has taken him far from Veredor. He is out there somewhere beyond the Cosmic Gate.'

'Then we will have to go out there and keep searching for him,' said Red, looking like he was ready to go at once.

'I believe Cassiel will be all right,' said Eben, reassuring Red. 'There are others who need him now. When the time is right he will return to Veredor again.'

'Who told you these things?' asked Baftel, intrigued that Eben could know so much about Cassiel and yet not have found him.

'I met a giant falcon with the voice of a man in the Desert of Eternal Loneliness.'

Baftel nodded and smiled, knowing the one who Eben spoke of. 'There is a legend about such a creature and an old song from the Forgotten Age. Most of the words of the song have been lost in the passage of time, yet a small fragment remains.' Baftel then began to recite the song: 'Over the moon and beyond the sun, Pilgrim flies to serve the one; into places beyond the deep, he will go and courage keep; the hand of peace reaches out, across the stars without a doubt; with falcon wings and a mind of light, old Pilgrim's heart shines forever bright; for a broken body he understands, is the path of every man;

and when darkness falls on the land, fear not when Pilgrim is close at hand.'

'He told me his name was Pilgrim.' said Eben.

Baftel nodded knowingly. 'Pilgrim was a friend to the Astarians before they arrived in Veredor. He was the one who gifted the Seven Relics to the Astarians. The Three Swords, the Star of the North, the Chalai, the Silver Leaf, and the Sun Stone were given to the Astarians by Pilgrim. He is a champion of peace and truth. If Pilgrim told you these things about Cassiel then we have nothing to worry about. Cassiel indeed has a path that will lead him elsewhere, and when the time comes he will return home to Veredor.'

CHAPTER FIFTEEN

Eben stood with Princess Apherah on the banks of the Adira River. They had found a quiet place where several large willow trees grew up beside the water. It was the first time he had been alone with her since his return. He was transfixed by Apherah's beauty. Her hair fell like silk beside her face, and her ocean blue eyes stared up at him with a shining brightness that only added to her beauty.

'I knew you would come back,' she said softly, reaching out and taking his hand. 'All the people of Irvaria are calling for you to be named the Ecorian Emperor. The Ecorian Empire will return. Truth and justice will govern all the lands of Veredor. King Ignis and Prince Armida agree with the people. You will be the Ecorian Emperor, Eben.'

Eben looked from Apherah out toward the slow flowing water. Even though he knew what she was saying was true he still did not feel that he could rule an empire. In his heart all that he wanted was a simple life. He had no desire for power or to rule the lands.

'I'm not sure if I can be an emperor. I don't know the first thing about ruling an empire. I grew up in a small village, far away from the courts of kings. All I want is a simple life.'

Apherah moved closer and smiled. 'That is why you should be an emperor, Eben. All men who desire power do not deserve it. Power should only be given to those who do not want it, because it is such people who have the strength to rule justly. I grew up in a royal court. I will always be by your side.'

Eben drew her closer, and just as they were about to kiss he caught sight of movement in the water. Suddenly five figures emerged and glided across the surface toward the bank. Eben knew instantly they were mer and were the same mer he had met beneath the ocean with Casimir. Apherah was startled. A moment later Casimir arose out of the river and walked toward the bank. He was surrounded by glowing light and looked vibrant and full of energy. The mer followed the Astarian.

'Eben Ecorian, we have come to show our appreciation,' said Casimir as he reached the shore.

'Casimir, I wasn't sure if I would ever see you again.'

Casimir bowed and smiled. 'I believe this will be the last time that we meet in Veredor.' He looked to Princess Apherah. 'I am pleased to meet you, Princess Apherah,' he said as he bowed again.

'This is the Astarian Casimir, and these are my people, the mer,' said Eben.

'I am delighted to meet all of you,' said Princess Apherah.

'And we are honoured to meet you,' said a beautiful mermaid.

'It seems that Veredor has passed from the Astarians to men and mer. Fiora's Bridge was crossed,' said Casimir. 'I no longer can pass through the Cosmic Gate at will. Veredor has now formed a relationship with men and mer. You found the secret to Fiora's Bridge and saved our world from the Prince of Shadows.'

Eben nodded and smiled. 'Did you know this would all come to pass, Casimir?'

Casimir shook his head. 'How you managed to cross Fiora's Bridge still remains a mystery to me, yet I knew, in my heart, that you had a gift, Eben, and I can see this gift will be handed on to your descendants. Alas, I will not be in Veredor to meet your children, for I must leave this world forever.'

'Where will you go?' asked Princess Apherah.

Casimir smiled with a twinkle in his eyes. 'My lady, there is a place far across the cosmos. I have only seen the fields of flowers which grow at the entrance; since my youth my heart has harkened for that place, and now I know the time has come for the long journey.' He looked from Apherah to Eben. 'Only the Ecorian can open the Cosmic Gate. Would you allow me to leave Veredor, Eben?'

'Of course, but I will be sorry to see you go,' said Eben, realising the significance of the last Astarian departing.

'The time of the Astarians has come to an end. A new age has arrived. Men and mer will prosper and Veredor will forever shine as a world of peace and hope in the cosmos.'

**

The streets and laneways of Faircastle were bustling with people. The victory celebrations were in full swing. Bright and happy music filled the city and people everywhere were cheering, dancing, and toasting to the victory over the Prince of Shadows and the return of the Ecorian Emperor. The liberation of Veredor was complete. Hundreds of Ecorian flags flew throughout the city alongside the flag of Irvaria.

Red and Stella sat beside each other at a table outside a bustling tavern just near to the palace gate and at the edge of the main square. Several musicians were playing fiddles and harps in the square, and the feeling in the streets was joyful to say the least. Red took a sip from his mug of Irvarian ale and smiled across at Stella. She smiled warmly back at him.

'Well, Stella, it looks like we will finally be able to settle down here in Faircastle,' he said with a smile from ear to ear. She leaned over and kissed him on the cheek.

'It's perfect.'

'There are no more dragons, draugs, and muckrons to fight,' he added. 'I guess the adventure is over,'

'No, Red, this is the beginning. We haven't really had much of a chance to be alone since our wedding. We have our whole lives ahead of us. Now that is going to be an adventure.'

Red nodded in agreement, and they kissed again.

In that moment a series of Irvarian trumpets blasted out across the city from the height of the palace. Red and Stella looked up and could see a crowd of nobles and knights were standing in a circle on a great balcony at the very height of the palace. Eben and Princess Apherah were with them and together they stepped forward.

'He did say to make sure we had a good view of the palace around midday,' said Stella as they both stood and looked up.

The people of Faircastle stared up in wonder. Eben and Princess Apherah stepped forward and they both held up the Ecorian flag. All the people throughout the city cheered when they realised what was occurring. Princess Apherah attached the Ecorian flag to a central flag pole and slowly the flag of the Ecorian rose up above the palace. The great purple flag depicting the white unicorn flew in the gentle breeze of the beautiful day. A hundred Irvarian trumpets sounded at once. All the people of the city cried out in joy and cheered as they knew Eben had accepted his role as the Ecorian Emperor.

'The new age has arrived! The Emperor has returned!' shouted a man in the main square. The people cheered. Red and Stella held each other close as they watched on.

The festivities continued throughout the day and into the night and didn't stop for many days to come. It was a long time before the people of Faircastle returned to their normal daily routines, and the feeling of joy and hope remained in the city for many years to come.

**

Three months later Eben and Apherah rode through the forest to the north of Clemensdale. Behind them rode the Royal Ecorian Guard which consisted of ten Tabarian Knights and two knights each from the realms of: Ortaria, Ateria, Irvaria, Vastoria, Scaldonia, and Iarthar. The leader of the Royal Ecorian Guard was Sir Conleth, a Tabarian Knight, who was a hulk of a man with a long red beard and a deeply weathered face.

Eben looked back to Sir Conleth. 'I would like to go on alone from here. I think that twenty fully armoured horsemen entering Clemensdale would unnecessarily frighten the village folk.'

Sir Conleth nodded. 'As you wish, Emperor.'

'Thank you, Sir Conleth.' Eben then looked across at the Empress who was riding a large white horse.

'We will discreetly protect the entrances to the village,' said Sir Conleth.

Eben then turned back to the Empress. 'Shall we go?'

They rode along the forest road until the forest came to a sudden end. Ahead of them were lush grass covered hills. The road followed the base of a shallow valley and passed by several small farmhouses. An old farmer, with hair as white as snow, was smoking a pipe and sitting on his wooden fence. He took the pipe from his mouth and waved.

'Is that you, Eben?' he asked as the horses approached.

'Hello Serg,' said Eben, riding slowly up to the old man.

'By Tiernan! I never thought I would see you again, my boy. Where have you been all this time?' asked the old farmer as he jumped down from the fence and stepped toward Eben and Apherah.

'I went to look for my parents.'

'Did you find them?' asked Serg as his bright blue eyes looked to Apherah.

'I travelled all the way to Irvaria searching for them. Unfortunately they passed away long ago.'

'I am sorry to hear that,' said the old farmer.

'Serg, I would like you to meet my wife, Apherah. This is Serg of Clemensdale. He has always been like an uncle to me.'

'Well, you look like a sweet young woman,' said old Serg, bowing low.

'I am pleased to meet you,' said Apherah, sweetly smiling at the old farmer.

'Oh, I am so happy you found yourself such a beautiful wife, Eben. Vera will be delighted. Let me get my pony; I want to come with you to town. This is the most exciting thing that has happened in years around here.' Old Serg spun around and ran back to his barn. A few moments later he reappeared and was riding on a shaggy old brown pony that looked a little too small for him.

**

Serg led Eben and Apherah into the village. Seeing the little cottages with their small flower gardens filled Eben's heart with happiness. The village folk were thrilled to see him and cried out greetings as they passed by.

Apherah looked over at Eben and smiled. 'Clemensdale is beautiful, Eben. You must have had a delightful childhood,' said Apherah, her eyes glowing with joy.

'Eben!' cried a man, running out of a store up ahead. Eben could see it was the baker, Gallus. Gallus ran over as Eben jumped down from Swiftwing. The old baker hugged him. Gallus was a short man with a large pot belly and a round happy face. 'We thought you would never return. I must tell Vera. Come with me; this is an occasion to celebrate!'

Apherah dismounted, and they followed Gallus to a small cottage situated directly behind the bakery. Gallus burst through his front door and shouted out. 'Vera. It's Eben! He's come home!'

A moment later Vera rushed from the front door, tears flowing from her eyes, as she dashed across to Eben. 'Eben! You really have come home!' Old Vera embraced him so tightly that he nearly tumbled over. 'I thought the worst had happened to you. I think I have to sit down.'

Vera and Gallus led Eben, Apherah, and Serg into the small cottage. Vera quickly tidied the small wooden table and pulled up some rickety old wooden chairs. Eben sat down with Apherah as Serg prepared some tea for the company.

'Eben, it has been much too long. Where have you been all this time?' asked Vera.

'I don't know where to begin, Vera. Before I tell you the story I would like to introduce you to my wife, Apherah.'

Vera warmly smiled and took Apherah's hand. 'Oh, what a lovely woman you found to marry. I think I am going to cry, Eben.' Vera wiped the tears away from her eyes.

'I am pleased to meet you, Vera,' said Apherah kindly.

Meanwhile Gallus poured them all some sweet Clemensdale tea from Vera's pot. 'Where have you been all this time? I'm sure you have a tale to tell.'

Eben looked across the table at Gallus and smiled. He took a sip of tea before beginning his story.

****

In the city of London, across from the entrance to Covent Garden Station, there is a place where three trees stand. On a mild summer day a tall young man in a long coat stood leaning against the trunk of the smallest of those trees. Cassiel watched the people pass by for a little while before moving on.

GLOSSARY

Alber – Alber is a kingdom situated in the north of Veredor. The Kingdom of Alber was founded in the First Age. The Kingdom of Alber, for the most part, remained distant from the affairs of the southern kingdoms of Veredor. Alber was often invaded and occupied by the Kaznor Empire.

Alblan – The people of the central kingdoms of Veredor are mostly descended from the Alban people who arrived in Veredor in the Forgotten Age and formed a colony in modern day Irvaria.

Astarians – The Astarian race were the original inhabitants of Veredor. Most Astarians, but not all, are similar to men and mer in appearance. They brought all the lesser creatures to Veredor and planted all the forests, but they never had the power to create life, only to nurture it. They were given Veredor as a new home by an even greater and mysterious being. Most Astarians could see the Cosmic Gate and cross between the realms of the cosmos. They do not die unless they are killed, and they are extremely powerful. Their skill with magic is far beyond the level that can be gained by men. Most of the Astarians were killed in the wars of the Forgotten Age.

BL – Refers to the ages before liberation and the return of the Ecorian Empire.

Blue Caps – Blue Caps are small humanoid creatures that look like miniature men. They came to Veredor with the Astarians at the time of the first arrival and were considered by Astarians as uninvited stowaways. They are ambivalent towards the Astarians, but they dislike men because men often exploited Blue Caps and forced them to work in mines as slaves in the first ages. They are commonly about two feet tall and live in tunnels and chambers deep underground. They form large communities in remote places and are extremely territorial. They will attack a trespasser always with the intention of capturing their opponent. When they capture men they take them deep underground and force them to work in mines until they die; however, they will often release captured women and allow them to return home as they have no traditional grudge against women.

Callidus – Callidus was one of the few Astarians who survived in Veredor until the time of liberation. He resided at the northern edge of the Great Mountains between the Kaznor Empire and the Kingdom of Alber. He had little to do with men and mer throughout history. The Prince of Shadows hunted Callidus on his return to Veredor. Callidus attempted to contest the Prince of Shadows but failed. The evil Astarian offered Callidus a place as his prime servant, above all others, if he would bow down and worship him as Lord of Veredor. Callidus accepted and gave his soul to the Prince of Shadows. He was given the Sword of Midlight as a reward for his service.

Carlin – The Fiorian Carlin was one of the most prominent Fiorians before the return of the Ecorian Empire. Carlin was a true hero and said to be one of the greatest swordsmen who ever lived. Carlin singlehandedly overwhelmed the Northern Sorcerer Azagord and imprisoned him beneath the Citadel of Zyran. Carlin remained in Ortaria after the birth of Eben Ecorian to protect the young Ecorian when Kaloren went north to rescue Elons Ecorian from Zarkanor. Carlin became aware of a secret threat to Ortaria by an unknown enemy who he suspected was an Astarian. He organised another Fiorian to take Eben Ecorian to be protected by Erako, a former Fiorian Knight. Carlin and several of his Fiorian companions were killed in an ambush set by the Astarian Callidus on the coast of Ortaria.

Casimir – Casimir was an Astarian who lived beneath the sea. He was a friend to the mer and ocean sprites. He was aligned with Fiora over the question of men and mer in the Forgotten Age. He opposed the Prince of Shadows in the wars of the Forgotten Age. His skill as a warrior was secondary to his great wisdom and knowledge of ancient lore. He remained with the mer beneath the sea during the later ages and was the last remaining Astarian who opposed the Prince of Shadows. He is also known as the Old Man of the Sea.

Chalai, The – One of the Seven Relics of the Astarians. The Chalai gives the carrier physical immortality. It played a major role in the wars of the Forgotten Age and a minor role thereafter. The Star King stole the Chalai from the Oran Oracle, and he attempted to use the power of the Chalai to open the Cosmic Gate. Kaloren threw the Chalai into a lake. It was later found by the mer and taken to the Astarian Casimir. Casimir hid the Chalai in the depths of the oceans.

Circle of Night, The – The Circle of Night were an assembly of powerful Northern Sorcerers and Skathean Knights who governed the Kaznor Empire from 401 BL until the sorcerers Baramak and Azagord rose to power in the year 28 BL.

Cosmic Gate, The – The Cosmic Gate is a mystical barrier forged from the essence of Veredor that protects Veredor from creatures of darkness. The Cosmic Gate was built by the Astarians at the end of the first wars of the Forgotten Age. Throughout most of history only the Astarians could pass through the gate at will. The Astarian Fiora sealed the Cosmic Gate against the Prince of Shadows at the end of the Forgotten Age.

Desert Knights – The Desert Knights were formed in the year 625 BL by Sir Grecob, a respected Vastorian knight of the time. Their original purpose was to free

Vastoria from Skathean influence and to bring peace and justice to the lands. The primary mandate of the Desert Knights is to protect the people of Vastoria. Desert Knights always wear black and cover their faces with metal masks. They exclusively use the curved single edged Vastorian sword in battle.

Dragons (Great) – There are three varieties of dragons. The first and most powerful were the Great Dragons (not to be confused with wyverns and lindworms). The Great Dragons of Veredor were allied with the Astarians in the Forgotten Age. There were originally dozens of dragons, but most died in the first wars of the Forgotten Age fighting against massive armies of wyverns and other lesser known creatures of darkness. At the end of the first wars of the Forgotten Age only five dragons remained in Veredor. The remaining five dragons withdrew from Veredor soon after the end of the Forgotten Age. The dragons instructed the first Northern Sorcerers.

Draugs – Draugs are described by the Astarians as dream shadows from the outer darkness. They do not exist in a physical body. They are living shadows that can move through solid objects and are often invisible to human eyes. Draugs can influence the thoughts of men. They can create dreamlike illusions. They can be killed by magic and flee from the goodhearted. Ri Draugs are particularly powerful draugs who can possess and enslave the minds of men and other creatures through temptation and desire. They do this to consume the essence of their victims.

Ecorian Arbiters – Ecorian Arbiters were the precursors to the later monarchies of Veredor in the time after the end of the Ecorian Empire. In order to rule Veredor justly, the Ecorian Emperor chose ten Ecorian Arbiters to govern the provinces of the empire. They were good and noble men who were revered by the people. They were all loyal to the Ecorian Empire. After the apparent death of Aluin Ecorian without an heir, the Ecorian Arbiters became the kings of the ten monarchies of Veredor and divided the Ecorian Empire. Several monarchies continued to claim lineage from the Ecorian Arbiters until the later ages. The bloodlines of the Ecorian Arbiters were considered to be truly noble and such a claim was often used to justify a right to rule.

Ecorian Emperors – The Ecorians are the direct descendants of Jeriel the Just who was the first Ecorian Emperor of Veredor. They were revered emperors who worked for the good of all. The Ecorian Emperors vanquished evil from the lands and worked closely with the Fiorian Knights. They were revered by all and good to all. The first two Ecorian Emperors carried the Sword of Light, but the sword was lost in the River Siarglas in Southern Iarthar. The last Ecorian Emperor was Aluin Ecorian. The continuation of the Ecorian line was unknown to the Ecorian Arbiters and hidden from them by the Fiorian Order, as by the time it was discovered the Ecorian Arbiters had already claimed power. The lineage of the Ecorians was protected and hidden throughout the later ages until the birth of Eben Ecorian.

Ecorian Empire – The greatest empire in the history of Veredor. The Ecorian Empire was formed by Jeriel the Just who became the first Ecorian Emperor. The Empire spanned all the Southern Lands of Veredor from the Eastern Ocean to the Merhome Sea.

Elons Ecorian – Elons Ecorian was born in the Gerish Highlands of Scaldonia. He was raised in a remote settlement by a Fiorian Knight named Roarna. Roarna was given the task of protecting the Ecorian lineage and the Sword of Midlight which was carried by the Ecorian. He trained Elons Ecorian in ancient lore and swordsmanship. As a young man Elons aided Roarna to infiltrate Kaznor in order to gain knowledge of the sorcerers Baramak and Azagord. Roarna and Elons later travelled south to Emeril. When Baramak invaded the Far Western Lands Elons went to the aid of the Irilian Order and the Kingdom of Iarthar. He was revered as a hero by all in the west and fought off the sorcerer Baramak's first attempt to take control of the Southern Lands. On his return to Emeril he met the Fiorian Kaloren who had recently become the Gatekeeper of Emeril. At this time news came that Ortaria was under attack by the Northern Sorcerer Azagord. Elons Ecorian went west with Kaloren and a group of Fiorian Knights. Elons and Kaloren fell in love and were married in Stonehaven. They continued on to Ortaria as husband and wife. They battled Azagord and forced him and his army out of Ortaria. News arrived that Baramak had renewed his attack in the Far Western Lands. Elons went west to contest Baramak, but he was captured by Baramak and Callidus. Elons Ecorian was then taken as a prisoner to the Dungeons of Zarkanor.

Emeril – Emeril is a fortress belonging to the Fiorian Order. Emeril was built in 1382 BL by Teodric as a home for the Fiorian Order. The secret path to Emeril is situated above the source of the Adira River. The fortress is built atop a mountain and has towers that reach high above a lush secret valley deep in the Great Mountains.

Erako the Hermit – Erako was a knight of the Fiorian Order and a friend of Carlin and Roarna. He was a great warrior who fought alongside Kaloren in the liberation of Vastoria. He grew tired and old and retired to Clemensdale, a remote village in the wilderness of southern Ortaria. He later became the guardian and adoptive father of Eben Ecorian; however, he never knew that he was protecting the last Ecorian.

Eriulan – The people of western Veredor are mostly descendants of the Eriulan colony. The Eriulan people settled in the land of Iarthar when men first arrived in Veredor after the first wars of the Forgotten Age.

Fiora – Fiora was the most noble and goodhearted of the Astarians. Fiora carried the Sword of Light and was the greatest warrior of the Astarian people throughout the Forgotten Age. She battled the first invasions from the outer darkness and led the Astarians to many victories. She was considered the greatest of the Astarians in battle. She was a friend to men and mer and convinced the Astarians to bequeath Veredor to the two races, as there were few Astarians remaining after the first wars of the Forgotten Age. She founded the Knights of Shidon which later developed into the Fiorian Order. She battled the Prince of Shadows at the end of the Forgotten Age and sacrificed her power and essence to seal the Cosmic Gate against his return. Soon after sealing the Cosmic Gate she left Veredor to men and mer and never returned.

Fiorian Order, The – The Fiorian Knights were founded by Toranah the Mystic in the year 2500 BL. Toranah was the last remaining knight of the Knights of Shidon. The Fiorian Order fought for the good of all people in Veredor and worked tirelessly against the powers of darkness throughout the ages. The Fiorian Knights focused their training on gaining a clear and true understanding of life. The Fiorian Knights use the same skills that were taught to the Knights of Shidon by the Astarian Fiora in the Forgotten Age. Fiorian Knights often live for hundreds of years due to a secret method of meditation taught to the Knights of Shidon by Fiora.

Fire Order, The – The Astarian Lumen saw the good that Fiora had done for men by forming the Knights of Shidon. Lumen decided to teach men Astarian magic. Men could use the method of the Astarians, yet not to the same degree as the Astarians. The Fire Order was founded by Lumen's students. They built the Tower of Fire at the northern edge of the Old Guardian Mountains at the sight of Lumen's former home. Throughout history they remained aloof and were rarely seen outside of their stronghold. They are considered the most powerful of the three southern orders due to their system being complete and mostly unchanged from Lumen's original teachings.

Gargoyles – Gargoyles were made by the Astarians in the first wars of the Forgotten Age. The primary role of a Gargoyle was to protect the abodes of the Astarians. They are not living creatures as they were formed by the magic and craftsmanship of the Astarians. Several Gargoyles remained until the time of liberation.

Ghouls – Ghouls are evil spectres who serve the Prince of Shadows. They were brought by the Prince of Shadows to Veredor when he first returned to Veredor after he spent an age wandering through the Desert of Eternal Loneliness. They were used by the Prince of Shadows to hunt down the Astarians who opposed his claim to rule Veredor. Ghouls were considered very powerful adversaries. They were also used as the personal guardians of the Prince of Shadows.

Irilian Order – Founded on the banks of the Iril River in the year 2220 BL by three former wizards of the Fire Order. The Irilian Order is one of the three major orders of wizards in the Southern Lands of Veredor. The Irilians generally focus their studies on understanding the natural world and working with men and other creatures for the good of all. They worked primarily throughout the Far Western Lands of Veredor and were revered in those lands. They also worked closely with the Fiorian Knights, the Tabarian Knights, and the monarchies of Dravania and Iarthar. They were often at odds with the Zyranian Order.

Irilian Star, The – The Irilian Star is a crystal amulet carried by the leader of the Irilian Order. In ancient times the Irilian Order learned how to store raw power inside crystals. Such stored power could be used at a later time making the carrier of the Irilian

Star many times more powerful than an ordinary wizard. The Irilian Star was built in the year 1675 BL.

Kaloren of Bergoth – Kaloren was the second last Gatekeeper of the Fiorian Order. She was born in the village of Bergoth in the land of Everdon. After a chance meeting with the Fiorian Roarna she undertook a dangerous adventure to return the Chalai to Emeril. She became a Fiorian and later aided the Irvarians in a war against the Skatheans in Vastoria. She led an army that liberated Vastoria from Skatheans who had taken hold of the lower regions of the Adira River. After the victory she was named Gatekeeper of Emeril and given the Sword of Light. Elons Ecorian visited Emeril and agreed to join a mission to help King Ignis liberate Ortaria from the Northern Sorcerer Azagord and his army from Kaznor. Kaloren was the leader of a group of Fiorians who went east to challenge Azagord. Kaloren and Elons married at Stonehaven. They went on to Ortaria and fought against Azagord, forcing the sorcerer to retreat across to Zyran where a final battle was staged at the gates of the Citadel of Zyran. Kaloren became pregnant and later gave birth to Eben Ecorian.

Kaznor Empire – Situated in the north of Veredor. The Kaznor Empire was never a part of the Ecorian Empire and was often at odds with the kingdoms of the South after the fall of the Ecorian Empire. The Empire is home to the Skathean Order and the Northern Sorcerers.

Lesser Creatures – The lesser creatures include but are not limited to: Foxes, Wolves, Bears, Deer, Jackals, Mountain Lions, Possums, Squirrels, Owls, Birds, Eagles, Hawks, Falcons, Owls, Horses, Cattle, Sheep, Goats, Badgers, Lions, Donkeys, Dogs, Mice, Rats, Bees, Insects, Spiders, and Fish.

Lumen – Lumen was an Astarian who instructed the first wizards in the ways of Astarian magic. He saw that men and mer were vulnerable to attack if the Prince of Shadows should ever return. He founded the

Fire Order to protect Veredor from such an invasion. Lumen left Veredor after completing this task.

Men – Men came to Veredor in the Forgotten Age to be the dwellers on land. They were invited to Veredor by the Astarians. The Astarians planned for men to inherit the land and the mer to inherit the sea. Men are capable of much good, but often their hearts are frail and they fear vulnerability. The fragility in their hearts makes other creatures afraid of them.

Mer (Merfolk) – The mer are a people of the sea. They came after the first arrival at the invitation of the Astarians. They are good natured humanlike people who live deep in the seas and oceans and have the ability to breathe underwater. Mer often live for hundreds of years. They occasionally venture into rivers and lakes. They are allied with the Astarian Casimir. When on land they appear as extremely beautiful women and very handsome men. They are rarely seen on land and only a few instances were recorded. The population of mer never increases because the mer can only have one son and one daughter. Eryna, a princess of the mer, married an Ecorian, and it is said that this was the reason that the Ecorian Emperors could only have one son or daughter. The marriage made the Ecorians into a bridge between the two races and provided the Ecorians with secret abilities, especially around water and the sea.

Muckron Bane Knights – Were an order of knights from the Far Western Lands of Veredor. They formed as an order to contest groups of muckrons that threatened towns and villages in Iarthar and Dravania. The order was completely destroyed in the final wars before the return of the Ecorian Empire.

Muckrons – Muckrons are large humanoid creatures that are often described as pig men. They stand between six and seven feet tall and have a head that resembles a wild boar or pig, dark fur, and clawed hands. They come from a world beyond Veredor where they were once the predominant species, but they consumed all the resources of their own world and journeyed through the cosmos searching for new worlds to consume. They played a lesser role in the first battles of the Forgotten Age. The Prince of Shadows encountered the muckrons in the Desert of Eternal Loneliness and later brought an army of muckrons to Veredor to serve him in his battle against Fiora and the Knights of Shidon. Most of the muckrons were killed in the battle, but some remained in the wilderness and caused trouble throughout the later ages.

Nodd Colony, The – The Nodd Colony was a very small colony of men that was founded in the land of Scaldonia in the Forgotten Age. It was so small that it was not considered one of the colonies that formed the people of Veredor. Little is known about the Nodd Colony; however, many people from Scaldonia still use names that are considered Noddian. It is said the Umblan Colony in Silvor was so successful that they eventually populated Scaldonia and assimilated the remnants of the Noddian Colony.

Northern Sorcerers – Before the dragons left Veredor they instructed several men in their magical arts. They did this in order to help men to protect Veredor from evil, but the dragons did not possess the wisdom to realise that their method was not suitable for men. The dragon magical arts relied on the ability to consume one's own essence. Men would often consume their own hearts and grow to be evil and fall into self-obsession and debauchery. The Northern Sorcerers were always considered the most powerful of all the magical orders.

Oracles – Oracles are Astarians who possessed the skill of seeing clearly into the future. There were three oracles in Veredor. They were all hunted down and killed by the Prince of Shadows upon his return to

Veredor. The Gerish Oracle (also known as the Scaldonian Oracle) revealed to the Prince of Shadows that the Ecorian line was not yet extinct and that only the Ecorian with the Sword of Light could stand in the way of his conquest of Veredor.

Prince of Shadows, The – The Prince of Shadows was a revered Astarian at the time of the first arrival. His former name was only known by the Astarians. He battled bravely in the first wars of the Forgotten Age. Only Fiora could match his ability in battle. He fell from grace in the Forgotten Age and led armies of monsters against the other Astarians. He killed many Astarians including Airleas, who was the carrier of the Sword of Midlight. The Prince of Shadows carried the Sword of Darkness. He was cast out of Veredor by the Astarian Fiora and had the Cosmic Gate sealed against his return.

Seven Relics, The – There were seven objects brought to Veredor by the Astarians at the time of the first arrival that were forged by a being who gifted Veredor to the Astarians. The Seven Relics were: the Three Swords, the Chalai, the Silver Leaf, the Star of the North, and the Sun Stone. All seven of the relics increased the power of the carrier in different ways.

Shapeshifters – Shapeshifters were brought by the Prince of Shadows to Veredor in the Forgotten Age. Shapeshifters can change their form at will and increase or decrease their overall size over time. They are a parasitic lifeform. They will take the form of the dominant creature in any given environment. They survive as parasites by infiltrating the social hierarchy. They can sense the presence of other Shapeshifters and can only breed with their own kind. They are manipulative and unpredictable and will only serve another out of fear. They possess a slightly higher level of intelligence than the average man. They have no other inherent magical abilities. They were used by the Prince of Shadows to infiltrate the societies of men, mer, and sprites in the Forgotten Age. A Shapeshifter was used by the Prince of Shadows to impersonate King Ignis of Ortaria in the last age.

Shidon – The Fortress of Shidon was built by the Star King at the end of the Forgotten Age to help Fiora overcome the Prince of Shadows. It is situated in a remote location at the northern edge of the Great Mountains on the Alber side. The Prince of Shadows laid siege to the fortress with a massive army of muckrons. He was defeated by Fiora and the Knights of Shidon and banished from Veredor. Because of its remote location very few people ever returned to the fortress.

Silver Leaf, The – One of the Seven Relics of the Astarians. The Silver Leaf was worn on a chain and provided the wearer with protection from all harmful attacks. It was worn by the wife of the Ecorian Emperors and later was given to Kaloren who wore the Silver Leaf when she challenged the Prince of Shadows in the Hall of Zarkanor.

Skathean Empire, The – The Skathean Empire was an evil empire that was formed in the Eastern Lands from the year 968 BL by the Skathean Brackin. The empire lasted until the year 686 BL. The Skathean Empire was ruled from the Isles of Dawn by a Skathean who carried the Sword of Darkness. The era is also known as the Dark Age of Veredor. The lands of the east greatly suffered under Skathean rule, and it is said by many that the Eastern Lands never fully recovered after the fall of the Skathean Empire.

Skatheans – The Skathean Order are an evil order of knights founded by the fallen Fiorian Krogin and the sorceress Scathea. They historically wielded considerable political influence in the Kaznor Empire and the Kingdom of Alber. They were the main antagonists of the Fiorian Order. Many battles were fought between the two opposing orders. The Fiorians prevented the Skatheans from gaining a foothold in the Southern Lands.

Sprites - Sprites are good natured creatures. They rarely reach a foot tall and they often have pale green skin and clothe themselves in fine linen. They are crafty and said to be good at making fine clothing and complex instruments. Most sprites wear long pointy hats that often nearly double the height of the sprite. They are very reclusive in nature. Sprites came with the Astarians as helpers in the time of the first arrival. Sprites have some limited magical abilities and they live in small family groups. There are three categories of sprites: The Water Sprites, who work with the mer; the Mountains Sprites, who live in high remote places; and the Earth Sprites, who often live underground or in forest glades, especially around mushroom patches. Sprites and Blue Caps are often adversaries.

Star King, The – The Star King was brought by the Prince of Shadows to Veredor at the time of the last wars of the Forgotten Age. He belongs to a rare race of cosmic builders and architects. He constructed the Fortress of Zarkanor for the Prince of Shadows in exchange for knowledge of Astarian magic. The Prince of Shadows revealed some magic to the Star King in exchange for finishing Zarkanor. After the exchange was complete the Prince of Shadows refused to return the Star King to his home world. The Prince of Shadows tried to force the Star King to continue building fortresses. The Star King refused and grew angry. He fought the Prince of Shadows in the grounds of Zarkanor. The Prince of Shadows prevailed and banished the Star King into the wilderness of Veredor. The Star King later aided Fiora in her struggle against the Prince of Shadows. He built Shidon as a fortress for Fiora and the Knights of Shidon. In the later ages he wandered the lands of Veredor seeking a way to return to his home world. The name Star King was given to him by men; his real name was never known.

Star of the North, The – The Star of the North is a relic of the Astarian people. Its powers are numerous and mysterious. The Star of the North was thrown into the sea by Artus Ecorian in the year 1700 BL.

Stone Horsemen – Stone Horsemen are humanoid monsters made from a combination of stone and fire. The Astarians believed that they were constructed by the Prince of Shadows using a similar method that was used to build the gargoyles. Stone Horsemen ride horses that are of the same stone and fire constitution. Thousands of Stone Horsemen were brought to Veredor by the Prince of Shadows to fight the Knights of Shidon in the final battle of the Forgotten Age. The Knights of Shidon destroyed all the Stone Horsemen in the army of the Prince of Shadows. They were not seen again until the wars of liberation.

Sun Stone, The – The Sun Stone was used by the Astarians to navigate the cosmos. The amulet is capable of opening gateways to any place in the cosmos. The Sun Stone was given to the mer by the Astarian Fiora before she left Veredor. It was treasured by the mer and they used its power to light the depths of the ocean; although they lacked the ability and knowledge to use it to travel beyond the Cosmic Gate. It was the only object that could open a way through the Cosmic Gate.

Sword of Darkness, The – The Sword of Darkness was one of the Three Swords of the Astarian people. The Sword of Darkness was originally a weapon used to defend Veredor. It became corrupted when it was used against the good creatures of Veredor by the Prince of Shadows. The Sword of Darkness was buried by the Fiorian Knights after the Prince of Shadows was cast out of Veredor. Krogin, the first Skathean, discovered the hidden location of the Sword of Darkness and took it for himself. He used the sword against the Fiorian Knights. For many centuries the Sword of Darkness was used by the strongest knight of the Skathean Order. The symbolic leader of the Skathean Order was always the Skathean who carried the Sword of Darkness. Upon returning to Veredor the Prince of Shadows killed the Skathean with the Sword of Darkness and instantly became the leader of the Skathean Order.

Sword of Light, The (The Ecorian Sword) – The Sword of Light was one of the three Astarian swords and also one of the Seven Relics brought by the Astarians to Veredor in the time of the first arrival. It was crafted by a being greater than the Astarians and given to the Astarians by the creature known as Pilgrim. The Sword of Light played a major role in all the battles of the Forgotten Age. It was used by the Astarian Fiora to contest the Prince of Shadows in the final battle of the Forgotten Age. The Sword of Light was later given to Toranah of the Knights of Shidon and later handed onto Jeriel the Just, the first Ecorian Emperor. It became a symbol of the Ecorian Emperors and was lost in the River Siarglas. It was later found by Saidrin the Great who joined the Fiorian Knights and later became their leader. After this time it was hidden and guarded by the Fiorian Order until the return of the Prince of Shadows when the sword was reunited with the Ecorian descendent.

Sword of Midlight, The – One of the Three Swords of the Astarian people. The sword was carried by the Astarian Airleas in the battles of the Forgotten Age. The Sword of Midlight was lost at the end of the Forgotten Age. In the year 931 BL the Sword of Midlight was found by Emer Ecorian. From that day onward the sword was always carried by the Ecorian descendent until the time of liberation. The Sword of Midlight was generally considered marginally less powerful than the Sword of Light and the Sword of Darkness.

Tabarian Knights – The largest order of knights in the Far Western Lands of Veredor. They were instituted by the Ecorian Empress Galiana in the year 1870 BL in order to protect the western borders of the Ecorian Empire from invasion from the Kingdom of Coran and Alber. They are allied to the Ecorians before all others. They later became a politically powerful order of chivalrous knights and remained until the time of liberation when they fought alongside the Irilian Order against the armies of muckrons that invaded the Far Western Lands.

Takalian Knights – The Takalian Knights are an order of knights founded by the adventurer Takal in the year 468 BL. Takal was a master of swordsmanship and a hero to many people in Veredor. The Takalian Order was distinct from other orders as the prime precept of the order was allegiance to the king of the land. This meant that at times Takalians would occasionally fight each other in battle when in the service of opposing monarchs.

Ten Monachies of the Ecorian Arbiters, The – The Ten Monarchies of the Ecorian Arbiters were the kingdoms that followed the end of the Ecorian Empire. They were mostly in the south of Veredor and included: Scaldonia, Ortaria, Silvor, Ateria, Vastoria, Irvaria, Dravania, Iarthar, Roven, and Glenia.

Three Swords, The – The Three Swords were the only weapons brought to Veredor in the first arrival at the beginning of the Forgotten Age. They were treasured by the Astarians. The swords were forged by an unknown maker in the time before Veredor was settled by Astarians. Each sword magnifies the ability of the one that wields it by a measure of the belief and strength of will of the owner. The swords also protect their owners from ill will and magical curses. They cannot protect the owner from his or her own evil thoughts. They were used extensively throughout the wars of the Forgotten Age and played a major role in many battles. After the fall of the Prince of Shadows the three swords became known as: the Sword of Light, the Sword of Midlight, and the Sword of Darkness.

Umblan – The people of eastern Veredor are mostly descendants of the Umblan people who settled in the land of Silvor in the Forgotten Age.

Veredor – In ancient times the world was called Veredord by men and later was simplified to Veredor. The world was given the name Veredor by the first men who arrived in Veredor. The Astarians use several other names to describe Veredor. It is thought to mean: the world of the true, or the fair and gentle world. All men throughout all the lands of Veredor use the term. The mer and sprites also refer to the world as Veredor.

Veredorian Language – The common language of men and mer is a close variant of the Astarian language. Originally there were three distinct groups of men that arrived in Veredor late in the Forgotten Age. Each group spoke their own language. The Eriulan Colony was in the land of Iarthar and originally spoke a distinct language; however, this language was lost at the beginning of the Forgotten Age and only remains in the names of places in the west. It is said the Irilian Order still maintain the ability to speak some old Eriulan. The second settlement was in northern Irvaria and was called the Alblan Colony who also spoke a distinct language that was completely lost over time. The third settlement was in the east in the land of Silvor and was known as the Umbralan Colony. The original Umbralan language continued to be spoken by people living in remote villages in Zyran and on some of the smaller islands in the Isles of Dawn until the return of the Ecorian Empire.

Wyverns – Wyverns are small dragons that are sometimes referred to as orms or simply as dragons. They should not be confused with Great Dragons. Wyverns are extremely rare. Wyverns came to Veredor in the Forgotten Age. They were the main antagonists in the first wars of the Forgotten Age when thousands of them attacked the abodes of the Astarians. They vary in size from two to ten meters. There are two varieties of wyvern; the most prominent variety are smaller and have wings and are simply referred to as wyverns. The Lindworms are larger and wingless. Some wyverns possess magical abilities. Many wyverns can hypnotise their victims by making eye contact, especially if their opponent has a weak will. They possess a similar level of intelligence to that of men. They are often self-obsessed and lonesome creatures, but they will work together under a common leader if they see a personal benefit.

Zyranian Enforcers – Zyranian Enforcers are an elite group of warrior wizards formed by the Order of Zyran and under direct control of the Gatekeeper of Zyran. They were formed in response to Azer Ecorian attempting to reduce the Zyranian Order's influence in the Eastern Lands of Veredor. Zyranian Enforcers focus their entire training on the acquisition of magic that is useful in battle. Generally there were about a dozen Zyranian Enforcers at any one time.

Zyranian Order – The Zyranian Order of wizards was founded by Jeriel the Just in the year 2000 BL. The Ecorian Emperor gathered together many isolated wizards and encouraged them to work together for the benefit of all. He gave these wizards the Island of Zyran and they formed the Council of Zyran which governed the island and the Zyranian Order. The Zyranians focused their studies on the acquisition of knowledge. They heavily influenced the kingdoms of the Eastern Lands throughout the ages. For most of history they were the largest of the three southern magic orders and often found themselves at odds with the Irilian Order. They were also suspicious of the Fire Order. The Zyranian Order suffered greatly from several invasions of the Eastern Lands. The first significant invasion was when the Northern Sorcerer Ondtast conquered Zyran in 1658 BL. It is said that a curse remained in the Zyranian Order because many Zyranians willingly served Ondtast against the Ecorian Empire. The second major event that severely harmed the order was the Skathean Empire that ruled the Eastern Lands from the years 968 BL to 686 BL. The Skatheans turned the Zyranians to evil ways and for almost three centuries the Zyranian Order served Skathean overlords in the armies of the Skathean Empire. After the fall of the Skathean Empire the Zyranian Order returned to their original precepts, but a tendency toward evil remained in the order.

THE HISTORY OF VEREDOR

This is an account of the history of the men of Veredor from the end of the Forgotten Age to the birth of Eben Ecorian.

2515 BL – The Astarian Fiora banishes the Prince of Shadows into the outer darkness beyond the Cosmic Gate. Fiora hands the Sword of Light to Sir Toranah, the last remaining knight of the Knights of Shidon. Fiora is never again seen in Veredor.

2500 BL – Toranah the Mystic appears in the west by the Crystal Lake and gathers a group of young men and women together to form the Fiorian Knights.

2450 BL – Toranah the Mystic with his followers cross the Great Mountains through the ancient pass and expand the Fiorian Knights.

2435 BL – The Fiorian Toranah dies in Silvor.

2350 BL – The Astarian Lumen instructs a group of men in the magic ways of the Astarians. His students form the Fire Order. Lumen leaves Veredor.

2340 BL – The Fire Order build the Temple of Fire at the northern edge of the Old Guardian Mountains at the place where Lumen lived.

2310 BL – The Fiorian Order battles the Dark Clans in Southern Iarthar. Many Fiorians die. The Dark Clans are destroyed.

2305 BL – The seven remaining Great Dragons teach their magic ways to the people of the north. The powerful students of the dragons become known as the Northern Sorcerers.

2300 BL – The Kaznor Empire is formed as the clans in the north gather under one emperor.

2280 BL – The Northern Sorcerers turn to evil around this time. In the land of Kaznor they discover the Star of the North, one of the Seven Relics of the Astarians. They seek to rule Veredor using the Star of the North.

2240 BL – The Fiorian Order discovers the existence of the Star of the North. It is known as the Great Weapon by the people of the time. The Fiorians plan to destroy the Star of the North. A group of mighty Fiorians storm the stronghold of the Northern Sorcerers at Lagad on the shores of the Bay of Night in Kaznor. They take the Star of the North and scatter the Northern Sorcerers.

2237 BL – The Fiorians attempt to destroy the Star of the North but find it cannot be ruined.

2220 BL – Several wizards leave the Tower of Fire and go west to form a new order. They establish the new order in Dravania by the Iril River. They later become known as the Irilian Order.

2190 BL – The Kingdom of Coran is formed in the Far West.

2170 BL – The Blue Caps of Vastoria and Ateria rebel against men. From this time onward the Blue Caps see men as a threat.

2150 BL – Tribes from Vastoria attack Ateria and occupy it for many years.

2110 BL – A flood in the Far Western Lands causes much suffering and destruction. The Irilian Order comes to the aid of the people which gives the order fame and favour for many years.

2100 BL – Jeriel the Just is born in the village of Fairlight (later Faircastle) in the land of Irvaria. End of the First Age.

2090 BL – Tribal wars become prevalent in the Eastern Lands.

2080 BL – Jeriel learns the ways of the Fiorians from Lorcan the Mystic, his mentor and friend. Jeriel is gifted in the Fiorian arts but refuses to enter the Fiorian Order.

2075 BL – Fairlight is raided by Vastorian clans. Lorcan is slain attempting to protect the village. Jeriel inherits the Sword of Light from Lorcan. The survivors of the raid on Fairlight flee north into the Endora Mountains where they live for ten years. Jeriel is said to have spent most of this time alone high in the mountains living in a cave.

2065 BL – Jeriel leaves the Endora Mountains and travels to Dravania and settles for some time by the Crystal Lake. He befriends the people of Dravania, and they are impressed by his nobility and wisdom.

2063 BL – Jeriel falls in love with Adira the Graced of Dravania. They are married this same year.

2061 BL – Jeriel has a vision of Lorcan and afterward begins his mission for peace in the Eastern Lands. He gathers many good men and several Fiorian Knights to aid him in his quest to bring peace to harmony to all the lands of Veredor.

2055 BL – Jeriel, riding with his followers, brings peace and casts out evil from the lands of Irvaria, the Irvarian lowlands (Everdon), and Vastoria.

2045 BL – Jeriel brings peace and unity to Ortaria, Silvor, Ateria, and the lower regions of Scaldonia.

2040 BL – Jeriel marches across the Ancient Pass through the Great Mountains and enters the land of Dravania. He befriends the Irilian Order and with their help brings unity to the Far Western Lands.

2030 BL – Jeriel returns to Irvaria and begins the construction of the great city of Faircastle on the site of his home village that was destroyed years earlier.

2010 BL – Jeriel ventures across the Endora Mountains to the forests of Kaznor and is given the Silver Leaf by an Astarian named Acelin who once lived deep in the forest.

2008 BL – The Ecorian Empire is formed and Jeriel is elected emperor of all the lands he helped to bring unity and peace to. The Empire is later named the Ecorian Empire.

2007 BL – Jeriel the Just has a vision of an Ecorian Emperor riding a union across a field against an army of monsters. The field is named Jeriel's Field. From this day onward Jeriel takes on the white unicorn as the symbol of the Ecorian Empire.

2000 BL – The Ecorian Empire is peaceful and strong. The Ecorian encourages his empire to value peace, honour, and truth. He gathers together many isolated wizards throughout his empire and forms the Order of Zyran, a powerful assembly of wizards who work for the good of all and they make a home on the Island of Zyran in the far east of Veredor. Jeriel forms an accord with the Fire Order. The Fire Order agrees to be allies of the Ecorian Emperor and to aid the Ecorian Emperor if a request is made.

1995 BL – Jeriel the Just dies in Faircastle and Adira dies seven days later to follow her love.

1994 BL – Aldis Ecorian, Jeriel's son, is crowned Emperor of the Ecorian Empire. He works with all his might for the good of all men. He is revered by all.

1990 BL – Aldis Ecorian sails from Everdon to Ortaria to see his empire. He is shipwrecked on the southern coast of Ateria and rescued by a mermaid named Eryna. He is spellbound by her beauty and requests for her hand in marriage. The mer are outraged by the request and refuse. Eryna does not heed the warnings of her people and leaves the sea and goes to Aldis. They marry that same year and form the only union between men and mer in all of history.

1985 BL – The Fiorian Order diminishes and is seen less frequently among men.

1980 BL – All those who are sick are mysteriously healed throughout all the lands of Veredor. The year 1980 becomes known as the year of healing (The Year of Light). An autumn festival is celebrated among some of the people of Veredor (especially the Jeanians, Empyrians, and Irvarians) in memory of the Year of Light right up until the return of the Ecorian Empire.

1955 BL – A dark and mysterious force comes to power in the land of Roven, turning the people to evil ways. It was later said to be a Ri Draug from the Forgotten Age. As an older man Aldis Ecorian leads an army across the ancient pass through the Great Mountains and defeats the shadowy enemies at Laravin on the Siarglas River. To the sorrow of the empire Aldis Ecorian is slain in the battle. The Sword of Light, once held by Jeriel the Just and Lorcan the Mystic, falls into the river and is not recovered. After the death of Aldis Ecorian his true love Eryna returns to the sea to live with the mer.

1954 BL – Tiernan, the son of Aldis and Eryna, becomes the Ecorian Emperor. He strengthens the armies of the empire.

1949 BL – An oracle appears in the Far Western Lands and takes refuge in the Oran Mountains.

1938 BL – Tiernan seeks to recover the Sword of Light from the Siarglas River but fails in his task.

1920 BL – Fiorians become extremely rare around this time.

1912 BL – Bandits ravage the land of Scaldonia. Tiernan goes north to destroy the armies of bandits. Tiernan Ecorian decides to live in a cave in the Deep Desert of Vastoria. He lives with the people who are called the Jeanians. He becomes known as Tiernan the Silent.

1905 BL – An oracle appears in the Eastern Lands and takes refuge in the Gerish Highlands of Scaldonia.

1901 BL – An age long war begins between the tribes of Alber and the Kaznor Empire.

1892 BL – Creatures of darkness appear in the Cold Lands of Scaldonia and gradually migrate south. Tiernan sends an army to destroy them.

1889 BL – Tiernan searches once again for the lost Sword of Light but again doesn't find it.

1881 BL – Tiernan returns to Faircastle and dies. His only child Galiana Ecorian becomes the Empress.

1875 BL – The Kingdom of Coran raises an army under King Ravadrin the Proud and invades Dravania. Galiana leads an army against the Coranese force and takes victory near Jenrind on the Star River in Iarthar.

1871 BL – An oracle appears in the north and takes refuge in the Eranai Mountains near the Silver Lake in Kaznor.

1870 BL – Galiana establishes the Tabarian Knights. The Tabarian Knights are given the task of protecting the Dravanian border at the Tabarian River.

1860 BL – The Order of Zyran requests more independence from the Ecorian Empire. Galiana forms the High Council of Zyran to rule the island of Zyran in accordance with the laws of the Ecorian Empire.

1849 BL – Vastoria faces a terrible drought. Many people flee the arid lands.

1828 BL – Galiana is warned by an unknown mystic that a power from the north may one day destroy the Ecorian Empire.

1816 BL – Galiana falls deathly ill. A cure is sought after by many in the empire.

1815 BL – Edur the Unrelenting, a hero from Ateria, begins his journey to find the cure to Galiana's illness. He journeys into the Swamps of Scaldonia to consult the Gerish Oracle.

1809 BL – Edur ventures far and eventually comes to Alber. He discovers the cure in the Icy Lands north of the Anga forest.

1806 BL – Edur returns to Faircastle after a great adventure and passes the cure to the dying Galiana. Galiana is cured.

1800 BL – A statue of Edur is placed in main square of Faircastle and remains there throughout the ages.

1791 BL Galiana dies in Orelin where she lived the remainder of her days. Her son, Galeran Ecorian, becomes emperor.

1789 BL – Galeran searches for the Sword of Light in the Siarglas River. He fails in his task like his grandfathers did before him.

1779 BL – A war begins the west on the border of the Kingdom of Coran and Iarthar. The Tabarian Knights battle the Coranese forces and hold them back.

1774 BL – Galeran travels to Coran to make peace.

1773 BL – Galeran builds a friendship with Rogan the Iron Willed, the King of Coran. Peace returns between the Empire and the Kingdom of Coran.

1762 BL – Evil grows in Ateria. An evil army is formed which quickly sweeps across Ateria.

1760 BL – Galeran underestimates the dark enemies; his army is beaten at the southern edge of the Endless Wall Mountains.

1759 BL – The evil forces in Ateria begin building a fortress at the sight of their victory over the Ecorian army. They begin to stretch their influence into Vastoria.

1757 BL – Galeran raises an army in Irvaria Minor (Everdon) and leads his army through the Grey Pass and across Vastoria. A battle is fought at the gates of the enemy fortress and Galeran takes victory.

1756 BL – Ateria is freed completely from the forces of evil. Galeran returns into the west.

1749 BL – Galeran lives a Ghrian on the Merhome Sea with his wife and son. The Ecorian Empire is peaceful for some time.

1731 BL – Galeran dies at Ghrian. His son Artus Ecorian becomes emperor.

1730 BL – Artus settles in Faircastle, the city of his forefathers.

1728 BL – Artus searches for the lost Sword of Light in the Siarglas River, but he fails like his ancestors did.

1722 BL – The Zyranian Order find the Star of the North.

1718 BL – Artus travels around his empire seeking the approval of his people.

1715 BL – Artus seeks out the Fiorian Knights and finds few remain.

1706 BL – Artus seeks out the Gerish Oracle in the swamps of Scaldonia, but fails in his search.

1701 BL – Artus discovers that the Zyranian Order possess the Star of the North. He requests that they return the dangerous relic to its hiding place. The High Council of Zyran vote against returning the Star of the North. The Zyranians believe the Star of the North will bring them power above all others. They are corrupted by the great power of the relic. Artus Ecorian seeks the help of the Irilian Order. He asks them to recover the Star of the North from the Zyranians.

1700 BL – An assembly of powerful of Irilian wizards travel from Dravania to Zyran and demand that the Zyranians hand over the Star of the North. The Zyranians refuse and fight off the Irilians and force the Irilians back. Later in that same year the Zyranians send a force to avenge the earlier attack by the Irilians. A battle is fought at the junction of the Irilian and Oread rivers. The Zyranians use the Star of the North against the Irilians. The Irilian Order is scattered. Most of the wizards of the Irilian Order are killed in the battle. The battle sparks a feud between the two orders that lasts for many ages. Artus, angered by the Zyranians attack on the Irilians, takes his army to Zyran and overwhelms the Zyranian Order. Artus Ecorian takes the Star of the North and throws it from the side of his ship. The ancient relic was never again heard of by men.

1680 BL – A powerful and evil sorcerer named Kodren the Cruel appears in the Far Western Lands and comes to power in Roven.

1679 BL – Artus Ecorian leads an army to Roven and overthrows Kodren's rule. Kodren escapes on a ship and sails away to Alber. Kodren later becomes High King of Alber.

1678 BL – Artus falls ill and dies in Faircastle.

1677 BL – Lennox Ecorian becomes the Ecorian Emperor.

1675 BL – The Irilian Order reforms and builds a fortress at the junction of the Iril and Oread Rivers. The fortress is called the Iril Fortress throughout the ages. The leaders of the Irilian Order construct the Irilian Star to help prevent the Irilian Order from ever being scattered again.

1672 BL – The Star King steals the Chalai from the Oracle of the Oran Mountains. His hand is cut off by the Oran Oracle, yet he escapes with the Chalai.

1670 BL – A powerful Northern Sorcerer named Ondtast comes to power in the land of Kaznor. His power is unlike any other sorcerer seen before. He carries with him the secrets of the Northern Sorcerers of the First Age, and his power corrupts him.

1669 BL – Ondtast reveals his thirteen Athad who he has trained as sorcerer-warriors to serve him. They are: Singar the Terrible, Gammak the Grim, Korb the Fearsome, Ertch the Pale, Orgoth the Violent, Crymak the Insidious, Eschak the Bitter, Titark the Murderous, Vidgar the Slothful, Berok the Ugly, Sleshkak the Tempter, Hozkork the Maniac, and Fudo the Cunning.

1665 BL – Ondtast takes control of Kaznor and begins building great armies with thoughts of conquering all of Veredor for himself.

1663 BL – Lennox Ecorian searches for the Sword of Light in the Siarglas River but fails to find it.

1659 BL – Ondtast sails through the Icy Sea with a massive fleet and invades Scaldonia. He divides his Athad servants and sends them on different tasks to prepare for the coming of his new empire.

1658 BL – Singar the Terrible takes control of Alber as Hozkork the Maniac arrives in Dravania and seeks to take control of the land and its people. Lennox Ecorian raises an army to contest the invasion of the Ecorian Empire. Ondtast invades Ortaria and takes over Zyran. He turns many Zyranian wizards to his evil ways. Half the Zyranian Order escape from Zyran.

1657 BL – Ondtast occupies Silvor and Ateria and begins invading Vastoria. The Athad are feared throughout the lands. Lennox leads his great army to meet the invaders in the Vastorian Wastes, but his army is shattered and forced to flee west back across Vastoria. Ondtast pursues Lennox and his remaining men. Ondtast follows Lennox into the Grey Pass.

1656 BL – Ondtast plans to slay Lennox Ecorian and take over the Ecorian Empire. Lennox calls on the Fiorians for help and gathers a small but valiant army on the western banks of the Everdon River. The Fire Order, at the request of the Ecorian, come down from the Tower of Fire and join Lennox's army. He is also joined by three Fiorian Knights: Alart the Wanderer, Ademar the Gentle, and Oisin the Firm. They await the coming of Ondtast and his army. The Athad gather to fight with their master in Irvaria Minor (Everdon). A great battle is fought across the river and Lennox Ecorian, with the Fiorians by his side, challenges the Athad and Ondtast. Lennox and the Fiorians slay all the Athad and cast Ondtast into the river. Ondtast is never seen again.

1655 BL – Lennox works to rebuild all that has been destroyed by Ondtast. Lennox grows tired in his efforts and sorrowful at the extent of the damage.

1654 BL – Lennox steps down as emperor and hands the throne to his son Ultan Ecorian.

1653 BL – Lennox Ecorian leaves Faircastle with his wife Dahirian the Silent and retires in silence in the Southern Forest (later the Forest of Sorrows).

1652 BL – The Star King begins a personal war with the Mountain Sprites of the Great Mountains. The Mountain Sprites flee from the Star King, and he destroys many of the hidden abodes of the sprites. Later the Fire Order come to the aid of the Mountain Sprites.

1650 BL – Ultan Ecorian journeys to the Western Oracle in the Oran Mountains and seeks council. He then searches for the Sword of Light but fails to find it.

1638 BL – Ultan falls in love and marries Ciaran of the Irilian Order.

1634 BL – Ultan lives with his wife in Dravania City on the Iril River.

1626 BL – Aluin Ecorian is born in Dravania.

1625 BL – The Fire Stone and Pure Flame of the Fire Order from the Old Guardian Mountains is stolen. They seek the help of the emperor to find it.

1624 BL – Ultan discovers the Fire Stone has been stolen by thieves and has been taken north to Kaznor. He gathers a group of valiant men to go with him north to recover it.

1622 BL - Ultan sails up the eastern coast and across the Icy Sea to Kaznor with his small band of adventurers. He discovers the Fire Stone has been taken to Garovna. Ultan is imprisoned in the Dungeons of Zarkanor before he can recover the Fire Stone.

1620 BL – Ultan Ecorian escapes the prison and makes his way to Garovna with the fire wizard Kaldo the Magnificent. He is thought to have perished by all the people of the Ecorian Empire by this time.

1619 BL – Ultan Ecorian finds the Fire Stone in the Tower of Garov. A battle occurs and Ultan escapes with the Fire Stone and makes his way back to the Ecorian Empire.

1618 BL – Ultan returns to Faircastle and later to his wife in Dravania. The Fire Order thank him and reward him by making him a sword which they named, Fire of Day. He graciously accepts the sword, but still his heart harkens for the Sword of Light.

1611 BL – Ultan Ecorian journeys north to seek out the Fortress Shidon in the deep north. He goes only with his prized magical sword, Fire of Day.

1608 BL – Ultan Ecorian enters Alber and has a vision of the unicorn at Silvari on the Zarakini River. He then heads for the western coast of Alber.

1607 BL – Ultan Sails to the Island of Pa across the Tabani Sea. His ship is wrecked south of Pa. He alone survives because of being half mer in nature. He swims for many days to reach Pa.

1606 BL – Ultan Ecorian wanders throughout the Pa Mountains. It is said that he sighted a unicorn running across a mountain ridge. Ultan Ecorian returns south to the Ecorian Empire.

1605 BL – Ultan returns to Dravania and falls ill. A year later Ultan Ecorian dies in Dravania.

1604 BL – Aluin Ecorian becomes emperor and returns to live in Faircastle.

1603 BL – Aluin Ecorian grows restless of ruling the Ecorian Empire and seeks a simple life.

1602 BL – The Pegasus is sighted in the southern regions of Veredor.

1601 BL – Aluin Ecorian sets out to search for the Pegasus.

1600 BL – Aluin Ecorian finds the Pegasus on a small island in the Southern Sea. Aluin Ecorian mounts the Pegasus and asks to be taken beyond the boundaries of Veredor. Aluin doesn't return and there is no heir to the throne of the Ecorian Empire. The Ecorian Age ends.

1600 BL – Aluin Ecorian, believing that the time of the Ecorian Empire has come to an end, secretly lives out his life in Ateria as a woodcutter and marries a village woman.

1595 BL – The Ecorian Arbiters of the empire argue over who is to become the next emperor as there is no Ecorian descendent.

1591 BL – The Ecorian Empire is divided into the following kingdoms by the Ecorian Arbiters: Irvaria, Irvaria Minor, Vastoria, Ateria, Silvor, Ortaria, Scaldonia, Zyran (ruled by the Council of Zyran), Dravania, Iarthar, Roven, and Glenia.

1590 BL – The new independent monarchies begin with complete sovereignty. Each is governed by an Ecorian Arbiter.

1586 BL – Darkness creeps out of the swamps of Ortaria. Draugs appear in Ortaria.

1585 BL – The Merus River of Ortaria is poisoned as evil forces rise to power in the Altus Forest. Many innocent people die in Ortaria.

1582 BL – The evil forces build an army under a warlord named Toki. Toki leads his army to Sevadir and sacks the city.

1581 BL – King Redron of Ortaria leads a small army south to challenge Toki. Toki charms Redron and marries his daughter Livia.

1580 BL – Redron falls ill and dies. Toki becomes King of Ortaria and leads the people into evil ways.

1579 BL – Other kingdoms become concerned and forge an alliance to challenge King Toki's rule in Ortaria.

1577 BL – Scaldonia and Silvor invade Ortaria. King Toki is slain. Livia becomes queen of Ortaria and harmony is restored. Peace settles on the kingdoms of the south for some time.

1558 BL – The Council of Zyran begins to exert influence over the Eastern Lands.

1555 BL – A revolt occurs in Vastoria and the kingdom is divided into north and south for many years.

1551 BL – Varius the Mighty becomes leader of the Council of Zyran.

1545 BL – Varius builds a formal academy in Zyran and a great library in Zyran. A class of student wizards begins studying in Zyran.

1540 BL – Varius is poisoned by an unknown enemy and dies.

1539 BL – A battle occurs in the township of Zyran between good and evil wizards of the Zyranian Order. The evil wizards of the Zyranian Order are banished from the island.

1538 BL – Evil grows in the Eastern Lands as the expelled sorcerers exert their influences over the kingdoms.

1536 BL – The Isles of Dawn separate from Ortaria and Silvor and become an independent kingdom.

1531 BL – The city of Orani upon the main island in the Isles of Dawn is completed. Orani is considered the most beautiful city on the eastern coastline of Veredor.

1526 BL – The Fiorian Knights discover the Star King has built a castle high in the Great Mountains.

1525 BL – A group of Fiorians visit the Star King. The Star King forces the Fiorians from his home. From this time onward the Star King is seen as a threat by the Fiorian Order.

1521 BL – The Star King builds a kingdom in the Great Mountains. He befriends the Blue Caps. The Blue Caps revere the Star King as their king and attempt to help him discover a mechanism for opening the Cosmic Gate.

1515 BL – The Mountain Kingdom grows within the Great Mountains hidden away from the world of men.

1510 BL – Mer are said to have entered the Merhome Sea and taken refuge at this time.

1506 BL – King Lee the Solid of Iarthar marries Princess Emer the Star of Glenia, forging an age-old alliance.

1501 BL – The ancient pass through the Great Mountains which was used throughout the Ecorian times becomes treacherous around this year.

1495 BL – The Mountain Kingdom of the Star King continues to grow and prosper and remains hidden in the mountains.

1491 BL – Bandits ravage Irvaria Minor (Everdon) leading to a war lasting twelve years.

1490 BL – Prince Treli of Coran is shipwrecked in the Merhome Sea and saved by mermaids. They request his help to recover the stolen Sun Stone.

1489 BL – Treli begins his quest to find the Sun Stone.

1488 BL – Treli searches the Far Western Lands but fails to find the Sun Stone. The Oran Oracle tells Treli to seek out the Fire Order.

1487 BL – Treli and a Fiorian Knight named Riordan the Unfathomable travel across the Great Mountains to Irvaria to seek the Fire Order in the Old Guardian Mountains.

1486 BL – Treli crosses Vastoria and enters the Endless Wall Mountains and battles a great red lindworm that stole the Sun Stone from the mer. Treli is victorious and returns with the Sun Stone to the mer in the Merhome Sea.

1480 BL – Kertax the Tyrant sails from across the Eastern Ocean and first appears off the coast this year.

1479 BL – Kertax destroys and plunders twenty one ships this year.

1478 BL – The kings of Ortaria, Silvor and Ateria seek to capture or slay Kertax, but Kertax escapes them taking another fifteen ships this year. He is feared greatly by all seafaring folk.

1477 BL – Kertax takes thirty ships this year.

1476 BL – The coastal kingdoms call upon the Fiorian Order to help them rid the sea of Kertax the Tyrant.

1475 BL – One Fiorian Knight named Ronan the Benevolent seeks out Kertax across the sea. He finds Kertax and inspires Kertax to turn from his violent ways and return across the sea from where he came. Kertax takes his great hoard of treasure and leaves the coast of Veredor forever.

1468 BL – King Ansurr comes to the throne of Scaldonia and does much good throughout his kingdom. Scaldonia grows to be prosperous.

1460 BL – King Ansurr establishes the Council of Kings. The Council of Kings brings much peace and wealth to the Eastern Lands.

1452 BL – War grows in the west between Coran and Dravania.

1449 BL – King Treli overcomes the advancing Dravanians on the Caran River sending them fleeing back home to Dravania.

1445 BL – The Kingdom of Coran grows to great power under King Treli. The mer people are often seen in this time and dwell just off the coast of Coran in the Merhome Sea.

1437 BL – King Treli dies of old age.

1436 BL – The mer people leave the Merhome Sea and are rarely seen after this time.

1426 BL – Plague strikes Roven and Glenia and many people die. Many Irilian wizards travel south. The Irilians cure many of the sick.

1415 BL – An evil curse takes hold in Zyran.

1412 BL – Teodric the Builder appears in Kingdom of Ateria. His origins are unknown. Teodric takes news to the king of Ateria about the growing evil in the east. A Fiorian Knight named Odger the Swift and a sorcerer named Ennius of Zyran travel with Teodric. Together they discover that Zyran is under the control of descendants of the ways of Ondtast.

1411 BL – Teodric, Odger, and Ennius flee north from Zyran and sail up the coast to Scaldonia where they escape the Zyranian Order at Havet Bay. Teodric, Ennius, and Odger travel across Scaldonia and make for the Iron Gate Pass. They hope to gain the help of the Irvarians.

1407 BL – The armies of Zyran conquer Ortaria. They then cross the Iron Gate Pass and invade Vastoria. Most of Vastoria falls under the rule of Zyran. Irvaria and part of Vastoria resist the armies of the east. Teodric gathers a small band of valiant men. They include Fiorian Knights and exiled wizards of Zyran, and the descendent of the Ecorian line, Cassian Ecorian.

1406 BL – Teodric and his band of warriors push back the armies of Zyran to the Iron Gate Pass. The war continues at the Edius Plateau and reaches a stalemate.

1405 BL –Teodric travels to Irvaria Minor (Everdon), leaving Cassian Ecorian to command his army at the Iron Gate Pass. Cassian Ecorian holds back the might of Zyran's armies. Teodric defeats King Brodon of Irvaria Minor who is conspiring with the enemy. Teodric raises his own army in Irvaria Minor and crosses the Grey Pass.

1404 BL – Teodric crosses the wastelands and liberates Darancra. He divides his army into two assemblies: one to guard the Iron Gate Pass and one to march into Ateria to oust the enemy forces.

1403 BL – Teodric liberates Ateria.

1402 BL – Teodric falls in love with Princess Avina of Vastoria, the only heir of the Ecorian Arbiter. They marry. He then marches through the Iron Gate Pass and crushes the Zyranian army. Teodric, in alliance with the Irvarians, invades Ortaria. Teodric, with the help of Cassian Ecorian, overcomes the evil wizards of Zyran at Ancora.

1398 BL – Teodric is made first King of Everdon and lives in Lucaria with his wife Avina who is a descendent of the Ecorian Arbiter. Peace comes to the lands for many years. Teodric works to make Lucaria into a beautiful port city. The lands in the east prosper.

1393 BL – Teodric helps the Irvarians to build the Fortress of Elcalee.

1389 BL – Teodric secures the pass through the Great Mountains.

1382 BL – Teodric secretly constructs the hidden Fortress of Emeril high in the Great Mountains. Emeril is built as a secret place of council and a refuge for the Fiorian Knights.

1379 BL – Teodric builds the Star House of Dravania for the Dravanian people.

1374 BL – Teodric begins to build the one hundred great towers of Zyran and the Citadel of Zyran as a reward for the Zyranian outcasts who fought by his side in the war.

1359 BL – Teodric finishes the Citadel of Zyran and all the towers.

1355 BL – Teodric builds the famed royal palace of Vastoria in Darancra.

1350 BL – Teodric builds the Chamber of Light in Ateria at Aruna.

1346 BL – Teodric is named Teodric the Builder by the common people.

1340 BL – Teodric takes his rest. The lands prosper.

1335 BL - Teodric dies of old age and is always remembered as a great king of the people.

1320 BL – Many Fiorian Knights retire to Emeril.

1310 BL – The Mountain Kingdom of the Star King prospers.

1300 BL – Evil grows in the forests of Southern Iarthar. The people of Laravin on the Sedente River grow fearful.

1299 BL – A draug is said to have emerged from the forest and turned the hearts of many men to evil. Laravin becomes well-fortified.

1295 BL – An evil warlord named Grobo the Draug Friend comes out of the forest and gathers an army north of Laravin. Grobo's army terrorises the villages north along the Siarglas.

1294 BL - Grobo and his host of evil men attack Laravin. Grobo declares himself king of all the lands between the Great Mountains and the Sea of Grass. The people of Laravin and the Siarglas River are heavily oppressed under Grobo's rule.

1292 BL – A small army sets out from Dravania to challenge Grobo's army at Laravin. Grobo destroys the small army and extends his borders further north into Iarthar.

1289 BL – A young oppressed fisherman's son named Saidrin draws the Sword of Light out of the sea whilst casting fishing nets in Laravin Bay. He takes the sword home with him, but he doesn't know the nature of his find.

1286 BL – Grobo gathers a large army in Laravin and plans to march on the town of Heida. Saidrin is forced to join Grobo's army.

1285 BL – Grobo marches with his army to Heida. Grobo is slain along the way by Saidrin in a duel. Grobo's men scatter without a leader. The power of the draug is removed. The people of Laravin are thankful to Saidrin. The draug that controlled Grobo seeks to destroy Saidrin, but it fears the Sword of Light.

1284 BL – Saidrin leaves Laravin. He travels across the Sea of Grass to Iarthar where he joins the Jenrind garrison and becomes a great swordsman. Saidrin becomes popular in Jenrind among the locals.

1281 BL – Saidrin leaves Jenrind and travels along the Star River to the Crystal Lake. He then journeys to the quiet village of Vorade.

1280 BL – Saidrin joins the watchmen of Vorade. The watchmen are impressed with his skills and knowledge.

1278 BL – Saidrin labours hard for the people of Vorade becoming respected by many.

1275 BL – A young adventurous maiden named Einin comes to Vorade out of the Verad Wild. She befriends Saidrin and is impressed by his amazing skill and nobility. She leads Saidrin into the Great Mountains to the hidden Fiorian Fortress of Emeril. Saidrin discovers that his sword is none other than the Sword of Light, the ancient sword of the Ecorian, Jeriel the Just, and the sword of the Astarian Fiora. Saidrin stays at Emeril with the Fiorians and begins training in the ancient ways of the Fiorian Order. Einin also begins training to be a Fiorian Knight.

1270 BL – The Star King's kingdom grows in the Great Mountains. The population of Blue Caps continues to grow. The Blue Caps become enemies of the mountain sprites. An ongoing war begins between the Blue Caps and the mountain sprites.

1264 BL – An army of bandits appears in Glenia and ravages the land. Evil grows again in Laravin on the Sedente River. The draug returns.

1257 BL – Saidrin is accepted as a knight in the Fiorian Order.

1256 BL – Einin is accepted into the Fiorian Order.

1255 BL – Saidrin travels back to Laravin and finds that the evil has grown strong again in and around the city. Einin travels into the east to Ortaria.

1254 BL – Saidrin travels into the forest around Laravin and encounters the draug. With the Sword of Light Saidrin is victorious. Saidrin returns to Emeril.

1253 BL – Saidrin travels to the Eastern Lands.

1250 BL – The evil and secret Guild of the Red Foot grows strong in the east and emerges in Silvor.

1248 BL – Evil grows strong in Larien. Larien becomes known as the Shadowy Harbour by seafarers and is generally avoided by sailors.

1247 BL – Duke Tral of Larien is slain by assassins. His son Constal takes control of Larien.

1246 BL – Constal supports the Guild of the Red Foot.

1245 BL – The Red Foot takes control of Talis. Later in the year the Red Foot takes full control of Silvor.

1244 BL – Einin comes to Talis and meets with King Constal. Constal fears Einin when he discovers she is a Fiorian Knight. He seeks to get rid of her. The Red Foot plans to assassinate Einin, but Einin escapes through the Red Pass to Ortaria. Einin takes her concerns to King Quintus of Ortaria at Ancora. King Quintus consults the Council of Zyran and then chooses to do nothing about the evil in Silvor as he does not perceive it as a threat to his kingdom. Einin disagrees and travels west to the Iron Gate Pass. Much to her joy she meets with Saidrin in a small village just east of the Golden Plains. They travel to the Iron Gate Pass to Sabulo in Vastoria and then onto Faircastle.

1241 BL – Constal raises an army under the influence of the Red Foot.

1240 BL – Constal invades Ortaria via the Red Pass. He marches to Sevadir and easily takes control of the city. The Red Foot spreads its influence across southern Ortaria.

1239 BL – Quintus leads an army to meet Constal's army. A great battle is fought near the Clarus River. King Quintus is forced to retreat to Ancora. Constal marches on Ancora and lays siege to the Ancora.

1238 BL – The siege of Ancora continues. The Council of Zyran fears Constal and the Red Foot. Constal continues to build and prepare his armies in Silvor and plans to invade the Isles of Dawn.

1237 BL – King Quintus and his family flee to Zyran. Constal takes control of Ancora declaring himself High King of Silvor and Ortaria. Saidrin and Einin make their way to Ateria to warn King Valens of Savadan about the threat in the north.

1236 BL – Constal invades the Isles of Dawn by sea, but a fleet challenges him from Ateria. Constal's fleet is forced back to Silvor.

1235 BL – The Red Foot grows tired of Constal and seek to remove him from the throne and replace him with someone more agreeable.

1234 BL – The Red Foot attempt to assassinate Constal. Constal escapes the assassins. A war begins in Silvor between those loyal to Constal and those loyal to the Red Foot. Constal seeks to destroy the Red Foot completely.

1233 BL – Constal loses control of Ortaria as the people rebel against his oppressive armies under the guidance of Saidrin and Einin.

1232 BL – Constal is betrayed into the hands of Red Foot assassins and is slain. Zyran takes the opportunity to rid Silvor of evil. The Council of Zyran gathers an army of men from Zyran, Ortaria, the Isles of Dawn, and Ateria. Saidrin and Einin go with the army. The Zyranian army later occupies Talis and Larien by sea. The Red Foot flees from the cities and becomes a secret society with little real power.

1231 BL – Prince Darlion of the Isles of Dawn is placed on the throne of Silvor under the authority of the Council of Zyran. Saidrin and Einin return west to Emeril.

1221 BL – An Alber warrior named Finn crosses the Endora Mountains from Alber to Dravania. He is imprisoned by the Irilian Order as he is deemed a troublemaker.

1219 BL – A Irilian wizard named Ronan the Sound befriends Finn. Ronan and Finn leave Dravania to seek out the Silver Leaf of the Astarians.

1216 BL – After searching the lands of the west; Ronan and Finn cross the Great Mountains and journey into the east to search for the Silver Leaf.

1214 BL – Ronan and Finn travel through Scaldonia. They seek out the Scaldonian Oracle and are told that the Silver Leaf was given to the Knights of Shidon and traditionally worn by the wife of the Ecorian Emperor. They are told that it was returned to Shidon after the fall of the Ecorian Empire. Ronan and Finn travel across Kaznor and through the pass to the west into Alber.

1213 BL – Finn and Ronan seek out Shidon in the distant icy north. They battle a powerful lindworm and Finn is slain. Ronan travels on alone to Shidon and finds the Silver Leaf. He is never again seen in the Southern Lands.

1205 BL – Saidrin becomes the Gatekeeper of Emeril and begins to instruct hopefuls in the ways of the Fiorian Order.

1201 BL – Einin travels east again.

1185 BL – Saidrin becomes known as Saidrin the Wise.

1179 BL – Einin wanders continuously through the lands and becomes famous for her courage and bravery.

1170 BL – Saidrin instructs a gifted young man named Krogin in the ways of the Fiorians.

1163 BL – Krogin becomes a Fiorian Knight and travels west to the Kingdom of Coran and then south to the Oran Mountains to seek out the Western Oracle. He discovers that the Sword of Light was found long ago and is in the hands of a Fiorian.

1159 BL – Krogin meets with an evil sorceress named Scathea the Tempter. Scathea did not claim her linage through any of the four known magic orders of Veredor as most wizards do. It is thought that her capability was gained through some other unknown origin. Krogin and Scathea travel north to Scathea's abode in the forests of Coran. They later marry and Krogin turns to evil ways.

1155 BL – Krogin takes on several students and begins teaching the Fiorian secrets to them. His teachings are a perversion of the Fiorian way. The Order of Skatheans is formed.

1149 BL – Krogin, with ten Skatheans, travels south to the Coran city of Kredon. Krogin gains control of the city.

1148 BL – The Fiorian Order becomes concerned and several knights travel to Kredon and discover Krogin has turned against the Fiorian Order. A battle is fought in the palace of Kredon and only one Fiorian escapes the Skatheans to return to Emeril.

1147 BL – Krogin seeks out and finds the Sword of Darkness.

1146 BL – The Fiorians gather at Emeril to discuss the threat of the Skatheans. They send ten powerful knights to Kredon to destroy the Skatheans. A battle is fought at Kredon and the remaining Skatheans are scattered. Krogin is enraged and escapes north to live at Scathea's hidden abode deep in the forest.

1142 BL – Krogin teaches his ways to a new group of students. Krogin desires the destruction of the Fiorian Order.

1140 BL – Krogin and his Skatheans assail Emeril and a great battle is fought. Saidrin slays Krogin with the Sword of Light and the remaining Skatheans flee. The Sword of Darkness is sealed into a hidden vault deep in the mountain beneath Emeril. The Skatheans who survive the battle gather together and flee north to Kaznor.

1134 BL – Einin combats a Skathean at Orelin and is victorious.

1128 BL – Saidrin instructs Gomer of Ateria in the ways of the Fiorians.

1121 BL – Gomer becomes a Fiorian Knight.

1116 BL – An evil sorcerer, Walok the Shadow, comes to power in Ateria. He was once a Zyranian and was cast out of Zyran because of his desire for power over others.

1113 BL – Walok enters Aruna and turns the town into an immoral pit of debauchery. All the good flee and those who remain make Walok their lord.

1111 BL – Gomer travels to Aruna and is shocked at how terrible the situation is. Gomer is captured by Walok and chained up in prison. Gomer soon escapes and travels to Savadan. Gomer falls in love with Princess Aalina of Ateria. He romances Princess Aalina and forgets his concerns about Walok's growing evil in Aruna.

1110 BL – Walok uses his sorcery to manipulate the rulers of Ateria. Walok becomes the master of King Dawi, Aalina's father. Walok's evil spreads to Savadan. Gomer challenges Walok in the court of King Dawi but is thrown into prison and tortured. A plot is developed by Walok to make everyone believe Gomer is responsible for all the troubles afflicting Ateria. Most people believe that Gomer is the evil instigator of all their misfortunes. Walok seduces Princess Aalina and marries her.

1108 BL – Gomer, in despair at losing his true love to his mortal enemy, escapes from prison and flees Savadan by ship to the Isles of Dawn where he is given sanctuary by the Fiorian Einin. Gomer returns to Savadan with Einin in secret. Gomer and Einin secretly form a resistance against the rule of Walok. Walok's troops storm the stronghold of the resistance movement and Einin is killed saving Gomer's life. Walok flees north into the Kaven Forest and meets Hergald, a wise hermit.

1107 BL – Gomer learns from Hergald. Walok's evil spreads into the Dry Plains.

1105 BL – Gomer emerges from the wilderness and infiltrates Walok's palace in Savadan. A great battle is fought and Walok is slain by Gomer. Gomer returns to the deep forest to live as a hermit.

1101 BL – The Skathean Order gathers power and grows in Alber and Kaznor.

1093 BL – The Star King has a disagreement with his legions of Blue Caps. The Blue Caps attempt mutiny, but they underestimate the power of the Star King and are forced to retreat from the Great Mountains. The Blue Caps of the Great Mountains make their way into Vastoria and build underground kingdoms in the Deep Desert.

1085 BL – The Skatheans cause much trouble for the people of Kaznor and Alber.

1080 BL – King Fredrin of Irvaria makes his kingdom exceptionally wealthy.

1076 BL – King Fredrin holds a tournament and invites all the greatest knights in all the lands to contest the right to court his daughter, Roseia the Graceful. A young peasant named Wiscard wins the tournament because of his pure heart.

1071 BL – Bandits block many of the ways in Everdon whilst burning villages and taking great hoards of wealth from their victims.

1066 BL – An army of bandits march north toward Faircastle. Fredrin raises an army and marches south to battle the bandit army. Fredrin is mortally wounded and dies south of Elcalee. The bandit army is completely destroyed.

1065 BL – Wiscard becomes ruling Duke of Irvaria with his wife Queen Roseia.

1055 BL – A great drought covers Vastoria. The Adira River almost completely dries up for two years.

1049 BL – Saidrin dies of old age. A Fiorian named Ornai becomes the new Gatekeeper of Emeril. Ornai inherits the Sword of Light from Saidrin.

1041 BL – The Great Mountains become extremely difficult to cross. The east and the west gradually become more cut off from each other.

1037 BL – Creatures of darkness slither out of the swamps of Scaldonia and cause trouble for the people of Orelin. The surrounding lands are heavily afflicted.

1033 BL – Packs of muckrons appear in the wild regions of Dravania.

1029 BL – The Star King grows old and tires of other creatures. He becomes very reckless and dangerous.

1020 BL – The Skatheans come to power in Kaznor and forge an allegiance with the Kaznor Emperor.

1015 BL – The Skatheans extend their influence into Scaldonia but have little success in Alber.

1011 BL – The Skatheans move south.

1004 BL – A Fiorian named, Lilian the Gentle, battles four Skatheans and is slain in Ortaria.

1001 BL – The Sword of Darkness is stolen from Emeril by the Skatheans.

1000 BL – Ornai sends two Fiorians to recover the evil sword. Dresia the Strong and Quinral the Swift seek the evil sword.

998 BL – The two Fiorians discover the Sword of Darkness in the possession of a Skathean. They are led into a trap and Dresia is slain. Quinral flees to Emeril, and the Sword of Darkness is taken north beyond the reach of the Fiorians.

996 BL – King Almod of Scaldonia becomes known for his great kindness and compassion.

989 BL – The Clans of Alber gather under a warlord named, Yarinai the Mighty. They invade Kaznor through the mountain pass in the north.

987 BL – After two years of conquest, Yarinai takes the throne of Zarkanor. He expels the Skatheans and outlaws them throughout his empire of Alber and Kaznor. Many Skatheans flee into the Southern Lands.

985 BL – Evil grows in Ortaria, Vastoria and Scaldonia. Skatheans heavily afflict the people of the southern kingdoms. The Fiorians are sent out from Emeril to contest the Skathean menace.

977 BL – The Skatheans assassinate King Almod of Scaldonia and place a puppet on the throne. King Almod's family flee to Ortaria.

975 BL – Scaldonia becomes a cursed land.

973 BL – An army is gathered by the Skatheans in Scaldonia. The Scaldonians reluctantly are forced to fight for their Skathean rulers.

972 BL – The Skatheans lead their army south and take control of the Iron Gate Pass. They then invade Ortaria and destroy all resistance. Brackin the Vicious, a Skathean, becomes Emperor of Ortaria and Scaldonia. The royal families of Ortaria and Scaldonia flee to Ateria.

970 BL – Brackin enslaves the Zyranian Order. He also slays the Skathean with the Sword of Darkness and takes it for himself.

969 BL – Brackin invades Silvor by sea.

968 BL – Brackin invades the Isles of Dawn and makes the magnificent palace of Orani his home and the centre of his growing empire. He names his empire the Skathean Empire.

967 BL – Brackin invades Ateria but is repulsed. The royal family of Silvor is murdered by Brackin.

966 BL – Brackin invades Ateria again and is victorious. He institutes a strict class structure in the conquered Eastern Lands. Brackin formally declares himself Emperor of Veredor. The royal families of Scaldonia and Ateria are captured and imprisoned. The royal family of Ortaria flees into the west.

965 BL – The lands of the east suffer greatly under the new rule.

964 BL – The Fiorians warn Irvaria and Vastoria of the grave threat of the Skathean Empire.

962 BL – Brackin invades Vastoria but his invading army is destroyed by the fierce Vastorian northern clans. Emperor Brackin fears the might of the Vastorians.

960 BL – The Star King prevents travellers from crossing the Great Mountains. He becomes a problem for the Fiorian Order.

955 BL – Irvaria and Vastoria form an alliance and invade Ateria. They are forced to retreat by Brackin's southern armies.

952 BL – The armies of Irvaria and Vastoria attempt to take the Iron Gate Pass to Ortaria. They are forced back in a furious battle.

950 BL – The Star King battles a group of Fiorians. The Fiorians chain him to a mountainside and convince him to stop harming other creatures. He repents of his recklessness and retreats into a hidden cave high in the Great Mountains and is not seen for centuries.

948 BL – A young woman named Emer begins a secret underground gang involved in organized disruption of the Skathean Empire in and around the port city of Talis.

947 BL – Emer's gang becomes a powerful force in Talis. Emperor Brackin orders the gang to be uncovered and destroyed, but they prove difficult to find among the masses.

945 BL – Emer is captured by Brackin's bounty hunters. She is brought to the city of Oranai in chains and thrown into the deepest dungeon.

941 BL – Emer escapes and secretly boards a merchant vessel bound for Vastoria. Emer arrives in Vastoria safely and works on a farm on the banks of the Adira River.

939 BL – Emer joins a band of desert wanderers and learns the harsh ways of the Dune Desert.

937 BL – Emer becomes a famous desert warrior. She battles bandits, villains, and raiders from the east whilst wandering all over Vastoria.

934 BL – A Fiorian Knight named Eoghan the Tall is sent east to help contest the power of Brackin.

932 BL – The Tabarian Knights battle groups of muckrons on the border of Dravania.

931 BL – Eoghan travels through Vastoria and meets with Emer. Emer and Eoghan seek a way to defeat the evil emperor Brackin and the Skathean Empire in the east.

930 BL – Eoghan and Emer are told by a mystic in the desert that they must find Shidon if they are to defeat Brackin. Eoghan and Emer travel north to Kaznor and cross into Alber. Emer and Eoghan are ambushed by Skatheans in Alber. Eoghan is severely wounded and cannot continue the quest to Shidon. Eoghan stays in the south of Alber as Emer travels north through the Icy Lands to Shidon. Emer eventually finds the ancient fortress and takes sanctuary there for seven years. She finds the Sword of Midlight hidden in the ancient fortress. Emer finds the hidden abode of the Astarian Callidus. It is revealed to Emer by Callidus that she is the only remaining Ecorian in Veredor. Callidus was not aware that Emer had found the Sword of Midlight.

923 BL – Emer leaves Shidon and returns south and finds Eoghan who lived with the Alber people for seven years. Emer and Eoghan return to the Eastern Lands and work against the Skathean Empire.

921 BL – The Tabarian Knights suffer greatly at the hands of muckrons that emerge out of the forests near the border of Coran and Dravania.

915 BL – Emperor Brackin greatly taxes the lands of his empire. The people of the east are impoverished.

909 BL – Bands of muckrons ravage Dravania and Iarthar. Many towns and villages are destroyed by the monsters.

906 BL – An army of brave men gather together in Southern Iarthar. The army marches north to destroy the muckron hordes. Many men die fighting the monsters. The muckrons are forced back into the wilderness.

905 BL – Emperor Brackin begins to believe that the Skathean Order is conspiring to overthrow him.

903 BL – An outcast of the Zyranian Order, Eliali the Flame, appears in Scaldonia. Eliali becomes extremely powerful and seeks to use her power to overthrow Brackin.

896 BL – Eliali travels to Oranai and infiltrates the palace disguised as a servant. She learns of Brackin's fear of the Skathean Order. She forges a letter with a Skathean seal in order to create a rift between Brackin and the Skatheans. After Brackin receives the letter he outlaws the Skathean Order.

894 BL – A group of Skatheans infiltrate Oranai and assassinate Brackin. A new emperor, Rocklat the Terrible, takes the throne of the Skathean Empire. Eliali flees Oranai and is never seen again.

892 BL – Emperor Rocklat proves to be even more oppressive than Brackin. He begins building massive armies and swears an oath to destroy the Ecorian Arbiter descendants who still rule in the west.

888 BL – Rocklat's armies invade Vastoria and occupy the southern part of the country. A massive Vastorian army is gathered together at Darancra to contest the invasion. Rocklat's army is completely destroyed.

883 BL – The Tower of Iron is built in the land of Glenia by King Murtagh.

876 BL – A group of cutthroat bandits take control of the Kingdom of Roven. Several Fiorian Knights travel west to restore the Roven royal family to power.

870 BL – Muckrons appear in Dravania. They terrorise small villages and towns.

866 BL – Princess Ilia of Dravania is kidnapped by muckrons. Many Dravanian and Iartharian knights begin the quest to rescue her. A young man named Davin goes into the wilderness to rescue her.

865 BL – Davin rescues Ilia from muckrons in the wild regions of Dravania. They fall in love and are married later that year.

859 BL – A serious drought afflicts Glenia and Southern Iarthar.

858 BL – A fire sweeps across the Sea of Grass and many small villages are burned to the ground. The people of Southern Iarthar blame the fire on muckrons.

850 BL – Around this time the secret way to Emeril in the Great Mountains is hidden from all but the Fiorian Knights.

842 BL – The ancient way through the Great Mountains becomes impassable. This cuts off communication between the east and west.

837 BL – The Irilian Order open a formal academy for training wizards at the Iril Fortress in Dravania. They only take on three students a year.

829 BL – Unak the Insane, a powerful Northern Sorcerer, appears in northern Dravania. He takes over several villages on the banks of the Oread River.

824 BL – King Trale of Dravania, the son of King Davin and Queen Ilia, sends a small army to destroy Unak. The Dravanian army is destroyed by Unak and his followers.

823 BL – Unak takes over all the towns along the Oread and Iril Rivers and Dravania City. Unak captures King Trale and slays him. Unak lays siege to the Iril Fortress but is held back by the Irilian Order.

821 BL – King Trale's cousin, Duke Tierney the Unrelenting, raises an army in the south. He marches north against Unak's followers. Unak leads his army to meet Duke Tierney's force, and the two armies clash south of the Iril River. Tierney's army is forced to retreat.

819 BL – For two years Duke Tierney prepares a new army. Tierney marches north again and faces Unak on the banks of the Iril River. Tierney takes

victory with the help of the Irilian Order. Unak escapes and flees north to Kaznor. He never returns south again.

815 BL – The Skathean Emperor Rocklat is poisoned by an unknown adversary. Kanrad, a powerful Skathean, becomes emperor of the Skathean Empire.

811 BL – Kanrad raises a massive army in Ateria. He builds many warships. He prepares to invade Vastoria.

809 BL – Kanrad leads his massive army across the Dry Plains and destroys the army protecting the port city of Kavacas. He takes over the city and prepares to march north to Darancra.

807 BL – Kanrad sails with his army up the Adira River and attacks Darancra. A massive battle is fought. The city is taken by Kanrad and Vastoria becomes a province of the Skathean Empire.

805 BL – King Ernald of Irvaria raises an army and prepares for a possible invasion. He forms mounted brigades in the sunset hills to protect the borders of his kingdom.

803 BL – The tribes of the Empyrian Hills seek help from King Ernald of Irvaria. King Ernald refuses to help the Empyrian tribes as he thinks that matching the huge armies of Kanrad would be an impossible task.

801 BL – Kanrad sails his warships up the Adira River and prepares to invade Irvaria. Kanrad's ships reach the Sunset Hills. A great battle is fought just east of the Sunset Hills. The Irvarians fight bravely, but they are no match for the much larger army from the Skathean Empire. The tribes of the Empyrian Hills come to the aid of the Irvarians. The battle is won by the Irvarians and Empyrian tribes. Kanrad is forced to retreat south. From this time onward the people of Empyrian Hills become the traditional allies of Irvaria.

798 BL – Kanrad lead his army across Vastoria and attacks the Grey Pass in the Old Guardian Mountains.

The Everdonians hold him back at Hawkwatch with the help of the Fiorian Order. Queen Catriona of Everdon prepares an army to match the threat from the Skathean Empire. She builds many warships in the port city of Lucaria.

796 BL – Kanrad sends a second army north and invades Irvaria. He lays siege to Elcalee. The Irvarians hold the city. Queen Catriona of Everdon takes the opportunity to send her warships to Kavacas. The Everdonians capture the port city of Kavacas. The Irvarians force Kanrad's army back to Darancra.

795 BL – The Irvarians, with the help of the Empyrian tribes, invade Vastoria. The Everdonians move north along the Adira River. The Irvarian, Everdonian, and Empyrian armies lay siege to Darancra. Kanrad is caught up in the battle and slain by the Fiorian Knights. Vastoria is handed back to the Vastorians. The Vastorian royal family, who were living in exile in Everdon, retake the throne in Darancra.

794 BL – The Skatheans battle each other for control of the Skathean Empire. A Skathean named Slagen takes the Sword of Darkness and the throne of the Skathean Empire.

790 BL – The Irvarians, Everdonians, and Vastorians prepare a great army in order to invade the Skathean Empire.

788 BL – The Irvarians, Everdonians, and Vastorians assail the Iron Gate Pass. They destroy the Skathean army guarding the pass and force them back into Scaldonia. Simultaneously a second united army invades Ateria. The united army continues into Ortaria, but they are forced back to the Iron Gate Pass. The united army in the south takes back all of Ateria.

785 BL – Slagen has a dark vision that the Prince of Shadows will return and lead the Skatheans to victory over the people of Veredor. Slagen takes a large army south and pushes the united army out of Ateria. He

takes no prisoners and crushes the united army in Ateria. Slagen invades Vastoria. The united armies in Vastoria battle furiously to hold back the Skathean Empire forces. The Skatheans are pushed back to the border of Ateria. A stalemate is reached.

779 BL – Muckrons attack several villages in Dravania. The Irilians hunt down the muckrons and push them north to the Endora Mountains.

761 BL – A warrior named Wyn becomes general of the third Irvarian northern army.

759 BL – Wyn leads his army through the Iron Gate Pass and into Ortaria. He battles against the armies of the Skathean Empire and holds the Golden Plains of Ortaria for several months before being pushed back to the Iron Gate Pass. Wyn's Irvarian army hold the Iron Gate Pass and fortify the Edius Plateau.

757 BL – Wyn again invades Ortaria. He pushes across the Golden Plains and captures Riverside. Wyn quickly liberates all the lands west of Riverside and prepares to march further east. Slagen sends an army to reinforce his army at Ancora.

756 BL – Wyn leads his army east and lays siege to Ancora, taking the city by the end of the year. Slagen escapes by sea and sails back to Orani on the Isles of Dawn. Meanwhile the Vastorian army cross the Iron Gate Pass and invade Scaldonia.

755 BL – Wyn completely liberates Ortaria. The Fiorian Order assists the Irvarian army. Wyn builds a fleet of warships at the port of Ancora.

754 BL – Wyn sails for Zyran and liberates the island.

752 BL – Slagen plans to have Wyn assassinated. Slagen strongly fortifies the port cities of Silvor and Ateria.

750 BL – The Vastorians completely liberate southern Scaldonia from the Skathean Empire. Wyn prepares to send an army through the Red Pass to Silvor.

749 BL – Wyn leads his main army through the Red Pass. The battle is fierce. General Wyn is injured in the battle and the army retreats back to the Clarus River.

747 BL – Wyn again attempts to take the Red Pass to Silvor, but his army is forced to retreat again.

746 BL – A Shapeshifter infiltrates the ranks of the Irvarian army in Ortaria. Wyn is assassinated by the Shapeshifter. After Wyn's death Slagen leads his army across the Red Pass and invades Ortaria. Slagen retakes the port city of Sevadir.

745 BL – The Skathean army takes control of most of the lands south of Ancora.

741 BL – Acelin, a close friend of Wyn, takes control of the Irvarian army in Ortaria. He prepares to face the Skathean army in the south of Ortaria. Many battles are fought around the region of the Clarus River.

740 BL – Slagen sends his fleet to Zyran and retakes the island. Acelin prepares for full scale war. The Irvarian army invade the south of Ortaria and push the Skathean army back across the Red Pass. The Irvarians retake Sevadir. They also send a fleet to fight off the Skatheans in Zyran.

739 BL – Acelin assails the Red Pass and invades Silvor. He successfully occupies all the land in the north around the Cerulean Lake. Acelin prepares his army to take the coastal ports. Acelin falls in love with a young Silvorian maiden from a village on the banks of the Cerulean Lake. He is distracted by his love and delays the invasion. This gives Slagen time to muster his strength in Talis. Slagen leads his army from Talis to the Cerulean Lake and attacks the Irvarian held position. Slagen completely destroys the Irvarian army and takes Acelin away in chains to the dungeons in Talis. Slagen destroys all the Irvarian held positions in Silvor and retakes the Red Pass.

738 BL – Slagen invades Ortaria. The reduced Irvarian forces retreat west. Slagen captures Ancora

and Zyran. By the end of the year Slagen completely forces all the Irvarians out of Ortaria through the Iron Gate Pass.

737 BL – Slagen sends his fleet to Scaldonia and contests the Vastorian armies in Orelin. The Vastorians force the Skathean army back to the coast. Scaldonia remains out of the grasp of the Skathean Empire. Slagen returns to the Isles of Dawn.

715 BL – The Skathean Emperor Slagen dies. The empire is taken over by the Skathean Kerzar the Slough. Kerzar takes the Sword of Darkness.

709 BL – Kerzar greatly taxes his empire. He lives in complete luxury in his palace overlooking the city of Orani. Kerzar has little interest in military affairs and focuses his full attention on worldly pleasures.

705 BL – Bands of muckrons appear in the wilderness of Southern Iarthar. They destroy many of the villages in the south and terrorise the people.

703 BL – A group of young men from Iarthar form a new order of knights. The new order is called the Muckron Bane Knights.

700 BL – The muckrons are forced back into the wilderness by the Muckron Bane Knights. Many young adventurers join the new order.

695 BL – Very few muckrons are seen again in the Far Western Lands.

694 BL – Kerzar the Slough heavily taxes his empire. He takes pleasure in watching slaves battle each other in arenas. The murderous sport becomes commonplace around this time.

691 BL – The Irvarian army gathers strength and prepares for a renewed invasion of the Skathean Empire. Kerzar takes no notice of the Irvarian plans. He is preoccupied with his focus on pleasure.

690 BL – The Irvarian army invade Ateria. They quickly crush all resistance. Within a month they completely liberate Ateria. Kerzar sends an army to meet the Irvarians. The Skathean Empire army is

completely obliterated. Kerzar prepares for the Irvarians and gathers a fleet at Orani.

689 BL – The Vastorians and Scaldonians invade Ortaria through the Iron Gate Pass. They capture all the land west of Lantern Hill. The Skathean armies in Ortaria are forced back to the coast.

688 BL – Ancora is captured by the Vastorians and Scaldonians. The Irvarians prepare a fleet at Aruna in Ateria. Kerzar fortifies the ports of Silvor and the Isles of Dawn. Zyran is taken by the Scaldonian army.

687 BL – The Irvarians sail for Orani. Kerzar's fleet sail to meet them and a great battle is fought at sea. Hundreds of ships on both sides are destroyed. The Irvarians retreat to an island south of Orani. The Vastorians and Scaldonians invade Silvor through the Red Pass; they capture Talis. The Skathean army falls back to Larien.

686 BL – The Vastorians and Scaldonians, with the help of the local freed Silvorians and Ortarians, attack the Skathean army near Larien. Larien is taken, and the Skathean army is destroyed. The Irvarians rebuild their fleet and again set sail for Orani. The Irvarians attack the city. A great battle is fought on the beaches. Kerzar is slain in the battle. The Isles of Dawn are liberated. The Skathean Empire is completely overthrown. The Sword of Darkness is taken by an unknown Skathean who escapes into the northern countries.

685 BL – The Ortarian royal family retake the throne of Ortaria. They are the only royal family who survived the occupation of the Eastern Lands by the Skathean Empire. They retake the throne of Ortaria based on the right of being descended from the Ecorian Arbiters. In the years that follow new monarchies, that are not descendants of Ecorian Arbiters, appear in Scaldonia, Ateria, the Isles of Dawn, and Silvor. The only Ecorian Arbiters royal families who remain at this

time are the Irvarians, Vastorians, Ortarians, Dravanians, and Iartharians.

675 BL – The Muckron Bane Knights are rewarded by the people for overthrowing the bands of muckrons that had terrorised the western kingdoms.

669 BL – The Irilian Order increase their academy intake to six a year.

665 BL – The Eastern Lands prosper after the fall of the Skathean Empire. Skatheans are not seen in the south again for many years.

661 BL – Many Fiorian Knights return to Emeril and take rest.

658 BL – The Far Western Lands prosper after the destruction of the muckron menace. The muckrons are thought to be extinct by people in the west.

650 BL – King Baznod of Alber sends a massive fleet south to invade Coran. Coran is quickly conquered by the Alber army. The Alber army moves eastward toward the Tabarian River.

649 BL – The Alber army battles the Tabarian Knights near the banks of the Tabarian River. The battle is fierce. The Tabarian Knights are forced to retreat north into the wilderness. Few Tabarians Knights survive. The Muckron Bane Knights hold a council in Ghrian. They prepare to meet the invading Alber army. The Alber army divides into two large armies. One army sails south to the coast of Southern Iarthar whilst the other prepares to invade Dravania.

648 BL – The Muckron Bane Knights gather an army and march south to meet the Alber army in Southern Iarthar. The Muckron Bane Knights are overwhelmed and forced back to Ghrian. Later in the year the Alber army captures Ghrian. The Muckron Bane Knights are scattered. The Irilian Order helps to prepare the people of Dravania. Queen Ida of Dravania prepares a massive army to contest the Alber invasion. A young woman named Anna becomes friends with Queen Ida. Anna is the Ecorian descendent and carries

the Sword of Midlight (The fact that she was the Ecorian was only known by the Fiorian Order). Anna helps Queen Ida prepare the Dravanian army.

647 BL – The two Alber armies join together and invade Dravania. Anna Ecorian leads the Dravanian army against the larger Alber army. The Alber army is forced back to Ghrian. Anna Ecorian leads the Dravanians against the retreating Alber forces. The Alber retreat to the sea and Ghrian is freed. The Alber army returns to Coran and fortifies the kingdom against a Dravanian invasion. King Baznod places his brother Duke Almhock on the throne of Coran. Anna Ecorian completely liberates Iarthar.

640 BL – The Tabarian Knights revive their order.

638 BL – Two hundred Tabarian Knights, with the support of five thousand Iartharian soldiers, and ten Irilian wizards, invade Coran and capture Duke Almhock. The Coranese monarchy is restored.

631 BL – A group of twenty Skatheans travel south from Kaznor and enter Vastoria. They plan to rebuild the Skathean Empire. The gather a small army in the Sandy Lands of the south and convince several small tribes to follow their rule.

630 BL – The Skathean army attacks Darancra, but they are repelled and retreat into the Deep Desert. Sir Grecob, a knight of the Vastorian throne, gathers together a group of brave young men to go after the Skatheans. Grecob travels through the Deep Desert and is ambushed by a dozen Skatheans. Half his men are killed. Grecob escapes with a dozen men into the north. They are pursued by the Skatheans until the reach the Empyrian Hills. Grecob and his men hide in the Empyrian Hills. They meet an old man named Huchon the Mystic. Huchon teaches Grecob a new method of swordsmanship using a single edged curved sword. Sir Grecob becomes a master of Huchon's method and teaches his men. Huchon's method is the original

method taught to Grecob; Grecob's method is a simplified version of Huchon's method.

628 BL – Grecob and his men travel south and search the desert for the Skatheans. A battle is fought between Grecob and his ten men and the ten Skatheans. Grecob and his men are victorious. Grecob returns to Darancra.

625 BL – Grecob is made Lord of the Deep Desert. Grecob forms a new order of Vastorian Knights based in Darancra. He calls his new knights the Desert Knights.

621 BL – Another group of Skatheans enter Vastoria with plans to avenge the Skatheans who were killed by Grecob and his men seven years earlier. The Skatheans assassinate most of the Desert Knights when they are off duty. Grecob attempts to hide the identity of his men by covering their faces so the Skatheans will not be able to recognise them when they are not bearing arms for the kingdom. From this time onward the Desert Knights always cover their faces with black cloth or a mask when they are in the role of knight.

615 BL – The Order of Zyran reopens the ancient academy. The order begins to grow strong again.

601 BL – Zyran begins to exert influence over the lands of the east. Scaldonia, Atera, and Silvor all fall under direct influence of Zyran; however, at this time the Zyranian intentions were not entirely evil.

598 BL – Zyran places wizards as advisors to the kings and queens of Scaldonia, Silvor, the Isles of Dawn, Ateria, and Vastoria. The Zyranian Order grows strong.

591 BL – A Fiorian Knight, Wyon the Gentle, visits Zyran to hold a council with the Gatekeeper of Zyran. The Zyranians fear the Fiorian Order and refuse to take counsel from the Fiorians. The Zyranians think of themselves as superior to all the other orders of wizards and knights in Veredor. Wyon leaves Zyran.

585 BL – The power of Zyran extends further. A Zyranian wizard becomes an advisor to the Irvarian throne. They directly influence all the lands of the east. The Fiorian Order begins to grow concerned about the extent of Zyranian power.

579 BL – A group of Zyranians cross the Great Mountains and seek to exert influence over the kingdoms in the Far West. Five Irilians come face to face with a dozen Zyranians in the court of King Conor of Iarthar. A feud begins between the two orders as the Irilian see that the Zyranians seek power over all the monarchies of Veredor. King Conor accepts a Zyranian advisor.

578 BL – A second group of Zyranians arrive in Dravania. They enter the court of King Niall of Dravania and seek to influence King Niall. King Niall accepts a Zyranian as an advisor. The Zyranians begin to seek out a way of ridding Veredor of the Irilian Order.

576 BL – The Zyranians attempt to convince King Niall of Dravania to restrict the Irilian Order. King Niall passes a law that does not allow the Irilians to instruct any new apprentices. A group of twenty Irilian wizards face the ten Zyranians in Dravania. A battle is fought between the two orders. The Irilians are victorious. The Irilians then move to remove the Zyranians from Iarthar. The Zyranians resist at first and then flee into the east because they are outnumbered.

571 BL – The Zyranians prepare to return to the Far Western Lands to avenge themselves against the Irilians. Forty Zyranians assail the Iril Fortress. The Irilian Order holds back the onslaught, but many Irilians are slain in the battle, and their order is much reduced. The Zyranian force returns to Zyran. Carrig, the leader of the Irilians, plans a counterattack.

568 BL – Twenty Irilians secretly cross the Great Mountains. They enter Irvaria and remove the

Zyranian counsellor to the King of Irvaria. They then do the same in Everdon. The Zyranians are outraged and declare war on the Irilian Order. One hundred Zyranians set out to fight the Irilians in Everdon. The Irilians cross the Vastorian Wastes and enter the Iron Gate Pass. The Zyranians arrive in Lucaria to find the Irilians are long gone. The twenty Irilians cross Ortaria and remove the Zyranians from Ortaria. They then sail to Zyran. The Irilians attack the unguarded Citadel of Zyran and ruin the academy of Zyran and damage the citadel significantly. The Zyranian Order returns to Zyran and are outraged by what they find.

567 BL – The Zyranians chase the Irilians across Ortaria and catch them in the Iron Gate Pass. A battle is fought at the Edius Plateau. Carrig holds back the Zyranians using the Irilian Star. The Irilians escape into Vastoria. For the first time the Zyranians fear the Irilians because they do not understand how one Irilian wizard could be so powerful. Ten more Irilians cross the Great Mountains to help in the fight against Zyran. Thirty Irilians battle seventy Zyranians just east of the Sunset Hills. The Irilians are forced to retreat over the Great Mountains. By this time only twenty five Irilians remain in the Irilian Order.

566 BL – The Zyranians gather one hundred wizards and prepare to completely destroy the Irilian Order. They cross the Great Mountains and attack the Iril Fortress in Dravania. Many Irilians die in the battle. The Tabarian Knights come to the aid of the last wizards of the Irilian Order and push the Zyranians back from the Iril Fortress. Many Tabarian Knights are killed in the battle. The Fiorian Order decides to intervene. The Gatekeeper of Emeril, Siobhan the Graced, holds talks with the Zyranians and the few remaining Irilians. An agreement is reached that prevents both orders from crossing the Great Mountains ever again. The Zyranians agree because they feel that they have all but destroyed the Irilian

Order anyway. They also feel threatened by the Fiorian Order and do not want to battle the Fiorians. The Zyranians return to Zyran after the accord is signed.

560 BL – The Zyranians reinstitute their regime of advising and controlling the kingdoms in the east.

549 BL – The Zyranians attempt to influence the Fire Order in the Old Guardian Mountains. The Fire Order sends the Zyranians away from the Tower of Fire. Later in the year a group of twenty Zyranians attempt to assail the Tower of Fire. The Fire Order destroys the Zyranians and all twenty Zyranians die in the battle. The Zyranians decide not to interfere with the Fire Order again.

541 BL – Three Northern Sorcerers, the Northern Triad, come south to Dravania and cause havoc in the kingdom. The few Irilians who remain do not have the power to stop the sorcerers. The Muckron Bane Knights gather a small company to challenge the three sorcerers. The company of Muckron Bane Knights is destroyed. King Lollan of Dravania attempts to negotiate and is taken prisoner by the three Northern Sorcerers.

539 BL – A hero named Azer appears in Dravania. Azer is the Ecorian descendent. Azer seeks out the sorcerer's stronghold in the Tabarian Mountains and singlehandedly defeats the three sorcerers with the Sword of Midlight. Azer rescues King Lollan. Azer returns King Lollan to his palace. Azer becomes known as a hero in Dravania.

534 BL – After spending several years in Dravania, Azer crosses the Great Mountains into Irvaria. He becomes a friend of King Farman of Irvaria. Azer influences King Farman against the Zyranians (Azer was mentored by the Irilian Order and knew of all the suffering the Zyranians had caused the Irilians). King Farman banishes the Zyranian Order from Irvaria. The Zyranians are angered and discover that Azer was behind the motion.

531 BL – Azer Ecorian confronts three Zyranians near Sabulo in Vastoria. Azer defeats the Zyranians. The Zyranians suspect that Azer is not an ordinary man as they know that no single man could defeat three powerful Zyranians without magic. Azer does not fear the Zyranians and makes his way to Ancora in Ortaria.

530 BL – Azer convinces King Ennius of Ortaria to break his alliance with the Zyranians. The Order of Zyran forms the Zyranians Enforcers to deal with Azer. Azer confronts a group of Zyranian Enforcers on the banks of the Merus River. Azer is forced to retreat and flees the Zyranian Enforcers. The Zyranians chase Azer and attempt to cut him off at the Northern Pass; Azer escapes into Scaldonia. Azer finds the Scaldonian Oracle and discovers many secrets.

526 BL – Azer seeks out the Fortress of Shidon in the north.

520 BL – Azer appears again in Irvaria. He discovers that the Zyranians are again influencing the Kingdom of Irvaria. Azer again convinces King Farman to rid his kingdom of the manipulative Zyranians.

515 BL – Azer Ecorian builds the house of Stonehaven. He marries a noble Irvarian woman and settles in the beautiful house he built in the Sunset Hills.

511 BL – Stonehaven is attacked by Zyranian Enforcers. Azer is killed. Azer's wife and daughter, Alia Ecorian, escape and take sanctuary at Emeril in the Great Mountains. The Sword of Midlight is taken by the Zyranian Enforcers to the Citadel of Zyran. The Zyranians realise that they have taken one of the three swords of the Astarians. They never knew that Azer was an Ecorian.

507 BL – The Irilian Order slowly recovers in the west. By this year the Irilian Order has nearly thirty wizards.

501 BL – The Tabarian Knights grow in numbers. The Muckron Bane Knights also recover.

497 BL – Alia Ecorian studies swordsmanship with Fiorian Knights as a teenager. She becomes a brilliant warrior.

492 BL – Alia Ecorian travels into the Far Western Lands and befriends the Tabarian Knights. She studies swordplay with the Tabarians Order.

490 BL – Alia Ecorian speaks with the Oran Oracle. Alia learns that the Zyranians are holding her father's sword, the Sword of Midlight, in the Citadel of Zyran. She also learns that the Zyranian Enforcers hunted down her father and murdered him when she was an infant. Alia swears to avenge her father and reclaim the Sword of Midlight for the Ecorian line.

487 BL – Alia travels to the Tower of Fire and seeks the help of the Fire Order. The Fire Order is reluctant to help Alia as she does not reveal that she is the Ecorian. Anchier the Magnificent, a wizard of the Fire Order, agrees to help Alia Ecorian.

486 BL – Anchier helps Alia infiltrate the Citadel of Zyran. Alia, in disguise, gains the trust of several Zyranians. Alia steals the Sword of Midlight from the Gatekeeper of Zyran. She slays the Gatekeeper of Zyran and battles her way out of the Citadel. Alia escapes Zyran with the help of Anchier. They flee across Ortaria. The Zyranians Enforcers are sent after Alia and Anchier.

485 BL – The Zyranian Enforcers ambush Alia and Anchier at Eaglemere in Everdon. Anchier faces the Zyranians and dies fighting them. Alia escapes after the battle and flees back to Emeril in the Great Mountains. The Zyranian Enforcers follow Alia to the gates of Emeril and threaten the Fiorian Order as they see the Sword of Midlight as a great prize worth fighting for. The Fiorians face the Zyranians. A fierce battle is fought on the doorstep of Emeril. The Fiorians and Alia Ecorian are victorious. The Zyranian

Enforcers flee back to Zyran. Alia rests in Emeril and falls in love with a Fiorian Knight named Thim the Strong. They marry in Emeril.

473 BL – Dravania falls under the rule of General Ultuck, who is an advisor to King Fergus. Ultuck becomes the ruler of Dravania through his control over the King. The people of Dravania suffer greatly.

471 BL – Takal, the son of the Duke of Marraw in Everdon, leaves his home to travel the lands of Veredor. Takal sails the Southern Sea and learns swordplay from the sailors. He then enters the Vastorian deserts and learns Grecob's Sword Method which heavily influences Takalian methodology.

470 BL – Takal furthers his studies in Irvaria and becomes known as a great swordsman. He crosses the Great Mountains and enters Dravania. Takal sees all the horror of the rule of Ultuck. Takal joins the resistance to Ultuck and battles Ultuck's henchmen. Within a year Takal faces Ultuck and defeats him in a duel. Dravania is freed from the evil influence of General Ultuck. Takal travels south to Iarthar.

468 BL – Takal travels to Glenia and remains there for some time. He teaches his method of swordsmanship to a group of young Glenians. His followers build a small fort on the shore of the Merhome Sea. The Takalian Knights are formed.

466 BL – Takal is challenged by Sir Darragh of Roven. Darragh is said to be the greatest swordsman in all the Far Western Lands. Takal faces Darragh. The battle is fierce and Takal takes victory over his opponent. Takal's fame spreads across the lands of the Far West.

463 BL – Takal journeys onward to Coran and then to Alber. He studies the Alber method of swordplay and takes all challenges. Takal is undefeated. Takal's fame spreads across Alber. Takal hears of mighty warriors in Kaznor and crosses the Great Mountains. Takal battles a group of Skatheans in Kaznor. He slays several

Skatheans in the battle, but he is captured and brought to Zarkanor in chains. Takal spends five years in prison and uses his time in the Dungeons of Zarkanor to perfect his sword method.

458 BL – Takal escapes the Dungeons of Zarkanor and flees to Scaldonia. He aids the Scaldonians in their ongoing skirmishes at sea with the Kaznor Empire. He trains a second group of Takalian Knights in Aldokan.

456 BL – Takal travels south to Zyran. The Zyranians are very impressed by his skill and ask him to become the leader of the Zyranian Guard. Takal refuses and continues on to Ateria. He builds a third branch of his order in Ateria.

453 BL – Takal returns to Marraw and becomes the Duke of Marraw. The Takalian Knights become popular throughout the lands. Branches of the order appear in Iarthar, Vastoria, Silvor, and Ortaria.

450 BL – Takal relinquishes his authority over the Takalian Order. He tells his knights to serve the king of whichever kingdom they are based in. The Takalian Order branches maintain loose connections with each other. They describe themselves as having a respectful affiliation. The order's branches are recognisable by the fact that they use the Takalian method of swordplay and follow the Takalian training regime.

439 BL – A draug appears in the Endora Mountains between Ortaria and Scaldonia. The monster makes a home in the Astrum Chasm at the height of the Northern Pass. Many knights attempt to kill the draug but none return. The Northern Pass is cut off.

437 BL – The Zyranian Order sends three Zyranian Enforcers to kill the draug. All three Enforcers are killed by the draug. The Zyranians fear the power of the draug.

432 BL – The Skathean Order takes power in Kaznor. The power of the order is based in Zarkanor.

425 BL – A group of Northern Sorcerers challenge the Skatheans for power in Kaznor. The Skatheans are

forced out of Zarkanor. Northern Sorcerers take over Zarkanor and spread their power throughout the Kaznor Empire.

421 BL – The Northern Sorcerers form an alliance with the Skatheans.

412 BL – The people of Kaznor suffer greatly under the rule of the Northern Sorcerers and the Skatheans.

404 BL – The Fiorian Order grow concerned about the growing power of the Skatheans and Northern Sorcerers in Kaznor.

401 BL – A group of Northern Sorcerers and Skatheans form the Circle of Night. The Circle of Night rule Zarkanor and begin to build an army. They plan to invade Scaldonia as a stepping stone to conquering the kingdoms in the Southern Lands of Veredor. The Skatheans hope to rebuild the Skathean Empire of old.

398 BL – The Circle of Night invade Scaldonia with a massive army. The Scaldonians fight back furiously. The Takalian Knights of Scaldonia save Aldokan and hold off the Kaznor attack. Zyran send wizards to help resist the invasion. The Kaznorians retreat back to Zarkanor and prepare for a second attack.

397 BL – The Circle of Night send an army to Alber. They face staunch resistance in Alber.

396 BL – The Circle of Night again invade Scaldonia. The Kaznorians capture Aldokan and force the entire population of the city to retreat south. The Scaldonian army falls back to Orelin. The Takalians gather their forces. The Zyranians send a host of wizards. The Kaznorians are halted at the walls of Orelin. The Scaldonian army forces the Kaznorians back toward Aldokan, but they suffer heavy casualties. The Kaznorians fortify Aldokan.

392 BL – King Eric of Scaldonia calls on the Ortarians to help liberate the north. The Ortarians send a small army to assist. King Eric prepares to attempt to retake Aldokan. The Circle of Night sends a

second army to Scaldonia to secure their captured territory. They also invade Alber again.

391 BL – King Eric marches north with his army and attacks the Kaznorian positions near Aldokan. The Scaldonian army is pushed back to Orelin after six months of brutal skirmishes in the north of Scaldonia. Most of the small Ortarian army are slain in the battles.

386 BL – The Zyranians realise that the threat of the Circle of Night is growing. The Zyranian Order uses their influence in the Eastern Lands to gather an army to assist in the liberation of Scaldonia. The allied army is sent to Orelin. The army consists of Ortarian, Silvorian, Aterian, and Vastorian soldiers.

385 BL – A battle is fought north of the Gerish Highlands. Both sides suffer greatly. The Scaldonians are victorious. King Eric leads his army into Aldokan. The Circle of Night is infuriated at the loss. They draw their armies out of Alber to send them east to Scaldonia.

383 BL – The Zyranians, Scaldonians, and Takalian Knights prepare for another invasion. They build ships and ready themselves for a war over water. The Kaznorian army are intercepted and most of the Kaznorian ships are sunk before they reach the shores of Scaldonia. The loss of the fleet prevents the Circle of Night from moving another army to Scaldonia. The Scaldonians celebrate their victory.

382 BL – The Circle of Night begin the slow process of building a new fleet.

373 BL – The Kingdom of Alber invades Kaznor. The Circle of Night sends their army to contest the invasion. The Kaznorians hold off the Alber invasion.

368 BL – King Zain of Vastoria breaks contact with the Zyranian order. He replaces his Zyranian advisors with Desert Knights. The Zyranians discover that Desert Knights have been working against them in Vastoria.

365 BL – The Zyranians send the Enforcers to teach the Desert Knights a lesson. The Enforcers slay a group of Desert Knights in the Dune Desert. The Desert Knights assemble. Over two hundred Desert Knights attack the small group of Zyranian Enforcers. All the Zyranian Enforcers are slain. The Council of Zyran is enraged and prepare for a counter attack. The Zyranians also spread false rumours about the Desert Knights throughout the Eastern Lands which endure for many years.

364 BL – A group of twenty Zyranians enter Vastoria to challenge the Desert Knights. King Zain sends an army and captures all twenty Zyranains. King Zain imprisons the Zyranians in Darancra.

362 BL – The Zyranians send a second group of Zyranians to Darancra. The imprisoned Zyranians escape and burn the city of Darancra to the ground. They slay King Zain and many Desert Knights die in the battle.

351 BL – The Circle of Night sends a new fleet east. The fleet sails to southern Scaldonia and attacks Havet Bay. They capture the city and invade Scaldonia. The Ortarians send a fleet to Havet Bay to challenge the invasion. The Ortarian fleet is completely destroyed. The Kaznorian army crosses Scaldonia and lays siege to Orelin. The city is captured. King Cicero of Ortaria fortifies the Iron Gate Pass and prepares the coastal villages and towns for a possible invasion.

350 BL – The Kaznorian force in Scaldonia holds off an attack from the Scaldonians. They prepare to invade Ortaria through the Northern Pass, thinking that the draug will not pose a problem. The Kaznorian army marches up the Star Steps and many men die at the hands of the draug. The army cannot pass through the Astrum Chasm. The army retreats back to Orelin. A group of Northern Sorcerers and Skatheans return to the Northern Pass to hunt down the draug. The entire company never returns. King Cicero of Ortaria

prepares to invade Scaldonia through the Iron Gate Pass. He prepares a plan with King Leif of Scaldonia.

349 BL – The Ortarian and Scaldonian armies both attack simultaneously. The Kaznorian army is mostly destroyed. Orelin is recaptured. The Kaznorian garrison at Havet Bay hold the Ortarians back for some time before retreating to the sea. The remaining Kaznorians return to Zarkanor.

341 BL – A Northern Sorcerer called, Fazmak the Good, holds talks with the Irilian Order. Fazmak hopes to build a bridge with the Irilians and seek knowledge of magic. The Irilians learn some new skills from Fazmak who is a student of all wizardry.

337 BL – Ari Ecorian travels with Fazmak to the Fortress of Shidon. They both seek the secret knowledge. Fazmak and Ari Ecorian discover the secret home of Callidus at the northern edge of the Great Mountains. Callidus is one of the last remaining Astarians in Veredor. Callidus does not care much for the men of Veredor, but he allows Fazmak and Ari to stay at his secret abode and tells them some of the ancient history of the Forgotten Age. Callidus asks Ari Ecorian for the Sword of Midlight in exchange for a gift of immeasurable worth. Ari Ecorian refuses the exchange as he thinks of the Sword of Midlight as a symbol of the Ecorians in exile and the Sword of Light as a symbol of the Ecorian Empire.

331 BL – Ari Ecorian and Fazmak enter Kaznor and go to Zarkanor. The Circle of Night fear and respect Fazmak, and they do not know that Ari Ecorian is carrying the Sword of Midlight. Ari Ecorian sees the terrible oppression that exists in Kaznor. He vows to free Kaznor from the Circle of Night.

330 BL – Ari Ecorian and Fazmak part ways. Ari Ecorian crosses the Eranai Mountains to Scaldonia.

325 BL – Ari Ecorian marries Princess Emony of Orelin. Ari Ecorian holds a council with his father-in-law, King Harold. Ari hopes to lead an army to Kaznor

to destroy the Circle of Night. King Harold agrees to allow Ari to raise an army of any willing young men in the kingdom. Ari Ecorian begins to build his army.

323 BL – Ari Ecorian has ten thousand men. He gains the support of the Takalian Order in Scaldonia. Ari Ecorian buys twenty ships in Havet Bay and prepares to invade Kaznor.

322 BL – Ari Ecorian's army sails for Zarkanor. Ari's troops lay siege to Zarkanor; however, the Northern Sorcerers and Skatheans tip the balance in favour of the Kaznorians. Ari Ecorian's ships are sunk in the harbour of Zarkanor. Ari Ecorian, with his remaining troops, retreats south through Kaznor. The Circle of Night pursues Ari Ecorian and his remaining five hundred men. A great battle is fought between Ari's army and a Kaznorian force many times the size. Ari's army is vanquished. Ari is slain on the battlefield. The Circle of Night takes the Sword of Midlight back to Zarkanor.

319 BL – The Northern Sorcerer Fazmak secretly enters Zarkanor and steals the Sword of Midlight. He takes the sword back to Scaldonia and gives the sword to Princess Emony in Orelin. Princess Emony keeps the Sword of Midlight for her infant son, Wymar Ecorian, who continues the bloodline of the Ecorians.

314 BL – A group of bandits form an army in the southern lands of Iarthar. They raid villages and terrorise the kingdom.

313 BL – The Fiorian Order, with the assistance of the Muckron Bane Knights, faces the army of bandits and completely obliterates them.

305 BL – A great famine strikes the Far Western Lands of Veredor after crops fail for two seasons. Many people in Coran, Iarthar, and Dravania starve. The people suffer greatly. Bandits and pirates take advantage of the vulnerable people. The weakened monarchies struggle to maintain law and order.

302 BL – The Irilians, Tabarians, Muckron Bane Knights, and Takalians become the arbiters of law and justice in the Far Western Lands. King Turlak of Roven builds his army and prepares to invade the famished lands. Roven becomes the foremost power in the west because it is mostly untouched by the famine.

301 BL – Roven invades Iarthar. The Roven army quickly sweeps across the land and conquers all the major towns and settlements.The Iartharian royal family is taken back to Ferdia in chains. King Turlak declares himself King of Roven and Iarthar. The Irilians hold a council with their old allies the Tabarian Knights. The Tabarians move east to protect the Dravanian border.

300 BL – Wymar Ecorian crosses the Great Mountains and visits the Iril Fortress in Dravania. Shortly after Wymar's arrival the Roven army makes a move on the Dravanian border. The Tabarian Knights ride to face the army. The Tabarians suffer a large defeat and are forced to retreat. The Roven army enters Dravania and faces the main Dravanian army. The Dravanians are also forced to retreat. Half of Dravania falls into the hands of King Turlak. Wymar Ecorian joins the remaining Dravanian army and helps to bring a sense of hope back to the troops. King Turlak requests the support of the Irilians; his request is refused. King Turlak invades Glenia and successfully conquers the small kingdom. King Turlak declares himself Emperor of the West.

299 BL – Wymar Ecorian and the Irilians help to prepare five thousand Dravanian soldiers for the coming invasion of northern Dravania. An army of thirty thousand Roven troops invade Dravania and are held back at the Iril Fortress. Wymar and the Dravanian troops force the Roven army south toward the border. King Turlak is shocked at the defeat and loss of territory. Wymar pushes the Roven army back toward the Merhome Sea.

298 BL – King Turlak brings every soldier in his empire to Ghrian. He prepares for a renewed attack on Wymar's army and Dravania. Wymar Ecorian leads his army to Ghrian. King Turlak takes forty thousand men to meet Wymar's five thousand. Wymar, with the support of the Irilians, Tabarians, and Muckron Bane Knights takes victory over King Turlak's army. King Turlak is taken prisoner by the Irilians. The monarchies of the Far Western Lands are restored. Roven is made a territory of Iarthar.

291 BL – The Circle of Night send a fleet to invade Scaldonia. The Scaldonians hold Aldokan, but they lose most of the coastal villages and towns to the Kaznorian invasion. Wymar Ecorian travels to Irvaria with his Iartharian wife, Princess Niamh.

290 BL – The Kaznorian forces capture Aldokan and prepare to invade the Southern Lands. The Circle of Night sends a massive army to hold the northern lands of Scaldonia. Wymar Ecorian hears of the invasion when he is in Faircastle.

289 BL – The Zyranians use their influence again to raise an army to assist the Scaldonians against the Kaznorians. Most of the Zyranian army are soldiers from Ortaria. The Ortarians and Scaldonians face the Kaznorians north of Orelin. The Kaznorian army is victorious and lays siege to Orelin. Orelin is captured later in the year. The Kaznorians capture the Iron Gate Pass and send small brigades into Vastoria. Wymar travels to Darancra.

288 BL – The Ortarians hold the Kaznorian invasion at the Iron Gate Pass, but they cannot regain control of the Edius Plateau. The Kaznorians invade Vastoria and meet little resistance. The Kaznorian army crosses the Deep Desert and attacks Darancra. Wymar Ecorian fights with the garrison at Darancra. The Kaznorians fall back to Sabulo.

287 BL – Wymar Ecorian, leaving Princess Niarm and his daughter in Darancra, rides east with an army

of Vastorians. They attack the Kaznorian force that holds Sabulo. The Vastorians army is vanquished and Wymar Ecorian is captured by the enemy. Wymar Ecorian and the Sword of Midlight are taken back to Aldokan and then on to Zarkanor in Kaznor. Wymar is thrown into the Dungeons of Zarkanor and the Sword of Midlight is taken again by the Circle of Night.

286 BL – The Kaznorians capture Darancra. Princess Niarm and Una Ecorian escape back to Faircastle. The Order of Zyran influences the Aterians to help in the struggle against the Circle of Night. The Aterians prevent the Kaznorians from capturing Kavacas, and they hold the southern regions of the Adira River against the Kaznorians.

275 BL – The elderly Northern Sorcerer Fazmak helps Wymar Ecorian to escape the Dungeons of Zarkanor. Wymar and Fazmak flee south without the Sword of Midlight. Wymar Ecorian returns to Faircastle with Fazmak. Wymar Ecorian convinces King Erart to raise an army to liberate Vastoria.

274 BL – The Irvarian army invades Vastoria and captures Darancra. Wymar and King Erart lead the Irvarians onward to Sabulo. They capture Sabulo and attack the Kaznorian positions in the Iron Gate Pass. Wymar Ecorian is killed by an arrow whilst fighting high in the Iron Gate Pass.

271 BL – Una Ecorian travels north with Fazmak. Together they cross the Endora Mountains and enter the forests of Kaznor. Fazmak leads Una to Zarkanor. Una infiltrates the fortress and steals the Sword of Midlight. She escapes with Fazmak's help. Fazmak is killed defending Una against the Circle of Night. He is remembered always as one of the few good Northern Sorcerers throughout history. Una hides out in the wilderness of southern Kaznor. She later lives in a small secluded Kaznorian village.

269 BL – Una Ecorian returns to Irvaria. She marries an Irvarian knight and lives in Stonehaven with her husband.

263 BL – A rebellion begins in Scaldonia. The people rise up against the Kaznorian oppressors. Orelin is liberated by the rebellion. The Zyranians send troops to support the rebellion, and the Kaznorians are forced back to Aldokan. The Ortarians, Zyranians, and Scaldonians push north to Aldokan. A mighty battle is fought south of Aldokan. The allied force is victorious. The Kaznorians are removed from Scaldonia.

258 BL – The Ortarians send a small brigade of brave knights to vanquish the draug in the Northern Pass. None of the knights return.

255 BL – A band of Vastorians from Sabulo dig a silver mine in the Vastorian Wasteland. They come across a massive colony of Blue Caps. The Blue Caps capture many of the miners. The Vastorians send a group of soldiers to recover the lost miners. The Blue Caps battle the soldiers in their tunnels deep beneath the desert. Many Blue Caps are killed.

254 BL – A massive swarm of Blue Caps attack Sabulo. They smash down much of the wall that surrounds the city and capture over one thousand men of Sabulo. They take their captives deep beneath the ground to work as slaves in the Blue Cap mines. The Vastorians fear upsetting the Blue Caps and leave them alone.

251 BL – Una Ecorian travels to the Blue Cap abode in the Deep Desert. The Blue Caps negotiate a deal with Una Ecorian. Una, also being of the mer people, gains the confidence of the Blue Caps who are traditionally opposed to men; however, they have no issue with the mer or women. The Blue Caps release the men of Sabulo on the condition that their home is left alone. Una of Stonehaven is revered by the Vastorian people after this event. The fact that she is an Ecorian is never revealed.

247 BL – A group of Skatheans unexpectedly attack Emeril. Many Fiorian Knights are killed in the raid. The Fiorian Order manages to hold back the attack. The Skatheans retreat.

244 BL – A group of Skatheans arrive in Coran. They quickly take power and assassinate all the ruling royal family.

243 BL – Groups of farmers in Coran rise up against their Skathean overlords. The Skatheans quickly put down the Farmer's Rebellion.

240 BL – The Skatheans rule Coran with an iron fist. The people suffer greatly. The Tabarian Knights with the help of the Fiorian Order prepare to invade Coran to challenge the rule of the Skatheans. The Tabarians build an army of ten thousand men who are mostly from Iarthar. The Tabarians invade Coran and meet the Skathean force close to the coast of the Merhome Sea. The Tabarians suffer heavy losses whilst taking victory over the Skatheans. Coran is liberated. Duchess Roisin of Iarthar becomes Queen Roisen of Coran.

237 BL – The Star King leaves his cave and seeks out the Sun Stone of the Astarians. He discovers the Sun Stone has the power to open a gate to any place in the cosmos.

234 BL – The Star King discovers that the Sun Stone is held by Casimir beneath the sea. He attempts to build a craft to take him beneath the ocean; however, he fails in his task.

232 BL – The Star King asks Callidus to request the Sun Stone from Casimir. Callidus contacts Casimir beneath the sea for the first time in thousands of years. Casimir refuses to give the Sun Stone to the Star King because the power of the Sun Stone is used to light the mer cities in the deep. The Star King grows angry and thinks Callidus and Casimir are conspiring to stop him from returning home. He battles Callidus at the northern edge of the Great Mountains. The

outcome of the battle is inconclusive, neither the Astarian nor the Star King are victorious. The Star King returns home to his cave high in the Great Mountains.

226 BL – By this time the Zyranian Order fully control the southern kingdoms east of the Great Mountains. Irvaria is the only kingdom that is not entirely under the influence of Zyran. The Fiorian Order considers the kingdoms east of the Great Mountains to all be part of the Zyranian Empire.

215 BL – An Irilian, Gael the Brave, crosses the Great Mountains to hold talks with the Zyranians. She hopes to build a bridge between the two orders. She is captured in Everdon and taken to Zyran in chains. The Zyranians attempt to extract the secrets of the Irilian Order from Gael. Gael sends a small black bird to Irvaria to tell her order of her imprisonment in the Dungeons of Zyran.

214 BL – An Irilian, Sean the Great, with four other powerful Irilians cross the Great Mountains in secret. They travel across Vastoria and through Ateria. Eventually Sean and his company arrive in Zyran. Their presence is undetected by the Zyranians. Sean instigates a plan to rescue Gael. Three of the Irilians are killed, but Sean and Gael escape Zyran and sail back to Everdon. From Everdon they cross the Great Mountains and return to the Iril Fortress. The Zyranians are enraged by the Irilian incursion. They declare war on the Irilian Order.

213 BL – Twenty Zyranian Enforcers cross the Great Mountains to attack the Iril Fortress. A group of fifty Irilians meet them in western Dravania near the Crystal Lake. The Zyranians are forced to retreat and several are slain in the battle. Zyran prepares for a full scale attack. The Irilians seek the assistance of the Fiorian Order. The Fiorian Knights do not want to get involved in the long running feud between the two orders.

212 BL – The Zyranians send fifty wizards to destroy the Irilians once and for all. Most of the wizards of the Irilian Order, about seventy wizards, leave the Iril Fortress to meet the Zyranians high in the Great Mountains. A great battle is fought with neither side able to take an advantage. For months ongoing skirmishes between the two orders occur high in the Great Mountains. Eventually the Zyranians give up after having sustained great losses. The decision is made mostly because they cannot maintain their influence over the kingdoms of the east whilst maintaining a war with the Irilians. The Irilians consider it a victory over the Zyranian Order.

207 BL – The Circle of Night send a fleet to attack Aldokan. The Kaznorian army is mostly destroyed by the Scaldonian garrisons protecting the city. The Scaldonians capture most of the ships of the Kaznorian fleet. The Zyranians see an opportunity to invade Kaznor. The idea of extending their influence into Kaznor grows over the course of the year.

206 BL – The Order of Zyran begins to build an army with the help of all of the kingdoms of the east. By the end of the year their army has over one hundred thousand men. The army gathers at Aldokan.

205 BL – The Zyranian fleet sails for Zarkanor. The fleet lands close to the city and captures all the surrounding territories. The Circle of Night sends an army to face the massive Zyranian force. Both armies suffer great losses but the Zyranians take victory. The Circle of Night retreats from Zarkanor. The Zyranians capture the city and the fortress.

204 BL – The Circle of Night, based in Garovna, begin to gather troops from the west of Kaznor. Meanwhile Zyran brings more soldiers from the south to bolster their forces around Zarkanor. The Zyranians also begin to tax Kaznor and send the wealth back to Zyran.

201 BL – The Circle of Night attacks the Zyranian positions around Zarkanor and completely obliterate the Zyranian force. The Zyranians pull back all their forces to Zarkanor and attempt to hold the fortress against the massive army of the Circle of Night. The Circle of Night army assails Zarkanor and not one soldier of the Zyranian force escapes Kaznor. The power of the Zyranian Order is much diminished by the loss.

198 BL – King Barat of Irvaria calls for all the knights of Veredor to take part in a great tournament. He sends word to all the knights of all the orders and all the kingdoms to come to compete for the right to court his daughter, Princess Bethia of Irvaria.

197 BL – The tournament takes place in Faircastle. Knights come from all over Veredor to take part in the tournament. The Takalian Knights, the Desert Knights, and the Muckron Bane Knights also send representatives. A Takalian knight from Scaldonia, Otis the Red, wins the tournament after defeating all other challenges. Princess Bethia falls in love with Otis and the two are married later in the year. Otis the Red becomes Duke Otis of Irvaria. The Takalian Knights gain a reputation as the most formidable fighters in Veredor after the tournament.

192 BL – Duke Otis, thinking he is the greatest warrior in Veredor, publically challenges a Fiorian, Liam the Silent. Duke Otis believes he will be revered as the greatest warrior who ever lived if he can defeat a Fiorian Knight. The duel takes place in the Great Hall of Faircastle and many dignitaries come to watch. Liam the Silent defeats Duke Otis with ease, shocking the entire audience. Otis is greatly ashamed of his loss and never wields a sword again.

187 BL – A draug appears in the forest south of the Crystal Lake. Many village folk are killed by the draug. The Irilians send a group of wizards to kill the draug. Five Irilians die fighting the draug, but they force the

draug to flee into the Great Mountains. The draug escapes and crosses the Great Mountains into Everdon.

185 BL – The draug appears in the Table Lands of Everdon. Many village folk and farmers suffer at the hands of the draug. King Galot of Everdon sends his knights to fight the draug. Most of his knights are killed by the draug. King Galot calls on the Fire Order for help but they refuse.

184 BL – A young village woman, Ismena of the Table Lands, takes up her dead father's sword and challenges the draug in the forests of Table Lands. Ismena kills the draug because of her pure heart.

182 BL – Ismena becomes the first female knight of the Kingdom of Everdon.

179 BL – The Gerish Oracle warns of the return of the Prince of Shadows. The Fiorian Order heeds the warning.

175 BL – A civil war breaks out in Kaznor between two factions of the Circle of Night. The Skatheans make up most of one faction and the Northern Sorcerers make up the other. The Skatheans are forced into subservience by the more numerous Northern Sorcerers.

171 BL – Many Skatheans decide to leave the Circle of Night and flee to Alber. Some Skatheans enter the Southern Lands of Veredor.

168 BL – A group of Ortarian miners accidently disturb a lindworm's den in the Red Mountains. Many of the miners are killed by the Lindworm. Several Ortarian knights attempt to slay the lindworm. They are all killed by the beast. The Lindworm forces the closure of all the Ortarian silver mines in the Red Mountains. King Claren of Ortaria seeks a way of killing the beast. He calls on all the orders of knights to assist him in the task. Two Desert Knights attempt to slay the beast but they are both killed.

165 BL – A knight of the Fiorian Order, Edolina the Wise, travels from Emeril to Ortaria to face the

lindworm in the Red Mountains. Edolina battles the beast, but she is forced to retreat due to an injury. The Zyranians send three Enforcers to kill the dragon. All three wizards are killed in the battle.

163 BL – Edolina seeks out the lindworm again. She slays the beast and later returns to Emeril.

159 BL – Packs of muckrons appear in Alber. The people suffer greatly. Vesrak the Stern of Alber calls on the Muckron Bane Knights of the Far Western Lands to save his people from the muckron menace. A group of eighty Muckron Bane Knights travel by ship to Alber. They free the Alber people from the muckron menace. A small contingent of Muckron Bane Knights remains in Alber at the request of King Vesrak.

154 BL – The Circle of Night prepare a fleet to sail east from Kaznor.

152 BL – The Kaznorian fleet sails around Scaldonia and attacks Zyran directly. The Zyranians fall back to the Citadel of Zyran where they take a stand against twenty five thousand Kaznorians soldiers. The Kaznorian army begins a long siege of the Citadel of Zyran.

151 BL – King Marc of Ortaria sends a fleet from Ancora to Zyran. The Ortarians battle the Zyranians in the Bay of Zyran and on the beaches surrounding the Citadel of Zyran. The battle is fierce and the Kaznorians retreat to the north side of the island. The Silvorians send a small army to assist. The two armies attack the Kaznorian positions in the north of Zyran. The remaining Kaznorians retreat back to Zarkanor. Zyran is liberated.

146 BL – The Oran Oracle warns of the return of the Prince of Shadows.

143 BL – Garin Ecorian travels to Emeril to study with the Fiorians.

140 BL – A powerful Northern Sorcerer, Fizzakar the Tyrant, appears in Roven. He quickly destroys all resistance and takes the throne of Roven. The Irilians

send ten wizards to remove Fizzakar. Fizzakar destroys the ten Irilians and rules Roven unchallenged. Fizzakar divides the nobles of Roven and conquers the entire kingdom.

137 BL – Garin Ecorian travels to Ghrian. He gathers a group of young warriors and prepares to take on Fizzakar. He attempts to gain the support of Queen Branna of Iarthar. Queen Branna refuses to help. Garin Ecorian travels to the stronghold of the Tabarian Knights to seek their assistance. The Tabarian Knights refuse the request. Garin Ecorian then goes on to request the help of the Muckron Bane Knights. They agree to help to liberate Roven by sending fifty knights with Garin Ecorian. Garin Ecorian at this time has one hundred and fifty men under his command.

136 BL – Garin Ecorian requests the help of the Takalian Knights. A small group of Takalians join his force. Three Irilians join Garin Ecorian's army. Fizzakar raises an army of eight thousand men in Roven and moves to attack Iarthar. Queen Branna prepares to defend her kingdom. Fizzakar leads his army across the border. Queen Branna's army is forced to retreat back to Ghrian. Garin Ecorian arrives at Ghrian and saves the city from Fizzakar's army. Fizzakar retreats back to Roven. Queen Branna helps Garin Ecorian to build an army to challenge Fizzakar.

135 BL – Garin Ecorian invades Roven. He quickly reclaims the conquered territory. Garin Ecorian liberates Roven and captures Fizzakar. Fizzakar is taken back to the Iril Fortress in chains. He is placed in the dungeons of the Iril Fortress and is never released.

131 BL – The Northern Sorcerers of the Circle of Night face turmoil within their own ranks. The Circle of Night is greatly weakened.

127 BL – The Eranai Oracle predicts the return of the Prince of Shadows in the age to come.

123 BL – Garin Ecorian enters Irvaria and marries Countess Orella of Elcalee.

119 BL – The Zyranians begin a feud with King Huggett of the Isles of Dawn. King Huggett refuses to allow any of the Zyranians to enter the Isles of Dawn as he sees that they are manipulating the monarchies of the east. He also prevents Zyranian ships from passing his islands on their way to Ateria.

117 BL – The Zyranians threaten King Huggett and attempt to influence King Vin of Silvor to send a fleet to conquer the Isles of Dawn. King Vin refuses to get involved in the feud.

115 BL – King Huggett is assassinated by an unknown assailant. Prince Hector commands the powerful fleet of the Isles of Dawn to attack any ship owned by the Zyranian Order. Many Zyranian ships are destroyed on the high seas. The Zyranians are outraged by the actions and claim to have had nothing to do with the assassination of King Huggett. Prince Hector is made King of the Isles of Dawn.

112 BL – The Order of Zyran persuades King Vin of Silvor to send his fleet to challenge the fleet of the Isles of Dawn. A great war on water is fought between the Silvorians and the Isles of Dawn with neither side taking an advantage. The war is ongoing.

110 BL – The Aterians decide to side with the Isles of Dawn. Ortaria and Scaldonia side with Zyran and Silvor. Ateria sends ships to reinforce the fleet of the Isles of Dawn.

109 BL – A fleet of Ortarian and Zyranian ships meet with the main fleet of the Isles of Dawn in the seas off the coast of Silvor. The Zyranian fleet is victorious and most of the ships of the Isles of Dawn are destroyed in the battle.

108 BL – The Isles of Dawn fall to the Zyranians with the help of the Silvorians and Ortarians. King Vin places his brother Prince Lucen on the throne of the Isles of Dawn. Prince Lucen becomes the King of the Isles of Dawn. Prince Hector is taken to the Dungeons of Zyran. Ateria remains defiant.

107 BL – Queen Avis of Ateria threatens to continue the war if King Hector is not restored to the throne of the Isles of Dawn. The Zyranian Order rejects the demands of the Aterians. The Aterians begin building a massive fleet and training a great army.

104 BL – The Aterian fleet sails for Zyran. The Aterians lay siege to Zyran. The Zyranian Order remains trapped in the Citadel of Zyran. The Ortarians attempt to break the siege but fail. The siege of the Citadel of Zyran lasts for seven months. The Zyranian Order agrees to the terms of the Aterians and release King Hector.

103 BL – King Hector retakes the throne of the Isles of Dawn.

100 BL – Clari Ecorian, the daughter of Garin Ecorian, travels east to Scaldonia to consult the Gerish Oracle. Clari remains in Orelin for several years.

97 BL – Several Skatheans from Kaznor attempt to infiltrate Scaldonia. Clari Ecorian faces three Skatheans north of the Iron Gate Pass. She defeats the three Skatheans with the Sword of Midlight.

94 BL – Clari Ecorian travels to Vastoria and meet with the Desert Knights. Clari falls in love with Sir Aldo of the Desert Knights; they marry in the Deep Desert. Clari remains in the desert.

91 BL – Gawyn Ecorian is born in the Deep Desert.

87 BL – A Fiorian named Miles of Emeril travels from Emeril to search for Shidon.

85 BL – Miles battles a group of Skatheans in the Icy Lands of Alber. Miles is victorious. Miles finds Shidon and later stumbles across the home of Callidus in the Great Mountains. Callidus warns Miles of the return of the Prince of Shadows and the downfall of men and mer.

84 BL – Miles returns to Emeril.

81 BL – Emeril is attacked by a large faction of Skatheans. The Fiorians hold back the attack. Many Fiorians die in the battle. The Fiorian Order is

weakened as a result. Miles becomes the Gatekeeper of Emeril and makes plans to expand the Fiorian Order.

78 BL – Miles seeks out the Star King in order to ask him about the possibility of the Prince of Shadows passing through the Cosmic Gate. He speaks with the Star King who still lives in his hidden cave high in the Great Mountains. The Star King reveals to Miles why and how the gate is sealed against the Prince of Shadows.

75 BL – Miles is assassinated by a group of Skatheans on his way to find the Gerish Oracle.

73 BL – The Skatheans attack Emeril again. The Skatheans almost capture the fortress. The Skatheans fall back and begin an organised extermination of the Fiorian Knights. The Fiorian Order is severely reduced.

71 BL – A Skathean faction known as the Haunted Shadow enters Vastoria and spread their evil influence throughout the kingdom.

70 BL – The Desert Knights attempt to remove the Haunted Shadow from Vastoria. Many Desert Knights are killed in the campaign, and the Haunted Shadow increases their power in Vastoria.

69 BL – Gawyn Ecorian travels to Scaldonia to find the Gerish Oracle. He searches for the elusive oracle for several years to no avail. It is later discovered that the Gerish Oracle deliberately avoided being found by Gawyn in order for him to live out his destiny of settling in the Gerish Highlands.

67 BL – Gawyn Ecorian settles in the Gerish Highlands and marries a local Scaldonian villager. Lilion Ecorian is born. Gawyn Ecorian is content to remain in the Gerish Highlands with his family.

65 BL – The Haunted Shadow continue to expand their influence in Vastoria. The Desert Knights lose control of much of the desert regions of the kingdom. The Desert Knights are forced to move their stronghold near to the Old Guardian Mountains.

62 BL – The Haunted Shadow infiltrates Darancra and run a group of street gangs that terrorise the city.

59 BL – The Haunted Shadow takes control of Darancra and effectively controls the whole of Vastoria. The Zyranians begin to see the real threat that the Haunted Shadow pose to the Southern Lands of Veredor. The Zyranian Order fears the return of the Skathean Empire.

58 BL – Three Fiorians travel to Vastoria to help the Desert Knights battle the Haunted Shadow. The Haunted Shadow gradually develops their street gangs into a well organised militia.

57 BL – Prince Edric of Irvaria is born.

56 BL – The Haunted Shadow assault the stronghold of the Desert Knights. The Desert Knights are scattered and lose much of their remaining power in Vastoria.

55 BL – The Haunted Shadow place Hervi the Idiot on the throne of Vastoria. Hervi is a close ally of the Haunted Shadow and a distant relative of the former royal family. Hervi claims a right to rule Vastoria through being a descendent of the Ecorian Arbiters. The Haunted Shadow continues to expand their powers in Vastoria and build an army.

54 BL – Prince Ignis of Ortaria is born.

53 BL – King Ernis of Ateria becomes concerned about the events in Vastoria. He calls King Hervi to a council. King Hervi refuses and deliberately insults King Ernis in a letter. King Ernis threatens war.

52 BL – Several small border skirmishes occur on the Vastorian border with Ateria. The Haunted Shadow attempts to draw King Ernis into a war with Vastoria. The Zyranian Order warns King Ernis of the threat and the plot of the Skatheans. King Ernis holds off invading Vastoria.

50 BL – The Haunted Shadow build a massive army in Vastoria. King Garit of Irvaria begins to build and army to protect Irvaria from invasion.

47 BL – Elons Ecorian is born in the Gerish Highlands of Scaldonia.

44 BL – Kaloren is born in Bergoth in the Kingdom of Everdon.

43 BL – The Haunted Shadow attempts to invade Ateria. The Aterian border army holds back the Haunted Shadow attack. The Haunted Shadow conduct organised raids into Irvaria. The Brigades of the Sunset Hills patrol the Irvarian western borders and are involved in numerous conflicts.

41 BL – Carlin, a young Iartharian warrior, becomes a Fiorian Knight. Carlin travels to Zyran to hold a council with the Zyranian Order. Carlin encounters a group of three Skatheans in the Ortarian wilderness. Carlin is almost slain but is saved by a huntsman named Erako. Carlin becomes friends with Erako and agrees to train Erako in the ways of the Fiorian Order. Carlin and Erako go to Zyran together.

40 BL – Carlin and Erako return to Emeril.

37 BL – Erako becomes a Fiorian Knight. A Fiorian named Roarna becomes the Gatekeeper of Emeril. King Hervi and the Haunted Shadow prepare to invade Irvaria.

36 BL – The Haunted Shadow invades Irvaria and attacks Elcalee with their massive army. The fortress holds off the attack. The Haunted Shadow sends their massive army north to assail Faircastle. Carlin, Erako, and Roarna go to Faircastle and help to hold off the Haunted Shadow invasion. The Haunted Shadow army is pushed back toward the border. Carlin, Roarna, and Erako help the Irvarians rid their land of the Skatheans.

33 BL – Carlin, Roarna, and Erako work tirelessly against the Haunted Shadow. The Desert Knights begin to reappear in Vastoria. They hide among the people and form an underground resistance against the Skatheans.

29 BL – Roarna seeks out the Gerish Oracle. Roarna is told to seek out the Chalai, the ancient Astarian relic that is held by the Star King. Roarna begins a quest to find the Chalai. Erako retires from the Fiorian Order and returns to the wilderness of Ortaria.

28 BL – The Northern Sorcerers Baramak and Azagord appear near the Bay of Night in Kaznor. They quickly gain recognition as incredibly powerful Northern Sorcerers. Their method and power has not been seen since the time of Ondtast. Baramak and Azagord travel to Zarkanor. The two Northern Sorcerers call a meeting with the Circle of Night to challenge the ruling group of sorcerers. Baramak and Azagord destroy the Circle of Night and take control of Kaznor. Baramak and Azagord divide Kaznor. Baramak rules the west of the empire and Azagord rules Zarkanor and the east.

27 BL – The Prince of Shadows breaks through the Cosmic Gate and appears in Kaznor. He quickly recovers the Sword of Darkness from the Skathean who carries his sword. The Prince of Shadows takes control of the Skathean Order. The Prince of Shadows conceals his real identity and is only known as the Master. The Prince of Shadows challenges the Astarian Callidus. Callidus attempts to battle the Prince of Shadows but fails. Callidus becomes a servant of the Prince of Shadows. The Prince of Shadows challenges Baramak and Azagord. Baramak and Azagord are made into slaves of the evil Astarian.

26 BL – The Haunted Shadow invade Irvaria. Several fierce battles are fought over the border regions of Irvaria. King Ignis of Ortaria marries Countess Clara of Talis. The Prince of Shadows begins to train armies of Skatheans in Kaznor. The Prince of Shadows seeks out and kills the Eranai Oracle. The Prince of Shadows also kills the Oran Oracle. The Prince of Shadows seeks to kill the Gerish Oracle, but the Gerish Oracle manages to avoid being captured.

Roarna and Kaloren take the Chalai from the Star King. Roarna dies near Bergoth. Kaloren inherits the Sword of Light from Roarna. Kaloren leaves Bergoth in Everdon and takes up the quest to return the Chalai to Emeril. Kaloren meets Dorn of Everdon. Kaloren and Dorn travel north to Irvaria. Kaloren helps the Irvarians battle the Haunted Shadow. Kaloren leads an army to Darancra to challenge the Haunted Shadow. Darancra is liberated. The Desert Knights assist Kaloren in the battle. Kaloren is revered for her bravery. Kaloren begins to train as a Fiorian.

23 BL – The Haunted Shadow is completely removed from Vastoria. The Desert Knights grow strong once again.

21 BL – A brigade of Fiorians attack Zarkanor. The brigade is slaughtered by the Prince of Shadows and his Skatheans. The Prince of Shadows sends an army of Skatheans to attack Emeril. The Fiorians, led by Kaloren, expect the counterattack and manage to hold back the Skatheans with the help of several Irilians and a small group of Tabarian Knights.

20 BL – The Prince of Shadows sends Baramak and Azagord south to seek out the last Ecorian and to recover the Sword of Light. Baramak attacks Coran with an army of highly trained soldiers, Skatheans, and Northern Sorcerers. Baramak conquers Coran. Azagord lands in Scaldonia and destroys Havet Bay. Elons Ecorian, with the Sword of Midlight, travels to the border of Dravania and Coran to help the Tabarian Knights battle Baramak's army. A fierce battle is fought on the border and Baramak is held back. The Tabarian Knights suffer great losses. The Muckron Bane Knights come to assist the Tabarians. The Prince of Shadows conquers Alber and sends a large army of Alber men to assist Baramak. The Dravanians and Iartharians send an army to help the Tabarian Knights in the war against Baramak. Elons Ecorian travels to Emeril to request the help of the Fiorian Order in the

war with Baramak. Elons Ecorian meets Kaloren, the Gatekeeper of Emeril. Meanwhile Azagord attacks Ortaria. King Ignis battles Azagord and the Ortarians suffer heavy losses. King Ignis sends a request to Emeril for help. Azagord lays siege to Ancora. Kaloren gathers a group of Fiorians to go east to help King Ignis. King Ignis' wife and family are assassinated by Skatheans. Kaloren and Elons Ecorian marry in Stonehaven. Kaloren (with the Sword of Light), Elons (with the Sword of Midlight), and four Fiorians (including Carlin) and one Irvarian Knight, Sir Dorn, arrive in Ancora. The Fiorians fight back Azagord and his army. Ancora is saved. Azagord takes his army to Zyran and attacks the Citadel of Zyran. Kaloren becomes pregnant. Kaloren gives the Sword of Light to Carlin to continue the battle with Azagord in Zyran. Carlin defeats Azagord with the Sword of Light and imprisons the sorcerer in the Dungeons of Zyran.

19 BL – Terrible news regarding the war in the Far Western Lands reaches Kaloren and Elons in Ancora. They learn that Baramak has taken much of Dravania and Iarthar. Kaloren sends Elons ahead to help the Dravanians, Iartharians, Tabarians, and the Irilians. Kaloren remains in Ancora. Elons Ecorian is captured by Baramak with the help of Callidus. Elons Ecorian is taken back to Zarkanor in chains. The Sword of Midlight is returned to Kaloren in Ancora. Callidus encounters six Zyranians in northern Scaldonia. Callidus persuades and tempts the six Zyranians to be servants of the Prince of Shadows. Among the six Zyranians are: Zarceler, Baltac, and Trebax. Callidus teaches the six Zyranians new powers and sends them back to take control of the Zyranian Order. Eben Ecorian is born in Ortaria.

ADDITIONAL MAPS OF VEREDOR

MAP OF NORTHERN SCALDONIA

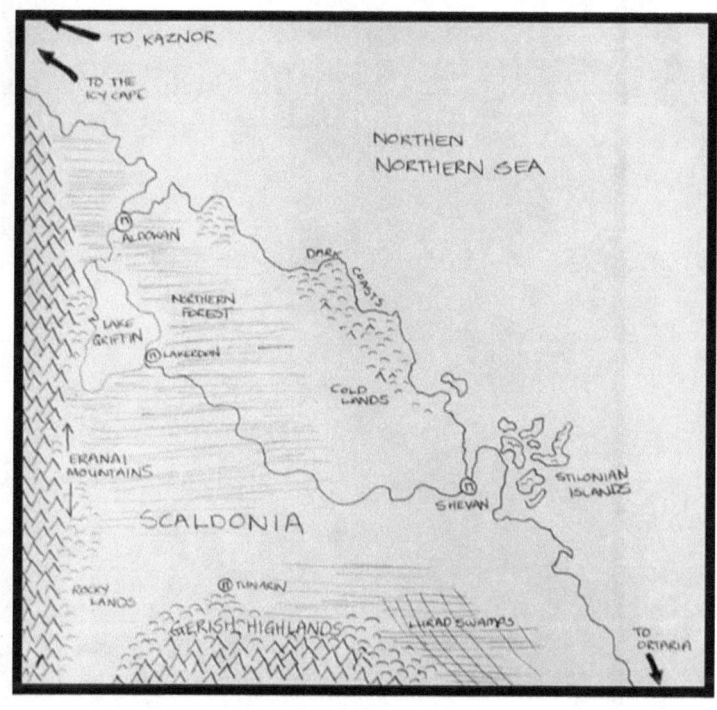

MAP OF THE FAR WESTERN LANDS

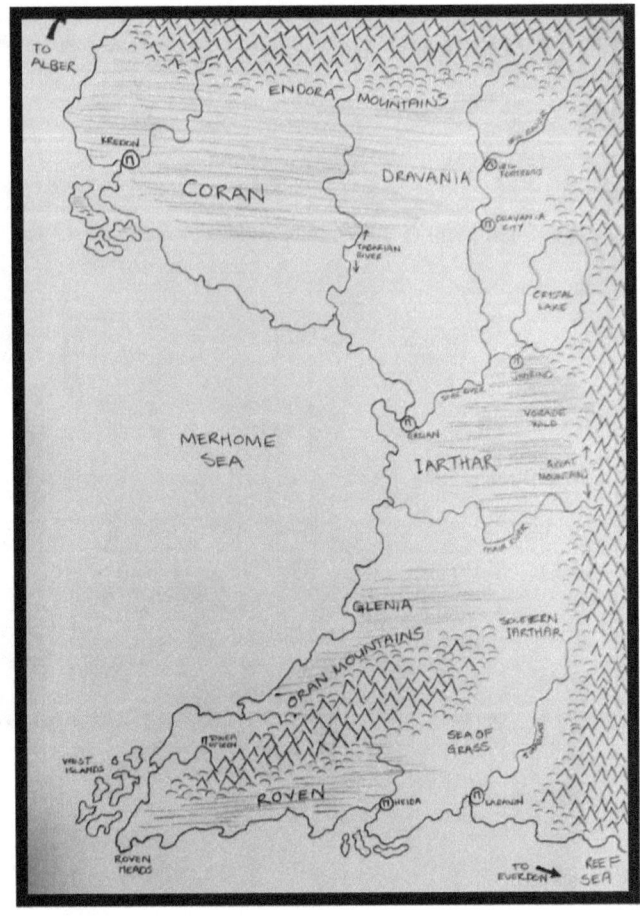

MAP OF ATERIA

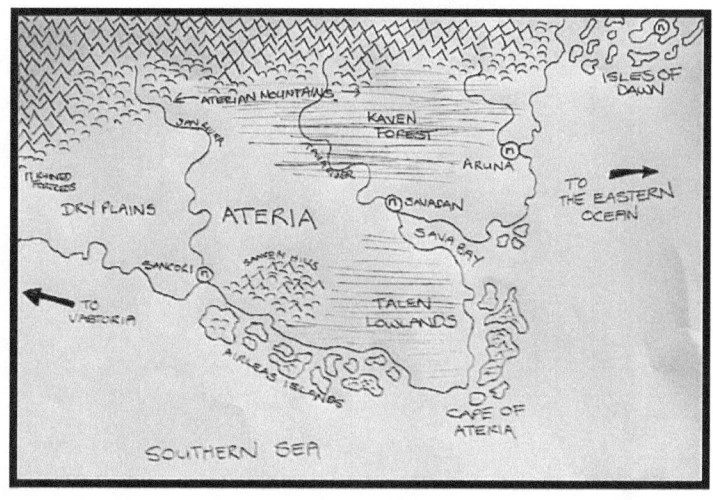

MAP OF KAZNOR

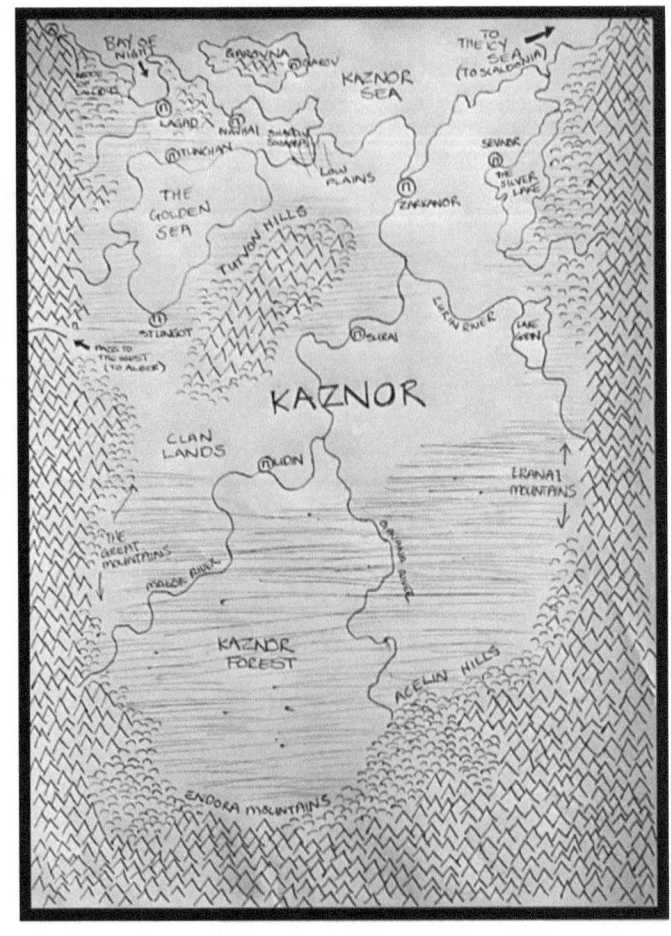

MAP OF ALBER

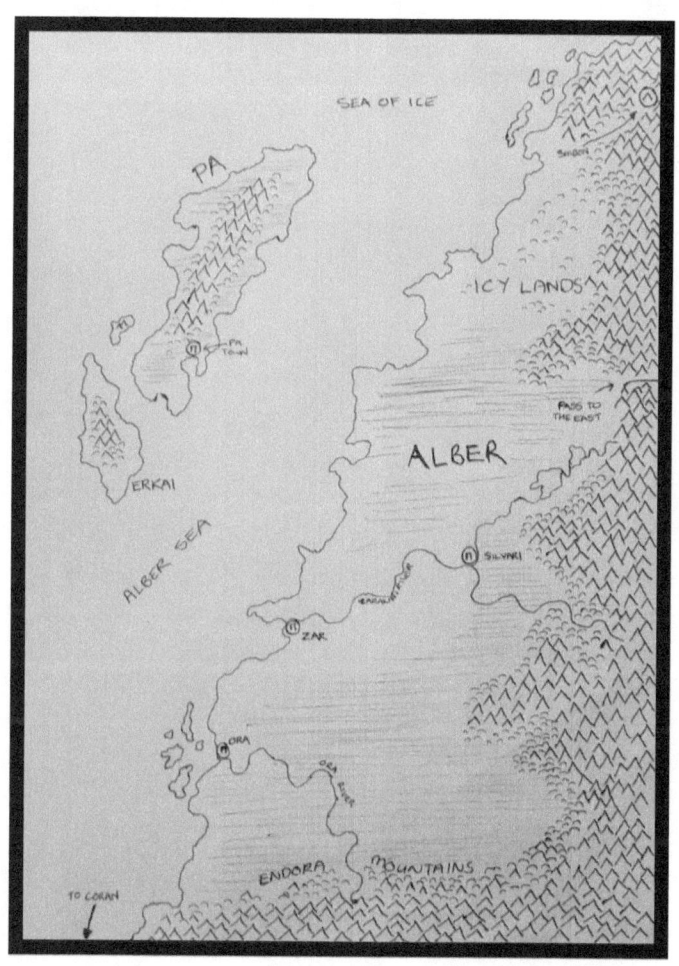